The Mammoth Book of

PARANORMAL
ROMANCE 2

Also available in the Mammoth series

Constable & Robinson Ltd
3 The Lanchesters
162 Fulham Palace Road
London W6 9ER
www.constablerobinson.com

First published in the UK by Robinson,
an imprint of Constable & Robinson, 2010

A copy of the British Library Cataloguing in Publication
Data is available from the British Library

UK ISBN 978-1-84901-370-3

1 3 5 7 9 10 8 6 4 2

First published in the United States in 2010 by Running Press Book Publishers
All rights reserved under the Pan-American and International Copyright Conventions

9 8 7 6 5 4 3 2
Digit on the right indicates the number of this printing

US Library of Congress number: 2009943389
US ISBN 978-0-76243-996-6

Running Press Book Publishers
2300 Chestnut Street
Philadelphia, PA 19103-4371

Visit us on the web!

www.runningpress.com

Printed and bound in the EU

The Mammoth Book of

PARANORMAL
ROMANCE 2

Edited and with an Introduction by
TRISHA TELEP

ROBINSON

RUNNING PRESS
PHILADELPHIA · LONDON

Contents

Acknowledgments

"To Hell With Love" © Jacqueline H. Kessler. First publication, original to this anthology. Printed by permission of the author.

"Princes of Dominion" © Ann Aguirre. First publication, original to this anthology. Printed by permission of the author.

"Spirit of the Prairie" © Shirley Damsgaard. First publication, original to this anthology. Printed by permission of the author.

"The Demon's Secret" © Nathalie Gray. First publication, original to this anthology. Printed by permission of the author.

"Marine Biology" © by Gail Carriger. First publication, original to this anthology. Printed by permission of the author.

"Zola's Pride" © Moira Rogers. First publication, original to this anthology. Printed by permission of the author.

"In Dreams" © by Elissa Wilds. First publication, original to this anthology. Printed by permission of the author.

"The Gauntlet" © Karen Chance. First publication, original to this anthology. Printed by permission of the author.

"The Getaway" © Sonya Bateman. First publication, original to this anthology. Printed by permission of the author.

"Mr Sandman" © Sherri Browning Erwin. First publication, original to this anthology. Printed by permission of the author.

"The Sin-Eater's Promise" © Michele Hauf. First publication, original to this anthology. Printed by permission of the author.

"Fragile Magic" © Naomi Lester. First publication, original to this anthology. Printed by permission of the author.

"NightDrake" © Lara Adrian, LLC. First publication, original to this anthology. Printed by permission of the author.

"The Sons of Ra" © Helen Scott Taylor. First publication, original to this anthology. Printed by permission of the author.

"Eve of Warfare" © Sylvia Day. First publication, original to this anthology. Printed by permission of the author.

"The Majestic" © Seressia Glass. First publication, original to this anthology. Printed by permission of the author.

"Answer the Wicked" © Kim Lenox. First publication, original to this anthology. Printed by permission of the author.

Introduction

Welcome to the most mammoth Mammoth ever!

Well, it *was*.

OK, OK, I got a little carried away. You see I am a huge fan of contracting great writers and letting them do whatever they want, write the story that their heart desires, that they haven't had the chance to write yet, that's always been in the back of their mind, looking for a home, a chance to be written. I feel that's when you often get the greatest stories. I think that if you burden writers with too many rules and guidelines, you can end up with a story that is just a little . . . flat. OK, so those are my ideas. This freedom-loving, write-what-you-want, to-hell-with-rules attitude also extends to word count and sometimes (now, for instance) I forget to keep an eye on just how mammoth my Mammoth is getting. And, oh, they can really grow, and very quickly. And, suddenly, instead of having a brick-like doorstop of a book (like any other garden-variety Mammoth), you have a book that needs to be published in three (or four) separate volumes. And that's what happened to me with this book.

It was 100,000 words over. Yes, you read that right. How did I allow that to happen? What kind of editor am I? Well, I think I just got a little excited and overwhelmed: so many wonderful writers, so many neat stories. You'd have trouble too (you really would). There were originally 25 stories in this collection, see, and to hit the word count I had to cut (wait, not *cut*, but *move* in a cunning fashion) eight fantastic stories by phenomenal writers. Here is a list of authors, along with their story titles, who were *originally* supposed to be in this book:

Sharon Shinn *Can You Hear Me Now?*
Robin D. Owens *Heart Story*
Laura Ann Gilman *The Rat King*
Dru Pagliassotti *Ghost in the Machine*
Maria Lima *The Song Remains the Same*
Catherine Asaro *The Pyre of New Day*
Toni Andrews *Nativitas*
Elle Jasper *Curse Me Wicked*

See my dilemma?
Now, obviously, these stories are not disappearing. I just had to do a little creative shuffling (talking to authors, begging for their consent, trying to find new books to put them in) and they will all be appearing in upcoming Mammoths (so watch for them!). The Shinn and Pagliassotti stories will be in the upcoming *The Mammoth Book of Ghost Romance* because they are fabulous and romantic ghost stories and are just the perfect fit. The Andrews story is set in a future world so it is just right for the new anthology of futuristic romance (can't wait to do this one!) that I'm putting together soon. The Lima story is a wonderful paranormal romance set in a hospital emergency room – lots of those bleeping cardio-respiratory machines, creepy life support systems, kick-ass nurses from hell and gorgeous paranormal males in those hospital gowns that just don't tie up properly at the back . . . Anyhow, all the stories have a home, you will be pleased to know. Whew!

So, I thought it might be fun in this introduction to confess my sins and reveal to you how much trouble you can actually get into when putting together a Mammoth if you don't keep your eye on the ball. In my exuberance, I took my eye off it for a moment, and look what happened. Chaos! Mayhem! I must admit that I am susceptible, as are most chronic readers, to getting carried away by a good story and losing hours, days, weeks in a great tale. That's just the way it goes. It's a book-lover's curse, I'm afraid.

But the seventeen stories that *are* in this book are going to knock your socks off. As well as a novella prequel from the amazing Karen Chance (with a word count that almost killed me – but how in tarnation could I say no? Oh, I am weak . . . so weak . . .), you'll get to grips with some great, gritty, sexy urban fantasy, some fast-and-furious paranormals, some hilariously fun magic and, of course, endless other-worldly beautiful men stretching as far as the eye can see!

Trisha Telep

To Hell with Love

Jackie Kessler

People have the oddest ideas about witches. They should be green-skinned. They should fly on broomsticks. They should have black cats as constant companions. Caitlin Harris blamed Hollywood for all the misconceptions. When it came to Caitlin, the truth was that her skin was pale, she flew only in airplanes and she was allergic to cats.

She could also throw magic like snowballs, reshape specific portions of universal memory, and brew a potion to transform demons into humans. But just because she *could* nudge probability on its backside and magic up her favourite movie on television whenever she wanted didn't mean she *should*. Magic had a price. And DVDs had been invented for a reason. Caitlin used to hear that all the time from a man who had once meant everything to her: magic was too important to be used for frivolous things.

Of course, without the remote control, the DVD was just a big dust collector. She used to tell that to the man in return – even as he'd pluck the remote out of whatever crevice it had fallen into. But his lesson still stuck, even two years after she'd told the man goodbye. So there Caitlin was, in the middle of tossing her sofa cushions around for the umpteenth time to find the wayward remote, when her phone rang.

Growling, she stomped into the kitchen to pick up the receiver. After the call, she'd give into the inevitable and use magic to locate the clicker. What she really needed, she thought as she answered the phone, was a GPS for her remote control. Maybe she could magic one up . . .

"Caitlin? It's Paul Hamilton."

Her eyebrow arched. Paul was her twin sister's boyfriend. Nice enough guy, from what Caitlin knew, although he was a little too Captain America for her taste. Still, he was good for her sister – and Goddess knew that Jesse Harris needed good influences in her life.

"Hey, Paul," Caitlin said, trying not to sound too weird. She and Paul had never actually spoken before. Everything she knew about him had come from Jesse . . . and from Caitlin's under-the-radar scrying. It wasn't being nosy. Really. She just had to keep tabs on her sister. "How are you?"

"I need your help."

Caitlin rather admired that Paul didn't waste time with social niceties. "What's wrong?"

"It's Jesse. She's in trouble."

Of *course* she was. Caitlin's twin had a penchant for trouble. "Could you be a little more specific?"

"She's unconscious and glowing."

Yes, that would be trouble. "Tell me everything."

He did so, calmly and coherently, even though tension laced his words. He'd come home at six-thirty, right after work. He'd been surprised to see Jesse's bag on the kitchen table; she should have been at her job since four. He'd called out hello, but there'd been no answer. At first, he hadn't seen her sprawled on the living room floor because the coffee table had partially blocked his view. When he found her lying prone, he'd rushed over to her. She was breathing; that much he could see. But she was also glowing with a pale blue light, so as much as he'd wanted to touch her, he'd held back.

"That was the right decision," Caitlin murmured. When mundanes fooled around with magic, the results were unpredictable at best.

"I can't tell if she's hurt," Paul said, the anger all too clear in his voice.

"Touching her might have triggered something even worse. Tell me what else you see. Any marks? Anything out of place?"

"There's a small box in her right hand. Looks like a jewellery box, made of wood. It's open."

"Don't touch that, either," Caitlin said, frowning. "Just in case it has something to do with her condition."

"Figured that part out all by myself." He paused, but Caitlin heard the wordless snarl of him blowing out an exasperated breath. "Sorry. I'm just . . ."

"It's okay," she said. "Anything else you see?"

He cleared his throat. "There's a padded envelope. Torn. It's on the floor near the sofa. Jesse's name is on the envelope, written in black marker. But there's no address, no postage. And no return address."

"Don't—"

"Touch it. Yeah. I didn't." He took another breath. "I don't know what to do, Caitlin. I can't call 911. I can't touch her. She's not waking up, no matter how loud I yell her name. Tell me," he said, a plaintive note creeping into his voice. "Tell me what to do to wake her up."

Well, she wouldn't be magicking up the remote control after all.

"Sit tight," Caitlin said. "I'll be right there."

A pause, and then Paul stammered, "You're in Boston. We're in New York City."

Actually, she was in Salem, but she didn't bother correcting him. "For family, I break out the big guns. I just have to lock up. Be there in a few minutes."

"Um. Okay. You have the address?"

"Don't need it."

"Right. Of course not. Um. See you soon."

Caitlin hung up, thinking that all things considered, Paul had sounded all right. That was something. Usually, mundanes didn't take too well to anything extraordinary that interrupted their lives.

But then, her sister wasn't a mundane human, so Paul had some experience under his belt.

Caitlin pulled together her travel bag, complete with basic spell ingredients, a small version of her Book of Shadows with its various magic recipes, and a portable ritual box. Then she slipped on her shoes and a jacket, grabbed her purse and locked the door. With a whispered word of power, her magical security system clicked on – enough to scare away the casual burglar as well as discourage any other practitioners or supernatural critters from entering her territory without permission. One experience of coming home to a houseful of fairies was enough for her, thank you very much.

Purse strap on her shoulder and travel bag in hand, she raised one arm and closed her eyes. She thought of her twin, and she felt the bond between them, the one that linked their souls together. Grasping that bond, she cast a silent prayer to the Goddess, asking Her to deliver her to Jesse's side.

The Hecate responded: power danced through Caitlin, pulling her skin taut until she was crackling with magical energy. She inhaled deeply, and then she *stepped*.

Caitlin always equated *stepping* through reality to swimming under water – space thickened around her, slowing her down. She could see when she *stepped*, but everything was distorted, and looking too long stung her eyes. She couldn't breathe when in Between places, and even with a lungful of air before *stepping*, she always felt like she was smothering. After, Caitlin would desperately want to shower, to wash away the remnants of Between from her skin. It didn't itch, exactly, but it felt wrong, and reminded her of just how precarious existence really was. Caitlin would be the first one to say that it was far more enjoyable to take a plane first class – and that the plane ride would be significantly cheaper than the cost of *stepping*.

But as she had said to Paul, when it came to family, Caitlin pulled out all stops. And Jesse, for whatever else she was, was family.

Well. Sort of.

She *stepped*; she arrived. The world rippled around her for one dizzying moment. Then air became less oppressive, and she released the breath she had been holding. Caitlin blinked until the world settled back into its normal pattern of existence. Shapes sharpened. Colours brightened and sank within their lines. She found herself staring at an entertainment centre overstuffed with DVDs and CDs. A television roughly the size of an elephant took up most of the unit. A few framed Nagels decorated the walls. A battered coffee table stood in front of Caitlin, littered with magazines. To her right sat a plush sofa that promised to be comfortable.

It was easy to see that this was a room that enjoyed being used. She could easily picture Paul and Jesse spending many an evening cuddling on the sofa, watching a movie, their fingers brushing as they both reached for the popcorn.

But then, knowing her sister, Caitlin thought the sofa was probably used for other, less passive, activities.

"Wow," a man's voice said behind her. "I believed you. But still. Wow."

Caitlin turned – slowly, because she was still a little dizzy – to face Paul Hamilton, the man her sister had sacrificed so much to be with. Light brown hair that was a little too long; small hazel eyes that had seen too much. Broken nose. Good smile. Had Caitlin been into big and brawny, she probably would have thought Paul had a great body.

"Hey, Paul," she said, dropping her travel bag and handbag to the floor. "Nice to finally meet you."

"Same here." He flicked her a polite smile. "She's over there."

He walked past Caitlin to the other end of the coffee table. She followed him, and there her sister was, sprawled prone on the floor. Most of her face was hidden by the unruly black curls of her hair, but Caitlin still knew that face intimately. Jesse's eyes were closed, but Caitlin knew they were bright green and sparkled with mischief; Jesse's mouth was slack, but Caitlin was well aware that when Jesse grinned, she had a slight overbite. Caitlin knew everything about how Jesse looked, down to her birthmarks.

She had been there two months ago when Jesse had first stolen Caitlin's looks. And her credit cards.

Caitlin stared at her sister in flesh: Jesse Harris, the former demon Jezebel.

For a long moment, Caitlin fought the urge to kick Jesse. Hard. But no matter how she felt about her twin, she had to protect her. All witches did, by the decree of the Hecate. That was why Caitlin had given the one-time succubus her name after turning her into a mortal two months ago: names had power, especially when offered freely.

She hadn't told Jesse why the Hecate was so invested in her. Caitlin wanted to give her sister more time as a normal human first – a couple of years, maybe, for her to be together with Paul, to learn how to truly love. Then she would tell Jesse about her destiny.

But first, Caitlin had to figure out why Jesse was unconscious and glowing.

She squatted next to Jesse and created a magical probe, one that would tell Caitlin more about the magic in play. It shimmered, lit up like a miniature nova, and incinerated. She murmured, "The spell that did this is still active."

"The glowing sort of tipped me off," said Paul.

She ignored the sarcasm. "Between the faintness of the glow and the colour, it looks like this has to do with dreams."

Paul hunkered down next to her. "You're saying she's sleeping?" He squinted at Jesse's face as if he could will her awake.

"No." Caitlin peered at the small open box in Jesse's hand. The patterns in the wood were intricate and beautiful, etched by someone with skill. Staring at those symbols, Caitlin remembered the last time she had seen anything like them before.

She felt the blood drain from her face.

Stop, she told herself. *Don't jump to conclusions.*

The torn envelope was on the floor next to Jesse. As Paul had said before on the phone, the package was padded and white, with only MS HARRIS on the front. No address. No information about the sender.

Ms Harris. Not *Jesse Harris*. Ms Harris. Written in black marker – by a hand that Caitlin recognized.

"Caitlin? What is it?"

Grimacing, Caitlin said, "This package wasn't intended for her." She turned to face Paul. "It was supposed to go to me."

He stiffened.

"That's a memory box she's holding," Caitlin said, pointing at the open box in Jesse's hand. "When the proper recipient opens a memory box, that person gets to experience a particular memory like it was happening now. It shouldn't open for the wrong person. Technically, it can't. It's made specifically for a particular recipient."

"But Jesse opened it," Paul said slowly.

"Maybe it's because she's my twin." More likely, it was because Jesse had been made Caitlin's twin by magic. "The spell wasn't meant for her, so what should have been passive instead became aggressive."

Paul's mouth pressed into a hard line. "Once more, this time in words I can understand."

"She's trapped in a memory." Caitlin gritted her teeth. "The spell within the box became corrupted when she opened it. If you'd touched her, you would have been sucked into the memory too."

"Can you help her?"

"Not without also getting pulled into the spell."

Something dangerous flashed in Paul's eyes. "We have to do *something*. We can't just leave her like this."

"We won't," Caitlin said, dreading her next words. "There's someone I can call. He's proficient in memory magic." Goddess knew, he'd said that very thing too many times to count. "If anyone can free Jesse, it's him."

"Who is he?"

Caitlin sighed and closed her eyes. "My ex-husband."

Aaron Lighter had intended to spend a quiet night at home – just him, a couple slices of pepperoni pizza, a few beers, and both volumes of *Kill Bill*. Nothing like artful slaughter to cheer him up. He'd been in a funk ever since that afternoon, when he'd finally made the decision to send Caitlin the memory box. He'd crafted it months ago, from selecting the proper solid cedar board and making the initial cuts to bend the corners all the way to etching the outer designs with complex wards.

Every cut he'd made, Aaron had thought of Caitlin Harris.

Adding the memory had been the easy part; he was no master woodworker, but his subtle magicks were his strong suit. And memory was extremely subtle. Malleable.

Maddening.

He laughed bitterly as he popped open the beer bottle. Sending the memory box was supposed to be cathartic for him. Cleansing. Instead, it had left him feeling oddly hollow, and painfully lonely.

Which, when he thought about it, was no different from how he'd felt when he'd been married to Caitlin.

No, that was unfair. She'd been the one to leave him, after all. One too many fights, and both of them too proud to admit their egos had smothered their affection. She'd left him, and he'd thought at the time it was good riddance. Two years later, she had still infected his heart.

When you compared love to a disease, it was time to take drastic measures. And so, he'd crafted the memory box.

He was on his second bottle and his second slice when his cellphone rang. He checked the number and took a healthy swig of beer before he answered. Of course she'd be calling. Probably to thank him, and then make some small talk, ask how his rituals were going, that sort of thing. That's all she was to him now: small talk. If he told himself that enough, he might actually believe it.

Swallowing his beer, he took the call. "Caitlin," he said by way of hello.

"Aaron." She said his name like she was spitting nails. "I know you sent the memory box."

He wasn't the sort of man to think *Well, duh*. But in this case, it was damn close. "Given the memory that was inside, I'd certainly hope so." He'd chosen it specially, out of all the time they'd had together. Goddess knew that after twelve years, there had been quite a few choice memories.

She let out an exasperated sigh. "Aaron . . ."

"Listen, you caught me right in the middle of something, so enjoy the present." He really wanted to watch some righteous murder right about now. Uma Thurman in a tracksuit was a bonus. Not that he was into tall, blond women with a thing for swords; he was much more about small brunettes with untamable curly hair.

He wondered if Caitlin still kept her hair pulled back in a ponytail, or if she let it go loose around her shoulders.

"Don't hang up," Caitlin snapped. "You messed up, Aaron. The box didn't go to me."

Aaron rolled his eyes. He didn't *mess up*, not when it came to memory boxes. While he enjoyed working various subtle craftings, the one area he truly excelled in was memory. Current actions defined a person only for the moment; memories defined them forever. "Of course it went to you," he said. "I was very specific when I crafted the package. I infused it with the essence of your dazzling smile and sharp tongue, dearest."

She sighed, clearly exasperated. "Aaron—"

"It couldn't *not* go to you. Besides," he added with a smile, "I felt it when you opened it."

Oh, he'd felt it, all right: the initial surprise, then a flood of lust so powerful it had given him a raging hard-on. He hadn't known Caitlin could feel *any* emotion that strongly. Maybe he wasn't the only one doing without sex.

"That wasn't me," Caitlin growled. "*Jesse* got the envelope. *Jesse* opened the box."

Her words hit him like ice water in the face. His mouth worked silently for a moment, until he finally spluttered, "You're joking."

"I wish I were. But I'm looking at Jesse right now." Caitlin paused, and Aaron could hear her grind her teeth. "She's trapped. Something went wrong, and she opened the box, and now she's trapped."

Aaron ran his fingers through his hair. Of all the possible ramifications he'd thought of when he had first crafted Caitlin's memory box – and he'd thought of just about everything, from Caitlin despising him to Caitlin throwing herself at his feet and begging for another chance – this scenario hadn't come up. Hell, this scenario should be impossible. But then, he admitted to himself, when it came to Caitlin's pseudo-sister Jesse, "impossible" didn't really exist.

He said, "Tell me everything."

She did.

By the time she finished, Aaron was sweating and his heartbeat was erratic. Caitlin had been wrong – he hadn't merely messed up. He'd fucked up, hugely. What was supposed to be a gift for his former wife had turned into a potentially lethal weapon against the one person the Hecate's followers had sworn to protect. The old saying was true: no good deed went unpunished.

"I need your help," Caitlin said.

Well, *that* had to kill her to admit. The thought made him smile. "I'll be there in twenty minutes," he said.

"It doesn't take that long to *step*."

"No, dearest. But it does take that long to get a cab." He paused. "I'm right here in New York, Caitlin. I left Salem after you walked out on me."

"Don't," she said, her voice sharp.

Caitlin never had liked hearing the ugly truth when it came to their relationship. Some things would never change. "Fine," Aaron said. "I'll get there shortly. Just don't touch her."

She snorted. "Tell me something I *don't* know."

"The address would be nice."

After Caitlin gave him the address, she said, "You could just *step* here and be done with it."

"Unlike some," Aaron said pointedly, "I don't like throwing around power when something more mundane does just as nicely."

"*Aaron—*"

"And taking a cab," he added quietly, "doesn't cost me a year of my life."

There was a long pause before Caitlin said, "Just get over here, Aaron." With that, she hung up.

Aaron dumped the leftover pizza and beer and turned off his television and DVR. He wasn't surprised that she had *stepped* all the way from Salem, even with such a high price to pay. Of course she'd come running to her sister's side. It's what Caitlin had been handpicked to do. Jesse was part of her life now – and Aaron was not.

The thought was distressingly bitter.

Steeling himself to work with his ex-wife, Aaron went to flag down a cab.

"I was starting to think that witches didn't travel like regular people," Paul said as Aaron took off his jacket.

"Female witches might not," Aaron confided. "But male witches tend to be more practical. We even ask for directions."

Caitlin bristled. She hated that Aaron looked so damn good, from his hazel eyes to his mop of sandy hair to the dimple in his left cheek. He wore all black, of course, from his button-up shirt to his slacks to his socks and shoes. His underwear – if he were even bothering with any – would also be black. She remembered that far too well.

Damn it. Stop thinking about him in his underwear. Or not in his underwear.

She did not find him attractive any more. Absolutely not. They were exes, formers, already-done-thats. She wasn't sorry that she was wearing her comfortable, baggy sweater with its shredded collar, or her well-worn sweatpants. No, not sorry at all.

He was by her side now, flashing his teeth. "Dearest," he said, offering his hand.

She wanted to wipe that smug grin off his face, but she forced herself to remain calm. Calm, calm, calm. She took a cleansing breath and blew it out slowly.

Yes. She was perfectly calm.

"Call me 'dearest' again," she said sweetly, "and I'll curse your hair to fall from your scalp and grow on your back."

Aaron threw back his head and laughed. "Still the charmer, Caitlin."

"Still a pompous ass, Aaron."

"*Hey.*"

Caitlin tore her gaze from Aaron to look at Paul, who was glowering at the both of them.

"Fight later," he said, his voice dangerously soft. "You're here to help Jesse. So make with the helping. *Now.*"

Caitlin felt her cheeks flush, but she ignored it. Paul was right. "Take a look at her, Aaron."

Her ex-husband walked over to where Jesse lay on the floor, and he squatted next to her. His lips moved as he cast a silent spell – Caitlin used to joke that if he were ever gagged, he'd never be able to work magic – and then white sparks flew from his outstretched hands and covered Jesse's form. After a few moments, the lights faded. The glow around Jesse's body remained a steady, soft blue.

"It's as you said. She's trapped in a memory. But it's not yours, as I would have thought." He glanced at Caitlin. "It's hers."

Oh . . . crap. Caitlin sank down on to the sofa and held her head in her hands.

"What?" That was Paul, sounding worried and angry. "What does that mean?"

"Jesse was a succubus for 4,000 years," Caitlin said grimly. "Three guesses what sort of memory she's stuck in."

"And the first two don't count." Aaron let out a strained laugh. "Sex and demons. This is going to be fun."

"Don't forget that she's an exotic dancer now," Caitlin added with a groan. "So that could be in there too."

"Sex, strippers and demons," Aaron corrected. "What's not to like?"

Oh, Goddess. There was no way Caitlin was going to survive this with her dignity intact.

"So," Paul said slowly, "what are you going to do? How can you help her?"

"We have to enter her memory and pull her out," said Aaron.

"You're making it sound simple."

"Hopefully, it will be." Aaron paused, and Caitlin felt his gaze on her. "She knows you, so I suggest that I anchor you."

Caitlin looked up at him. He was still smiling, but it looked forced. And what she had first taken as haughtiness sparkling in his eyes now looked more like worry. Not that she blamed him. The worst that could happen to her if she failed to find or free Jesse would be getting stuck in Jesse's memory. But the worst thing for an anchor, should the rescue go awry, would be death. Caitlin was a strong anchor, though. Chances were, she wouldn't die, even if things went terribly wrong.

"You're better at navigating memories than I am," she said. "Maybe it should be the other way around."

"Won't work. Jesse doesn't know me, so she won't trust me enough to shake her loose from the memory."

Caitlin couldn't help it; she barked out a laugh. "You think she'll trust *me*? She hates me, Aaron."

His smile slipped into something warmer. "That doesn't mean she won't trust you."

He had a point. Sort of.

"She's your sister," Paul said to her. "She'll listen to you."

Caitlin's lips twitched. For all that Paul was a good man, sometimes he was horribly naive. Even though he knew about Jesse's sordid history, he still believed she was a good person. He loved her, despite her faults. Paul and Jesse made it work, even though it shouldn't. A former succubus, in love with a mortal man bound for Heaven? Impossible. And yet, there they were, Paul and Jesse. Together.

"Together," she said to Aaron. "We can go in together."

He frowned at her. "That's not how it's done. One to enter, one to anchor. It can't be any other way."

"Just because it's not done that way doesn't mean it can't be done. Think about it," she said, imploring. "You're a strong navigator; I'm a powerful anchor. If we join, we can be both navigator and anchor, with all our strength combined. If we do it together, we have a better chance of getting to her quickly and pulling her free."

Aaron asked softly, "And how do you suggest we join, Caitlin?"

She blushed again, but she refused to look away. "I brought my ritual bag. We can call upon the Hecate to bless us and join us."

"Or we could do it the old-fashioned way."

Her eyes narrowed. "In your dreams."

"You mean, in her dreams." Aaron motioned to where Jesse lay.

"It doesn't have to come to that," Caitlin said tightly. "We're strong. We can fight it."

"Fight what?" Paul asked. "What are you talking about?"

"Sex," said Aaron, sounding horribly chipper. "Sex magic is the ultimate way to join essences. And sex is the only thing to expect when we enter the memory of a succubus."

"If I didn't know better," Caitlin said, "I'd think you were looking for a quickie."

"Strictly here for a rescue mission," he said, throwing his hands up in a universal Don't Hurt Me move.

Get a grip, Caitlin scolded herself. Maybe Aaron was her ex-husband, but he was also the best person to help her rescue Jesse. And that's what mattered right now: freeing her sister. She could deal – or not deal – with Aaron after.

"We're calling on the Hecate," Caitlin said, rising to her feet. As for what would happen once they were in Jesse's memory, well, they'd tackle that then. She moved to get her travel bag, and she pointedly did not think of having sex with her former husband, or how long it had been since she'd last had a lover.

Or how she still missed Aaron's touch.

"Terrific," said Aaron. "Nothing like getting a little Goddess-inspired bliss to really kick off an evening."

"Paul, you might want to go out," Caitlin said as she rummaged for her ritual kit. "There's no way to tell how long this is going to take."

"I'm staying right here," he insisted.

"I like a man who's into voyeurism," Aaron said with a grin.

Caitlin ignored him. "Then I'd appreciate it if you could please take your phone off the hook."

"Done," said Paul, marching into the kitchen to take care of it.

Caitlin glanced at Aaron. "Well then," she said. "Let's make some magic."

Aaron offered to help Caitlin set up the altar, but she was persnickety about anyone other than her touching her ritual items. Gosh, what a shock. He grinned as a memory flashed: the first time they were participating in their coven's circle, sky-clad by the light of the moon, the sound of a crack as an eighteen-year-old Caitlin Harris slapped his hand away from the ritual chalice. "For the Goddess," she'd said tartly. "No shit," he'd replied, chuckling even as he rubbed his hand. She'd glared at him, and he'd winked at her.

Three months later, they were dating. Two months after that, they were lovers.

She hadn't been his first. But by the Goddess, she'd been the best.

As Caitlin set up the items on the portable altar, Aaron worked on his breathing to help him prepare. *Pure thoughts*, he told himself. It would have been easier – and more fun – if instead of a formal ritual, Caitlin had agreed to have sex with him. She'd always been the perfect match for him, the high priestess to his high priest. When their bodies moved in concert, all in celebration of the Goddess, there was nothing they couldn't do.

But that had been back when she'd loved him. Anything that happened between them now would be strictly for the purpose of making magic. And that meant no sex. Caitlin wasn't into casual sex. Never had been, not even when the other coven members had taken advantage of sky-clad rituals and joined beneath the stars.

No, for Caitlin, making love had never been casual.

Feeling sad and bittersweet, Aaron breathed.

Next to her sister, Jesse lay prone, the memory box yawning open in her outstretched hand. *So much trouble*, Aaron thought, *for something that was supposed to be a gift.* Seated on the couch behind Jesse, Paul watched everything with curious, haunted eyes. Aaron didn't envy the man. Being in love with any woman was heartache enough. But in love with a former demon? That had to be a nightmare.

But then, given that Jesse had been a succubus, Aaron guessed the sex was damn terrific. That had him thinking about Caitlin again. Biting back a frustrated growl, he worked on his breathing.

Soon, everything was ready. Set on the altar were a silver chalice, pewter bell, a small metal cauldron, a bronze pentacle, a besom, a wooden wand, a black-handled athame, candles, a censer filled with incense, and a bowl of salt. Aaron usually didn't bother with such trappings, but given that they had to beg a blessing from the Hecate, he admitted it couldn't hurt to follow at least some of the protocol.

"Paul," Caitlin said, "some of what you hear and see may sound strange."

Paul grunted. "Lady, you stepped here out of thin air. My girlfriend is glowing blue. My definition of 'strange' is being rewritten even as we speak."

Aaron chuckled. He liked this guy. "Let's get on with it, dearest, so the intrepid boyfriend can get back to his regular life with his not-so-regular girlfriend."

Caitlin glowered at him. "Follow my lead."

"Ladies first," he said with a wink.

They began by casting the circle of protection, with Caitlin using the athame to draw four pentacles in the air, north and east and south and west. Aaron scattered salt in a large circle as Caitlin placed the candles in the directional points. She lit them from east to south to west to north, and Aaron felt it as she grounded the energy in the centre of the circle – a tickle of sensation dancing along his flesh.

He was very glad they weren't sky-clad now. Nothing like a boner to undermine the seriousness of the ritual.

Shaking away such thoughts, he invoked the directions and the elements, and Caitlin followed with an invocation of the

Goddess herself as she cradled the cauldron in her hands. Then the two of them raised their voices in song, praising the Hecate and asking to receive her gift of union.

What had started as a tickle soon became stronger, a gentle stroking, back and forth, like waves undulating over his skin. He was hyperaware of the sounds of his breathing, of his heartbeat, of the smells of burning candles and the scent of anticipation. He and Caitlin sang, their voices intertwined.

And then he felt Her presence – between them, around them. *Inside* them. The Hecate filled Aaron, infusing him with Her blessing. He threw back his head as his body reacted to his Goddess's seductive touch – his breath caught in his throat, even as his erection strained against his pants. Awash in pleasure, Aaron's senses stretched until he felt Caitlin's presence as well, from the fine trembling in her upraised arms to the sweat dotting her brow to the building desire that pearled her nipples and licked between her legs.

Blessed be, whispered the Hecate. And then She vanished.

Shaking, Aaron commanded himself to breathe. Goddess, he was ready to blow! The twin sensations of his and Caitlin's arousal made it impossible to think. He gritted his teeth, and he breathed.

"Now," Caitlin said, her voice thick.

Aaron and Caitlin clasped hands, his left and her right, and then together they reached over to brush their fingers over Jesse's head.

The shock was immediate – a surge of energy like none Aaron had ever felt before, a torrent of emotion and intention flooding him. Overwhelmed, he felt himself dragged under. He opened his mouth to shout, but he was drowning in magic, burning in Hellfire, lost in the power of the Hecate and the Underworld and sucked into a former demon's dream . . .

And then Caitlin yanked him back up, anchoring him in the here and now.

But it wasn't as simple as that. Yes, they were in Paul and Jesse's apartment, seated on the ground, their hands touching . . . but they were also floating in a world of grey, the colour somewhere between a soft dove and a winter sky, surrounded by thousands upon thousands of mirrors. They were both in the

Real and on the cusp of the Surreal, the place where memories and dreams mixed like cocktails. He blinked, and the real world was an after-image behind his eyelids.

Aaron, with his expertise in memory magic, was used to the Surreal. But he wasn't used to navigating the Surreal while still being anchored in the Real. It was damn disconcerting.

As was the sight of Caitlin's naked body.

Because they weren't grounded in reality while in the Surreal, her form was more of a sketch of Caitlin nude, all bold outlines and pale skin and black hair, with no contours to give her depth. Her eyes flashed emerald; her lips were a splash of cherry red. She reminded him of the Nagels in Paul's apartment, and Aaron wondered if Caitlin had been influenced by the art.

If so, he must have been as well. From the little he saw of himself, his flesh was just as white as hers. And as nude as hers.

Then again, it was possible he just had sex on the brain.

He shook his head to clear it. "That," he said hoarsely, "was not at all fun."

"I've been through worse." Caitlin sounded nonchalant, her expression giving nothing away. But Aaron was joined with her, so he didn't need his eyes or ears to tell him that she had been caught off-guard by the rush of magic and that even now, she was floundering. He read her emotions as easily as a scrying bowl: Caitlin was discovering that being both a navigator and an anchor was slightly overwhelming.

What was more unsettling to her, though, was how she was still sensitive to Aaron's touch, how just a nudge right now would send her over the edge and leaping into rapture.

Aaron, never the fool, pretended he didn't know. And he pretended he didn't care. "I'm sure you have, dearest. After all, you were married to me."

That got sliver of a smile out of her. "You read my mind."

No, not that. But he had her emotions down cold. And since she was joined with him, she had to know how he was feeling. What he was feeling.

How he wanted to touch her, hold her, kiss her.

"Well then," he said abruptly. "Let's get this rescue started, shall we?"

★   ★   ★

Caitlin had been in the Surreal before, many times. But she much preferred to be the anchor: firmly entrenched in the Real with only a cursory awareness of the miasma of winking mirrors that made up the Surreal. Those polished surfaces flashed hypnotically, beckoning to her.

Caitlin felt Aaron's impatience before he spoke – a benefit (or not) of being joined. "Don't look at the mirrors. Walk only where I walk."

She sniffed. "You just want me to watch your ass."

"It's a great ass, you have to admit."

Caitlin gave him her best Wicked Witch stare, and she firmly did not think about how great his ass really was.

His grin slipped. "I'm serious, Caitlin. Don't look at the mirrors. With the spell on the memory box distorted by Jesse opening it, the mirrors may not be passive."

Reluctantly, she nodded. If things had been normal – as normal as they could be in the Surreal – she could have gazed within any of the mirrors for as long as she liked, and she would have been treated to a view of a particular memory. But given how Jesse herself had been sucked into a memory, neither Caitlin nor Aaron could assume that they could look within and be unharmed. "You can find which mirror she's in?"

"Yes. Just let me concentrate, and then follow me." He frowned, then turned to the right. "This way."

They walked for what felt like forever, their footsteps whispering along the grey nothingness. To either side, and above and below them, mirrors glittered like diamonds. Aaron strode confidently, taking turns without hesitation, as he sussed out which memory had captured her sister.

She had to admit, he *did* have a great ass.

Caitlin turned her head away so that she'd stop looking at how his buttocks moved as he walked and stop thinking about how she had enjoyed caressing him, letting her fingers trail across his bottom and slowly make their way to his front. She had to stop thinking about him, damn it. She had to stop remembering how good he had made her feel, how easy it would be to just touch him, kiss him . . .

No. Stop, stop, stop.

Glancing over her shoulder – nowhere in sight of Aaron's terrific ass – she gasped as a mirror sparkled in front of her. And within, she caught a glimpse of her own face.

Not Jesse's copy of her face, no, but her own face – hers, Caitlin Harris, smiling. Not a reflection, but a memory. And Caitlin watched herself open her mouth and . . .

. . . *she says, "If you want another favour, Jesse, then you need to give me something in addition."*

The demon Jezebel stands before her, wearing a copy of her form, and she gives Caitlin a tiny, helpless smile. "You're right," she says. "I'll give you something."

And Caitlin feels that something *settle over her, a subtle tickle of desire. She sneezes once, and then she looks into Jezebel's face, her amazing face, and Caitlin feels her lids become heavy and her breathing quicken. Jezebel licks her lips slowly, suggestively, and Caitlin's lips part in return. She feels invisible fingers skimming over her body, and a sound escapes her mouth – the softest of ohhhs. Heat kindles in her belly and lower, blooms over her chest until her nipples are hard, ready to be suckled.*

Caitlin slowly unfastens one button of her flannel nightshirt. And then the next.

Jezebel's voice is soft as silk. She purrs, "Say my name."

Caitlin's fingers fumble the third button open, and her right breast pokes out from the gap in her nightshirt. In a breathy whisper, she says, "Jezebel."

And now she's lost in Jezebel's touch . . .

Until pain shattered the memory.

Gritting her teeth to keep from shouting, she stared daggers at Aaron. She pulled her arm out of his grip. The man had nearly dislocated her shoulder! How dare he . . . !

And then she realized what had happened.

She blushed fiercely. One slip. One small slip, all because she hadn't wanted to stare at Aaron's backside any longer. She could still feel the ghost of Jezebel's fingers travelling along her body, tracing her curves, heating her blood. The memory had been from two months ago, right after she'd brewed the potion that would transform the demon Jezebel into the mortal Jesse. Jezebel had tricked her, bespelled her.

Seduced her.

Caitlin gingerly rubbed her shoulder as Aaron glared at her. Rage was stamped on his features – but through their joining, she felt the fear that gnawed at his gut. He was furious with her, but also terrified by what had nearly happened. "When I say 'Don't look in the mirrors'," he snarled, "that damn well means don't look in the mirrors!"

"It was an accident," she said, hating how lame her words sounded.

"Penicillin was an accident! This was intentional!"

Her eyes narrowed. Yes, he was right to be angry with her; even so, she wouldn't be his whipping post. "Stop yelling at me."

She felt his emotions dance in quick succession: fury, frustration, relief, and something else, something she couldn't – or wouldn't – name. "Fine," he said quietly. "Keep your head in the game, dearest, or a memory will try to eat you again." He whirled around and stomped off, leaving Caitlin to hurry after him.

Stupid, stupid, stupid! She mentally slapped herself for being careless, and she slapped herself again for having to be rescued by Aaron. He'd never let her live that down. Damn it.

Well, at least he *had* rescued her. And now she was too mad to think about his ass. So that was all right.

Aaron came to a halt in front of a mirror. He was careful to keep his gaze on his feet as he reached out with his magic to confirm that this was it. And . . . yes, there. Jesse's spirit was somewhere within. He was amazed by how similar her soul felt to Caitlin's, and he wondered, not for the first time, if Caitlin had given Jesse more than mortality and a shared name two months ago.

Did they share a soul? If so, no wonder the memory box had gone awry.

But as he recognized Jesse's spirit, he also noted that it was too solid, too present within the memory. He frowned. Whatever she was reliving, it would be real to her. And it would loop continuously, keeping her sealed within while her body starved. Soon enough, she would die in the Real. Her soul would either fade or be locked within the Surreal – all because she had opened a memory box not intended for her.

It was an insidious trap. If he had done it on purpose, he would have been terribly impressed with himself.

"Got her," he said, turning to face Caitlin. Like him, she was purposely not looking at the mirror. "Remember: we go in, you go up to Jesse and wake her up. Do it fast, before the memory overwhelms you."

She nodded curtly.

"As soon as she wakes up, the memory will shatter. We'll launch ourselves out before everything winks out. Be ready for a hasty exit."

Again, she nodded. And then she did something that nearly dropped him on his ass: she kissed him. It was sudden, and passionate, and over far too quickly. A moment of heat and promise, and then she pulled away, leaving him rather dazed. "For luck," she said softly.

"Luck," he agreed, his head spinning. He steadied himself, then said, "Ready?"

Face pale, she nodded.

Then they stepped into the mirror . . .

. . . *and Aaron flinches from the intense heat baking his skin. The ground is flat and hot beneath his feet; he takes in a startled breath and he feels his throat char. And he knows in his soul that he's in Hell.*

Not me, *he tells himself.* This isn't happening to me.

Ahead of him is the biggest wall he's ever seen, and a pair of wrought-iron gates. Muffled sounds echo beyond the wall – screeches and moans and laughter and snorts and more, so much more, a cacophony of exclamations that make him want to clasp his hands to his ears. But this isn't real.

Not real.

In front of the gates, two demons are groping each other. Satyrs, both of them – the woman bald with cherry red skin and a curly black pelt, the man a bright turquoise and blond. Fire-red horns jut out from beneath his golden hair, and his eyes flash amber as he grins at the woman – the succubus. "Patience," the incubus says as he wraps his arm around her waist and crushes her against his chest. "Just a little taste first."

Not real.

He kisses her, hard, and Aaron sees, feels, their passion as she kisses him in return. Now the incubus is licking his way down her chin, tracing the lines of her jaw, teasing her collarbone with his mouth. She arches back, exposing her breasts, telling him with her body exactly what she wants him to do.

Not . . .

Aaron wants to pull his gaze away. But he can't. He watches as the demon sucks one of her nipples until she is writhing in his arms, her delighted groans like music. Now the incubus attends her other nipple, working on it with his lips and tongue, blowing on it.

Aaron is groaning, too, as the demons play. He feels their arousal, their need, and it sinks into his skin, setting him on fire. Panting, he watches the demons and slowly loses himself to lust, thinking of Caitlin as he wraps one hand over his shaft and begins to pump.

Hurry, *he thinks, but whether it's for Caitlin to hurry over to Jezebel or for himself to come, he couldn't say.*

The succubus' hands tangle in the demon's hair, and her hips roll as he sucks her, back and forth, first one nipple and then the other. His hand reaches down, snaking over the curve of her belly. Down more, trailing his fingers over her mound. Stroking her sex. She lets out a throaty growl – insistent, demanding, hungry.

Aaron growls, thinking of Caitlin, wanting her like never before. He wants to pin her to the ground and fuck her senseless. He wants to hear her squeal as he pounds her again and again.

Caitlin . . .

And now Caitlin is rushing past him, dashing over to where the incubus is prodding the succubus to orgasm. She throws her arm back and cracks her palm against the female's cheek. "Wake up, you stupid succubus!"

The incubus keeps fingering the female demon, who is looking at Caitlin with heavily lidded eyes and a lazy grin. "Heya, Sis," she says thickly. "Come here often?"

"Jesse Harris," Caitlin says in the way that siblings have mastered over the millennia, "you stop this right now!" She slaps the succubus again. "Come on, Jesse – it's time to wake up!"

No longer grinning, the succubus blinks. "What?"

"You heard me," Caitlin says, preparing to strike her again. "This isn't real."

This time, the succubus catches Caitlin's arm. For a moment, it looks like she might rip the limb from Caitlin's body. But then she cocks her head and looks at Caitlin, and then at Aaron, and then she considers the incubus, who's still playing her body like a fiddle.

"You're right," she finally says to Caitlin. "If this were real, Daun would be at least four inches bigger."

And like that, the succubus disappears in a puff of brimstone.

Aaron feels the lust recede just as everything around him fades out. Caitlin launches herself at him, tackling him to the ground . . .

. . . and Aaron opened his eyes. He was in Paul's living room, seated on the floor, Caitlin's hand in his. He stared at Caitlin, and he shivered from the vestiges of lust that danced along his body. He wanted to pin her to the ground and fuck her senseless.

No. That hadn't been real.

Yes. Yes it had.

Embarrassed and flustered and horny, he opened his mouth to say something, anything. But that's when Jesse propped herself up and said, "Sweetie, you look much better with your clothes off."

The coffee shop was fairly empty, which, for Manhattan, was a small miracle. Caitlin murmured her thanks as Aaron handed her an environmentally-friendly cup filled with steaming liquid caffeine. He sank into the chair opposite her, and for a few minutes neither of them said anything as they drank their coffee. No longer joined, Caitlin couldn't feel Aaron's emotions. There was no need; the damage, if that's what it was, had already been done.

She still wanted him. And she knew that he wanted her just as much.

But lust wasn't love. And love with Aaron hadn't worked.

Maybe it could work again . . .

No. And no.

With a sigh, Caitlin drank her coffee.

"So," Aaron said, "when are you heading back to Salem?"

She shrugged. "After this, I guess."

He gazed at her, drinking in her features. "You're drained, Caitlin. *Stepping* now isn't just a frivolous waste of a year of your life. It's potential suicide."

"I could do it," she insisted.

His mouth quirked a smile. "Of course. The great and power-ful witch Caitlin Harris would never risk casting a spell strong enough to bend the Universe's rules when she was falling-on-her-face exhausted."

"So dramatic," she said with a sniff. And never mind that he was right.

He reached over and touched her hand – hesitantly, even shyly. "Stay the night," he said, his voice soft. "I'll give you the bed, and I'll take the couch. But stay. Rest. And tomorrow, travel the old-fashioned way. I'll even drive you to the airport."

Her head swam. Aaron had no business being chivalrous, not when she was already on the precipice. He needed to be a jackass, a pompous jerk who thought the world revolved around himself. "You don't have a car," she said.

"Well, I'll put you in a cab." He squeezed her hand, once, then snatched his hand away. "If you don't want to stay with me, can you go back to Paul and Jesse's and stay there overnight?"

She shuddered. "Ugh, no. Jesse didn't even wait for us to leave before she started attacking Paul."

Aaron's eyes sparkled with mirth. "They were still dressed when we snuck out of there."

"A temporary condition, I promise you."

They shared a laugh.

"Stay," Aaron said. And Caitlin agreed – but only for the night. And as long as Aaron took the bed; she'd take the couch.

As Caitlin finished her coffee, Aaron put the memory box on the table. He'd grabbed it before they had made their unobtrusive exit – carefully ignoring how Jesse was eating Paul's face – and he'd carried it tucked under his arm as he and Caitlin walked to the coffee shop. Caitlin had noticed Aaron's fingers brushing it as she worked on her latte, saw his lips move silently. Now she stared at the ornately carved wooden box, and she marvelled how something so small and so beautiful could be so dangerous.

Aaron slid the box over to her.

"I fixed it," he said quietly. "It got all messed up when Jesse opened it, but it was easy enough to nudge everything back into its proper place."

Caitlin arched a brow and said nothing.

"It's just a memory box," he said. "Nothing nasty inside. No wicked surprises. It's for you."

She looked at Aaron, scanned his face for any hint of deception. What she saw made her feel horribly sad and tired and, damn it all, hopeful. She saw not the arrogant man but the young warlock she'd married, the man she'd once thought she'd love forever.

"Caitlin," he said. "Trust me."

And she did. With trembling fingers, she opened the box.

It's a summer night in the park, and grass is tickling Caitlin's bare feet as the tree leaves make music with the wind. She is eighteen and immortal, and she's intoxicated with the power of participating in the coven's circle. Thirteen witches, sky-clad in the moonlight and linked hand in hand, sing their praises to the Hecate, thanking Her for the gift of magic. Aaron's hand is so large, it swallows Caitlin's completely.

After, as the coven members dress or pair off to make their own sort of magic, Aaron and Caitlin linger in the clearing. His hand is still in hers, and he presses her knuckles against his lips, his tongue darting between her fingers. She blushes, both from the attention and from the way heat blooms in her breasts and belly. It's been two months since she and Aaron have started dating – two months of sweet kisses and curious hands, of a slow awakening of her body. She's not a virgin, but the boy who had taken that piece of her had been rough and uncaring. That boy had dumped her a week later to move on to the next girl, leaving Caitlin to wonder what she had done wrong.

Aaron is far from uncaring. In the eight weeks they'd been together, he'd made her laugh and made her furious. He is as passionate as she about magic, and he is funny and smart and sexy. But he is also cocky and arrogant, completely sure of himself even when he has no idea what he's talking about. Caitlin had been stunned to discover that she liked that about him . . . and even more stunned when she realized that he liked her as well.

Their first kiss still makes her lips tingle even after two months.

They had gone slow, with him letting her set the pace. Trust built, and attraction deepened, bringing them to tonight, to this moment – to Aaron, naked in the moonlight, kissing her hand and flicking his tongue against her knuckles.

Nervous, eager, she smiles at him and leads him across the clearing to a more secluded section of the park. She finds a spot near a cluster of trees, private and yet inviting, and she wraps her arms around his shoulders and stands on her tiptoes as she pulls his head down to hers.

The kiss begins softly, tenderly, as Aaron embraces her. His mouth is warm against hers, and she slowly melts in his arms. Now his tongue is nudging between her lips. She opens her mouth to him and his tongue rolls against hers.

His hands leave her waist to travel up her back, caressing, stroking. Warmth turns to heat as she feels those touches in other places, small sparks along her arms and chest and lower.

Caitlin moans, but the sound is eaten by Aaron's kiss.

Now his mouth is moving down her jaw, her neck, along the curve of her shoulder, his kisses damp on her skin. Back up along her throat, and now the shell of her ear, licking and teasing, kissing and nibbling, making her pant.

She wants this – just her and him, together, tonight. She wants him to touch her all over. She wants to explore his body and discover what he likes – what he loves.

She wants him.

Caitlin lowers her arms until they're circling his waist. As he's kissing along her jaw and her other ear, her hands move lower until they're skimming along his bottom. Lower still, until her fingernails graze the backs of his thighs.

His erection pokes her belly.

"Caitlin," he whispers in her ear, his voice husky. "Tell me. Tell me when to stop."

One hand still playing along his backside, she reaches up with her other hand to cup his chin. Her gaze locked on his, she says, "Don't stop."

He licks his lips before he asks, "You sure?"

"I trust you."

Something dances behind Aaron's eyes – excitement or arousal or maybe something else completely, and he says, "I trust you too, Caitlin." And then his mouth is on hers again, pressing hard now, bruising her lips with his own. Lower now, down her neck again until he's licking between the swells of her breasts.

Caitlin is breathing heavily, her chest thrust out, feeling her body flush. Aaron's mouth latches on to her nipple, and her knees buckle. He catches her, supports her back as his tongue licks that sensitive nub. Now the other nipple, coaxing it until it's as hard as its twin.

Deep inside her, something begins to coil, a delicious ache that quickens her breathing and makes her say his name.

His hand leaves her back, glides its way along her hip until it's resting on her belly. And he's sucking her nipples, first one and then the other, now kissing the swells of her breasts, mouth and tongue working against her skin. His fingers stretch down, whisper over her pubic hair.

She's rocking against him, panting, telling him with her body to do more. The ache within her increases to an insistent pressure, building as his hand moves farther down – slowly, so very slowly. Too slowly.

"Aaron," she breathes. "Don't stop."

His fingers slide between her legs, and she gasps. He's inside her now, probing, stroking, and she's bucking against him, her head thrown back and her eyes closed. And then he hits a spot that makes her blood catch fire. The coil winds tight tight tight . . . and she cries his name as the orgasm takes her.

Aaron slides his hand out, and now he's lowering her to the ground, and she barely feels the grass along her shoulders and back and bottom because she's still floating in bliss so sweet she never wants it to end. She hears something tear, like foil, and she looks up to see Aaron fumbling a condom over his erection. She tries to imagine which spell he'd used to make it appear out of nowhere but her mind is foggy and her body is pulsing with aftershocks, and Caitlin can't really think at all.

He pauses for a moment, standing over her as he drinks in her form, and the way he's looking at her makes her feel like the most beautiful woman in the world. "You sure?" he asks, his voice raspy.

She smiles up at him. "Yes."

Triumph shines in his eyes as Aaron climbs on top of her, and now he's kissing her and kissing her and kissing her as he moves on top of her, slides inside her, nudging that spot that makes sparks shoot behind Caitlin's eyes. Aaron is pumping inside her and she's moving with him, hips together, bodies fluid, up and down and up and faster and faster now as he's thrusting and she feels that amazing pressure build again, yawning up like a tidal wave inside her, up and up and up and just as she thinks she can't take it anymore, Aaron shouts her name and thrusts one final time and as he shudders against her, the wave crashes over Caitlin and she spirals down in rapture.

He sags against her, spent, grinning like a fool and laughing. "Caitlin," he says like a song. "Caitlin. Oh my Caitlin."

"My Aaron," she says, her voice thick and sleepy.

They lie there for a time, limbs entwined like pretzels, as their sweat cools beneath the glow of the moon. Caitlin has never been more at peace. She wants to thank him, but what she actually says is, "I love you."

And by the Goddess, Aaron replies, "I love you too."

It's the first day of what assuredly will be the rest of their lives together . . .

Caitlin blinked away tears as the memory ended. Closing the lid, she looked at Aaron, and the man she had once loved so very much, and she asked, "Why? Why this memory?"

A long pause as Aaron gazed at her, his eyes sad, the lines on his face suddenly prominent. And he said, "Because it hurt me too much to keep it any longer."

This time, Caitlin can't stop the tears.

"I still love you," Aaron says softly. "I wish I could just turn it off, or that it would have faded away. I wish I could say I'm not the same man I was when you left me, that I've changed. But I am who I am, Caitlin. And all the magic in the world won't change that."

She closed her eyes and remembered the boy she had loved.

She opened her eyes and saw the man who loved her still.

The man she still cared for, still wanted.

Still loved?

She bit her lip and reached over to take his hand. "We travelled to Hell to save my sister. Why is this the hard part?"

Aaron's lips twitched in acknowledgment, but he said nothing as he waited for her to pass judgment.

With her free hand, she brushed away her tears. "I don't want you to change, Aaron. I don't know what I want. But . . ."

When her voice faded, he prompted, "But?"

Caitlin took a deep breath. "But maybe we can both sleep in the bed tonight, and then take it from there."

Aaron's eyes shone, and he lifted her hand to kiss her knuckles. " 'Maybe' has never sounded so good."

Caitlin, smiling through new tears, had to agree.

They left the coffee shop, hand in hand. And soon they were making new memories together.

Princes of Dominion

Ava Gray

One

Just one glimpse. Camael knew it was unwise. He had been warned more than once and yet he found himself helpless to resist. Her beauty struck him on a level deeper than pleasure, deeper than pain. And so he stood on the other side of the Veil, hidden from her sight, and watched her brush out her long hair beside the river.

Most women bathed in company. Soft laughter and splashing would accompany their ablutions, but not hers. She was quiet, almost sombre; it did nothing to lessen her loveliness. Her hair shone like polished onyx, streaming down her shapely back in a swathe of dark silk. Sometimes she sang, and he closed his eyes, buoyed up by the melody. But not today.

For the first time, she spoke. "I feel you."

She could not possibly mean him. Camael held his silence.

"I know whenever you are here," she went on. "At first I took you for one of the river spirits, and I left gifts. But they went untouched."

Should he have accepted her tokens, then? She had left him seashells and beads, prettily strung. But he had no use for such things. He stilled, uncertain.

"Show yourself," she commanded.

His brethren would do worse than talk of folly if they witnessed what he did next. But he could not resist the urge to speak with

her. It went against every edict. Passing the Veil, he shimmered
into her world and donned a human body. She rose in a silver
ripple of water and turned to face him, clad only in her hair.

"What are you, river spirit or demon?"

"Neither," he said.

"Why do you watch me?"

"Because you are beautiful."

Such a simple answer – and yet it appeared to please her.
He could not have expected that, given how exotic she seemed
and how little he knew of mortals. Camael only knew that he
enjoyed watching them; they always seemed so much freer than
he, unconstrained by the rules of heaven.

"My father would cut off the head of any man caught dishon-
ouring me so." She tilted her head, speculative. "But you . . .
you are not a man."

"No."

"What then? You wear a man's form. Are you a devil come to
seduce me?"

Again, he said, "No."

But a flicker of interest stirred in him for the first time. It
was impossible to look on her silken skin without curiosity – to
wonder how it would feel to smooth his hands over her body.
And she sensed it; a smile curved her lush mouth.

"Pity," she said softly. "I do not think I'd mind. I am Rei."

"Camael." He found speech strange.

In the divine sanctum, they shared thoughts as a matter of
course. There were no secrets. But now, of course, he had one.
And that troubled him. Not enough to make him step away,
however. Not enough to send him fleeing through the Veil and
to find his archangel and beg for forgiveness. He was only a foot
soldier, he reasoned, one who followed orders. Nobody would
notice this breach. Nobody would care.

The woman pulled her long hair forward, so it cloaked her
breasts. He wished he were those tresses, teasing her nipples
with each breath she took. The force of the longing astonished
him; this must be the reason they proscribed wearing flesh.
With it came such shocking need. This was the first time he
had broken the taboo, and he reeled with inundation from all
his senses.

Warmth blew across his skin. With some shock, he realized he'd not clothed his form, perhaps because she wore nothing. In the realm from whence he came, such things were not needed. Everything was light and shadow and complete intimacy with every other scion. And somehow that still felt impersonal compared to the heat of the sun overhead, the chirp and buzz of insects and the soft whistle of wind in the reeds.

It was too much, and he stumbled, dropping to his knees. Beauty stepped towards him, concern overcoming her amused caution. "Are you ill?"

"Merely . . . overwhelmed."

"You truly do not spring from our world. Are you a god?" She seemed untroubled by that possibility.

Perhaps in her mythology, the gods regularly walked among humankind. Camael knew people entertained myriad theories about what beings populated the spirit world and the after-life. None of them was correct, but it did not stop them from building complex theologies and rituals. Such practices offered comfort.

"No."

"A messenger, then, for one of them."

Near enough. Explanations would require more concentration than he could muster at the moment. He nodded.

"Is that why you've watched me? Need you to deliver me a message?"

"That I did for pleasure alone."

"You would have me believe I own a beauty so great it distracted you from divine endeavours?"

"Yes." And it was true.

Even now he longed to touch her, with a need so great it burned like an endless fire in his veins. His fingers curled. He had no experience with self-denial. In the sanctum there were no such desires. In comparison, sanctum existence was pure and sterile, all ideas with no passion to fuel them. He had never noticed the lack before.

He must pass the Veil again before he changed irrevocably. It would be uncivil to vanish without a word, but better than the alternative. Better than—

Oh.

Rei touched him. Her soft hand on his bare shoulder drove all thoughts from his mind. Longing surged through him in a maelstrom of bewildering heat. He had never been touched before. It did not matter that his physical body was only energy held together by his will. He still felt it, and that caress altered him forever.

"If that is so," she murmured, "then surely I must reward you."

His head spun, and all thought of escape fled his mind. "How?"

She pushed him back gently; it did not occur to him to resist. The bank beside the river cushioned him with soft grasses and moss. The tall reeds hid them from sight. Overhead, the sun shone gold, sweet and hot on his skin, and the sky blazed with a blue so fierce it filled him with wonder. He had watched her in innocent fascination, and she had caught him, against all expectation.

She gazed down at him, eyes dark and hooded. "You are quite pleasing too."

Her hands travelled his body, stroking him with sweet surety. He gasped in shocked pleasure as she bent her head and set her lips on his skin. Camael had no words for how it made him feel. A soft sound escaped him, part arousal, part encouragement. He wanted – he did not *know* what he wanted.

But she did. She eased on top of him, slim and graceful in the sunlight. "You are passive for a godling. By rights you might have taken me as soon as I caught your fancy. Why do you hold back?"

Whatever he might have said, it was lost as her mouth claimed his. She was the goddess in this encounter, so sure of herself, so expert as her lips toyed with his. He did not even know how to respond, but she taught him with inexorable, rising excitement. When they broke away, she was breathless, her face flushed.

"I know," she whispered. "*Now* I know. I am your first."

"Yes."

"Give me a son. With your blood in his veins, he will conquer all he surveys."

Camael meant to tell her that was not possible, but she curled her hand around his shaft. The throb of pleasure nearly undid him. And this was only a close facsimile; how much more intense might he feel if he were, in truth, flesh and blood? He lifted up, pushing into her fingers.

She raised her hips and then sank down, claiming him with her fierce heat. The world broke apart and then reshaped itself. Like a force of nature, she rose and fell on him, head thrown back. He gazed up into her face, memorizing her features. Surely no creature had ever been so lovely.

"Rei," he gasped.

"Touch me too." She raised his hands and showed him how.

It was like being given a key to a secret kingdom. He belonged to her now as surely as if she had created him. She took him to a place where only her touch had any meaning, and by the time they both stilled, he knew he would never be the same.

She lay down on him, trembling, and he wrapped his arms around her back. Her hair felt cool in contrast to her heated skin. He closed his eyes and drank in her clean river scent and her womanly musk. He would remember this moment as only one of the host could – forever indelible.

"I must go," he whispered. "They will be looking for me."

"Camael. Come to me again." It was a plea, but it settled into his spirit as a command.

"Yes. As soon as I may."

Leaving her felt as though he had ripped himself in twain and left the other part, perhaps even the greater part, in her keeping. Yet he rose because he must – and duty drew him back to the divine sanctum. For the first time in Camael's memory, he did not wish to return. It was no homecoming; it was a burden.

Two

"You are late," Kenzo said.

Rei had never liked him, though he professed to want peace. His sire had killed her mother in the last raid, not that her father seemed to mind. Isuke was already looking at village girls for a replacement, some younger than Rei herself. It was disgusting, but it was also the way of the world. He needed to sire a son instead of a worthless daughter. Now Kenzo was here on diplomatic terms, talking to her father, who was village chief, about a permanent solution.

She had only been a widow for four months. It was too soon to turn herself over to another man's keeping, but she lowered her head as he fell into step with her, knowing she had little say in the matter. Rei led the way toward the wooden huts, the largest of which she shared with her father.

"Answer when I speak to you," he persisted.

"I lost track of time at the river."

"Have you taken a lover, Reika?"

How she hated for him to call her that. It was an endearment, and yet he dirtied it. Rei meant *lovely* and ka meant *flower*, but he meant it as a possessive, not a compliment to beauty. Her left hand curled into a fist and her nails bit into her palm.

"Would you not smell another man on me?" she asked in mock-humble tones. "Are you not the greatest warrior the Tanaka village has to offer? Surely your senses are superior to those of other men."

"You would do well to remember it. One day, you will belong to me, Reika. Your father will not listen to your sighs and your tears forever."

She smiled. "But today is not that day."

It angered him when she gave him her slim back and went into the house, where her father waited for his dinner. Courtesy dictated that she should have invited him in, but he was not her guest. Isuke could fetch him, if he wanted Kenzo's company.

"Have you given the marriage any thought?" her father asked, later. "Kenzo will rule Tanaka someday, and it would be good for our village, too. No more raids. No more death."

"Perhaps not from Tanaka," she said, stirring the pot. "But there is always death."

Three

The others had already assembled. Camael found Raziel waiting for him, impatient as always. His kinsman wore a frown. In the divine sanctum one could shape the energy however he wanted, and today Raz was tall and thin, the better to loom over one he perceived as derelict in duty.

Where have you been? he demanded. *Seraphiel has been looking for you. We have a new assignment, given by the Most High.*

But the moment Raziel's thoughts touched his own, they stilled. Incredulity radiated between them. He did not even try to hide his actions. There was no point. The host kept no secrets between them.

Cam . . . what have you done? You are—

Different, he supplied.

They will cast you out for this. It is not done. Not since Gabriel. All knew how that had ended. After the Morning Lord, Gabriel had been the first to fall in eons. He had done so, not out of hubris or ambition, but for a reason they found baser and more inexplicable – for love, for a human woman who would crumble to dust. So pointless, such a waste. Yet Gabriel's half-breed children had risen up to challenge mankind. The nephilim wars had required the host itself to intervene; such a march had never been seen on earth.

In light of that history, it rendered Camael's behaviour even more incomprehensible to his kinsman; this, he knew. He wished he could blame the woman – call her a sorceress – but what magic she owned came from her skin and her hair and her wiles, not some nebulous force. He understood now why Gabriel had given it all up. Here, one could shape the world to suit him. If he wished, he could recreate the river where he had lain with her, or he could stand in the hanging gardens of Babylon. Anything he could conceive, he could create. Despite that majesty, part of him – the half he'd left with Rei – still yearned towards Gabriel's path, even knowing it heralded disaster.

Raziel paced. *You cannot face Seraphiel like this. He will sense the stain on you immediately.*

Nor can I conceal it.

His kinsman acknowledged the truth of his statement. *That is why I am calling Nathaniel and Ezekiel.*

The other two who comprised their host arrived almost immediately. One could always recognize Ezekiel because he always painted a black circlet about his arm, still mourning Gabriel's loss. Everyone else preferred to forget, but Ezekiel had loved him. Once he had called Gabriel the best and brightest. Now Ezekiel refused to speak the Fallen's name, but he eternally wore the black band, not as an accessory but as an integral part of him.

Nathaniel favoured red, and so his hair glowed like a sunset. Though they could resemble anything they wished here, most often they kept to recognizable forms. Not that such meetings were necessary, but Seraphiel preferred them as a means of guaranteeing he had his audience's full attention.

As Raziel had done, the others saw the stain immediately. Nathaniel explored his memory, and Camael wished he had a way to prevent it. For the first time, he owned a thing he wanted to keep private. Then shame marked him at the impulse. They both drew back, shocked stillness in their thoughts.

And then from Ezekiel: *So I am to lose another brother.*

Not necessarily, Raziel countered. *We must teach him to shield.*

Nathaniel drew back, appalled. *That is not permitted to our host. Only the Thrones may—*

It is that, or lose him, Ezekiel interrupted.

Raziel faced their superior, as did Camael. As Ezekiel had the charge of them, it would be his choice, whether they attempted this forbidden thing. He would have faced his punishment alone, gladly, but joy suffused him that he did not have to. His host would not forsake him, no matter his transgression.

Can it be done so swiftly? Raziel asked.

By his expression, Nathaniel wondered the same thing. If Seraphiel grew impatient enough, he would touch their thoughts and summon them directly. Distance was nothing in a realm shaped by mind alone. The leader of the Seraphim, which took its name from him, could port them, should he so desire, and their wills would be unable to stand against him, for he was Seraphim, and they were mere foot soldiers.

Yes, their leader replied. *I once had occasion to commune with one of the Thrones. Because they mediate between the Most High and the rest of us, they must know how to shield, so they do not yield more knowledge than we are permitted to possess. I took that knowledge when I broke the bond.*

Why? Raziel asked.

Camael knew the answer even before Ezekiel gave it. *To save Gabriel. But he would not even try. He was proud of his sin. He wished not to hide his love.*

That boldness made Camael feel small. Was he so much less than Gabriel? Apparently he was, for he did not feel ready to confront Seraphiel and confess.

Let us have this thing done, Nathaniel said, some of his bright spark dimmed. *We must needs all learn to shield, for we all share Camael's secret now.*

Perhaps Nathaniel wished that were not so. It was too late for regrets; his host had made their choice. He felt the warmth of their acceptance, though it came without understanding. None of them could fathom his choice. And yet he regretted nothing.

In the end, it was simple: a shift, a twist, and the mind divided in two. This, one showed the divine sanctum. That hidden thing remained crouched like a beast, behind the brighter part. The ease made Camael question what the Thrones might be hiding. What if the Most High were not made of perfect goodness and boundless justice? What awful darkness might his most trusted servants conceal from the rest? Once tasted, doubt burrowed into his spirit, leaving hollows.

Let us go to Seraphiel, Ezekiel said.

And, as they had always done, they followed him.

Four

Time wore on.

Though Rei often went to the river alone, she did not see her golden god again. Her excuses about why she could not accept Kenzo and cement peace between the Tanaka and Nakamura wore thin. In her heart, she hoped their enemy's son would lose interest, or find someone younger. These days, she could no longer be considered in the flush of youth. She no longer danced in the cherry blossoms with the young virgins. Instead she sat silently weaving with the old women.

At length, Isuke married his bride of choice. The girl had sixteen summers . . . and she was silly. Hana did not know how to cook rice or clean a home, or how often the straw needed to be changed for use in bedding. She only knew how to smile prettily.

That would not be enough. If she did not give him a son, then she would go as Rei's mother had done. In the dark of night, she sometimes wondered whether her father had asked his enemy to rid him of the wife who bred nothing but girls and dead babies. None of Rei's sisters had survived to adulthood.

Still, it was too beautiful a day for such dark thoughts. Rei watched the dancers and listened to the trilling flutes. The smell of roast meat wafted on the summer wind, carrying the scent of hydrangeas. By this time, the azaleas were in bloom as well, like a stormy twilight. Rei strolled away from the festivities, avoiding the pantomime and the boy begging for sweets with tugs at his mother's robe. It was good to see everyone in the village happy, even if such carefree days were coming to an end for her. With an inaudible sigh, she curled up beneath the purple fringe of the wisteria tree.

Kenzo found her, as he always did. There had been no attacks from Tanaka since he had been paying court – with her father's approval. Now that Isuke had wed Hana, he would want her out of his house, and their old enemies would take it badly, should she give her favours elsewhere. No, there had long been an understanding. Rei only needed to make peace with her fate, and say farewell to what had been nothing more than a girl's foolishness, lost in dreams by the river. Only in sleep could she have found such perfection.

The real world offered pots to scour and fields to tend and oxen to track down when they went astray. And Kenzo. The world offered her Kenzo as a husband. In truth, there were no other suitors. Too long had passed.

He sat down beside her, darkly pleased with himself, and set his hand on her arm. His touch filled her with revulsion, but soon he would have the right to do with her as he chose – beat or kill her – at his pleasure. Rei had no doubt he would brook no repudiation of his will. Kenzo would offer no choices. Most likely, he would also make her suffer for keeping him waiting so long. As the Tanaka's firstborn son, he loathed being denied what he believed to be his due.

"When?" he asked softly.

She did not pretend to misunderstand. "It will be an autumn wedding, when all the leaves turn red."

Kenzo offered a sharp look, for red was a dual color. But he did not demur. "So it shall be, Reika."

Five

To convey his displeasure, Seraphiel greeted them in a huge cavern with a ceiling so high it appeared to be made of darkness. Jagged streaks of lightning crashed overhead, highlighting the stark rock. Other times, this place might appear to be all white, formed of nothing but marble pillars. The leader of the Seraphim was not to be crossed lightly.

First he kept them waiting, and then he manifested in a font of golden light. *When I call, I expect obedience.*

Apologies, Ezekiel offered.

It took considerably longer to appease Seraphiel, and for every moment, Camael expected him to know, but the shields held. And Ezekiel intended for them to maintain this deception for eternity? Impossible. He already felt sick and shaken, not by his actions, but the subsequent efforts to conceal them. No matter the regulations, touching Rei did not *feel* like sin.

At length, they took their orders and went from the divine sanctum. They shook the mountains and painted the sky red, as instructed. It seemed like a great deal of effort in order to change one man's mind, but they did not question instructions handed down through the hierarchy. Even Seraphiel did not know the reasons behind the commands he gave.

Afterwards, he followed the rest of the host. Once – not long ago – privacy mattered not at all. Now it was crucial. As he watched, Ezekiel shaped the wards that would keep others away. Let them think they discussed some secret orders given by Seraphiel, handed down by the Thrones.

Despite their success, Ezekiel wasn't pleased. *We must live this way forevermore. You all accept this?*

The alternative is losing him, Nathaniel responded.

Raziel kept even his thoughts to himself, but of them all, he had been closest to Camael, and he could read his kinsman's brooding silence. He was blisteringly angry. *I never asked for help*, Camael thought. *I would have taken my punishment and left you out of it.*

And you truly think I could allow that? Raziel demanded. *Of us all, you would be destroyed down there. Did you know people call you Camael the Innocent, even here, where* all *are pure?*

He hadn't known that, and it angered him. *Innocent I may have been, but I am not helpless.*

No, Raziel responded. *Just stupid.*

Enough. The force of Ezekiel's thought silenced them both. *We acted to preserve your secret. You must go now to this human woman. Tell her whatever you must, but there will be an end to it.*

He had watched the Morning Lord's fall, once the most beloved and beautiful. Later, he had seen Gabriel willfully turn his back on his host. Neither hurt so much as the prospect of this – and he did not know why. Only that an ache throbbed deep in the core of him at the prospect of bidding farewell to a beauty he had hardly known.

I will attend to it now.

With a twist of his will, he left them. It was too much to hope he would find her where he had before, and yet that was the first place he looked. Camael matched his appearance to what she had seen before; otherwise, how would she know him? The river had risen since his last visit, which signified rain. How much time had passed? He stood quietly, listening to the water tumbling over the rocks. The trees were a little thinner, somewhat less green, and the air carried a chill. This was the dying season, when the leaves fell, and the world spun toward winter.

It was too cold for bare skin and he thought clothing into existence to cover himself. Not because he felt discomfort on any crucial level, but if another traveller came upon him here, they would call him demon or worse, finding him tarrying so. For the first time, it occurred to him he did not know how to find her. While he could focus on her essence and port to her, it might prove awkward if she were in company. He did not want to cause problems for Rei, or offer trouble she could not explain away.

And so he sought shelter in a cave not far from the river, where he built a fire. It was easy work, a matter of laying wood and willing it to kindle. He could have had fire without fuel, but that too would alarm human travellers. Camael wanted to blend in as best he could. Once he had created a tolerably comfortable space, he sat and sent the call. If Rei felt anything for him, she would be compelled to seek him out. The delay gave him time to accustom himself to her world. This time, he would not be helpless and overwhelmed by so many physical sensations.

On the third day, she found him. She looked different, less girlish. He had no way to gauge the passage of time here.

"It's you," she breathed. "And you have aged not even a day."

He'd wondered if she remembered. He had wondered if he ought to come and tell her there could be nothing more. Perhaps she already knew. But his conscience would not permit him to share such intimacy and then offer only silence thereafter.

The right words – words of farewell – trembled on his tongue and yet he did not speak them. "Did you miss me?"

"Yes," she said softly. "But when I did not quicken, I thought I dreamed you."

Would that were so – then he would not feel the awful sensation of being torn in two. He carried Ezekiel's orders like a weight in his heart, but for the first time, he struggled against them. Camael did not want to obey. He craved a few more moments with her.

"I cannot get you with child," he said, instead of good-bye.

"Because you are truly not of my world."

He inclined his head.

"Then it is safe for us to be together." Before the fire, she began to disrobe. "I relived that afternoon so many times. Nothing ever felt so good or so right."

This was where he *must* tell her. But instead, he admired the curves of her body, no longer sylph slim, but rounded and succulent. "Rei . . ."

"You make my name sound like singing. No one ever did before."

When she threw herself into his arms, he was lost, oh, so lost. Camael wrapped his arms about her. He had not touched her thoughts as he did with the host, and it mattered not at all. He knew her. The ache he hadn't been able to explain before intensified into longing, and then he recognized it.

"I missed you." Such longing for an absent person; it was wholly new to him.

Six

"And I, you."

It had been almost five years since she'd first felt him watching her, nearly three since she had lain in his arms. Yet she had never been able to forget him. Rei wondered now whether she was mad. Her father had at last broken down her will to refuse the marriage, and in two weeks' time, she would become Kenzo's bride. An alliance between the two villages would improve life for all concerned.

No more raids. No more burning houses or dead livestock. Thus she had been told, over and over again.

So what was she doing here, breaking her vows for a golden dream that had come to seem no more real than the touch of the breeze upon her skin? The answer was simple: she could not deny him. He lived in her blood, like a fever. Yet she could not blame him for what had passed between them. She had seduced him, and if she were honest, that sense of power offered great allure. In her village, she had little, even as chieftain's daughter. But she had bewitched this impossibly powerful male – and that certainty was heady.

Just once more, she told herself. *Kenzo will never know.* He had not been promised a virgin bride, after all. Rei had married young, and her husband perished of fever. She had been a widow for some months before she encountered Camael by the river, else she would not have known how to seduce him.

But this time, it was different. She sensed it even before he put his arms around her. He was more centred, more sure of himself. Rei did not yet know what that change signified.

He kissed his brow to hers. "I want to know you."

Rei thought it a poetic way of asking to make love to her again, so she nodded. Suddenly her mind filled with him, every small shame and unworthy secret – he possessed them all. The moment she tried to resist, he went away again, leaving her alone, and that might be worse.

"What—"

"I thought you gave permission."

"For *that*?" It seemed wholly more intimate than sharing her body.

"I wanted to know you this time, before . . ."

Before they made love. She understood the impulse, though in her experience, such knowledge came in small trickles, not in a single brush of their minds. But she knew him now, too, and he was unquestionably alien. He had touched no women in this world or any other. Rei could not have explained why that excited her; only that it did. It lit a fire unlike any she'd ever known.

But even so, she wasn't the aggressor. This time, she could tell he knew what he wanted. His mouth claimed hers, tender but implacable as well, as if his kiss branded her. Madness. Though she had been free three years ago, she was no longer. And yet she could not refuse him. Did not desire to, no matter the cost later. She had been like a shade, echoing the memory of life after vitality had fled. Only in his arms did she kindle beyond that pale shadow.

As he kissed her throat, she shivered. When he stroked her inner thigh, her legs fell open in welcome. There was nothing so divine as a godling slaking his desire. Her breath hitched as he traced the curve of her hip and nibbled behind her ear. Then he slipped his hand around her body, playing with her right breast.

But he wasn't as sure as he pretended. In the firelight, his oddly innocent eyes asked reassurance. "You like that?"

Mutely, she nodded, not sure if she could speak. Rei's husband had never taken such care with her. Sometimes she wanted the mating, and sometimes she didn't; it had all been the same to him. In her world, men most oft felt so. They held all the authority. Despite his otherworldly power, the same did not hold true with Camael. She marvelled at that, even as he caressed her. It seemed to her she had never truly known free will before.

He paused, holding her arms to the light. "Who did this?"

"Kenzo."

The Tanaka's firstborn saw no reason to be gentle with a woman. He used his strength instead. Camael bent his head and pressed his lips to the marks. As she watched, they faded with a god's power to heal. Rei wanted to weep, but instead she answered with a kiss to his throat.

The firelight permitted her to see his response – awe gilded his beautiful face, even as much as the fire did. He revelled in her pleasure and his own ability to invoke those feelings. His lips followed his fingers: full of delicacy, demand, and burgeoning confidence. The heat against her skin was delicious and unexpected; his mouth sliding along her curves made her scrape

the soles of her feet against the rock. Groaning in response, he
licked until her nipple stood erect, begging for his attention. She
cried out when he sucked it into his mouth and teased her with
his teeth.

"Tell me what you want now," he murmured, sounding odd
and hoarse.

Unbearable tension rose within her as his golden head surged
between her breasts. She did not notice when he slid the robe
completely away, baring her body. Aware of a momentary lapse
in contact, her senses swam as she tried to focus and received
only the sweet shock of his hot skin against hers.

Dipping his fingers into the slick, swollen folds of her feminin-
ity, he stroked her, making her hips lurch up to meet him. He
found a place that felt to her as if he held lightning against her
flesh. Rei tested him in turn, fingers stealing down his abdomen
and curling around his man's flesh. He bucked, strain evident
in his face. For long moments, he worked against her cupped
palm, moaning with each push.

Oh, now, my love. Now.

She was ready, so ready. But to her surprise, he did not cover
her. Instead he slid lower. Since he was innocent, he must have
taken this from her darkest and most secret fantasies. No man
would stoop to perform this intimacy for a woman. But a god
would. Only such a one could possess the self-assurance to
humble himself so.

"Camael!" she cried as his mouth found her.

Rei clutched his head, fingers tangled in his gilded hair, and
rocked against his mouth. He licked her, just so. Climax shook
her, head to toe. Giving her no chance to recover, he slid up and
pushed inside. Once, twice, thrice, he thrust, making her moan.
He wrapped his arms about her hips, dragging her up to meet
each push and she locked her legs about him. His fierce beauty
almost hurt her eyes, seeing his intensity so focused on her body.

Her second peak crashed almost as hard as the first, coming
in relentless spasms, and it drove him over the edge. Though
her own satisfaction had been staggering, she still knew when
he shook in the familiar response. But she had never been so
fiercely glad of it before. Her husband had used her body,
but only Camael made her feel *this* way, and she took visceral

pleasure in maddening him in the same fashion. He offered no accompanying gush of seed, however, and she regretted the lack. It was the only imperfect part of their union.

She did not protest when he rolled to the side and wrapped himself about her for warmth. With him at her back and the fire at her front, she felt the cold beyond their private haven not at all. But the world would intrude soon enough.

"I heeded your summons this last time," she said softly. "But I can come to you no more. I have made promises to others, now."

"Yes. I saw that in you."

Of course he would have. How could he *permit* it? Why wouldn't he take her away, back to his godly palace, and keep her there for himself? Yet those were not questions she could ask, and so she swallowed the pain like a shard of broken pottery.

"Rei . . . according to the rules of heaven, this is wrong. I am not to have you. Not to do what I have done. Twice now. Twice the sin." He did not sound as though he felt guilty, though, merely sad beyond bearing.

"So you will not call to me again, either."

"No." He laid his head on her breast, ear to her heart, as if listening to what she could not say. "But *if* I did, if I found a way, would you give up everything for me, Rei of the River?"

"Yes." There was no hesitation in her, only a broken kind of longing, because the fierce desperation of his arms about her in this moment did not speak of hope. Instead it betokened an impossible love and inevitable ending.

Seven

Did you end it? Ezekiel asked.

They awaited his return together, converging as soon as they felt him. Camael did not need to answer. As soon as he let them touch his mind, they knew. Nathaniel filled with sorrow while Raziel boiled with anger. From Ezekiel, he sensed nothing, not even surprise. Doubtless he saw only history repeating itself. He had walked this road with Gabriel.

You endanger all *of us with this madness,* Raziel accused.

Nathaniel stared at him, sombre as he rarely was. *He is right, brother. Do you think Seraphiel will forgive our involvement?*

I shall not, the Seraphim intoned, manifesting.

The time had come, then. For himself, he cared remarkably little. Camael only wanted to return to Rei before she married the man who had put the bruises on her arms. He cared nothing for the dramas of heaven any longer. Still, he could not let his host suffer for his sins. He had to try.

I acted alone, he told Seraphiel. *They knew nothing. Only I must Fall.*

The leader of the Seraphim sent angry amusement arcing into his thoughts like a lightning bolt. It stung, as intended. *Do you take me for a fool? I saw through your shields immediately. I only wanted to see how complete the conspiracy. And so I have. Your whole host is corrupted. They will pay.*

A flaming blade appeared in Seraphiel's hand, rippling with awful blue fire that gave no heat: the Sword of Judgment. With it, he tapped Ezekiel on the shoulder. *Ezekiel, your loyalty to your host proved greater than your love for the Most High. I know you yet mourn Gabriel's loss, so I bear good tidings.* The grim glee that accompanied the thought sent a wave of horror through Camael. *You may now join him, as the leader of these Fallen. If you can find him. If he yet survives. I know you, Ezekiel. You feared the Fall as nothing else. For our kind, it is the closest thing to death. And so I give you dominion over it. I give to you power over death and transformation. They will beg you for clemency, those dying and doomed, and you will offer none. May it bring you nothing but pain to be known as the Merciless Archangel when your secret heart is so tender.*

Camael thought he would run Ezekiel through then, but no. They had conspired together; thus they would die together. And the Seraphim had not finished sentencing them for their crimes.

Seraphiel spun to face Nathaniel. *To you, Fallen, I give responsibility for fire. This force can be used for cleansing or destruction. You will spend eternity weighing the difference, judging what must burn, what should rightly burn. Since you were the gentlest of us all, it will be a just punishment, and for each wrong judgment, you shall receive a scar. You will know agony* beyond imagining, *Nathaniel.*

And you, Raziel. The Seraphim pointed the Sword of Judgment. *Who first plotted to hide this transgression from me. I find it fitting to give to you the mantle of mysteries. From this day hence, you will be charged with keeping divine knowledge from the mortal world. They must not know of us, see us, or hear of us. You do so love your secrets, do you not? And this responsibility will give you the most contact with humans – and I do know how you love them. You will clean up for them forevermore.*

Finally Seraphiel came to a stop before Camael. He stood straight and steady against the terrible threat of the sword. *You had carnal knowledge of a human woman and sought to hide it. You put base pleasure before your vows to the Most High. So then, Camael, I charge you with joy.* That did not sound terrible, but then the Seraphim continued. *You will be responsible for making sure the world stays in balance – that those who ought to be happy, are, even when* you *are not. In time, it will become . . . excruciating. I only wish I could be there to see the moment when you realize I have placed upon you the heaviest burden of all. You craved the pleasures of earth, and so I bestow them upon you. You were once princes of heaven; now you are only princes of dust, princes of your small dominions. You are exiles, henceforth, never again to know divine peace. Go forth, Fallen. I cast you out!*

Seraphiel swung the Sword of Judgment in a wide arc, and the fire cut them wide open. Beneath their feet, a chasm opened, and then they fell. Pain became Camael's only awareness. The world washed red.

Eight

As Hana plaited her hair, Rei faced the truth. He was not coming. She had been a fool to place her hopes in a god's hands. Surely she should have learned by now that they did not care. If anything, they saw this world as a place to come and play, where pleasures might be shared and then forgotten.

He had not promised; he'd only said *if I find a way.* It seemed impossible that there existed a force that could hinder the will of a god, but then, he had also said he was only a messenger. So perhaps he was not important enough to break free whenever he chose. Perhaps he too had responsibilities.

She bore fresh bruises on her back, but her wedding clothes hid them. Kenzo had tried to take his rights as a husband the night before, and she'd fought him. Not before tonight. And so he'd taken his satisfaction of her in another way – with his fists. He truly might have killed her if Hana had not heard her cries and tiptoed to see. Though she was a silly girl, she was not heartless and she had run to fetch Isuke.

"She is not your bride yet," her father had said. "While she remains in my house, you will treat her with respect."

For a long moment, she'd dared to hope her father would call off the ceremony. But no. He needed the Tanaka alliance, so he must abide by the agreement. This was no more than a temporary respite, as Kenzo stormed out. They both knew she would pay dearly for her final night of peace.

"I am sorry for you," Hana said then. "I wish he was a kind man, like Isuke."

"It will help the village. I am only one woman, after all. And if I die in Kenzo's care, Father will have a legitimate grievance. The Tanaka will owe him blood money, so my death may serve better than my life."

"All the same," her stepmother said. "It is not my wish for you."

"Nor mine. But we cannot have our dreams come true."

If she could, a golden-haired godling would come to smite her enemies and carry her away to his palace in the sky. Instead she sat still while Hana finished her hair and pronounced her ready. "There has never been a prettier bride."

Untrue. But she forced a smile; she would not wear her misery openly. She was the only living daughter of Isuke of Nakamura, and she would honour him by going to her fate with courage. As Kenzo's wife, she would not live long. She had antagonized him and shown she had too much spirit, too much of her own mind.

It was hard to contemplate her own death. Rei stood, raised her chin, and followed Hana out of the hut. But as she trod the petal-strewn ground, she heard the call for the second time, like a flute inside her head and trilling in her veins.

He had come. Against all odds, he had come. If she fled with him, the village would suffer. They needed her to seal the peace with Tanaka. Rei shook her head; she had never craved the role of martyr. Then she lifted the hem of her wedding robe and began to run.

Nine

Death. In an agonizing eternity, Camael felt all he was cease to be. The cessation of his divine self hurt more than he could have imagined; as though Seraphiel had rammed the Sword of Judgment through the middle of his soul and he'd come away lesser and smaller. That might be an apt comparison.

Covered in blood, he pushed shakily to his feet. As before, he was naked, and it was cold. But this time, he felt it. The flesh he wore felt heavy and awkward, a meat cage that housed his spirit. Camael took stock of his surroundings, and with some amazement, he realized he'd Fallen beside the river, where he first saw beauty. Of the others, he found no sign. Were they to be punished then by spending an eternity of exile alone with their sins? He longed to see the rest of his host and beg their forgiveness for what his desire had cost them.

He had no way of knowing how long it had been, how long he had suffered in earthly terms. It might have been years, again. She might have forgotten him. He knelt beside the water and washed as best he could. That done, he knew he could not leave this place without learning the truth. Rei was the reason he was here. It was unthinkable to go into exile without knowing.

Now, he needed a fire for warmth instead of comfort, but time might be short. Closing his eyes, he sent the call. While he waited, the chill sank in, raising bumps on his flesh. How he wished he had something to cover himself. He had once thought humans did it to hide their shame, but now he saw there was a more practical reason.

The waiting seemed endless.

And then he heard the soft crackle of dry plants crushed beneath running footfalls. Camael was in no condition to fight, but he recognized her movements even before she burst into sight around the bend in the river. Rei wore a complex robe, layered in sashes, and her hair had been intricately arranged.

"We must go quickly," she said, breathless. "I will be missed soon."

Go where? She knew more about this world than he did. Camael had no idea where they might be safe from her pursuers. The only place he could find readily would be the cave where they had sheltered together and made love. Though he was vague on the concept of distance, that would not be far enough away. His whole body burned with cold, and he could not think.

She drew up, staring at him with furrowed brow. Her dark eyes raked him head to toe, taking in the differences. "You're real this time."

"Yes," he said. "I will not be leaving you again."

Rei froze, terror dawning on her lovely face. "I need you to take me away from here. They will kill you. And me." But it was clear from her expression, she feared more for him.

Camael went to her then, his uncertainty easing. He took her in his arms. "Fear not. Though I have Fallen, I am not powerless."

In his heart, he sensed the scales Seraphiel had inflicted on him, weighing the generosity of her spirit against the circumstances surrounding her. The verdict was clear; Rei deserved to be happy – and she was not. Camael sensed the bruises on her back, more serious than the ones he'd healed on her arms. Someone had hurt her and would do worse, if he permitted it.

But *he* could make her happy. Perhaps he twisted the spirit of the intent, but the Seraphim had given him room to make his own judgments. And so he would.

But before he could make any plans, he heard the sounds of pursuit. These footfalls were unfamiliar to him, but Rei stilled in his arms. Her upturned face reflected pure dread; she thought him helpless.

"Run," she begged.

The man who burst into sight carried a curved blade. Like Rei, he was dressed in formal regalia, his long black hair upswept. And Camael knew he was also the monster who hurt her. Guilt and fury bled from him in red-black rays, surrounding him like a tainted sun. This one did *not* deserve joy – and Camael had the power to sever him from all possibility of attaining it.

"I knew you had taken a lover," the angry beast spat. "And he is not even of our people. You shame your father, Reika."

She glared at him. "Do *not* call me that, Kenzo! You have no right."

"How will you stop me? I have all the power. I am the Tanaka's firstborn, and I have been wronged. No one will speak a word in protest when I order the two of you executed. See how your beloved cowers."

Camael stepped away and gently set her from him. He spoke to Kenzo. "You have brought nothing but misery, even to your father. Your mother died bearing you. You are the very soul of grief."

For the first time, the other appeared shaken. But he rallied, raising his sword. "Words. You have only words." And Kenzo charged.

Camaek raised his arm and plucked the air with his fingers, latching on to the immortal part of the man who hurt Rei and took pleasure in it. Instead of silver or gold, his life-thread unravelled black and red like the aura blazing around him. This was the right thing; the scales in his heart agreed. It was a fair judgment. With one final tug, he drew the soul out and set it wafting in the air. Its weight would decide its final destination. As with all mortal spirits, it tried to soar, but sin weighted it down, and Kenzo's soul drifted down into the earth and beyond his knowledge. His body fell, empty and lifeless. The sword clattered to the ground.

"There will be war." Rei sounded numb. Not with grief, but shock. "What magic have you that you can slay a man with a turn of your wrist?"

"Only that of judgment. He stood in the way of your happiness."

"And you think his murder will bring me contentment? What manner of monster are you?" She backed away, her slippers sliding on the damp grass.

"Did you love me better when I was not real?"

"I think I did not know you at all."

"Yet I Fell for you. I gave up everything. You said you would do the same. Did you lie, Rei?"

A sob broke from her. "I – no. No matter what you have done, no matter what it costs me, I love you still. My heart beats for you, whatever dark thing you are."

Camael smiled, aching for her. She was still – and always would be – the most beautiful woman he had ever seen. "It will cost you nothing. Watch."

He knelt beside the dead man and touched his fingers to his face. It was a simple task, hardly more than a flicker of energy.

When he stood, he *was* Kenzo. He stripped the robes, dressed, and took the man's sword, and then he nudged the body into the river. The water claimed it.

"You will take his place," she breathed. "There will be peace."

"None will ever know but you. Does this bring you joy?"

"Yes. I never imagined I could keep my home *and* be with you. I thought there would be a terrible choice."

There was, Camael thought. *And I made it for you.*

She kissed him with all the passion she had given him before. Now he could have it for a lifetime. *Her* lifetime. He would accept the consequences later; he knew now what punishment Seraphiel intended for him. His damnation would be deferred. In centuries to come, he must find the rest of his host – and possibly Gabriel as well – but he would make her happy while he could. Such a short time. How diabolical the leader of the Seraphim – and how clever. But today was not for suffering. Not today.

"Let us marry," he said aloud to Rei. "I think that is why we are dressed so."

Her smile nearly blinded him with its delight. Taking his hand, she led him towards the village and their life.

Spirit of the Prairie

Shirley Damsgaard

R.J. Baxter stood on the bluff overlooking the waving prairie grass and cursed fate. A reporter for *The News Courier* in Michael's Creek, South Dakota, her editor had sent her out to do yet another "fluff" story. The opening of a cultural center on the Talltree Reservation stretching out before her.

She'd done her research. She knew all about the "lost generation" of Native American children – children who had been rounded up back in the 1940s and carted off to schools run by white missionaries. It had been an attempt at forced assimilation into the white culture and had failed. Its victims were left with feelings of not belonging to either society. When they were finally allowed to return to their people, they knew nothing of their heritage or language. Alcoholism ran rampant. Now their grandchildren were trying to change all that by instilling pride in the next generation, and the new cultural center was the means.

R.J. didn't need another human-interest story. She needed a juicy murder, a natural disaster, a political scandal – anything to get her out of the bush leagues and bring her work to the attention of a major newspaper. She had talent, but it was wasted writing endless stories about church bazaars and one-candidate elections whose outcome was long decided before the first vote was ever cast.

Ambition sizzled through her as she looked to the heavens and raised her fist. "Give me something, anything," she cried to the endless stretch of sky.

A crack of thunder drew her attention to the far horizon. Boiling clouds rolled across the prairie as lightning flashed sideways. If she didn't get back to town and the motel that she'd spotted nestled amid the pawnshops, the bars and the convenience stores, she'd be caught in the rain storm.

With a hurried step, she turned then paused. Her scalp tingled. Someone watched her. Whirling, she searched the landscape. Nothing. Empty except for a lone pine tree to the right of the bluff.

Suddenly its branches trembled, and a huge white owl emerged from behind the thick needles. Unblinking yellow eyes glowed across the distance. Seconds ticked by as it stared at R.J., then with a screech, it lifted its massive wings and launched itself skyward. The storm forgotten, R.J. watched while it soared higher and higher, becoming smaller and smaller, until it disappeared completely into the dark clouds. Shaking herself out of it, she rushed to her Jeep and sped off down the road while the clouds chased after her.

When she reached the town sitting at the edge of the reservation, she whipped into the only motel in sight, bouncing across its empty parking lot. *Not the best place she'd ever stayed.* The neon sign flickered hypnotically – on and off, on and off, on and off. The doors to each unit looked like they'd recently received a coat of new red paint, but the rest of the building was faded and peeling. With a shrug, R.J. grabbed her purse and ran into the motel office.

A young man sat at an old desk located behind the counter. Holding some kind of computer game in his hand, at first he was oblivious to R.J. When he did notice her, a flare of expectation lit his face only to die instantly.

"What do you want?" he asked in a surly voice, taking in her dark brown hair and brown eyes.

"A room, please," she replied, approaching the counter.

With a frown, he returned his attention to his game. "We're full," he said while his thumbs moved quickly over the keyboard.

Smacking her purse on the counter, R.J. leaned forward. "Then where are all the cars?"

"Sorry."

Great, the storm was almost upon them – the kid wasn't going to rent her a room. What did she do now?

She hadn't reached a decision yet when a door at the back of the tiny office opened. An older man strode out. He took one look at the kid, one at R.J., then noticed her Jeep visible through the office windows. His hand shot out and he gave the kid a whap on the back of his head.

"Put that thing away," he said, glaring down at the young man. "Can't you see we have a customer?"

"But Gramps, you said not to rent rooms to—"

Another whomp to the kid's head silenced him. "You idiot. They don't drive Jeeps with out-of-county plates." The man looked at R.J. and gave her a toothy grin. "Sorry about my grandson," he said, sidling up to the counter. "He'd rather be playing that damn game than doin' what he's paid for. Go fold those towels in the back room," he called sharply over his shoulder.

Without a word, the teen stood and shambled out the back door.

"Need a room, Missy?" the older man asked hopefully.

R.J. thought about telling him he could take his rude grandson *and* his seedy motel and shove it, but another crack of thunder changed her mind. The idea of searching for another motel during a deluge was less appealing than staying here.

"Yes," she replied, pulling out her driver's license and credit card.

The man studied it, comparing the picture to R.J. "Ruth Baxter from Michael's Creek, hey?"

"Actually, I go by R.J." She picked up a pen and read the form. "I'll need it for at least three nights, maybe more."

Avarice shone in the man's eyes. "*Three* nights?" He swiftly ran her card and handed it back to her. "What are you doin' in this neck of the woods for three nights?"

"I'm a reporter for *The News Courier*," she said quickly, filling out the form.

"A reporter, huh? What's around these parts worth reportin' on?"

Man, this guy was chatty. But what could it hurt letting him know why she was here?

With a sigh, she handed him her registration. "The new cultural center."

A frown crossed his face. "Yeah? Would've been better for everyone if old Jon Swifthawk and that grandson of his would've left well enough alone and let them build a casino."

Her reporter's curiosity perked. "A casino?"

"Yup. A casino would've brought a lot more tourists than some ratty cultural center. But oh no, Swifthawk had to convince the Council that gambling would only corrupt the young." He gave a mean snort. "Like they need any—" He suddenly broke off and handed her a key. "Number nine, the one clear at the end." His eye twitched in a wink. "That way you won't be bothered by all the comin' and goin' next door."

She wasn't interested in the bar in the next building, whose parking lot, unlike that of the motel, was full. No, she wanted to hear more about Jon Swifthawk. Taking the key, she glanced down at it, before giving the man a speculative look. "Tell me more about this Jon Swifthawk? Is he someone important?"

"Humph, thinks he is," he exclaimed, "And his grandson. If you ask me . . ." He paused and a look akin to fear crossed his face. "Hey wait a second – you're not goin' ta quote me are you?"

"Not if you don't want me to," R.J. assured him. "You were saying – Jon Swifthawk's grandson?"

He turned away from the counter and crossed back to the rickety desk. "Never mind. None of my business about what goes on out there," he said firmly. "Enjoy your stay."

Giving up on quizzing him further, she hurried out the door and to her Jeep. She had just parked in front of her room when the first raindrops hit. She reached in the back seat, jerked out her laptop and ran to the door. Once inside, she placed the laptop on the small desk and flipped on the light. Her heart dropped. This was worse than she'd expected.

The room smelled musty and unused, and the floor was carpeted wall to wall in avocado green. Several suspicious dark stains stood out against the putrid color. R.J. refused to let her mind contemplate what might have caused them. A mismatched bedspread was flung across what looked like a very uncomfortable mattress. Above it hung a reproduction of some Frederick Remington print. If the picture had been meant to give the room a touch of class, it had failed miserably. Cheapened by the rest of the décor, it only looked sad.

With a shudder, R.J. crossed the room to take a look at the bathroom. A stool, a shower, a sink in a vanity scarred by cigarette burns met her gaze.

"Won't be any chocolate mints on the pillow in this dive," she muttered to herself.

The sudden ring of her cellphone startled her. Crossing to the bed, she pulled it out of her bag. Her lips twisted in a frown. *Mom.* With a sigh, she flipped it open.

"Hi."

"Where are you?" her mother asked without preamble.

"I explained last week," she answered, trying to hide her exasperation. "I've been assigned to write a story about—"

Her mother broke in. "You're going to be home in time for your sister's baby shower, aren't you?"

"I'll try."

"Trying isn't good enough. You know how important this is to Dee." Her voice took on a distinctive whine. "Do you realize how disappointed she'll be if you're not there? And the neighbors? What will they think if—" She stopped. "What did you say?"

"Nothing," R.J. mumbled into the phone. The truth was Dee could not care less if she attended her shower, and R.J. had inadvertently said as much, but thankfully her mother had been too busy with her rant to catch it.

Her mother sniffed. "Well, I expect you to be there. Your aunts have gone to a lot of trouble organizing this. You should've helped, but you were too busy."

R.J. rolled her eyes. "Look, Mom, I have a life and a job. I can't drop everything just because Dee's—"

Her mother didn't let her finish. "We'll expect you at two on Saturday."

"Mom," she began, but her mother had disconnected.

She looked at the silent phone in her hand. "Nice talking to you, too, Mom," she said, tossing it on the bed.

One of these days, when she finally had the chance to show what she could do, maybe it wouldn't be "Dee, Dee, Dee" all the time. Her mother would be proud of her, too.

A loud boom reminded her of her suitcase, still out in the Jeep. Crossing to the door, R.J. flung it open and was immediately hit in the face by raindrops, sharp as needles. She winced as she darted into the storm. By the time she'd retrieved her suitcase and hauled it through the door, she was soaked. Wiping the water out of her eyes, she turned to shut the door.

It was half-closed when she heard the noise.

Somewhere, above the sound of the pounding rain, an owl hooted in the night.

The old man stood in the protection of the lean-to while his eyes roamed the storm-tossed sky. Wind whipped at his braids and water poured down in a curtain from the sloped tin roof. Finally he sensed what he'd sought. Stepping out of his shelter into the rain, he extended a leather covered arm and braced himself. The weight of the bird landing made him stumble as sharp talons clung to his arm. With a quick movement that belied his age, he swung around and ducked back under the cover of the roof.

The bird, spotting his perch, leapt with a flutter from the old man's arm and settled himself. Spreading his immense wings, he ruffled his feathers and shook. Droplets of water flew while his yellow eyes focused on the old man.

Tsking, the old man picked up a towel and gently dried the bird's white feathers. "I worried for you," he mumbled softly, dropping the towel.

The owl, his eyes never leaving the old man's face, bobbed his head twice in response.

With perfect understanding, the old man sighed and glanced back into the storm.

"Ah, it is as I feared," he whispered.

A chant to welcome the morning sun rang through the meadow. Two voices – one young; one old – melded together in an ancient rhythm while the sky lightened first to grey, to rose, to pink shot with gold. A breeze, sweet from last night's rain, blew around them and made the cottonwoods shiver.

The younger man's heart filled with peace. Tipping his head back, he closed his eyes and lifted his arms high. His voice rose, almost drowning out that of his grandfather. Then as the warmth of the first rays touched his face, he let his voice slowly fade. Opening his eyes, he saw Jon Swifthawk watching him. With a smile, his grandfather placed a hand, almost in a benediction, on his grandson's auburn hair. Pride shone in the old man's eyes.

"Come, Akecheta," his grandfather said, calling him by the name he preferred.

With an arm around the old man's shoulders, Akecheta and his grandfather walked together towards the lean-to.

Jon went directly to his workbench and, removing the cover, looked lovingly at his tools in their neat, straight line. Picking up a twist of sage, he lit it and one by one smudged each tool and a long piece of cedar before sitting on the battered work stool. Taking up a whittling knife, he slowly stroked it down the wood that would become the stem of a sacred pipe.

Akecheta leaned against a post and found comfort in watching his grandfather's still strong hands slice away slivers of cedar. He'd been only fourteen and suddenly alone when this man had given him a home.

A cold spot formed in the pit of his stomach as he remembered those days and the terror he'd felt on the bus ride from Las Vegas to South Dakota. Just a kid, he'd stepped into a culture he knew little about and into the arms of a man he'd never met.

"Disturbing thoughts serve no purpose, grandson," his grandfather said without lifting his head.

Pushing away from the post, he shoved his hands in the pockets of his jeans. "I was just thinking about Mom and—"

"We don't speak of them," his grandfather said, cutting him off.

His grandfather's insistence on not mentioning the dead irritated him. He could never share the good memories of his childhood – his mother's shy smile so different from his father's boisterous ways. He didn't know if his grandfather clung to the old custom out of belief, or because his grandfather had hated the man who'd lured his beloved daughter, Dawn, away from her people and into the white world. Either way, it left him feeling that a large part of his life was locked away. A life his grandfather wanted to pretend never existed.

Turning from his grandfather, he stepped out of the lean-to and walked a short distance into the clearing. Over the past twenty years, he'd grown to love his grandfather and this land. As his eyes roamed the clearing, he thought of another land, another clearing eleven years ago. Not dappled with early morning sunlight like it was now. No, it had been scarred with freshly overturned dirt. His heart lurched at the memory of that mass grave and its victims. Dozens of bodies dumped without ceremony. Clenching his jaws, a feral smile twisted his lips. The men responsible had paid. He'd used his talent to hunt them down and – suddenly his grandfather's voice broke into his thoughts.

"Excuse me?" he said, returning to the lean-to.

His grandfather had placed his tools back on the bench and sat watching him intently. "It's not good. The reporter – the *white* woman," he said, almost choking on the word *white*.

Akecheta tugged the thin streak of white hair at his temple in frustration. "We've been over this, grandfather. I know you don't want her here, or the tourists her story will bring, but we need them if the Center's going to pay its own way."

A grunt answered him.

Grabbing a broom, Akecheta carefully swept up the wood shavings to be used later as kindling for the fire. "The gift shop will bring revenue to the tribe," he said, making the same argument he'd made a hundred times. "Our people can sell their crafts there instead of peddling them along the road, or worse, in town next to the bars."

His grandfather's mouth tightened in a stubborn line. "Nothing good has ever come from the whites."

The words *"what about me?"* almost popped out of his mouth, but respect for his grandfather stopped them. Placing the broom against the wall, he knelt before him. "Would a casino have been better? At least the Center will educate our young. Give them a place to go and celebrate our culture."

His grandfather shook his head sadly. "She brings trouble."

"We've trouble already." His gaze drifted toward the empty perch above his grandfather's head. "But we'll be warned in time."

"They'll use her against you."

"I won't let them," he answered.

Cupping Akecheta's face, the old man stared into his amber eyes. "I don't know if you can stop them."

R.J.'s tyres spun as she hit the gravel in the Center's parking lot. Man, she was late. If some jerk hadn't let the air out of her back tyres, she'd have been on time. Coming to a sliding halt in a cloud of dust, she noticed a man pacing back and forth in front of the new building.

Tall with auburn hair, his light blue chambray shirt clung to wide shoulders and his jeans fit his legs like a second skin. He looked like he'd be more at home on a horse than a place dedicated to Native Americans.

Spotting the Jeep, the man scowled and started down the stone path toward her. *Had he been waiting for her?*

R.J.'s interest kicked up a notch. With an attractive man like him hanging around, being stuck out here in the boonies for the next few days wouldn't be so bad after all. She quickly glanced in the mirror and fluffed her hair. She needed a little more lip gloss, but swiping some on would be too obvious. Grabbing her backpack, she slung her camera around her neck, but before she could open her door, the cowboy beat her to it.

"Hey, cowboy, are you waiting for me?" she said flirtatiously, giving him a wide-eyed look and a flash of her dimples.

The dimples didn't work. The cowboy's scowl deepened.

"R.J. Baxter?" the man asked in a brusque voice, "you're late."

"Sorry." Defeated, her smile faded as she jumped out of the Jeep and the man turned, and with long strides, headed back up the path. She ran to catch up with him. "Somebody let the air—"

"Here." He stopped and shoved four pouches in her hand.

"What—"

"Tobacco." Taking her arm, he hustled her forward. "When I introduce you, give one to each of the elders."

Perplexed, she glanced down at the pouches. "Why?"

"It's a sign of respect," he replied with a disgruntled look, "but in your case, it's an apology for keeping them waiting."

R.J. skidded to a stop and jerked away. She'd had enough of being yanked around. Holding the tobacco in one hand, she placed the other on her hip and glared up at him, towering over her. "Look, I'm sorry I was late, but just who the hell are you?"

"Sean O'Brien. I'm the tribe's liaison. Any questions, ask me."

Smart – hiring a white to interact with the press. Too bad he was so abrasive.

Eyeing her camera, he frowned. "No pictures without permission. Don't touch any of the displays. And remember you're a guest here. Act accordingly."

She didn't appreciate the lecture.

"Any other rules?" she asked, not keeping the sarcasm out of her voice.

He spun and walked away, his boot heels clicking on the polished wood floor. "Not at the moment."

Wait a minute – she wasn't following two steps behind. After catching up with him, she matched her strides with his. Noticing her huge steps, a small smirk played across his face. When they reached a doorway at the back of the Center, he motioned her inside.

The room was large. Long windows stretched across the far wall, and above each window hung brightly painted shields. The opposite wall was decorated with paintings depicting the Native American way of life two hundred years ago. Four men, with their hands clasped in the front of them, stood looking very solemn. Long braids hung over their shoulders, and their weathered faces reminded R.J. of old sepia photographs. A feathered staff hung on the wall behind them.

Sean stopped and drew R.J. forward. "George Eagle Feather, Art Walker, Grady Crow Wing, and Jake Swift," he said with a slight bow to each man. "R.J. Baxter from *The News Courier*."

R.J. stepped up to the first man, and handing him the pouch of tobacco, smiled. "Thank you for inviting me."

The man's features softened as he took the gift. "Welcome."

She repeated the process with the remaining three. Once introductions were complete, her eyes were drawn back to the staff. It was wrapped in strips of white, black, yellow and red cloth. Eagle feathers, attached to the cloth by beadwork, gracefully draped down its length. Intricate carving adorned the top.

She moved past the Elders to get a better look. Pausing, her breath hitched while her fingers longed to stroke the soft feathers. She took another step, pulled closer by its beauty. Of its own accord, her hand lifted toward the staff.

Suddenly Sean was beside her.

"This is sacred," he said softly with a slight shake of his head. "Only warriors may touch it."

The spell broken, her hand dropped. "May I take a photo?" she asked in a voice that sounded distant to her ears.

Sean cast a glance over his shoulder and the four Elders nodded in unison.

After rapidly shooting several photos, R.J. turned back to the group of men. "Would you mind answering some questions?"

The men exchanged looks before motioning to one of the long tables lining the far wall. When all were seated, the Elders on one side with Sean and R.J. on the other, R.J. removed her pen, notebook and tape recorder from her backpack, placing them on the table.

The recorder caught their attention and they stared at it as if it were a coiled snake. Four pairs of eyes turned to Sean and seconds ticked by as unspoken words seemed to pass between them. Finally, George Eagle Feather spoke, pointing to the recorder. "Yes, we will answer your questions, but you may not tape our voices."

"Okay." With a shrug, R.J. tucked the recorder back into her bag and picked up her pen. She'd start out with a few warm-up questions to put them at ease. "Who designed the Cultural Center?" she asked, directing the question to George Eagle Feather.

"A young architect in Minneapolis – Edward Little Bear," Sean replied.

"A Native American?" R.J. asked, scribbling the name in her notebook.

"Yes, we wanted a designer who understood the culture," he answered.

She ignored Sean and focused on George Eagle Feather. "How long did it take to complete the project?"

"We broke ground ten months ago," Sean replied, launching into an explanation. "All the materials are from the reservation and from renewable resources. During the construction, the entire tribe participated in some way." He pointed to the shields and the paintings, hanging on the walls. "These were all made by people here on the reservation, as were many of the displays that I'll show you later."

R.J.'s pen paused while irritation shot through her. This – some carefully crafted script that anyone could write – wasn't the story she wanted. Not if she wanted a major newspaper to notice her. It was time to hit him with something from left field.

Cocking her head, she studied him. "Why a cultural center instead of the casino that some of members of the tribe wanted?"

Her question hit its mark. Without glancing their way, she heard the Elders shift in their seats while Sean's amber eyes flared.

He recovered quickly and gave her a tight smile. "There's always two sides to every question, but the important thing is, in the end, the tribe came together to build this." Rising, he motioned to the door. "Come, I'll show you the rest of the building."

Reluctantly, R.J. stood. She would love to get one of the Elders aside and grill him about any dissention that might have existed, but Sean wasn't going to give her the opportunity. Maybe she'd have her chance later.

After voicing her thanks to the Elders, she followed Sean into the display area. While they strolled along, he gave a running monologue, describing each display and its significance. They paused in front of photos showing families standing in front of tar paper shanties; dancer displays with elaborate costumes and beautifully beaded moccasins; tribal implements used hundreds of years ago when the people still roamed the plains following the buffalo.

Interesting, but R.J. had finally had enough. She stopped short in front of a large stone plague. "I appreciate the tour, but if you really want to draw tourists, you've got to give me a better angle than this."

"What do you mean?"

"What makes this place different than every other Native American museum in the country?"

"I told you – it's made of material from the reservation; the entire tribe worked—"

R.J. cut him off with a wave of her hand. "So? You think anyone really cares about that stuff? Readers want to know more than just facts and figures. They want the human story."

"Such as?"

"Well, one question that springs to mind – why did the Elders hire a white to represent the Center?"

He stiffened. "I'm not white."

"But with a name like O'Brien, I assumed—"

"You assumed wrong," he said, cutting her off. "My father was white, but I was raised here."

"Don't you know who this is?" a voice from behind her called out.

R.J. turned to see a man standing a few feet away. Shorter than Sean and barrel-chested, he wore a dark shirt and jeans. A pair of sunglasses dangled from a pocket embroidered with the words "Tribal Police".

He crossed the short distance and held out his hand. "You must be the reporter. I'm Charlie Two Horses. Welcome to the rez."

Shaking his hand, R.J. stole a look at Sean who'd taken a step back. "Thanks."

Charlie turned toward Sean and smiled. "So our boy here didn't tell you about himself, huh?"

Sean shuffled uncomfortably. "This isn't necessary, Charlie."

"Of course it is," he replied turning back to R.J. "This here's Sean Swifthawk O'Brien, grandson of Jon Swifthawk. Raised you didn't he, Sean, after your parents were killed?"

"We don't need to go into that, Charlie."

Charlie's face took on an expression of innocence. "But I heard her say she wanted a 'human' story, and just think how yours would tug on the heart strings . . . the son of murdered parents; a poor half-breed kid shipped off to the rez to be raised by one of the most important men in the tribe?"

"My family background doesn't have anything to do with the Center," Sean said in a clipped voice.

"Sure, it does, Sean. You and your grandfather were the ones who talked the tribe into building it—" He stopped and looked at R.J. "Sean was also the one who got white investors to put up the money."

"I organized a few fundraisers."

Charlie snorted "A *few* fundraisers? How much did you get? A cool—"

"That's enough, Charlie," Sean said, his hands clenched at his side.

Charlie took a step forward. "What's wrong, Swifthawk," he spat out the word. "Don't want to give her too—"

"Not now," Sean began, his chin rising. "She doesn't—"

"Doesn't what?" Charlie interrupted, moving closer.

R.J. squirmed. A fight breaking out in the Cultural Center *would* make a better story, but she really didn't want to see them come to blows. "What's this?" she asked quickly, trying to diffuse the rising tension.

"Ah that," Charlie said, suddenly forgetting Sean and stepping up to the plaque. He ran his finger down the carved names, stopping on one near the bottom. "It's in honor of our warriors. All who've proudly served in the Armed Forces." He tapped the plaque. "Here's *my* name," he finished proudly.

R.J. read down through the names. "Where's yours, Sean."

Charlie gave a bark of laughter. "He didn't serve, did you, Sean?"

"Not in the Army," he replied curtly.

Charlie shrugged. "That's right – you went off to college instead." He shrugged again. "Not everyone's cut out to be a warrior." Taking his sunglasses out of his pocket, he settled them on his face. "Nice meeting you, R.J." With a slight sneer, he glanced at Sean before returning his attention back to her. "If there's anything I can do, be sure and let me know."

R.J. watched Charlie march down the hall before turning back to Sean. "Ah," she began, but the words caught in her throat.

His eyes – for a split second, she could've sworn they changed from amber to yellow.

It was late afternoon by the time R.J. returned to the motel. After Charlie had left, Sean had continued his tour of the Center. He'd been articulate and at times even charming. She would've needed ice flowing through her veins in order not to have felt the tug of attraction, especially when he smiled. *Man, he had a great smile.* And the pride he felt in the Center would've been kind of cool had she not known he was only using her as a means to an end. She had cooperated. She'd taken a ton of photos, learned all about life on the prairie, and could quote exactly how many stones they'd used in constructing the Center.

No doubt about it – this story was going to be just another piece of fluff, she thought, slapping her hand on the steering wheel in frustration. The only thing that had been remotely interesting, other than staring at Sean, was the animosity between him and Charlie Two Horses. But was that a lead she wanted to pursue? She remembered the look on Sean's face as he watched Charlie walk away. She wasn't a coward, but the idea of coming up against Sean Swifthawk O'Brien made her shiver. *And* not in a good way.

She'd almost made it past the bar, when suddenly someone stepped out between two parked cars and waved her down.

Charlie Two Horses.

Rolling to a stop, she cranked down the driver's window.

"Hey, good to see you again," Charlie said, approaching her door then motioning toward the bar. "How about a beer?"

She debated with herself for a moment. She wasn't an idiot – this guy had an agenda and he wanted to use her to achieve it. But on the other hand, she had her own agenda – a better story than the one she was being forcefed. What could it hurt to at least talk to him?

With a nod, she pulled into an empty parking space.

From inside the bar, the jukebox whined with the sound of steel guitars and a singer lamenting how "she'd done him wrong". Above the bar itself, hung an old TV with the volume shut off. Some sporting event flickered across the screen. Taking her arm, Charlie held up two fingers to the bartender then guided her past the pool tables to a booth in the back. They'd barely settled when a waitress with the biggest beehive R.J. had ever seen slapped two bottles of beer in front of them. Without a word she turned and sauntered back to the bar.

Charlie lifted his bottle, saluted R.J., then took a long pull. Scooting back, he stretched an arm across the back of the bench. "So? What did you think of the Center?"

She thought for a moment before answering him. The best way to play this was close to the vest, sound non-committal, let Charlie do all the talking.

"It's nice," she replied, in a neutral voice.

"But not much of a story, huh?"

She lifted a shoulder in a shrug.

Dropping his arm, he shifted forward. "I could give you a better angle than the one Swifthawk shoved on you."

This guy really did want to dish the dirt. Regardless of her trepidation about Sean O'Brien, R.J. felt a tickle of excitement. "Like what?" she asked, keeping her face calm.

He downed his beer and motioned to the waitress for another. Sliding the empty bottle to the side, he crossed his arms on the table. "See here's the deal – the rez needs money. I could show you homes that are no better than squatter shacks and the Center isn't going to change that." He stopped as the waitress smacked another beer in front of him. He waited until she was out of earshot before continuing. "A casino would."

"A little late for that, isn't it," R.J. replied. "The tribe chose to build the Center, not a casino."

"They were misled." His eyes darted to the side before returning to R.J. Leaning forward, his voice dropped. "Swifthawk and his grandfather didn't want a casino and persuaded them it would be easier to finance the Center."

"And Sean raised the money?"

"Yeah." He sipped on his beer. "Him and his white buddies."

"Then convince him to raise the money for a casino."

His mouth twisted in a bitter line. "Swifthawk won't do it. Him and his grandfather want to cling to the old ways. They want our people to live as they did 200 years ago. It can't be done." His expression lightened. "But here's the beauty of it – now we don't need him. The Center's paid off and it could be used as collateral to finance a casino."

R.J. threw a hand in the air. "There's your solution."

"No," he said with a shake of his head. "Like I told you – they don't want a casino and they'll do everything they can to stop it."

"I don't see how I can help you."

His eyes narrowed and he gave her a smug grim. "If you dig below the surface, you're going to find Swifthawk's motives aren't as pure as he'd like the tribe to believe."

"You want me to discredit him."

"No, I want you to write the truth."

"Which is?"

"How Sean's sold out to white investors." He moved even closer. "I can give you names – people who'll tell you the truth about Swifthawk."

A million ideas bounced through her mind and she longed to whip out her notebook and begin taking notes. But that would seem too anxious. Much better to let Charlie think he needed to convince her.

"How do you know they'll talk to me?"

"Oh, they'll talk, if you ask the right questions," he answered cryptically.

"How can I? I don't know anything about Sean and his grandfather."

Charlie's lips pursed. "You won't get much on the old man. Going back as far as I can remember, people on the rez have always been reluctant to talk about him." He shook his head. "Even my own grandfather – I did hear him say something once, but my grandmother shushed him."

"What was it?"

"I can't recall his exact words," he replied, scratching his chin. "But it wasn't about Jon Swifthawk. It was about his father."

"Sean's great-grandfather?"

"Yeah . . ." he paused, trying to remember. "He said something about animal totems."

"What are they?"

"Never mind – we're talking forty years ago." He picked up his beer, drank it in one long gulp then stood. Throwing a piece of paper on the table, he stared down at her. "I'm telling you – if you want a 'real' story, take a closer look at Sean."

The dying sun cast long shadows in the clearing. In its centre, Sean stood before the fire, watching the rocks glow red. He removed a pinch of tobacco from the pouch dangling at his waist. Holding it high, he turned to the north and let it fall from his fingertips. He shifted to the east, to the south, to the west, repeating the process as he offered the sacred herb to Mother Earth. Finished, he turned back to the fire and grabbed a pitchfork. Using it, he carried the hot rocks one by one into the canvas-covered sweat lodge and placed them in the fire pit.

Satisfied the stones were aligned, he exited the lodge and quickly pulled off his boots, his socks, his jeans, until finally he stood naked in the gathering twilight. Turning he entered the lodge.

It was like walking into an oven. Instantly sweat popped from his pores and snaked down his face, chest and arms in tiny rivulets. Moving to the blanket woven by his grandmother, he sat cross-legged and reached for a ladle of water from the nearby bucket. He cast water on the shimmering rocks, making the air hiss with steam.

Hot, so hot. It felt like the spit inside his mouth was ready to boil. With a sharp intake of breath, he picked up the drum at his side. He shut his eyes and began beating a slow rhythm on the taut deer hide while he focused on the spot deep inside where his heritage lay.

He needed guidance. The confidence he'd shown his grandfather had been false and, at times, the special burden he bore threatened to crush him. He knew his power and the temptation to control it was a constant fight. How could he help his people win their battles if he couldn't even win his own?

He beat the drum harder.

The brush of wings seemed to graze his cheek while, softly, the distant whisper of his ancestors began to echo in his ears. Images flickered in the recess of his mind. A buffalo thundering across the plains, a lone wolf darting through the cottonwoods and, finally, a white owl soaring into the heavens. He felt connected to all that had gone before him and the heaviness in his heart eased with each beat of the drum.

He *would* help his people towards a better life. He *would* win against those who plotted his downfall. He *would* stop them from using the woman.

The woman. His hand faltered and he felt his connection slip. She had tried to charm him, slip under his defences. She'd almost succeeded, but it wasn't her dimples that had drawn him, but her refusal to be intimidated.

It was a new experience for him. Most of the people on the reservation had always steered clear of him – either due to the rumours that had circulated about his family, or because they didn't trust him. Whatever the reason, it no longer mattered to him. His only concern was saving their culture.

He needed to remember that. He needed to remind himself even though she might look like a Native with her dark hair and dark eyes, the heart that beat beneath the pretty exterior was white. He'd sensed her ambition, her self-serving attitude. He knew she wanted more than he was willing to give.

What of her reaction to the sacred staff? He knew she wanted to touch it and would've had he not stopped her. Why? Was it just the need to handle something "unique", or had the staff called to her?

Her face took over his mind, chasing away the buffalo, the wolf, the snow owl. The whispers died. *No!* His questions hadn't been answered.

He pounded the drum harder; pounded until his fingers ached, trying to banish thoughts of the woman and to regain his link with his ancestors. *No good.* All he saw in his mind's eye was her face smiling at him, and all he felt was the pull of a culture he'd left long ago.

Laying the drum aside in frustration, he rose and left the lodge.

The sun had set and the evening star shone in the night sky above the cottonwoods. Gleaming with perspiration, he paused and glanced toward the trees while steam rolled off his naked body. His eyes were sharp and he saw what the darkness hid. Night creatures – like him – hunting their prey. A longing to join them came over him. To run free and wild. To forget the woman, forget his questions. He tamped it down. He'd bent to bundle his clothes when he felt the air stir. He looked up. Above him white wings glistened in the starlight.

"Little Brother," he murmured acknowledging the owl, then with heavy steps walked away from the lodge.

Like a disembodied spirit, the white bird hovered over him, guarding his back.

The thin drapes did little to block the wavering light of the motel sign outside R.J.'s window. It flashed like a strobe light across the yellowed ceiling. She lay on her back and watched while thoughts of half-remembered dreams lingered in her mind. She'd been on the prairie, walking through tall grasses blooming with yellow, purple and white flowers. In the distance, from a branch in a tall cottonwood, a white owl seemed to beckon her. Her steps had quickened. Then . . . nothing. Whatever had happened next in the dream eluded her. Baffled, she flipped over on to her stomach and buried her face in her pillow. "Forget it, go to sleep," she mumbled. But she couldn't. Not when her pillow smelled like a hunk of month-old bread. She rolled back over and stared at the lights once again.

She had to reach a decision. Did she pursue the information that Charlie Two Horses had given her, or did she write the story Sean O'Brien expected of her? If the first story was as juicy as Charlie hinted, it could be THE ONE. Her toes curled at the thought of what such a story could bring into her life. Recognition, respect, money.

But what would an exposé do to Sean O'Brien's life? If what Charlie said was true, and he had sold out, then he had it coming. So what if he *was* one of the best-looking men she'd ever seen? Hormones had no place in journalism. She was a pro, not some simpering female blinded by a guy's smile.

A prickle of conscience hit her. Even the truth could come in shades of grey and, as a pro, she knew she could spin the story any way she wanted. She had the power to make Sean O'Brien either the hero or the villain of the piece. Which would it be?

Tossing the covers to the side, she swung her legs off the bed and pulled jeans over her gym shorts. She grabbed her sweatshirt and threw it on, too. She couldn't think straight in this musty, smelly room. She needed fresh air. A drive would clear her mind.

Moments later she was flying down a black ribbon of highway, while the moonlit prairie whizzed by her open window. Without knowing why, she found herself back at the same spot where she'd stood and watched the storm roll in. She shut off the ignition and scanned the landscape. Yesterday, she'd felt eyes upon her. If she got out of the car, would she feel it again? It was the middle of the night and she was alone. How did she know what might be lurking in the tall grass?

"You're nuts, R.J.," she muttered, her hands gripping the wheel. "Go back to the motel."

She remembered the haunting dreams, the stale room, the flickering lights. A tightness squeezed her chest and she took a deep breath to ease it. The scent of sweet grass and wild clover seemed to fill the Jeep and she looked longingly across the plains. *So fresh and clean.*

"Quit being a ninny." She pushed the door open and climbed out. "It was only a stupid owl," she whispered with a glance at the lone pine tree.

High grass brushed against her pant legs as she tromped up the hill and, in the stillness, it sounded as loud as a troop of soldiers marching. At the top of the rise, she stopped and took a deep breath. Nothing but miles and miles of heaven and earth. No houses, no lights, no fences. A strange feeling of aloneness came over her and with it a sense of freedom. Is this how the Native Americans once felt, wandering a land with no boundaries?

A sudden whoosh followed by the soft rustling of grass made her spin round. Her eyes scanned the ground between her and the Jeep. *As empty as the space behind her.*

She turned back to the endless landscape. Quit dithering she told herself, thinking of the paper Charlie had given her. It wouldn't hurt to meet a few people, ask a few questions. She wouldn't let Charlie use her any more than she intended to let Sean O'Brien. She could—

"What are you doing here?" a voice behind her whispered.

She twirled so fast she almost lost her balance while her heart seemed to stutter in her chest. In the moonlight, she recognized Sean, climbing the hill towards her. Her temper flamed.

"What am *I* doing?" she asked, her eyes narrowing. "What are *you* doing, sneaking up on me?"

A small smile tugged at the corner of his mouth as if he were pleased that he'd startled her. It vanished. "It's not smart to be out here alone. People have been known to disappear."

She lifted her chin a notch. "I'm not afraid."

"Maybe you should be."

"Are you threatening me?" she shot back.

"Of course not. I'm well aware of the power of the press." A real smile flashed in the dark. "I wouldn't dream of threatening a woman who buys ink by the gallon."

Damn, he could turn on the charm when he wanted and she felt her anger soften. "You didn't answer my question."

"What am I doing here?" He lifted a shoulder. "Like you, I couldn't sleep."

"How did you—"

His low voice cut her off. "Look over there." He pointed to a spot on the left. "Do you see them? A mother coyote with half-grown pups."

R.J.'s eyes searched the prairie, trying to see what he did, but she only saw waving grass. "I can't."

He stepped away from her. "Ah, well, I come out here a lot at night." He hesitated. "I guess my eyes are accustomed to the dark."

"I'll say," R.J. said, still trying to pick out the coyote. "I can't see a—"

"I love it out here," he said, suddenly changing the subject. "At night, I can imagine how it must've been two hundred years ago."

"The freedom."

He glanced at her, surprised. "You felt it too. I didn't realize you were so perceptive."

She recalled Charlie's words about their way of life. "You can't go back, you know."

Moving a few paces away, he bowed his head for a moment before squaring his shoulders and facing her. "I know. We have to go forward if our culture is going to survive."

"The Center."

"Yes . . ." his voice trailed away. "Charlie talked to you, didn't he?"

It was her turn to be surprised. "How did you know?"

He gave a soft snort. "I've known Charlie a long time. He's using you."

R.J. crossed the distance between them. "Please. Don't insult my intelligence by stating the obvious. I know he has an agenda." She stopped and looked up at him. "But then again, so do you."

"My only goal is to help the tribe have a better life."

"Not according to Charlie."

"What did he say?"

"Oh, that's not the way this works," she said, cocking a hip and shaking her head. "If you want information from me, you have to reciprocate."

He lifted an eyebrow. "Seems Charlie and I aren't the only ones with agendas."

"Damn straight!" she exclaimed. "I'm tired of writing stories that any eighth-grader could write."

"Regardless of the truth?"

"Of course not," she replied with heat in her voice. "I don't want lies – I want the real story."

"No one would believe it," he murmured more to himself than her.

Her breath quickened. This guy was weakening. If she played it right, if she could convince him to be honest with her. She took a step closer. "Sure they would. I'm good, really good," she insisted. "Give it to me straight and that's the way I'll write it. Cross my heart."

He startled her by placing a hand on her cheek. "I can't," he said sadly. "There are some things that can never be revealed. Forget about the story, Ruth Baxter, and go home. We'll find another reporter."

Looking into his eyes, she felt the full force of his magnetism and, without thinking, moved in until they were almost touching.

She heard his sharp intake of breath and time seemed to slow. His eyes glowed in the night with desire and with something else. A wildness that she'd never seen before. His face lowered to hers.

When his mouth touched hers, she felt the thing that had been coiled inside of her for so long smooth. Her driving ambition faded and her entire focus was on the mouth pressing against hers. Stealing her hands up his arms, they settled on his shoulders and pulled him closer. Her lips parted and she felt, more than heard, his groan. She tasted him while his scent surrounded her. The strangest feeling came over her. It was if she were gliding toward the heavens, no longer tied to the earth. Suddenly his mouth left hers and began a trail across her cheek, down her neck, to a place right below her ear. Heat shot through her as his tongue began to trace lazy circles on her sensitive skin. She tipped her head to the side and gripped his broad shoulders. His hand stole down her back, cupping her bottom and bringing her closer.

This is crazy registered somewhere in the corner of her mind. She'd known him less than twenty-four hours and she wasn't even sure she liked him. Yet all he had to do was kiss her and she turned into a wild thing.

Abruptly he released her and jerked away.

Dazed, R.J. tottered while a cool breeze chased away the heat.

"Wh-wh—" she stuttered.

Grabbing her arm, he began to drag her down the hill toward the Jeep. "We have to leave."

She stumbled. Sean righted her. When they'd reached the vehicle, he opened the door and tried to bundle her in. The rush down the hill had cleared her thinking and she dug in her heels, refusing to budge.

"Wait a second. What's going on? One minute you're all over me like a rash, then—"

"I don't have time to explain. I'm needed at the Center."

The expression on his face told her not to argue. She shoved the keys into the ignition and jerked her head at the passenger side. "Let's go."

"No, you go back to the motel—"

"No you don't," she interrupted, "you're not ditching me. Get in."

"But," he said with a glance over his shoulder, "I can travel faster if I—" His hand hit the side of the Jeep. "Damn!" Slamming the door shut, he ran to the other side and jumped in. He barely had his seatbelt fastened when she hit the gas and sped off down the road. Minutes later, they were at the Center. They opened their doors at the same time, but before she could leap out, his hand restrained her.

"You stay," he hissed, jabbing a finger at her. Without giving her a chance to answer, he was out of the Jeep and running into the Center in loping strides. He disappeared inside.

Fuming, R.J. gripped the steering wheel. Every instinct told her she was missing out on the action, but what? *Only one way to find out.* Leaning over, she grabbed her can of mace out of the glove compartment then, exiting the Jeep, quietly stole up the walkway. Inside, she paused and let her eyes adjust to the shadows. Slowly she crept down the hallway, one finger on the trigger of the mace while her other hand trailed the wall, guiding her.

She stopped halfway and listened. Silence. She began to feel foolish. What was she doing sneaking around in the middle of the night, hanging on to a can of mace like her life depended on it? That Sean O'Brien was playing her. He ran hot then cold. Next he scares her into thinking that something big is happening. Nothing was happening. And he was just plain weird.

Turning on her heel, she started back the way she came. She'd leave him here, go back to the motel, write the stupid story, then blow this place. Her mother would be happy. She'd be home in time for the baby shower. So what if this story didn't pan out as she'd hoped. One of these days—

A loud crash followed by a shriek startled her. Spinning, she ran down the hall to the Council room and skidded to a stop inside the door.

Moonlight streaming through the windows lit the scene playing out before her. Two men crouched in the middle of the room with arms stretched over their heads, weaving and bobbing, while a white owl circled above them. With a screech, the owl extended its talons and dive-bombed the men. The bird sliced at their faces. One man cried out. Wheeling, it soared back towards the ceiling, getting ready to make another run.

R.J. turned to race away but an arm, shooting around her neck, jerked her backwards. She slammed into a body and her adrenaline surged. Without thinking, she lifted her heel and brought it down full force on the foot next to hers. His grip loosened while his yelp joined the cries of his buddies. Pivoting, she sprayed him in the eyes with the mace and fled. *She had to get out of there. She didn't know what was going on, but she didn't want any part of it. Some reporter!*

She was almost to the door when she heard the beating of wings behind her.

Shit, the damn owl was after her *now.*

Hearing a thump, she whirled, ready to give the owl a shot of mace.

Up close, it was huge. Staring at her with yellow eyes, it expanded its wings until they stretched wider than a man's body. R.J. gasped and in the blink of an eye, the shape in front of her changed.

The owl disappeared and Sean O'Brien stood in its place.

Staggering back, she hit the wall and felt her face turn white. The can of mace slipped from her nerveless fingers and rolled down the hall. Her eyes, never leaving Sean, watched him bend and snag it.

He took one step.

Knees buckling, her last thought before hitting the floor . . . *what a story!*

The not-so-soft tapping on the side of her cheek was the first thing she felt. She opened her eyes to find herself sprawled on the floor with Sean kneeling beside her. Sitting up, she scooted until her back hit the wall. "What hap—"

"You tripped and hit your head," Sean said quickly, cutting her off. Standing, he offered her his hand.

She brushed it away and scrambled to her feet. A wave of nausea hit her. She clutched her stomach and took a deep breath. "No, I didn't." Straightening, she looked him square in the eye. "An owl was chasing me – only it wasn't an owl – it was—"

"Don't be ridiculous." He gave a quick glance over his shoulder. "You need to leave."

She crossed her arms over her chest and held her ground. "No way. Not until I get some answers."

"There are no answers," he spat out and marched to the door. Flinging it open, he waited for her. "The Center's been vandalized and the men escaped. You have to leave before Charlie and his goons show up." Reaching out, he grabbed her arm and pulled her forwards.

Yanking away, she glared at him. "Why? We can explain what happened."

"And what are you going to say?" he asked, his eyes drilling into hers. "How are you going to explain what you, a white woman, were doing at the Center in the middle of the night?" He pointed toward her Jeep. "Go."

Giving up, she followed him down the path. Her mind felt muddled. Did she see the owl change into Sean? Like he said, it was ridiculous. Things like that just didn't happen in the real world. Sean had been in the shadows. She'd been scared. Her eyes had played tricks on her. When he stepped out, it only appeared that the owl transformed.

But what had happened to the owl? She opened her mouth to ask, but before she could speak, Sean opened the Jeep's door and hustled her into the driver's seat. Slamming it shut, he turned back toward the Center.

"Wait," she called out. "Aren't you coming with me?"

With a deep sigh, he shook his head. "No, I'll be needed here." He faced her. "It would be better for both of us if you left and forgot this place."

Sean stood before the Council and tried not to look at Charlie Two Horses, sitting at the end of the table. He longed to shred the smug grin from Charlie's face as he spun his lies to the Elders. With a will of their own, Sean's fingers curled talon-like at his side, but he remained still. Next to him, his grandfather, rigid with indignation, glared at the tribal leaders.

"Akecheta stopped the vandals," his grandfather insisted.

"Did he stop *them*, or did I stop *him*?" Charlie asked before any of the Elders could speak. "When I arrived, the place was a shambles and he was alone."

As his grandfather focused the full weight of his stare on Charlie, Sean felt a small wave of pleasure when Charlie squirmed, but he kept his face blank.

"That makes no sense," his grandfather said with a wave of his hand. "Akecheta worked hard to build this place. Why would he want to destroy it?"

"Insurance," Charlie replied.

His grandfather shifted his attention from Charlie to George Eagle Feathers as if Charlie's words had no importance. "Only a foolish man says foolish things."

Rebuffed, Charlie's face lost some of its smugness while he leaned forwards and addressed George. "I checked. There was no sign of a break-in and, other than the Council, Sean is the only one who has keys. If there were three men as he claims, how did they get in?"

Moving past Sean, his grandfather stood directly in front of Charlie and, placing his hands on the table, leaned in. "I know what you're trying to do—"

A sudden commotion at the door interrupted him. All eyes turned toward the sound and watched R.J. blunder into the room.

Sean suppressed a groan. *Ah hell, what's she doing here?* Steeling himself, he didn't look her way when she came to stand beside him.

"I apologize," she began, focusing on the Elders and ignoring Charlie, "I don't mean to intrude in private matters, but when I heard Sean had been accused, I felt I needed to help."

"Why?" Charlie barked. "You barely know him."

Shifting her attention to Charlie, she gave him a stiff smile. "True, but I know for a fact he isn't responsible."

"How?" Charlie scoffed.

Turning back to the Elders, she showed her dimples. "I was here, too."

From behind him, Sean heard his grandfather's gasp.

Charlie shifted forward. "Really? Why?"

"I recently received some information," she replied, giving Charlie a pointed look, "and I wanted to give Sean a chance to respond." She turned her attention to George. "When we arrived, there were three men . . . at least I think it was three . . . it was dark." She glanced at him as if she expected him to confirm her story. When he didn't, she gave a shrug and glossed over what really happened. "They saw us and ran off."

George's eyes shifted from R.J. to Sean. "Is this true? Why didn't you speak of her?"

Sean's jaw clenched and unclenched. He appreciated R.J. coming to his defence, but in reality she'd only made the situation worse. He'd kept an eye on Charlie during R.J.'s explanation. Speculation had played across Charlie's face the whole time. Not good. By aligning herself with him, she'd just made an enemy. He had to get this inquisition over quickly and get her out of town.

"I didn't think it right to involve her in tribal business." He finally allowed himself to look at her. "She has her story and will be leaving town today," he said, with emphasis on 'today'.

R.J. refused to meet his eyes.

George placed his hands on the table and stood. "Thank you for stepping forward. If you'll excuse us?"

She took the hint. And after casting a triumphant look first at Charlie then at George, she left the room.

It didn't take long for the Council to dismiss Charlie's allegations. Relieved, Sean and his grandfather quietly walked to the door. Sean could feel the disapproval rolling off his grandfather in waves and he wasn't looking forward to the explanations he'd have to make. He'd acted foolishly last night, letting the woman distract him. Only by luck had he won this battle. If he were to continue to win, he had to forget her and step up his guard.

His grandfather didn't wait long to jump him. They stepped into the hallway and he pulled him to the side.

"What were you thinking," his grandfather hissed. "Why did you bring the woman here? Did she see—"

Sean held up his hand, stopping him. "Yes, but I think I convinced her that she imagined it."

His grandfather exploded. "You think? For god's sake, she's a reporter – a *white* reporter."

"Grandfather, I mean no disrespect, but who would believe her if she wrote the truth? A story like that would destroy her reputation as a reporter. And trust me, she'd never risk her career."

Slightly mollified, his grandfather continued down the hallway. "Maybe, but stay away from her," he cautioned.

"Don't worry, I w—"

The words died as he stepped outside and saw R.J. waiting by her Jeep.

Shit.

When she came running up to them, he had no choice but to introduce her to his grandfather. "R.J. Baxter," he said, indicating her. "R.J., this is my grandfather, Jon Swifthawk."

"It's a pleasure to meet you," she replied, rummaging around in her bag. A second later, she withdrew a pouch of tobacco and handed it to his grandfather. "I've heard a lot about you."

Reluctantly, he accepted her gift, while Sean felt a glimmer of pride that she'd remembered their custom.

"Miss Baxter," his grandfather said gruffly. "Thank you for defending my grandson."

With a shy smile, she nodded. "I appreciate the time he's given me."

"Hmm," his grandfather said with a steely look his way. "I must get home – Sean?"

"I'll be there in a minute," he said, "I need to discuss something with R.J."

She waited until his grandfather had reached his pickup then leaned in.

"He doesn't approve of me," she whispered.

"It's not personal, it's—" his voice faltered. "Look, I don't have much time. I want you to leave today. You'll no longer be welcome here." He made a move to join his grandfather, but she shifted to the side, blocking him.

"Wait, I need to talk to you."

He made a move around her. "No you don't. You have your story."

"Do I?" Her eyes narrowed. "You want me to write about what happened last night?"

"Go ahead," he answered with a shrug. "We stopped a break-in. That's it."

She cocked her hip and gave him a long stare. "Yeah? Well call me crazy, but I think there was a little more to it than that."

"Such as?"

"Such as . . . who were they? How did they get in? What was their motive?" she replied, ticking off her questions. Her voice dropped and she stepped closer. "And, last but not least – how in the hell does an owl change into a man?"

"That's impossible. The blow to your head must've addled your brain," he scoffed.

"Really?" She touched the back of her scalp. "If I hit my head, why don't I have a bump? Now what about that owl?"

"There wasn't an owl," he insisted.

Her eyebrows lifted. "Tell that to the grandson of the guy who owns the motel." She whistled through her teeth. "Man, you should see the gouges on the side of that kid's face—"

"A white boy? I thought—" He stopped and, taking her arm, pulled her around the side of the building. "You recognized him from last night?"

"No, but I can recognize claw marks when I see them."

He plucked on the white streak at his temple. Great, what did he do now? This woman was too clever for her own good – for his own good. He gave her arm a shake.

"Thanks to your butting in today, they now know you were with me," he said through clenched teeth. "It's not safe. You have to leave today. Go back to Michael's Creek. Forget about the story. I'll square it with your editor."

Her face took on a mutinous look. "I don't want to forget."

"I told you," he hissed, "people have disappeared on the prairie. You could be next."

"I'm not afraid," she blustered.

"You should be. There are ravines deep enough to hide a body until next spring. Do you want to wind up a pile of bleached bones?"

She gulped. "Not really."

"Then leave." He spun on his heel, but her hand on his arm stopped him.

"Listen. I'll leave. Tomorrow. Meet me tonight," she pleaded, "I can't walk away without answers. I promise I'll keep my mouth shut . . ." she hesitated. "I just need to know I'm not nuts."

His mouth formed in a grim line. "You're not, but I am. Meet me at eleven."

Leaning her head against the driver's window, R.J. waited for Sean. She glanced at the dashboard clock. He was late. Was he standing her up? He'd better not. If he tried, she'd hunt him down like a dog. She wasn't leaving town without answers.

Regardless of what he'd said, R.J. still had a problem wrapping her mind around what she'd seen. Lying awake last night and staring at the ever-blinking lights, she'd gone over and over the scene in her mind. It had happened so fast. First there was the owl then there was Sean. Being a reporter, her life had brushed up against a lot of odd things and she'd become convinced a long time ago that life really was stranger than fiction. But this?

Only when the first rays of morning lightened the sky had she decided it hadn't been her imagination. Old legends were true. Sean Swifthawk O'Brien was a shapeshifter. And she wanted him to confirm it.

But first she needed more information. Before she confronted him, she had to learn all she could about shapeshifting and Native American lore. She'd tried going online but she couldn't find a connection from her crappy motel room. It was when she'd gone to the motel's office to ask where the nearest Internet connection might be that she'd seen the kid. And overheard him and his grandfather discussing the accusations against Sean. The discussion ended the instant they'd seen her and the kid had hot-footed it out the back door, but not before she'd seen the marks on his face.

How they'd known about Sean so early in the morning was anyone's guess. She had her suspicions. No proof, but plenty of suspicion. She longed to dig deeper and find the truth, but Sean's remark about bleached bones gave her pause. Nope, the best she could hope for was an explanation from Sean about his peculiar abilities. After he gave her one, she'd cut her losses and get out of town.

The irony of it all? She'd be walking away from a story bigger than she could've imagined. Only no one would believe it and if she tried to convince them, her credibility would be ruined. She'd be laughed out of the newspaper business. She'd find herself working for some rag, writing about alien abductions and crop circles.

Sean was right. She should go back to her life in Michael's Creek and forget everything. Well, maybe not everything. She doubted she could ever lose the memory of his kiss. Thinking about it now made her feel all soft and gooey inside. She shoved the feelings away. He wasn't for her. Even if they hadn't come from two different cultures, she'd seen his type before – a selfless do-gooder out to change the world.

Good luck with that one.

She'd go back to Michael's Creek and focus her energy on landing a story that everyone would believe. Sooner or later one had to come along.

Sitting up, she stared out the window. My god, it was spooky out here tonight. Last night, moonlight had lit the landscape but now clouds chased across the moon, dimming its light. The Center sat like a hulking beast and even the air felt heavy. Her hand stole over to the passenger's seat and the jack-handle lying there. She wasn't a fool. She'd lost her mace last night, but she wasn't going to go traipsing around in the middle of the night without some kind of weapon. Just in case. The jack-handle seemed like a good choice. Settling her head against the window again, she placed the handle on her lap as the lack of sleep overtook her.

What seemed like only moments later, a sharp rap on the window made her jump. Sean. Her eyes flew to the clock. My god, it was four o'clock in the morning.

She pushed the door open, still hanging on to her weapon. "I thought you said eleven? Where have you been?"

"Something came up." He eyed the jack-handle. "Planning on using that?"

She snorted. "You were the one who said it wasn't safe."

Without commenting, he turned and headed towards the hill beyond the Center. R.J. ran after him. At the top of the rise, he suddenly whirled on her.

"What do you want to know?"

Caught off-guard, the words stumbled out, sounding silly even to her. "Are you a shapeshifter?"

"Yes."

Shocked at his honesty, R.J.'s jaw dropped and she waited for him to continue. He didn't.

"That's it? 'Yes'?"

A wry grin twisted the corners of his mouth. "I think that word covers it."

Frustrated, she kicked a clod of dirt. "Not bloody likely, mister."

"I suppose you want to know the 'who, what, when, and where'?"

"Damn straight I do," she exclaimed.

Sean sighed deeply. "My gift, talent, whatever the whites would call it, runs in my family."

"Your grandfather, too?" R.J.'s eyes widened.

"No, not him, but his father." He stopped and looked up at the sky as if trying to decide what to say. "This is hard," he said finally. "Not even our people are aware. They know that my family has powerful medicine, but they've never questioned what it might be."

"Have you always been able to shift?"

"No. It started shortly after I came to live with my grandfather. I was lucky in a way that I'd come here. Because of what he'd learned from his father, he recognized what was happening to me and was there to guide me through it."

"Does it happen . . . um . . . well . . . you know . . . whenever the moon–" she broke off, feeling foolish.

"Are you trying to ask me if I only change during a full moon?" he inquired, not hiding the humour in his voice.

Irritated, her chin hiked. "According to movies and literature–"

"In case you haven't noticed," he cut in, his humour gone. "We're not in a movie – this is my life we're discussing. No, it's not only during a full moon, I can change at will. At first, when I was a teenager, it'd happen whenever I experienced high emotion."

"Must've happened a lot."

"It did. After the first change, my grandfather took me out of school for about a year and taught me at home. During that time, he showed me how to manage the changes."

"Are you like–" she paused, trying to think of the right word, "well, invulnerable?"

"We're back to the movies, huh?" He shook his head. "No, I can be killed just like any other animal. It wouldn't take a silver bullet." Tugging on his bottom lip, he studied her. "I've never had to explain this to anyone and I don't really know if I can. When I'm in animal form, there is still a part of me that's human but I feel the freedom of being a wild thing."

"Last night, when you were fighting those men, why didn't you become something other than an owl? Something a little bigger with a few more teeth?" she asked, playing with the jack-handle still in her hand

He gave a rough bark of laughter. "You really don't know anything about the legends, do you?"

She pulled herself up and glared at him. "Nope, sorry, never saw the need to do research on shapeshifters," she replied sarcastically. "If I'm not asking the right questions, you'll just have to forgive me."

"I can only become an owl – it's my totem. I told you that, as an owl, part of me is still human?"

She nodded.

"As a human, the owl is always with me, too."

"I don't get it."

"I can move silently whenever I need to, I can see things in the dark that are invisible to others, and my hearing?

Unbelievably sharp." He came close, looming over her. "*And* I will do everything I can to defend and protect my family and my territory."

She swallowed. "I'm not going to write about this," she insisted.

"I believe you. It wouldn't be in your best interests."

"You think I'm selfish, don't you?" she asked defensively.

He stepped back. "I think you're so driven by ambition that you'd do anything to succeed."

"What's wrong with that?" she huffed.

"Nothing . . . in your world. In mine, we're worried about surviving."

"And you're using, what did you call it? Medicine?"

"Trying to." His eyes roamed the landscape. "There are those who've been seduced, lost interest in the good of the people. They see only their own desires."

"Charlie Two Horses."

"He's one. There are others."

"Why do they want to ruin the Center?"

"There are several reasons. People with little else have donated possessions that have been in their families for years. To see them destroyed would be destroying the heart of our people." He focused on R.J. "People without heart, who've been beaten down, are easier to manipulate," he said sadly. "Then there's the money. The Center is heavily insured, so if something happened to it, a large sum of money would be paid to the tribe. That money could be used for other things."

"Like a casino?"

"Exactly. Some people lose enough of their money in town; they don't need easy access to gambling here."

"Have you made this argument to the Elders?"

"Of course but it's not that simple. My grandfather has a lot of honour in the eyes of the tribe, but I'm still a half-breed."

She saw lines of weariness tighten his face. "They don't trust you?"

"Not completely."

Moving close, she dropped the jack-handle and laid a hand on his arm. His muscles quivered at her touch. "Then why are you fighting for them? Why not leave this place and start a new life away from all of this?"

A look of regret crossed his face and he opened his mouth to speak. Abruptly, his features hardened. His lips closed and he shook his head. "I can't. My place is here."

The sadness in him reached out and swamped her. Putting her arms around him, she laid her head on his chest and felt him shudder. His hand stole up to her face and he tilted her chin, looking deeply into her eyes. Her breath caught in her throat when she saw the fire burning inside of him. Unblinking, he began to lower his face to hers. Suddenly in the depths of his eyes, a yellow spark flamed.

"Down!" he whispered harshly, pulling her off her feet.

"Wha—"

He clamped a hand over her mouth. "Quiet," he hissed, crouching beside her. "You'll give away our position to the men down there."

Her eyes strained against the darkness, trying to see what he saw, but all she could make out was the dark shape of the Center.

He released her arm and began to steal away. "Stay here."

"Oh no you don't, Bird Man," she said softly, picking up the jack-handle. "You're not leaving me behind this time."

"Bird Man?" he sputtered. "You make light of my medicine?"

"Hey, I'm just going with the flow," she murmured, "and happy I'm not insane after all."

She felt him tense and saw the conflicting emotions race across his face. She almost sensed what he was thinking: how many were there? Should he leave her here unprotected? What if he lost the fight?

Finally, he made his decision and motioned her to follow. "Quietly," he cautioned as he crept ahead.

R.J. tried to mimic Sean's stealth. He hadn't been kidding when he said he could move silently – the tall grass barely stirred as he edged forward. He led her to the side of the building and moved her into the shadows. Laying a finger on his lips, he pointed to the ground with his other hand, indicating she should stay put. Then without a word, he disappeared around the side of the building.

Flattened against the side of the Center, her heart hammered in her chest and sweat beaded in her armpits. Visions of bones scattered across the prairie danced in her mind. Could she make it to the Jeep without giving Sean away? She could go for help – but where? And who could she trust? *No*, she thought with a shake of her head, *for once she'd obey and pray that the owl wasn't outmatched.*

Suddenly she heard the sound of voices. Shrinking back into the shadows, she strained to listen.

"Shut up," one voice rasped.

"I'm telling you – that's her Jeep sitting there," A second voice whispered. "What if she comes back and catches us?"

"Do what I tell you and she won't."

"What if she's inside?"

"That's her problem, not ours."

"But—"

"Just do it."

A shift in the breeze lifted a strand of R.J.'s hair and with the breeze came a strange odour. Her nose twitched and she felt a sneeze building. Grabbing the tip, she pinched until the feeling passed. Letting go of the breath she'd been holding, she inhaled deeply. Oh my god, she smelled gasoline – they were going to torch the place. *Where in the hell was Sean?*

She slunk around the corner of the building and saw three shapes huddled on the ground by the long windows of the Council room. Close enough to make out what they held in their hands, she saw a glass bottle with a rag trailing down its side. *Great, a molotov cocktail.* She smelled the sulphur as the match struck and watched in horror as the flame drew near the rag. She had to do something.

But then, the flame abruptly died and the man holding the spent match flew into the air as if yanked by an invisible rope. A foot shot out and knocked the bottle from the next man's hand. A second hit to his jaw had him sprawling backwards. He didn't move. The third man scrambled to his feet and took off at a run towards a stand of cottonwood. A screech rent the air, and a white owl soared above the running man's head, outdistancing him.

At least now she knew where Sean was. Relieved, she fell back against the building, until a quick movement on her left had her standing at attention.

A fourth man. With a gun. As if in slow motion, he raised it, training it on the white shape headed for the cottonwoods.

"Hey!" She pushed away from the building and, raising the jack-handle high, rushed him.

Surprised, his gun wavered, giving R.J. time to bring the jack-handle down with full force on his wrists. Bones snapped and dirt flew when the shot went wide. Holding his arms tightly against his stomach, the man wheeled and ran.

R.J. thought about giving chase, but a noise from the stand of trees caught her attention. She turned just in time to see the man make it to the trees . . . but the owl had made it first. It waited on a low branch, and as the man ducked under the limb, the owl disappeared. Sean swung down and planted both feet on the man's chest. He staggered back, trying to gain his balance, but Sean was on him in a flash. The thud of fists hitting flesh lasted only a few moments.

The man went down for the last time.

Sean watched Charlie Two Horses bundle three of the vandals in the back of the tribal police car.

"They'll be set free," his grandfather said softly from where he stood beside him.

"I know." Sean's mouth tightened in a grim line. "They're white *and* they're barely eighteen. I imagine if they're tried at all, it will be as juveniles and the charge will be malicious mischief. Not much of a penalty for that."

"Did you recognize them?"

"One is the grandson of the man who owns the motel. He was also involved in the vandalism last night, but we can't prove it."

"You came close to losing this time, Akecheta."

He gave his grandfather a nudge. "But we didn't." His eyes travelled to R.J., leaning against the side of her Jeep. "She helped."

His grandfather stiffened. "What if she tells her story?"

"She won't. She gave me her word."

"Ha! The word of a white woman."

"She saved my life, grandfather," he replied in a quiet voice.

The tension in his grandfather's stance eased. "Hmm, we'll see."

"I'm going to go say goodbye."

R.J. pushed away from the Jeep as he approached. A soft smile twitched at the corner of her mouth. One dimple showed.

"Got to say this for you, Swifthawk," she said, shoving her hands in her pockets. "You sure know how to show a girl a good time."

"And you, R.J. Baxter," he answered with a smile and a tap to the end of her nose, "don't know how to follow instructions." He sobered. "And I'm glad you don't. Thanks for saving my life."

Her face tinged with pink. "No problem." Shifting her attention to the patrol car slowly leaving the parking lot, she gave her head a shake. "What will happen now?"

"Nothing."

"What do you mean 'nothing'?" she asked, indignant. "They tried to burn down the Center."

"They're white. Charlie will turn them over to the sheriff and at most, they'll get a slap on the wrist."

"That's not fair."

He lifted his shoulder in a shrug.

She watched the patrol with a speculative look. "I could do a story about the injustice of it all?"

"Don't," he replied, placing a hand on her shoulder to draw her attention away from the departing vandals. "It won't do any good. We know them now – they'll be watched."

R.J. crossed her arms over her chest and arched an eyebrow at him. "I'll agree you have some pretty unusual talents, Bird Man," she said in a low voice, "but you and your grandfather can't be everywhere."

"There are others."

Her eyes flew wide. "What?" she hissed, "Some secret society of shapeshifters?"

Sean allowed a smirk. "Let's just say we have 'friends'."

"But—"

The hand on her shoulder squeezed lightly, cutting her off. "Let it go, R.J."

She glanced towards the Center with a light glinting in her eye. "Okay, I won't write about the plot to destroy the Center," she said, slapping him on the arm, "but I'll tell you what I *am*

going to do – I'm going to write a story that'll make this place
sound better than Disneyland." She chuckled and gave a quick
nod. "And I can do it. You're going to have so many tourists to
fleece, the tribe won't know what to do with all the money."

"I hope you're right."

"Yup," she said with a broad smile, "this place is going to be
so popular that whoever's behind this attack won't dare try and
destroy it again." Her smile fell away. "You really can't leave,
can you?"

He shook his head, almost with remorse.

"Well," she said, and shot a glance towards his grandfather.

Then, before he could react, she grabbed the front of his shirt
and, standing on tiptoes, planted a kiss that shook him to his
core. With a satisfied smile, she turned and hopped in her Jeep.
Starting the engine, she winked. "See you around, Bird Man."

He watched as she slowly pulled away and turned on to the
highway.

"Did she call you Bird Man?" his grandfather asked in
shocked tones.

"Yes," Sean answered with a low chuckle.

His grandfather scratched his head, his attention on the
retreating Jeep. "Even for a white, she's a strange woman. It's
good we've seen the last of her."

"I wouldn't be so sure," Sean replied, more to himself than
his grandfather. With a jerk of his head, he motioned towards
the rise. "Come on, let's go home."

Together, they walked across the prairie as the sun brightened the horizon. At the top of the rise, they looked down at
the highway winding its way out of the reservation and the Jeep
speeding away.

Above it, in a golden sky, a white owl circled.

The Demon's Secret

Nathalie Gray

One

Demons usually didn't take so many bullets to die.

"Damn. I don't have all night," Cain muttered.

He emptied his magazine into the flying monstrosity as it swooped past, and scowled at the horrid smell that hit him like a slap of hot wind. Pausing only to slam in place a spare drum magazine, he leaped from one building to the next. The *boom-boom-boom* of his shotgun thundered in the winter night. Nickel-plated, custom-fitted, this combat shotgun was nicknamed "the jackhammer". Who the hell *named* guns?

Around him, snow-covered east end Montreal rooftops resembled clouds. Like running in heaven. Except he'd never be allowed in heaven. There were books written about him, even *the* Book mentioned him.

If Cain didn't kill the spawn, that'd make him look bad. And weak. In his line of work, looking weak invited all kinds of bad press and the attention of some beings even worse than he was. His own master would love nothing better than to punish him.

"Come on," he hollered. "I'm freezing my nuts off!"

The demonic spawn came back for another dive, hoping perhaps Cain was too busy trying not to fall off the building. Cain straightened his arm, took aim and didn't let his finger off the trigger until a sizable chunk of the creature had been blown off. The monster crashed on to a tin roof, tumbled several times and sent a geyser of snow ten feet high before stopping in a flailing, writhing heap. Cain skidded to a halt, pinned one of the demon's ruined, leathery wings beneath his Italian shoe. The magazine was empty, so he methodically hand-loaded one of the special shells.

He called these rosaries.

"Next time you come after me, you piece of hell-shit, bring a few buddies along, okay?" Cain aimed at the creature's neck and fired.

The shot dispersed in a stainless steel wire, dotted with silver-plated ball bearings. Like a flying garrote, it hit the creature across the neck, severing it. Black blood sprayed outwards and melted snow over a foot-wide radius. Like an overripe melon bursting. The smell of sulphur and smoke stung Cain's nose. The black creature's glistening body caved in on itself and then broke in several smouldering embers that blew away in the wind. No traces of it remained except for despoiled snow.

Not much could hurt those demonic creatures. Holy water, silver, gold, direct sunlight and a couple of other things he never would've guessed before becoming . . . Whatever he was now.

Cain checked his watch. Maybe he wouldn't be too late for the harvest.

After retracing his steps to the private clinic's roof, he opened the door leading into the service stairwell, knocked his feet, one by one, against the jamb to dislodge what he could of snow – and black, viscous blood. Heat like a wave greeted him when he climbed down the stairs to the second floor. He hadn't realized how cold he was. His fingertips tingled, as did his toes. Cain smoothed down his felt coat, pushed the door leading to the second floor and, staring straight ahead amidst the oblivious staff, returned to the room where he'd first spotted the spawn as it tried to get in through the window. The door was still ajar. Cain slipped in and just by smell he knew he wasn't too late. The man still lived. Barely.

"Am I going up or down?"

Cain snapped his gaze to the man's face, where a pair of old but vibrant blue eyes stared at him. *Directly* at him. Cain had forgotten what it felt like to have someone look at him this way. The only ones who could see him were demons, their spawns – like the one on the rooftop – the angels that still gave a damn, and the lunatics. And of course, the dying. But they were rarely happy to see him.

"Up."

A look of relief passed over the weathered face. He nodded imperceptibly, except to Cain – because he knew what to look for and already waited for the sign.

"You? You from above or below?"

"Above," Cain lied. He approached the bed, placed a hand on the man's wrist. A weak, arrhythmic pulse throbbed against his cold fingers. Not long now. The machine agreed with him and began to bleep.

The man closed his eyes for the last time, Cain knew. He went to work quickly, efficiently. He'd done this thousands of times throughout the centuries. He pulled a gold pillbox from his coat pocket, clicked it open and placed it near the man's mouth. The last breath created fog on the metal surface. Cain narrowed his eyes when the soul emerged, a manifestation that resembled a thin tendril of silver smoke coiling upward. Within the thin mist glittered tiny white flakes like snow. Cain could never get over how many secrets people kept. This man had *dozens*. Big ones, little ones, some darker and heavier and others that floated like tiny feathers.

Before the soul could rise further – the lucky man indeed was going "up" – Cain passed the pillbox through the soul several times. He shivered every time his skin came in contact with the gossamer stuff. He tucked his hand against his chest and clipped the box shut. Several of the dead man's secrets were now stored safely inside. Berith, Great Duke of Hell and almighty asshole, would be happy. And when Master Berith was happy, it meant one more day on the mortal plane, harvesting secrets from the dying, instead of roasting back home down on the seventh level of hell. The special place of those who'd done violence against others. Or themselves. Plus, the more he collected secrets, the more souls Berith could buy, and someday, if he brought enough, Cain would be set free. That was the deal.

Cain was out of the clinic by the time the staff came rushing into the dead man's room. His car waited on the corner, looking forlorn and broody with its black body and tinted windows.

Sunlight didn't agree with Cain – neither did water and a whole slew of things that never bothered him back when he was . . .

When he was a human. So long ago.

He gunned the engine and tore up the street. His breath rose in front of him. Without bothering to warm up the car, he just drove it to his temporary home at the foot of the Jacques-Cartier bridge. Graffiti and detritus covered the brick walls and uneven streets. Montreal was like a bipolar city – elegance and beauty on one side, pestilence and corruption on the other. He parked the car near an abandoned foundry, slipped between the chain link fence doors and then cursed when he splashed cold mud into his shoes. The many locks and chains barring his door meant he had to stand outside as it began to snow. It seeped into his hair, down his collar. Cain was shivering when he pushed the door closed behind him, and repeated the process in reverse order. But at least, he was indoors.

Neon light flickered to life when the motion sensors caught him. Part armory, part gym, part derelict industrial kitchen – the only place in the building that still had running hot water – his home shared nothing with the one he'd left behind all those years ago.

"Forget it. That life is over."

"Life? Barely," came a voice behind him. "Existence would be the correct term."

Cain twitched. "I hate it when you sneak up on me."

"Life entails a soul," the voice went on, as if he hadn't spoken. "So 'existence' is definitely a better word for you, Damaged One. One can still be damned and *exist*."

His demon master had chosen the body of a young woman to possess that night, all slender limbs in the pale grey suit, and shiny black hair. Maybe Berith had developed good taste after all. "You almost look good tonight, Berith."

The woman's smile accentuated. "If you were not my favourite secret keeper, I would personally escort you to the eighth level."

"Maybe I'd be better off with liars and thieves."

Berith approached him, leisurely caressed the lapel of his suit. Cain curled his upper lip and stared hard.

"Did you do good work tonight?"

"That's what you call it?" Cain snarled.

The demon rolled her eyes. "Don't be so damn melodramatic. You work for hell. Get over it."

"And some day I'm going to take your damn job and shove it."

A dangerous glint shone in Berith's eyes. "But in the meantime, you belong to me." She stuck her hand out, palm up.

"Fuck you." Cain fished the pillbox out of his pocket and slammed it into the small hand so incongruous to the demon's true form.

"You should not toy with me so, Brother Cain."

"Don't call me that." No one had called him that since . . .

"Ashamed of your past? You should not be. It was what drew me to your soul. So grey, so close to turning. But it was his fault, he took credit for something you did. As always."

The hurt and confusion in his brother's eyes. Cain would never forget it.

He gritted his teeth hard enough to hurt his jaw. "You didn't hear me the first time, demon? Fuck. *You.*"

Maybe if he pushed the creature far enough, he'd kill Cain once and for all. Oblivion. He could taste it.

Berith whispered a word that caused Cain to drop to his knees in searing agony. His chest constricted, his head throbbed so intensely he feared the skull wouldn't take the pressure, every nerve ending felt on fire, bile rose up his throat and, in the blink of an eye, he was no longer in his temporary home in the slums of Montreal.

He was back in hell.

Ashes and glowing embers flew in twisters around him as the voices of the damned rose in complaints and cries. Everything was dead or dying. People, animals, things. Falling apart, collapsing, burning up in black smoke that choked the crimson sky and created heat vortices darker than night. Black holes in the blood-red sky. Spawns like the one he'd killed earlier that night swooped down on him, lashed his naked back with their talons, cawed in parody of his roars of pain.

In all his squalid grandeur, Berith towered before him, wisps of hair flying in the burning wind, shreds of skin falling off the massive skeleton. But the eyes were intact, always remained

intact no matter the body's decay. They stared at Cain, right
into his core. Rage and terror and pain closed in on him.

"What was it about my 'job'?" Berith asked, leaned over. He
smiled as he delicately pressed a rotten finger through Cain's
shoulder.

His world vacillated. And Cain screamed.

They said if a man hurt enough, his body would shut down. In
hell, that theory didn't apply.

Cain flopped to the concrete floor back in Montreal when
Berith summarily dismissed him in the middle of a quartering.
Lucky someone had interrupted the demon because the last
time Cain had pissed Berith off, he'd paid for it dearly. Even by
hell standards.

"I need—" He coughed, cleared his raw throat. He *really*
needed a drink.

His clothes hung in tatters and one of his shoes was gone.
He shivered, raked a hand through his sweaty hair. Ashes still
clung to his eyelashes and lips. Any moist part of him was like-
wise covered in the stuff. A dull, familiar pain radiated from the
inside of his left forearm. Rolling on to his back to cool that side
against the concrete, Cain raised his arm in front of his watery
eyes. As with any other job, the name of his next "client" was
carved in his flesh. It'd disappear. Not because the skin would
heal, but because after he'd deliver the secrets, Berith would
erase the name. Only to carve another. Then another.

But this one gave him pause. The name of a well-known
politician.

"Shit."

Other demons would want that woman's secrets, like gold
coins to the denizens of hell. *Everyone* wanted someone else's
secrets, demons included. They could buy souls with the stuff.
And nothing was more important to a demon than the number
of souls under his or her command. Maybe if Cain harvested a
good number, Berith wouldn't continue where he'd left off.

He showered to get the stench of Berith off him and, once
again in a dark suit and Italian shoes – his armour – fired up
the laptop to access tax records made available by another of
his boss's many "employees". The demon had in his charge

accountants and artists, politicians and activists, men, women, young and old, of every nation that existed and some that no longer did. Every demon had at least as many as Berith, some more, others less. He'd had to fight through hordes of rival demons' spawns and secret keepers to get the jobs done. One in particular, Belial, employed only the most vicious and degenerate and commanded legions of lesser demons, spawns, humans and even a couple of renegade angels. No one wanted to mess with him, except Cain. He just didn't care anymore.

With a triumphant ping, the search yielded a full legal name, an address and more information than Cain could ever use. He noted the address on a piece of paper – since the name was carved in his flesh – and tucked it into his coat pocket. Because he'd never been the positive type and suspected shit would hit the fan again, he loaded up on ammo and weapons, slipped a pair of throwing knives in their sheaths strapped to his calves. He might look like a banker but he hid an arsenal worthy of any specops operative, complete with little sachets of holy water and bullets made of gold and silver.

As he walked out, he caught a glimpse of himself in the mirror. From tall, dark and handsome, he'd turned into tall, dark and haunted.

But first, a drink. He knew just the place and, if he was lucky, he might even meet the closest person he had to a friend.

Half an hour later, Cain pulled the dirty door to a hole-in-the-wall tavern named after the dead proprietor's wife. It'd changed hands three times in the last fifty years. Cain could name each bartender since the place's opening.

An older woman in a corner booth caught his attention. So he wouldn't drink alone that night.

Cain slipped into the booth. "Sister."

"You look like shit," she said in rapid-fire sign language. The gold cross resting on her mint-green cardigan gleamed when she raised her hand, three fingers extended. "Eat something."

The bartender came over and set down an open bottle of Canadian rye whisky and a pair of thick-bottomed tumblers. With a dip of his chin to the woman, the bartender returned to his bar.

The first swallow scorched Cain's already raw throat all the way down then spread in a nice warm wave in his belly. He inhaled deeply, was about to take another swallow when the bartender returned, this time with a plate of smoked meat sandwich and fries.

Out of habit, Cain thanked the man, remembering too late, as always, that not many would remember him two seconds after talking to him. It'd taken him centuries to get used to it – of people looking through him as if he wasn't right there in front of them. But the in-between state had its pluses – especially when it came to gunfights. Ha. Yet the solitude had been crushing at first. Then he'd become accustomed to the shroud that seemed to cover him, used it to his advantage. Those like him who didn't belong on the mortal plane, who'd had their turn and left, were no longer part of the equation. Like ghosts.

He wondered why the Sister *could* see him though. She'd accosted him a few years ago as he walked across a park. It'd been so long since he'd spoken to someone that he'd temporarily forgotten what it felt like for a person to look straight *at* him. A real, living person. The dying could see him all right. But she hadn't been dying – and still wasn't – neither was she a demon, spawn or angel, that he could tell, anyway (angels had always been sneaky). She must have been a lunatic then. Not that he'd ever tell Sister Evangeline to her face. The woman ran a men's mission near the old port and no one willingly messed with her, not even the mayor. The thought made him smile.

"I didn't even know you had them," Sister Evangeline said. A mocking lift to her mouth rounded her ample cheek.

"Had what?" Cain bit into the sandwich. Juices triggered by the meat and hot mustard forced him to focus on the meal and not the conversation. He wolfed the thing down in four bites.

"*Teeth*. I didn't know you had teeth. Never saw them." She stole a fry from his plate.

"It doesn't bother you he thinks you're talking to yourself?" Cain nodded in the bartender's direction. The man seemed oblivious to Evangline's gestures as he watched a snowy little TV screen set on a soccer game.

"He can think whatever he wants." Still holding the fry, she managed to sign at the same time. "It's you I worry about. I swear to God, you look worse every time I see you. Are you sick?"

Cain pushed the plate away. He wasn't hungry anymore. But he was still thirsty, so he poured them both a second glass.

She grimaced. "Fine, be the mysterious jerk. If you think it makes you look cool, think again, *mon garçon.*" Only Evangeline would ever call him a boy. He was older than she was, by a few millennia, too. He'd lived through the Great Flood and listened live on the radio as the Hindenburg burned.

He caught her looking down at his chest and realized the butt of his Luger stuck out of his coat. With his elbow, he surreptitiously slipped the holster back a bit. His forearm throbbed like a neglected wound quickly infecting. He had to get to work.

"Remind me again what you do for a living?" Her eyebrows moved as much as her hands when she talked.

He stood, slipped money from his pants pocket and placed it on the table, drained another glass that didn't burn half as much as the first two. "I never told you what I do for a living, Sister."

"Do you know your scripture?"

"What makes you think I'm Catholic?"

She smiled. "You wear guilt and shame like a pair of well worn gloves. So, *do* you?"

"You know what they say about curiosity. 'But his wife looked back from behind him, and she became a pillar of salt'."

Sister Evangeline's French-Irish temper came out in explosive hand signals almost too fast to follow. Cain had always thought the sign word for "asshole" was funny as hell. A reversed version of the symbol for "OK".

Grinning, he left the seething woman to finish the fries.

Two

Cain felt trouble long before he caught the first whiff. Spawns, a lot of them. The night sky took on a more sombre quality, as if it was thick with activity he couldn't see. But hear it he could. Hissing, growling, sucking sounds, the flap of wings and scrape of talons against concrete.

Snow fell slowly, in small flakes that didn't melt when they landed on Cain's shoulders and coat sleeves. A twister of debris roiled along the sidewalk a few feet away. In front of him like a gargantuan sentinel, stood a tall and thick stone mansion surrounded with a high wrought-iron fence. He checked behind him, noted nothing above the rooftops except for the faraway silhouette of the Olympic Stadium, Montreal's white elephant, and its inclined tower.

Yet he could feel *them*. Growing closer. It hadn't taken them long to sniff him out. Sometimes, he suspected spawns had nothing else to do than wait for a gate to open so they could swoop down on whatever came out.

Movement exploded left, right, above. Snow flew in thick ribbons that lashed and whipped him like tiny grains of salt.

"Here we go," he snarled.

Cain cocked his shotgun a second before the first spawn swooped down to his left, missed and hit the pavement a couple of inches in front of him, creating a tiny but messy crater. This surprised him. They rarely missed their aerial attacks. They were being careless, therefore desperate. They'd make mistakes. Bad news for them. Very good news for him.

He pumped a quick pair of specialized maximum shredding rounds into the fiend. Each minced a wing and part of its torso and, on a long and angry hiss, the thing lay still. Others replaced it. They always did in his world of in-between – not on Earth, not in hell. Both at once, yet in neither place.

One landed right on top of him, sent him to his knees, dug talons and claws into his back and shoulders. It wailed in his ear a split-second before he aimed the AA-12 straight up and fired. A shower of gooey bits fell around him and burned like acid wherever the stuff touched. The burn of its claws spread to his body. Hellish fever. Cain ran across the deserted street, fired as he went, rounds hitting targets and downing them, others ricocheting on bony ridges and creating scuffs against the stone fence. To mortal eyes, nothing would show, no sound would be heard.

On a run, he leaped on top of the hood of his car, then on to the roof, where he whirled on himself and dispensed death at five rounds a second. One spawn thudded against the trunk, trashing and flailing. One of the wings caught Cain on the arm. His shotgun went sailing ten feet high and landed in the snow bank.

"Shit," he snarled. His breath was ripped out of his lungs when a spawn struck him with its wing. The talon lacerated his coat across the chest. Despite the adrenaline, he heard a button land on the frozen sidewalk.

Cackling in delight, the spawn raised its misshapen, clawed hand. The final hit. This one would hurt. Cain only had time to pull his Luger out of its holster at his chest. Gold bullets with silver cores dipped in holy water. His best ones, usually reserved for full-fledged demons. Such a waste.

He levelled it at the thing's chest, fired just as both its wings spread for the coming attack. The shock sent it flying back in a geyser of embers and ashes, sent it colliding against a hydro pole. It bent with the violent collision. Sparks coursed along the wires.

Burning pain exploded in his lower back.

Cain looked down, more shocked than hurt, and spotted a long, glistening claw coming out of his belly.

"Damn."

Dying meant a split second of suspension where he'd be catapulted back to hell, where no wound was too great to "heal", then another split second to be sent right back up to the mortal plane as if nothing had happened. Where half a dozen spawns waited for him. The circus would never end. Not until he'd accumulated enough secrets for Berith's taste. The demon had told him that some day, when Cain had brought enough secrets to sell for souls, he'd be sent up to the purgatory. Still in hell, but a world better than the seventh level.

He aimed back and fired a bullet into the spawn that had backstabbed him. And then he died. Again.

Ashes and smoke, the smell of sulphur and charred flesh, cries and lamentations, crimson sky, black sun, and abruptly, snow replaced it all. It grated against his face as Cain realized he'd come back facedown into the street, where a spawn stood over him, no doubt ready – and delighted – to send him back for another spin downstairs.

"Oh, for Christ's—"

BOOM.

The explosion drowned the spawn's shriek just as a wave

of energy traversed the air a couple inches above Cain's head. Gunshot followed the detonation. A *lot* of gunshot. Someone had their finger on the trigger and wasn't letting up. He floundered to his hands and knees, ashes choking him, still reeling from his short trip to hell, and turned in time to catch a scene that tore a curse from him.

A lone woman stood in the middle of the street, blond hair in a punk cut, dressed in white vinyl from head to toe except for black military boots that reached up to her knees and an assortment of belts that crisscrossed her muscular frame. Bethany Simard, infamous keeper for one of the most powerful demons, Asmodeus, pain in the butt extraordinaire and probably Cain's one and only weak spot.

Great timing.

He couldn't help giving her a good, long look. Hot *and* dangerous.

"I'm easy on the eyes, huh?" She cracked an irreverent grin. "Behind you, handsome."

Cain whirled around, thanked his lucky star he still had his gun. A gold and silver bullet took off half of the fiend's head. The rest hit the fence, dissipated in glowing coals and ash.

Movement registered in the corner of his eye. He turned back to the street. Bethany was gone. Mocking laughter, rapidly diminishing, floated to him from the other side of the fence.

"Shit."

He took a moment to fish his silvery shotgun from the snow bank before chasing the woman over the fence. He knew exactly where she was going, and he intended to prevent it. Velvety silence greeted him once he landed on the other side of the fence. Cain circumvented the mansion, his heart thumping. Ahead into the gloom, he spotted a figure darting left and right amongst the skeletal bushes separating the mansion from its neighbour. He lengthened his paces, pumped his gun-free arm hard and fast. Cold air burned his lungs. From a tiny darting figure, the woman's silhouette grew clearer. She'd reached the back porch. Bethany had always been *fast*. Thankfully, he was a *tiny* bit faster. Cain caught up to her just as she flipped back a sling strapped across her shoulder like a postman bag. A matte black MP5 submachine gun hung from the sling.

He gripped it, yanked sideways and sent the woman crashing against the stone wall. With a yelp, she extended a hand, caught herself against the balustrade. Cain used his long arms to seize her by an arm, whirled her around and pinned her there with the barrel of his shotgun pressed against her wrist.

"Hey!" She cocked her free arm to punch him, he caught that wrist, too. He knew her too well to let her have a free arm around him.

They stood face to face, their breaths mixing in puffs of steam. He'd neutralized both her arms, but that meant he didn't have one left either. Cain angled one foot back so she wouldn't get any ideas to kick him.

"That's how you thank me?" Bethany twisted one arm then the other. "I thought you were one of the good ones."

Cain squeezed harder. Her neck tendons corded like violin strings as she struggled to free herself. He wouldn't hold the diminutive Valkyrie in place for much longer. "Why are you here?"

"Why are *you* here?" she snapped.

He glared at her. "Don't make me send you back, Bethany."

Black eyes heavily rimmed in kohl flared in fear a brief instant, then bravado replaced it. "You're not like that."

"You'd be surprised. Your master sends you, or are you on one of your 'goodwill' hunts?" He'd had to answer to a very displeased Berith once because of her. Demons didn't like the idea that lowly keepers would do freelance hunts for others. Or that other keepers didn't turn the renegades in.

"It's one of his."

"Well, you can go back, because this one is mine."

Bethany smiled, batted her eyelids dramatically. "Maybe we can share?"

"And have Berith after my ass like the last time I 'shared' something with you? I don't think so."

"Aw, come on, it wasn't all bad."

It hadn't been all bad. In fact, he'd enjoyed working with the cheeky woman. Even damned as she was, she still had a verve for life that he found very intriguing. And appealing. Plus, no one ever talked to him, not with his reputation and "charming" personality. Evangeline and Bethany were basically his entire social circle.

"It *was* bad. You're a pain in the ass." The smudged mascara, crazy hair and attitude didn't deter him at all. He suspected he found her attractive *because* of it and not in spite of it.

"But oh-so-irresistible and brilliant. Come on, Cain, we got another kick at the can, we should make the most of it." She gave him a pronounced once-over, actually winked in a very suggestive way. Simply unflappable.

"I wouldn't turn my back on you for a second, never mind taking my guns off." A smile escaped him. "Plus, you're not my type."

Liar.

Bethany grinned. "I bet you've always been a heartbreaker, even before . . ."

"Before I was damned?"

She shrugged. "Call it what you want. I call it a second shot at life."

"It's not *life*, Bethany. Not even close. We're on borrowed time, with our own personal demons yanking on the leash."

She lost her smile. "Party-pooper."

"Look," he began, regretting the words as they came out. She *was* his weak spot. Dammit. "Some day, maybe . . ."

A sparkle made her dark eyes look like coffee beans. Smile lines appeared at the corners of her eyes and mouth. She arched her hips off the wall and pressed herself against him. Her heat seeped into his clothes. "Maybe what, hm? You'd like to see *more* of me?"

"Yeah, I'd like to see 'more' of you."

Bethany's eyes sparkled.

Damn, he couldn't think when she pulled that shit. "Look . . ."

He must have relaxed his hold on her arm and saw his slip too late. The top of her head struck him on the chin. Pain exploded in his brain. His grip failed as he bent over.

And she was gone again, her boots thumping madly.

Cain stumbled into the house through the back door she'd left open. Careless, loud, obnoxious. He could've followed her progress from outside the house. Good old Bethany. Two by two, he took the stairs, followed her by the smell he'd come to associate with her – vinyl and body lotion. Up to the third floor, down a carpeted hallway lined with thick frames of dead people. Someone walked by – oblivious to the two gun-toting bounty hunters racing down the hall – as if moved by unseen hands into the place Cain had just occupied a split-second before. He'd always wondered what would happen if a mortal occupied the same space he did? Would they feel him?

There, at the end of the hallway. Light filtered out from underneath a door. Cain gripped his shotgun tighter as he silently pushed against the panel. There she was, his "saviour", bending over the dying politician, a wizened Asian woman. In the golden glow of a baroque lamp on the dresser, his competitor resembled an elf. But armed to the teeth. Bethany was too busy fishing around in a tiny leather purse strapped to her belt to pay much attention to him.

Cain sneaked up just close enough to press the barrel against her nape. "Don't make me send you back."

She froze.

"Start running, Bethany. I'll give you ten seconds head start."

"I need this," she whispered, turned her head slightly so she could look up at him. Tears welled in her eyes. Her chin trembled. He'd never seen her that way, so vulnerable, so afraid. He'd never seen her afraid despite some pretty serious fighting and crappy odds. He could only imagine what a woman went through at the hands of a demon. "Okay? I *need* this, Cain. Please, I'm not yanking your chain."

Staring into those pleading eyes wasn't as easy as he would've thought.

"Asmodeus . . ." She stopped, swallowed. "He's going to send me down another level if I don't bring him this one. You know what that means . . ."

Cain twitched in spite of himself. If Berith's reputation for viciousness was well known in all levels of hell, another demon beat him by miles and bounds. Asmodeus, king of demons, with untold legions at his command. Cain wouldn't want to be anywhere *near* the Tormenter if he'd failed to do his bidding. And being sent down another level was dying all over again. She'd have to start over. He could only imagine the horror. No wonder Bethany looked desperate.

But it wasn't any of his business. Or his problem.

The woman straightencd, slowly, turned to face him with her hands at shoulder level on either side of her. "What level are you on, Cain?"

"Seventh."

She nodded. "So you have a temper, huh?"

"You have no idea."

"Look, I'll help you with something else. Anytime, anywhere. But please, let me have this one here." She turned toward the older woman on the bed who lay with her eyes closed and a rosary tucked in her joined hands. Except for the ones his ammunitions contact made for him, he hadn't seen a real rosary in over thirty years. Traditions were dying at an alarming rate.

Cain shook his head. "And you think Berith will be happy to see me when I go back empty-handed?"

"I have connections, you know I do. I'll help you. I swear, okay? Name it." She grinned wide. "Anything for you my cutie patootie."

"Don't push it." Cain cursed under his breath. "*Anything*?"

Her gaze hardened. She lifted her chin defiantly. "Yeah, anything, even that."

He wasn't thinking about *that*, but preferred to keep the dangerous woman on her toes. "You *owe* me."

Since when did he give breaks to people? Was he losing his edge? Would Berith keep him in hell instead of sending him back to the mortal plane for another job? Damn that woman!

Bethany blew him a kiss, turned to the dying woman and pulled out a tiny black lacquered box when she noticed the telltale sign of the woman's passing. She collected the secrets – a whole cluster of them, he was so in shit over this – slipped the box back into its home at her belt and backed to the door.

"Would you have helped if it hadn't been me?" she asked.

"Why do you care?"

"Is that a no?"

"Just get the hell out. You owe me, Bethany. Big time."

She agreed with a nod. "In all the years we've known each other, you never once asked what level I'm on."

Cain sighed long and hard. This was turning out to be a very bad day. He hated bad days. They invariably ended with his butt in hell, being tortured and taunted then tossed back up. "I don't give a shit."

"Yes you do. You're just too proud to admit you care." She winked. "I'm on the eighth."

Before Cain could process the implications, she was gone.

The eighth level of hell was reserved for usurpers and swindlers. And *liars*.

The one time he gave someone a break and this was what happened. That woman would be the end of him.

"Bethany, you trouble-making little shit."

He took off after her. She was easy to follow if only because of the racket she caused. As if she didn't care if he followed. Or maybe she didn't *mind*.

Winter air blasted him across the face when he burst out on to the back porch, ran along the fence and cleared the mansion corner just in time to catch Bethany leaping over the fence. While running, he aimed more or less in her direction and fired once. The shot clanged against the iron fence, busted the closing mechanism, and Cain only had to dip his shoulder as he ran into the opening.

As Cain chased the little liar down Avenue Pierre de Coubertin, the air filled with the flap of wings. A leathery *fap-fap-fap* that presaged nothing good for either of them.

"Give me the box!"

He was out of time. She could disappear down below whenever she wanted. She just ignored him and kept on running.

A city bus on its lonely night run temporarily obscured her when she crossed the wind-swept street. The stadium loomed in front. If she lost him in the maze of concrete ramps and walkways, he'd never find her again.

Three silhouettes suddenly rose near the underground parking entrance. Cain only had time to mutter a curse when Bethany ran right past them. In her haste, she must not have spotted them. Bright muzzle flashes preceded the thunder of several firearms. With a yelp, the woman stumbled, managed to fire a shot before she crashed against the concrete ramp. Like vultures, the three attackers jumped from their perch to finish the job. By that time, Cain had silently caught up to them. Wind drowned what little noise he made as he crept up behind the trio of men.

"Do not kill her yet," said the man to the right, a tall fellow with a dark coat that reached the ground. His courtly speech pattern tickled Cain's memory. "There is no reason to be hasty, is there?"

Bethany used the ramp for support as she gingerly climbed back to her feet. "Guys, guys, it's just a misunderstanding. We can work through this, right. Just hear me out."

Cain levelled his shotgun at their backs. He could have given them fair warning, a chance to step away and get lost. He might have felt a bit more lenient toward them if Bethany hadn't already wasted what little goodwill he possessed. As it were, he'd already lost too much time. Plus, the kind of men who ganged up on a woman wouldn't be missed if they suddenly exited the gene pool.

He opened fire.

Two collapsed right away, the air instantly filling with the smell of sulphur and the acrid taste of ash. He should've known. Keepers. They'd be back within seconds, "resurrected" by their demon masters, just like Berith had done for him earlier that night. Bethany nimbly jumped on the other side of the ramp.

It figures.

The third man, however, growled in pain but seemed otherwise unaffected by the silver slugs dipped in holy water. So, not a keeper then. And not a human either.

Cain understood why when the man whirled around. Massive wings shredded the long coat, spread high and wide. Contrary to popular belief, angel wings weren't feathered but made of tough hide like those of demons. In fact, the only distinguishing factor between the two – other than their disposition – was the smell. Cain swore under his breath. He didn't have time for this.

"Thanks for the hand," he growled for Bethany's benefit. No doubt she was already long gone.

Grinning, the angel began to pull a sword from within what remained of his coat. Cain didn't wait to see the tip before he emptied his magazine. Each slug propelled the snarling angel back a step. Barely. When Cain knew he'd just chambered the last shell, he slipped his Luger out. A gold bullet ought to do the trick.

With a smile, the angel bowed slightly. "Wait."

"Oh? Okay."

Cain fired twice. Both times, the angel used his blade to smack the bullets away. Deafening metal-against-metal clangs made Cain's teeth hurt.

"I can help you, monkey-man," the angel said.

"Shutting up would help."

The angel smiled. A bit too wide, a bit too forced. Mimicking humans. They could never get it right and could never understand it wasn't about the mouth. It was all in the eyes. And theirs never smiled.

"I can help you get back."

Cain aimed straight between the thing's eyes. Maybe he'd get lucky and blind it long enough to slip his last rosary shell in his shotgun. "Get back where?"

"Here." The angel's grin widened, as did his wings. Like a hawk trapping its prey. "You could have another chance at life. If you give me what she stole."

"Life? I tried it once, it wasn't all that." *Liar.* He'd do anything for another shot. "Plus, why don't you take the soul yourself? Oh, that's right, you can't, it has to be freely given."

"You wasted yours away," the angel snarled. Greed and anger blasted out in a furious wave that hit Cain in the chest. "You took His gift, and threw it back at Him. But I can help you get back in His good graces, monkey-man. He is forgiving."

The wall of rage dissipated and Cain shook his head. "You're no more in his good graces than I am, so quit flapping your wings."

"Hey." Bethany slowly walked around the concrete ramp, hands well in view. A little black pouch dangled from one. "Here, take it."

Cain couldn't believe she'd returned. Maybe she wasn't all bad. Just *mostly* bad. "Bethany, don't—"

"Freely given?" The angel cut Cain off and turned slightly in Bethany's direction. Avarice narrowed his eyes. His fingers twitched by his side. The sword tip wavered just the slightest bit. For an angel to get his hands on a bit of human soul was like an addict finding half a pound of cocaine. Jackpot.

"Yeah." She flicked a quick glance at Cain. "I don't want to go back to the eighth. Please, okay, please give me another chance. Here, that soul is yours."

The pouch dangled invitingly at the end of its cord. Bethany's hand trembled.

His nostrils and eyes flared, the angel bent over to take the little pouch from the much smaller woman.

Cain wouldn't get another chance like this.

Years of practice kicked in. Within a second, a rosary shell was loaded into the shotgun. Thunder reverberated when he shot the renegade angel. For a split second, he thought he'd missed as the thing straightened, rage and hatred disfiguring the handsome face and making him even more imposing. Everything slowed, time itself ticked away one grain at a time. The silvery wire spread, each dot like a silver teardrop, flew at the angel's neck, where it bit into the flesh, sliced right through and embedded itself into the concrete wall behind. The wings shook with a spasm. Bethany cursed. Cain barely had time to protect his face with his arm when ashes and embers swirled like a mini twister, higher, wider, peppered him with burning bits, disintegrated into black smoke until only a scuff marked the angel's spot. Through the smoke, Bethany's face was like a tiny white moon, eyes huge.

Cain slipped his Luger into its holster. "You're a good liar. You had *me* going with that pouch. That a decoy?"

She beamed. "Smart *and* beautiful. I have it all."

He aimed the shotgun at her. "No more tricks, Bethany. Give me the secrets."

In the distance, the flap of wings heralded the spawns' return, their cackling and shrieking growing louder. Shit.

A blast of wind fretted her hair. She backed against the ramp. "I wasn't lying to you. I need this."

"Argh, come on! You think I'm—"

Cain froze and looked up into the sky. He felt them clearly now. Close. *Very* close. By the sound, he knew there were hundreds of them. Carrions. He wouldn't have time to make it to his car.

She approached despite the barrel of the gun digging in her chest. "We need to work together. If we make it to dawn, we'll be okay."

He checked his watch. 04:33 glowed aqua-green. "Shut up. Let me think."

Unfortunately, Bethany was right. No time to reach his car and lose them in narrow alleys. Even less time to find the temporary sanctuary of a church and wait for daylight. They'd have to fight them out here in the open, in the dark. If he died before getting the secrets, he'd go back to Berith empty-handed. He should've stayed in bed.

"If you stab me in the back again . . ."

To his astonishment, she winked. "I may not be a good woman, Cain, but I'm a smart one."

"What do you have left?" He had one magazine left for his shotgun, some incendiary magnesium shells, the four gold bullets that remained in his Luger, and his knives. Not that these would help much against spawns, only against fellow keepers. He threw her a dark look. Maybe he should get rid of her now and hope to get lucky with the demonic hordes. Yeah, his luck had been so *good* so far . . .

She checked her various straps, winced. "I don't have enough."

The first spawn landed not ten feet away, spread its wings wide and let out an ear-piercing shriek of triumph.

A very bad day, indeed.

Three

Other shrieks echoed around them, a dozen, a hundred, more. Countless demonic wings flapped in the night sky, creating snow twisters that temporarily blinded Cain and sent icy pellets into his eyes and mouth. They abraded his skin when they sliced into his ruined coat and exposed hands. Growling, he charged into the underground parking, Bethany on his heels. Booms reverberated as she peppered their escape with bullets.

"Don't waste your ammo!"

Fluorescent tubes fluttered to life when they triggered the motion sensors, but immediately blinked out as the demonic hordes followed them underground. They couldn't do anything against daylight, but artificial light and fragile conductors were no match against the vile presence. Yellow placards flashed by, parsing the Olympic grounds into sectors and levels. A maze of concrete. Cain tried to read as best he could as he sprinted down the gentle incline, gripped the corner of a metal handrail and leaped over it so he could open the door leading to the stairs. The concrete well leading upwards smelled of urine and humidity. Behind him, Bethany cursed under her breath. Two by two, they climbed up to the first level. He was about to get out that way when she grabbed his coat and yanked him back.

"Wait!" she panted. "Dawn. It's close. Let's fight. Outside."

"Too late!" He yanked his coat out of her hand and would have kept on going when a faint sound stopped him cold, all but froze the blood in his veins. It came from inside the stairwell, below them. Close.

"Brother Cain," called a man. The whisper grew to chuckles. "I know you are here."

Berith had found a human to possess.

Bethany pointed her submachine gun into the space between the handrail and arched to get a better shot. "I can see him," she mouthed silently.

The urge to take the secrets from her almost overtook him. It'd be easy. The pouch was right there at her belt, not four feet away, and contained the little black box. He was stronger, he could take it by force and push her into the void. By the time Asmodeus brought her back, Berith would have the bit of soul he wanted. Maybe their deal wouldn't be over.

But it wouldn't change a damn thing, would it? Berith would find some other reason to torture him. He never lacked imagination that one. Fuck him. If he wanted to get the secrets, he could move his demonic ass and come get them.

Cain shook his head *no* at Bethany – this was an innocent man possessed by the demon – and resumed climbing the stairs. Bethany followed but clearly would have preferred putting a few bullets in their pursuer.

"There." He pointed to the third line of text on a nearby placard. *Tour de Montréal*.

He opened the door, let it clatter against the wall then soundlessly began to climb to the next level. Grinning, his impromptu ally followed, passed and afforded him a very nice view of her body clad in white vinyl and black straps. He'd always wondered what she'd done to end up in hell.

Their ploy must have worked because the door opened and closed below them, noisily, the sound like gunshot. While Berith searched that level, Cain would be on his way to his true destination – the Tower of Montreal. It'd give them a couple minutes tops before Berith sensed, even in his diminished form, he'd been duped. If Cain was going to piss off his demon master, he might as well go all the way. Plus, Bethany was right. Dawn wasn't that far off, so if they could make sure to be outdoors when the sun crested the horizon, the spawns wouldn't be able to tolerate the light. Neither would Berith. Cain could buy a few precious hours of peace before . . .

For the first time in his second life – his *existence*, Berith had called it – he was sick of it all. Sick of always running, always fighting, always dying. Again and again and again. He'd love to just *stay* dead one time. Life just wasn't worth it. Not when he ended up in hell every time.

But then again, after what he'd done, he *deserved* to fry.

She must have guessed their destination because Bethany planted an index finger on the placard. Dark eyes stared back at him to wait for confirmation. Like a team player. He hadn't been on any "team" in ages, if ever. When he'd been a living, breathing man with a soul, a lot of people had looked at him for guidance, for instructions and directives. He'd been the older brother, the firstborn son. Until that day he'd found out his brother had betrayed him – or so Cain had thought. The rage had been too much to contain.

Cain pushed the memories down and nodded to Bethany.

A tic pulled at her cheek. Maybe she was trying to work the situation to her advantage. He wouldn't put it past her to try to double-cross him, even with untold spawns on their heels and a demon in corporeal form within shouting distance. Cain gripped his shotgun a bit tighter. He didn't want to hurt her, for some strange reason didn't want to be the one to send her for another trip downstairs. Not Bethany. She might be a pain in the butt, but for a keeper, she wasn't all that bad.

She flashed him a smile and rolled her finger by her temple. "As cute as you're crazy," she whispered.

Yeah, crazy, damned, and soon, back in hell.

When they arrived on the main level, Cain pressed his open hand on the door, pushed just enough to get a glimpse of what waited for them on the terrace. He couldn't see anything, couldn't smell anything either. But across the large concrete expense, reflections in the mammoth glass walls flitted back and forth, like vultures circling a dying beast. The spawns must have flown up to a safer height – for them – to get a better look.

A warm body pressed against his side as Bethany squeezed into the embrasure so she could get a look, too. His breath caught. It'd been so long.

"We have half a chance." Bethany pulled back. Cold replaced warmth and made him shiver. "If that."

"It's better than sitting on our hands and waiting for it." He checked his pockets to make sure he'd counted the shells right the first time. Not enough. Not nearly. This whole thing wasn't going to end nicely for either of them. Berith already knew Cain was fucking with him, so there'd be no break that way even if he managed to take the secrets from the other keeper. But Asmodeus didn't know anything yet. Bethany still had a chance to bring the secrets back to her master. It was only logical. Unless he was going soft for her again, thinking with his dick instead of his brain.

Cain leaned back against the wall as he checked and rechecked his ammo supply and the silvery shotgun's functionality. "Go. I'll keep them busy."

"*What?*"

"Don't make me repeat something so stupid, okay?"

Bethany planted herself in front of him, close enough for Cain to feel her warmth again. But it was more than warmth he saw in her expressive face. White-hot anger. "You think I'm that kind of woman?"

"Says the girl who lied to my face about ten times in the past two hours."

"I won't let you take the hit for me."

"I would if it were me."

"Bullshit. You're a decent guy, even if you work very hard at playing the asshole."

Cain peeled his back from the concrete wall. As much as arguing with the pain in the butt made him feel more alive than he'd felt in years, they didn't have time for this. "Fine. Stay here and get a faceful of spawn. Just don't call me asshole again. Ever."

She cracked an irreverent grin. "Then stop acting like one."

"Ready?"

Bethany lost her smile. She shortened the sling on her sub-machine gun so it rested directly on her chest, pulled a fresh magazine – her last that Cain could see – from her belt and clipped it on her harness. To Cain's shock, she fished a gold-coloured grenade from her jacket pocket.

"What?" she asked. "You don't use these?"

He would've loved having a bit of time to ask where she got her gear. In fact, he would've loved just spending some time with her without having half of hell trying to make ribbons of them. "The glass wall across the terrace, the funicular to the tower is there. I'll make us a door as we run for it."

Before he could react, Bethany fisted the front of his ruined coat, hoisted herself up to him and kissed him square on the mouth. "I don't care what they say, I like you."

It took him a good five seconds to get his wits about him once more. The timing couldn't possibly have been worse. He took a long breath, nodded.

"Here we go."

Cain kicked the door wide and ran out.

They barely made it ten feet when the first few spawns to catch a whiff of them wailed and screeched a warning to the rest of the horde. Like fingernails on blackboard. The sky became alive with black wings as the air filled with the smell of ash and sulphur. Concrete chunks rained down around them, broken loose by talons and claws, or ridged wings hitting walls as the spawns spiralled downwards to catch their prey. Cain fired ten shots out of his thirty-two magazine before he'd taken ten steps. The glass wall was still at least 300 feet away. By his side, Bethany's small black MP5 *tack-tack-tacked* death at eleven bullets a second. He hoped the trigger-happy woman would keep a few for later because some-thing told him they were in for more "fun".

As if the power of his thought alone had made the real thing manifest itself, gunshot that was neither hers nor his echoed around them. Muzzle flashes to the right registered in the corner of his eye. More keepers. Dammit.

"Cain!" Bethany yelled. "Door!"

Just as Cain aimed his shotgun in front of him and fired, a giant spawn landed ahead of them, blocking their access to the tower base. Cain fired half a dozen slugs into the spawn. He'd never seen one so big. Leathery wings made miniature tornadoes of snow when it raised itself to its fullest. The thing must have been twenty feet tall!

A small golden item arced ahead of them.

Bethany skidded to a halt, gripped his coat tails, which barely slowed Cain. He understood a split second before thunder temporarily deafened him. He only had time to turn his face away. The detonation happened right between the spawn's legs. It blew up in a giant geyser of gooey chunks and thick, dark liquid that splattered in a wide radius. Bethany and he were pelted with debris both hard and soft, liquid and solid. More spawns landed around them. Some seemed more interested in feeding off their brethren's remains than in attacking the two humans, but others came for them. One in particular made a beeline for Bethany. She turned her MP5 to it, let fly bullets that slowed the beast. But didn't stop it.

Cain could do nothing but watch from the corner of his eye as half a dozen smaller spawns came at him, wings spread and talons out. His shotgun recoiled with each shot. His wrist throbbed but he kept going.

When Bethany screamed – pain had a universal sound, no matter the victim's location, age or culture – Cain whipped around, thinking he could pump a few into the spawns after her. Too late.

Like in a slow-motion movie, the demonic fiend struck in an arc. Bethany caught the taloned appendage in the side, bent over the limb before being projected sideways. More gunshot from the other keepers erupted in tiny concrete volcanoes around him. They had seconds before the enemy closed in enough to place their bullets with more accuracy.

While Bethany tumbled to a stop, Cain pumped one, two, three, four shots into the advancing spawn. Finally, he hit its head. He didn't wait for it to hit the ground before he ran to Bethany, who struggled to stand.

"I—I'm good." She slung her submachine gun in front, stumbled forward. "I'm good."

Together, they ran at the wall of glass panels. As he'd said he would, Cain fired a single shot at the connection between two panels. For a second, the wall turned milky-white. Just when Cain was considering wasting another round on his "door", the wall disintegrated into a cascade of cubic diamonds. Broken tempered glass crunched like gravel when Bethany and Cain rushed into the base of the tower. A counter curved away from the wall and would provide temporary shelter as they waited for the funicular elevator. Bullets hit the marble wall on either side of the steel doors. Cain crawled amidst the raining debris, mashed the button on the access panel.

Through the window, the sky was taking on brown and orange hues. Dawn couldn't be far off. He checked his watch again. Half past five or so.

"It's here." Bethany's voice sounded higher-pitched than usual. She popped up above the counter, emptied her magazine through the broken wall then crouched back. A riposte several seconds long made ribbons of decorative banners, swiss cheese of partitions and clanged against the waiting area's aluminium poles. Cain pulled the empty magazine, dropped it, loaded the last three shells he had. The incendiaries.

The doors slid apart. He didn't need to urge her to be quick about it when she passed him at full sprint. He backpedalled into the giant funicular made of bay windows and steel beams. Spawns had begun to land around the broken glass and scrambled inside the tight opening. Like vultures trying to squeeze in through a doggy door. Gunshot accompanied them. The keepers were close, too.

Cain fired the first of the incendiary shells. Magnesium and flint cores, they'd been meant to penetrate the target and blow it up from the inside. The closest spawn caught it in the belly. Its bony ridges and skeleton triggered the charge. As the elevator pinged its arrival, the spawn exploded. A firestorm that reached the cathedral ceiling. Flames leaped out in all directions. Because he wouldn't be able to use the incendiary shell up in the tower, he fired a second one into the lobby. The conflagration turned the air desert-dry and oven-hot. Gunshot stopped. Wails and shrieks drowned even the swoosh of blood flow in his ears. As the doors closed, a wave of heat buffeted the cabin.

At the rate of seven feet a second, the funicular took them up towards the tower's apex. Around them, Montreal had begun to wake. Deep orange slashes crisscrossed the sky. Dawn was less than an hour away.

"We need a plan." Cain turned to her, caught the look of pain she quickly masked beneath her usual bravado. "Ideas?"

"Lemme think, okay." Bethany leaned against the wall, closed her eyes. Cain wasn't fast enough to keep her from sinking to her butt. Her rictus of agony cut through his temporary shell shock.

"Where are you hurt?" He leaned over so he could take a look.

"I'm good," she replied through her teeth. "Nothing to it."

Bright red blood seeped through her fingers as she pressed a hand to her hip. Cain knelt by her side. "You're not good, a spawn got you."

"Not for the first time." She grinned, grimaced. "We should start our own biz, you and me. It'd be fun."

"Fun like tonight? No, thanks."

Cain peeled her fingers off the messy wound. An injury from a spawn's demonic touch wouldn't heal unless cleansed with holy water. Fever would set in, infection, hallucinations. For this woman, a long and agonizing death that could take years before another trip downstairs. At least she had a run of secrets to show for it. Asmodeus might leave her alone and send her back up right away. *If* she were very lucky.

"You know how it goes, Bethany. You know how it always ends for those like us."

"I know. I just . . ." She cleared her throat. "I wanted it to be different."

As soon as they reached the top, Cain slipped his arms under Bethany and carried her just outside the door. She winced when he deposited her back on to the carpeted floor. He then dragged a metal garbage can from the landing, dropped it in the funicular doorway so none of the keepers or Berith's unfortunate host could call it down to them. The doors closed with a ping, hit the garbage can and slid back out again. And again. The funicular would stay at the top. Plus, if all went well – and his luck suddenly turned for the better – they'd need a ride down.

The sky was turning orange and mauve, with bands of brown and amber across the horizons. Daylight was minutes away. Not fast enough.

"Hold still." Cain pulled out of his coat pocket a handful of the little bags of holy water. They looked like fast food packets of ketchup. He tore one open, dribbled some between her fingers, then more right into the wound while she held the torn vinyl wide. Blood and holy water turned her white outfit pink.

The spawn's talon must have dug deeper than he'd thought. There was so much blood. Too much. He used all his holy water to make sure the wound was clean. Working on the gash also meant he didn't have to meet her gaze, which she kept on his face the entire time. Neither stated the obvious futility of cleaning a mortal wound.

"Would you stay?" Bethany asked.

He knew what she meant.

"Yeah." He sat by her side, knees drawn up. She'd pulled herself to a sitting position along the wall. A more dignified way to go.

Fresh blood continued seeping through her fingers. "It's too bad."

"What is?"

"Timing," she grunted. "I – I would've . . . asked you out . . . like on a real date. Been meaning to for years." She smiled despite what must have been terrible pain. "You won't . . . b– believe this, but I'm kind of shy."

Cain laughed. Couldn't help it. "Yeah, shy. We can always plan for next time." He didn't know if either of them would be sent back to the mortal plane after such a huge fuck-up. He knew for a fact Berith would want some time to play with him before he shot him back up to earth. *If* he did.

"I just wish . . . I – I just wish things were different."

He patted her knee. Heat seeped into his cold hand and he found taking it off her was much harder than it should have been. So he left it on her leg. She pressed her own hand over his. Blood coated their skin. A bond made of pain.

"Take them, okay."

Cain shook his head. "It's your only bargaining chip, without them, Asmodeus—"

"He would anyway. And I d – don't give a shit." She grimaced as she reached into her belt. "Take them."

Earlier that night, he would've done anything to get his hand on the little black box Bethany presently proffered. But as he looked at it now, he didn't have the heart to take it from a dying woman's hands. Especially Bethany's hands. "It won't make a difference for me. I pissed him off too many times."

Bethany rested her head on his shoulder. "Lied to the cops. Wrapped my car . . . around a telephone pole." She pulled her hand away from the wound, rubbed her crimson fingers together. "Killed t–two others . . . was drunk."

Cain understood then why she'd been sent directly to the eighth level. He'd always wondered about that, because if the woman was a major pain in the butt, she didn't look like a hardened criminal. But liars, cheaters and usurpers populated the eighth. And drunk drivers who pretended to be sober.

"You?"

Cain swallowed hard. "I killed two people, too. My brother Abel, then later, myself."

"I knew . . . y–you were *the* Cain."

What was there to say? He acquiesced with a nod.

She pressed the little box in his hand. "D–don't be a hero." Her voice grew weak, her eyes closed. "I hope . . . see you . . ." Her head lolled on her chest.

He knew she still lived because her body hadn't yet burst out in ashes and glowing embers. But he checked for a pulse at her neck, wanting it to be steady and strong. Weak, shallow. Barely there. She wouldn't be waking again.

Cain took the little black box, slippery with Bethany's blood, and turned it around in his hand. He'd watched Berith gorge on secrets, all at once like a glutton, or savour them one at a time, placing the fragile gold paillettes on his tongue. He'd seen demons sell them for more damned souls like Bethany and him. Like cards on a poker table.

He was done being played.

Around him, the Montreal skyline turned brighter. Almost dawn.

Four

Don't be a hero.

He hated them right now, demons and spawns, angels, too, even the good kind. They couldn't stop meddling with people's lives, trying to pull the blanket on to their side. Jealous freaks, the lot of them. They didn't have souls, and it burned them to think monkey-men had them, when clearly, they were inferior. Like animals.

Cain couldn't have been less hero material. But that didn't mean he intended to make it easy for hell to get its claws back into him. They wanted the secrets, they could come pry them out of his dead fingers. Fuck them. Fuck Berith.

"Wait here, okay," he murmured, even though he knew Bethany couldn't hear him any longer. "After it's all done, I'll come find you."

He gently laid her down on her side and stood. After he gathered what ammo Bethany still had strapped to her, he straightened and caught movement in the reflective glass to his left. Cain only had time to whirl around. A split second later, something resembling a giant bat crashed against one of the glass walls. A spawn. Shudders traversed the floor. Ominous cracking sounds reverberated along the ceiling and down the concrete half walls. Dust floated around him like tiny snowflakes.

Through the windows, more spawns circled the leaning tower. The sky filled with them. Another hit the glass walls, then another. Like birds hitting a windshield. Wails and shrieks made Cain's ears hiss.

He had to put as much distance as he could between Bethany and him, if only to spare her the sordid violations those keepers had in mind for her. He wouldn't let them get their hands on her, even dead.

He *couldn't.*

Time slowed. Noise came to him dimmed and dulled like standing across the street from a pounding discotheque. The smell of sulphur choked the air. There were two ways down from here. He couldn't go back the way he'd come for fear of the other keepers getting their hands on Bethany. His sacrifice wouldn't make that much of a difference in where she'd wake up, but at least they wouldn't go after the defenceless woman. It'd at least buy her a serene death.

Cain jumped on to the glass ledge. Two feet wide, he stood directly on it, well away from Bethany.

"Come get me," he growled through his teeth. "You fuckers."

Cain aimed his Luger down between his feet and fired his second to last bullet. The shot went through the tempered glass and widened the spider web already there. Lines crackled outward, turned milky white like a small frozen puddle. But instead of hitting the frozen ground, when this "puddle" shattered nothing but air caught him. With a growl, he fell through the hole.

Spawns converged on him. They hit and slashed him with their serrated claws and scalpel-sharp fangs. Something gave in his shoulder. In his descent, he managed to twist face-up. Such a pretty sky. A spawn dived for him and grabbed Cain by the torso. He felt his skin perforating. Wet warmth spread. Blood everywhere, falling up from him in a reversed crimson rain. Wind howled but couldn't drown his laugh. Cain was dying. He shot his last bullet right into the monster's face. It wailed and dropped him.

What a fucking way to go.

Out of nowhere a bright white glow sliced the air.

What the—?

Spawns screeched. The light reached him with the speed of a bullet. Something caught him, and Cain humphed with the sudden deceleration that squished his innards back along his spine. Whatever – whoever – had caught him couldn't be seen for the brilliant glow that enveloped the stout form. All he knew was that as soon as the being caught him, spawns had flown away in a flurry of leathery wings and frustrating shrieks. Wind abated, the angle changed, and Cain was gently deposited to the ground where he collapsed to his knees, forehead against the concrete and hands splayed on either side. Too weak to stand, barely strong enough to lift his head to look at his saviour.

The being straightened up. A pair of feathered wings like golden horns thrust heavenward on either side. Cain understood. Of all the weird things he'd witnessed, this took the prize. What the fuck was going on?

The glow abated, the wings folded behind a pair of stooped shoulders and a head clad in a hand-knitted cap he would've recognized anywhere. He couldn't believe his eyes.

"You're heavier than you look," Sister Evangeline said. Her hands moved rapid-fire.

Cain struggled up to his knees, panting and gagging. He patted his side where the spawn had sliced him. Nothing. Not even blood. Jesus on a cross . . .

"What have you done?" he panted. "You're an *angel*? Why didn't I see you as you really are?"

She sucked her teeth. "You're welcome, *mon garçon*."

Cain sat on his heels because he couldn't stand. Not because of his injuries, as he couldn't seem to find a single one, despite being cut and shredded and sliced in many places during the two-second fall from the funicular. He took a few deep breaths, closed his eyes. When he thought he wouldn't stumble around like a drunk, he stood slowly, cautiously, as if trying on a brand new pair of legs. Everything felt different somehow and he couldn't place why. Even the cold against his exposed skin felt sharper. He shivered.

Reality pressed back on him. He was only delaying the inevitable. Berith was waiting for him. "It won't change anything."

"It will," she retorted. "Plus, you wouldn't have survived the fall."

"It doesn't matter. He would've sent me back. After playing a bit with me first, of course. I pissed him off really good this time. Those secrets were worth a fortune in souls." Fucking with Berith was worth the pain, though.

Sister Evangeline shook her head. "Not this time. You would have died. You would have squandered that life, too, just like you did the first."

Cain took a moment to process the last part. "What—?"

She smiled and his theory was busted – because her eyes reflected the joy, unlike the other angels he'd met (not that they'd been the good kind, only fallen ones or hybrids).

A shiver tickled up his spine. "Do you mean . . . ?" He couldn't even force the words out. It couldn't be. He'd never heard of it. He was seeing things, or Berith was playing a cruel joke on him.

She nodded. "He's all about second chances, you know. Even if people whine all the time and waste the years away."

He couldn't believe what was happening. "How? I . . . I killed my own *brother*! How can he forgive me? What did I do?"

"Abel forgave you a long time ago, Cain. Live here and now. You could have left with the secrets, or you could have let the demons take her when they first caught up. Instead, you put the bull's eye right between your own. You jumped to save her."

Cain could hardly process the chain of thought. It was all a blur in his mind. It couldn't be. He'd never have to go back there again? He'd never have to look into Berith's ugly face? He was free from hell?

His elation quickly crystallized. "What about her? She belongs to Asmodeus."

The older woman's kindly eyes glowed white-hot for a moment and terrible, godly anger once more swelled her wings with glacial wind. Her hair stood on end, crackles of electricity joined her splayed fingers. Cain took a step back. "Do not speak their name!" Then the smile was back again as she seemed to deflate to her normal appearance. As if nothing had happened.

Sneaky angels.

Cain looked up at where the funicular light gradually descended to ground level. His heart leaped. What the hell was going on? Had one of the keepers snuck up there? Was Bethany still alive, in the hands of some hell-bought thug?

"Why do you worry about her?" The Sister's hands flashed rapidly. "You like her?"

His first reaction was to snort a denial. Instead, what came out was a strangled, "Yeah, so?"

Sister Evangeline winked. "You think He'd bring you back to true life, only to make it miserable? She was going to get a second chance, eventually. But you." She dropped her hands before starting to sign again. "You're the one who surprised us all. Even Him."

The Sister's wings gradually receded, until nothing showed. She was once again an older woman with a messenger bag slung across her shoulders and a hand-knitted wool hat screwed on low. "Keep her out of trouble. I'm not going to pull you out of the roaster again. Already lost a few feathers for you two."

"Yeah, I thought you guys didn't have feathers."

"Are you comparing me to the scum who turned their backs on Him? *Merci beaucoup*. That's because you'd never seen a *real* angel. Until now."

She turned and walked away before he could reply. Not that he had anything to say.

A faint sound caught his ear. He instinctively reached for his shotgun, which wasn't there but somewhere between the base of the tower and the stadium itself. Shit. Wouldn't that be grand to lose it minutes after being granted a new chance at life? Adrenaline shifted when he spotted the source of the noise. Boot heels clacking on concrete.

Bethany was coming at him. Not stumbling or floundering or even walking, despite the injuries she'd just suffered. The blond was running for him like a sprinter after the shot went off. And she didn't seem to have any intention of slowing down either. Such spirit. How the hell had she managed that?

He squared his stance a second before she reached him, grabbed the front of his ruined jacket and planted a kiss that landed like knuckles. He had his arms around her before the thought registered he was killing his reputation. He didn't give a damn. Not any more. Not around her.

Bethany pulled away, panting, tears in her eyes. She smiled, shook her head. "What the *hell* is going on?"

"We got another chance."

He'd never been one for theatrics and big declarations. Get to the point. Life was too short for bullshit.

Her megawatt smile warmed him right down to his gut. "I'm hungry."

"Yeah. A steak would be nice. Lots of blood and gravy."

"Who said anything about food?" Bethany chuckled.

Cain could get used to that sound. In fact, he intended to do just that.

Marine Biology

Gail Carriger

The problem, Alec thought, swishing a test-tube full of sea-water about gloomily, *is that I'm unexpectedly alive. To be unexpectedly dead would be simplicity itself. After all,* he made up the statistic on the spot so that he would sound more learned in his own head, *half of all deaths are unexpected. One is, to a certain degree, prepared to die unexpectedly. But when one expects to die at eighteen and instead finds oneself unexpectedly alive at twenty-four, there's nothing for it but to be confused about everything.*

He sighed, put the test-tube into its cradle and dragged his thoughts forcibly back to the sample's acidic content. Which was unexpectedly high. *There's global warming for you.*

His phone rang. After a brief flurry of scrabbling about, he fished it out from underneath a massive book on nudibranchs – *how had it migrated there?* – and glanced at the caller's name before flipping it open. His stomach twisted. *Great, what's Dad doing calling me at the lab?*

"Yes?"

"Your problem is that you never got used to being alive."

"I hate it when you do that. Hold on." Alec pushed his protective goggles up into his spiky hair and rolled his eyes at his boss on the other side of the lab table. "Family emergency," he mouthed.

Janet, who was the best kind of boss – a relaxed one – merely waved him off to the fire escape.

Alec trotted over and pushed out into the cold grey day. The lab coat was little protection against the biting wind but he didn't notice. He didn't really get cold, not since his eighteenth birthday.

"How are you calling me, Jack? You're non-corporeal."

The ghost's tone became petulant. He did not like being reminded of his disability. "Voice dial, of course."

"Of course. Do you know what kind of heart attack that gave me, seeing Dad's number?"

"You've got to get over this thing with your father."

"He's a dick, I'm passive aggressive and you're the one who's haunting because of it."

"We were talking about your problems, remember? You can't take being alive."

"So you call me at work to tell me something I already know?"

"No, but I thought if I started out reminding you how well I know you, you might refrain from arguing with me for the next twenty minutes over the thing I actually need to ask you. I always win these arguments, in the end."

"Jack, you're making me nervous." Alec could feel his canines starting to emerge. "You know what happens when I get nervous."

"Yoga breaths, darling, yoga breaths."

Alec breathed in deeply through his nose and then out. The telltale teeth retracted slightly. And the rest of the pack wondered how he functioned so smoothly in laboratory-land. He tried to imagine them doing yoga, and that made the teeth entirely vanish. Alec's fellow pack members were mostly large and hairy and took to being both with enthusiasm. It was as though they were trying to be as stereotypical as possible, working in construction, riding motorcycles, barbequing a lot. Not the yoga types. Unless the yoga somehow involved leather chaps and brisket.

"Fine, yes, so, what's going on?"

"Party, darling, tonight. My place."

"Oh, really, must I?" Alec ran a finger under the collar of his polo shirt.

"'Fraid so. Fifi's calling in and Biff's bringing the beer. You know what that means."

"Pack meeting?"

Alec looked nervously up at the gloomy sky, as if it were night-time already. "Is it full moon? Did I forget it was full moon? I hacked one of those female cycle programs for my computer, it's supposed to remind me when I'm due."

Jack interrupted his panic. "No, something else is going on."

"Crap, what?"

"Can't tell, darling, can't tell. But it was made clear that your presence, specifically, is required."

Alec swore. "Jack? Jack, you're supposed to be my friend."

"Dead men tell no tales."

"Tales or tails?"

Silence met that pun.

Alec's canines were back. "You know, if you weren't dead, I'd kill you."

"But you'll be there?"

"Clearly, I have to be there. If my brother's bringing the beer, I'll bring the salad."

"No one will eat it."

"It's either that or seafood, and I'd rather not remind them how far I've strayed away from the family business."

"Well, that was easier than I thought. I guess you didn't have a date for tonight?"

"Jack, I never have a date."

"Pathetic. Even I have a date and I'm dead."

"You're telling me."

"It won't be me doing the telling."

"Oh, shit. That's not what this meeting is about, is it?"

"Just show up, Alec, and bring your damn salad."

Then the phone went dead. Alec looked at it with an expression of profound disgust, as though the cell were what was wrong with his life. *How had Jack managed to hang up without hands?*

Alec sighed, flipped the phone shut and slouched back into the lab.

Janet took in his hangdog expression and immediately knew what was required of her as friend and confidante. "Oh no, what happened?"

"Family thing tonight that I didn't know about."

"Need me to be your date?"

"Not this time, but thanks."

"You know, I've never met your family. I find it odd to think you came from somewhere."

"Well, if you met them, you'd find it odder."

"That bad, huh?"

"The worst. I think they might be staging an intervention."

"But Alec, you're perfectly sober. A fine upstanding citizen. I don't think I've seen you drink even a glass of wine. Unless, of course, it's your addiction to the whole Atkins diet they're worried about."

Thank goodness for Dr Atkins – the perfect excuse for a cultured werewolf to eat nothing but meat. Before the good doctor came along, Alec had been forced to hide his shameful rare burger habit.

"With my luck, they're pulling me out of the closet."

No one – really, no one – especially not Alec, had expected him to survive the Bite. The only person in existence less qualified to become a werewolf was Richard Simmons. Not that people wandered around calling Alec effeminate, not to his face anyway, but under no circumstances could he be described as either large or hairy.

His Dad was beta to the local pack, with four strapping, football playing, monosyllabic, *Playboy*-touting sons – and Alec. Alec was the middle child and there'd been some talk about "looking like the neighbour" when he came along. Skinny, even after the whole big feet, eat everything, smelling-like-a-goat, phase. He also read books – not the backs of cereal boxes – and he preferred post-modern literature of all horrible things. He joined the swim team, not the football team, and that only because his father insisted he undertake some kind of sport. High school saw him wallow in typical teenage depression, except that he *knew* he was going to die. He didn't have to don eye make-up and write bad poetry. The local werewolf alpha was set to try and change him into a supernatural creature on his eighteenth birthday and there was simply no way he'd survive the transition.

Until he did.

And spent the next six years trying to figure out why, and what to do with his life, and how to reconcile the monthly slavering beast he would become with his still skinny, still post-modern-reading self.

The yoga helped.

Alec's Dad, the aptly named Butch, owned the house that Jack haunted. That was, in fact, the reason Jack haunted it. It was a popular misconception that a ghost haunted the man who killed him. In actual fact, they tended to go for the person who pissed them off the most in life. Jack, their former next-door neighbour, had hated Butch. There'd been an argument over the sprinkler system and the next thing they knew Jack was stuck forever haunting his neighbour. In a classic ironic twist, the pack now called Butch's house Jack's Place. This made Butch livid. Which was one of the reasons the pack did it. The other reason was that Jack wasn't the kind of ghost who wafted around mist-like in the background. Oh no, he was the kind of ghost who organized parties and criticized your shoe choices. Which is why the parties were always at Butch's place – Jack liked to get up in everyone's business. The werewolves thought this was a great joke, that the pack had a pet ghost. Jack could get away with insulting them, because he was already dead and large hairy men didn't scare him anymore. Quite the opposite, in fact.

Alec marched in, head high, still wearing his lab coat defiantly, and slammed his store-bought salad down on the rickety kitchen table.

"Hi, Ma."

"Hi, baby. Salad? I was hoping you'd bring sushi. Still, very thoughtful dear. At least you brought something, which is more than I can say for your brothers." His mother tossed peroxide blond hair out of her eyes.

Alec leaned his hip against the refrigerator. "Well, be fair, they brought their wives. Pam, at least, is useful."

"Not tonight they didn't. Pack only." Both mother and son paused to look out the window at the backyard where a large collection of beefy men milled about drinking beer.

"Where you going, Ma?" Alec snagged a wedge of raw beef before his mother could stick it on the skewer.

"It's lady's poker night over at Sharon's."

Out in the back yard a couple of the men roared their approval as a great gout of fire flared up off the grill.

"Ugh. Why do they bother? Everyone eats it rare anyway."
Proving his point, Alec nibbled on the cube of meat he was
holding.

"Oh, sweetie, men and fire, you know how they get. Doesn't
matter if they're werewolves or not."

"Any idea what's going on?"

"Sorry, baby. Can't say."

She hefted the platter of kebabs and carried them out into the
backyard. Alec trailed after her.

His mom placed the meat down on a dilapidated picnic table.
"Right boys, there you go. Cook it or eat it fresh, it's not my
problem. Just do it out here and don't mess up my kitchen. You
know I hate coming home to find blood all over the floor; it's
hell on the linoleum. I'm off. You know where the beer is kept."

A chorus of polite "yes, ma'ams" met that remark.

Alec watched her disappear back into the house.

Jack wafted up next to him like a mercurial little genie. "Not
a bad sort, your mother."

"'Cept she's throwing me to the wolves."

They stood at the fringes of the gathering, Alec tense and
nervous, Jack bobbing up and down softly.

"So," Jack had *that* tone in his voice, the tone that said gossip
was imminent. "Did you hear Biff's wife left him?"

"I can't imagine why. All that lively conversation."

"Hey now, a man can say a lot using only monosyllabic grunts.
Did you bring sushi?"

"No, salad, I told you I would. Don't you remember?
Everyone mocks me when I bring sushi, so I thought I might as
well give them a real reason."

"That's your problem Alec—"

"Oh, another one?"

"—you're just obtuse enough not to play their very simple
game with any skill. You could. You just have a death wish."

"Oh, thank you for the psychoanalysis, fly boy."

"Speaking of sushi, how's the sea life?"

"Still not grunting."

"You're no fun."

"I don't like surprises Jack, what the hell is going on?"

"Oh, you're gonna like this one, I think."

One of the Neanderthals in front of them tore himself away from a scintillating conversation and lumbered in their direction. He had a massive scar on one cheek, a skull bandana around his head, and the exact expression a pit-bull wears when he catches some other dog peeing in his yard.

"My father could give lessons on stereotypical biker behaviour."

"Butch is a man of culture and sophistication," was Jack's helpful comment before he drifted away. He couldn't get too near to Alec's father – classic case of ghostly Tourette's. Jack would start lunging and swearing at the man who kept him tied to the world. It made for an interesting living environment.

Alec stood his ground.

"Son," Butch spat the word out like it tasted bad in his mouth. "Did you bring your usual sushi?"

Alec gave his father a funny look. "That's the third time I've been asked that since I arrived. Why? You hate sushi, no one ever eats it when I bring it, and you all make stupid jokes about 'the other white meat'. Despite the fact that the new place by Bruno's is really good." Butch made Alec nervous and when Alec got nervous he babbled. "I don't think the owner is actually Japanese, but that doesn't seem to matter."

Disappointment, a common emotion when talking with his middle child, crossed Butch's face. "You *would* fuck it up this time."

"Christ, Dad, if you wanted sushi why didn't you email me? Or I could just go out and get the darn stuff right now. It'll only take five minutes." He turned towards the house, any excuse to leave.

"Oh, no, really, don't bother." That was a new voice. And a new smell. A briny, salty, fishy smell. Not unpleasant to the nose of a marine biologist, even if it was an extra sensitive werewolf nose.

Alec turned back.

To be confronted by one of the world's most beautiful people – slender, high cheekbones, big blue eyes, straight white teeth, webbed fingers . . . *Wait! Webbed fingers?*

"Whoa, you're not a werewolf."

"I should certainly hope not." The woman smiled at him. *Really, very beautiful. Bummer about the gender.*

Butch was watching Alec's reaction carefully, so Alec slid in slightly and took the beautiful woman's hand in one of his. Trying to pretend attraction. *Right, webbed fingers.*

"You're a mermaid?"

The woman gave him *that* look. "Merwoman, please!"

"Sorry, we don't get many of your kind in these parts."

"You do, you just don't realize it," that was another new voice – mellow, masculine.

Alec turned. *Ooo.* Still blond, only taller and definitely male. Mer*man*. Alec suddenly lost access to the part of his brain that housed the English language.

The man gave him a slow smile. "Nice to see you again, Alecanter."

At a loss, Alec stuck his hand out.

The merman's skin was cool to the touch, the webbing between his fingers soft and rubbery.

Alec could feel himself start to blush. *Crap, why'd I end up the only fair-skinned one in the family?* "Do I know you?" *Face like that – hell, body like that – I'm not likely to have forgotten.*

That smile didn't waver. "Picture me with dyed black hair and lots of eye make-up."

Alec nearly swallowed his tongue. *Could the man get any sexier? Oh wait.* He mentally took off about fifty pounds, all muscle, from the merman and dressed him in a torn black T-shirt emblazoned with the name of some obscure band. "Marvin?" *Weirdo goth-boy from high school? No way!* "But you wouldn't even join the swim team." There'd been some teasing about that, because Marvin used to come and sit and smoke in the bleachers pretty regularly, watching the swim practice. He'd always taken some secret amusement from it.

"Home surf advantage. We merpeeps aren't allowed. Can't have the monkeys getting suspicious."

"That explains why you always wore gloves. I thought it was some weird Goth thing."

They were still shaking hands, well, still holding hands. Alec let go.

Marvin lowered his own hand slowly and sidled almost imperceptibly closer. "You noticed what I was wearing?"

Alec's danger warning system went off and he glanced around

at the pack. His father was paying awfully close attention to their conversation and frowning. So was the mermaid. *Sorry, mer*woman.

Alec backpedalled. "You used to watch me, at swim practice. Never thought you'd see a wolf in water?"

The merman wasn't going to let it go. "You weren't a wolf yet. But, yeah, that was one of the reasons."

Alec's tongue came out to wet suddenly dry lips. He angled towards the merwoman. That's what straight men did, right? *Pay attention to the hot female.* "So, what's your name?"

"Giselle. And before you ask, we're siblings."

Alec wasn't gonna but, "Oh, good," slipped out anyway.

Marvin's grin widened.

"So, you two are the reason for the pack meeting, huh? And the sushi obsession." Alec grappled for civilized thought.

"You could say that."

"And don't worry about the sushi. You can totally take me out for some later." Marvin wasn't particularly subtle. Alec glared at him, *Don't you dare* out *me, that's the last flipping thing I need right now.*

The merwoman glanced around, taking in Alec's sudden tension and Butch's avid interest in their conversation. "You can take *us* out later," she qualified her brother's statement.

Alec gave her a grateful look. "So, what's the meeting for then?"

"Pack protocol," growled his father, "think we better let Fifi tell us."

Hearing his name, the alpha looked up from the tri-tip he was tearing into and wiped the blood off his massive beard with his sleeve. "Yeah, let's get this over with so we can really eat." The alpha was big and furry even in human form, with a ruddy pockmarked complexion. If he wasn't a werewolf Alec would have described him as yak-like.

The pack pulled into a loose circle with Fifi, the two merfolk, Alec, and Butch at its centre. This made Alec nervous. He usually tried to stay, as much as possible, out of pack focus. Half the pack seemed centred on Fifi but most of the younger members were looking at Alec. This made Alec even more nervous. It had been happening more and more recently, and he was beginning to wonder if they knew something. If perhaps Jack had told someone something he shouldn't have.

Fifi gesticulated with what was left of the hunk of meat. "This here's Marv and Grissy."

"Giselle, please!"

"Grissy," said Fifi firmly, "they's in town on official business. Been ordered to meet with us so as we can provide back-up if needed. We gotta assign them a pack liaison, make sure they don't fuck-up. Alec here's closest thing we have to a fish guy, so he's taking the job."

A chorus of groans met that statement. Giselle was a tempting liaison prospect.

I am? Okay. Well, there's that explained. Alec couldn't suppress a little thrill of his own.

"We," stated Giselle very firmly, "are *not* fish!"

"And I specialize in micro-organisms anyway. But I wouldn't try to explain the difference if I were you," advised Alec.

Butch casually, and without much attention to detail, back-handed Alec across the face. "Don't be a smart-ass," he barked at his son.

Pain blossomed in one cheek. Alec had to clamp down on the visceral response to launch himself at his father. It would be so easy just to morph into his wolf head and tear out his dad's throat. Butch was stronger but it'd be worth it for that first bite.

Marvin lurched forward, expression shocked.

This snapped Alec out of his violent fantasies. He made an almost-imperceptible stopping motion at the merman with one hand. Then he shook his head to clear it and spat blood. Good thing he'd heal quickly. *So much for trying to impress the cute boy with clever talk.*

Fifi brought everything back into line. "Now Marv, you tell us what's going on."

Marvin crossed his arms and arched an eyebrow. "Think I'll let my sister do that."

"What are ya, pussy-whipped?" asked Butch.

That's my father for you, so fucking classy.

Marvin didn't miss a beat. He smiled an ironic little twist of a smile. "Nope, fin-whipped. We're a matriarchal society, four-legs. No point in fluffing your ruff at me."

Giselle said, "Would you two like to go piss in a corner somewhere?"

Alec hid his own grin at that. This was kind of fun to watch.

His father actually growled. At that, Fifi grabbed Butch by the ponytail and tossed him back towards the circle of other pack members. Butch was a big tough guy, but Fifi was bigger and tougher and everyone knew it. Pack dynamics had some benefit. Butch left, still growling low in his throat.

"So we're here to follow up a lead from a West Coast investigation," said Giselle, getting right to the point. "Seems the Irish mafia are in town."

Alec couldn't help himself, "There's an Irish mafia?"

Giselle gave him the same kind of look his father gave him. Apparently she wasn't used to being interrupted. "Well, yeah. We got a couple of selkie to bark to our song, over in San Francisco. Said there's some kind of money-laundering scheme going on round this coast. You know, offshore accounts."

"Selkie! What are they doing mixed up with the Irish mafia?"

Giselle, patted him on the arm condescendingly. "Darling, the selkie *are* the Irish mafia."

Alec looked around at the pack. "Great, what are we? A sleeper cell for the KGB?" *There goes my smart mouth again.*

Luckily, unlike Butch, Fifi didn't seem to mind it much when Alec went off. The alpha grinned. "CIA, pup. Canines In Action."

Very funny.

The pack laughed obligingly.

"Right, so, Alec, you stick with these two. I trust you'll tell me anything I need to know." Fifi seemed to think that was settled.

"Yes, sir."

"Good, let's eat."

Fifi wandered off and the pack went back to milling about the barbecues, gulping down booze and meat in equal measure.

Alec turned to their two guests. "So, sushi and further details?"

Marvin smiled brightly. "Perfect."

Giselle wrinkled her nose. A number of the pack members were ambling in her direction with leers and puffed-up chests. "Definitely."

Alec and the two merfolk made their way towards the house.

Alec's oldest brother, Biff, grabbed his arm and pulled him aside before he'd gotten very far.

Alec tensed automatically. He couldn't be sure but he thought he saw Marvin start back towards him. Giselle put a hand on her brother's arm.

"So, Bro."

"Yeah, Biff?" Biff wasn't so bad, as brothers went. Almost as big as their father and just as tough but a lot less mean. Didn't say all that much as a general rule, but he had spent some time as a kid pulling the other three brothers off of Alec's scrawny ass. Alec always felt he owed him for it.

"I recommended you'd do for these two, seeing as your job's, you know, with the ocean and all. Thought maybe you'd heard something."

Alec tried to look flattered. *I didn't know Biff had so much sway with the pack these days.* "Supernatural? I'm afraid not. I'm a marine biologist, not a wave psychoanalyst. I look at tiny creatures in a laboratory. Even if I did do mammals, selkies are well outside my expertise."

His brother shrugged massive shoulders. "Yeah, well, I thought maybe something fishy would be right up your alley. Hot, huh? And you like that sea stuff."

"I study *micro-organisms*."

Biff was looking at Giselle's fine ass climbing the steps into the house. "I wouldn't say no to getting hold of her micro-organisms."

"Uh, Biff. Everything okay with you and Pam?"

"Just saying, Bro. You seem to have a little chemistry going on with them fishes there. I'd tap that, if I were you."

Alec swallowed down on some bile. He'd rather have his dad yelling at him than his brother giving him sex advice. "Biff, did Mom put you up to this?"

Biff gave him a very serious look out of his craggy Neanderthal face. "Pack's talking, Bro. Why you not doing your duty by us? How long you gonna hold out? You need to settle."

"You think a werewolf and a mermaid can breed? What, some kind of sea-wolf?"

"Hey now, what's so bad about being half-fish off dry land? It's not like you're showing interest in any other kind of tail."

"Cute Biff, real cute. Didn't know you could be witty and all."

Biff frowned. "Alec, all I'm saying is I recommended you for this job. Don't fuck it up, unless it's to fuck. We clear?"

"As a Dutch hooker. Ah shit, Biff, I gotta go, our guests are talking to Jack."

"They are? Fuck."

Jack was doing his worst. "Alec, this here is Marvin."

"Yes, we've met. And Jack, we really gotta go."

"Marvin thinks you're cute."

Giselle started to laugh. Marvin didn't look at all embarrassed. Alec could feel his ears starting to burn.

"Jack," Alec hissed, "not here!"

The ghost swivelled toward the merman. "Alec thinks you're cute, too."

"Jesus Jack, what are you, twelve?"

Marvin laughed and then added, "He's right, you know, I do."

Aw shit. Alec lost track of things for a moment. *You do?*

"And Biff did kind of set this whole thing up," cheeped Jack, helpfully. "Could be he approves."

Alec glared at the ghost. "I don't think Marvin was the one my brother intended me to get to know."

Giselle nodded her agreement. "I'm thinking the fuzzy one is right, brother dear."

Marvin sidled in close to Alec. "Ah, you're not out, are you?"

When did briny get to be such a sexy smell? Alec looked between brother and sister. "And you are?"

In this Giselle seemed content to let her brother do the talking, merely watching their interaction with amusement.

Marvin shrugged. "Hey, I live in a world run by women. I was outed by household gossip before I'd even acknowledged I was gay to myself."

"Nice life, but we really should be having this conversation somewhere other than my incredibly homophobic father's kitchen." Alec glanced nervously around the empty room.

"Werewolves not so down with it, huh?"

"Well, just look at them."

A tussle had started in the back yard, Biff and one of the other youngsters. Punches were being thrown. Any second now the combatants would be ripping off their clothing and fighting, teeth and claw. Alec turned to watch, interested despite himself.

Jack said, "When you gonna just fight Butch?"

Alec shrugged.

"What, afraid you might win?"

"Shut up, Jack."

Marvin came up and pressed partly against Alec's back. Alec felt suddenly very warm.

"It seems like a pretty cool situation, if you like 'em big and hairy. You get like that, pretty boy? With the whole growling and tearing off of your clothes? Not that that's really my thing. I'm kind of liking this lab coat look. I mean, how hot is it that you're *actually* a marine biologist?"

Well that is a new one. Usually, guys get off on my being a werewolf, not a scientist.

Marvin petted Alec's arm as though Alec were some skittish animal.

"So here I am, a marine mammal, and I got biology. I was thinking I might work my way on to your sample chart."

Alec laughed and turned to look down at the man next to him. *This is really a bad idea, with the pack right out there.* Nevertheless he couldn't help but lean into the petting. "Didn't you just hear me telling Biff? I specialize in micro-organisms."

Marvin shrugged. "Probably got a few of those too."

"Ew, not sexy."

"So, date sometime?"

Who knew sea mammals could be so aggressive. "Aren't we supposed to be heading out to sushi?"

"I'm thinking a date *without* my sister along."

"I can't."

"Why not?"

"Pack."

"So?"

"Don't you have, oh I don't know, a school or something you have to keep happy?"

Giselle interrupted them at that. "My pearl, we'd be happy to see him dating anyone. It ain't healthy for our kind to go on for such a long dry spell."

Now it was Marvin's turn to look embarrassed.

Alec was intrigued. *A man as hot as Marvin?* "Really?"

"Oh yeah, been carrying a torch for some young stud since high school."

Wow, blonds sure can blush.

"Awe, Giselle! Must you." Suddenly the two merfolk were acting like true siblings.

Alec arched his eyebrows at the merman. "High school, huh?"

Marvin's blush got, if possible, deeper. "Hey, you were this hot jock."

"Wait, *me*?" Alec practically squeaked.

"I had to grow out of being that weird skinny Goth kid."

Alec was incredibly flattered. "Well, allow me to say, you did it beautifully."

"Yeah?"

"Yeah." *My god he has gorgeous eyes.*

Jack's voice interrupted what was looking to be a very interesting progression to the conversation. "Boys! Not that I ain't enjoying the show, but we got company."

Alec practically leaped all the way across the kitchen. His teeth sprang out, and he felt his eyes start to shift.

Marvin watched this action with interest. "I don't know whether to be insulted or turned on."

Alec growled at him. Instinctive response.

"Ooo, definitely turned on."

"Oh, shut up, Marvin," said his sister. "You got no idea what kind of pack dynamics you're messing with."

"Yeah? Well I know which ones I'd like to be messing with."

The kitchen door swung open and Fifi marched in.

"Still here? Thought you guys were off to catch a meal."

"We got a little distracted by the architecture," Giselle jumped into the breach. "House designs always intrigue me. As a sea person, you know?"

Nothing could be calculated to turn Fifi off the scent quicker. The alpha's eyes glazed over. "Yeah, well, whatever floats your boat." He gave Alec's ruffled appearance a curious look. "You're always so tense youngling. Think perhaps your brother's right. You need to get laid."

Alec sputtered.

Marvin muffled a snort of laughter.

"Uh, yes sir." Alec started inching towards the hallway. "'K, we'll be off now, sir."

"Carry on."

Alec shepherded the two merfolk out of the house.

Jack's voice whispered in his ear just before the door slammed shut behind them, "Now you're under orders from your alpha."

"Fuck off, Jack."

"Not before you."

Alec's favourite sushi place was pretty crowded for so early in the evening. But Giselle's looks and charisma got them a table pretty darn fast, and Alec was a regular – popular with the staff.

"Where's your girlfriend?" asked the waitress, twinkling down at them all. She was a pretty dark-haired girl with big brown eyes who'd always had more than just a nice smile for Alec. Alec, had, of course, never noticed.

"Oh, Janet? Uh, not with me this evening."

Marvin gave him an accusing look as soon as the woman had taken their orders.

"Girlfriend?"

"Naw. Janet is just my boss down at the lab. It's easier to just—"

Giselle interrupted, "Of course, avoidance is the hallmark of all gamma werewolves."

"Who said I was a gamma?" But Alec muttered it so softly the other two didn't seem to hear. *Merpeople,* Alec figured, *probably aren't all over the supernatural hearing. Not something particularly called for under water.*

Marvin cocked his golden head to one side, thoughtfully. "So, how deep in the closet are you?"

Alec gave him an expressive look. "Honey, I shit mothballs."

They paused while the waitress put down their tea.

"Your pack is really that bad?" Giselle asked politely.

"It's big and restless. Not the type of environment for a sudden revelation as to my sexual orientation."

"You sure? They don't seem all that bad. Well, except your father. He's a piece of work."

Alec didn't take that bait. "Hmm. Pack should have splintered before we got to such numbers. But no one from my generation has claimed alpha. Biff's got promise, and I know he's courting a few of the youngsters, but I'm not sure he's got it."

"Got what?" Marvin leaned forward, interested.

"You know, *it*. That thing that alphas have."

"I have no idea what you are talking about."

Alec shrugged. "That's because I'm trying to teach a fish to ride a motorcycle here."

"Hey, I'm pretty good on two wheels." Marvin smiled at him.

"And still – not fish," added Giselle.

Alec decided to try a new line of conversation. "So the West Coast, huh? Is that where you went after high school?"

Marvin nodded. "Oh, yeah, you know, pod migration. Being a merman is almost as bad as being an army brat, we move around."

"And this investigation of yours?"

Giselle jumped in. "We've been tracking this racket for a while. Ocean's our jurisdiction, as I'm sure you know. But there seems to be some kind of land connection with this one. Selkies can be a problem. Slough off their skins and suddenly the trail dries right up."

"What's this one done? Murder? Kidnapping?"

"Nothing violent like that. Pure white-collar action. Some funding collected by one of our nonprofits disappeared. We have this ocean reclamation and coral rescue operation, suddenly half the bank account vanished along with this fellow and his family."

"Mmm," Alec nodded. "How much are we talking here?"

"Three point two million dollars."

Alec coughed into his green tea. "All that for coral?"

Giselle shrugged. "The non-profit fronts a dummy account for our pod to run day-to-day integration operations. You know how it gets for us supernatural types. Trying to keep everything hidden from the monkeys. We contracted out a few delicate bits of business to a reputable selkie agent and the next thing we know . . ."

"Tough break. What makes you think it ended up here?"

The waitress reappeared with their sushi and a very wide-eyed look. Alec wondered if she had overheard any of their conversation.

"Those informants we told you about."

"Oh, yeah, I remember." Alec bit into a piece of tuna happily. It wasn't quite as good as fresh red meat, but there was something appealing about fish. He was a little sorry the rest of the pack were so down on it all the time. They were really missing out. "So, where should we start?"

"How about when? Tomorrow morning, your place?"

Alec agreed and gave them his address. They enjoyed the rest of the meal accompanied by pleasant inanities and mild flirting. Alec returned home feeling, for the first time in a long while, as though it was okay to be unexpectedly alive.

They met the next morning at Alec's tiny apartment.

Marvin brought Alec a tin of sardines as a courting gift.

"How do you know I'm not the kind of guy who likes whole salmon?"

The merman gave him a look, and then, despite the amused presence of his sister, leaned in and kissed Alec full on the lips.

Alec was startled but not unwilling. It was early for such shenanigans but the way his love life had been lately he'd take what he could get. Marvin tasted amazing, far better than the sushi of the night before. And that had been really good sushi. *Salt and sea and something else. Something chemically addictive and sexual.* It rather derailed Alec's thoughts. Especially as Alec wasn't much of a morning person anyway.

Marvin pulled away first, licking his lips. "You know I've been waiting about ten years to do that?"

Alec rediscovered his attitude. "Self-control not one of your strong points?"

"Oh, someone is snarky today. You always like this in the morning?"

"Wouldn't you like to find out?"

"Absolutely."

Giselle brushed past the two men in the doorway and took in Alec's small apartment at one glance. It was neat and tidy and masculine without any further pretensions towards style or fashion.

"Well, this is certainly no indication of your sexual orientation."

Alec arched his eyebrows. "What were you expecting, pink leopard print couch covers and a gilded floor lamp?"

Marvin grinned. "She has weird ideas about you land people. You'll have to excuse her assumptions on the grounds of ignorance. It's only us mermen who get sent in to attend dry schools. Our females cause too many problems. Especially with teenagers."

Alec watched Giselle sway about his living room, long thick blond hair just touching her undulating hips. "I can't imagine why."

"Hey!" A pair of cool fingers pulled Alec's chin around to look into Marvin's face.

Alec smiled, swooped in and gave Marvin a full-on kiss. *There it was again, that addictive taste, delicious.* It would have been all too easy to continue, so Alec pulled back. The merman was left looking agreeably speechless. "Purely an aesthetic observation I assure you. So, where are you two staying?"

Giselle returned from her perusal. "Little place down by the docks, of course."

Ask a silly question, reflected Alec. He went to pour himself some coffee. Caffeine didn't do much for the werewolf constitution but he enjoyed the ritual of it and the lab insisted on a near constant supply. He waggled the pot at his guests but both shook their heads.

"Got any clam juice?" Marvin asked.

"Should I open these sardines?"

Marvin looked hurt. "Those are a gift, special just for you, don't be crass."

Alec smiled, and put the sardines carefully on to the counter near his toaster. "Very thoughtful."

Giselle seemed to think it was time to stop the flirting and get on to business. "So we're thinking the best way to hide the money would be to feed it into some kind of local business." Giselle pulled out a sheet of paper. "Here's a list of businesses started over the last few months. I'll try all the clothing stores. You two try the restaurants."

"You sure you'll be okay on your own?"

The merwoman gave Alec a look that should have turned him to stone on the spot.

In fact it did.

Alec felt his body involuntarily seize-up. His feet felt like they'd been super-glued to the floor. The merwoman continued to stare at him, something deadly in her big turquoise eyes, and Alec couldn't for the life of him move a single muscle.

Finally she turned that aquamarine gaze away and Alec felt his body come once more under his control.

"Wow, impressive."

Marvin looked mildly amused. "Natural defensive mechanism," he explained. "Ever heard the myth of Medusa, turning people to stone? That's where it comes from."

"Can you do it too?" *That'd make for an interesting relationship.* "Nope."

"What about the whole siren song thing?"

Giselle grinned. "Oh, we can both do that."

Marvin added, "But not around werewolves. What's alluring to monkeys causes you guys to bleed out of the ears."

"Sensitive supernatural hearing?"

"Exactly."

"Okay then."

They left Alec's apartment and set off on a strange kind of tour of new businesses about the city. Alec found Marvin an amiable companion. The merman was a horrible flirt, but mostly harmless about it. They made an effective pairing, what with Marvin's open and engaging ways and Alec's natural reticence. But they had no success, and met with a sulky Giselle later that night to find that she too had had no luck. She waved them off to the sushi restaurant without her, insisting that all she needed was a long bath and a can of clam chowder.

Back at Alec's favourite sushi place, the dark-eyed waitress took their orders and then vanished, wearing a skeptical look.

"She doesn't like me," commented Marvin, idly watching the girl's retreating back.

"And why should she have an opinion?" Alec hadn't really noticed.

"'Cause she likes you."

Alec was genuinely surprised. "She does? That was unintentional."

"It's one of your more endearing qualities."

"Unintentionality?"

"Mmm. I remember you in high school, cutting a swathe through all those cheerleaders – no idea how much arguing there was over the presence or absence of your interest."

"Oh yes, of course. Scrawny old me. The ladykiller."

Marvin brushed aside Alec's sarcasm. "You had this incredible attractiveness and you never even realized it."

"I did?"

"You do."

"Flatterer." Alec could feel himself blushing. He sipped tea to hide his self-consciousness.

"Not at all. So, why are we dodging around this thing between us?" Marvin slid his hand under the table and rested it casually on Alec's knee.

"You're a merman who's out and lives on the other side of the country?" Alec didn't react to the hand on his knee, but he didn't remove it either.

"Pah, insignificant details." The hand squeezed and then began a gentle exploration.

"Because I have this feeling you're just trying to satisfy some left-over adolescent curiosity?" The hand stilled its wandering and was removed.

Marvin pouted. "Why must you be so serious? Okay, fine. And what? You're looking for a lifelong commitment, when you can't even tell your family you're gay?"

"Touché."

The hand returned. "So our relationship has a few minor difficulties. What true love experiences smooth swimming from the start?"

Alec couldn't help but smile at that.

The waitress and her frown returned with their order.

"I hardly see that she should feel so strongly," said Alec, this time noticing the girl's gloomy expression. "It's not like I'm a regular or anything. This place hasn't really been open long enough to have regulars."

Marvin blinked at that. "New business? How new?"

Alec bit into a piece of sashimi. "Couple of months ago. And you know I wasn't going to try it, because I heard the owner wasn't even Japanese, but then . . ." Alec trailed off, following where Marvin's question had led. "Right time frame?"

The merman nodded. "And that waitress does have very large and dark eyes."

Alec really looked at the woman for the first time. "Fetching girl."

"What does she smell like?"

Alec shrugged. "Fish, but then, Marvin, this is a sushi restaurant. Everyone smells like fish."

"Let's finish up, shall we? I have a sudden need to investigate the kitchen of this establishment."

The waitress returned, looking hard and determined. "How's your meal, boys?"

"Delicious. But I'm afraid I must ask to see your kitchen." Marvin pulled out his wallet and flashed some sort of badge at the young woman. "Health inspectors."

The dark eyes widened and then narrowed. "Of course, sir. Right this way."

Marvin stood, grabbed his jacket, and followed. Alec, rather clumsily, glommed on to the merman's scheme and trailed after.

The kitchen was everything that a health inspector might wish, very clean and very modern, all the appliances shiny and new. It was also equipped with some very large and solid frying pans, which Alec's head discovered much to his surprise. Out of the corner of his eye he saw Marvin receive the same frying pan treatment, then there was nothing but blackness.

Alec was the first to awaken. Werewolf healing apparently beat out merman abilities in that arena. It didn't stop his head from hurting like the devil. There was a throbbing pain coming from the back of his skull. *What the hell?*

His sensitive werewolf hearing went into immediate overdrive. Not that he needed it – whoever was speaking was mighty close.

"Health inspectors, health inspectors indeed. I think not!" That was an unknown voice, deep and masculine and heavily tinged with Irish.

The sushi restaurant owner, I presume.

"Now, Da," that was the voice of the pretty dark-eyed waitress. "How can you be certain? Pure certain they aren't health inspectors?"

"Well, that one there's a web-handed tail-ended nark. Can't you tell from the hair and the cheekbones? Humans just don't grow that beautiful. Not outside of Denmark, anyway. Can't rightly place the pretty boy, but you can bet he's something we don't want reporting on our whereabouts."

"Shame really, he's been coming in to my section for weeks now. I kinda thought, you know . . ."

A snort met that comment. "Just goes to show where thinking will get you."

"He's also awake," said Alec, sitting up and testing the strength of the rope that bound his hands tight behind his back. The rope eased against his flesh. Not strong enough for a were of any breed, let alone a wolf. He cocked his head at his two captors. They really didn't know what he was. *Silly selkies.* Alec supposed he couldn't really blame them all that much, after all, he didn't look like a werewolf, not even slightly. For once his appearance was standing him in good stead.

Alec let them think they had the upper hand – or was it flipper? – at least while Marvin was still out of it. He looked sideways, down at his companion. The beautiful blond lay flopped, eyes closed, face abnormally pale. Alec frowned in concern. *What if they really have damaged him? Perhaps mermen can't recover from frying pans to the head.* Alec could feel his canines beginning to show in anger and agitation. *What the hell?* He wasn't in any immediate danger. Usually, his wolf side didn't take any kind of protective interest in others, not even in his friends, only in his own worthless skin. Alec heard Jack's voice in his head, *Yoga breaths, darling.*

Alec took several deep breaths while Marvin lay there, quiet and still. Alec's inner wolf remained unhappy about this and felt very protective despite the yoga. *Well, crap,* thought Alec, finally understanding his own feelings, *this is mating behaviour. Fantastic. I always knew I had this abnormal affection for fish, but really, Body, this is a ridiculous. Stop it.*

The teeth retracted slightly and Alec decided it would be best to look away from Marvin's comatose form.

So he glanced about his surroundings, to find that they were in some kind of storage room, possibly a cellar. The waitress sat over to one side, on top of an overturned plastic tub, and next to her stood a very fat, very fierce-looking man, with the most impressive moustache Alec had ever clapped eyes on. And Alec had hung out with the Hell's Angels on more than one occasion, so he was tough to impress.

"You didn't hit him hard enough, pup," said the man with the moustache to the waitress.

"Sure I did, Da!"

"Then why's he up and talking so soon?"

"Don't know, Da."

Alec saw Marvin twitch slightly out of the corner of his eye. *Awake and playing possum?* He had a moment of profound relief.

"So," said Alec casually, "Used the money to set up a Sushi restaurant, did you? I commend you, you have really good sushi."

"Well, what else were we to do?"

"Still, setting up this place can't have taken all of it."

"No, it didn't."

"So," Alec gave the moustache an opening.

"So?" The fat man was not so much of an evil Bond villain to fall for that trap.

"So where's the rest?"

The massive moustache twisted in annoyance. "Wouldn't you just love to know?"

Alec sighed. Marvin twitched again. The merman was shamming. Hoping Marvin would follow his lead, Alec decided to take a chance.

He shifted forms, the rope bonds dropping easily off of his now reconfigured body. His pants also fell away. Sadly, his shirt was not so accommodating. It got all tangled about his neck and forelegs and he ended up having to rip it off with an undignified wiggle. *Darn it, that was Armani.* Of course, Alec could have simply broken the rope bonds but he didn't feel the need to prove himself with any of that masculine tripe – that was more his father's speed. Shifting out of them was easy enough, and it put him in wolf form, which was far more practical for fighting.

He charged at the man with the moustache.

The man let out the most remarkable barking bellow but

didn't run, instead moving forward to meet Alec's flying furry leap with a crash.

The man was a hell of a lot stronger and more nimble then he looked, and he seemed to know a thing or two about fighting against a wolf. He went for the muzzle, wrapping one beefy arm about Alec's nose, clamping Alec's jaw shut, and jabbing at Alec's eyes with his other hand. Meanwhile the waitress leaped for Alec as well, grappling with his legs. She, too, was unexpectedly strong. *Crap, no one warned me selkies had superhuman strength.*

Alec scrabbled, sharp and fast, his back legs raking down the woman's face and neck. She let go with a cry of pain. Then he turned his attention towards the man. Alec scraped forward with his front legs, claws out and wickedly sharp, and at the same time he twisted and jerked back, managing to free his head. He whipped it around and clamped down with big sharp white teeth on the man's upper arm. He then put a concerted effort into tearing that arm right off. Alec didn't normally consider himself a violent man, but sometimes, arms simply needed to be removed.

While he was busy gnawing, he noticed two things. First, that Marvin was up and running frantically around the cellar, clearly looking for something. Second, that the moustached man's arm tasted rather odd. The normal bloody red meat taste of human flesh was absent. Instead the man tasted like salt-cream mixed with hazelnuts. It was quite pleasant, actually. Alec bit down harder. However, he didn't seem to be getting anywhere with the amputation agenda.

Marvin reappeared in his line of vision, carrying what looked like two scruffy fur coats. The waitress screamed in horror upon seeing them, and this diverted the moustached man's attention away from Alec.

"No!" he cried, as though that would stop the merman.

"Oh, yes," replied Marvin. And then he threw one of the ratty fur coats over the man's head and the other over the waitress's.

Alec had seen many shape changes in his day. Werewolves, after all, were all over that shit. But he'd never seen any quite so fast, involuntary, and undignified as the two that resulted from Marvin chucking those fur coats.

The arm he'd been chewing away at vanished as the fat man collapsed back on to the floor in a yelling, shivering, convulsing

blob. This quickly resolved itself into a barking shivering convulsing brown blob with outrageously long tusks. It still sported a
large and impressive moustache. *A walrus selkie? Huh, who knew.*

While Alec's animal form served him well on land, the
selkie were handicapped by their alternative duds. The waitress (who seemed to be some kind of harbour seal) and the
walrus could do nothing more effectual than a sort of awkward
worming in Alec's direction, which was more ridiculous than
threatening.

Alec converted back into his human shape. Being wolf
seemed a little much given the enemy's current state. He poked
about, looking for his discarded jeans. Despite the fact that most
of Marvin's attention was on their undulating opponents, the
merman still seemed to have plenty to spare for Alec's naked
form. Unfortunately, the walrus flopped over and tried to tusk
at Alec's ankle before he could get hold of his jeans, so Alec took
refuge up a little stepladder. Marvin, with a decided twinkle in
his eye, joined him. The diminutive nature of the stepladder
made for an agreeably intimate relationship. Marvin was quite
as thrilled by the lack of jeans as Alec was troubled.

"Their skins?" Alec asked, over the barking sounds as the
two blubbery beasts wiggled viciously against the base of the
stepladder.

"Yes."

"How long do they have to stay – uh – floppy?"

"Once they are in seal form they must visit the ocean, only
then can they remove their skins and return to dry land as
humans."

"Bummer."

"And you thought you werewolves had it tough."

Alec shrugged.

"You make a very handsome wolf, by the way. Though I'm
thinking I like this form best of all." One of the merman's
webbed hands formed a newly intimate relationship with Alec's
posterior.

Alec blushed. He'd always thought his wolf form a little bony.
Speed was his best trait, not brawn. "Thanks."

"Beautiful, even." Marvin shifted against him and tilted in,
going for a kiss.

Alec obliged him, though it was not the most romantic of moments – atop an unstable stepladder with two angry seal-type creatures barking up at them.

Marvin seemed interested in pressing matters further, and a tentative tongue tip touched Alec's lip.

Well, fuck it, I might as well show him everything. Which was when a different part of Alec's wolf side came to the fore, and Marvin learned a thing or two about what kind of wolf he was attempting to court.

Alec modified the kiss, rising up on his toes and pressing bodily downwards against the merman, slanting his head and diving his tongue aggressively into the other man's mouth.

Marvin gave a little squeak of surprise, but acquiesced willingly enough, melting easily against Alec's aggression. Alec gave a little growl of approval and grabbed that tempting long blond hair with one hand, and yanked the merman's head around to exactly the right angle. *Now, that's a kiss.*

Then he stopped.

Marvin, for once, seemed to have nothing to say. His mouth went open and then closed for a little while in shock. He looked like – well – like a fish. Finally he said, eyes wide, "So that's how it is?"

Alec, blushing a little at his own temerity, pretended a casual shrug. "You thought I was submissive?"

Marvin nodded, but recovered from his surprise enough to snuggle up against him.

Alec explained. "You thought I was in the closet just because I was gay? Not me, I got far more problems. I'm a closet alpha too. I just act the gamma around the pack, makes things easier. I'm a non-confrontational kinda guy." The stepladder tilted dangerously at a particularly hard whack from the walrus. They would have to deal with the selkie situation soon.

But Marvin was more interested in the implication of Alec's kiss. "You telling me you're an alpha in everything?"

"Do you even know what that means?"

"Apparently not."

"Well, for one thing people are always trying to follow me places without my actually doing anything. Can get pretty hairy in a gay bar, let me just say. And I am so not into bears."

Marvin blinked at him.

"I was trying to be funny." Alec sighed. "So, technically, yes. I'm alpha. That's kind of what started all my problems. I always knew, you see? Since right after they changed me. You just kind of do know, once you're a werewolf. Know where you sit in a pack, I mean. But, can you imagine the hell I'd have to pay if it became known by anyone else? My dad already suspects, and I think Biff might too."

"I thought they suspected you were gay."

"Possibly. But that'd just be the excuse to fight me. I might be able to take a couple hits now and again, but a real fight? It's in my nature to have to prove things. That'd just be bad. So I avoid it."

Marvin looked at him. "You just don't want the responsibility of your own pack?"

Alec shrugged. "Maybe."

Marvin blinked long blond lashes at him in a parody of a fifties housewife. "Honey, are you telling me I'm in love with a single dad?"

"If you count about seven grown-up bikers. Yup."

"That's how many you think would follow you?"

"If I won alpha, sure."

"I always wanted a big family." Marvin didn't seem to mind this possibility.

"You're a loon, you know that?"

The most remarkable high-pitched yet melodic keening wail cut through both their conversation and the seal barking. Alec flinched. The sound was so sharp it almost tore through the delicate drum of his hypersensitive ears.

"What the hell?"

Marvin grinned. "I believe my sister has arrived. Cover your ears."

Alec did so. Marvin threw back his head and let out a correspondingly painful yet lovely sound.

A few moments later a loud banging commenced and then the door at the top of the cellar steps crashed open, breaking the bolt. Giselle appeared. She was shadowed by three large and bulky figures who seemed to have done the brunt of the damage to the door.

Alec sniffed suspiciously. *Eau de Dad, brother, and alpha. Just wonderful.*

Giselle and the werewolves crashed down the stairs and then paused, confused, at the bottom. For there were Marvin and Alec, clutching each other on the top of a rickety stepladder while at their feet two large furry sausages writhed about in an entirely unthreatening manner.

"Uh," said Giselle.

"Marvin found their skins and incapacitated them."

"Makes them mighty difficult to interrogate though."

"But not so much of a threat," Alec defended.

Marvin shrugged. "Bundle them up in a couple of tarps, take them back to Alec's place and dump them in the bathtub with a bit of salt. Should do the trick."

"Oh, now really. Must it be my apartment? My tub isn't nearly big enough for a walrus." Alec protested.

"We'll be careful. It's the only way to get a confession out of them. Need to trace the rest of that money."

"What the hell are you doing on a stepladder with a merman? Naked!" Butch asked in *that* tone of voice. Apparently, he had finally taken stock of the situation.

Alec sighed. Suddenly he was very tired of hiding everything all the time. His mouth tasted like seal blubber, the man of his dreams was in his arms, and the future just didn't seem all that bad anymore.

"Kissing him, if you really must know."

Butch sputtered.

Giselle grinned.

"Would you like a demonstration?" Alec offered. *Might as well go for broke.*

"No need to press the matter, pup," warned Fifi in his alpha tone of voice.

Butch, ignoring the walrus, the seal, and the merman, charged down the steep wooden stairs into the basement and leaped at his son, changing form midair in a spectacular display of werewolf prowess. His clothing fell to the floor with a sad little *fump*.

"Oh, well, that's just great," said Alec, falling off the stepladder with his father's jaw wrapped around his shoulder.

Then he too changed.

★   ★   ★

Alec had never actually fought his father before. After he became a werewolf he'd fought his brothers, one at a time, and several at once. None of them talked about it, but Alec had kicked their proverbial furry butts. But his Dad was pack beta. And very very big.

He was also, Alec soon found, a tad out of shape and beginning to feel his age.

Alec never understood how any werewolf could lose his human sense along with his human form. It seemed silly simply to let the slavering beast take over. So Alec fought smart, using his intelligence as well as his wolf body. With his father mindlessly attacking, tearing for the throat and scrabbling at his jaw, Alec – quick and nimble – fended off his attack and steered him in a furry, slathering, growing tumble around the basement towards a promising-looking fish tank.

His dad took a particularly nasty nip to the side of the face, under one eye, and backed away, circling his son warily for a moment.

Alec seized the opportunity to dart in at exactly the right moment, and instead of going for a ruff-grabbing bite as one might expect, he nosed under his father's belly, and heaved upwards, using leverage and supernatural strength to simply flip the wolf over and into the fish tank. There was a tremendous splash and then the glass shattered under Butch's weight.

Butch took a moment to recover, shaking the glass and water from his coat. He was just about to charge his son again, and Alec was beginning to wonder how he could end this without actually killing Butch, when both Fifi and Biff stepped in.

"Enough, Butch," said the alpha. "The fight is done. Consider yourself rousted. He's fighting smart, and we both know what that means."

Butch crouched down among the remnants of the fish tank and glared at his alpha.

"He's always fought smart, you just never bothered to ask any of us why we stopped picking on him after he changed. You thought we didn't test him?"

Marvin and Giselle were occupied trussing up the two barking sea mammals in a couple of tablecloths they'd unearthed from the kitchen stores. But, drawn by the conversation, Marvin wandered over.

Giselle, apparently tired of all the barking, glared the walrus into silent stone stillness. Without him, the harbour seal seemed far more amiable.

"What's it mean, fighting smart?" Marvin bent down and began scratching Alec's ears. Alec leaned into the caresses. It was a little lap-dog degrading but it felt wonderful.

"It's an alpha trait, keeping the brain with the change, as it were."

"Oh, I thought "alpha" had to do with dominance and size."

"Size, sometimes. Dominance, definitely. But that has to do with smarts and how you use them."

Fifi looked down at Alec. "Enough playing, pup."

Alec sighed and shifted back to human. He found and pulled on his jeans before Marvin could say or do anything rash.

Marvin gave him a very significant look.

Alec looked to Fifi. "So, now that it's out, what are you going to do about me?"

Fifi shrugged. "I've been waiting for you to get your crap together and take on responsibility for your half of the pack for a couple years now. Couldn't understand what was holding you back."

Alec winced.

Biff looked at his brother, head cocked to one side thoughtfully. "I can."

"What's your interest in this matter?" Alec wanted to know.

"Didn't you realize it? I'm your beta."

Alec took a closer look at his brother. It would explain his protective behaviour over the years. "Oh." *I guess he always knew he was a beta, just like I always knew I was an alpha.*

"So?" Fifi demanded, one heavy foot resting casually on Butch's still lupine back, as if he were afraid Alec's dad would leap up and begin attacking once more.

Biff shrugged, looking significantly at Alec and then Marvin, who'd sidled up behind him and wormed one hand into his.

Alec puffed out his cheeks. "So, I'm gay."

Butch twitched and growled under Fifi's foot but did nothing further.

Fifi shrugged. "So?"

"You're not mad?"

"You're not making a pass at me, are you? Why should I be?"

Biff said, "We all, well, kinda already knew."

Alec turned to his brother, voice rising, "Oh really? How long?"

Biff raised both eyebrows. "Well, there was that thing when you were six. I was gnawing on one of Ma's shoes but you took if away from me because it was Italian."

Alec's jaw dropped. "You don't care?"

Biff shrugged. "Why should I?"

"You aren't worried about your alpha being, well, you know . . ."

"Alec, I just think it's time you settled down, came out as an alpha, took your piece of the pack, and relocated us. We've waited long enough, we're restless."

"None of the others care?" Alec was thinking of his brothers and the rest of the younger pack members.

"The ones that do will stay with Fifi. The rest of us don't give a damn. New generation, Alec, it's just not an issue anymore. We're, you know, modern. Though, I don't know how they'll feel about the in-laws smelling like fish."

Marvin grinned at him.

Alec turned to look down at the merman. "So, I come with a bit of baggage."

Marvin grinned. "Every relationship has its little hurdles."

"Little? Who you calling little?" Biff glared.

Marvin ignored Biff, nuzzled up against Alec's neck and gave it a little lick.

Alec jumped slightly. "Behave." He turned back to Fifi and Biff. "So what do we know about the Bay Area, any packs roaming there?"

Fifi grinned. "Not that I know of. The general feeling on San Francisco, amongst the older pack leaders, is that there are too many, well, you know . . ." He trailed off.

Alec shrugged. "Guess I'm the right kind of alpha for the area then."

Biff grinned. "So you're in? You'll do it?"

"Do I have a choice? At least there are still marine biology labs over there."

Marvin slid an arm around his waist. "Plenty. I may even have influence with one or two of them."

Alec smiled and looked down at the merman's blond head. "I suppose to be unexpectedly in love is a nice change from being unexpectedly alive."

The merman stood up on his toes and kissed him.

Alec wondered what Marvin looked like with a tail. "Man, this is going to be one weird relationship."

"All the best ones are," replied his merman boyfriend.

Zola's Pride

A Southern Arcana Short Story

Moira Rogers

One

He was going to get the cops called on him if he wasn't careful.

Walker Gravois dropped his second cigarette, crushed it under his boot and turned his attention back to the wide window across the way. Fluorescent light streamed through the glass, doing more to illuminate the narrow street than the lamp over his head. Inside the dojo, a woman with chocolate skin blocked a punch, then paused to correct her assailant's form.

She didn't have to be facing him for Walker to recognize her. *Zola.* Every line of her body tugged at memories he thought he'd banished years ago, and he couldn't help but compare the woman before him with the one he remembered.

She'd been thinner then, just as strong but not as curvy. The wicked flare of her hips drew his gaze, and he licked his lower lip to ease the tingle of curiosity.

Walker checked his watch with a quiet curse – half past ten. He'd been standing there for close to an hour. In this part of the Quarter, it wouldn't take long for someone to phone the police about the pervert loitering outside the dojo, watching the students kick and lunge in their tiny T-shirts and Lycra sports bras. Unfortunately, the neat letters etched into the glass window that listed closing time as nine o'clock seemed like more of a guideline than a rule.

And he desperately needed to talk to her.

He'd just begun to entertain the notion of simply walking in when Zola stepped to the front of the room and turned to address her gathered students. Clearly, she was preparing to dismiss them, so he shoved his unlit third cigarette back into the pack and crossed the street.

Man up, Gravois, he told himself. *She'll either hear what you have to say . . . or she'll kick your ass clear across the river.* The hell of it was that he had no idea which she'd choose. Normally, he wouldn't worry – he could handle whatever fury Zola unleashed on him – but he had more to think about now than himself.

So he'd let her scream at him, get out whatever lingering old hurts plagued her, and then he'd make sure she heard him.

He could do this.

He had to.

The evening class had run long again.

Zola never minded. Friday night was reserved for her private class, the class made up of girls and women who walked among the supernatural denizens of New Orleans as daughters, sisters and wives. Some had powers of their own, like Sheila, a gangly, sweet-faced wolf on the cusp of womanhood, all arms and legs and uncertain strength. Some were psychics and some were spell casters, witches and priestesses who twisted magic and read minds.

Some were human, and they were the most vulnerable of all.

The soft murmur of feminine voices drifted through the dojo as the last few students lingered in the warmth of the building, catching up on the latest gossip or making plans to meet later in the week. February had brought an unseasonable cold snap, the kind of chill that settled in Zola's bones and made her long for the unforgiving deserts of her childhood.

The floor creaked behind her, and Zola looked up from re-arranging a stack of punching targets to catch sight of Sheila's reflection. The teenager had a jacket zipped up to her chin and a knitted hat pulled low over wild corkscrew curls, leaving just her pale face uncovered. "Zola?"

She looked worried, and Zola tensed. "Yes, Sheila? There is a problem?" Even after all these years, English didn't come naturally. The words tumbled out in an order that always made others laugh, but she'd spoken too many languages in too many countries to worry now.

Sheila was so accustomed to Zola's linguistic oddities that she didn't blink. She did, however, speak in her own nearly indecipherable dialect. "There's a guy lurking outside. I mean, he's hot and all, but the lurking is pretty creeptastic and a little pervy."

Zola didn't need to understand the words to decipher their meaning. She turned and squinted through the broad windows, her vision hampered by the darkness outside and the glare of the dojo's lights. Even a shapeshifter's enhanced senses had their limits.

"Stay," she murmured, already crossing the room. The hardwood floor was cool beneath her bare feet, but she ignored it, just as she ignored the bite of freezing air against her uncovered arms as she pushed open the door.

The scent of the French Quarter hit her in a rush, a hundred smells that would take hours to untangle. Strongest was the coffee from the shop next door, rich and bitter, undercut with the sweetness of freshly baked cookies.

Then the wind shifted, and she smelled *him*.

Shock held her frozen in place, a statue of ice that might shatter at any moment. Cigarettes. Leather. Lion. *Male*. His musky cologne should have changed in ten years. The way it heated the blood in her frozen heart should have changed.

Zola turned to face the women who had fallen silent and watched her now, wary and uncertain. She opened her mouth to reassure them and French came to her tongue, so easily she almost bit the tip to keep the words from rolling out.

He'd whispered his words of love in French, under a full moon and ten thousand stars.

She fought for English and it came out choppy and abrupt. "Time for leaving. To leave. Time to leave. Next week, I will be seeing you all?"

They flashed her confused looks but left, filing out into the dark night. Zola watched little Sheila until she met her older brother, who lifted a hand in silent greeting. Zola acknowledged him with a nod, then turned abruptly and strode back inside.

Her visitor would follow.

Follow he did, but not so quickly or so brashly as he would have in her youth. Zola had time to slip her feet into her soft house shoes and don a sweatshirt over her tight tank top before Walker Gravois walked back into her life.

His scent hadn't changed, but he had. Hazy memory had declared him beautiful, with full lips and cheekbones sharp enough to cut, a youthful warrior painted with all the colours of a clear day on the savanna, golden skin and eyes like the sky. But time had left its mark, put sorrow in his eyes and lines on his face.

Jeans and a leather jacket couldn't hide the strength of him, and instinct twisted inside her, turned a visit from an old acquaintance into something darker. Lion shapeshifters were rare in the States, so rare that she'd carved out her own territory that spanned most of Louisiana. Walker Gravois was an interloper – and maybe lethal enough to drive her from her home.

Sometimes history did repeat itself.

He didn't greet her, just dropped his bag and leaned against the small counter near the door where she took care of the trappings of business. "You look good, Zola."

English. She'd rarely heard English from him, though it was his native tongue. Responding in kind would reveal her difficulty with the language, a weakness she felt too unsteady to reveal. So she replied in French, short and to the point. "Why are you here?"

He followed her lead. "I came to see you. I have some news."

She'd been so recklessly distracted by his presence that she hadn't considered what it must mean. Walker had been the youngest of her mother's bodyguards, sworn to her inner-circle with more than the bonds of loyalty holding him. If he was here, alone . . . "She is dead."

Walker shoved his hands into his pockets. "She was killed last week. I'm very sorry."

Maybe she truly was a woman of ice, with a heart long since frozen beyond melting, for the words stirred nothing but gentle regret and guilty relief. Perhaps surprise that it had taken so long – the madness that claimed most Seers had started its work on Tatienne's mind a decade earlier, when she'd looked on her only daughter and had seen nothing but a rival.

Walker's face mirrored her guilt, but there was nothing relieved about it. "That's not the only reason I came."

Of course not. Seers were the most powerful creatures to walk the earth – when had the death of one ever come without pain and trouble for those left in the rubble of their broken lives? "Tell me."

He shifted his weight from one foot to the other. "Is there someplace we can talk?"

She could take him next door, to the coffee shop, but she imagined nothing he had to say could be said in the presence of humans. Bringing him to her home was too trusting, too intimate – but denying him felt like cowardice.

Pride had always been her folly. "Come upstairs. I'll make you some coffee."

Walker had thought that nothing about Zola's present life could shock him. She'd always been a free spirit, and he'd had to acknowledge at the outset of his search that he had no idea where or how he'd find her, which was predictable in its own way. But the one thing he hadn't seen coming was that she might have run back to New Orleans. "I didn't expect you to be in Louisiana."

No one who didn't know her would have noticed the tiny flinch, the way her shoulders tensed up and squared, a telling defensive gesture. "New Orleans is a good place for a cat. The wolves ignore me."

"I know." He'd grown up in the bayou, south of the city. "I guess all the stories about my old stomping ground made it sound irresistible."

The coffee cup she'd pulled from the cupboard smashed into the counter hard enough to fracture, and she hissed her frustration. "I didn't come here because of you," she said stiffly as she shoved the cup aside and reached for another. "And why I am here is irrelevant. Why are *you* here?"

Easy enough to answer, and it still might get him kicked out of her apartment. "I need your help."

Zola didn't seem surprised. "Yes, Seers rarely die quiet deaths. I suppose she left a mess behind?"

That was one way to put it. "Tatienne ran into some trouble with a mercenary group in Portugal. It was bad."

"How bad?"

"Bad enough for them to follow us." Bad enough for them to kill most of the pride.

She turned slowly, eyes narrowed, face tight. "Why me? Why throw yourself on *my* mercy when not one of you had a sliver of compassion in your hearts when she drove me out? I am not a martyr, not for any man. Not even for you."

Yes, she would assume no one had cared, because the truth was an unthinkable horror, one he would never reveal to her if he could help it. "I cared, Zola. You have to know I did."

"Maybe." She turned again, gave him her back – this time in a clear show of disrespect. "Maybe not enough."

There was nothing to say, no soothing words to offer. "The pride is mine – what's left of it, anyway – and all I want to do is keep them alive. Keep them safe."

"You want to move them here?" Disbelief painted the words. She spun to face him, and her fingers twitched toward her palm, a warning sign that her temper burned hot. Ten years ago she would have followed through, formed a fist and struck him. Her passions had always ridden close to the surface, but maturity had clearly tempered them with restraint.

"New Orleans is the safest place," he told her calmly. "Surely a half-dozen lions who only want to keep to themselves won't get in your way."

"Oh, are we civilized now? Are we *human*?" She abandoned the coffee she'd poured for him and stalked across the hardwood floor to slam a hand on the table next to him. Then she leaned into his space, filling the air with the angry sizzle of a shapeshifter challenge. "I will not be forced from my home again."

Keeping a leash on his own reaction cost him dearly. There were few ways to react to such a challenge, and they all ended in violence or sex – neither of which was an option, not if they both wanted to keep their heads on straight. "I'm the only one left, Zola. The only one who stood by while Tatienne drove you out. And I'll – I'll leave as soon as the rest of the pride is settled."

She recoiled, leaving only the lingering scent of her skin. "You're asking me to lead."

A frisson of irritation made him grit his teeth. "Those are

your options, Zola. Lead or follow. You can't stay alone in your territory forever."

"I don't—" She bit off the words and paced away from him, leashed energy vibrating with every step. "You haven't told me enough. Why do you need to come here? Why are there only a half-dozen of you left? My mother had more followers than all of the lions in this country combined."

The truth was uncomfortable because, willing or not, he'd been a party to it. "She did, and now they're all dead."

She reached the far wall and pivoted, meeting his gaze across the space that separated them. "Are you still being hunted?"

"Yes." Walker waved to the other end of the sofa. "Sit down, and I'll explain everything."

Two

Zola did the only thing she could. She sat.

A half-dozen lions. At its height, her mother's pride had numbered in the forties, lions from every continent flocking to kneel at the feet of the generation's only lion Seer. To imagine that strength reduced to just a handful – and all strangers. No one would look at her and see a vulnerable girl.

Perhaps she could lead them after all. If she had to. "Was it my mother's madness?"

"I don't think so, not at first." Walker sipped his coffee. "There were a lot of mouths to feed, and the pride needed money. Tatienne said lions made the best warriors, the fiercest, so she started looking for underground fights."

Bloodsport. Not the same as a clean challenge, not when magical cheats were common and death was all but guaranteed to anyone who fought long enough. It *was* madness, no matter what Walker claimed.

Worse was knowing whose fighting skills she would have bartered first. "You fought?"

"Yeah. Mixed martial arts stuff, but only the invitationals for supernaturals. I'm not a cheat. Some of the others weren't so picky."

So they'd died. But surely not so many, so quickly. "And after the fights?"

"Your mother found other kinds of work, mercenary stuff."
Walker glanced at her, his eyes tight with shame. "Mostly body-
guarding or lift jobs, sometimes intimidation. She sent a couple
of the newer guys out once for what I was pretty sure was a hit,
but she knew better than to tell me so."

Morality had slipped from her mother's grasp along with her
sanity. Zola's stomach knotted at the sheer disgrace of it. Unfair,
perhaps – she could hardly be held responsible for the actions of
the mother who'd driven her away – but she'd always cherished
her memories of an earlier time. Of the woman whose mind
hadn't been consumed by magic, who had soothed a daughter's
childish hurts and taught her to be strong and fierce.

But the Tatienne she'd known had died many years ago.
"Why did you stay with her?"

He didn't deny that he'd wanted to leave. "By the time I realized how far gone she was, I couldn't abandon the others."

"How far did it go?"

"Too far." He set his cup on the table with a clatter. "She
was already dancing close to the edge, and Portugal was the last
straw. She'd managed to move in on another group's territory,
was stealing their commissions. That got their attention, but
what held it was Tatienne."

Walker hurt. His pain dug hooks into her heart, tore at the
scabs of wounds she'd thought long since healed. Words of love
hadn't been the only kind they'd whispered on long nights in
the desert. She could remember all too easily the way her chest
had ached as her mother turned cold, how Walker had taken
her in his arms and comforted her after each argument, each
fight.

Every one but the last, and that stood between them, a wall
she couldn't knock down. It wasn't her place to touch his cheek
or his hair, to give him that gift, that knowledge of belonging. All
she could do was coax him to finish the story, though she could
guess the end. "They targeted her because she was a Seer?"

"They call themselves the Scions of Ma'at," he answered.
"They're mercenaries who work in basic pair groups – a shifter
and a spell caster. They train together, live together, you name
it. Each pair is considered one entity. One fighter. They're all
about balance and order, and Tatienne's nature offended that."

The name tugged at a memory, but it slipped away before she could grasp it. "But they've killed her. They've killed so many. Why are they still hunting you?"

"Because they haven't settled the score yet. We—" Walker rose and paced to the other side of the room. "We killed even more of them."

"And they seek vengeance?"

"An eye for an eye," he muttered grimly. "That's their idea of balance. Of justice. Maybe they're not wrong in theory, but the people I brought over had nothing to do with what happened."

And only six yet lived. "How many lives do they demand?"

He turned and met her gaze. "All of them. All of *us*."

Her lips parted to give voice to the protest growing inside her, one born of instinct and ancient feelings, not logic. Years might have passed, but she remembered what it was like to feel the familiar press of his power and know he was *hers*.

She shielded herself with logic. "Surely they'll be cautious about chasing you into this country. The wolves' Conclave might not always be efficient, but they can be ruthless against outsiders."

"I'd hoped as much," he admitted, "but I can't rely on the Scions' willingness to shy away from enraging the wolves. For all I know, they don't give a damn."

There was one way to find out, and it was probably the reason he'd come to her in the first place. "You want me to call Alec Jacobson."

"I hear he's the one in charge around here."

"He's the one in charge of the wolves." A distinction Alec didn't always understand, but one she had no intention of letting anyone forget.

Walker scratched the back of his head in a familiar gesture. "Then he's in charge, Zola. The wolves run the States, or have you forgotten?"

He'd been gone a long time, long enough that he might not know how petty the leaders of the wolves had become. "The Conclave might unite against an outside enemy, but they're weakened. Not what they were. As long as I don't confront them, they do not try to rule me."

He shrugged. "Then I'll leave it up to you. All I care about is getting the ball rolling. I need to make sure my people are safe."

"I'll call Alec Jacobson." A concession, but not as big as the one she was about to make. "You should stay here tonight."

Walker tilted his head to one side. "You don't have to do that, Zola. I know it isn't – I have a place to go. I'll be fine."

She wouldn't be. She couldn't close her eyes to sleep, knowing he roamed the city and might disappear before she'd pried the truth from him. Before he'd given her the closure she deserved, the final balm to the heart he'd broken so long ago. "Stay. We have things to discuss. You owe me this, in exchange for my help."

Some of the tension faded from his stance. "Are you sure?"

Zola couldn't help but smile. "Sure that you owe me? Yes."

"Sure that you really want me to stay."

Yes. "You're sleeping on the couch."

A slow smile curved his lips. "I expected nothing less."

The smile spoke of wicked confidence and lingering heat, evoking a strong enough reaction to drive her from the couch in search of her phone. Calling Alec would give her time to catch her breath, to find her balance. Perhaps time to fool herself into believing that she'd invited Walker to stay in search of closure, when the truth seemed so much more damning.

Her rebellious heart wasn't trying to close the chapter of her life dominated by Walker Gravois. It was trying to start a new one.

Walker sat behind the dojo's small front desk and fielded another inquiry about class schedules and rates. The phone had been ringing nonstop all morning, making it clear just how successful a business Zola had built for herself.

But she needed help. There was a whole level between the ground studio and her apartment on the third floor, a single cavernous room where clients worked out or sparred between private lessons. Right now, it sat empty. Someone could be up there teaching a second class. And if she had someone working the desk—

Knock it off, Gravois, he told himself firmly. *It's her business, not yours.*

A particularly enthusiastic *kiai* drew his attention back to the floor, where Zola ran herd over a dozen supernatural children.

Most knelt in a ragged circle, fidgeting with the abundant energy of youth, while one tiny wolf with bouncing pigtails barrelled through *taikyoku shodan* so fast it looked like a blur instead of a *kata*.

Separate classes for humans and supernaturals, another thing that had to complicate her scheduling. She definitely needed help, and he had to remember that he was the last person who should offer it.

Zola murmured encouragement to the girl as she corrected the position of her arms, then watched her execute a few vigorous punches. "Better," Zola said, raising her voice. Her gaze caught Walker's across the room, and she smiled a little. "Up, all of you. Along the far wall."

One or two of the children groaned, but they still formed a staggered line against the mirrors. Zola moved to stand beside the desk and nodded. "Sprints. Thirty. Boys, then girls, then boys, then girls. *Go!*"

The seven boys took off toward the far wall, the shapeshifters outdistancing the one child who sparked with magic instead of feral power. Zola turned her back on the spectacle and switched to French. "I cancelled my afternoon classes. When the little ones are gone, we'll be able to concentrate."

"It's a nice place, Zola."

Pride shone in her eyes. "Yes. My place. My home."

And he'd stumbled back into it. Guilt raked at him, and he had to force a smile. What if her involvement went beyond allowing him to use her contacts? If he'd brought his fight to her . . .

He'd never survive if his mistakes hurt her.

She read his turmoil in the fake smile. "I wasn't helpless, even as a girl. Whatever comes, I'll handle it."

He should have known he wouldn't be able to fool her. "You shouldn't have to. That part's on me."

One dark eyebrow swept upwards. "You think I need your protection?"

Careful, Walker. "I think it's my responsibility if I bring my trouble to you."

"Only if you're better at handling that trouble than I am." She smiled in teasing challenge as the doorbell jingled, announcing the arrival of the first of the parents returning to retrieve their children. "Perhaps we'll see later."

Definitely a challenge. "You looking to fight me?"

"Just a friendly sparring. I'm sure we've both learned new tricks since the last time."

So many layers of meaning, even if Walker was fairly certain she'd meant the words innocently. "Can't wait," he murmured, lowering his gaze so she wouldn't see the awareness there.

Zola slipped away to resume watch over her charges, running them back and forth as more parents and guardians arrived, until the front of the dojo was crowded. More than one of the wolves cast curious glances his way, but no one approached him, not even when Zola sent the last of her students stampeding toward the exit.

She closed the door and threw the deadbolt. "The children are my favourites. They haven't learned to be afraid yet."

"But they're aware." They'd recognized him as out of place.

"New Orleans is safer. Not safe."

Another thing that hadn't changed in the years he'd been gone. "My half-brother still lives here." Better to get that out there, to let her think it had influenced his decision to come back, even if it wasn't true. After all, he hadn't dragged his ass into John's restaurant past closing time, asking for help.

No. He had come to her.

She brushed her fingers over the light switch, leaving the dojo lit only from the broken light slanting through the blinds on the front window. "Yes, I remember." Her footsteps took her towards the stairs, as if she expected him to follow. "I enjoy his cooking."

Surely John would have said something if Zola had taken pains to introduce herself. "Have you met him?"

"Of course." She hesitated, then turned while balanced on the first step, putting her eyes level with his. "I told him only that I'd met you during my travels, and that I'd considered you a friend. He never indicated he knew otherwise."

Because his brother had never been a meddling bastard, and it was a dozen kinds of wrong for Walker to regret it now. "John's the quiet type."

"Mmm. Some say the same of me." A smile played at the corners of her lips. "So. Do we spar?"

So that was what had her in such an all-fired hurry to get upstairs. Walker acquiesced with a shrug and one raised eyebrow. "If you think you can handle me."

Laughter was her only answer as she spun and launched herself up the stairs. He had to follow at a run, and barely ducked a swing when he made it into the open room above.

He circled out of reach, keeping a sharp gaze on her centre of gravity. "That wasn't quite fair, honey. Cheap shots are beneath you."

"No such thing." Her weight rested nimbly on the balls of her feet, and she swayed a little, smiling. "Never start a fight you don't intend to finish, no?"

"The cardinal rule," he agreed. "But you know dirty fighting exposes weakness."

"So does friendly banter." She darted forward, a feint obvious enough to be easily avoided. "Play with me, Walker."

He kicked off his shoes and rushed her once. Instead of meeting her straight on, he pushed off on her shoulder, using the momentum to spin them both around. She went with it, flowing into the turn so fast she whipped around in a tight circle and nearly struck his back.

He broke away and let her come at him, ready to pin down her technique. She didn't have one; she had at least a dozen, drawing on elements from various martial arts so quickly, so fluidly, he could barely catalogue them.

There was more than a little capoeira influence in the way she moved, especially when she crouched to avoid a blow and immediately retaliated by bracing her weight on one arm and launching into a *meia lua pulada*. Her legs kicked through the air, spinning so fast they almost blurred, and he barely dodged.

Walker managed to get her on the mat, but she hooked her feet under his legs and threw him off immediately. He landed with a thump on the mat, and she sprang up in another flurry of kicks.

Walker rolled and swept her feet from under her. She went down again – barely – and he threw one leg over her and wrestled her wrists to the mat above her head. "Should we count it off?" he panted.

"I don't submit," she snarled, but something other than anger laced the words. Desire. Heat. A heat reflected in her eyes, in the way her body twisted beneath him, not so much testing as teasing. "It has been too long since I fought for survival. I am becoming soft."

He only wished that were true, that she'd reached a point – found a place – where she could afford to let go a little. "You're tough as nails and you know it, Zola. I'm just stronger, that's all." Stronger but stupid, because he couldn't help responding to the soft press of her body.

"I'm faster. Speed should balance strength." Her voice dropped to a husky whisper that invited him to test more than her strength. "It would have, too, if the lion didn't wish to be caught. She does not have my pride."

Blood thundered in his ears as sense memory overtook him. He'd had her under him like this before, a mostly innocent situation that had turned to painful awareness in a heartbeat. She had kissed him that time, the awkwardness of the advance eclipsed by her eagerness – and by his own desire.

Memory clashed with adrenaline and the feel of her body against his, and Walker's dick hardened. He would have rolled away, but that hot invitation in her eyes kept him motionless. Riveted.

The world upended in a surge of sleek muscle. She moved fast, rolling them in a tangle of limbs that ended with her straddling his hips, hands planted on either side of his head. Echoes of that same memory were reflected in her eyes, along with wariness. "If you want that innocent girl, you won't find her here. I'm a grown woman."

He hadn't wanted to want that innocent girl any more than he wished to complicate Zola's life by desiring her now. "I know who you are."

"No, you don't." She nuzzled the line of his jaw and back toward his ear, her cheek smooth against his face. Her breath blew warm over his earlobe just before her lips brushed his skin, an electric contact. "If you stayed, you could learn. All the things you used to know, and the things you never discovered."

The most dangerous issue of all was how Walker wanted to respond to the sweet temptation of her offer. He *could* stay. He had—

No idea what the fuck is going to happen, he reminded himself coldly. He'd be risking her heart again if he promised something he couldn't deliver, though his body didn't care. It yearned towards her, desperate to augment his memories with a thousand things he'd never felt. "Zola."

She closed her teeth on his throat with a purring growl.

Heat streaked through him, and Walker flipped her without thinking. He pinned her hips with his and almost returned the sharp, instinctive caress. Instead, his mouth descended on hers.

He hadn't known he was going to kiss her until he did, his tongue parting her lips before slipping into her mouth. He'd missed this the most, but instead of trembling under him like she had all those years ago, she bit the tip of his tongue with a needy little snarl and kissed him like she'd forgotten how to do anything else, teeth and tongue and desperate gripping hands, pulling him closer.

They *didn't* know each other anymore, but that could change in a moment. A heartbeat. And it would be all too easy to lose himself in her.

Walker tore his mouth from hers and struggled for control as he panted against her bare shoulder. "We have to stop this."

"Alec will be here soon," she said, and it might have sounded more like agreement if her body wasn't still hot and pliant under his.

He rocked back to his knees, scrubbing both hands over his face. "Are you hungry?"

A rough knock sounded from below before she could answer, and Zola sighed and rolled away. "That will be him."

Resenting the other man's intrusion was ridiculous, especially since he'd only come to help. Walker rose, his body still painfully tight. "Later, we need to talk about this."

"We'll see." She came to her feet in one graceful movement, hands already smoothing her dishevelled clothing. Trying to erase any visible sign that he'd touched her, though it would take days for his scent to fade from her skin.

It pleased him more than it should have.

Another impatient knock rattled the front door. Walker bounded down the stairs two at a time and dragged it open to find a tall, imposing wolf with dark hair, dark eyes and a dark scowl that faltered when he dragged in a deep breath.

Confusion flickered through his eyes, then he tilted his head, eyeing Walker with obvious appraisal. "So. I hear you're John's half-brother. Didn't realize you were so friendly with Zola, too."

He held out his hand. "We go way back. I'm Walker Gravois."

"Alec Jacobson." The wolf had a firm handshake, strong, but not overly aggressive. "Zola here?"

"Upstairs. She'll be down in a second."

"Ah." A knowing little smile. "Can I at least come in? You and I can talk."

"Yeah, sure." Walker locked the door behind him and pulled the shade tighter. "Did you manage to reach the Southeast council?"

"Skipped them." Alec leaned against the desk. "Got some hush-hush info from the Conclave instead. Your group – the Scions? They've already petitioned the Conclave for permission to extradite you."

"I'm not surprised." If he'd gone straight to Conclave sources, he had to be more connected than Walker had realized. "What about the rest of the pride?"

"They seem focused on you, for now. The Conclave . . ." Derision filled Alec's voice. "Well, off the record? They're spinning their wheels. Some of them want to hand you right over, and the rest don't want to get involved at all, because it's not a wolf matter. Right now, they're looking for an excuse to say it isn't their business."

He'd already thought of it. "Like if the pride belonged to someone else. Someone who'd never crossed the Scions."

"Like if the pride belonged to Zola." Alec nodded shortly. "Here's the deal, Gravois. The Conclave might order that we give you up, but they know we won't. Not if Zola doesn't want us to. New Orleans is pretty much off the grid right now, and the Conclave isn't ready to force a confrontation. But they can't exactly admit to your Scions that they're so powerless that they *can't* hand you over. So if they've got a reason to stay out of it – like Zola being in charge and you being one of *her* people now . . ."

"Then they'll stay out of it." Walker's gaze drifted to the stairs. "The Scions will come anyway. For me, at least."

"Does she know?"

"I told her they're not going to give up." Walker squared his shoulders and turned to face Alec. "I protected Tatienne when they came for her. She may have been nuts, but she was one of us. I killed a few of them, and now the Scions have a personal score to settle with me."

The stairs creaked behind him, and he marked Zola's passage easily by the whisper of bare feet on hardwood. "I am hearing you both quite clearly," she said when she reached the ground level.

Alec responded to her irritated tone with a lazy grin. "Never figured you couldn't. Just catching your friend up on the lay of the land, darling."

He addressed her with irritating familiarity, but it was the way Zola reacted to the endearment that made Walker grit his teeth. She stared at Alec, flat and hard. "Behave."

The wolf raised both eyebrows in a clear *What did I do?* expression. Zola snorted and turned to Walker, speaking in French. "He's testing you. He tests everyone. He seems to think it makes him very clever." She looked to Alec and switched back to her deeply accented English. "We do not have time to play your wolf games, Alexander Jacobson."

"You're the one who's always telling me that cats play better than wolves."

"Yes, because cats know when play is appropriate."

Alec held up both hands. "I told your man how things stand with the Conclave. If you take over the pride, the Conclave'll tell the Scions to fuck off, and hell, they might even listen. The wolves have managed to keep it under wraps that they don't quite have control of their pet Seer anymore, so most of the supernatural world's still trembling in their boots."

Walker had heard about Michelle Peyton, just like everyone else. The fact that she was the wolf alpha's daughter had kept her alive when other Seers had been killed. "They'd better hope it stays that way, or she'll become a target. The Scions think Seers are an abomination, and they'll only stomach their existence as long as they're under control."

Alec pushed off the desk. "There's not much else to tell. You two need to talk. If Zola wants to declare herself the leader, all she needs to do is call me. I'll pass it on to the Conclave."

"Thank you." The words didn't come easily. Having so little control over his eventual fate scared the hell out of Walker, and it made him unfairly pissy. "Thanks, I mean it."

"Thank me by not stirring up too much trouble. We're between crises." He prowled towards the door with an easy arrogance that made Zola's fingers tighten on Walker's arm. "You two have a good afternoon."

When he was gone, Zola blew out a breath. "I do not always care for him. He's useful when there's trouble, but the same traits that make him useful make him aggravating."

She'd slipped into French again, and this time Walker followed her. "As long as he gets things done, right?"

"Perhaps." She moved away from him and locked the door, then closed all the blinds, blocking out the early afternoon sun. "It is always about power with the wolves. Accepting their help is acknowledging their dominance. He knows I will do no such thing. So he plays his games, and I must play too. Tiring."

"Seems like it might not be the only game he wants you to play."

Zola's lips curled into a tight, amused smile. "Yes, a fact that might be flattering if Alexander Jacobson were capable of keeping his pants on. I'm not interested in a man who falls into bed with a different woman every night."

Her declaration would have been reassuring – if he'd been jealous. But Walker wasn't stupid, and blind jealousy wasn't an option when the scent of her skin lingered on him, and the memory of her body against his stirred arousal even now. "He's not a lion – which helps me not want to punch him in the head."

She laughed, warm and delighted. "Believe me. Prolonged exposure will make *anyone* want to hit him. Unless they want to sleep with him." One dark eyebrow arched. "Do you?"

He pretended to consider it. "Tempting, but I'll pass."

Amusement glinted in her eyes as she tilted her head toward the stairs. "I can't cook as well as your brother, but I'll make do. Let's have lunch . . . and talk."

He folded his hand around hers. "That sounds good."

Three

Lunch turned into a mess. Zola tried to remain casual while lion and woman fought a fierce battle inside her. Walker seemed willing to stick to safe topics, telling her about those who remained in the pride as she crashed about in the kitchen. She tried to listen, but her gaze caught too often on the strong line of his shoulders or the firm curve of his full lips. Desire had settled to a low simmer, one that flared at the most inopportune moments.

She burned their meal while imagining his hands on her skin, his mouth on her throat, his hard body between her legs. Even abandoning the meal and dragging him out to a local cafe didn't help. With their future so uncertain, the lion judged every woman who smiled at him to be a threat, and Walker's beautiful eyes and sharp cheekbones attracted a good deal of feminine appreciation.

Mate. Such a foolish word, one with which the wolves were endlessly obsessed. Her mother had not allowed formalized matings amongst the pride, too concerned that loyalty to a mate would supersede the loyalty she thought her due.

Mate. A foolish word, but one that plagued her, tickled her mind and wiggled under skin until tension had her strung tighter than the finest bow.

If she didn't take Walker to bed soon, it might be the death of her sanity.

Assuming he'd accept such an invitation. That he wanted her was not in question. She'd felt proof of that fact hard and hot between her thighs on the practice room floor, so good she could have rocked up against him and driven herself to bliss without his assistance. But oh, how good his assistance would be . . .

Unfortunately, business could only wait so long. Zola showered while Walker made calls to wherever he'd stashed his people, some place in Mexico where a witch enhanced the spells woven into a charm Zola's mother had given them. The last gift of her fractured mind, magic that hid their presence from the Scions.

Magic that wouldn't last forever. Zola braided her hair and gathered her willpower. They'd spent precious hours circling. Stalking. Neither was ready to commit to the one conversation they needed to have.

It was time to stop playing.

Zola stepped from her bedroom and found Walker in the living room studying the framed photos on her walls. "You studied with DeSilva?"

"Four months." Her gaze drifted over the rest of the wall, over a dozen framed photographs of her with her many teachers, some of her most prized possessions. She'd honed her craft under the greatest masters who would teach her, flitting from country to country for six years after her mother had driven her from her pride.

She stepped forwards and lifted her hand to brush the frame of a photograph of her standing next to a man who barely came to her shoulder. "I stayed longest in Okinawa. With Nakamura. He's a psychic. Precognitive. Just a few seconds, but that's all he needs. I've seen him take down shifters twice his size."

Walker laughed. "You don't need bulk when you know what the tank coming at you plans to do."

Her preternatural speed had been of no use against Nakamura, who had left her with her fair share of humility – and a healthy respect for psychics and spell casters. "I've only been in New Orleans for a few years. It didn't feel safe to settle in one place at first. I didn't know if my mother might change her mind and come after me. Or if her enemies might."

He didn't argue with that. "Did you enjoy your travels?"

She gave him the truth, because she'd be demanding plenty of it from him soon enough. "Not at first. I was young. Scared. But my teachers gave me confidence, and I grew."

His voice roughened. "You did all right."

"Yes. I did." *No turning back now.* She pivoted to face him, and worked to keep her voice even. "I will take your people under my protection. I will reform the pride. But, in return, you will tell me the truth."

Walker stepped back, such a small movement that she wondered if she realized he'd done it. Retreat had never been in his nature, any more than it was in her own. Nor was the wariness in his voice. "The truth about what?"

Zola braced herself. "Why did you let her drive me away? Why didn't you follow me?"

She saw the moment he decided to tell her, and she knew it would be the truth. His eyes shadowed, and he sighed. "I couldn't stop you, and I couldn't follow you. Not without putting you in danger."

"Because of my mother?"

"Because of your mother's orders."

She hadn't realized hope still lived until it fluttered weakly in her chest. "What would she have done to you if you'd followed me?"

"Tatienne said that if any of us went with you, she'd have to assume we meant to start our own pride. A rival pride." He met her gaze. "She would have killed you, Zola."

Zola closed her eyes as pain rose, bringing the sharpness of memory with it. Tatienne as a younger woman, pale skin bronzed by the relentless sun, her auburn hair streaked with gold. Zola had inherited her colouring from her father, chocolate and twilight, but her mother had been all the colours of a desert sunset. Power had sung in her mother's veins, but so had love. Love for her daughter, for her pride.

The Conclave's Seer was heavily pregnant. Would sweet little Michelle Peyton lose the gentleness in her nature? Would the son she carried beneath her heart turn some day to find his mother had vanished, lost to the ravages of a power too great for one body to contain?

"Hey." Walker urged her face up with gentle fingers under her chin. "I know it's horrible. That's why I promised myself I wouldn't do this to you."

Too late, she scented salt. Her cheeks were wet with traitorous tears, revealing the depth of her helpless vulnerability to the one man who'd always had the power to lay her heart bare.

She recoiled, stumbling back two steps before turning and scrubbing away all evidence of her lapse from her cheeks with two shaking hands. "She loved me once. She loved all of us. Whatever monster she became, whatever she did to the people she had sworn to protect – it is not our fault. It is no judgment on us. A Seer's power consumes them."

"That's all true." He cupped her shoulders, rubbed his cheek comfortingly against the top of her head. "Doesn't mean it can't hurt."

Tatienne had betrayed him too. Zola leaned back and let his warmth and strength curl around her, along with the wonderful *belonging* that came from being with one of her own kind. "If it had been your choice? Would you have followed me?"

He released a long, slow breath that stirred her hair and tickled her cheek. "In a heartbeat. Nothing else could have kept me away."

Truth had a scent. A feel. Bitter, sometimes, but always solid and implacable. Tension that had lived inside her for a decade slowly unknotted itself. "Then it's behind us. I like who I've become. I have my freedom."

He stiffened, just a little. "I wish I could say the same."

Zola slid her hands up to cover his. "The past is the past. You're fighting to protect your people. I like who you've become."

"You won't if I have to go." His hands slipped down and tightened around her waist. "I'd do it to protect you."

He expected her to be shocked. Perhaps she *should* have been, or outraged, or even angry. Some male shifters smothered their mates with a blind protectiveness that carried an unpleasant aura of chauvinism. But if Walker had such unsavoury prejudices against women, he wouldn't have willingly followed Zola's mother.

Zola smoothed one hand up his arm and shoulder, curling her fingers around the back of his neck. "I would do the same to you. We protect the ones we—" *Love.* "—care about. Which is why I'll take your people under my care. I'll call the Conclave tonight and declare them my pride, and the people in New Orleans will help me keep them safe."

A beat. "Where do I fit in?"

The warmth of his body made it so easy to move closer – and hard not to rub against him like a cat in heat. "You can lead with me, or you can leave. I won't blackmail you into my bed by holding their safety over your head."

His laugh vibrated against her skin, less amused than wondering. "That's the last thing you'd have to do to get me in your bed."

Instinct whispered that he wouldn't make the first advance, so she did, rocking up on her toes to close the distance between them. His lips were warm and firm and tasted like bitter coffee mixed with cinnamon from the pastry he'd had for dessert, and underneath it all *Walker*. Lion. Male.

Mine.

Her back hit the wall and Walker pressed closer, lifting her a little as he eased between her thighs and ground against her. "I won't stop this time. Not until I'm inside you."

She'd had plenty of men in her bed, in her body. But never another lion. Nothing could have prepared her for the satisfaction that roared up from the deepest place inside, washing away reason in a wave of primal hunger. She got both legs up around his hips, trusting him to hold her as she pulled at his shirt.

With his hips bracing her weight, he leaned back and yanked his T-shirt over his head. "You're positive?"

Such a foolish question. She answered by working a hand down until her fingers cupped the hard weight of his cock. "I told you. I'm not an innocent girl anymore. Can you keep up with me now?"

Walker hissed in a breath and nibbled her, the sharp press of his teeth on her jaw just short of savage. "Ask me again later, if you can still think."

Thought was already fighting a hopeless battle. She got her fingers around the button on his jeans and ripped it off in her haste. "Hurry."

"No." He slid his hands under her ass and hoisted her up. "First door, yeah?"

She'd take him into her now and glory in every thrust as he fucked her against the wall. Some dangerous alchemy of lust and instinct turned her wild, and only the promise of seeing him twisted in her sheets made it possible to find her voice. "Yes."

It took him only a few quick steps to reach the bedroom – and the bed. He dropped her on it and slipped his hand under her shirt, his eyes blazing. "I missed you."

Warm, callused fingers stroked over her stomach. She arched into the touch, eyes falling shut. "You don't need to miss me any more."

"No, I don't." He palmed her breast through her sports bra. "Take off your clothes."

Easier said than done. Her T-shirt tore under her frantic fingers. She let the cotton slip to the floor and wiggled her way out of her pants more carefully.

By the time she lay in her bra and underwear, Walker was watching her, his hands clenched by his sides. "This is the first time," he whispered. "You've been mine for so long that it seems surreal, but this is the first time."

Their first time, and relief rose that it wasn't *her* first time. At fifteen, she'd fallen in girlish love with a youth of twenty-one. At nineteen, she'd trembled beneath the careful kisses of a man who'd held himself back, too aware of her innocence.

At thirty, she was a woman who knew what she wanted, and she took it, rising to her knees and sliding her palms against the incredible heat of his strong chest. "The first time. Not the last."

"No." He slid his fingers into her hair and tilted her head back. "What do you like?"

Zola laughed and scraped her nails down his arms, letting power rise in her, the best kind of challenge. "Figure it out."

"Uh-huh." He arched an eyebrow. "You're not naked yet."

With the button from his jeans gone, it was easy to slide the zipper down. "I'm distracted. If it's important to you, maybe you should help."

He caught her wrists in an iron grip, and it was only then that she realized how tenuous his control was. "If you want me to take my time," he rasped, "then you're going to have to *let* me."

Wildness seethed just under the surface, and she wanted it. Needed it. With her wrists pinned she used her teeth to drive home her point, biting his shoulder with a low growl. "Take your time later. Now, we fuck."

Walker surged over her with a growl, as if some leash holding him back had snapped. "Should have just said so." The stretchy fabric of her bra yielded under his hands.

It was too fast to savour, but she wouldn't have been able to appreciate finesse with blood pounding in her ears and hunger narrowing the room to his touch. Callused fingers, fast and frantic until she revealed a weakness with an arch or gasp, then so intense he had her panting as he toyed with her breasts. She moaned when he added his mouth, his rough tongue and sharp nips of his teeth.

He teased his thumb under the edge of her panties. One gentle tug and then he ripped those off, as well, baring her to his touch. He didn't hesitate, just rocked the heel of his hand against her and groaned when pleasure shattered through her so hot that she cried out.

If he worked his fingers inside her body, she'd come and he'd take her and it would be good, but it wouldn't be what she needed. Using all the strength in her trembling limbs, she broke free and rolled to her stomach, then came to her knees. "*Now.*"

Walker growled his pleasure, but he didn't touch her again until his bare skin brushed her ass and the backs of her thighs. He leaned over her, strong arms braced beside hers, and kissed the back of her shoulder. "Now."

He drove into her, and the world tumbled end over end in a dizzy spiral that tightened along with her body. In ten years of running she'd never belonged anywhere as much as she belonged here, beneath him, around him.

Part of him, as she'd been since the first day she'd loved him.

Her fingers fisted in the blankets as she rocked back, taking him deeper until pleasure gained a sharp edge that sliced through her, laying everything bare. That edge cut deeper as he nudged her hair off the back of her neck and bit her, then began to move, slow and strong.

Perfect.

She wanted it to last forever, but of course it couldn't. Zola closed her eyes and revelled in the slick thrust of his cock, the heat of his skin, the flex of his muscles. Too soon, she was trembling.

He whispered one dark, quiet entreaty. "Come."

She did, with a helpless moan that didn't drown out the sweet sound of their bodies slamming together as she tumbled into bliss. He bit her again, arms shaking as his thrusts sped until he went rigid and followed her over the edge with a choked sigh.

Her name.

I love you. The words echoed in her mind, but she collapsed in a sweaty, trembling tangle of limbs without giving them voice. Too fragile. Too old *and* too new. So she pushed them down and ignored the lion's unhappy rumble.

Walker would be theirs soon enough. She wouldn't let him go a second time.

Four

Walker woke with Zola draped over him, a living dream that had haunted him for years. His third time of waking and reaching for her, and she came to him as readily as the first, wrapping her legs around his hips.

"Slow." More than a whispered promise to her, it was a pledge to himself. They'd both waited so long, and they deserved to have each other in every way imaginable.

He kept his pledge until she bit his ear and whispered, "Mine."

He lost himself then, surging deep. *Mine*. More than a word – a claim, one that matched the way her body welcomed his. Pleasure overwhelmed him, pure instinctive satisfaction.

Completion.

He belonged here, exactly where he was.

Afterwards, he licked the sweat from the hollow of her throat and smoothed her hair back. "Do you have classes tomorrow?"

A sleepy shake of her head as she stroked his back. "Never on Sundays."

One of a hundred tiny little details he didn't know, and he relished the opportunity to learn everything about her. "Just us, then?"

"Unless we want to start making arrangements to bring the pride to New Orleans." Her fingers slid up to tease the back of his scalp. "I have money. We can find them a place to live."

Money was the least of it. "So do I. The problem is how much red tape is involved with a move like this. That's part of why I wanted the wolf council's help."

She chuckled. "I did not immigrate . . . naturally. There is a thriving business in New Orleans that focuses on nothing but making red tape disappear."

"And if they're like all the other thriving businesses like that all over the world, you don't just walk up to them with an envelope of cash."

"No," she agreed, laughter still bubbling in her voice. "You send Alexander Jacobson. He will do it, because I've recently taken on a young woman of his acquaintance as a private student, and he's feeling very grateful."

He joined in her laughter. "I see how it is."

"Mmm." Her hand stilled as she yawned, then nuzzled his chin with sleepy affection. "Rest. You'll need it if we're to do this again in a few hours."

"I need you more than I need sleep." He kissed her temple and slid out from under the covers. "I'll be right back."

Walker made his way down the hall towards the bathroom in the dark. As he approached the half-open door, his skin prickled, the hair on the back of his neck rising.

Something was wrong.

Though he could see well enough, he wasn't that familiar with Zola's apartment to notice anything visibly out of place, and he heard nothing. Not a damn thing to fuel his indefinable sense of *wrong*.

Still, it remained.

He flipped on the bathroom light, and his blood chilled. A bag of dirty black cloth dangled from the mirror by a length of coarse twine. A gris-gris, maybe, one that Zola definitely hadn't placed.

The bag clinked as he yanked it free. He smelled flowers and copper, two scents that exploded in his nose as he upended the bag on the counter. Rose petals and pennies tumbled out, along with a small bottle of whiskey and a slim dime that seemed to spin in time with his pounding heart before finally settling on the slick tile.

Just like that, he was back in the bayou, watching his mother bury another wax doll baby under the raised edge of their ramshackle porch. She'd always whispered words, low, mellifluous entreaties that faded in the heavy air, rising to blend with the rustle of Spanish moss in the trees.

Not a gris-gris. Flowers, nine pennies, whiskey and a Mercury dime. Everything a rootworker would need to buy graveyard dirt from the departed.

It was a message and a warning, all wrapped up in bits and pieces of his past. The Scions had come in while they slept, or even while they made love. Under cover of magic, they'd violated the safety and sanctity of Zola's home.

And yet, no blood had been shed.

Walker swept the contents of the black bag into the small wastebasket beside the vanity. The Scions wanted nothing to do with Zola, either because of her connections or because she'd been blameless in Tatienne's affairs – but they'd hurt her if they had to. To get to him, they'd mow down anyone and anything in their way, and damn what the Conclave had to say about it.

He made a cursory check of the apartment, but found nothing. He hadn't expected to. No one remained stealing about the rooms under cover of magic. They had no need for it.

The Scions had accomplished their mission and left their message. They knew Walker, knew what lived at the very heart of him – and the lengths he would go to in order to keep Zola safe.

And *he* knew where they'd be waiting.

Walker parked his borrowed bike at the end of the long driveway. Someone had taken a swing at the rusted out mailbox, and it dangled precariously from its wooden post. He righted it before he set out for the house on foot, though he had no idea why.

No one lived here and, unless his half-brother tired of city life, no one would.

It had been years since he'd walked the mostly-dirt path. Grass had grown up in the middle of the road, between the packed ruts, and the heavy canopy of live oaks and cypress overhead blocked out the light of the moon.

The path lightened, and he could see the house at the end of it. Walker had barely cleared the thick cover of the trees when a voice spoke from the sagging porch. "So. You come alone."

Walker studied the simply dressed man and shrugged. "I assumed that was what you wanted."

A soft footstep made the porch creak, and a woman appeared at the man's shoulder. "It is easier not to have to contend with the Seer's get, but we were not sure you would abandon her."

Abandon. The word rankled, shamed him. "She has nothing to do with this."

The man laughed, rusty and flat. "No, I suppose not. Taking her from you might right the scales, but she's more trouble than she's worth . . . as long as you come with us quietly."

"Just me." Walker shifted his weight, instinct demanding a fight – though there would not be one. "The rest of the pride is hers now, and my life is yours."

Gravel crunched behind Walker, and the two Scions on the porch stiffened. The woman tilted her head and gazed past him. "Does *she* know that?"

Damn it. Walker turned to find Zola standing there, eyes narrowed. "I thought I might have gotten away with it."

She raised both eyebrows, silently asking if he'd *really* thought he could, then looked past him toward their enemies. "I know what's mine. The pride is mine, as is Walker Gravois. Are you here to challenge me for them?"

The woman paused at the top of the porch steps. "Gravois is coming with us. He must answer for what he has done."

Zola strode forwards until she stood at his shoulder, then reached down deliberately and curled her hand around his. "He stays. You leave."

She was strong, beautiful. Defiant.

His.

Walker gripped her hand and looked down at her, his chest aching. "They fight as one," he whispered, "but so do we."

"Always." Her fingers tightened until her grip bordered on painful. "Do you challenge us, Scions?"

In response the man pulled a gun and levelled it at Walker's head, finger already squeezing down on the trigger.

Walker released Zola's hand and ducked into a roll as magic surged through the night. One kick to half-rotted wood brought down the corner of the porch, and the Scion stumbled and dropped his gun.

He dived for it, but Zola was faster. Her first kick sent the gun skittering under the groaning porch, and her second swiped the man's legs out from under him, spilling him into the too-tall grass. A second later the woman – the shapeshifter – leapt from the crumbling steps and tackled Zola.

Zola bucked and rolled, using the Scion's own momentum to throw her aside. Walker caught the woman off-guard, drawing her attention away from Zola. As the child of a Seer, Zola's natural resistance to magic made her a better adversary for the spell caster.

And she pressed that advantage, coming to her feet just as the man fisted both hands and raised them. Magic cut through the cool air, prickling along Walker's skin, but the brunt of the power rolled off Zola as she spun again, lightning fast, and clipped the wizard's jaw with her heel.

His grunt of pain made his partner turn for a split-second, and Walker slammed his elbow into her temple. She staggered, and he caught her around the throat. "Will you go?" he demanded. "Leave and never come back to New Orleans?"

She replied with a snarl and a knee driving into his groin as magic snapped again, this time slamming into *him*. His vision blurred as pain and magic mingled, and he lashed out, instinct driving him.

He struck her in the throat with the blade of his hand. The delicate bone protecting her airway snapped and she fell back, choking for air in loud, heaving gasps.

It wouldn't take her long to recover. Walker struggled to focus, to shake off the spell so Zola wasn't left to fight alone.

The sharp crack of gunfire echoed around him, a second before a warm body crashed into him. Zola's, by the scent and feel. She bore him to the ground and rolled them until his hip bumped into the collapsed end of the porch.

"He's got the gun," she whispered, a breath of sound against his ear. "Firing from under what's left of the stairs."

"The other support beam." The porch had been rickety even in his youth. One more well-placed blow might bring the entire thing down on the hidden Scion.

"Can you get to it if I distract them?"

He was still seeing double, but he nodded. "Get the shifter. I'll handle this guy."

Her lips brushed his cheek in a whisper-soft caress, and then she was gone in a swirl of near-silent footsteps across the untamed grass.

One shot fired into the night, but a second later he heard the Scion shifter's grunt of pain as Zola pounced on her, tangling them up so the wizard wouldn't get a clear shot at her.

As Zola grappled with the shifter, Walker eased around to the edge of the porch. A shot whistled past, and he cursed. Without rounding the house, there was no way to sneak past the spell caster under the porch.

Screw this. He scrambled up the collapsed side of the porch, the wood creaking under his weight. Another loud report, this one accompanied by a blaze of pain in Walker's arm.

He'd been shot, and he didn't give a damn. He roared his anger and punched down through the boards to close his hand in the man's hair. He managed to slam his adversary up against the wood three times before the listing porch collapsed.

"Walker?" Zola's voice, edged with worry. "Are you all right?"

He closed his fingers around the gun and groaned as he rolled on to his back. "Peachy. You?"

An uncertain pause, and she echoed the word back to him in her accented English. "I am hoping that means good."

"It means I'll make it."

The sound of flesh on flesh followed, a muffled grunt and then silence. "She is alive. Unconscious, but alive. I will call the Conclave. The Scions. Offer her for your pardon. A life for a life, yes?"

A life for a life. How could the Scions refuse, when the woman's defeat rendered her life forfeit? "I think that'll work out just fine." Underneath him, the shattered boards shifted, and the spell caster groaned. "Maybe even twice over."

Zola rose and crossed the yard, the moonlight glinting off her features. "Are you injured?"

"Just a scratch." Walker rolled off the flattened porch and landed on his knees. "My jacket's ruined, though."

"Fool." Her fingers slid into his hair and down, cupping his neck. Her words drifted to French, low and intimate. "I love you too much to lose you to stubborn pride. But if you walk into another trap without me at your side, I will kill you myself."

"I screwed up, but never again." Leaving her was, without a doubt, the most idiotic thing he'd ever done. Zola didn't need his protection. She just needed *him*, and he knew the feeling. "We fight together?"

"As one. Always." Her lips seized his in a breathless, desperate kiss, over almost before it began. "And now we call Alec Jacobson. He has a cage in his basement for situations like this. I'm afraid you will find they happen more often than not, if you stay here."

He couldn't help but laugh. "I grew up around here. I know the lie of the land."

"Then you know it will never be boring."

Living in a plastic bubble wouldn't be boring as long as Zola was with him. "Are you sure you can forgive me for sneaking out on you?"

A hint of laughter bubbled up as she reached into her pocket for a phone. "This time. But only if you take over my class full of adolescent male shifters. Perhaps a weekly reminder of the crippling effects of male ego will teach you a valuable lesson."

It was far more than he deserved, but there was no way he'd squander a chance to make up for the hurts he'd visited on her in the past – the distant and the not so distant. "Make your call, Zola. The faster we get these two out of here, the faster we can be alone."

The faster he could convince her she'd made the right choice.

Epilogue

". . . so after the Scion representatives struck their deal with you, the Alpha escorted the whole mess of them back to New York on his jet. Got a call from him last night to let me know they'd left the country."

Zola made a non-committal noise, only half of her attention on Alec's voice as it spilled out of her phone. There were only six students in her adolescent shifter group – only males, because she refused to teach them in a mixed class when their hormones would be driving them to posture and preen for their classmates' feminine attention. Any urge they might have had to fight for *her* attention had been knocked out of them within their first week, leaving a moderately serious group of youths on the cusp of manhood.

Manageable enough, until confronted with a shapeshifter male in his prime. Zola hid a smile behind her hand as Walker deftly handled another borderline challenge, patiently but firmly, setting the boy in his place without damaging more than his ego.

Alec was still talking, and Zola made a conscious effort to drag her attention back to the conversation in time to hear, ". . . all taken care of, then. Paperwork for the pride should be ready in a few days. If you need help getting them across the border—"

"We will be fine." Considering all the trouble Alec Jacobson got himself into, owing him *too* many favours could prove to be an uncomfortable situation. "Thank you."

She ended the conversation just as Walker ended the class, sending the boys out into the cool New Orleans evening. When the door swung shut behind the last one, she lifted an eyebrow. "Well?"

He flashed her a hint of a smile as he cracked open a bottle of water. "Well what?"

"Nothing." Impossible not to admire the beauty of him, sweat-sheened golden skin and hard muscles and those eyes she'd now seen glazed with passion. Making love to him was new, but loving him was like remembering a move so ingrained it was instinct. *Muscle memory*, an amused part of her noted as she crossed the room to slip her arms around him. *The heart is just another muscle*.

Walker wove his fingers through her ponytail and pulled her closer, tilting her head up for a slow kiss, his open mouth teasing over hers. Hot, perfect, even before she parted her lips on a moan and realized he was determined to kiss her within an inch of her life.

Which made it even easier to catch his leg with her foot and spill them both to the ground. A breathless moment later she was straddling his waist with her hands on either side of his head. And because English was *his* native language, she ignored her self-consciousness and her odd accent and spoke from her heart. The words, in any case, were simple enough. "I love you."

"Love you too." He slid one hand to her hip, the other around to her back, cradling her close. "That's why we're stronger together."

"And you should never forget it," she whispered, before leaning in to kiss him again. Soft and slow, like she had all the time in the world.

Because she did.

In Dreams

Elissa Wilds

Time didn't exist here. Not in this place. Not in these moments. Here, the air held an electric charge that swept through Anna when her feet touched the soft-as-silk sand and made her limbs shiver with excitement. Here, she breathed in the salty ocean air instead of city smog and the exhaust fumes of rush-hour traffic. No worries touched her mind. Nothing of the two-dimensional world she called reality could penetrate to this realm.

Which was a good thing.

The whole reason she'd decided to attempt astral travel was to escape from an unbearable reality. From a world where her husband was dead and she was alone. Two years had passed since Richard's death, but it seemed to her a lifetime.

In the astral realm, a quiet peace filled her being and made the world she called home seem but a dream. A sad, unnecessary dream.

Anna glanced around with a quiet calm she had only recently developed. The first few times she'd attempted to astral travel, she'd been nervous and uncertain. She'd read books on the subject, but as much as the authors of those books reassured that nothing could hurt her here, it had taken a few successful trips for her to believe them. She'd learned quickly. With the slightest focus Anna could create what she wanted to see and experience. So of course, she came back here. To her dreamtime beach.

She loved the beach, but hadn't seen much of it since she'd accepted the job in D.C. She'd been anxious to get out of Santa

Barbara. To go anywhere as long as it was far away from her life in California and the life she'd shared with Richard.

But running had proved pointless. *Wherever you go, there you are.*

Anna dug her feet farther into the sand and stared at the water rippling along the shore. Light flickered off the tourmaline blue waves. She wandered closer to the shore and knelt, catching her reflection in the water. Her dirty blond hair sparkled gold and her face was worry-crease free. She smiled with the realization once again that in the astral realm she was her brightest, most radiant self. The few extra pounds she'd gained over the holidays were irrelevant. Here, her slightly rounded hips and shorter than average frame was exotic, beautiful.

A slight breeze brushed over her skin, not too cool, not too hot.

"Perfect," she murmured.

"Of course," a deep voice spoke at her side. "All is perfect in the astral realm."

Anna started, but before the sensation of fear could creep into her gut and send her hurtling back to her body – a lesson she'd learned the hard way the first few times she'd encountered another being during one of her astral trips – she forced herself to calmly turn and face the individual who'd spoken.

Her breath caught. He was tall and lean. Dark hair curled over the nape of his neck. He wore white pants and nothing else. The material hugged him in all the right places and shimmered as though the cloth were threaded with tiny diamonds.

The man stared, his emerald gaze studying her, his lips curved into a half smile.

"I know you," he said.

She shook her head. This was not a man she'd soon forget. "No, I don't think so."

He circled her, his limbs moving in that soft, unfocused way in which everything moved in the astral realm. Images, places, things, seemed to shift on a sigh. Anna still found the process disorienting. *He* was disorienting.

He was behind her. She shivered as his hand touched her hair and he fingered the strands lightly. "Your hair shines like gold."

He trailed his fingers over her shoulder and arm, then her back. His touch was soft, fleeting, yet it seemed to Anna that there was fire beneath his fingertips. A heat that made her insides quiver and dance in a way they hadn't in a long time. Another time, another place, she would have yanked herself away from this man, this stranger who approached her with such strange familiarity. But she didn't have to follow normal convention here. She didn't have to behave with propriety. In this hazy place of no time, she could do exactly as she wished . . . without concern for consequence.

And it had been so very long since she'd been touched by a man.

He stood in front of her again, hands at his sides. Anna frowned, wanting those large, elegant hands on her body again, caressing her. The stranger tilted his head to the side and studied her, his expression curious and confused. Then he leaned in close. His face nuzzled her neck as he breathed in deeply.

"Ah," he murmured. "You smell so good. Like fresh honeysuckle. So sweet . . ."

His breath danced over her skin, tickling her flesh. "I – I love the smell of honeysuckle," she managed to gasp out, struck by the inanity of her words. How she smelled of this, she didn't know, but anything was possible in this place. It delighted her to know that her scent pleased him.

Hot lips touched her neck with the slightest of caresses. Desire arched through her body and dipped between her thighs. "Oh!" Her breath hitched. She certainly hadn't experienced a reaction like *this* to anyone in a long time.

His face hovered in front of hers, his eyes filled with a certain knowing, a confirmation of sorts. Of what? She wished she knew.

"You enchant me. You must be a witch. Or an angel? Who are you?"

She opened her mouth to tell him her name, but he halted her words with one finger to her lips. "No, don't tell me. I will call you Angel. Your beauty rivals a being from the heavenly realms, and I'm told that any number of various and sundry creatures travel through these planes." He smiled, his full lips pulling across straight, white teeth. His finger traced her mouth. It took all of her self-control not to let her tongue snake out, not to nip at his finger playfully.

Odd, she thought. *I don't even know this man, yet I want to do something so intimate with him?* The internal thought was both question and statement. An image flashed through Anna's mind. The stranger's finger in her mouth. His other hand between her thighs. Her lips clutching his finger, mouth suckling the digit in rhythm with the hand that touched her sex.

Oh! Intimate, indeed!

"Yes," the man continued as though oblivious to her sensual thoughts, "I'll call you Angel. My Angel. And although I've never before seen your lovely face, my body knows yours. I think, perhaps, we have kissed before." He removed his finger, and leaned in, his lips hovering over hers. "And I ache to do so again."

He was so close she could taste his breath, could inhale his scent. He smelled like chocolate and burgundy wine and everything decadent.

Her flesh hummed from his nearness. Her stomach muscles quivered, taut with anticipation, waiting. He cupped her arms, his hands hot, searing her skin through the thin cotton shift she wore. Anna's lips parted in invitation, and her eyelids fluttered shut.

And yet, the stranger hesitated. "The anticipation is so very sweet . . . isn't it?" he murmured. He tilted his head to the side, allowed his cheek to brush hers ever so slightly, then dipped to her neck, nuzzling, inhaling sharply, breathing her in. Then, before she could fully register the gamut of emotions trilling through her, his gaze met hers once again, and his lips parted into a half smile.

She couldn't take this. She had to touch him. She had to kiss him. Taste him. She had to—

His mouth pressed hers, stealing her thoughts. His lips teased her with slow, sensual movements that whispered of a deeper, more intimate joining. His fingers left her arms and caressed her neck, twined through her hair, and left her own hands free to roam.

And roam they did. To his lean waist, over his bare, flat stomach and his hard chest. He touched his tongue to her lips with a quick, tentative exploration. Just enough to stoke the fire burning in her belly and send licks of flame between her thighs. Anna gulped air, her head swirling. The kiss deepened and became more aggressive. She suddenly couldn't feel the sand beneath her toes, couldn't hear the water lapping at the shoreline. The stranger's heartbeat beneath her fingertips accelerated. She could feel his heart beating, frantic and erratic. So was her own. The two beats grew louder, filling her head, making her dizzy with want and need.

Anna's body seemed to melt into the stranger's. They were as one being. The sensation was erotic and exciting.

And then suddenly, the man was gone. Cool air brushed her lips and wove around her empty arms. Anna's heart plummeted as disappointment washed through her. *No!* A white void surrounded her. And she was falling, falling . . .

Anna gasped as she slammed into her body. The return was so fast and unexpected this time that she couldn't move for several long moments. She struggled to reorient herself. Then she felt it. The hot tongue licking her face. The loud, persistent purring in her ear. The ten pounds of fur perched on her chest.

She groaned and rolled over in her bed, sending the cat tumbling to the pillow next to her. She blinked one eye open to stare at the orange tabby and the bedroom door he'd obviously found his way through.

"Emerson, how do you do it? You don't even have opposable thumbs."

The cat scooted closer to her and licked her cheek. *"Meow,"* came his reply.

She scratched him behind his ears, eliciting more purrs, and sighed. She'd started locking Emerson out of the bedroom at night because he had a habit of affectionately attacking her in her sleep and disrupting her nocturnal travels. Tonight was one night Anna really wished Emerson wasn't such a clever little feline.

Anna immediately fell back into a deep, dreamless sleep. Sometime in the middle of the night, she awoke for no reason and could not fall back asleep. After glaring at Emerson who was snoring beside her, oblivious to her insomnia, she rose and went to the bathroom to dig out some melatonin from the medicine cabinet.

A half-hour later, still wide awake, she decided a hot shower might help her plight. She took her time with her shower, enjoying the sting of the hot water and the delicious aroma of her goji berry and chocolate scented body wash.

Anna stepped from the shower into a thoroughly steamed up bathroom and wrapped herself in a fluffy towel. After opening the door to let out some of the steam, she turned to the sink to find her comb.

Her eyes went wide and her breath caught. The comb hit the tile floor with a *clickety-clack*. Tears spiked and trickled over her cheeks. There, on the mirror, written as though a ghostly finger had reached out from beyond the grave to scribble the words on the steamed-up glass, was a message.

I am sending you love. Love is in the air. R

The next day was Saturday. Anna had not slept more than an hour after finding Richard's message. They'd joked once that whoever of them died first would find a way to get a message to the other and let them know they were okay. But it had been two years since Richard's death, and as much as she'd wanted to feel him near, to know he was alive and well somewhere beyond the veil, she hadn't had the slightest paranormal experience to breathe life into that hope.

Why? Why now? Was he concerned that it had been so long since his death and she'd yet to start dating again? Possibly. Maybe he wanted her to know he was all right so that she'd have an easier time letting him go.

Was it a coincidence that his message came the very same night she'd met the handsome stranger in the astral realm? Anna frowned. What if Richard's motivation was just the opposite? What if he was angry she was moving on, even in this small way? She immediately pushed that thought away. No, that didn't sound like Richard. Richard had always been more concerned about Anna's well-being than his own.

And what exactly had happened tonight? Who was the stranger? Why was she so drawn to him? She couldn't stop thinking about him, about his mesmerizing eyes, his titillating touch.

She spent most of the afternoon pouring through her dense library. Always an avid reader, after her husband's death, Anna's fascination with the afterlife and all related phenomenon had filled her spare bedroom with books, books and more books.

"One of these days, I'll organize everything," she muttered to herself while scanning the jam-packed shelves. It was a familiar vow. And one she'd yet to find the time to honour. She didn't know exactly what she looked for, but something told her that during one of her recent impulse book buying sprees, she'd picked up a book that would be useful; that might explain her experience last night and the man with whom she'd shared that experience.

Whoosh! A white paperback with purple lettering literally flew off the second shelf and landed on her foot, spine first, sending a sharp zing of pain through her big toe.

"What the hell?" She bent and scooped up the book. The title was *Astral Love*. Anna frowned. She didn't remember buying this particular book, but she could hardly overlook the fact that it had catapulted itself from the bookshelf.

She flipped through the pages, overcome with curiosity. She sank into the beanbag chair tucked into one corner of the room and immersed herself in the book. Hours later, the sun dipped low, casting shadows across her small office. She blinked and glanced at the clock on her desk. Had she really been reading that long? The crick in her neck and the grumble in her stomach confirmed she had. She set the book aside, having read most of it, and made her way to the kitchen to fix a sandwich.

She'd read a couple books on astral travel before attempting the procedure herself. She had not come across anything like the information in *Astral Love*. Apparently, one could actually meet others on the astral plane and connect with them for love-making. There were many tips and tricks relayed by the author on how to go about attracting the right type of astral lover and how to avoid unpleasant characters. Just as on the Earth plane, not all beings travelling the hidden realms were kind and scrupulous.

Anna spread mayo on her wholewheat bread and thought about her interlude with the sexy stranger. Had he gone looking for a lover and discovered her? Did he intend to make love to her? She wondered what that would feel like. Just the thought of him touching her intimate places, of his hands and mouth on her bare skin, created a tingle of desire between her legs.

It had been so long . . . her heartbeat accelerated as her mind wondered about what the stranger might do to her.

Her cell phone emitted her 1970s dance tune ringtone and Anna jumped, startled. She hurried to the coffee table where she'd left the phone. She glanced at the number. Her best friend, Tina. Tina was fifteen years older than Anna, a die-hard hippy who studied all things metaphysical. It was Tina who'd introduced Anna to astral travel.

"Hey," Anna said into the phone. "What's up?"

"What's up? I've been calling you all day. You didn't get my messages?"

Anna glanced at her phone. Three missed calls and two text messages. *Whoops.* "I'm sorry, I was reading and I got so caught up in my book I didn't hear the phone."

"Yeah, I know how that is." Tina did understand. She was more of a bookworm than Anna. "There's an independent film festival going on this weekend at that theatre I was telling you about. The old one with all the cool architecture that they just renovated? Thought you might want to go see the movie playing tonight."

Anna frowned. While she did want to see Tina, if she went to the movie she knew she'd get back too late to attempt any travelling. She'd be so tired she'd just want to sleep. And suddenly, she was very, very eager to get back to her possible lover.

"Um, not tonight Tina. I'm already having my dinner, and I'm sort of tired." She didn't bother to tell Tina why she was tired. She wasn't ready yet to share the details of her nocturnal liaison or Richard's message.

"Are you sure? You know if you're not there, I'll be forced to keep any attractive guy I meet for myself." Lately, Tina's mission had been to help Anna find a man. She'd decided Anna had been depressed and dateless for long enough. Anna knew that Tina was right, of course, but she just didn't have it in her to make menial small talk with strangers while wondering whether her lipstick was on her teeth or the jeans she'd chosen made her butt look big. The few times Tina had dragged her to spots where she thought Anna might meet a guy, the men Anna had met were anything but interesting. She wanted someone who shared her interests. Unfortunately, her interests of late were slightly outside the norm. So far, no luck.

"I'm sure. Try to go easy on the boys. Next time, okay?"

Tina sighed. "Alright, but I'm holding you to that!"

"Deal. Have fun. Bye."

Anna closed her phone and returned to the kitchen to finish making her sandwich, the phone call quickly forgotten as she planned her evening.

This time, Anna took precautions. She set a very put-upon looking Emerson out of her bedroom and shut – and locked – her door. Following the advice in *Astral Love*, she had already showered, brushed her teeth, applied a bit of ruby red lipstick, and dressed in her favourite silky number. The book admonished those who sought an astral lover to be sure to treat their pursuit seriously. You wouldn't go out on a date with poor hygiene or messy hair, the author had insisted.

Although she'd felt a bit foolish getting all glammed up to lie on her bed alone, Anna had followed the directions anyway. She didn't want to take any chances that she wouldn't find the stranger again tonight on the astral plane.

Anna let the soothing, New Age feel-good tunes she'd chosen to listen to drift over her and lull her into that calm, relaxed state of semi-consciousness where you hovered just on the edge of sleep, but had not yet stepped off the ledge into unconsciousness.

She focused on sensing her energy body, the part of herself squatting inside her physical form and, after a few moments, she could feel her spirit body moving and vibrating. Her whole body was starting to shake and twitch and a rushing sound filled her ears, like a jet engine revving for take-off.

Out, she thought. *Out and up.* With one swift jerking motion she lifted off and out of her body. Immediately, the roaring sound stopped, and she envisioned herself on her favourite beach. The place where the sexy stranger had first contacted her.

She had been standing on the beach for what seemed like mere moments when he appeared beside her. Just as Anna, he was clad in the same attire as the last time they'd met. Which was a good thing, because the man's chest and abdomen were just too beautiful to hide. She ached to bury her face there and run her lips over his skin.

She blinked and tried to focus her thoughts on talking to him. All she could think of was touching that delicious golden skin of his again.

"Angel," he murmured, brushing her face with his fingertips. "I'm glad you came back."

"Of course I came. I've been travelling these realms for some time now."

He flashed a rakish smile. "Ah, I see. So you would come here regardless of my presence?"

She nodded.

The stranger leaned close and nuzzled her neck, causing a riot of goose bumps to break out over her arms. "But you did hope to see me, didn't you? At least a little bit?" He trailed his fingers over her arms, feeling the telltale bumps. Her nipples hardened in response.

"Your body is happy to see me," he said.

His lips trailed her neck feather-light; for a moment she thought she imagined the touch. Then he leaned back so their eyes met. "Angel, there can be no pretence between us. Not here."

Anna sighed, suddenly wondering why she'd felt the need to be coy. "I did hope to see you here."

His eyes twinkled with delight. "And you have thought of me since we last met?"

She nodded. "I daydreamed . . ." That was an understatement.

"What did you think of . . . exactly."

Anna swallowed. There was no way she could be less than truthful. Not with those mesmerizing green eyes of his staring into her own as though he could read her every thought and divine her deepest, most sensual desires.

"I thought of you kissing me."

He pressed his lips to hers. The kiss was sweet and tender, and it wasn't nearly enough.

"What else?" he prodded.

"I imagined you touching me," she managed to get out on a breathy murmur.

He ran his hands over her shoulders. "Here?"

She nodded.

His fingers stroked her inner arms. "Here?"

"Yes."

His hands circled her waist briefly before he moved upward and his palms closed over her breasts. "How about here?" He rubbed his palms against her sensitive peaks.

"Oh, yes, there." She sucked in a deep breath, assaulted by an onslaught of desire. Heat writhed beneath her skin and shot from her breasts to her sex.

His mouth lifted and his gaze darkened with mischievous intent. "I'd imagine that this came up in your daydreams?" One of his arms snaked around her waist and with his free hand he lifted her dress ever so slowly. The material slid up her thigh, silky cool against her heated skin. Her pulse beat erratically. She was eager for his hand to reach its intended destination.

Finally, his fingers brushed her naked sex. The stranger's fingers teased her already swollen flesh. With a start, she realized she wore no panties. *Panties are unnecessary in the astral realm.* The silly, errant thought made her giggle.

"This is amusing?" His movements halted.

"No, no it's not." She desperately wanted him to stimulate her again. "Please, don't stop what you're doing."

He resumed his ministrations. His touch was making her crazy with need. She wanted much more than this. But some part of her held back and wouldn't let her ask him for more. Not yet. She didn't even know this man. And then, there was the issue of Richard . . .

"I don't even know your name," she gasped in between waves of pleasure.

"What do you wish to call me, Angel?"

What should she call him? She could hardly think straight. How was she supposed to produce a fitting name for such a beautiful, mouth-watering creature? He looked like something straight out of mythology, a god. He reminded her of a painting she'd once seen while on an art walk in Santa Barbara of the Greek god Aether, god of the upper sky, space and heaven – right down to the piercing emerald eyes.

"Aether," she murmured.

He smiled. "I like that." His mouth captured hers, kissing her with such intensity she became dizzy with her desire. First one, then two fingers entered her. Her inner muscles spasmed in ecstasy. They were no longer strangers, she told herself. It was acceptable to make love with him. Besides, it wasn't as though she were loving him with her actual physical body.

With that thought, any further concerns about Richard fled, and Anna gave herself over to Aether. Aether, sensing her surrender, waved away their clothing and lowered her to the sand. His hands, lips and tongue left no part of her body untouched. He seemed to be everywhere at once, his hard, lean form one minute hugging her own, the next hovering over her, just his mouth caressing her. She allowed her hands to roam over him, to feel his smooth skin and the muscles rippling beneath.

Her entire body tingled with anticipation as he spread her legs and entered her in one smooth stroke. She cried out her pleasure. Waves of heat and longing washed through her. The sensations were all so real, so vivid. She momentarily forgot she was in the astral plane.

Anna clutched Aether to her body, tilting her hips to meet his every thrust. Something was building inside of her, a fierce ache, a spiral of energy that started at her toes and travelled to the top of her head.

"Oh, Angel," he groaned, "you are heaven."

A moment later her entire body arched and rocked in Aether's arms and she was spinning, twirling, overcome with pleasure so intense, so rapturous, it bordered on pain. Aether shuddered his release, calling her name and then, his voice sounded very far away, fading as she spiralled away from him and crashed into her body.

The next two weeks passed in a blur. Anna went through the motions of going to work and performing her duties but no matter how she tried to push him from her mind, Aether occupied the majority of her thoughts. And each day, she hurried home from work, eager to have dinner, feed and pet Emerson, then resolutely lock the cat out of the bedroom so that she could travel back to that place between worlds where Aether waited for her. And he was always waiting for her. He made love to her each and every night, and the bliss she experienced in his arms was like nothing she'd ever known.

Tina called a number of times, inviting Anna to go out but Anna always had an excuse for why she needed to remain at home. When she began to run out of excuses, she just stopped answering Tina's phone calls.

During the beginning of the third week, Anna had just finished eating a modest meal of canned soup and grilled cheese, when Tina appeared at her front door, hands on hips, worry creasing her pretty face.

"Where have you been?" Tina demanded, brushing past Anna into the house. Tina's broomstick skirt made a swooshing sound as she paced the floor.

"I've been here, and working," Anna responded lamely.

Tina huffed and crossed her arms. "Don't you think for a minute I'm letting you off that easy. I've been calling you for weeks. Why are you avoiding me?"

Anna sighed. "I'm not avoiding you, Tina. I just haven't felt like going out, and I knew if I told you that you'd show up here and drag me out anyway."

"Damn right, I would. No more moping around the house depressed. I'm going to drag you into your healing if I have to do it with you kicking and screaming."

Suddenly, Tina stopped short, and her eyes narrowed as they washed over Anna and her red silk robe and the matching negligee that peeked out from underneath. Anna's stomach dropped, and she willed Tina not to go into her bedroom. She cringed at what she knew Tina would find there.

But Tina was way too intuitive by far, and she craned her neck toward the bedroom, and seeing Anna's nervous expression, promptly marched down the hall. Tina flung the bedroom door open. Anna bit her lip, taking in the scene as Tina must be seeing it, knowing she was going to have some serious explaining to do. Incense curled from a Buddha-shaped burner on the bedside table, candles flickered from various surfaces in the room, and soft, sensual music filled the silence.

Tina spun around to face Anna, eyebrows raised. "Well hell, girl, when were you going to tell me you'd found a man? Is he hiding in the closet? Or hasn't he made it here yet?"

Anna's face grew red and heated. She hoped Tina wouldn't notice her flush in the dim lighting. Her embarrassment gave way to annoyance. So what. So, she'd taken the advice in *Astral Love* to heart. And it had seemed to ensure that she met Aether each and every time she returned to the astral realm. Maybe it was all in her mind, but there were worse things than preparing yourself and your surroundings as though you were meeting your astral lover in the flesh . . . Weren't there?

"It's not what you think," Anna said.

Tina frowned. "Why don't you explain it to me?"

"Let's go sit down, and I'll tell you everything."

The two returned to the living room and an hour later, Tina knew the whole story. And regarded Anna with even more concern in her eyes than when she'd first arrived.

"I know that look," Anna said.

Tina's brow crinkled. "This is not good, Anna."

Anna's spine stiffened. "How can it be bad? I'm having the time of my life!"

"That's just it. The time of your life is being had with a phantom in your dreams."

Anna shook her head. "He's not a phantom."

"He's not a real, flesh-and-blood human male," Tina pointed out.

"Maybe he is. I mean, the books said that although all sorts of beings pass through the astral realm, so do plenty of humans just like me."

Tina sighed. "Let's say he is a real person, like you, exploring astral travel. You can't have a relationship, not a *real* one, with someone you meet in your sleep."

Anna crossed her arms and bristled at Tina's words. She didn't want to hear this. She didn't want to listen to what she knew, deep down, was the truth.

Tina gestured to the living room. "Look around you. You haven't cleaned your house in weeks, have you?"

Anna blinked, taking in the discarded clothing, newspapers and take-out food containers. The room was littered with trash and clutter. And she hadn't noticed.

"And what about Emerson? This cat hates me normally. What the heck is he doing to my leg? Are you spending any time with him at all anymore?" As if to lend emphasis to Tina's words, the tabby cat was rubbing himself all over Tina's legs and feet, purring, then stood on his hind legs and batted at her knees, begging for attention. His eyes rolled back into his head with pure pleasure as Tina rubbed him behind his ears.

A pang of guilt swept over Anna.

"And beyond all that," Tina continued. "From what I gather, you haven't left your house except to go to work since this whole thing started. And I'll bet your work progress is less than stellar right now."

Anna frowned. Tina was right.

Tina scooted closer to Anna and wrapped one arm around her shoulders. "Sweetie, I am really worried about you. You're obsessed. You're never going to find love again this way. And this is not healthy. You yourself know that it's not good for you, don't you?"

Resigned, Anna nodded. "I need to end it."

"Yes."

"I'll go back to see him tonight and tell him it's over and then—"

"No," Tina interrupted. "You should not see him again. You need to quit. An alcoholic does not allow himself just a little drink to remind himself not to drink."

Disappointment rained over Anna. Tina was right. She was completely right. And Anna hated that her friend was right. She already felt a pang of despair at the knowledge she'd never see Aether again.

"Okay," Anna agreed.

"Okay, what?"

"I'm done. No more astral travelling. No more sexy dream guy."

Tina hugged her. "Good. And this weekend, we are going out and you are going to meet a real, live hot-as-hell man, and you'll allow him to sweep you off your feet and live happily ever after, right?"

Anna allowed herself a small smile. "If I must."

After giving Emerson one more quick scratch behind the ears, Tina rose and headed toward the door.

"Tina, what do you think Richard meant?"

Tina paused with her hand on the front door handle and thought about the question. "I think he was trying to lend you strength so you could move on, that's what I think."

"And the whole 'love is in the air', thing?"

Tina shrugged. "Wasn't he always writing you bad poetry? Perhaps his talent hasn't improved much in the afterlife." Tina's grin was infectious.

Anna returned the smile. "See you later."

"See you this weekend," Tina insisted.

"I agreed, didn't I?"

Tina lifted her eyebrows as if to say she wasn't sure Anna's word could be trusted. Then, she gestured toward Emerson who had followed her to the door. "And pay attention to that cat, will you? I'm no good as a stand-in. I can feel my allergies acting up already."

To show his gratitude for Tina's concern with his plight, Emerson promptly coughed up a fur ball on to her foot.

True to her word, Anna did not attempt another meeting with Aether. She forced herself to accompany Tina on at least one night out on the town per week. They frequented places Tina strategically chose for man-hunting potential. Anna actually found herself having fun during these outings. She flirted, got flirted with and gave out her phone number a time or two. She even entertained the idea of returning the phone call of a handsome lawyer who'd called.

Her house was clean, her work was caught up and Emerson was happy to have regained his side of the bed. But late at night, when she was supposed to be sleeping, Aether filled her thoughts. And a fierce, aching need swept through her.

Then, one Friday evening after a long, gruelling day at the office – an evening when Anna really would have rather backed out of Date Night with Tina – something truly magical happened.

Anna stood next to the bar in the latest, hippest club, watching people in various modes of attire get their groove on atop the strobe-lit laden dance floor. She sipped a glass of Pinot Grigio and waited for Tina to return from the restroom. Just as she was finishing her last swallow of the wine, a very broad shoulder bumped her arm. She glanced up into familiar green eyes – and choked.

"Are you okay?"

The man who'd bumped her patted her lightly on the back. When she'd calmed down and gathered herself, Anna wiped the wine from her chin and nodded.

Same wavy, jet hair, same chiselled features, definitely the same arresting gaze. How could this be? Was she losing her mind?

Say something, she told herself. *Say something, anything*. But she could barely breathe, let alone speak. The man didn't seem to notice. He was studying her, too.

"You seem familiar," he said. "Do I know you?"

She opened her mouth to answer but then his hand touched her arm and shivers of delight burst over her skin. She stifled a moan of pleasure.

"I'm so sorry about bumping you. This place is really crowded tonight."

Anna swallowed and finally found her voice. "It's okay."

If he only knew just how *okay* it was.

"I haven't seen you here before. Are you local?"

"I live just a few blocks from here," she told him.

"Really? Me too." He tilted his head to the side. "Man, I could swear we've met before. What's your name?"

"Anna," she said. "And yours?"

He stuck his hand out. "Aether. It's a pleasure to meet you, Anna."

Anna's pulse sped and her legs grew weak. It was him. She wasn't crazy. It was really him. "Aether?" she repeated, incredulous.

He gave her a shy smile. "What can I say? My dad is a professor who specializes in Greek mythology and my mom is an artist. She even painted me once as the Greek god, Aether."

"Greek god?" Anna repeated, realizing she was starting to sound like a broken record but unable to stop herself.

"Yeah, you know, the god of Air?"

And suddenly everything made perfect, beautiful, crystal clear sense. Her sudden interest in astral travel, meeting Aether and their intense connection. And especially, Richard's message on the bathroom mirror.

I'm sending you love. Love is in the air.

Moisture welled in Anna's eyes. Her heart swelled with elation. *Richard, you truly are the most wonderful man. I will never forget*

you. Thank you for loving me. Thank you for looking out for me.
The words whispered through her mind, unspoken. Somehow
she knew that wherever Richard was, he heard her.

"Let's go get you a new glass of wine, shall we?"

Anna smiled. "Thank you."

"It's the least I can do."

He took her hand and led her toward the bar. Anna happily
followed him, suddenly aware only of the tall man in front of
her, of the feel of his large hand covering hers, of the scent of
his woodsy cologne. She tuned out the other people pushing in
around them and the loud music blaring through the space.

When they reached the bar, Aether quickly made his order,
then placed a fresh glass of wine into Anna's free hand. Tingles
spread from the hand Aether held and travelled up her arm. A
current of delicious, sensual heat followed.

Aether sucked in his breath and glanced down at their joined
hands. Then he smiled at her, flashing straight white teeth
and a set of dimples she hadn't noticed during their nocturnal
meetings.

"Let's go sit outside where we can talk. It's too noisy in here."

"Yes," she agreed, "Let's."

They wound their way to the exit. The tables scattered around
the outside eating area of the restaurant-turned-nightclub were
full. Anna's heart sank. Then a couple to their right vacated
their table, and Anna and Aether quickly snatched it up.

Once they were seated, Anna expected Aether to release her
hand but he did not. Instead, he turned his hand palm up and
traced a lazy pattern over her fingers. His gaze sparkled with
mischief.

"Anna, I'm almost positive we've met before."

She smiled a mysterious smile. "Perhaps."

He chuckled. "Well, I want you tell me everything about
yourself. I want to know all there is to know about you, Mystery
Lady."

Anna's brows rose. "That could take awhile."

Aether pressed a soft kiss on her hand. A jolt of desire shot
through her.

"I've got a lifetime."

The Gauntlet

Karen Chance

Chapter One

The sound of a key turning in the rusty old lock had everyone scurrying forward with hands outstretched, begging for food, for water, for life. Gillian didn't go with them. Trussed up as she was, she could barely move. And there was no life that way.

The burly jailer came in carrying a lantern, with two more dark shapes behind him. To her surprise, he didn't immediately kick the women aside with brutal indifference. Instead he let them crowd around, even the ones who had been there a while, whose skeletal hands silently begged with the others.

"This is the lot, my lord," he said. "And a sorry one it is, too."

"Why are some of them gagged?" The low, pleasant tenor came from one of the shapes she had assumed to be a guard. The speaker came forwards, but she couldn't see much of him. The hood on his cape was pulled down and a gloved hand covered his face, probably in an attempt to block the stench.

She smiled grimly and let her head fall back into her arms. It wouldn't work. Even after two days, she hadn't become inured to it: the thick, sickly-sweet odour of flesh, unwashed and unhealed.

"Some are strong enough to curse a man to hell otherwise," the jailer informed him, spitting on the ground.

"Show me the strongest," the stranger said, and Gillian's head jerked back up.

The jailor grumbled, but he ordered his men to drag the bound bodies that had been shoved to the back of the room to the forefront. The stranger bent over each one, pushing matted, filthy hair out of their eyes, as if looking for someone. Gillian didn't watch. She concentrated everything she had on biting through the remaining mass of cloth in her mouth, her eyes on the open door behind men.

The guards came only once a day, doling out water and a thin gruel, and she didn't know what kind of shape she would be in by tomorrow. Even worse, she didn't know how Elinor would be. She glanced over at the child's huddled form, but she hadn't moved. Not for hours now, a fact that had Gillian's heart clenching, part in fear, part in black rage.

If those whoresons let her daughter die in here, she'd rip this place apart stone by stone. Her arms jerked convulsively against the shackles, but they were iron, not rope. If she couldn't speak, she had no chance of breaking them.

It didn't help that she hadn't had water in more than a day. The guard assigned to that detail last night had been one of those she'd attacked on arrival, in an aborted escape attempt. He'd kicked her in the ribs as he passed and waved the ladle under her nose, but not allowed her so much as a drop. If he'd followed orders, he might have noticed what she was doing, might have replaced the worn woollen gag with something sturdier.

But he hadn't.

"That one's dead," the jailor said, kicking a limp body aside. He quickly checked the others, pulling out one more before lining up the remaining women at the stranger's feet. Most were silent, watching with hollow, desperate eyes above their gags. A few struggled weakly, either smart enough to realize that this might be a way out, or too far gone to understand what was happening.

"What about this one?" A hand with a square cut ruby ring caught Gillian's chin, turning her face up to the light.

"You don't want her!" the jailer said, aiming another kick at her abused ribs.

"The agreement was, 'in good condition'," the stranger said, blocking the booted foot with his own.

Gillian barely noticed. Up close, it was obvious that she was in even more trouble than she'd thought. The fact that the stranger was dead wasn't a good sign. That he was still walking around was worse.

Vampire.

They stared at each other and he smiled slightly at her start of recognition. He had a nice face – young, as if that meant anything – with clear, unmarked skin, a head of dark brown curls and a small goatee. The last would have been amusing under other circumstances, as if he was trying to make his pleasant face appear more sinister.

She wondered why he didn't just bare his fangs.

"I don't see as it makes a difference, if you're aiming to feed off her," the guard said, angry, but smart enough not to show it.

Those liquid dark eyes swept over her. "What I do with the woman is my affair."

"Ahh. Some sport beforehand, then. I'd not risk it, meself. One of my men tried the night she was brought in and the bitch cursed him. He's in a bad way, still."

"How tragic," the vampire sounded amused.

The guard must have thought so, too, because his already florid features flushed even darker. "See if you're laughing with a pillicock the size of a pin!" he spat.

The vampire ignored him and put a hand beneath Gillian's arm, helping her to stand. "I'd let you out of those, but I'm afraid you'd hex me," he said cheerfully, nodding at her cuffs. "And I like my privities the way they are." He glanced at the guard. "Tell me about her."

"One of them that's been operating out of the thicket," the man said resentfully, referring to Maidenhead thicket on the road between London and Bristol, where Gillian's group had had some success relieving travellers of their excess wealth.

"Ah, yes. I met a robber there myself, not long ago." The vampire smiled at her. "He was delicious."

Gillian just stared. Did he always talk to his food this much before eating it?

"But I must say," he commented, his eyes on her worn gown, greasy red hair and dirty face. "For a member of one of the most notorious gangs of thieves in England, you do not look very prosperous."

Maybe I would, she thought furiously, *if I didn't have to spend most of my time avoiding people like you.*

Once, she'd had protection from his kind. She'd been a member of one of the Druid covens that had ruled the supernatural part of the British Isles for time out of mind. But that had been before the arrival of the so-called "Silver Circle", an ancient society of light magic users who had brought nothing but darkness to England.

They had arrived in force ten years ago, as refugees of a vicious war on the continent. The religious tensions that culminated with Spain launching the Armada had offered an opportunity to one of the Circle's oldest enemies. A group of dark mages known as the Black Circle had joined forces with the Inquisition under the pretence of helping to stamp out heresy. And by all accounts, they had been brutally efficient at hunting down their light counterparts.

But their suffering hadn't made the Silver Circle noticeably gentler on anyone else. They had but one goal in mind – to rebuild their forces and retake control of magical Europe. And they intended to start with England.

Gillian's coven was one of those who had refused their kind offers of "protection", and preferred to continue determining their own destiny. In return, they had been subjected to a witch hunt mightier and more successful than anything the Inquisition had ever managed. By the time they realized just how far their fellow mages would go to support the idea of a unified magical community, the covens had been decimated through deceit, betrayal and murder.

But they haven't killed all of us, Gillian thought viciously. Not yet. It was a fact that would some day cost them dear.

The vampire had been watching her with interest. She didn't know how he could tell anything past the folds of the gag, but apparently he saw something that amused him. His smile became almost genuine.

"See my man about payment," he told the guard, his eyes never leaving her face. "I'll take this one with me."

"Take her?" The guard's scowl became more pronounced. "Take her where?"

"That is my affair," the vampire repeated.

"Not if ye're planning to make off wi' her, it damn well isn't! No one will much care if she doesn't last long enough for the rope, but it's as much as my life is worth to let her go beyond these walls. She's dangerous!"

"I do truly hope so," the vampire said oddly.

A beefy hand fell on his shoulder. "If ye want to make a meal off her, that's one thing. But all the gold in yer purse won't save me once they discover—"

In an eye blink, the guard was slammed against the wall, held several feet off the floor by the slim hand around his throat. "Perhaps you should be more concerned about your immediate future," the vampire said softly.

Gillian didn't wait to see who would win the argument over which one would be allowed to kill her. The soggy threads finally came apart in her mouth and she spat them out. But with no saliva left, and a throat still throbbing from the elbow blow it had taken days ago, she couldn't speak. She swallowed convulsively and concentrated everything on making some kind of sound – anything.

An incantation rolled off her tongue. It was a dry whisper, but it was enough. With a rusty creak, the shackles parted around her wrists and ankles, and she was free.

Her limbs were stiff and uncoordinated and her head was spinning from the power loss. But then she caught sight of Elinor and nothing else mattered. She lurched forward in a scrambling crawl, making it a few yards before rough hosed legs blocked the way.

"Where d'ye think you're going?" the other guard demanded, grabbing her by the back of the collar. She slung a spell at him, but the angle was off and it missed, exploding against the low ceiling of the room.

Had the roof been in proper repair, the spell would have either dissipated or ricocheted back, depending on how much power she had been able to muster. But whoever owned this heap of stones before the Circle had skimped on repairs and the once stout wood had seen one too many winters. What felt like half the roof suddenly rained down on their heads, sending her stumbling back and burying the guard under a pile of weathered beams.

Gillian clutched the wall, blinking in the wash of brilliant sunlight that streamed through the ruined roof. It was blinding after two days of almost complete darkness and the struggle with the guard had disoriented her. She was no longer sure where Elinor was, and when she tried to move, she was battered by screaming, panicked women, on all sides.

"Elinor!" she yelled as loudly as her parched throat would allow, but there was no answer.

Her eyes finally adjusted and she caught a glimpse of her daughter's slight form huddled against one wall. She was rocking slightly, staring at nothing, her hands bound to an iron ring. Gillian crawled over and started to work the leather bindings on her wrists off. They were so tight that the circulation to her hands had been partially cut off and her small fingers were swollen like sausages.

Elinor didn't fight her, although she couldn't have seen much through the glare or heard her mother's whispered assurances over the din. She was trembling from a combination of exhaustion, shock and fear. Dark blue rings stained her eyes and her beautiful blond hair hung limp and lifeless, like her expression.

The last stubborn strap came loose and Gillian pulled her daughter into her arms. She started to rise when one of the bound figures on the floor rolled into her, struggling in vain to throw off her bonds. The old woman was in irons and gagged, as Gillian had been, with no chance to escape if she couldn't speak.

Gillian pulled a disgusting scrap of cloth out of her mouth, to give her a fighting chance, while scanning the room for any way out besides the door. "Release me," the woman gasped, on a rattling breath.

"Release yourself, old mother," Gillian told her distractedly. "I need what strength I have left."

She could already hear soldiers on the run, thudding their way up the tower's wooden steps. There was only one way down – and it was the same path the guards were taking up. She might make it alone; she had that much pent up rage. But not with Elinor.

"Mind your manners, girl!" she was told, right before

wrinkled, age-spotted fingers reached out and gave her a pinch.
Gillian grasped the woman's hand, intending to pry it off her
flesh. But then she looked down – and stopped cold.

Crisscrossed by delicate veins and almost buried under a layer
of grime were faint blue lines, etched on to the woman's inner
wrist. Gillian stared at the curling, elegant pattern, one older
than the walls that imprisoned them, older than almost anything
else in these isles, and felt her skin go cold. The three-pointed
triskelion was worn only by the leaders of the great covens.

A cannon ball had landed a dozen yards from her once, and
it had felt like this, like being knocked flat even though she
hadn't moved. She had never really believed that it might work,
this plan of extermination. The covens could be hurt, but they
would come back, as they'd always come back, through every
war, invasion and black time that littered their past. But if the
Circle could reach even to the heart of them, could reduce one
of the Great Mothers to this . . .

They could destroy us, she thought blankly. *They could destroy
all of us.*

Chapter Two

Another pinch interrupted Gillian's thoughts, this time feeling
like it took a hunk of her arm along with it. "Stop daydream-
ing," she was told tetchily. "And do as you're told!"

It wasn't a request, and obedience to the elders was ingrained
from birth. The requisite spell all but leaped to her lips. But the
iron was corroded, or perhaps her power was fading, because it
took a second application before the old hinges finally gave way.
And by then, reinforcements had arrived.

Gillian could hear them in the corridor, being hit with spells from
the few witches still capable of throwing any. Someone screamed
and a body crashed into the heavy wooden door, slamming it
shut and momentarily interrupting the attack. But it would be a
moment's reprieve at best. And when the guards broke through,
she didn't think recapture would be their main concern.

The Great Mother latched on to her arm with a strength
she hadn't thought the woman had. "There." She pointed to a
corner of the room that had emptied of prisoners. A splash of

sunshine, mid-afternoon and richly golden, highlighted a patch of bare worn boards. They were old and slimy, scattered with rat bones and smeared with human waste. But unlike the roof, they were solid.

"I can't," Gillian confessed. She knew without trying that she didn't have the strength to destroy the floorboards. They were good English oak, as hard as the stones that made up the tower's walls, and just as immovable. "We have to find another—"

"Stop arguing," the eldest snapped, cutting her off. "And take me."

Gillian took her. She didn't know what else to do. They were trapped.

Even worse, the vampire was standing off to the side, casually observing the chaos. She scowled; she should have known that sunlight wouldn't kill him. If he was that weak, he'd have come at night. He'd retreated further into the hood of his cape, leaving him a long column of black wool, but otherwise appeared unconcerned.

He didn't move, but Gillian carefully kept the sunlight between them nonetheless. She pulled Elinor and the eldest along the wall, hoping the glistening beams would provide some kind of protection. His head turned, keeping them in view, but he said nothing.

"In the middle. There!" the Great Mother gasped, and again Gillian followed orders, only to have her arm gripped in a steel-like vise. Cloudy blue eyes met hers, almost sightless, but some-how penetrating all the same. "In times like these, we do what is needful – what we must to survive, for us and our folk. Do you understand, girl?"

No, Gillian thought frantically. What she understood was that the door was about to open and they were all going to die. That was pretty damn clear. "I do not think they mean for any of us to survive," she said, her throat raw.

The Great Mother's grip became positively painful, arthritic fingers digging into the flesh of Gillian's arm. "It matters not what they mean! Will you *fight*, girl, for what is yours?"

"Yes," she said, confused. What did she think? That Gillian planned to simply lie down and die? "But it is not likely to be a long one. I have little power left, and the Circle—"

"You will find that you have all the power you need."

Gillian didn't understand what she meant and there was no time to ask. The door burst open, but she barely noticed, because the frail body on the dirty boards had begun to glow. Power radiated outward, shimmering beneath translucent skin like sunlight through moth wings. It flooded the ugly room, gilding the old bricks and causing even the guards to shield their eyes.

Elinor made a soft sound and hid her face, but Gillian couldn't seem to look away. For one brief moment, the Old Mother looked like an exquisitely delicate statue, a fire-lit radiance flowing under the pale crepe of her skin. And then Gillian's own skin began to heat, the flesh of her arm reddening and then burning where the thin fingers gripped her.

She cried out and tried to jerk away, but the Old Mother stubbornly held on. Her skin was shining through Gillian's hand now, so bright that the edges of her flesh were limned with it. But she couldn't feel her anymore. She couldn't feel anything but the great and terrible power gathering in the air, power that whispered to her, wordless and uncontrollable.

It exploded the next moment in flash of brilliant fire. Gillian threw her body over Elinor's, trying to shield her from the searing heat and deadly flames she expected. But they didn't come. And when she dared to look again, the old woman's body was gone – and so was half the floor.

The thick oak boards had dissolved, crumbling into nothingness like charred firewood, leaving a burnt, smoking hole looking down into the room below. Gillian crouched beside it for a moment, her heart pounding, knife-edged colours tearing at her vision, until a glance showed that the guards had fled in fear of magic they didn't understand.

She didn't either, but she recognized an opportunity when she saw one.

Elinor was clinging to her neck, hard enough to strangle. It was far from comfortable, but at least it meant she didn't have to try to hold her as she lowered them on to one of the remaining rafters of the room below. It was the gatehouse, where a contingent of mages usually stayed to watch the front of the castle and to guard any prisoners in the room above. No one was there now, everyone having run up the stairs to secure the door or having scattered after the escapees.

For a brief moment, they were alone.

Gillian's arm throbbed under the burnt edges of her sleeve, but she ignored it and started making her way along the beam to clear the pile of smoking shards below. Yellow sunlight struggled through the haze, enough to let her see stone walls spotted in a few places by narrow, arrow slit windows, a few stools and a flat-topped storage trunk that was being used as a table. The remains of someone's lunch was still spread out over the top.

There were no obvious ways out. The only door let out on to the ramparts, which were heavily guarded. And even if they had been able to fit through the tiny windows, the main gate was protected by two towers filled with archers. Anyone trying to leave that way would have to traverse a quarter mile of open fields, the local forest having been cut back to give the archers a clear shot.

Gillian thought that she could just about manage a weak shield, but not to cover two, and not to last the whole way. And Elinor couldn't help or even protect herself; she was barely seven and her magic had yet to manifest. The eldest should have saved her sacrifice, she thought grimly. They weren't going to get out of this.

"Could I be of assistance, at all?"

Her head whipped up to see the vampire's curly mop poking through the charred edges of the hole. She threw up a shield, silently cursing him for forcing her to use the power, and jumped to the floor. Shards of wood and a few old iron nails dug into her bare feet, but the pain was almost welcome. It helped to push away the gut-wrenching panic and let her think.

A guard was sprawled on the floor nearby, half hidden by the fall of wood and debris. He wasn't moving, and one hand was a bloody mess – he must have used it to try to shield himself. The other gripped a long piece of wood that was partially concealed by his body. She crouched beside him and started tugging on it, while keeping a wary eye on the creature above.

"My earlier jest may have been . . . ill-timed," the vampire offered. "I do not, in fact, intend to dine upon you. Or your lovely . . . daughter, is it?"

Gillian's head jerked up. "Touch her and they will never find all the pieces," she snarled, pulling Elinor behind her.

But the creature made no move toward them, other than to spread his hands, showing that he held no weapons. As if he needed any. "I assure you, I pose no threat."

"A harmless vampire." She didn't bother to keep the mockery out of her voice.

"To you." A smile came easily to that handsome face. "In fact, I work with a party in government charged with maintaining the security of these lands."

"You lie. Vampires work for their makers."

"Yes, but in this case, my mistresses' interests align."

"And what would those interests be?" Gillian asked, not because she cared, but to buy her time to find out if the item in the guard's hand was what she thought it was.

"The queen's enemies are not composed of humans alone," he told her, as easily as if he carried on conversations upside down every day. Which maybe he did, she thought darkly, images of bats and other unsavoury creatures coming to mind. "Ever since England became a refuge for the Silver Circle, she has been a target for the dark. And the assassination attempts grow with each passing day."

"And why should a vampire care about such things?"

"We must live in this world, too, Mistress—"

"Urswick," she panted. Curse it – the guard weighed a ton!

"I am pleased to make your acquaintance, Mistress Urswick," he said wryly. "I am Chris Marlowe, although my friends call me Kit."

"You have friends?"

"Strangely enough, yes. I would like to number you among them, if I could."

Gillian was sure he would. But while she might be a penniless thief, her coven ruined, her friends scattered or dead, neither she nor her daughter would be feeding him this day. "Don't count on it," she snarled, and jerked the slender column of wood free.

It was a staff as she'd hoped, but not of the Circle's make. The surface was satiny to the touch, worn smooth as stone from centuries of handling. The oil from all those hands had cured it to a dark mahogany, blending the black glyphs carved along its length into the surface. She traced one of the ridges with a fingertip and didn't believe it, even when a frisson of power passed through her shields to jump along her nerves.

Her fingers began to prickle, black fury rising in front of her eyes, as she stood there with a Druid staff in her hands. It wasn't enough that they were persecuted, imprisoned and murdered. The Circle had to steal what little of their heritage they had been able to preserve as well.

"At the risk of sounding discourteous, may I point out that you are in no position to be choosy?" the vampire said, right before the door to the room slammed open and half a dozen guards rushed into the room. And then blew back out as the staff turned the door and half the wall into rubble.

"Perhaps I spoke too soon," he murmured, as she pulled a white-faced Elinor through the red bite of heat and the smell of smoke to the now missing door.

Outside, the castle's walls hemmed them in on all sides, grey stone against a pewter sky. A battle was going on to the left, with the prisoners trying to get down the stairs. They looked to be holding their own, with one witch's spell sending a guard flying off the battlements into the open courtyard. But that was about to change.

Reinforcements were already running toward the battle from either side. And they were the Circle's elite corps – war mages, they called them – instead of the talentless scum employed as jailers. The witches from most of the covens were well trained in self-defence, but their weapons had been confiscated when they were taken. Without them, they wouldn't last long.

Of course, that could prove true of them as well. A group of the Circle's dark robed mages broke off from the main group and started their way. And in front of them was a lethal cloud of weapons, iron dark against the pale sky.

Gillian didn't try to run; there was no time and nowhere to go. Against the Circle's harsh alchemy of steel and iron, she called Wind, and it answered far more quickly than usual. She was only dimly aware of a blizzard of debris behind her back and the mages' squawks of alarm as their weapons went tumbling back at them.

For a long moment, the roar of her element filled her senses in a heady rush, billowing out her tattered gown, matting her hair and blowing into her eyes. She didn't bother to brush it away. It felt good. It felt like power.

But it didn't last. Within seconds, the wind was already dying. The staff was magnifying her strength, but she had so little left. And when it gave out—

"My offer of assistance remains open," the vampire said casually. He'd jumped down from the second floor and was leaning against the shattered wall, watching the chaos with the mildly interested glance of someone at a bear baiting with no money on the outcome.

"It's well known that your kind helps no one but themselves!"

"Which is better than attacking and imprisoning our own, would you not say?" She didn't see him move, but he was suddenly beside her, the wind whipping his curls wildly around his face.

"Why should you want to help me?" she demanded harshly.

"Because I need yours in return."

Despite everything, Gillian almost laughed. He stood there in his fine clothes, smelling of spices and sporting a jewel worth the price of a house. And she was supposed to believe that he needed anything from the likes of her?

"'Pon my honor," he said, seeing her expression.

"You may as well swear on your life! Everyone knows that vampires are selfish, base, cruel creatures who only want one thing!"

"And everyone knows that coven witches are weak, treacherous and easily corrupted," he shot back. "Everyone is often wrong."

Gillian started to answer, but a harsh clanging echoed across the keep, cutting her off. A small group of witches had cleared the stairs and made a break for the gates. But the heavy iron portcullis guarding the entrance had slammed down before they could reach it, trapping them in the middle of a sea of enemy mages. Her hands clenched at their desperate cries for help, but there was nothing she could do but die with them.

And she had Elinor to think about.

She spun on her heel, brushing past the vampire and racing back inside the small gatehouse. The trunk was still there, with its bit of stale loaf. She brushed it aside and threw up the heavy lid, hoping for weapons – charms, potions, protection wards – anything designed to hold a reservoir of magic for use in times like these. But there was nothing, aside from a few rat droppings.

She slammed the trunk shut in frustration, wishing she had the strength to throw it at the wall. The guard must have taken the staff as a trophy. Because wherever the Circle was storing their weapons, it wasn't here.

"The other gate is still open," the vampire said, from the doorway. "And I am skilled at *glamourie*. Let me inside your shields and I can hide you and the girl. We can walk out of here while the fight distracts the guards."

"Why should I trust you?" she demanded harshly, desperate for a reason, any reason.

"What choice have you?"

Gillian didn't see that they had much either way. Getting outside the walls would do them little good if it left her drained and defenceless, and at the mercy of a creature whose kind were well-known to have none. But with no weapons and her magic all but exhausted, staying here would mean certain death at the hands of the Circle.

The vampire's head suddenly came up, reacting to something beyond the reach of her senses. "Help me and I'll help you," he said urgently, holding out his hand.

Gillian hugged Elinor against her, every instinct she had screaming that she was mad to put their lives in the hands of a creature who saw them merely as prey. But if her only choice was between dying now and dying later, she would take later. "If you betray me, I will use my last breath to curse you!"

"I would expect nothing less."

Gillian licked dry lips. She didn't believe him, didn't think for a moment that he really wanted to help. But the wind had died and booted feet were pounding up the stairs, and she was out of options. She readied a curse, hoping it wouldn't be her last. And dropped the tattered remnants of her shield.

Chapter Three

This was typical, Kit thought sourly, slamming them back against the wall as a mob of mages rushed in. Find the perfect candidate and, naturally, everything went to hell before he could get away with her. Unfortunately, his lady was not one to understand unforeseen difficulties. He really did not want to think of the reception he was likely to get if he returned empty-handed.

Of course, at the moment, he would rather settle for returning at all.

"Search every inch," his dark-haired leader snapped, and Kit silently cursed.

He'd been hoping for a group of slow-witted guards who might have assumed that the witch had somehow slipped past them in the confusion. But judging from their windblown hair and murderous expressions, these were the men she'd attacked outside. And he couldn't take a half-dozen war mages on his own.

At least, he didn't think he could, having never before tried. And he discovered that he wasn't all that keen on finding out. He decided some subtlety was in order and started shuffling his little party towards the ruined door.

He thought their chances of making it out undetected were reasonably good. He'd used one of the talents he'd manifested since becoming a master and gone dim as soon as he heard the men approaching. Dim wasn't invisible – he could still be seen if someone was looking right at him. But even then he'd be only a faint, indistinct outline, like a haze of black smoke. And with all the real smoke choking the air, who was going to notice?

A war mage, apparently. He'd almost reached the door, where only a single mage stood guard, when one of the nearby searchers suddenly changed direction and grabbed a fold of his cloak. "Sir! They're—"

So much for subtlety. Kit seized the man's arm and slung him into the mage guarding the door, hard enough to send them both staggering backwards off the ramparts. Then he snatched the child into his arms, grabbed the witch by the waist and bolted.

It wasn't the most elegant escape he'd ever made, but a lifetime of close scrapes had taught him not to be picky. He dodged a spell that came blistering through the air after him, sidestepped a small battle, and headed for the stairs. And then pulled up abruptly and spun them back against the wall.

"What is it?" the witch demanded. "Why are we—" She stopped, catching sight of the same thing he had.

The stairs were choked with guards and the courtyard of the castle had turned into a particularly colourful hell. The flimsy wooden shacks that housed the kitchen, stables and blacksmith had caught alight and were burning merrily, with spell-fire tinting the billowing smoke in glowing colours. Horses were neighing, people were screaming, and spells were exploding on all sides.

In other words, it was the usual battlefield chaos, which was what gave him pause. On any given battlefield on any given day, there were about a hundred ways to die – and that multiplied tenfold if it was a magical battle. He was going to have to—

A spell he hadn't seen coming hit them broadside before he could finish the thought, sizzling against the shield the witch had managed to raise before flaming out in a burst of acid green sparks. And while no one might have been able to see them, that spectacle had been all too visible. Even worse, the effects didn't dissipate; instead, a glowing nimbus pulsed in the air around them, like the corona of the sun on a foggy day.

"Marker," the witch gasped, before he could ask. "They used it to hunt us in the forests, to make it impossible for us to hide. You can't conceal us now and I cannot protect all three of us!"

She started struggling, probably deciding to use her remaining strength to save herself and the girl. But it wouldn't be enough and Kit knew it. They had to stay together, and they had to get out that gate, but the stairs were impossible. He could probably survive the assault of the guards but not the witches.

That left only one option.

"Hold on," he said grimly, renewing his grip on them.

The witch was quick; he'd give her that. "Are you mad?" she stared from him to the chaos below and back again. "We can't go down there!"

"And we cannot stay here! We're sitting ducks. The smoke should hide us."

"Hide our bodies, mayhap," she snarled, struggling to get away.

Kit held on and dragged her to the edge of the rampart, trying to spot the least lethal landing place. But mages were converging

on them from all sides, and there was no more time. He jumped,
right before a bolt of pure power tore through the air he'd just
vacated.

It hit the side of the stairs behind them, blowing a hole in the
stone and sending sharp shards raining down on to the crowd
below. The screaming and cursing and spell-throwing from the
surrounding witches increased four-fold, but Kit barely noticed
because at that moment, something hit him full in the face.

It wasn't a spell, unless the mages had invented one that
smelled like burnt feathers and tried to peck your eyes out.
He cursed, but couldn't do much more with his arms full
of witches. But whatever-it-was went into a frenzy anyway,
squawking and flapping its wings wildly, as if he was attempting to murder it.

And then the ground tilted under his feet and he landed on
his arse.

It took him a few seconds to realize that he hadn't hit the
ground at all, but the edge of a cart full of woven cages of chick-
ens. Half of them had been broken open in the battle and the
contents were floundering around in the mud or getting roasted
mid-flight by the spells crisscrossing the air. Except for the one
that had somehow gotten its claws trapped in the wool of his
doublet.

The witch had righted herself and her daughter and was
hunkered down beside the cart, watching in disbelief as he did
battle with the guards' dinner. Kit had the distinct impression
that his credibility might have just taken a knock, especially
since he seemed to be losing. And then wounded dignity was
the least of his problems when a dark-haired mage jumped off
the stairs and landed on the cart's other end.

Kit went flying into him, bird and all, and the three of them
tumbled off the back of the cart. The mage was cursing and
trying to raise a shield, while Kit attempted to drain him before
he could manage it. They were both half successful. The mage
snapped his shields shut, but they didn't completely stop the
flow of blood Kit was leeching out of him through the air.

In a panic, the man sent out a cluster of magical weapons.
Half of them collided with crazed birds while the rest attempted
to bury themselves into Kit's flesh. He swatted at them, but like

a storm of angry bees, they kept buzzing around, rushing in to stab at him whenever they got the chance.

"You're losing as much blood as you steal, vampire!" the mage crowed, attempting to gut him with a sword.

"But I can replace mine," Kit said sweetly, sending the sword spinning across the fight with a well-aimed kick. "How about you?"

"Well said," the man replied, and kicked him square in the groin.

Kit stumbled back, fervently wishing that padded codpieces hadn't gone out of style, and landed in the cages of squawking fowl. His impact burst most of the ones left intact and sent up a whirlwind of flapping wings and clawing feet. He fought his way free, finally tearing his own damned passenger loose and tossing it aside. But by the time he got back to his feet, the mage was gone.

And so was the witch.

"God's Bones!" he hissed, staring around wildly. But she and the girl were nowhere in sight. That could mean that a mage had her, but he doubted it. The spells the Circle's men had been casting weren't the kind they used when they wanted to take prisoners, and he didn't see her body.

No, it was a safe bet that she'd run off somewhere while he was distracted. The question was, where?

He glanced at the secondary gate, or what he could see of it through drifting clouds of smoke. It was temptingly close, and the mages hadn't yet managed to lower the portcullis. It looked like they'd tried, but the witches had hit it with something that caused the metal to run like honey. And enough had dripped into the crevices of the track to cause the gate to stick partway down.

There looked to be room to squeeze out underneath, but that required getting to it first. And that didn't look likely. The Circle had placed a double line of guards across the opening to act as a human buffer, leaving their own men free to slowly decimate the witches who were gathering in force nearby. In between the two groups was a hell pit of smoke, spells and running, screaming people.

If she'd headed that way, she wouldn't last long.

It had seemed such an easy task, Kit thought grimly, as he ducked and dodged his way through the melee. Interrogate Lady Isabel Tapley, a coven witch lately apprehended by the mages who was suspected of being in league with the Black Circle. There were rumours that another plot was brewing against the queen, whom the dark blamed for sheltering their enemies, and Kit had been sent to find out if there was any truth to them.

But nothing had gone right from the beginning – Lady Isabel had poisoned herself before he arrived, leaving him to question a corpse, and not the animated kind. The fact that she'd resorted to such extreme measures made him that much more convinced that the plot was genuine, but she'd left no papers behind and her servants knew frustratingly little about their mistress' plans. The only thing he had been able to glean was that she had a meeting in three days' time with several men newly arrived from Spain.

And that one of them shared the name of a noted Black Circle member.

Kit needed to be at that meeting. And for that, he needed a credible Lady Isabel. But young, redheaded coven witches were a little thin on the ground these days, thanks to the Circle. And his request to be allowed to borrow one had been flatly refused. He had therefore gone to the source and bribed the guards, only to land in this mess.

The more sensible side of his brain offered the observation that, really, there had to be other witches who fit Lady Isobel's description. And some of them might be found in somewhat less trying circumstances. The other part of his brain, however, the one that was always getting him in trouble, was dead set on this woman. He'd bled for her; he would have her. And the Circle would not.

Assuming he could find her before they did.

Chapter Four

So much for my knight errant, Gillian thought, watching her rescuer getting beaten up by a half-roasted bird. She was about to rescue the creature when one of the war mages dived off the side of the ramparts, flinging a curse in front of him. She acted on instinct, dropping her all-but-useless shields and throwing up a *declive* instead. It took most of her remaining strength, but it worked; the protection spell acted like a mirror, reflecting the caster's magic right back at him.

It caught him in the middle of his leap, popping his shields and sending him crashing headfirst into the cart. The vampire had landed on the other end, and the 200-pound mage crashing down at the edge of the cart caused him to go flying, chicken and all. And then she didn't see any more, because strong arms clapped around both of hers from behind, lifting her completely off the ground.

She tried to mutter a curse, but found she couldn't draw a breath. The guard – and it had to be a guard, because she was still alive – was doing his best to squeeze her in two. She couldn't aim the staff with him behind her, so she brought it down on his foot instead, as hard as she could. The man bellowed and dropped her and Gillian scrambled away, only to be dragged back by the ankle.

She rolled over to try to free herself and then had to roll again as a knife flashed down, ripping through her gown and missing her by inches. As he wrenched it out of the ground, she caught a glimpse of Elinor behind him, her face pale and her eyes huge. And then the guard dropped his knife and started screaming.

Gillian scrambled to her feet, ready to grab her daughter and bolt, assuming he'd been hit by a stray spell. And then she realized – it was a spell, but it hadn't gone astray. A coiling ribbon of reddish gold flame had snaked out of a burning hut and hit the man square in the back.

At first she thought Elinor must have done it, despite the fact that it was years too early for that. But a searing pain in her arm caused her to look down, and she saw the fire glyph on the staff glowing bright red. She stared at it in disbelief, because she couldn't call Fire.

All coven witches had to specialize in one of the three great elements – Wind, Fire or Earth – when they came of age, and hers was Wind. She'd never been able to summon more than one; no one could except the coven Mothers, who could harness the collective power of all the witches under their control. But she could feel the drain as her magic pulled the element through the air, as she called it to her.

She just didn't know how she was doing it.

And she didn't have time to figure it out. The guard had made the same assumption she had and spun, snarling, on Elinor. Gillian had a second to see him start for her daughter, to see his fist lash out—

And then she was looking at the hilt of a knife protruding from the burnt material of his shirt.

The smell of the charnel houses curled out into the air, mixing with the tang of gunpowder and the raw-lightning scent of spent magic. The guard fell to his knees, the blood gushing hot and sticky from a wound in his side, wetting her hand on the hilt of his blade. She let go and he collapsed, a surprised look on his face and blood on his lips. And then Elinor was tugging her away, shock and pride warring on her small face.

Gillian didn't feel pride; she felt sick. She wiped her sticky hand on her skirts, feeling it tremble, like the breath in her lungs, like her roiling gut. But the guard's death wasn't the cause. She pulled her daughter into her arms and hugged the precious body against her, her heart beating frantically in her chest. She'd almost lost Elinor.

She crouched down beside a nearby well, the only cover she could find that wasn't burning, and stared around desperately for some opening in the crowd. Panic was making it hard to think, but she shoved it away angrily. She couldn't afford weakness now. Weakness would get them killed.

A group of nearby witches was attacking the stables, but Gillian couldn't see the point. The horses' faster pace might get them beyond range of the archers before their shields gave out, but that was assuming they made it out at all. And while the portcullis wasn't completely down, a mob of guards and who-knew-how-many protection spells stood in their way.

No. No one was getting through that.

But they might cause a great deal of commotion trying.

She blinked, her heart drumming with sudden hope. She stared from the battlefield to the high, grey walls surrounding it. And then she scooped up Elinor and took off, weaving through the remaining sheds and outbuildings that hugged the castle walls.

She stopped when they reached the far side of the castle, squatting beside a wagon piled with empty barrels, and breathing hard. She didn't think they'd been seen, but she couldn't be sure. There were guards here, too, although not as many. Most had joined the fight and the rest were staring at it, as if watching her people being slaughtered was great entertainment.

She probably had a few minutes, at least.

She tugged Elinor behind the wagon and started working on the ropes holding the barrels, tearing her nails on the tight knots.

"What are you doing?" Elinor was looking at her strangely.

"Getting us out of this place!"

"There's no door here," Elinor said, staring past her at the carnage.

"Don't look at it," Gillian told her harshly. "And no door doesn't mean no exit."

But not getting one of these barrels loose might. The knots must have been tied before the previous night's rain and they'd shrunk. Try as she might, she couldn't get them loose, and while it would be easy with magic, she didn't have it to spare. She was ready to scream from frustration when she spied a little barrel on one edge of the cart that no one had bothered to strap down.

She rolled it on to the ground and stood it on its end, glancing about. She didn't know if she could do this once, but she certainly couldn't manage it twice. The moment had to be perfect.

It came an instant later, when the guards on the ramparts above them reached the farthest end of their patrol. It left a brief window with no one on the walls directly overhead. Gillian stepped back, pointed the staff at the barrel and cast the strongest levitation spell she could manage.

For a long moment, nothing happened, the small container merely sat there like a stone. But then, as she watched with her heart in her throat, it quivered, wobbled slightly and sluggishly lifted off the ground. She breathed a brief sigh of relief and jerked the staff towards her. The barrel followed the movement, but slowly, as though it weighed much more than empty wood should. But she didn't start to worry until it began to shake as if caught in a high gale.

And then it started cursing.

A stumpy little leg suddenly poked out the bottom, with a big toe sticking out of a pair of dirty, torn hose. Then a plump arm pushed through the side and a head topped by wild red curls appeared where, a moment before, the round wooden lid had been. The head was facing away from her, but the barrel was slowly rotating, so it wasn't but a second before a small, furious face came into view.

It had so many freckles that it was almost impossible to see skin, but the militant glint in the hard green eyes was clear enough. "Goddess' teeth! I'll curse you into oblivion, I'll gouge out yer eyes, I'll cut off that bald-headed hermit twixt yer laigs and feed him to—" She paused, getting a good look at the woman standing in front of her. "Gillian?" Her gaze narrowed and her head tilted. "Wot's this, then?"

"Winnie," Gillian said hoarsely, her brief moment of hope collapsing as the barrel resolved itself into a stout, four-foot-tall woman in a green Irish kirtle. "I didn't recognize—"

"I should demmed well hope not," Winnie said, flexing her small limbs. She gently floated to the ground while rooting around in her voluminous skirts. "'Ere. You sound like you need this mor'n I do."

Gillian took the small bottle her friend proffered and downed a sizeable swallow before realizing it wasn't water. Now she couldn't talk *and* she couldn't breathe. "What?" she gasped.

"Me special brew."

"Didn't they take it from you, when you came in?" Elinor asked suddenly. Seeing a familiar face seemed to have done her good, and she had always liked Winnie.

"Naw. Made it look like a growth on my thigh, I did. Hairy." She nodded archly. "Lots o' moles. The guards din' want ter get too close."

Elinor looked suitably impressed.

Gillian gave Winnie back her "brew" – her wits were addled enough as it was – and she tucked the possibly lethal concoction away. "Right, then. Wot's the plan?"

"The plan was to levitate one of these and ride it out of here!" Gillian croaked. "There's about to be an assault on the front gate. If it draws enough attention, we might be able to slip away while the guards are—"

"Don't matter," Winnie broke in, shaking her head. "The Circle's got charms on the walls, don't they? Try ter go over and poof," she gestured expressively. "The spell breaks and ye fall to yer death. Saw a witch try it a minute ago."

So much for that idea, Gillian thought, swallowing. But Winnie's plan wouldn't work, either. "They'll check for those in hiding," she said, trying to keep the panic out of her voice. "As soon as they've rounded up those who chose to fight!"

"Aye," Winnie said, imperturbably. "And mebbe they'll find me and mebbe they won't. But fightin' war mages is nothin' but a quick death – if yer lucky."

"If we had our weapons, they wouldn't kill us so easily!" Gillian said passionately.

"But we don't. They're up there," Winnie pointed at a nearby tower. "And ain't no reaching 'em."

"What?" It took a moment for her friend's words to sink in. And then Gillian turned her face upwards, staring at the massive cylinder of stone that loomed above them, blocking the sun. "They're right there?"

"Don't go getting any ideas," Winnie told her, watching her face. "I know how ye are about a challenge, but this one's a beggar's chance. There's a mass o' guards on the door and probably more inside. I heard a couple talkin' about bein' kept on duty to help secure the place."

"That's never stopped us before," Gillian murmured, feeling a little dizzy at the sudden return of hope.

"This ain't a job, Gil," Winnie said, starting to look nervous.

Gillian rounded on her, eyes flashing and colour high. "No, it's not *a* job, Winnie. It's *the* job. Our last, if we don't do this!"

"But we can't—"

"It's just another robbery! Only we need this one more than any gold we ever took."

Winnie put a small hand on her arm. "Gil, stop for a minute. Stop. Yer're not gettin' through that door."

"Oh, don't worry," Gillian told her, staring upwards. "I'm not planning on it."

Chapter Five

Kit reached the hell pit only to have to jump aside to avoid a group of stampeding horses, which some enterprising witches were using to try to storm the gate. And then a rogue spell blistered past, caught the edge of his woollen cape and set it on fire. He flung off the now deadly garment and started to stamp out the flames, when he caught sight of a nearby guard.

The man had taken a break from combat in order to besport himself with a pretty blond. He had the struggling girl on her back, her dress over her head and his knee between her thighs – until Kit tossed the length of burning wool over his head. It was rather more pleasurable, he decided, stamping out the flames this way, although the guard didn't seem to agree.

The girl did, though. She scrambled to her feet and kicked the man viciously before sprinting off. But after only a few yards, she turned around, came back and kicked him again. Then she looked at Kit, dropped a small curtsy and fled.

He stared after her, shaking his head. Witches. He was starting to think they were all a bit addled.

And then he was sure of it, as he caught sight of his own particular lunatic attempting to ride a levitating barrel over the walls.

For a moment, he just stared, sure his eyes were playing tricks on him. Until he spied no fewer than five mages heading for the cask and its glowing cargo. Devil take the woman! He sprinted across the battle, cursing, as his witch floated gently to the top of the East Tower.

About halfway across the courtyard, he realized what she was doing. That tower was used as the armoury, and it was a safe bet she was trying for the weapons. But he didn't give much for her chances. The Circle surely had a ward on them, if not on the—

It was on the window. He watched her reach the only one on this side, an elongated type barely wider than the average arrow slit, and cry out. Then a burst of power flared and the barrel shot away from the tower like a ball out of a cannon.

It went sailing off through the air with the witch's slumped form miraculously still attached. Not that that was in any way positive. She'd have been better served had she fallen off; she might have only broken a bone or two that way. As it was, she was headed straight for the heart of the battle.

Kit's eyes flicked around, even as his brain told him that it was over, that there was nothing to be done, that this was *not going to happen*—

And then he was running and leaping and grabbing for her as she shot past. Because he'd obviously gone mad at some point and hadn't noticed. But at least it couldn't get any worse, he thought, as he hit the side of the cask and held on for dear life.

And it rolled over and he ended up dangling upside down.

The only reason they weren't spotted immediately was the thick smoke cover, but there were alarming gaps in it and a hovering cask with two glowing riders was a bit hard to miss. But, on the positive side, his impact had caused their mad conveyance to change course slightly, allowing them to miss the thick of the fight. On the negative, they were now careening for the west wall of the castle at an alarming rate.

He tried to grab the witch and jump off, but she wouldn't budge. It took him a vital few seconds to realize that she'd lashed herself in place with rope, and by then, it was too late. A huge grey expanse filled his vision and, even with vampire reflexes, they were out of time. He threw his body to the side, causing the barrel to spin – right into the wall.

The impact didn't break the wood, because it never hit the cold, unforgiving stone. Kit did, at a rate of speed not recommended for vampire-kind. For a moment, it felt like his body had actually merged with the rock, and he wasn't sure it hadn't. Because when the barrel suddenly jerked and pulled away from the wall, he was sure some of his hide stayed behind. There was no time to check, because they weren't slowing down. The impact should have absorbed most of the forward momentum, but they hadn't simply wobbled off a few yards and stopped. Instead, the barrel seemed to have a mind of its own, and it was quite obviously demented.

Kit held on, fingers clenched white against the wood, as they swooped around the edge of the ramparts, causing several of the guards who had remained at their posts to have to hit the ground face-first. But others retained their dignity – and their ability to fire. The barrel rolled and plunged, weaving in and out of the cover of smoke, as a rain of arrows shot by. One of them grazed Kit's arm, leaving a stinging track across his skin, while another buried itself in the wood between his spread legs.

He stared at it wildly – there were certain things he was not willing to sacrifice for queen and country – only to have the witch start kicking at him. It looked like she wasn't dead, after all, he thought, as a dirty heel smashed into his nose. He grabbed it, trying to see past the blood flying in his face, and caught sight of wild red hair and glaring grey eyes.

"Let go!"

"Do you promise not to kick me again?" he demanded thickly.

"Yes!"

He released her and she jerked her foot back, only to bury it in his throat a moment later. Kit would have cursed, but he thought there was an outside chance he might never talk again. And then a mage jumped him.

Their manic ride immediately took them into the open air once more, the mage holding on to one of Kit's boots as the vampire tried to kick him off. He finally succeeded, losing a fine piece of footwear in the process, only to have another mage jump at them from the ramparts. Kit tensed, ready for a fight, but the barrel suddenly stopped dead and the man sailed on by, more than four feet off-course.

Kit turned his head to grin at the mage and received another kick upside the jaw.

"I'm trying to help you!" he told the witch indistinctly.

"It's a weak charm! You're going to wear it out!"

Kit personally thought that would be a vast improvement, particularly when the crazed cask suddenly went into convulsions. He held on, feeling rather like he was trying to break a particularly cantankerous horse, as it bucked and shuddered and shook. And then it suddenly flipped and dived straight for the ground – with him underneath.

He cursed as he was dragged across the battle, though the sides of burning sheds and over piles of debris. The fire worried him most – he'd lost his cloak and his doublet was quickly being shredded, leaving little barrier between the deadly embers and his skin. Thankfully, the barrel didn't seem to be the patient sort, and a moment later they were back in the air.

Kit decided that enough was enough and snapped the rope holding the witch, preparing to leap off with her, only to be smashed in the face by something huge and heavy. It took him a moment to realize that it was the side of the tower. They had circled back to where this whole crazy ride had started.

And then the equally crazy witch lunged for the spelled window ledge again. "Are you mad?" he asked, grabbing her.

"Let me go!" Her elbow caught him in the stomach, but he grimly held on.

"You'll get yourself killed! The ward—"

"Is down," she gasped, struggling. "It expended its energy last time – I can get through now!"

"You can get trapped now," he shot back. He didn't understand enough about magic to fully follow what was going on, but the guards running for the base of the tower were all too familiar. As was the spell that hit him in the back a moment later.

For an instant, he thought the witch had thrown it, but she wasn't even facing his way. As soon as the stun loosened his hold, she grabbed the window ledge and, with a wriggle and a twist, squeezed through. Kit slumped over the barrel, staring blearily down at a red-headed dwarf at the bottom of the tower, who was pointing the witch's staff and glaring menacingly up at him.

There was little he could do if she chose to hit him again, but instead she glanced behind her at the approaching guards, grabbed the little girl's hand and towed her away. Kit concentrated on not falling off the barrel, which he might survive, into the forest of guards, which he probably wouldn't. His head was numb and his fingers clumsy, but he managed to grab the window ledge on the third try and somehow slithered through the opening.

"You complete *ass*!" The woman looked at him as he collapsed to the floor. "Did you push it away?"

"Push what away?" he asked thickly, trying to figure out which way was up. The stunner had been a strong one, and while he could throw it off, it would be a few minutes. And he wasn't sure they had that long.

"The barrel!"

She leaned dangerously far out the window, and cursed. A moment later, he managed to sit up, only to have the blunt end of a pike hit him upside the temple. It was a glancing blow, but it slammed his head back into the wall. He sat there, watching the room spin, as several witches fished out the window with the sharp end of the pike.

They resolved themselves into one madwoman a moment later, about the time he heard the approach of far too many mages on the stairs. Of course, in his condition, one might be enough to finish him. Kit staggered to his feet and started towards the door, only to have the witch flap a hand at him. "I warded the room!"

"It won't hold them for long."

"It won't have to." She'd hooked the barrel – Kit could see it bobbing outside the window – and was in the process of loading it with the contents of a large trunk. "Well, don't just stand there!" she said frantically. "Help me!"

"Help you do what?"

For an answer she shoved a double handful of wands, charms and bottles of odd, sludgy substances into his hands. He didn't know what half the things were, but although some of them buzzed, chimed and rang like a struck tuning fork against his skin, nothing appeared to be attacking him. For a change.

"Put them in," she said impatiently.

"Put them in the barrel?" he asked slowly, wondering if he was following this at all.

"Yes! By the Goddess, are you always this slow?"

Kit thought that was a trifle unfair, all things considered. But then the door shuddered and he decided to worry about it later. He threw the weapons into the cask, turned and almost bumped into the witch, who was right behind him with another load.

He sidestepped and dragged the heavy trunk over to the window, earning him a brief glance of approval. "I don't see what good this is going to do," he pointed out, as they finished cramming the barrel full of the trunk's contents. "The fight is halfway across the courtyard—"

"As this is about to be." The witch started to climb out of the window, on to the overstuffed cask, when a spell came sizzling through the air. Kit jerked her back and it exploded against the stone, leaving a blackened scar on the tower's side.

"God's Bones, woman!" he cursed, fighting an urge to shake her.

"It wasn't meant to happen this way," she said, staring blankly at the window. "I planned to have the weapons out before anyone noticed."

"They appear to have noticed," Kit said grimly, looking for other options. Unfortunately, there didn't seem to be any. The room was small and wedge-shaped, with but one door and window, both of which the Circle was now guarding.

She rounded on him. "You should have stayed out of it! If you hadn't jumped on board they might not have spotted me!"

"If I had stayed out of it, madam, you would be dead," he snapped. "And I was not the one sending us careening about like a drunken hummingbird."

"Neither was I!" Grey eyes flashed like lightning. "Winnie thought you were attacking me. She was trying to shake you off."

"Winnie would be the demented dwarf?"

"She isn't either," the witch said heatedly. "And say that sometime in her hearing!"

"I will, should I live so long," he replied, as the door shuddered again.

The witch stared at it, and then back at the barrel. And then she snatched a wand from the chest and aimed it at the fully-loaded cask.

"What are you doing?" he demanded, grabbing for her arm. But the stun had made him clumsy and before he could knock it aside, their only way out of this death trap went flying off like a bullet.

"Giving us a fighting chance."

"That was our chance!"

The witch shook her head violently. "None of us has a prayer if they don't get that gate open!"

"And now what?"

"Now this." She rotated her wrist and far away the barrel followed the motion, spewing its contents across the smoke-blackened scene.

"That wasn't what I meant!" Kit said, giving into temptation and shaking her. "How do you plan to get out of here?"

She licked her lips. "We fight."

"With what? You've just sent our only weapons to the other side of the castle!"

"Not all of them," she protested, glancing at the pieces that lay scattered across a nearby table. "As long as it's only guards, we should be—"

The sound of a heavy fist, pounding on the door, cut her off. "Open in the name of the queen!"

"She isn't my queen!" the witch yelled.

There was a pause, and then another voice spoke. "Then open in the name of the Circle."

Chapter Six

Gillian stared at the vampire, who looked blankly back. She didn't have to ask if he had any ideas. His face was as pale and tight as hers felt.

Outside, someone's spell smashed the barrel into a thousand pieces, but too late. There was a huge shout from the crowd as the witches realized what had just rained down on them like manna from Heaven. And then the fighting resumed, far more viciously than before.

It was what she'd wanted, what she'd worked for. There was no way of getting Elinor out of here if the gate stayed closed, and no chance to break through without weapons. But the plan had been to ride the barrel back down before sending it off into the fray. Not to get trapped five storeys off the ground with the Circle on either exit.

"Master Marlowe," the mage's voice came again. "We know you are in there with the witch. Send her out and you may leave peacefully."

"Peacefully?" The vampire snorted. "Your men attacked me!"

"Because you were protecting the woman. Cease to do so and we will have no quarrel with you. We promised your lady safe passage and we will honour that agreement."

Gillian braced herself, sure he would take them up on the offer. She had friends who would have abandoned her in such a situation, and she wouldn't have blamed them. And this man owed her nothing.

But he surprised her. "I have need of the witch," he said, gripping her arm possessively.

"Then you can petition the council."

"Would that be the same council that sentenced her to death?" he asked cynically.

"Send her out, or we shall come in and take her."

The menace in the man's voice made Gillian shiver, but the vampire just looked puzzled. "Why?" he demanded. "Why risk anything for a common cutpurse? She is of no value to you, while my lady would reward you handsomely—"

The mage laughed. "I am sure she would! Do not think to deceive us. A common cutpurse she may have been, but the guards saw what the old woman did. We know what she is!"

The vampire looked at her, a frown creasing his forehead. "What are you?" he asked softly.

Gillian shook her head, equally bewildered. "Nobody. I . . . nobody."

"They appear to feel otherwise," he said dryly. Sharp dark eyes moved to the table. "I don't suppose any of those weapons—"

"Magical weapons are like any other kind," Gillian told him, swallowing. "Someone has to use them."

"And I'm not a mage."

"It wouldn't matter. Two of us against how many of them? No weapon would be enough to even the odds, much less—"

A heavy fist hit the door. Gillian jumped and the vampire's hand tightened reflexively on her arm. It shouldn't have been painful, but his fingers closed right over the burn the Eldest had given her. She cried out and he abruptly let go, as the mage spoke once more.

"Master Marlowe! I will not ask again!"

"Promises, promises," the vampire muttered.

Gillian didn't say anything. She'd pushed up her sleeve to get the fabric off the burn, but no raw, red flesh met her gaze. Instead, she found herself staring in confusion at an ancient, graceful design etched on to her inner wrist.

Her fingers traced the pattern slowly, reverently. It wasn't finished, with only two of the three spirals showing dark blue against her skin. But there was no doubt what it was. "The triskelion," she whispered.

"The what?" the vampire asked.

She looked in the direction of his voice, and found him sprawled on the floor, his curly head pressed against the dusty boards. Her own head was spinning too much to even wonder why.

His eyes narrowed. "A moment ago, you claimed to be of no importance, and now you tell me you're a coven leader?"

"But that's just it, I'm not! At least . . ." Gillian had a sudden flash of memory, of the Great Mother's hand gripping her arm, of how she had refused to let go even in death – and of the ease with which the elements had come to her aid thereafter. She had put it down to the staff magnifying her magic. But no amount of power should have allowed her to call an element that was not hers.

"At least what?" he asked, getting up with a frustrated look on his face.

"I think there's a chance that the Great Mother . . . that she may have—" she stopped, because it sounded absurd to say it out loud – to even think it. But what other explanation was there? "I think she may have passed her position on to me."

She expected shock, awe, disbelief, all the things she was feeling. But the vampire's expression didn't change, except to look slightly confused. And then his head tilted at the sound of some muttering outside. It was too low for her ears to make out, but he didn't appear to have that problem.

"They've sent for a wardsmith," he said grimly. "Before he arrives and they rush the room and kill us both, would you kindly explain what that means?"

"They offered you safe passage," Gillian reminded him.

"And I know exactly how much faith to put in that," he said mockingly, hopping up on to the table. "Now *tell me*."

She took a deep breath. "Every coven has a leader, called the Great Mother or the Eldest. In time of peace, she judges disputes, allocates resources and participates in the assembly of elders at yearly meetings. In time of war, she leads the coven in battle."

He'd been trying to press an ear against the ceiling, but at that he looked down. "And you agreed?" he asked incredulously.

"She asked if I was willing to fight for my own," Gillian said defensively. "I thought she meant Elinor, to get her out of this . . ."

"So of course you said yes!"

"I didn't know she was putting me in charge!"

"That is why the mages marked us," he said, as if something had finally made sense. "I wondered why they were focused on you when there were dozens of prisoners closer to the gates."

Gillian shook her head. "They don't want me, they want this." She held out the arm with the ward.

"For what purpose?"

"The triskelion gives the Great Mother the ability, in times of danger, to . . . to borrow . . . part of the magic of everyone under her control," she said, struggling for words he would understand. "It's meant to unite the coven in a time of crisis, allowing its leader to wield an awesome amount of power, all directed toward a single purpose. It's why the Circle fears them so much, why they've hunted them so—"

She broke off as her voice suddenly gave out. The vampire frowned and pulled a flask from under his doublet, bending down to hand it to her. She eyed it warily, thinking of Winnie and her brew, but it turned out to be ale. It was body-warm and completely flat, and easily the best thing she'd ever tasted.

He balanced on the edge of the table in a perilous-looking crouch, regarding her narrowly. "If the ward is that powerful, why did the jailers not take it off the witch once they had her in their grasp?"

"They didn't know who she was," Gillian gasped, forcing herself to slow down before she spilled any of the precious liquid. "I didn't even know. She was dressed in rags, her hair was dirty, her face was haggard – she must have been in disguise and was picked up in a raid."

"But do not magical objects give off a residue your people can feel?"

"Yes, but the ward isn't like a charm – it holds no magic itself when not active. And non-magical items can occasionally be missed in searches."

"But if it's so powerful, why didn't the witch use it herself?"

"She was gagged," Gillian said, thinking of the disgusting scrap of cloth she'd pulled from the Eldest's mouth. "And by the time I freed her, she was too weak to fight. Goddess knows how long she was in there."

"So in return for your help, she saddles you with the very thing most likely to get you killed," he said in disgust.

"She wanted to save her people, and she needed someone strong enough to use the ward!"

"Then I suggest you do so. There are four guards in the chamber below and at least five in the corridor outside – and that is assuming no one is hiding under a silence shield. Above us is the roof of the keep, guarded by four more men who can be called down if needed. And then there's the two below the window, who are doubtless hoping we'll poke our heads out again and get them blown off!"

"*Fifteen men?*" Gillian repeated, appalled. That was three times as many as she'd expected, especially with an escape in progress. What were they all doing here?

"Fifteen war mages." He smiled grimly. "There is a price to be paid for breaking into the most secure part of the prison."

"But . . . but how do we get past so many?"

"We don't. I can take three, possibly four with your help. No more. We need a diversion to draw the rest away to have any chance at all."

Gillian licked her lips, staring at the blank space on her arm where the third spiral of the triskelion should have been. The ward looked oddly lopsided without it, the pattern disjointed and incomplete. Like the connection it was meant to make.

"I . . . don't think I can," she confessed.

"I beg your pardon?" the vampire asked politely.

"This isn't a complete ward," she explained. "The triskelion should have three arms, one for each of the three great elements. And this has but two. The other hasn't manifested, and until it does, the ward won't function."

The vampire jumped off the table and grabbed her arm. "You're sure it had three, when you saw it on the old woman's wrist?"

"Her title was Eldest and yes! They all do."

"Then where is the other one?" he demanded suspiciously.

"Well, I don't have it hidden in my shift!" she said, snatching her arm back. It throbbed with every beat of her heart, a pounding, staccato rhythm that was getting faster by the minute. But she couldn't afford to panic. Not here, not now. She had to figure this out, and there was an answer – she knew it. Magic had rules and it followed them strictly. She just had to find the ones that applied here.

The vampire must have thought the same, because he straightened his shoulders and took a breath. "How is the sigil usually passed from person to person?"

"There's a ritual," she said, trying to concentrate. "The last time it happened in my coven, I was a child. My mother wouldn't allow me to attend – she thought it too gruesome—"

"Gruesome?"

Gillian hugged her arms around herself. "The new Mother has to run a gauntlet, to prove her fitness to lead. She must summon each of the three elements to her aid, and each time she calls one successfully, that element becomes active on the sigil."

"What is shocking about that?"

"If she fails, she dies," Gillian said simply, her chin lifting. Her tone challenged him to denigrate the covens' traditions as the Circle constantly did. Barbaric, they called them, and backward and crude. But it was for instances like this one that the ritual had been instituted. Only someone with a firm belief in her abilities and an utter devotion to the coven could pass the gauntlet, because only someone with that level of commitment could lead in times like these.

That was the kind of woman the Eldest had been, capable and strong, in spirit if no longer in body. But Gillian wasn't that person. She wasn't anything anymore.

"And then what?" the vampire demanded.

"Nothing, I . . . that's all I can remember. Call the elements and the sigil activates."

"Well, you must have called two already," he said, pointing to the two arms of the triskelion. "Which ones?"

"I remember calling Fire," Gillian told him. "It was in battle. I looked down because my arm hurt and saw the glyph glowing on the staff. I wondered why I was able to summon it when I never could before."

"And the other?"

"That has to be Wind – my own element. It didn't hurt, so I can't be sure, but I think it came in when the Circle's men attacked us the first time."

"When you blew their weapons back at them."

"Yes."

"Then which one is missing?"

"Earth," she whispered, her eyes going to the window as the full implication hit.

His eyes narrowed at her tone. "Why is that a problem?"

"Because Wind comes from air and I was standing right by a burning hut when I called Fire!"

"And?"

"And I need to be near an element to summon it."

His own eyes widened as comprehension dawned. "And we're five storeys up."

Chapter Seven

Gillian didn't have a reply, but she couldn't have made one anyway. Because the next moment, the assault on the door resumed. Only this time, it sounded like a battering ram had been brought up. The door shuddered under massive blows, the ward around it sparking and spitting.

The vampire swore. "I didn't think they would find a ward-smith so quickly."

"They didn't, or they wouldn't be trying to batter their way in! They were probably lying before, hoping you'd hear."

"Then we're safe for the moment?"

"No," she admitted. "Wards like this are tied to the integrity of an item. Just as a shattered charm loses its magic, the ward will fail as soon as the door suffers enough damage."

"And when will that be?"

She stared at the tiny fractures already visible in the wood and swallowed. "Not long."

"It doesn't make sense," he said angrily. "If you were going to use the sigil, you would have done so before now. They must know that you can't. Yet half the war mages in the prison are here, instead of at the gates!"

Gillian shook her head. She'd had the same question, and he was right, it didn't make sense. She couldn't direct the fight from here, not that anyone was likely to listen to her anyway. The witches had fled before the Eldest died; they hadn't seen what had happened.

She was, she realized with sudden clarity, about to die for a position nobody even knew she had.

"You've already sent most of the weapons that were here to the battle and the Circle has men watching the window in any case," the vampire fretted. "They can't be concerned about you sending more. Why waste this many men on a single woman who isn't even a threat?"

Gillian started to shake her head again, but then she stopped, staring down at her wrist. And just like that, she understood. "They're not," she said blankly.

"They're not what?"

Her hand closed over the ward, but she could still feel it, carved into her flesh like a brand. "They're not aiming for one witch," she said, looking up at him as it all came together in a rush, like a riddle that had needed but one final clue. "This is about destroying all of us!"

"I don't understand."

"There is no such thing as a one-way street in magic. Anything that can give power can also be used to take it!"

"You're talking about the triskelion."

She nodded frantically. "It links all the witches under the Eldest's control. If the Circle gets their hands on it, they can use it to bleed each and every one of them dry! It doesn't matter if they run, if they hide—" she broke off abruptly, thinking of Winnie. Gillian had given her the staff, hoping its power would allow her to hide herself and Elinor. But if the Circle obtained the ward, it wouldn't matter how well they were hidden.

They could be killed just the same.

Gillian felt her blood run cold.

"But the ward isn't complete," the vampire protested. "If you cannot use it, how can they?"

"By putting me under a compulsion, by forcing me to call the last sigil – and then using me to drain every last person here!"

"But surely, not everyone here was a member of the same coven."

"It doesn't matter! Magical objects follow simpler rules than humans do. And a coven, in the loosest sense, is a group of magic workers under the leadership of an elder. And she was the most senior witch here."

"You're saying that the ward thinks the whole prison was her coven?" he asked doubtfully.

"Which she passed on to me," Gillian said numbly, staring at the window. The setting sun was shining through drifting clouds of smoke, casting a reddish light into the room. She couldn't see the battlefield from where she stood, but it didn't matter. The real battle wasn't going to be fought down there.

It seemed hopeless. The Circle held all the cards; they had from the start. There were too many of them and too few coven witches, and unlike the Great Mothers, the Circle had no sense of community, no reverence for ancient ways, no respect for a magic so different from their own. They had never meant to work with anyone. From the beginning, their strategy had been subjugation or destruction.

It was their game, and they had already won.

But they wouldn't win completely.

"Kill me," Gillian said harshly, as the pounding on the door took on a strange kind of rhythm, like the furious drumming in her chest.

"What?" The vampire had been staring at the window, too, as if in thought. But at that, his eyes swivelled back to her.

"I won't let them do it," she told him flatly. "I won't let them use me to destroy everyone else. I can't save myself, but I'll die on my own terms, as the old Mother did. A free coven witch and damn them all!"

"And yet you'll still be dead," he said sharply.

"Nothing can stop that now."

"Perhaps, perhaps not. If you will give me but a moment to think—"

"We don't have a moment," she said, grabbing his arms. "Do as I ask or it will be too late!"

"You don't understand," he told her, and for the first time

since they'd met, he looked unsure of himself. "The thought occurred to me, as well, but it isn't that simple."

"Your kind does it all the time!"

"We do no such thing!" His dark eyes flashed. "Those who join us are chosen very carefully. Not everyone is fit for this life, and it does little good to go to the trouble of Changing someone merely to have them—"

"Changing?" It took her a moment to realize what he meant, and then her fingers dug into his arms. "You're saying that – you mean you can—" she broke off, the implications staggering her.

He was talking about making her into one of them, about turning her into a monster. She shuddered in instinctive revulsion, her skin going clammy at the very thought. Walking undead, drinkers of blood, merciless killers – every horror story about the breed she'd ever heard rang in her mind like the clanging of a bell. She *couldn't*—

But it would work. Coven magic was living magic, based on the deep old secrets of the earth. And its creations were living things, tied to the life of the one who bore them. If she died, the ward died with her. It was why they had to be passed from Elder to Elder before death, or new ones had to be created.

And it didn't get much deader than a vampire.

It was the only way to survive this. The only way to see Elinor again, to be there as she grew up, to protect her. It wouldn't be anything like the life she'd hoped to have, the one she'd dreamed of for them. But it would be *something*.

And that was more than her own kind were willing to offer.

"Do it," she told him. "Make me one of you."

The vampire scowled. "As I informed you, it is not that easy. And there is a chance that it could make things even worse."

Gillian severely doubted that. "The Circle promised you safe passage if you ceased to protect me," she reminded him. "If they find me dead, there's a good chance they'll leave you alone rather than risk making an enemy of your mistress. They have enough of those as it is!"

"That isn't the point—"

"Then what is?" she demanded desperately. The wood of the door was starting to splinter. They had minutes, maybe less, and she wasn't sure how long the process took.

"The point is that I am not sure how," he admitted, with faint spots of colour blooming high on his cheeks.

"But . . . but you're a master," she said, bewildered. "You have to be! You've been running about in broad daylight for the last hour!"

"Yes, but . . ." he sighed and ran a hand through his curls. "It is too complex to explain fully, but essentially . . . my Lady *pushed* me."

"Pushed? Wha—"

"It is done when a master wishes to elevate a servant's rank quickly. A great deal of power is . . . is shoved through a subject all at once," he told her, swallowing. "It is rarely done, because many times, the subject involved does not survive. But the threats against her Majesty were grave enough to make my Lady decide that she needed someone on the inside, and no one in her stable was qualified. But a newly-made vampire has many weaknesses that—"

"Newly-made?" Gillian grasped onto the one thing in all that which made sense. "How new?"

He licked his lips. "A few years."

"A few *years*?"

"If you round up."

Gillian felt her stomach plummeting. "You're telling me you've never Changed anyone before?"

"I never had cause," he said, looking defensive.

"Didn't they train you?" she demanded, suddenly furious. She had found a way out of this, against all the odds, she had found a way. And he *didn't know how*?

"It is rather like sex," he snapped. "The theory and the practice being somewhat different!"

"You have to try!"

"You don't understand. It is a little-known fact that newly-minted masters, even those who took centuries to reach that mark, often have . . . mishaps . . . before they succeed in making their first Child. If I do this incorrectly—"

"Then I'll be dead," she said harshly. "Which is what I will be when the Circle finishes with me in any case." She took off her kerchief, baring her neck before she could talk herself out of this. "Do it."

For a moment, she was certain he would refuse. And why shouldn't he, she thought bitterly. It sounded like masters changed only those who could be helpful to them in some way, and she'd been little enough use to anyone alive. Why should being dead be any different?

But then he swallowed and stepped closer, his hands coming up to rest on her shoulders. There was fear in his eyes, and it looked odd on that previously self-assured face. Like the bruises purpling along his jaw and cheek, wounds his kind weren't supposed to get. Her hand instinctively lifted to touch them, and found his skin smooth and blood warm, nothing like the stories said.

She stared at him, wondering if his kind felt pain, if they felt love, if they *felt*. She didn't know. She didn't know anything about them but rumours and stories, most of which, she was beginning to realize, had likely been fabricated by people who knew even less than she.

"Try to relax," he murmured, and she wasn't sure whether he was talking to her or himself. But then his eyes lightened to a rich, honey-gold, as if a candle had been lit behind them. The pounding on the door receded, fading into nothingness, and the cool breeze flowing through the window turned warm. Incredibly, she felt some of the stiffness leave her shoulders.

For a moment – until his lips found her neck and she faltered in cold panic, the soft touch causing her heart to kick violently against her ribs. Her hands tightened on his sleeves, instinct warring with instinct – to push him away, to pull him closer, the will to live fighting with the need to die.

"I'm not doing this correctly," he said, feeling her tremble. "You should not feel fear."

"Everyone fears death, unless they have nothing to live for."

"And you have much."

She nodded, mutely. She hadn't realized until that moment how focused she'd been on all that she'd lost, instead of on what remained. She didn't want to die. She wasn't *supposed* to die, not here, not now. She knew it with a certainty that was at war with all reason.

"I cannot do this if you fight me," he told her simply. "Humans tell stories of us forcibly Changing them against their will, but that rarely happens. It is difficult enough when the subjects are willing, when they want what we have to offer."

"And what is that?" she asked, trying for calm despite the panic ringing in her bones.

"For most? Power, or the possibility of it. Wealth – few masters are poor, and their servants want for nothing. And, of course, the chance to cheat death. Quite a few transition in middle age, when their bodies begin to show wear, when they realize how short a mortal life really is."

Gillian shook her head in amazement, that anyone would throw away something so precious for such scant reward. "But few become masters, isn't that right?" He nodded. "So the power is in another's hands, as is the wealth, to give or withhold as he chooses. And as for death—" This didn't feel like a cheat to her. It felt like giving up. It felt like the end.

The vampire smiled, softly, sadly. "You are a poor subject, Mistress Urswick. You are not grasping enough. What you want, you already have; you merely wish to keep it."

"But I'm not going to keep it, am I?" The terror faded as that certainty settled into her bones. She had one chance, here and now, and it would never come again. She could let fear rob her of it and die, or she could master herself and live. A strange life, to be sure, but a life, nonetheless.

"Do you wish to proceed?" he asked her, watching her face.

Gillian took a deep breath, and then she nodded.

Chapter Eight

He didn't tell her again that this might not work. He didn't tell her anything at all. But golden threads of a magic she didn't know suddenly curled around her hands where they rested on his arms. She had always thought vampires were creatures of the dark, but the same bright magic shone around him as his hands came up to bracket her face.

"I don't know your first name," he whispered, against her lips.

"Gillian," she told him, hearing her voice tremble.

"Gillian," he repeated, and her name in his voice was full of so much longing that it coiled in her belly, dark and liquid, like her own emotion. And perhaps it was. Because when he suddenly bit down on her lower lip, the sensation left her trembling, but not with fear.

He made a low noise in his throat and pulled her close. The same strange magic that twisted around them sparked off his fingers wherever they touched her, like rubbed wool in winter. The tiny flashes of sensation had her arching helplessly against him, one hand clenched on his shoulder, the other buried in the heavy silk of his hair.

She could taste her own blood, hot and coppery, on his tongue as he drove the kiss deep, and it drew a sound from her, something animal and desperate. She gulped for air when he pulled back, almost a sob. She wanted – she wanted more than this; his hands on her body, his skin against hers, his tongue tracing the tiny wound he'd made—

But when he returned, it wasn't to her lips.

A brilliant flash of pain went through her, like a shock of cold water, as his fangs slid into the flesh of her neck. She drew in a stuttering breath, but before she could cry out, a rush of rich, strong magic flooded her senses, spreading heat through every fibre of her body. She'd always thought of vampires as taking, but this was giving, too, an impossibly intimate sharing that she'd never even dreamed was—

He didn't move, but it suddenly felt like he was inside her, thrusting all that power into her very core. She shuddered and opened to him, helpless to resist, the vampire shining on her and in her, elemental and blazing and gone past human. The pain was gone, the magic driving that and everything else away, crashing over her like ocean waves, an unrelenting and unending tide. She screamed beneath it, because it couldn't be borne and had to be; because there was no bracing to meet it and no escape; and because it would end, and that would be even harder to bear.

"Gillian." It took her a moment to realize he had drawn back, with the tide of magic still surging through her veins. It felt like the sea, ebbing and flowing in pounding waves that shook the very foundations of—

She blinked, and realized that it wasn't just the vampire's magic making the room shake. It wasn't even the pounding on the door, which seemed to have stopped in any case. She frowned and watched as the few remaining charms jittered and danced off the table, all on their own.

"What is it?" she asked, bemused. The vampire pulled her to the window, and leaned out, dangerously far. "What are you doing?" she tried to pull him back. "They'll kill you!"

"I don't think so," he said, his voice sounding as stunned as she felt.

"Why not?"

"Because I believe you may have completed that ward, after all."

He backed away from the window and she moved forward, in time to see what looked like a black wave crash into the side of the tower, shaking it to its very foundation. She blinked, dizzy from blood loss and still burning with strange energy. And then another wave started for them, rising out of the earth of the courtyard, and she understood.

"In defence of your life," the vampire said, with quiet irony.

Gillian looked down to see the third spiral of the triskelion, glowing bright against her wrist. She traced it with a finger and power shivered in the air for a moment, before melting back into her skin, joining the tide swelling within her.

"I think it might be best if it didn't hit," he said, glancing from the approaching wave to the cracks spidering up the old walls. "Can you stop it?"

"I don't want to stop it," she told him, flexing her fingers and feeling the warmth of deep rich soil beneath her hands, the whisper of the age old magic of the earth in her ears. But there was something else there, too, alien and strange, but powerful, all the same. It wasn't the vampire's rich, golden energy, but colder, more metallic, more—

She laughed, suddenly understanding what the old Mother had meant. "You'll have all the power you need," she repeated.

"What?"

"The Mother didn't just link the witches into her coven," she told him delightedly. "She linked the mages, too!"

He stared at her, and then back at the awesome power of the land rising to meet them. "That's . . . very interesting, but I think we had better jump before the next wave hits."

"Let the Circle jump!" she said, and pushed *out*.

The magic flowing along her limbs followed the motion – and so did the earthen tide. It paused almost at the tower base, trembling on the edge of breaking like a wave about to crest. And then it surged back in the other direction.

Masses of black soil rippled out in concentric circles from the base of the tower, flowing like water towards the old fortress walls. They hit like the surf on the beach, crashing into stone and old mortar already riddled with tiny fissures from years of neglect. The fissures became cracks, the cracks became gaps, and still the waves came. Until the earth shifted beneath the foundations and the stones slipped loose from each other and the walls crumbled away.

There were shouts and curses from the guards who fell with the walls, and from the bewildered mages who suddenly found themselves at the centre of a pile of spread-out rubble. But the witches were eerily silent, turning as one to look up at the tower for a long, drawn-out moment. And then they gave an ancient battle cry that raised the hair on Gillian's arms.

And charged as one.

Chapter Nine

"Nope, nothing." The distant, muffled voice came from somewhere above him, right before something was slammed down through the dirt, barely missing his head.

Kit swivelled his eyes to the side to stare at it. It was wood, as thick around as his wrist and pointed slightly at one end. A fine specimen of a stake, he thought, with blank terror.

"Are you sure you saw him over here?"

That was the witch, Gillian. He tensed at her voice, trying to force something, anything past his lips. He wasn't sure if he succeeded, but the stake was removed.

"Aye, although I don't know why ye care," the other voice said. "He's a vampire. He'll just feed off ye again."

"He didn't feed off me the first time," the witch said. "I told you, he was helping me."

"Strange kind 'o help that leaves ye pale and sweating," the other voice grumbled, right before the stake was slammed down again – between his legs.

His alarmed grunt must have been audible that time, because the witch's voice came again, closer this time. "Don't move, Winnie."

Kit lay there, his heart hammering in his chest in the rapid beats that his kind weren't supposed to have. But then, they weren't supposed to panic, either. And that was clearly a bunch of—

"Found him!" Gillian's excited voice came from just above him, and there was a sudden lessening of the weight of the earth pressing down on his limp body.

It took ten minutes for them to haul him out, either because the witches had expended their magic destroying the jailers, or because no one cared to waste any on a vampire. Certainly the sour-faced dwarf who finally uncovered his head looked like she'd much rather just heap the dirt back where she'd found it, possibly after using her massive stake one more time. But the Gillian got hands under his arms and pulled him out of the hole in a series of sharp tugs.

She laid him on the ground and bent over him, her unbound hair falling on to his filthy face. "Are you all right?" she asked distinctly.

Kit tried to answer, but only succeeded in causing his tongue to loll out of his mouth. He tasted dirt. She pushed it back in, looking worried.

"What's wrong with him?" she asked the dwarf, who was suddenly looking more cheerful.

"One too many stun spells, looks like to me," she said cheerfully. "And he didn't get out 'o the way fast enough when the tower came down." She poked at him with her toe. "Be out of it for a while, he will."

She moved away, probably off to terrorize someone else, and Gillian knelt by his side. "We can't stay," she told him, trying to brush a little of the caked dirt off him. "The Circle probably knows about this already, or if they don't, they soon will. We have to go while we still have a head start."

Kit coughed up a clod of dirt from lungs that felt bone dry. He strongly suspected that he'd swallowed a good deal of it, too, but mercifully, the witch had found his flask and filled it with water. He gulped it gratefully, despite the unpleasant sensation of mud churning in his stomach.

It managed to rinse enough soil loose from his vocal chords for a dry whisper. "You . . . came back," he croaked.

She brushed dirty hair out of his eyes, causing a little cascade down the back of his ruined shirt. "Of course. What did you expect?"

"I . . . wasn't sure." He licked his lips and drank a little more with her help. "We . . . had a deal, but . . . many people . . ."

She frowned slightly. "What deal?"

"I help you . . . you . . . help me."

"I did help you," she said, the frown growing. "Winnie wasn't the only one who wanted to stake you."

He shook his head, sending a cloud of dust into the air. "No. You promised . . ."

"I'm not going with you," she told him flatly. "I have a child to think about. I have to get her out of England."

"You . . . you're Great Mother now," he protested. "You can't leave."

"Watch me," she said viciously. She gestured around at the tumbled rubble. "This is what the Circle brings. Nothing but ruin and destruction, everywhere they go. I'm not raising a child in constant peril!"

If he'd had any saliva, Kit would have pointed out that the Circle hadn't turned a perfectly good, if slightly dilapidated castle into a pile of rocks. But he didn't, and she didn't give him the chance in any case.

"And as for the other, you cannot have a coven of one. And I'm shortly going to be the only one left. Everyone else is going back to their own people, to regroup, to plan, to hide . . ." she shrugged. "It's a new world, now that the covens are gone. And we each have to find our own role in it."

He lay there, watching the last rays of the setting sun blaze through her glorious hair. And wished his damn throat would unfreeze. He had a thousand things to say and no time to say them. "If you're not . . . going to stay. Why look for me?" he finally managed.

She bent down, her face softening, sweet lips just grazing his. "To say thank you," she whispered. "Winnie will never understand but . . . I was there. I know. You could have finished what you started."

"Not . . . unwilling."

She smiled, a little tearfully. "And if ever anyone was to convince me . . ."

He caught her hand as she started to rise. "Stay," he said urgently. "You don't . . . I can show you things . . . wonders—"

"You already have."

She kissed him, with feeling this time, until his head was spinning from more than just the spells. She didn't say anything when she drew back, but she pushed his hanging mouth closed with a little pop. Then she jumped to her feet and ran for the distant tree line.

But after only a few yards, she stopped, paused for a moment, and then ran back. And relieved him of his ring. "Travelling money," she said, with a faintly apologetic look. And then she took off again.

Kit stared after her until the gathering shadows swallowed her up. Witches. He'd been right all along. They were completely mad.

He smiled slightly, his lips still tingling from her final touch. But what glorious madness.

The Getaway

Sonya Bateman

If there was one thing Jazz hated more than birthdays, at the moment, it was Gavyn Donatti – ex-thief, current boyfriend, and completely hopeless co-navigator.

She nosed the sedan to the top of the rise, tyres spinning in the muck. How they'd gotten on to a dirt road was beyond her. Rain battered the roof and sheeted down the windshield, the wipers at top speed barely affording a glance at the few feet of desolate nothing the headlights picked out. No signs, no lights, no goddamn asphalt. No miracle turn-off to this supposed dream cabin.

Only Donatti could get them this lost with a map and detailed directions. Hell, he'd get lost with a GPS and a personal tour guide.

"Your car's a piece of crap," she said.

Donatti slouched in the passenger seat. "Sorry, babe," he muttered. "Haven't had time to upgrade lately."

"Don't 'babe' me. We're lost."

"No, we're—" He straightened and peered out the windshield. For a long time. "Okay. We're lost."

"How perceptive." Jazz nudged the shivering car through a series of deep ruts, fighting the jerks and tugs of the wheel. Christ. She'd driven getaway cars at a hundred miles an hour with bullets tearing through the back end and had less trouble than this. The four-banger under the hood ground its gears and let out a couple of disconcerting clacks. "When's the last time you changed the oil in this thing?"

"Um."

"Jesus, Donatti. You've got to take better care with vehicles." She refrained from bringing up what he'd done to her van. He knew what she meant. "What happens if we throw a rod out here? I didn't bring a spare engine."

He flashed a quick frown. "I'll fix it."

"Oh, no. I told you, I don't trust that magic stuff."

"Jazz, come on. You know it's real. You've been—"

"No."

"What do I have to do, turn lead into gold?"

"Nothing. Don't do anything, okay? In fact, let's make this a magic-free weekend." She glared through the dark and the rain. Yes, she was being irrational. Donatti had just found out a few months ago that he was part djinn, and she'd seen him do impossible things. Like make himself invisible. And kill two thugs with one spell. But that didn't mean she had to like it. For God's sake, nobody believed in genies, any more than they believed in fairies and unicorns. "Promise me no magic."

"Fine. I promise." He let out a sigh. "Look, why don't you pull over a minute? I'll see if I can make any sense out of the map."

Jazz shook her head. "If I get off this mud-bog excuse for a road, we won't be able to get back on."

"All right. You're the boss."

"Damn straight." She allowed herself a smirk, but it faded fast. This was a mistake. Celebrating her birthday, which she didn't give a shit about anyway, at some remote frigging *romantic* cabin with the thief who'd gotten her pregnant and then vanished for three years, only to turn up again just in time to completely eviscerate the life she'd made with Cyrus.

Okay. Maybe not eviscerate. Disrupt, definitely. Donatti had smoothed things over pretty quickly, and Cy had taken right to his father like he'd been there all along. But between her and Donatti, there was just an old spark. She might have loved him once. Now she wasn't sure. Hell, she didn't know anything these days. Sometimes she wanted to strangle him with his own intestines . . . but he was adorable even in his incompetence, and she couldn't stay mad at him for long. He wasn't bad, really. Just unlucky as hell. And he'd turned out to be a good father, once she'd finally managed to inform him that he was one.

Speaking of Cy, it was late and she hadn't called to check on things at home. They were supposed to be at the cabin two hours ago. She pointed at the cell phone she'd plugged in to charge and said, "Can you dial the house? Put it on speaker."

"Sure."

Jazz realized she'd been gripping the wheel tight enough to cramp her fingers. She forced them to relax. Cy would be fine. She'd left him with Ian and Akila – Ian being the djinn who'd sprung himself on Donatti three months ago saying he was his great-great-great grandfather, or something. Akila, also djinn, was his wife.

The phone wasn't ringing. Wasn't making any noise at all. She looked sideways at him. "Did you forget the number?"

"Not exactly." He cleared his throat. "I'm not getting any bars."

"Shit!"

"Yeah. Listen, I'm gonna check the map again."

"You do that," she muttered, and shifted her concentration back to driving. She didn't expect him to find anything. Following directions wasn't one of his strengths. He was more the type to accidentally wind up in the right place – even if it was almost always at the wrong time.

The torrential downpour seemed to be slacking, and the road looked a little wider, a little firmer. That might've been wishful thinking. At least the car had stopped trying to fling itself kamikaze-style off the path. There was another little rise ahead. Maybe they'd find a new road on the downgrade. Or Atlantis. With Donatti around, she never knew.

Paper rustled sharply from the passenger seat. "Okay, so did we pass Loon Lake?"

"We passed a lot of lakes, Donatti."

"I think we did. And we're looking for Wolf Pond."

She blew out a breath. "A pond in the Adirondacks. Shouldn't be too hard to find."

"You're being sarcastic, aren't you?"

"You win a cookie."

"Chocolate chip?"

"Cut the wisecracks. I'm trying to drive."

He smirked at her. "Can't have that now. You'll get a DWL, and that'll go on your record forever. When they put you away, they'll make you watch Barney videos and listen to Rico Suave all day in your cell."

"DWL?" She arched an eyebrow. "Do I even want to know?"

"Driving while laughing. It's a serious offence in the great state of New York. Have you ever seen a trooper crack a smile?"

She smothered a laugh. Damn, he always managed to make her grin, no matter how bad things got. She actually envied his endless supply of optimism – he could whip out a smartass remark while he was standing at the wrong end of a gun. Maybe he was a little stupid sometimes, but he made up for it with buckets of brass fucking balls. She had to admire that. "Happy troopers? That'd scare the shit out of me," she finally said.

"Me too." He maintained the serious-like-a-church-service front. "I actually saw one, once. He was cuffing me at the time."

"Figures." She smiled and glanced at the speedometer. The sedan was doing a whopping 24 mph. At this rate, they might make civilization some time before New Year's. They cleared the rise – and Jazz eased the brakes down, practically gaping through the windshield. "Tell me I'm not seeing things," she said. "Is that pavement?"

"Yes, ma'am." Donatti grinned. "See any road signs?"

"Yeah, sure. Right next to that mini mall over there." She stopped with the front tyres on the paved surface, not in the mood to push this thing out of the mud. Trees to the left, and trees to the right. Nothing in either direction said head-this-way. She flicked the hazards on – as if anyone else would be out driving on East Bumfuck Mountain in this weather – and said, "Okay. Now what, Mister da Gama?"

He shrugged. "I don't know. Turn."

"Brilliant idea. Which way?"

"Hey, don't look at me." He folded the map in his hands a few times. "If I pick the wrong way, you'll kick my ass."

"I should probably kick your ass anyway. This was your idea."

Donatti stiffened and stared straight ahead. "Yeah," he said softly. "How stupid of me, thinking we might have a good time together."

I'm sorry. It was on the tip of her tongue, but she couldn't quite bring herself to say it. Instead, she popped the car into gear and eased into a left turn. "I think this way's down," she said. "At least we should hit a crossroad or a sign eventually."

"You're the boss."

Jesus. Did he have to sound like she'd kicked him in the balls? Irritated, more with herself than him, she took the car up to a decent speed and listened to the tyres slice over drenched asphalt. After a long silence, she coughed once and gestured to the radio. "You want that on? It might take a while until we get oriented again."

"Nah. If there are any stations in range, it's probably your choice of country, country and western." He dropped his gaze to his lap. "Jazz, I'm sorry I got us lost."

His apology where hers should've been sent a spark of anger sizzling through her. She managed to throttle it back. "It's not completely your fault," she said. "I'm driving."

"Yeah, well – holy shit. You see that thing up there?"

"What . . ." *Thing?* The rest of the question faded from her lips. The rusted hulk of an old car lay by the side of the road ahead, choked in tangles of weeds. She slowed when they passed it, and gave a low whistle. "That's a DeSoto. Well, it used to be. Back in the fifties. Jesus, it's crumpled to hell."

"Kind of weird, isn't it? All the way out here?"

"Yes. Weird." It was damned unsettling. Like finding a horse in a parking garage – or rather, the bleached skeleton of a horse.

The road curved, and when they rounded the bend something shivered in her gut. "There's another one," she said. A rusted, twisted auto body overgrown with brown vegetation. This one had come to rest after a collision. "A Mustang. Early seventies."

Donatti stared at it. "Okay, I'm creeped out," he said.

"I'm turning around. We'll go the other way." She tapped the brake.

The car sped up.

"What the *fuck*?" Jazz gripped the wheel and tromped on the brake. It didn't slip, shimmy or sink to the floor. Went down cushioned, like a normal pedal. But the sedan didn't slow. The speedometer climbed to thirty-five, forty, forty-five. She didn't dare take her eyes from the road.

"Uh, Jazz?" Donatti's voice shook a little. "We going for a Dukes of Hazzard turn here?"

"It won't stop." She managed to sound calm. "I changed my mind. Use magic."

"Right."

They flew past another wreck, too fast to make it out – but definitely a classic car like the rest. She knew it took him a few minutes to do anything magic. It had to warm up or something. The needle climbed. Fifty. Fifty-five. The wheel strained in her hands, and the car tilted.

Ahead, the road curved.

A string of curses refused to pass her lips. She grabbed for the emergency brake, hit the button, and the steering wheel lurched from her grip. She didn't even have time to shout a warning. With a squeal of rubber, the car spun out of control, rammed something on the shoulder and lifted, airborne.

Her body jerked like a whip, and her head smacked the wheel. The lights went out.

Sunlight and singing birds. The crisp, sweet smell of autumn leaves. All the ingredients for a beautiful fall day hovered just outside Jazz's closed eyes.

None of them were right. It was raining. Dark. And she'd crashed the car.

Her eyes snapped open, and a startled gasp escaped her. No broken glass or twisted metal. She was on a bed, in a room – not a hospital. Thick log walls. Cabin walls. To her right, french doors stood open on a wooden patio overlooking miles of picturesque mountain forest, red and gold and green. It would've taken her breath away if she hadn't already lost it.

Though her body ached, there was no real pain. She touched fingers to her forehead where she'd cracked the wheel and found smooth, unbroken skin. No bumps or gashes. Had she dreamed the accident? Maybe they'd made it to the stupid cabin after all. But if they had, where was Donatti?

Besides, it'd been too vivid for a dream. So maybe she was dreaming now, and she was actually lying unconscious in the wreckage. Not a cheerful thought.

She sat up slowly. Movement flickered in her peripherals, and her hand went reflexively for the piece she'd stopped carrying after Cy was born. She turned towards the motion, and a figure walked through the french doors.

Definitely not Donatti.

The guy was tall and solid. Dressed in jeans and a dark tee stretched over lean muscle, his steps were practically silent despite the sturdy black leather boots he wore. Shaggy red hair framed angular features and light brown eyes, almost gold, sparkled at her over a sexy-as-hell smile.

A hot guy in a cabin, in the middle of nowhere. This had to be a dream.

"I hope you're not too frightened," the guy said. He had a deep, soothing voice, as hypnotic as his eyes. "I couldn't leave you in your car."

"Christ, it really happened?" She shivered. *Impossible*. She'd damn near shattered her skull. Should've been in a lot worse shape than this. But she was uninjured and completely clean. Not a speck of dirt or rain anywhere. "Where's Donatti?"

His smile vanished. "Your friend," he said, and the sympathy in his tone punched her gut. "I'm afraid he didn't make it."

"No." Not a dream, but a nightmare. The world dimmed and blurred at the edges. She was going to faint. She pinched her arm hard, and the pain snapped everything into too-bright focus. A cabin. A bed. A stranger's face, lined with terrible sorrow. "He's not dead," she whispered. "Not Donatti. He always gets out of everything."

"I'm so sorry. You're in shock. I shouldn't have . . ." He hesitated, stepped closer to the bed. "I'm sorry," he said again. "There was nothing I could do for him."

Jazz closed her eyes. A sob lodged in her throat, but she choked it back. He couldn't be dead. She wouldn't believe it. The force of her denial calmed her enough to breathe evenly, and she focused on the stranger. "Who are you, and where is this?"

His smile eased back in, a tentative curl of his mouth. "My name is Seth, and this is my home. You crashed about a mile from here."

"But I whacked my head on the wheel." *Donatti's dead*. The words screamed through her, made her wince. She pushed them away. "And I'm not even hurt. Just a little stiff."

"You weren't injured when I found you. Only unconscious. Miraculous, really, considering the shape your . . . Donatti was in." Seth flashed a look of heart-melting sympathy. "Maybe you're remembering the accident wrong. The mind plays tricks when it doesn't want to recall something, especially trauma."

She shook her head. "No, I felt it. That's what knocked me out."

His brow furrowed. After a few seconds, his features relaxed with a sigh. "We should take things slowly. You're still a bit muddled," he said. "I've made coffee. Would you like a cup?"

He'd made coffee. Donatti, who'd sleep until noon every day if she didn't pull the covers off him, had gotten up before her and made the coffee the morning they'd left. She'd stumbled into the kitchen, where he'd greeted her with a steaming mug and that dangerous, adorable excitement – that usually got him into trouble – flooding his blue eyes and spilling into a crooked smile. *Road trip, babe*, he'd said. *It's been a while, hasn't it? At least nobody's chasing us this time*.

Yesterday. For fuck's sake, that was *yesterday*. And today he was—

Her stomach rebelled, and bitter bile scalded her throat. She bolted from the bed, pushed past a startled Seth and through the open doors, out to the patio railing. Leaned over and puked, emptied everything, dry-heaved again and again. *Donatti's dead*. Dee Eee Ay Dee. Deceased. Lifeless. Gone, for good this time.

Her knees buckled and she crumpled to the deck, aching like a sore tooth.

Strong arms went around her, drew her to her feet. "Easy, now," Seth murmured. "You're all right. I have you. You've got to breathe."

She let him hold her and tried to obey, snatching deep, shuddering breaths of air. Her head throbbed, the heavy acceptance of Donatti's death suddenly pushing against everything else she had to worry about – Cyrus, the ruined car, the fact that she was lost in the middle of nowhere with a man she didn't know. A man who was warm and comforting, and had probably saved her life.

"Bathroom," she murmured.

He drew back. "What?"

"I'm sorry. I think I . . . need a bathroom."

"Of course." He rubbed her shoulder, settled a hand at the small of her back and guided her gently inside. He pointed across the bedroom. "Through there, to the right. Can you make it?"

She nodded and hitched a watery smile. "Thank you."

"Any time."

Jazz followed his directions and closed herself in a spacious bathroom appointed in rustic splendour. Almost everything was wood, from the walls and floor to the cabinets enclosing the sink and the large corner bathtub. Even the toilet seat was polished wood. At the far wall, sheer curtains covered a block-glass window that stretched from floor to ceiling.

She relieved herself, and the fluttering nausea in her gut abated a little. She'd have to get it together fast. Get hold of Akila and Ian, tell them what happened. Somehow make arrangements to retrieve Donatti's body.

Jesus. They'd have to bury him. Have a funeral. The thought sent her stomach roiling again.

She fought it, stood and dressed. The shelves by the window caught her eye. Folded towels, soap, bottles of shampoo. And a . . . toaster? Frowning, she moved closer and stared. It was an old radio. A 1960s-style transistor, streaked with rust and dented near the top. Beside it was a scratched Polaroid camera with a cracked eye – not the plastic flip-out style, but a metal monster with an accordion lens. The kind that hadn't been made since the 1970s.

Her mind flashed to the decades-old wrecks they'd passed last night, and a cold splinter lodged in her chest. First classic cars, now this battered old junk. It didn't make sense.

Neither did waking up unharmed. She *knew* she'd smashed into the wheel.

She made her way to the sink and turned the faucet on with trembling hands. This was all wrong. And it wasn't a dream. She washed, splashed water on her face and glanced up, expecting to catch a glimpse of her own disturbed face.

There was no mirror.

With no concrete idea why that bothered her, she dried her
face and hands with the towel hanging by the sink and scanned
the room. No mirror on the walls or the back of the door. Block
glass window. The french doors in the bedroom had been mesh
screen panels, framed with more block glass. There were no
smooth, reflective surfaces.

The djinn could use reflective surfaces as transporters to
move them anywhere in the world that had a mirror or window
they could picture in their heads. Donatti could've used one to
get them home in a few seconds. If he wasn't dead.

The reminder dizzied her, and she grabbed the sink to keep from
falling over. *Pull it together, Jazz.* She had to get out of here, find
other people, phones, transportation. Get away from Seth, before
she found out what was wrong with him, with this place. Instinct
told her that once she discovered the truth, it'd be too late.

"Was he your husband?"

Jazz, seated at a table in a charming little kitchen that made
her want to puke some more, gripped the mug he'd given her
and avoided meeting Seth's eyes. She wanted to tell him not
to refer to Donatti in the past tense, but that wouldn't do any
good. "No," she said. "My . . . boyfriend. I guess."

Seth sat across from her. "You guess?"

"My son's father. We live together." *Lived together.* Grief
bubbled through her, and she blinked rapidly as her hands
around the coffee cup blurred. She'd never get used to this.

"You have a son?" he said.

"Yes. He's two. And I need to get home to him."

Seth didn't say anything. She looked at him, and the disturbed
expression on his face made her cold all over again. "I'm afraid
that's going to be difficult," he said.

"Why?"

"This place is a good fifty, sixty miles from anywhere. That's
a straight shot, not using the paths. And I don't own any transportation besides my feet."

"You're kidding."

"No." He sipped at his own coffee. "I grow or trap everything I eat. This coffee? Made from dandelion roots. Not bad,
either."

"But you have store-made clothes. Shampoo. Dishes." She wouldn't mention the radio or the camera. Not until she knew what the hell was going on. Not ever, if she could help it. She'd be long gone as soon as she got something useful from him. "You couldn't have made those."

"I have a deal with a couple of forest rangers. They come around once a month, bring me supplies, visit a while." He frowned again. "They were just here two days ago."

Shit. No way she'd hang around here for a month. "Well, you must have a phone, right? Or a CB or something. For emergencies. I know somebody who'd come get me." Much as she hated to admit it, roads or not, Ian could get here. He could fly.

He shook his head. "No reception towers in range. Even if there was, it's almost impossible to find the place."

"My friend could find it."

He gave a gentle laugh. "Maybe you did hit your head."

"Yeah." She had, damn it. So why wasn't she hurt? A horrifying idea occurred to her, one that made her lightheaded and nauseous all over again. "Seth," she said. "How long have I been here?"

"Just since last night." He smirked. "And I still don't know your name."

Last night. So she hadn't been unconscious for weeks, at least. For some reason that didn't bring much relief. "It's Jazz," she said.

"Jazz. With the beautiful eyes."

Her breath caught. She'd always hated her eyes – they were different colours. One brown, one green. Donatti had loved them. Called them her goddess gaze, with the same unmistakable husky tone Seth had just used. The one that said he wished for a private room and a few hours alone. She and Donatti hadn't gotten much of that since he came back. Now they never would.

"I'm sorry," Seth said before she could get good and annoyed. "That was uncalled for."

"I want to see the wreck."

He stared at her. "The what?"

"The car. The crash site. Donatti." Her throat closed around his name. "I just can't believe he's . . . gone. I have to see." And maybe she could salvage her cell phone. If she could, she'd walk the paved road, in the direction she should've chosen, until she got a signal.

Damn it. If she'd just turned around at the first sign of weirdness, that ghostly overgrown DeSoto, Donatti would still be alive. She'd killed him. And gotten herself more lost than he ever could have.

Her eyes burned with unshed tears. She should've apologized. She owed him that.

"I don't think that's a good idea." Seth spoke gently, as if comforting a child. "It's not pretty, Jazz. Not at all."

She glared across the table. "I want to see him. Take me there."

"Okay." He held up a hand. "I'll take you. But please, relax for a few minutes. Drink your coffee. I'll fix something to eat, and then we'll go."

She didn't want any goddamn coffee. She wanted to go home, to hold her baby and find some way to tell him his daddy was never coming back, to share her grief with someone who knew her, knew Donatti. But Seth had agreed to take her, and being pushy or demanding might change his mind. She'd never find it without him.

"All right," she finally said, and added, "Thank you," because it seemed appropriate.

He smiled tentatively. "Toast okay?"

"Perfect." She managed to smile back.

While he stood and walked to a cupboard, Jazz eyed the mug suspiciously. Dandelion coffee, huh? She half expected to see little yellow petals floating in it. But it looked like coffee, and smelled like coffee. She raised it to her mouth and took a tentative sip.

It tasted like heaven.

"My God," she murmured. Another swallow, and the taste coated her throat – silky smooth, nutty and sweet, better than anything Starbucks ever dreamed about serving. And somehow, familiar. "This is dandelions?"

"Mountain grown. The best kind," Seth said without turning.

"It's fantastic." She'd tasted this before. Impossible, but she knew the flavour. She drank again, trying to remember. It seemed important.

Her eyelids grew heavy. At once, she wanted nothing more than to stretch out, right here on the table, and close them. But she shouldn't want that. "Seth," she said thickly. "I think . . ."

He turned, and his concerned features appeared to distort. "Maybe you should rest before we go," he said. "Just for a little while. You've had such a hard night."

"Rest," she slurred. "I need rest."

You need to get out! He's drugged you!

Even if her mind had managed to grasp the warning, her body couldn't obey. She slid smoothly into sleep, the mug falling from her fingers and toppling on the table. An errant phrase, stark and baffling, imprinted on her thoughts just before she dropped into unconsciousness.

The nectar of the gods.

Somebody was banging on the door.

"Go 'way," Jazz muttered, pulling a pillow over her sickly throbbing head. Good lord, what had she done last night? This was one killer fucking hangover.

Killer. Last night, she'd crashed the car. Killed Donatti. And was in a remote, inaccessible cabin with a lunatic who'd drugged her to sleep.

She bolted upright. Same bedroom, same french doors, still wide open on an expanse of woods that glowed a rich gold in the slant of late afternoon light. Seth hadn't tried to lock her in. Probably because he knew she had nowhere to go if she ran. So he hadn't been lying about the miles-from-nowhere thing.

The pounding came again, from the front of the cabin. No sign of Seth answering the door. Maybe he was the one banging – but why would he knock at his own place? Sluggish hope stirred in her. She got up and headed out of the room, holding her breath. Maybe the rangers had found the car, and come back to see if Seth knew anything about it.

The bastard knew a lot about it. Too much.

She passed through a hall, the kitchen, a den and into a living room. Didn't see Seth anywhere. There, the front door. More knocking sounded as she approached it – shorter, weaker. Like whoever was out there had decided nobody was home, but they'd try one more time anyway.

Halfway across the room, she froze. She had no idea who or what was on the other side of that door. It could be a friend of Seth's, even an accomplice. She scanned the room for something useful and weapon-like, spotted a fireplace and a neatly corralled set of iron tools beside it. Perfect. She crossed to it, grabbed the heavy poker and went back to the door.

A thud from outside shook the house.

Drawing the poker back for a quick strike, Jazz turned the knob and yanked the door open. For a split second she saw no one. Then she spotted a bedraggled figure leaning on the outer wall, just to the left of the jamb.

Male, filthy, gasping for breath. Bruised and bloodied.

Donatti. Alive.

The poker fell from her numb fingers. She rushed out to him, unable to speak. Embraced him mud, blood and all. He was soaked, fever-hot beneath his torn clothes. But so real. So very not dead.

"Jazz. Thank God." He strained to speak, returned the embrace one-armed. "Knew I'd find you. Sorry it . . . took so long."

The thousand questions she wanted to ask would have to wait. "We've got to get out of here," she said. "Can you walk?"

He gave a rusty laugh. "Walked here. Would prefer to stop walking now."

"Sorry. Short version – the guy who lives here told me you were dead, and drugged me when I said I wanted to see the wreck."

"So . . . no hot shower, huh. No soft bed."

"No. And no mirrors or windows. Just block glass."

He focused on her, blue eyes filling with shock. "What?"

"Yeah. I didn't like it, either." She kissed him, fast and urgent. "I'm sorry, Donatti. Don't ask why. I'll tell you later."

One corner of his mouth lifted in a smirk. "You're the boss."

"Right." She hesitated, then moved to the door and picked up the poker. "I'm bringing this. Can you find your way back to the car?"

"Think so." He frowned. "Why? It's totalled. Can't even fix it with magic."

"My phone," she said. "Hopefully, it's not too busted. Maybe you can fix that if it is. And we'll just keep going until we get a signal, and call Ian."

"Good plan." He moved a step forward, groaned and dropped to his knees. "Then again, maybe not."

Jazz bit her lip. She hated to force him into this, ached to see him so battered, but they couldn't stay here. Seth obviously didn't want Donatti around. He'd left him for dead. "You got a better one?" she said.

"No." Jaw clenched, he struggled to one knee and got on his feet. "Let's go. I feel great. We'll run a marathon."

She blinked back tears and grabbed his hand. "You're a lousy liar, Donatti."

"Yep. Right this way, lady."

He led her off the porch, across a small lawn towards the beginnings of a thin forest. A worn dirt path, barely visible through dead leaves and browned pine needles, trickled between skinny pines and young maples. Donatti limped along at first, but managed to gain an almost normal walking pace.

Just as they set foot on the path, laughter rumbled and echoed through the air around them, as though it came from the mountain itself.

"That's Seth," Jazz whispered. "The crazy guy. How . . ."

"You survived," the rolling voice said. "How entertaining. Let the games begin."

A chill drizzled down her spine. "Oh, fuck," she said. "I remember now. The drink he gave me. The nectar of the gods." She swallowed, and it felt like a mouthful of rusted nails. "Akila made it for me a few times. Donatti . . . I think Seth is a djinn."

More cold laughter pelted them. "Run, rabbits. Find a hole and hide. I'll seek you."

Somehow, they ran.

It wasn't long before the flight was aborted. Donatti tripped over an exposed root, went down hard and didn't get up. "Gotta stop a minute," he muttered into the ground. "Sorry, babe."

Jazz glanced back. At least they were out of sight of the cabin. She crouched next to him, helped him crawl to the nearest tree and sit propped against it, cringing when he winced at her touch. "How bad is it?" she said softly.

"Don't know. Couple busted ribs, a bum arm. Don't think it's broken. Hurts like hell, though."

"Which one?"

He nodded at his left shoulder.

"Let me look." She eased the torn remains of his jacket down the arm and saw the problem. "It's dislocated," she said. "I can put it back. You'll feel a little better."

"Go for it."

She straightened his arm and bent the elbow up. "This is going to hurt."

He grunted. "Figures."

"Try to relax."

"Got any booze?"

"Fresh out."

"Okay. I'll just man up and faint." He closed his eyes and leaned his head back.

She debated doing it the fast way – a lot of pain, over quickly. But she didn't want to do any more damage if she could help it. The slow way was just as painful and drawn out, with a lot less chance of tearing muscle or ligaments. She grabbed his wrist, moved his hand against his chest and rotated arm and shoulder out slowly. He hissed through clenched teeth, let out a guttural shout when she hit full extension.

It took three tries to set the joint back. By the time she finished, sweat bathed his face and washed away some of the grime. "Oh, Christ," he gasped. "Thank . . . you . . ."

"I did warn you."

"No, I mean it's better. A hundred times better. Shit, I think I really can run a marathon now." He grinned at her. "Or at least walk one. Just have to . . . sit a minute."

"I'll join you." She plopped on the ground next to him and scanned the area, taking in the increasing density of the trees, the waning light. They had maybe an hour before full dark. Should be able to make a mile. Of course, they also had no idea what Seth was planning. "Maybe we should talk. Try to figure things out," she said. "Let's start with you."

Donatti pulled himself straighter. "Well, I couldn't make

anything happen to the car," he said. "I tried, but it was resisting or something. Then I got knocked out in the crash."

Jazz frowned. "Resisting?"

"Yeah. Pushing me back, kind of. Damn. Ian's really going to have to explain this magic stuff better." He paused, winced and pressed a hand to his ribs. "Anyway, when I came around, you were gone. I freaked out. Got away from the car – think I was screaming for you. And while I was flopping around in the mud, an animal attacked me. A fox. Big one." His brow furrowed. "Thing went straight for my throat. Not very fox-like. I thought maybe I was hallucinating."

She understood where his thoughts were going. The djinn were born into clans named after animals, because they could assume their clan's animal form. Ian was Dehbei, the wolf clan. She'd seen him go wolf once. Huge, beautiful, deadly wolf. And as a more-or-less human, he had shaggy, wolf-coloured hair, and a wolf's eyes. "Seth has red hair," she said. "And his eyes are . . . well, like a fox's."

"Motherfucker." His jaw firmed. "Djinn can only kill humans when they're animals. He told you I was gone because he thought I was. He sure as hell tried to make it that way."

"So how'd you get out of it?"

He smirked. "I played dead. You're supposed to do that with bears. Thought it might work for a fox. Apparently it works with a djinn, too." One hand went to his throat. "Bastard tore me a good one. Blood everywhere. I think . . . I tried to heal myself. Must've done something right."

"You're not completely hopeless."

"Coming from you, that's a compliment." He reached for her hand, and she gave it to him. "I could feel you," he said hoarsely. "That's how I found you. It was like you were whispering in my ear."

"Oh, yeah?" She squeezed his hand. "What was I saying?"

"Let's see. It was something like, 'Get your ass here, right now, before I kick it all the way back upstate.'"

Her own laughter surprised her. "Yeah, that does sound like me," she said.

"So there's my story," he said. "What's yours?"

She told him everything, from waking up in the cabin bedroom thinking it was a dream, to realizing too late that she'd been drugged. "Those things he has in the bathroom. The radio, the camera," she said. "They threw me when I thought he was just a guy who couldn't be more than thirty. But he's djinn."

"And djinn don't age," Donatti said. "He wrecked the car. That was the resistance. How much you want to bet he did the same thing with those other cars we saw?"

"Jesus," she whispered. "And the passengers . . ."

"Let's not stick around long enough to find out what he does with them."

The woods were strangely silent. Other than a faint wind rustling dry leaves and their own steps on the forest floor, there was nothing. Not a single creaking branch or calling bird. No signs of other life.

They'd been walking for about fifteen minutes when Jazz slowed and came to a stop beside a big fir tree. "Donatti," she said. "Does this look familiar to you?"

"No. It's a goddamn tree. We're surrounded by trees, and—" He looked closer. His gaze found what she'd noticed already, the lower branch that was broken and splintered at the trunk, hanging at a sharp angle, almost touching the ground. "We passed this before," he said.

"Yeah. We just walked in a big fucking circle." She kicked at the ground, spraying a cloud of dead needles in the air. "This is still the path you came up, right? So apparently it's changed directions in the past few hours."

Something rustled in the brush ahead. A flash of red fur darted between branches and vanished again. The bastard was following them.

"Son of a bitch." Jazz gripped the poker two-handed and strode for the brush.

Donatti grabbed her. "Whoa, killer," he said. "That doesn't work with djinn. Remember?"

"Yeah. I can't take him out. But it'll still hurt when I smash his fucking skull." She'd always taken care of herself, so being defenceless pissed her off. Regular people couldn't kill a djinn. In order to enter the human realm, they had to be bound to an object, a tether. And only destroying the tether would destroy the djinn. You could empty a machine gun into one and he – or she – would live through it. Since Donatti was only part djinn, he'd still die like a human.

Of course, *he* could destroy the djinn. With magic. That pissed her off, too.

"Don't," he murmured. "I've got a feeling we're going to need this guy."

"Why? You planning to make a coat out of him?"

"Let's keep walking." He tried to guide her ahead. She resisted. He frowned. "Jazz, please. Trust me."

Right. Trust the man who couldn't plan a takeout dinner without an instruction book and a personal coach. The man who'd ditched her, almost gotten her arrested, left her alone and pregnant, then damn near gotten her killed when he popped back into her life like nothing had happened.

The man who saved my life, and Cy's, when a djinn tried to kill us. The man I was just crying over a few hours ago when I thought he was dead.

Damn it. Maybe she did love him.

"All right," she said. "I'll trust you. This time."

"Your confidence is overwhelming." He led her back to the faded thread of the path, and lowered his voice to a whisper while they walked. "Listen, I don't want him to know about my . . . uh, abilities yet," he said. "I think we're gonna have to outsmart this guy."

"Great. We're dead, then."

"Thanks a lot." He scowled, but the expression changed to a smile when he caught the laughter in her eyes. "Anyway, I've got an idea. Hopefully it'll stop us from walking in circles."

"I hope it works fast," she muttered. "We're losing daylight, and —" Something rustled behind them. Jazz whirled around, reflexively bringing the poker back over her shoulder, ready to swing.

The fox sat on the path, twenty feet away, watching them with glittering eyes and a grin that was almost human. The thing was so big, it made her head hurt. There weren't any foxes the size of Saint Bernards. The longer she stared at it, the more she wanted to . . .

Go to him. Stroke his fur. Lie down on the cool ground and let him warm you, soothe you.

"Wrong way, babe." Donatti's low, urgent voice snapped her back. "Keep moving. Don't look at it."

For a few seconds her feet wouldn't obey the command to walk. She managed a step, then another, and the small victories shattered the remains of the trance. She moved. But she couldn't resist a quick glance behind them.

The fox was gone.

She shuddered. Should've been used to things disappearing by now, but it still creeped her out. "So, what are we doing?" she whispered.

"Well." He stared straight ahead, like he didn't want to tell her. "Djinn magic works on need, right? So I figured if I really needed to find the car, we'd find it."

"That's your big idea?"

"Yeah. You got a better one?"

She sighed. "No. Unless you've got a helicopter up your ass."

"I keep telling Ian we need one of those, but he won't listen. Maybe you can talk him into it."

"Right. And maybe I could convince Charles Manson to take up knitting." Ian had been royalty or something, back in the djinn realm before he came here. Nobody talked him into anything. Except Akila, and even she didn't win half the time.

They walked in silence while the sun slipped low and stuffed the woods full of deeper shadows. Still no sign of the road, or any indication of a break in the forest, but at least they didn't seem to be passing the same places. Maybe Donatti's crazy idea was working.

"Poor little lost rabbits."

Seth's voice broke the stillness. At least it wasn't a booming echo this time. Jazz glanced around, didn't see him anywhere. Then she faced forward and spotted him standing on a thick branch, halfway up a tree loaded with blazing red leaves. "We're not lost, asshole," she said.

Donatti elbowed her. "On't-day alk-tay im-hay," he muttered.

She gaped at him. "You're not serious. Pig latin?"

"Shh."

She rolled her eyes and shut her mouth. Looked back at the tree. No Seth.

"Oh, but you are."

This time the voice came from the right, and Seth popped into view perched on a moss-covered boulder. He laughed. "By all means, keep going this way. Have fun when you get to the gorge."

He was fucking with them. Had to be.

Didn't he?

"Jazz." Behind them now, his voice a seductive swirl. "You don't have to die out here with him. Come with me. I'll take care of you."

Donatti squeezed her hand. She kept walking. Didn't look back.

Seth materialized ahead of them. Grinning. "It's a long drop down the gorge," he said. "You won't see it in the dark. If you survive the fall, I hope you can swim."

"Fuck off," Donatti snarled.

Seth's mouth opened, and laughter oozed out like blood. He faded into nothing.

Jazz waited a few minutes. "I thought you said don't talk to him."

"So sue me."

"You're cute when you're jealous."

"Hmph." He coughed once, slowed and pointed ahead. A grin eased on to his lips. "I'm cuter when I'm right."

She followed the gesture – and saw the wide swath cutting through the trees, just visible in the fading light. It had to be the road. "I'll be damned," she said. "It worked."

"You can thank me later."

They made their way to the clearing. No stretch of pavement ever looked so beautiful. She would've knelt down and kissed asphalt if there wasn't a witness. "So the bastard was just trying to confuse us," she said. "Gorge, my—"

A strangled gasp from Donatti cut her mid-curse. She followed his stricken gaze, and saw the obliterated wreck down the shoulder on the opposite side of the road. Not the sedan, but a mid-1960s Impala, weathered and weed-choked. And bursting from the shattered windshield, lying spread-eagled on the hood with legs still inside the car, was an aged and decimated human corpse.

Jazz stared at her feet until she was sure she wouldn't vomit. "Well," she said in a choked rasp. "You did find a car."

★　　★　　★

They still had to get to the sedan. It was on the road somewhere. Even if there might've been a chance at finding something useful in the Impala, Jazz wasn't about to go looking through it. This time, she let Donatti pick the direction.

Of course, he decided they had to go past the dead guy.

As they walked past the wreck, Donatti wore a look she recognized, and wasn't too happy about. It was an echo of the look of furious determination Ian always wore right before the two of them headed off to destroy one of the evil snake djinn, the Morai. On such missions there was always a chance they wouldn't come back alive.

"You're thinking about being a hero, aren't you?" she said.

His mouth slashed a firm line. "He's killing people up here. We have to stop him."

"By ourselves?" It wasn't like she'd been opposed to the whole Morai extermination thing. She'd seen what they were capable of doing, to humans and to other djinn. Plus, they turned into snakes. She hated snakes. Hell, she'd more or less encouraged Donatti to help Ian when it turned out he was the only one who could. But Ian's magic was a lot stronger and more reliable. Of the few things Donatti could do, he'd only perfected invisibility. None of his spells ever went the way he planned them. "Maybe we should get Ian before we try to take this guy on," she said.

He didn't answer right away, but she could feel the anger radiating from him. Finally, he sighed and said, "I guess you're right."

She offered a sympathetic grimace. "You know, Donatti, I understand how it feels."

"What, chicks get penis envy too?"

She laughed. "Not exactly. I meant . . . being helpless. Not having what it takes and knowing it. It's frustrating as hell."

"Yeah. Nothing like a case of magic blue balls to get the blood pumping." He gave her a one-armed hug. "I'm sorry you have to go through this so much. Believe me, if I could give this stuff away, you'd have it."

"No, thanks. I like being normal."

"Babe, you are anything *but* normal."

"Is that a compliment?"

"Yeah." He grinned and rubbed her arm. "It is."

They rounded a curve and found the ruined sedan on the shoulder, its crumpled hood nosed against a tree. Broken glass, plastic fragments and snarled bits of metal sprayed across the pavement. The driver's side door lay on the ground in front of the car, hinges torn and twisted, its window and mirror completely shattered.

In fact, every bit of glass on the car had been reduced to pieces.

Trying to ignore the stone weight in her gut, Jazz leaned the poker against the side of the sedan and crawled carefully into the driver's seat. She grabbed the wheel to steady herself, and felt the tacky residue of what had to be her blood. She'd definitely hit it hard. At least she'd remembered that right.

The coiled charger cord was still plugged into the lighter socket. With the last faint light dying outside, she couldn't make out much else beyond shadows. She picked the cord up, already knowing from the non-weight that the phone wasn't attached any more, even before she saw the bare jack. It must've slid down on the floor somewhere. She hoped.

"Donatti," she called. "You have a flashlight in here?"

"Glove box. There should be a few of those packages of mini-donuts there, too."

She glanced back at him. "You're thinking about food? Now?"

"Hey, I haven't eaten since yesterday. I'm starving."

Her stomach rumbled suddenly, as though the idea of starving had kicked off a protest in there somewhere. She hadn't even thought about eating until he mentioned it. Practically salivating, she reached over, popped the compartment open and felt inside. It was empty.

"Fuck!"

"What, right now?"

"Can it, Donatti." She forced a giggle into a snort. There he went again, making her laugh when she wanted to cry. She backed out and brushed at the debris clinging to her jeans. "There's nothing in there. The box wasn't damaged in the crash, but the stuff's gone."

"Oh. That kind of 'fuck'." Frowning, he circled the sedan and stared at the trunk. "See if this'll pop?"

She reached down and pulled the release. There was a heavy clunking *sproing*, and the trunk eased open a crack.

Donatti wrenched it open and swore. "Okay, our bags are gone, too. So's the jack and tyre iron. And my gear. Damn it, I'm getting sick of re-buying that pick set."

"Gear? You're supposed to be retired."

"I am. I just . . . like to practice. Keep the skills up."

She folded her arms. "How can you *practise* stealing?"

"You still drive."

"That's different. And you didn't answer the question."

There was a hollow thump, and Seth appeared on the buckled roof of the car. "Are we having a lover's spat?" he said. "By all means, don't let me interrupt."

Jazz backed slowly towards Donatti, keeping the poker hidden behind her back. Hopefully he'd keep his mouth shut about the weapon. "We still ignoring him?" she said when she reached him.

"No. Where's our shit, mountain man?"

Seth gave an exaggerated shrug. "Could be anywhere," he said. "Lots of wild animals around here. Scavengers. Bears, wolves . . . foxes."

"Uh-huh. Every fox needs a cellphone, right?"

"Is that what you're trying to find?" Grinning, Seth leaped lightly to the ground. "I thought you might be looking for that interesting little set of tools in the black case. Thief."

"Ex-thief," Donatti said. "Retirement's great. You should think about retiring from the psycho racket."

"Oh, I'm not crazy." Seth's gaze fastened on Jazz, and dizziness washed through her. "It gets so cold on the mountain at night." He moved toward them, not sparing Donatti a second glance. "Come with me, Jazz. I'll keep you warm. We'll embrace in front of a roaring fire, you and me. Forever." In the near-dark, he seemed to glow.

Lip curled, Jazz brought the poker around and swung it full-force against his skull. He dropped like a rock. "Embrace that, asshole," she said.

Donatti coughed. "Whoa. Nice one, babe. Not exactly what I had in mind, but that'll work."

"What did you have in mind, insulting him to death?" She

lowered the poker, ran a hand through her hair. "Besides, he was going to change. And probably try to kill you again." All the djinn started glowing right before they transformed.

He grinned. "My hero."

"Shut up."

"Right." He glanced down at Seth, who hadn't moved. It looked like he wasn't even breathing – but he was far from dead. Eventually he'd come around and heal himself. And then he'd be really angry. "Guess we'd better get going before he wakes up," Donatti said.

"Uh-huh. And what's the plan now? We can't reach Ian, and it's fifty miles to anything."

"Not exactly. There's one place we can get to."

It took a few seconds to sink in. "You can't be serious."

"Easiest way to catch a fox is in its den."

She opened her mouth, closed it. "That might actually be a smart idea."

"Yeah. It's gotta be a fluke. Don't worry, it won't happen again."

Damn it, why did he have to be so frigging cute? As much as she bashed his constant, often ridiculous jokes, nobody ever made her laugh like he did. For the first time, she actually wished they had made it to the cabin – because right now, she'd be dragging him to the bedroom. If they made it that far. "Okay," she said. "But there's two problems. One, I can barely see you now, and it's going to be pitch black in a few minutes. Don't know about you, but my night vision's shot."

He cleared his throat. "Well, maybe I can do that flame-ball thing Ian does."

I doubt it. Since saying that wouldn't exactly boost his confidence, she opted for a cheerful tone that fell flat. "Can't hurt to try."

He fell silent. Probably trying to concentrate. After a minute, there was a dim glow that brightened steadily – not floating over his hands, where Ian usually formed a light, but coming from the front end of the wrecked car.

Brow furrowed, she circled around and looked. The intact left headlight burned at full strength, cutting a path through the darkness ahead.

Donatti came up behind her. "Guess my magic's a little more modern than Ian's."

"Hey, it's a light." She grinned at him. "Think you can keep it going if I take it out?"

"I hope so."

She crouched to take a look. It was an older car, with a one-piece headlamp instead of a halogen bulb and lens. It'd provide a more focused light than a bare bulb, but it might be a bitch getting it out. "You don't happen to have a dime, do you?"

He reached in a pocket, came out with a handful of coins and pinched a dime free. "Change from the donuts," he said. "Which I didn't even get to eat."

She took it and started on the first screw. "If we get out of this, I'll make you some donuts."

"You can *make* donuts? With ingredients and stuff?" There was something that suspiciously resembled awe in his voice. "Oh my God, I love you."

"I make a mean funnel cake, too."

"You're killing me. I'm going to drown in my own drool."

She managed to get all four screws out, and pulled the metal frame loose. The hood was already open a few feet, so she reached inside and yanked the plug free from the back of the headlamp. The light still shone. If she didn't know it was magic, she would've freaked a little. "Here," she said, handing it to Donatti. "All right. How long do you think he'll be out?"

He shrugged. "You put a nice dent in his head. I'd guess a while."

"Might not be long enough. We'll need time to do . . . whatever we're doing." She retrieved the poker from the ground. "Maybe I should whack him a few more times."

Donatti shuddered hard enough to shake the light. He'd always been opposed to violence. Didn't even like to swat flies. A strange trait for a criminal. "You sure you have to do that?"

"We've got to keep him from following us, for as long as we can."

"I guess." He frowned. "So the light thing's taken care of. What's the other problem?"

"He keeps finding us," she said. "If surprising him is the only advantage we have, we've got to keep him from expecting us at his place. Throw him off our . . . scent." She moved towards the car, a glimmer of inspiration forming. "He's a fox, right?"

"Yeah. So?"

"So he's probably tracking us by scent." She reached through the door-shaped gap in the driver's side and felt under the seat until her fingers brushed cool metal, and dislodged a black aerosol can. "Pepper spray," she said.

He laughed. "What are you doing with that?"

"Last resort for a getaway, in case I get pulled over and made."

"You're supposed to be retired."

"Why do you think I didn't break your teeth for hanging on to your pick set?" She smiled and gestured at the unconscious Seth. "So . . . dose him in the face?"

"Hell yeah."

"If he moves, I'm clocking him."

"Deal."

She strode over, spray in one hand, poker in the other. Holding the can a foot from the unconscious djinn's face, she pulled the trigger and held until the stuff covered him like a wet mask.

He moved. She clocked him, and he stopped.

She tucked the spray in a pocket and went back to Donatti, who was staring at the sky, the wreck – anywhere but at the bloodied figure on the ground. "I'm done now," she said, unable to hold back a smirk. "We can head out any time."

"Now's good." He grabbed her hand. "Don't let go, okay?"

"Never."

With the fading light and Donatti's slightly improved needing-to-find-something spell, they made good time back to the cabin. Seth had left some lights on. On the plus side, they'd be able to look around without arousing suspicion if he happened to come back. But the lights also meant that if he snuck up on them while invisible, he'd see them right away.

Donatti ditched the headlamp. They went to the front door, expecting to find it locked, but it opened right up. Surprised, Jazz took a closer look. There was no deadbolt, no chain, not even an entry latch on the knob. He couldn't have locked it if he wanted to.

Of course, he didn't have to worry about uninvited guests. The only people who showed up here were the ones he sabotaged.

"Okay. Here's what I'm thinking," Donatti said. "We find his tether and I threaten to destroy him unless he helps us get back to civilization. He's got to have some way to move. Then, we get Ian and figure out what we should do with this guy."

Jazz frowned. "How about we find his tether, you skip the threat part and just destroy him?"

"I'm not killing anybody if I can help it," he said. "This guy isn't Morai. I don't know enough about him to make that decision."

"And if he doesn't let us go?"

He closed his eyes. "Then I guess I'll have to go through with it," he said. "But destroying him is the absolute last thing I'm going to try."

"Fine. As long as it's somewhere on your list." Her conscience muttered a protest and she told it to shut up. She'd always held the opinion that if someone was about to kill you, you had every right to kill them first. And she'd exercised that right more than once. Lately, though, Donatti's insistence that killing could and should be avoided almost every time – coupled with the fact that he was still alive – had been chipping away at her beliefs. As if she didn't have enough guilt to deal with. "All right, what are we looking for?" she said.

"It'll be something metal and relatively small. Not a car or a fridge. Something that looks like it belongs in a museum."

"So it wouldn't be a 1960s radio."

He shook his head. "Djinn don't have radios. Whatever it is, it'll have come from their realm. A coin, a dagger, a piece of jewellery."

"Right."

They stayed together. The living room turned up nothing, in plain sight, under the furniture cushions, or buried in the ashes of the fireplace. In the kitchen, one cabinet held exactly enough dishes for two people, another was filled with cardboard canisters of salt and most of the rest were empty save for a few canned goods, a bag of flour and a box of sugar. The fridge and freezer contained plastic jugs of water and unlabelled lumps of foil-wrapped meat. Deer, Jazz told herself firmly. Anything else was unthinkable.

The only out-of-place items in the bathroom were the ones she'd noticed the first time. That left the bedroom. There, they lifted the mattress, shook out the pillows, opened and removed every drawer in the small dresser, poked and prodded a closet for hidden panels. Nothing. Not even a suspicious dust bunny.

"So much for leverage." Jazz sat down slowly on the bed. "Maybe we should start walking now. We could make fifty miles in a couple of days, if that road actually goes anywhere. And if Seth doesn't find us."

"He will." Donatti crossed to the screened french doors, closed against the cool night. "What's out here?"

"A deck, and a billion trees."

He opened the doors and walked out. She heard him clomping around on the plank floor, his steps moving away, pausing, coming back. He stuck his head in. "Think I found something."

"Tell me it's a Hummer." Christ, what she wouldn't give for an off-road vehicle right now. Anything, even a little puddle-jumper Jeep but she'd sell her soul for a Hummer.

"Sorry. You'll have to settle for the consolation prize. Come out here."

Reluctantly, she stood and followed him. He led her to the left side of the deck and gestured, over the rail and down. "Bet you a dollar there's something good in there."

It was a storm cellar. Double wooden doors angled up from the ground, held shut with a hasp and padlock.

Jazz smiled. "Race you." Before he could react, she vaulted over the rail and landed on the ground five or six feet below, bending her knees to absorb the impact.

"Do I look like Olympic-quality material to you?" Donatti practically groaned. "Guy's been here at least five decades. Should've built some goddamn stairs on this thing by now." He threw one leg over the railing, struggled to bring the other one around, and slid into the drop, stumbling when he hit the dirt.

"Can you make it to the doors, or should I fashion you a makeshift crutch out of sticks and vines?"

"Ha. Ha." He walked over to the cellar and inspected the padlock, then straightened and patted various pockets. "Gotta have something . . . ah. Have this open in a sec." He worked a slender length of metal free from the hem of his jacket. A lock shim. "Emergency supply," he said with a grin.

She watched him work the lock, mentally ticking off the time. When the arm popped, she said, "Twenty-two seconds. I'm impressed."

"I'd be impressed if I could figure out a way to close it back up from the inside." He slid the lock out, popped the clasp and replaced it on the hook. "Oh, well. Here we go."

He pulled one door open, then the other. Inside was a rough wooden staircase, descending into darkness beyond the pale wash of light cast from the bedroom. There was a darkened light bulb with a pull chain mounted at the top of the doorway. Donatti walked down steps until he could reach the chain, and turned the light on.

They descended to an opening framed with rough planks of lumber. Donatti had to stoop to get through, but Jazz had a few inches of clearance. Being five-foot-nothing came in handy sometimes. Through the doorway was a small, earth-cooled room. Enough light came in from the stairwell to make out the shapes of several dead animals hanging from the walls – rabbits, birds, a skinned deer. Seth's meat locker.

"Yummy," Donatti said. "Dinner."

"I'm not even close to hungry enough for raw meat." Jazz scanned the place for a switch or a bulb. Didn't see a light, but she did see the other door, knobless and detectable only by the small hinges set flush with the boarded walls. "There," she said, and pointed.

Nodding, Donatti moved to the door and pushed it open without resistance. The light wouldn't stretch through the doorway. He felt along the inside, flicked something, and a glow sputtered and steadied.

"Holy Christ," he said. "Seth must be part squirrel."

He walked through and stepped aside, giving her a view of the room. It was bigger than the meat locker, the wood walls sanded and stained. And it was full of . . . stuff.

She went in and closed the door behind her. It was hard to decide where to start processing everything in here. There was a stack of tyres arranged by size, biggest to smallest. An intact leather-finish bucket seat, probably from the DeSoto. Three mismatched bumpers mounted vertically on the back wall. A pair of fuzzy dice and a coon-tail antenna decoration. Four old suitcases arranged side-by-side on top of a steamer trunk. Three folding metal TV trays – one with pairs of sunglasses, another with wrist and pocket watches, the third containing rings, necklaces, bracelets and earrings. None of the jewellery was ancient or museum-worthy.

And then there were the dummies.

Six life-sized carved wooden figures lined up along the left-hand wall. Four female, two male. Each of them was dressed in clothing that wasn't sold in department stores any more. The mannequins wore 1950s and 1960s dress – bellbottoms, a crinoline skirt, shirts with ruffles and checked patterns and butterfly collars and tie-dye. One of the males wore a houndstooth suit.

This stuff sure as hell hadn't come from a vintage shop.

"Looks like this is the luggage department." Donatti was in front of the suitcases. He moved them to the floor and opened the steamer trunk. "Thought so. Here's our bags."

"See if my phone's in there." Jazz tore her gaze from the dummies and drifted to the stack of tyres, trying to shake off a serious case of chills. She wanted to believe that the clothes came from the suitcases, and not from the bodies of people who'd crashed up here; that the carvings were just random figures, and not likenesses of Seth's victims.

She concentrated on finding something that resembled a tether. All the tyres were mounted on rims, so he couldn't have stashed it inside one. While Donatti rifled through the contents of the trunk, she opened the suitcases one by one. All empty. She moved back to the TV tables and stared at the jewellery, as though she could intimidate one of the pieces into being what they needed.

"I found your phone," Donatti said. "Sort of."

She turned to him, and he held out a handful of plastic shards and broken circuitry.

"Son of a bitch," she said.

"Yeah. I think it's safe to say I can't fix it." He let the debris fall back into the trunk and glanced across the room. "Man, those things are creepy."

"At least he didn't stuff and mount the corpses." Frowning, Jazz looked at the mannequins again. Blank wooden eyes stared back at her, giving nothing away. Each of them was posed straight on, arms at their sides, except the third one in – a female in a flowered sundress, with one hand outstretched.

And there was something in that hand. Something metallic.

She walked over and slid the object free. It was a row of copper tubes, even at one end and varying length at the other in descending order, banded together with thin strips of silver. Panpipes. There were symbols, almost like Arabic lettering, etched into the tubes near the even end. The thing could've stepped out of a Greek myth. She turned and held it out toward Donatti. "I'd call this museum-worthy," she said.

He grinned. "Jackpot."

"Okay, we've got the tether." She went to him and handed it over. "Now we . . ."

"Wait for Seth."

"And what'll we do when he gets here?"

"Um. Tackle him?"

"Somehow, I don't see that working."

Donatti stared at the pipes, turned them over in his hands. "Wish I could read djinn writing," he said. "Maybe I can get Ian to teach me."

A muffled sound drew their attention. A bang, like a cellar door closing. Another bang followed. "You picked the wrong hole, rabbits," Seth called. "This one only goes down."

Donatti took a step back. "Queens," he whispered – and vanished.

Jazz might have loved him, but she didn't like him very much right now.

She knew exactly what he meant. When they were both still working, pre-Cyrus, they'd done a job in Queens lifting some electronics from a high-end specialty place. The owner had showed up in the middle of the gig, and Donatti had sent Jazz out to play the lost and horny distraction while he legged the rest of the stuff out the back. With one word, he'd just told her to seduce Seth while he did . . . whatever.

He'd better do whatever real goddamn fast. If she had to go any further than second base, she'd shove his picks up his nose. One at a time. Slowly.

Footsteps approached the door to the room. She debated throwing herself at him, telling him that he was the sexiest thing on two legs, but Seth didn't strike her as stupid. She'd have to play things a little less directly.

At the last second, she remembered something critical. She'd bashed his skull in – and she wasn't supposed to know he'd survive. Time to change tactics. She moved to the steamer trunk and started climbing inside.

The door banged open just as she was swinging her leg over. She stared at him and let out a startled cry. "You," she whispered. "I killed you."

Seth laughed, a harsh sound far from his earlier indulgent amusement. "You must not have hit me as hard as you thought."

"But there was blood. I saw it."

"A scratch." He walked closer, his gaze sweeping the room. "Where's your friend?"

She let herself shiver, put a tremor in her voice. "We got separated in the woods."

"So the thief taught you how to pick locks."

"We're both thieves. Retired. We were on vacation." She swallowed. "Why are you trying to kill us?"

"I wouldn't have hurt you, Jazz with the beautiful eyes." The beginnings of a smile eased across his lips. "Your friend was in the way. Sadly, he'll probably die in the forest. It's so easy to get lost out here."

"Lost," she whispered. Not all of her confusion was faked. Dizziness swirled around her, and her thoughts tried to centre themselves on Seth, on touching him, holding him. He was hypnotizing her again. *Come on, Donatti, do something.*

"Yes, but you're not lost any more." Seth closed more of the distance between them, his eyes practically flashing. "You've found me. And now you'll stay, won't you?"

Stay with you. It was an effort not to speak the words. Part of her wanted to cry out *yes!* and fall into his arms swooning, like some idiot woman in a herbal shampoo commercial.

Seth's smile dropped away. "I sense . . . impossible. You can't be."

"Do these things actually work?" Donatti popped into view across the room behind Seth, holding the panpipes. They were

splashed with blood – his own. One of the things he needed for
the spell to destroy them. "Not much of a musician myself, but
this seems pretty cool."

The moment Seth turned to look at him, Jazz felt normal
again. She held off on the sigh of relief, though. She still had
no idea what Donatti was planning, and if Seth was like Ian, he
could do just about anything.

"Lost in the woods, are you?" Seth glared at him. "Give me
those."

"Not until you tell us where your mirror is. I know you have
one somewhere."

"My . . ." Seth's brow furrowed in what looked like genuine
confusion. Then his expression shifted to mockery. "Ah, I see,"
he said. "A human who believes he knows something about us.
What do you think you're going to do with my pipes, human?
Make me grant wishes?"

Donatti grinned. "I'm not human," he said. "At least, not
completely."

"So you're a thief *and* a liar."

"Oh, yeah?" He stopped smiling. "*Ani lo'ahmar nar—*"

"Stop!" Seth cried.

A shiver went through Jazz, genuine this time. That was the
destruction spell. Damn. Donatti had gotten a lot better at
bluffing.

Seth took a few staggering steps and sat down hard in the
bucket seat. "Who are you?" he said hoarsely.

"Hold on." Jazz stepped out of the trunk and crossed the
room to stand with Donatti, giving Seth a wide berth. "Before
we get to the Q&A here, can't you do something to make sure
he doesn't throw any magic at us?"

"I don't have to. He's just about tapped." Donatti almost
looked sorry for him. "He would've had to transform to heal
himself, and then change back. That takes a lot."

Seth fixed him with an astonished stare. "How could you
know that?"

"Because I hang around with a couple of djinn. And I'm
descended from one."

"Who?"

"Gahiji-an, but we call him Ian."

"The Dehbei prince." All the colour faded from Seth's face. "I'd heard . . . he was supposed to have been killed. Centuries ago, when he was banished here."

Donatti grimaced. "Oh, nice. I'm sure he'll be thrilled to hear he's dead. I wouldn't tell him that, if I was you. He might kill you for it."

"By the gods." Seth looked away and slumped in the seat. "I don't believe this," he muttered. "All this time, and I . . . wait. You said there were other djinn. Who? Where are they?"

"Wait. First, it's your turn," Donatti said. "Who are you really?"

He looked at them with hollow eyes. "My name is Seti-el, of the Anapi clan," he said. "At least, I was. I'm sure my clan's disowned me by now."

"Just a guess, but I'm thinking Anapi means fox," Jazz said.

Seth nodded. "Tricksters and thieves, the lot of us. Some more than others," he said with a healthy dose of bitterness. "That's why I'm here, instead of in my own realm. I was tricked into an arranged marriage to someone I despised, someone who despised me and only wanted the bond so she could make me miserable forever. I couldn't change things, so rather than marry her, I came here. I'm sure you noticed I have no windows or mirrors in this place. It's so they can't find me and force me to come back."

A glimmer of sympathy passed through Jazz, and she swept it aside with the image of the wrecked cars and the corpse. "So you settled down and started killing people," she said.

"No! I've never killed anyone." Seth let out a shuddering breath. "The dead man on the road wasn't my doing. He crashed deliberately. Took his own life. I never came into contact with him." He looked straight ahead, and his gaze unfocused.

"Yeah, right." She frowned at him. "Even if that's true, it means you caused the other wrecks. And you tried to rip Donatti's throat out."

He shook his head and looked at Donatti. "I knocked you down, yes. But I only nipped you, and you passed out from your other injuries. The blood was rabbit's blood. I wouldn't have let you die."

"So I didn't heal myself? Damn." Donatti raised an eyebrow. "That's seriously fucked up. Why would you do that?"

"To see how you'd react." Seth stared at the floor. "I'd been here fifty years, alone, before humans started coming into the area. They were building that road. At first I only watched them, but when I realized whatever they were planning would bring them to my cabin, I . . . scared them off. Convinced them the place was haunted. And it was fun. The first entertainment I'd had in decades. Of course, after that it was years before anyone else came this way. A couple who'd gotten lost. So I decided to have some fun with them."

"Let me get this straight," Jazz said. "You crash people's cars and chase them around the woods because you're *bored?*"

He offered a miserable nod. "The first time, I didn't play with them long. I healed their injuries before they woke from the crash, 'miraculously' unharmed. I let them see the fox, and turned myself invisible to play ghost. I created a few small illusions. Nothing too terrible. And when I'd finished, I brought them to the nearest town with altered memories and enough money to replace what I'd stolen. Your money is easy to reproduce." A half-smile appeared and vanished. "But with each new arrival, I kept them a little longer, and played more elaborate tricks, until . . . well, you know what I've done with you."

"Yeah. You tried to make me think Donatti was dead so I'd sleep with you."

"I've been lonely," he whispered. "I'm afraid that's no excuse. But you are the most beautiful human I've ever seen and I couldn't resist trying."

Donatti made a disgusted sound. "Good thing it didn't work, or I wouldn't be able to resist kicking your ass. Not that I would've succeeded. But I'd try."

Jazz stopped herself from making a reflexive caveman comment. Usually she hated it when he went all defend-the-little-woman on her. Tonight, it didn't annoy her so much. "If you're so lonely, why didn't you just move somewhere else?" she said. "You know, somewhere with a population bigger than one plus a bunch of rabbits and bears."

"Djinn can't . . . I mean, it didn't seem possible that a djinn could live with humans, or form relationships with them. I thought I'd be an outcast. I'm already shunned by one realm, and I wouldn't do well if this one hated me, too." He blinked a few times. "But it obviously worked for Gahiji-an, or you wouldn't exist, Donatti. And the two of you are together."

"Yes, we are," Donatti said with a little scowl. "Very together."

A smile forced itself across Jazz's mouth. Damn, he was cute when he was jealous. "You'll do fine," she said. "There's plenty of people more freaky than you."

Seth almost smiled. "I believe you. But then . . . I don't know. It's such fun here, and I'm hardly hurting anyone. There are so many of you humans. If I had access to more, the temptation would be great to—"

"Don't even think about it," Jazz said. "I may be human, but I *will* kick your ass. And it won't be so easy getting up again next time."

Donatti gave Seth a withering stare. If she didn't know him, she'd be afraid of that look. "She will," he said. "And when she's done, I'm sure Ian's gonna be next in line. He will hear about you, and he's not going to like it. We'll be watching."

"Well, if you put it that way." Seth blanched and looked away. "I'll stop. Really."

"So it's settled, then," she said. "You're out of here."

"Maybe." Seth spent a few minutes staring at the floor. Finally, his features grew resolute and he stood slowly. "I think I will," he said. "Yes. I'll join the world. There are so many things I'd like to see. Disney World. The Sahara desert. Strip clubs."

Jazz laughed, and even Donatti cracked a smirk. "I guarantee you'll enjoy at least one of those things," she said. "But you have to stop fucking with people. Trust me, that isn't going to go over too great in civilization."

"I swear I won't hurt anyone. Just a few harmless tricks now and then."

"Really. And what, exactly, do you consider harmless?"

Seth grinned. "I was thinking of making Mount Rushmore disappear."

"Holy shit," Donatti said. "That'd be awesome! It'd drive so many people crazy trying to figure it out. The brilliant scientists, the conspiracy nuts, the FBI, the—"

"Donatti."

He coughed. "Sorry. I mean, don't do that. It's a bad idea. Very bad."

"All right." Seth made a show of crossing his heart. "No vanishing national monuments."

Jazz sighed. "I really hope we're not unleashing the eighth plague here," she said, and turned to Donatti. "I don't know about you, but I'm filthy and starving and exhausted."

"Ditto. Seth, please tell me you have something to get around with."

He nodded, headed for the back wall and stopped. "Before you go, could I please have my tether back?"

"I don't know," Donatti said. "I'm thinking maybe I should keep it for a while. Maybe mail it to you, or send it up with the park rangers. What's gonna stop you from fucking with us all over again if I give it back?"

The corners of Seth's mouth twitched. "You have my word," he said. "You're free to go, and I won't harm you."

Donatti frowned. "What do you think, babe?"

"I think he'd better show us how we're leaving first," she said. "Besides, we can always find the pipes again if he screws up. Akila can track those things."

Seth went still and blinked rapidly. "The Bahari princess?"

"Yeah. She's Ian's wife."

It took him a minute to recover. "You have powerful friends."

"We've got a few connections," Donatti said.

"Understood." Seth moved to the bumpers mounted on the wall and said, "I had to have some way to bring the people off the mountain." Reaching for the middle one, he grabbed it and pulled, and part of the wall swung out to reveal a recessed area with a tall shape draped in black canvas. He tugged the canvas away. Beneath it was a free-standing mirror. "I assume you know what to do," he said to Donatti.

"Yup. Blood, words and poof. Instant portal."

His features contorted for an instant. "My tether?" he said softly.

"Here." Donatti handed them over slowly. "Don't worry about the blood. I'm not contagious."

"Good to know." Seth accepted the pipes with a grateful nod. "I'll get your bags for you," he said. "I'm sorry for putting you through this. And I . . . thank you. For proving me wrong, and setting me free."

"Just don't make us live to regret it," Jazz said.

"You won't."

When he walked away, Donatti raised an eyebrow. "This guy's a little nuts," he said. "You really think he'll lay off the sabotage racket?"

"Probably. And like you said, we'll be watching him." She shivered and glanced across the room, where Seth was inspecting the trunk, grabbing loose items and tossing them in one of their bags. "I would've killed him," she whispered. "If I had the magic, he'd be dead. But you were right. He doesn't deserve to die."

"Hold on. Did you just say I was right?"

"Congratulations." She shook her head, smirking. Maybe a little of his optimism was rubbing off on her. And maybe that wasn't a bad thing. There was room for second chances – for Seth, for her and Donatti. Starting now. "So, this wasn't the vacation I expected," she said.

Donatti's shoulders sagged like somebody just laid the weight of the world on them. "Some getaway," he muttered. "Well, babe, I guess I'll take us home. You ready?"

"Home?"

"Yeah. You're exhausted, you're worried about Cy, and . . . well, you never really wanted to come out here with me, anyway. I know you're not big on romance." He gave her a smile so forced, he might as well have had a gun at his back. "So I'll take you where you want to go."

"Good. Because I want to go to a semi-secluded cabin on scenic Wolf Pond, for one remaining romantic night with the man I love."

If his jaw fell any further, he'd have to reattach it.

She smiled. "Get me to a bed, Donatti. We'll make all the magic you want."

Mr Sandman

Sherri Browning Erwin

When her life's usual chaos had suddenly balanced into a sense of order so perfect that it bordered on the supernatural, Eve Daniels should have seen it for what it was: a sign that things were about to go drastically wrong. Eve didn't do perfect. And yet . . .

Almost without effort, she'd finally lost that pesky twenty pounds she'd carted around since college. Her lingerie designs had caught the notice of some leading fashion magazines, drawing an elite crowd to her tiny Brooklyn boutique, leading to her dream move to trendier digs on Fifth Avenue. And at last, she'd met her tall, dark and handsome, (and rich) Mr Right, married him after a whirlwind courtship, and moved into his upper eastside penthouse apartment.

And then.

She came home one day to find Mr Right adjusting his personal antenna in front of his webcam, to the obvious delight of his latest chatroulette buddy on flagrant display through the twenty-six-inch flat screen monitor. Gay. She should have known.

"Not gay," her husband countered, reaching out for her. "Bi-curious, baby. You know you're the one for me. This is something we can explore together."

"Put your pants on," she said, not bothering to hide her outrage. "And we can explore our legal options. I want a divorce."

And then.

One of her high profile clients, sexy starlet Natalie Grant, claimed that the underwire in her Mighty Aphrodite Goddess bra (one of Eve's most consistent bestsellers) broke through the silk to puncture her left breast implant – and cost Natalie a lead role in Quentin Tarantino's latest blockbuster action film.

Natalie planned to sue Eve and Heavenly Body Lingerie, the tabloids said – "Millions in lost wages!" After two weeks and no word from Natalie's lawyers, no summons served, Eve realized Natalie was simply using her bra as a smokescreen to cover for the fact that she probably wasn't even considered for the role in the first place. But the damage was done. Word was out. Eve's expert workmanship was suddenly considered second-rate. Heavenly Body bras were potentially dangerous, and not in a "beware: deadly curves" kind of way. Business declined at an alarming rate and Eve was forced to close her doors.

And then.

The stress of losing her marriage, her sweet address and her livelihood caused her to turn to Ben and Jerry for comfort. A steady diet of Chunky Monkey with a Cherry Garcia chaser put the twenty pounds back on her five-foot-six frame in no time. Plus an additional ten.

And now.

It was a big relief, and a respite from staying on her best friend's couch, when her Aunt Mae called to say she needed someone to come watch her place while she went on vacation to Italy with her church group. Mae's "place" happened to be a bed and breakfast on Moody Beach in Wells, Maine. It was April, still off-season with no reservations on the books, so Eve imagined a quiet two weeks by the sea to regroup and find her bearings. So far, so good.

Eve, on her beach chair with her toes in the sand, looked out at the crashing waves. Mae told her she was welcome to stay as long as she wanted, but Eve knew that she would be taking up valuable space once Memorial Day came around. True, her aunt would never ask her to leave. But how could she stay once ocean view digs started commanding premium prices? Eve would have to head back to the city and look for a new apartment.

Of course, she couldn't afford a new apartment until she found a new job. She refused to take Alexander's money, no matter how generous he wanted to be to buy her silence. At last, she knew why he'd married her. True love? Ha! He'd wanted a beard to keep his secrets safe from his ultra conservative boss at Lerman and Schmidt Holdings.

Love. How could Eve have been so blind? So ignorant? One good-looking guy whispered sweet nothings in her ear and she let herself be swept away. Disappointed as she was in his transgressions, she couldn't judge him. She, too, had been living a lie. She'd never loved him, either. She loved his look. She loved his lifestyle. She was head over heels for the penthouse. But Alexander? Her first week out of the apartment, she missed Alexander's multiple jet bodyspray shower more than she'd given any thought to missing her husband.

Sure, tall, dark and handsome (and rich), had its advantages. But Eve had always preferred blonds. Big, burly blonds. Daniel Craig's head on the body of Dwayne "The Rock" Johnson. Matthew McConaughey on steroids. Dolph Lundgren as He-Man, Master of the Universe.

She stood up, picked a stray stick off the beach, and started drawing in the sand, a rough sketch of her perfect man. Very rough. It probably would have gone better had she not downed an entire six pack of Corona Light on her own, but what the hell. This was vacation. At least, if she called it vacation, it felt less like what it was: major life fail. She got one thing right, at least. Her sandman had one very obvious perk. If she was going to design her dream man in the sand, he might as well be well-endowed.

And blond.

With a six-pack.

Blue eyes that shone like a beacon through the heavens.

Solid pecs and knotty biceps.

Thighs as thick as tree trunks.

Did she mention that outrageous bulging . . . Oh. She felt dizzy. She lost focus. She thought she was going to throw up, but . . . everything went black instead.

Eve Daniels struggled to catch her breath and find her balance but she fell, splayed-out, to the sand.

*   *   *

Cold wet foam tickled her toes, waking her. She drew her feet up, curled them under her bottom and stretched her arms, not ready to open her eyes to the haze of the setting sun. She draped herself over the warm body at her side. Body? She ran her hands over the solid planes of a male chest. A man!

She bolted upright. A completely naked man filled the space on the sand next to her, right over the spot where she'd drawn the image of her dream guy. He was wet, as if recently coughed up by the ocean. But – she watched his chest rise and fall in steady rhythm. He was breathing. He was alive! Who – *what* – was he?

Her gaze involuntarily dropped to his – ahem. Yep. He fit the design brief, all right. With her eyes, she traced the trail of blond curls up to his navel, well-defined abs, nearly hairless broad chest, square jaw. She guessed his eyes were blue. Of course, she couldn't draw blue eyes and blond hair in the sand, but she'd said aloud that it was what she wanted. And here he was. Could it be?

No. *As if* the ocean just washed her fantasy man up at her feet? Ha!

She knelt at his side and shook him gently. "Wake up! Are you all right?"

No answer. She shook again, a little firmer this time.

"Sir?" She was prepared to perform mouth-to-mouth, just in case.

But suddenly, he rolled to his side, away from her, and coughed. The coughing lasted for several seconds. She began to wonder if he hacked up anything significant but she didn't want to look. She stroked his back instead. "That's it. Let it out."

At last, he turned to face her and her breath caught in her throat. He was, without a doubt, the most beautiful man she had ever seen. Gold-tipped lashes framed stunning blue eyes, one slightly half-closed with a scar across the lid. A break in the perfection. But it somehow made him more intriguing. A tad menacing. He was big. The most rugged, most manly of men.

"I beg your pardon," he said, his voice a velvet husk. "I don't seem to know – I mean, I – I'm at a loss."

"A loss?"

"I don't know." One large hand flew up to tangle in his gold locks. "I can't seem to remember anything, not even who I am or how I got here."

She breathed a sigh of relief. Not so menacing after all.

"You don't say." She had drawn him in the sand, and here he was. Her sandman.

"I just said." His brow furrowed.

"No." She laughed. "That's not what I meant. I—" She spied a crowd of teenagers strolling up the beach. "Let's get you inside before anyone sees you. Here." She stood, stripped off her windbreaker, and handed it to him. "Put this, er, you know."

"I think I do." He draped it over his bottom half.

"Can you stand? Are you hurt?" She reached for his hand.

"I don't seem to be injured." He moved and flexed everything in sight, took her hand and got to his feet, letting the windbreaker fall back to the sand.

Eve lost her breath all over again. She reached for the jacket and handed it back, careful to avoid lingering eye contact. He took a step and faltered.

"So weak." He seemed surprised by it.

"Who knows what you've been through, you poor man. Here." She looped her arm around his waist and encouraged him to lean on her. "I'll help you."

Somehow, they'd made it up the beach, into the house and to one of the ground floor rooms on the oceanfront side of the house. He'd practically fallen into the bed. She left him there while she went to run him a bath. By the time she returned, he was under the covers, sound asleep.

Should she wake him? Call someone? An ambulance? The police? What if he had a head injury? Amnesia was a sign of something not quite right. But instinct warned her to keep him to herself, for now, and just to keep an eye on him. She watched him as he slept. Before long, the Corona buzz took over and she was asleep in the chair at his bedside.

She woke again, a strong briny stench invading her senses. The sea? Nope. The smell of the sea on him. She should have insisted on that bath first. One look at the window revealed an ink-black, star-dotted sky. Night. How long had they slept? A glance at the clock told her they'd been out for three hours at least. She'd found him at sunset. It was now nearly eleven, but letting him sleep through the night was no option with that smell. Besides, she needed to wake him to make a health assessment.

"Adam," she said, the name an instinctive choice. "We need to get you cleaned up." She brushed a hand across his forehead, no fever, and swept sticky blond locks off his face.

He stirred, reaching for her with strong arms. It was impossible to resist him as he pulled her atop him on the bed.

"Ah, Hades, you've done it again." His eyes opened slightly, lids heavy over the shocking blue irises. He raised the scarred brow and tugged at the sleeve of the cambric shirt she'd layered over her tank top. It had been warm on the beach for April, but not bathing suit warm. "Still dressed, lass? This will never do."

"Hades?"

"Hm," he murmured, intent on his purpose of taking the shirt off her. She let him. He seemed skilled enough at the art of undressing a female, and she still had her tank top and khaki capris besides. "Mount Olympus is all well and good, but Hades keeps the best serving girls. You can't beat the Underworld for hospitality."

She sat up over him, straddling him. It was unavoidable that she could feel his erection under her, but at least she was in the position of power now. He seemed healthy enough, physically. As to his mental state, she had her doubts. "Look, dude, I'm not your serving girl and you're not in the Underworld."

With one powerful hand, he urged her off him to the mattress and rolled atop her. "My compliments to Zeus, then. He's finally upped his standards."

"I—uh," she began to protest, to try to explain, but he lowered his head to hers and crushed her mouth in a kiss. A mind-numbing, breath-stealing, toe-curling kiss. She forgot to protest, to worry about her beer breath and just gave in to the moment, taking his tongue between her lips and urging him on.

He laced fingers with hers, stretching her arms up over her head, leaving her body exposed to his whims. He broke contact from her mouth, blazing a trail down her chin and neck to her breasts. With his teeth, he grazed a nipple through her shirt. She moaned eagerly, but he stopped and shot up suddenly.

"What's that smell?"

She was grateful for the chance to recover her senses. "That smell is you, from the ocean. We need to get you a bath."

Once she had him in a tub full of fresh, steaming water, she explained to him where he was and what had happened. At least, as far as she knew. He took it all in with a shrug, remaining single-minded in his attempt to get her to join him in the tub.

"There's plenty of room. It's a little lonely. Plus, I might need some help scrubbing hard to reach places." He smiled a lazy half-smile, which looked all the more lecherous thanks to his scarred eyelid.

"I'm sure you can manage just fine. Or do you have someone to bathe you at home?" She moved to stand behind him in the claw-footed tub and got to work on shampooing the sticky salt water out of his hair.

"I assume so, though perhaps I prefer to bathe alone at Mount Olympus. I don't recall Zeus having any particularly tempting serving girls on hand."

"Unlike the Underworld." So he was back to the serving girls bit.

"And here." He reached up and caught her forearms in his. Even wet, his strength was outstanding. She couldn't move. "Come on, lass. I still smell the sea and I suspect the stench is no longer coming from me alone."

She sniffed. He was right. She must have picked it up from helping him inside. She doubted she could trust leaving the poor man alone long enough to grab a shower of her own. What if he left the house? He wasn't exactly in his right mind.

"Slip out of those clothes and get in." He released her arms, but did not turn to face her. "What's the harm? Is it a virgin's reputation you protect?"

She snorted. "Hardly. Not that it's any of your business."

"We're two consenting adults who share a mutual attraction."

"I never said I was attracted—"

He laughed. "It would be a shame to waste all this steaming water on me alone."

She *was* an environmentalist. At least, she preferred to be, when she remembered to think about it. His arguments all made sense. So what if she got in the tub? She'd already seen him naked. What if he had been sent just for her, a gift from the gods? Why, it would practically be a sin to turn him down.

She stripped off her clothes. "Slide back," she said, presenting herself at the other side of the tub. "Make room. I'm coming in."

A gleam of appreciation lit his blue eyes as he took her in from head to toe, and back up to the lush curve of her full breasts. Typical man. "Very nice."

She could feel the heat of a blush warming her whole body even as she stood barefoot on the cold tile. He reached for her hand as she went to grip the edge of the tub to get in. She met his gaze, those blue eyes twinkling with mirth and mischief, and she knew she was a woman lost. One time with him, this man of her dreams, would never be enough. She wanted it all.

A future. A whole new world at his side. Who knows, maybe he could take her to Mount Olympus, or the Underworld. When his arm wrapped around her and pulled her to his solid length, she felt her inhibitions slip away and she was ready to follow anywhere he would lead.

And he was quite ready to assume full command. Whoever he was, there was no doubt that submissive was not a part of his nature. He dominated her in the bathtub, and later, after towelling each other off, picked her up, slung her over his shoulder, and headed back to the bed.

She squealed with laughter. It felt good to lose control. "You're just like a conquering warrior."

"A warrior I am," he said. "And you're about to be conquered."

"Not in here. There's sand in the bed." She stopped him before he put her down. "Upstairs. To the—" she was about to say honeymoon suite, as Mae affectionately called the large corner room with the private bath and enormous king four-poster bed, but she didn't want to scare him. "To the room on the left."

Upstairs they went, with Eve still slung over the warrior's shoulder as if she weighed about as much as a sack of feathers. At last, he slung her down to the fluffy white bed.

"Prepare to be conquered," he said, his voice deep and unrelenting.

A thrill shot straight through her at his words. "My defences are already down. Do your worst."

He wanted to do his best by her.

This woman. A mere mortal, as pretty as a goddess and twice as voluptuously curved. Why did he want to impress her? "How old are you?"

"A woman never tells."

"Tell," his voice gruff, commanding. She wouldn't dare resist.

"Twenty-six."

He laughed. "A mere babe."

But legal, in her world. That much was important to him. He hated breaking mortal laws as much as he disliked bending the rules of Mount Olympus. But he had broken rules, hadn't he? At the back of his mind lurked a vague recollection of injustice, retribution. What had he done? Who was after him? He knew more than he'd told her, but she wasn't ready to hear. Mortals were rarely ready to accept that there were gods in their midst.

Or in her bed. He smiled again. Her skin was pink from the hot water. Practically glowing. His own little pearl from the ocean.

How he hated the ocean. Poseidon's domain. Yes, there was something about Poseidon.

She stretched like a cat, making her rosy nipples jut out, beckoning him. Remembering could wait. He was going to make love to his woman.

Eve lost count of how many times, how many ways, they'd done it. But she ached all over, in the best possible way, and she couldn't believe her good fortune. The perfect man, except for a few scars that only made him more perfect to Eve. In her bed. Making sweet, hot, animal love to her and now sleeping curled at her side, one arm draped protectively over her. His woman, he'd called her. She loved it.

But she had to extricate herself from his possessive hold and run to the powder room. A lady had needs. Plus, she wanted to check her hair, brush her teeth, and make sure she was completely presentable when he woke up. She felt his erection tickling at her backside. The man was insatiable! Would he want to do it again? She couldn't believe her luck.

Finally, she managed to pry his heavy arm up and roll out from under his hold. She rose on tiptoe and headed for the bathroom when she realized the shades were up. Dawn's soft violet rays filtered in through lace curtains. Once the sun came up, it would be too bright to sleep comfortably. After last night, they would both need their rest. She wasn't wearing a stitch, but who would be out on the beach at this hour? The few dedicated shell-hunters scouring the rocks for bounty deserved to get a peep for their efforts. She opened the curtains, reached for the shade, and drew back in surprise.

"Holy birds, batman!"

There had to be hundreds of them, tiny black birds, all on the stretch of beach directly in front of Mae's house. And she nearly jumped out of her skin when she turned her head to see two vultures poised like gargoyles on opposite corners of the balcony. Vultures? She'd only seen them in cartoons, or maybe at the zoo. But they were vultures all right. What was going on?

She looked at her sandman, sound asleep in her bed. The sudden appearance of the birds had to be connected to him somehow. She had no idea how. Maybe there was something to his talk of Zeus and Hades after all. She knew nothing about Greek mythology, but Mae had a computer downstairs. After freshening up, Eve grabbed her robe and headed down to do some research.

A look with search engines revealed some interesting information, but not enough to go on. She typed in gods and vultures, and Ares came up. After last night, she might have suspected god of love, but god of war? Hard to imagine. Though, he did say he was a warrior. A conquering warrior. The vulture was a sacred bird and frequent companion to Ares. And the little black birds?

She stood, went to the sliding doors, opened the shades, and gasped. The porch was full of them, so many little black birds that she couldn't see the tiles beneath them. She rapped on the glass, thinking to startle them away, but they wouldn't move. A few of them craned to look at her, but showed no signs of fleeing in fear. And their feathers? They looked like little daggers. She ran back to the computer and read the Wikipedia on Ares. Birds liked Ares. Not just vultures, but also owls and woodpeckers. And he was frequently surrounded by little black birds with dagger-like feathers they were known to shower down on Ares's rivals. Stymphalian birds. Her breath caught in her throat. She leaned back in her desk chair.

The god of war was sleeping in her bed.

The ring of the doorbell interrupted Eve's musings. She made a quick glance of Mae's calendar. The bed and breakfast wasn't due for any guests for at least three weeks. On her way by the window, she passed the porch door and did a double take. No birds. Where had they gone? And so suddenly?

No time to figure it out. She had to get the door before the caller gave up and went away. Not that it would be a problem if she missed a door-to-door salesman or meter reader. Or with her luck, another one of Jehovah's Witnesses eager to convert her to the flock. No thanks. Not this week. She had enough trouble with gods on her hands.

Though, when she thought about it that way, the whole idea just sounded really silly. God of war? Yeah. And Aphrodite's at the door.

She opened it. A gorgeous woman, svelte in what had to be a designer suit, stood outside, a black satchel in her hand. Yes, definitely designer. Eve recognized the black, body-conscious, fur-trimmed jacket and skirt ensemble from a Dennis Basso show, one of the last she'd attended as a thriving designer in her own right. The woman even had the matching pillbox hat, perched at a jaunty angle atop her Little Mermaid red curls. Eve didn't expect to see original Basso designs in Maine. What next, Karl Lagerfeld would stop by for a drink?

"Pardon me, but I believe you have what I'm looking for." She held out a gloved hand, as if meaning for Eve to take it, then pulled it back. "Amy Nethans."

"Well, I'm sorry Ms Nethans. We're closed for the season. We'll be ready for new visitors in a few weeks. Thank you. Try the Atlantic Motor Lodge on the Wells side." Eve started to close the door. Ms Nethans didn't exactly give her the warm and fuzzies, and she was eager to get back to Ares, er, Adam, er . . . she had to figure out what to call him. They hadn't even eaten together yet. He must be starving. She wondered if he liked eggs.

"You don't seem to understand." Ms Nethans pushed the door open and stepped in. "I think you found my husband last night."

"Your hu—" Eve took a breath. Ms Nethans eyes were softer now, a dark blue. She gnawed her lip as if concerned. Maybe Eve had misread her fear for aggression. "Your husband?"

"Hmm. He's really tall, built." She made a bodybuilder pose that won Eve over. No one too full of herself could resort to physical clowning in front of a stranger. "Blond hair. Blue eyes."

Eve just nodded along. *One enormous* . . .

"Mistake," Eve said, out loud. Then wished she could take it back. "I'm sorry Ms Nethans. Your husband?" She couldn't confess to the woman right then and there that she had spent the night, all beautiful night, with her husband. Suddenly, she felt underdressed, even though she was wrapped up tight in her plush apple-green Eden's Temptation robe, one of her favourite designs.

"He went missing from our yacht yesterday. We were anchored off Kennebunkport. Fell right over the edge, we suspect. Our captain traced the tide patterns and figured he might wash up here. He's a strong swimmer. We didn't see any reason to worry until we found no trace of him and then—"

"Then?" How could they have found him? What did he have, a computer tracking chip like Malomar, her best friend's maltipoo?

"Then one of your neighbours called the police and reported seeing a man with you yesterday. On the beach."

Eve blushed and looked down to the floor. Amy Nethans wore platform peep-toe Christian Louboutins. Last year's Louboutins. And there was a weird little feather stuck on one of them. A deliberate decoration? Or an accident? Either way, so much for style. But besting Amy Nethans didn't matter. She'd slept with her husband, for goodness sake. And someone had seen them! Probably that nosy Mr Plimpton. He was always at the windows, watching. He probably saw her passed out after her own little Corona-fest, too. But did he come help her? Of course not.

"And the police led you here?"

"They gave us some addresses to check out. They wouldn't get involved for another twenty-four hours, not enough time to care, they said. Like the love of your life suddenly disappearing from your yacht shouldn't be any reason to worry?"

Amy Nethans had a yacht. And a husband. *That particular husband.*

Eve struggled to catch her breath. She felt light-headed. As if her life hadn't crashed and burned spectacularly enough, now she was The Other Woman. Why hadn't she resisted the urge to get into that tub?

"Ms Nethans," Eve began, not knowing quite what to say.

"Amy. Please. Call me Amy." Amy gripped her arm, as if she needed the steadying. Eve was the last one to lean on.

"Amy, um."

"He's here, then? He's okay? I've brought his clothes." She held up the satchel.

"His clothes?" Of course the man had clothes. Not that it should come as a surprise. It was just that Eve had gotten to know him so well without his clothes that she couldn't begin to picture what he would wear. Beyond her silk Adam's Rib boxer briefs, specially designed for the man who likes to hang loose in style.

"Yes. He, um," Amy paused and nibbled her lush lower lip. "He sleeps in the nude. It was the middle of the night. He got up for a drink of water, and just – poof. He never came back. In the morning, we found his watch near the railing."

"So he sleeps naked. Except for his watch?" Eve raised a brow. His skin was bronzed, but she didn't remember seeing any tan lines where his watch would be. Someone as attached to a watch as to sleep in one, when he takes off everything else, would surely have a tan line. Maybe she just hadn't looked close enough.

Amy nodded. "And he sometimes just gets up in the middle of the night and doesn't come back to bed right away, so I wasn't alarmed. At first. By the time the sun started to rise, well – can you take me to him? Please? We'll get right out of your way in no time."

Eve paused. Maybe she should deny it, say he wasn't here? On the other hand, what reason did she have to suspect Amy

Nethans of anything hinky? Why would some strange woman just show up at her door after some strange man just washed up on her beach unless there was an honest connection? *His wife.*

The word landed in the pit of Eve's stomach like a big, barnacle-encrusted rock.

"He's upstairs. Asleep. He seems to be in fine shape. Just a little, uh, worn-out." Eve couldn't meet Amy Nethans' striking blue eyes. "And he's suffering from a bit of amnesia."

"Amnesia? So he doesn't know who he is?"

Eve shook her head. "No idea."

"And he doesn't know who I am?"

Eve felt the blush stinging at her cheeks again. "Um, I don't know."

"Take me to him. Please."

"Of course." Eve gestured toward the staircase, around the corner from the entry hall. "Right this way."

At the top of the stairs, Amy called his name. "Arthur."

Arthur? It seemed weird and foreign to Eve, not the right name for him at all. She pictured some grizzle-bearded wizard from Harry Potter, though that was Albus and not Arthur. Still, Arthur? It simply didn't fit.

"In here," Eve said, pointing to the door of the honeymoon suite. "Why don't you let me wake him for you?"

Amy's eyes widened. "Wake him? You? But he's not wearing a stitch!"

"Yeah. I noticed." Over every inch of him. Over and over again. "But he's all tucked in snug. He recognizes me now. I don't want to startle him."

"I'm his wife," Amy said, with some fire in her voice. "Step aside."

Eve sighed and moved out of the way.

Amy went in and shut the door. For a few minutes, Eve stood outside, trying to listen, wondering if Adam (Arthur?) would be shocked, would protest, would insist he belonged here, with Eve? But she didn't hear a thing. After ten minutes, she felt defeated as well as out of place, and just plain nosy, and she decided to go get some clothes on and putter around the kitchen until the happily married couple would finally emerge.

*   *   *

Forty minutes later, Amy appeared in the door of the kitchen, holding Arthur's hand and pulling him like a recalcitrant child along at her side. He wore a blue button-down shirt, tucked into khaki pants, with topsiders. Like a waiter at any of the seashore dives trying to pass themselves off as classy restaurants. Not what she pictured him in at all. The shirt stretched tight across his broad shoulders. It barely fit.

"We would like to thank you for your hospitality." Amy spoke for them both. "Say thank you, Arthur."

His hair was parted in the middle, combed neatly to both sides and tucked behind his ears. Again, it didn't fit. She wanted to run her fingers through to muss it up.

He cleared his throat, looked down. It was a bit of a surprise to see her big strong warrior, Mr Commanding, acting so sheepish and shy. It simply didn't fit. One thing Eve, a bra designer, knew was the importance of fit.

"Adam," Eve said loudly. She didn't give a damn what Amy thought about the name. "Adam, look at me. Are you okay? Do you know where you are? Who you are?"

He met her gaze, the formerly brilliant eyes clouded over. "I'm Arthur. You brought me in from the beach. Thank you. I'm going home with my wife now."

"Very well, Arthur," Amy said. "We've taken enough of your time. I've left enough for a night's stay on the bed upstairs. I wouldn't want to be a bother. Now we'll be on our way."

Eve rushed after them as they headed for the door. "But wait – breakfast!" She'd made eggs, reheated muffins. Mae's famous Maine blueberry muffins, fresh from the freezer.

But by the time she got to the door, they were gone. Absolutely gone. As if they'd vanished on the wind. The only thing left on her porch was – feathers? Eve crouched and picked up one of the hundreds of little black feathers that dotted the pavement. Sharp, like an arrow. And black.

"Stymphalian birds," she said aloud. "Stymphalian birds on attack." And she had a feeling that something was wrong, very wrong, with this picture.

That feeling was intensified when another hulking blond man suddenly appeared at the end of her driveway and made his way briskly up her walk. She stood transfixed. As he got closer, she could make out the differences in appearance between this new one and her bedtime warrior. This one was fair, while her sandman was bronzed. His hair was a dazzling platinum, while her sandman's was golden. Her sandman had the menacing scar across his eye. This one, no scar. Ice-blue eyes, she noticed, as he drew closer, close enough to look in his eyes. Eyes wide open. And challenging hers.

"Where are they? Where did she take him?"

Eve took a step back, his proximity overwhelming.

"I don't know."

"But you let him go?"

"Um," she gestured down the length of her body. She'd put on a sundress, a little cool for the weather, but it was a pretty colour that matched her green eyes, and had a flattering drape. It tied at the neck, downplayed her weight gain, and emphasized her assets, her full breasts and shapely legs. "I'm five four. How was I supposed to stop him?"

He followed her hands with his gaze. One blond eyebrow shot up. "I'm sure you would have found a way."

She found herself blushing again. "I—"

"We don't have much time. Give me your hand." She hesitated. "Give me your hand," he repeated in a more commanding tone. She gave it to him. He held it in his large warm grasp.

Suddenly she felt a shock, then a tingling sensation running up her spine to the base of her brain. And then she knew. *She knew.* "Eros."

"That's right," he smiled. "I'm usually more gentle, but we're in a rush. You've no idea what they're prepared to do to him."

"They – Aphrodite? Amy, I mean. She was Aphrodite, right? Was she jealous because I – because we – Ares and I? She knew?" She assumed Aphrodite, because she'd read about Aphrodite's affair with Ares in the Wikipedia entry.

"Not Aphrodite." Eros shook his head. "I guess our connection wasn't as strong as I'd thought. I usually have no trouble with women when it comes to connecting."

"Connecting? You mean that Vulcan mind meld trick?"

"Yes. It usually works best when there's some mutual attraction, but it's already too late for you. You're a goner."

"What do you mean?"

"For Ares. You love him. I don't know how it happened so fast, but you couldn't make a full connection with me because you're in love with him."

She was about to protest. He put a finger to her lips. "Trust me. I know."

"Of course. You're the god of love."

"And you prefer the god of war."

She shrugged. "I've always had a thing for chaos."

"Then you're in for some conflict. War is order, not chaos. But the most enduring love stories are filled with conflict."

"Enduring? Not exactly, considering he's already off with – whoever she was. Not Aphrodite."

"Tell me. What did she call herself? What did she look like?"

"She was tall, slender, but curved in all the right places. A beautiful face. Blue eyes. Long red hair like Ariel's."

"Ariel's?"

"Disney's the Little Mermaid? Never mind. Red, long hair. Slightly curled. She called herself Amy."

"Amymone." Eros nodded. "One of Poseidon's consorts."

"What do they want with Ares? You should have seen him, Eros. He seemed defeated and out of sorts."

"She must have drugged him. It's the only way he would have followed."

"But he was lost. He didn't know who he was."

"He knew. He might have been a little out of it, at first. But he knew. Come. We have to go. We must rescue him before Poseidon carries out his revenge."

"His revenge?" And before she knew it, Eros swept her into his arms and held her tightly. Time seemed to stop. Her lungs felt frozen, as if she couldn't breathe, but yet she was not panicked. She was at peace. Complete peace. Surrounded by a soothing white light. Her mind flooded with images.

Ares, enraged. A father's rage. And shame. He should have known. He should have been able to protect his daughter, his beautiful Alkippe. Alkippe, raped by Halirrhothios, son of Poseidon. Who could blame Ares for his brutal actions? Eve watched Ares lose control, wild with a dagger in his hand, stalking his weaker opponent, hovering over Halirrhothios. She felt his pain. He wasn't a killer, not really. This was justice. *Justice!*

She didn't even bother to ask how it happened, how she could see it all? Feel it as if she had been there? Some sort of magic. Why question the gods?

She opened her eyes and felt breath – blessed breath! – fill her lungs. Fog had closed in around she and Eros. When it cleared, she saw that they were on a small island in the middle of the ocean, a bare stretch of sand, little more than a sandbar with one lone palm tree. Ares was across the sand, tied to that tree, his head hanging, hair falling loose. Was that blood? Blood dripped from the side of his face. He wore only a small cloth around his middle. She could see the bruises all over his body. He had been beaten!

The important thing now was that she had to get to him, to let him loose and tend his wounds.

"Ares!" She launched into a run, not even caring that her robe opened.

"Stop!" Eros called, but it was too late.

The sand in the middle of the bar dissolved into water, and she crashed into the waves as they churned into a wild whirl-pool. She struggled against the water, but could not stay on the surface. Any minute now, her body would fail her. Her lungs would fill with water. She would die.

But all she could think about was Ares, and the future they would be denied. It didn't matter. As long as he was safe.

"Ares!" she called out. "I'll always love you."

She heard high-pitched feminine laughter. And then she could hear no more.

Ares looked up in time to see her go under. He ripped from his bonds, ran to the narrow pool and struggled to reach for her. The pool was too small for them both. He had no idea how deep. Instinct warned him it was a cleverly designed trap of Poseidon's. If he jumped in to save her, his weight would force her deeper and she would surely drown. All that was left, to try to reach her and pull her up and out. Eros, the fool, stood back and watched it all, a bemused observer.

"You idiot!" Ares hissed. "She's going to die! Why did you bring her?"

"I brought her because she's the only one who could save you."

"Clearly." He snorted, still struggling to grasp her hands, still reaching up through the waves. She was a fighter, his woman. How he admired her!

Admired? No. He loved her, he knew. He loved her! Ares had never known true love before. The feeling astounded him. "Make it stop! I love her! Take me, Poseidon. Take me instead!"

Poseidon and Amymone appeared at his side.

"Delighted to make the trade," Poseidon said, and pointed his sceptre at the pool. It turned into sand, bringing Eve to the surface. She was unconscious, but she—

"She is alive?" Ares asked.

Poseidon shrugged. "She will live."

Amymone laughed, a shrill and irritating noise. Even death would be better than a lifetime at Amymone's side. No wonder Poseidon was such an ogre.

"I mean to keep my bargain, then. Do it, Poseidon. Take my life. As I took your son's, the raping bastard."

Poseidon raised his sceptrre, as if about to inflict the final blow.

At last, Eros stepped forward. "Poseidon! The court's decision is final. You will not harm Ares on penalty of your own death. He has fulfilled our expectations. Aeropagos has concluded."

Aeropagos! The special court formed on Mount Olympus to determine Ares' guilt or innocence in killing his daughter's rapist. He had been acquitted, or so he'd thought.

"It was a conditional acquittal," Eros explained. "I was sent to see that you lived up to the condition."

"And the condition was?" Ares raised a brow, the scarred one.

"That you showed you could set aside your warring ways and sacrifice all for love. Why else would they send Eros? I know love more than anyone. And you did. You were willing to make the ultimate sacrifice, your life for hers."

"Anything for her," Ares nodded. "I love her. We've only just met, but I feel I've known her always, body and soul. I need her as I've never needed."

He approached and scooped her in his arms. "I want her as I've never wanted."

"Then we'll take the girl," Amymone said, a wicked smile on her pink lips. "It's only fair. To make up for the loss of our beloved Halirrhothios, you give up your beloved Eve to Poseidon."

"Halirrhothios got what he deserved. The court has determined justice in this case," Eros interrupted. "The girl is free. Ares is acquitted. Aeropagos is concluded. Let us go our separate ways."

Poseidon and Amymone, no doubt disappointed by the court's decision, disappeared as quickly as they'd come. Ares had no recollection of leaving Eve's bed. And now, she was limp in his arms.

Ares watched her, but Eve did not seem to be breathing. He leaned to her tender lips and offered her a breath of his own. "Breathe, my love! Live!"

Just as his heart felt squeezed to a pulp, she coughed, sputtered, and turned away from him to spew the water in her lungs to the sand. She was naked, her dress long lost, torn off in the force of the tide pool. He smiled at the coincidence. It was exactly how she'd found him, on her beach, the previous day.

"We'd better get you inside," he said, stroking a finger down her petal-soft cheek before taking her back in his arms. "Before anyone sees you."

He held her in such a way to protect her nudity from Eros's observance. Not that he hadn't already seen it all.

"Where's inside," she asked, once she regained her power to speak. "Where are we?"

"An island in the middle of nowhere," Eros answered. "And if we don't leave soon, Poseidon will send a storm to wipe us out."

"Do you want to go back to your house?" Ares asked. "Or would you do me the honour of coming to Mount Olympus and becoming my consort?"

"Consort?" She wrinkled her nose.

"He means wife," Eros interjected.

"You want to marry me?" Her voice lifted so that it sounded nearly angelic to Ares' ears.

"Indeed. I wish to marry you. I wish to be with you, always."

"And I want to go with you," she said. "There's nothing for me in New York. But – I promised my aunt Mae. I'm supposed to be watching her house."

"Consider it done," Eros said. "I've arranged for your cousin Candace to arrive for a surprise visit and stay with Mae awhile."

"How did you arrange that? She's married and living in New Jersey. Why would she just suddenly give everything up and go to Maine?"

"Her husband left her," Eros said. "When he came home and found her in a compromising position on chatroulette."

Eve laughed. "You don't say."

"I didn't," Ares said. "I didn't say a word."

Eve laughed harder. When Eve laughed, it was a lilting, lyrical sound that reminded him of cherubs singing. He could live with that laugh for eternity and consider it a blessing.

"I will marry you, Ares," Eve said. "And I'm dying to see Mount Olympus!"

"Then let's be off," Ares said. "What are we waiting for?"

"For you to kiss the bride," Eros said. "I consider you god of war, and wife."

And as Ares leaned to kiss her, the naked blushing bride, Eve felt the earth move and shake and rock, and her toes curled, and she lost all awareness of everything else – until she opened her eyes and found herself in a honeymoon bed on the clouds of Mount Olympus, with Ares about to make love to her.

Finally, life was perfect, so perfect that it was well in the territory of the supernatural. And Eve was not the least afraid to find out what would happen next. In fact, she couldn't wait!

The Sin-Eater's Promise

Michele Hauf

One

Blackthorn Regis released the soul that clung to his aura into the sulphur-laden atmosphere. Screams echoed. He told himself it was not the human soul screaming but rather a pleasurable sound made by the mercury-slick river that consumed them.

He remained impartial. It was not his place to discern if a man had lived virtuously or had inspired dread. He simply ferried souls Above or Beneath.

His trips Beneath were more rare than mortals would guess.

"Soul-bringer."

The Receiver of Beneath stood so high, Blackthorn could not see his face, yet he felt the menacing presence curdle his marrow. Not once had he fixed the creature in the gaping spaces where eyes should be. Blackthorn possessed no soul, yet surely he would still feel the soul-grinding weight of such darkness.

"You're missing one."

Blackthorn swore at the back of his throat. "It won't happen again," he offered, and bowed reverently before turning and shimmering away from Beneath.

There was only one way a soul went the wrong destination.

"There must be an infernal sin-eater working my territory."

Shimmering into a small Midwestern countryside, Blackthorn spied the culprit bent over double at the edge of a meadow. Dew spangled the scattered weeds and clover heads, and sparkled on fuzzy cat-tails spiking the nearby ditch.

Thick, black sin exploded from the mouth as it repeatedly heaved. It lifted its head to keep the fluid from spilling down the dress – dress? The sin-eater was *female*. Blackthorn's chest and throat muscles squeezed, matching the clench of his fists.

He marched purposefully across the field. "Leave it to a sin-eater to make enemies of not only Beneath but also Above."

Viscous sin spattered sprigs of white clover. Sin-eaters involuntarily purged following an eating or would forever cloud their soul with the sins of those they'd eaten.

Gagging and spitting, she sat back on her heels, clasping thin arms across her middle. Attired all in black, her pale flesh glowed with moonlight. She was startled as he grabbed her by the throat and dragged her to stand.

Shaky legs made her wobble before Blackthorn. But she quickly grasped her bearings and, bouncing on her black high-top sneakers, fists lifted in challenge, she jounced before him like a scrawny prize-fighter.

Seething, Blackthorn prepared to match the ridiculous challenge, yet though he was not human, mortal civility reminded him that one mustn't hit a woman. He flexed his fingers open.

The woman's wide grey eyes, surrounded by smeary black eyeshadow, flickered. He'd never seen eyes so bright and clear. So defiant. And sad. Her eyes pleaded for understanding, and then shoved him away for seeing that weakness.

All that in a scrap of flesh and stolen sin?

Rage settling, a smirking levity emerged. She was just a bitty thing. Not unappealing, either. Blackthorn slid a hand down his waistcoat. What to do with his hands if not choke her senseless?

"Desist," he growled darkly.

The woman stopped her aggressive bouncing. Sin dappled her lip. Starlight dived into her dark hair and waded iridescent within.

"Who the hell are you? I warn you, I can throw a mean left hook."

Blackthorn chuckled. The utterance was so odd to him that he abruptly ceased and cleared his throat. "I am Blackthorn Regis. Soul-bringer."

One of her dark brows assumed a chevron.

"You." He wagged a finger at her. "Are a nasty sin-eater."

She smacked a fist into a palm. "Sin does taste nasty, let me tell you. What do you want from me?"

"Stop eating sins."

"Stop?" She leaned into his space, wafting the sweet scent of cherries on a sugar-high under his nose. "This is my job. It is what I do."

"You are reviled, sin-eater." Though he didn't quite feel the revulsion himself. Odd.

She snapped her arms across her chest and lifted her chin. "Someone's got to do it."

"Not in my territory."

"Oh yeah? What's a Soul-bringer? Where do you bring them?" She slapped her palms together and exclaimed, "Oh, I get it. You're the guy who brings the decedent's soul to Heaven or Hell, right?"

"Above and Beneath. I ferry the newly dead."

"Cool. I've always wanted to meet a psychopomp."

"You steal my souls!" he announced, angered at his frustration.

The woman rolled her eyes sweetly and teased her tongue across her lips. "I hadn't considered that before. The stealing part. Of course, that's your opinion. I like to think I give hope."

"Every time you eat sins," he confirmed, "you steal from me."

"But you still get to take the soul. Just not to its intended resting place. Heaven is so much nicer, anyway – I mean, *Above*."

"I do not discern 'nicer'."

Blackthorn stepped closer. He ate very little, but he suddenly craved cherries, bunches of them glistening with fresh dew. Could he drink her skin as if it was the syrupy juice she smelled of? Such a delicious repast.

She thrust out her hand. "Name's Desdenova Fleetwood. Yeah, it's from a song. Blue Oyster Cult. But you can call me Nova. Blackthorn, right?"

"You do as I ask, Desdenova Fleetwood, and I may show you favour."

"Really? Favour? I can't wait." She clasped her hands before her chest and batted her lashes. It wasn't meant to tease but rather, mock. "You going to give me back my life? There's nothing I can do but eat sins. Do you know how many men like to date girls who eat sins for a living? Zero." She held up her fingers in a circle between them to emphasize.

Was she drunk? Blackthorn couldn't be certain. Surely, expelling so much sin must weaken her. "I have no concern for your personal life."

"Why not? Don't you think I'm pretty? Of course not."

"You are very pretty. Save for the sin you've dribbling down your chin."

He gestured towards her face. "Perhaps that is what frightens the men off."

She smeared the back of her hand through the black sludge. "Go away."

"Not until you promise to stop eating sins."

Slapping her hands together, she paced before him, kicking up dew in spittals before her. When she turned a look over her shoulder, a bright tease danced in her eyes. "I would give up sin-eating for a kiss," she whispered.

Blackthorn studied the pleading grey irises set within blackest streaks of make-up. In his myriad centuries of ferrying souls he rarely got involved with mortals. However, he did live on the mortal realm and he was like mortal men; he could appreciate a beautiful woman, and the feel of her skin under his hand.

This little girl lost only wanted a kiss?

And what did he want? *Did* he want? It had been so long . . .

"Give up sin-eating," he stated, "and then I shall reward you with a kiss."

"You're lying. Guys don't kiss girls like me."

"Perhaps it is because you dress to put them off."

"What's wrong with the garb? This is me." She fingered the hem of the black tulle skirt, worn over white and black striped thigh-high stockings. "If the world doesn't like it, the world can screw off."

"Is that so?" He sensed she'd prefer the world to lunge forwards and embrace her – Blackthorn checked himself. He didn't care. He should not care.

I want for nothing. I am . . . nothing.

"Mr Harvey's soul shouldn't have went Beneath anyway," she said. "He was a nice guy. I don't think his sins were too great."

"Says the girl who just vomited up heinous sin all over the meadow."

"Happens every time."

"In such copious amounts?"

She studied the ground, apparently realizing only now the output was an oddity. "He couldn't have done anything *that* bad."

"Murdered a child three decades ago," Blackthorn recited, knowing the details merely from the residue of the man's soul that yet clung to his aura. He shook his shoulders, dismissing the sludge.

Parted lips softened. She had no idea the affects of her actions.

"Desist," Blackthorn repeated.

"Very well," she said, still in a daze. "I quit and you'll kiss me?"

"That was the proposal, yes."

She presented her hand to shake. "Deal."

Grasping Desdenova's hand shocked his nervous system with a tender jolt of defiance, independence and need. He actually felt her need slide up his arm and squeeze at his heart. A heart of glass that could never pulse. But it could feel. And what he felt surprised him.

Tugging his hand from hers, Blackthorn turned and marched off across the field. Why hadn't he just punched her and threatened her life?

A kiss?

He slapped a hand over his chest. "It did not pulse. It could not have."

Two

Nova lived in a one-bedroom apartment in the uptown district of Minneapolis. She wasn't much of a people person, so instead of taking the elevator up to the third floor, she clattered up the iron stairs hugging the back of the building.

And no, she did not dress this way to keep people away. The

Soul-bringer was wrong about her. Mostly. It was easier to keep a distance when connection seemed an impossible dream.

But what he'd known about Mr Harvey iced her blood. She had eaten heinous sins in her lifetime, but she'd known Harvey. He used to serve on the board of his church.

That a person could never truly know anyone further reinforced her need to keep people at arms reach.

Shrugging off her soiled clothing and stockings, she then aimed for the bathroom, flipped on the shower, and peeked at her reflection. Sin drooling down her chin? How utterly embarrassing.

She laughed as she soaped up in the shower. *That* was all she was worried about? She'd just come face to face with a pissed-off Soul-bringer who had accused her of stealing from him.

Pissed, yet handsome. A strong, angular face had been underlined with a dark goatee to match his record-vinyl hair. The slim-tailored suit and vest was hip, a little Goth, yet he had carried himself with a confidence Nova had only noticed in older men.

"I've always wanted to stop," she sputtered into the water stream. "But what else would I do? How would I support myself? I have no viable nine-to-five skills."

She'd considered stopping before. Sin-eating was no life for a twenty-five-year-old who wanted to date, get married and have children.

Her mother would turn over in her grave if Nova stopped eating sins; it was a tradition passed through the female generations of the family. Nova had been eating sins since her thirteenth birthday. Families steeped in the ancient tradition of cleansing the soul before burial, hired her. And also atheists with deep, yet completely unfounded, fears of a Hell they shouldn't rightly believe in.

The job gave her indigestion and ostracized her from normal society. And talk about messed up? Try eating the sins of your parents and see how well you walk away from that surprising moment.

But stop? Seriously, what was normal? She was human, not immortal, or anything remotely similar. Yet humanity grew farther from her grasp with every sin she consumed.

Drying off and pulling on a fuzzy white robe, Nova tried the idea of *desisting* in her thoughts. The pros: no more ruined clothing. Sin was like tar; no laundry detergent or bleach could take it out. No more attending dismal wakes or funerals or meeting the bereaved at the morgue. Possibility of finally making friends.

The cons? She'd think of something.

Was a kiss from a stranger worth abandoning a notorious yet revered profession handed down to her through generations?

Nova sighed. "It shouldn't be."

Daily, Blackthorn made dozens of trips Above and Beneath. Yet he had a lot of down time. He liked to shoot billiards in scuzzy local bars and drink wine from glasses instead of goblets. And he read anything with an appealing title.

Add tracking a sin-eater to the list. He'd found her easily – only to feel his heart pulse. As if his body had reacted to her presence. As if she could make him think of things beyond bringing souls. Wondrous things, like kissing and holding hands.

"You're letting those dewy grey eyes of hers throw you off-balance."

That was the truth of it. No woman adjusted her life so monumentally for a mere kiss. She had been playing him. The desperate need he'd thought to see in her eyes? Must have been loopy after-effects from purging sin.

Prepared to shimmer out from Beneath and back to the mortal realm, Blackthorn paused when he sighted something charging toward him.

"Blackthorn Regis, do you bring all my souls?" the Receiver growled.

"Yes. I've taken care of the sin-eater."

"You had best be right. There's a blackened soul will be mine in a few days. So many it has murdered."

"If it is destined Beneath, it shall be yours."

"Not if your sin-eater snacks on its murders. If you do not bring that soul to me, Soul-bringer, then I shall take recompense in the sin-eater's soul."

"But you cannot." Blackthorn clamped his mouth shut.

The Receiver roared and inclined his shape so he met Blackthorn eye to fangs. "What did you say?"

"Only that you cannot force a soul your way until her time of death occurs."

"I can make anything happen."

Blackthorn had known that. Why argue for the mortal woman?

"And to make things more interesting, should I be denied this soul, I'll take your life, too. But not until after you've watched me lick the sin-eater's soul to shreds."

"You will not have the opportunity." Blackthorn squared his shoulders before the malevolent creature. "I will bring the killer's soul to you."

He shimmered away and landed in a dark alley in the depths of a city. Holding out a hand before him revealed shaking fingers.

Blackthorn held nothing dear, had no family, no ties to anything living, so he had no reason to fear. He'd never thought himself capable of fear.

It mattered little if the Receiver decided to take his life. But if he could get hold of Desdenova's life simply because Blackthorn could not convince her to give up sin-eating . . .

Glancing up, he spied light in the window he knew belonged to Desdenova. If she ate the killer's sins, the insurmountable evil consumed would crush her, and she would die.

One way or another, the Receiver would claim her soul.

Three

The voice on the other end of the phone receiver announced this collect call was from a federal penitentiary lockup and was being monitored, and then inquired if she would accept the charges.

Befuddled, Nova muttered, "Sure."

She didn't know anyone in prison, yet after replying she kicked herself for not hanging up.

"Desdenova Fleetwood." A man's ragged voice came on. She didn't recognize it. "It's been a long time since we were ten years old, Nova, but I had to speak to you one last time."

Ten years old?

"This is Scott," he said. "Scottie Weston from down the block?"

"Scottie!" Remembrance flooded her brain with sunny summer afternoons spent playing on the jungle gym, and of trekking down the alley, red wagon in tow, in search of dinosaurs and buried treasure. Heck, Scottie had even played Ken to her Barbie, but they had pinky sworn never to tell a soul.

An ominous cloud quickly covered those memories.

"You're um . . . in prison?"

"I am. I don't have more than three minutes to talk to you, Nova, so listen. Remember the promise you made to me under the apple tree after you told me how all the women in your family eat sins?"

She clutched her throat. Words did not form. The air hazed and her eyelids fluttered.

"I'm holding you to that promise, Nova. Come to the federal penitentiary on Saturday at twelve. Arrangements have already been made to allow you admittance. You have to bring ID. Can you do that for me, Nova?"

She had promised a ten-year old boy she would someday eat his sins. Because they had been young and silly, and she'd thought the whole idea of going into the family business sort of exciting, yet steeped in weird gothic overtones that involved religious persecutions and ostracization.

She'd also promised Scottie to give him his first kiss, marry him and jump naked into the Atlantic Ocean with him some day.

It's what kids do.

Nova did not lie or break promises. Never did she sin. It would prove detrimental to her immortal soul when she took her final breath. There was not a sin-eater in the world who would touch another sin-eater's sins.

"Sure, Scottie. Uh . . ."

The receiver clicked and the dial tone hummed.

She moved to replace the receiver. The plastic headset clattered to the floor just as someone beat on her front door. Scrambling to wrangle the phone, she slapped it to the wall cradle and rushed to the door.

The Soul-bringer leaned against the doorframe. The smartly fitted black suit was unbuttoned to reveal a gold-threaded black vest over a black shirt. He looked dapper, seriously, if not for the skater-boy goatee.

When common sense dictated she slam the door in his face and barricade it, she dumbly asked, "How did you know where I live?"

"Followed your soul path. Every mortal leaves one. The brightest, most lasting, belong to those who live good, abundant lives."

"Huh. So mine was pretty bright?"

"No." He bent his head around the doorframe and scanned her efficiency-size living room. "Would you invite me in?"

"Why?" Regaining some of her confidence, Nova stretched an arm along the wall. "Do you need an invitation? Are you like a vampire?"

He strode across the threshold. "No, but an invitation would have left you feeling in control. How are you today, Desdenova?"

"I'm great." She clasped her arms across her chest to allay the nervous jitter. Her heart still pounded after that weird phone call. "Why the visit?"

He strolled behind the purple velvet coach, drawing his fingers along the crushed nap. His eyes took in the abundance of clutter, silk scarves draped over windows and lamps, pillows, books, plants and Mucha lithographs on the wall.

"Quite the marvel," he mused. His crooked smile appealed to her. "But I don't see you in here. Of course, the ego always holds the soul captive."

"I don't have an ego." That was a lie. "I do," Nova blurted out the correction. "We all do."

"Yes. Only the newborn soul is pure. And the soul released from the body following mortal death."

"What about killers like . . ." Mr Harvey.

"Mortal sin does stain the soul irrevocably. There," he said, pointing out the crocheted snowflake tucked in the corner of a picture frame. "A bit of the real you. How intriguing."

"My grandmother taught me the craft. It was for my mother. She died before I could give it to her."

He placed a hand over his heart, which Nova thought reminded her of one of those Knights Templar who vowed to fight for king, country and lady, all in the name of honour.

She could so get behind having her own knight.

"So you think I'm intriguing?" she prompted. "Is that in a 'I'd like to take you out for coffee sometime way', or an 'I've never seen a chick barf up sin before' way?"

"A little of both."

Suddenly Nova grew an inch, and the control he had mentioned bubbled to the surface.

He trailed his fingers along the bookshelf where mysteries

and thrillers loitered with the lush pink and violet spines of romances. "You said last night you would give it up. I thought to stop by and ensure you'd spoken truthfully."

Nova sucked in her lip. Shoot. Last night she'd been playing with the idea of just that. But one phone call had changed everything.

Blackthorn tilted his head to study her face. She wouldn't meet his eyes. He'd see her conflict. And she would want to kiss him just to know his taste.

"So my soul trail isn't bright?"

"You are a thief, Desdenova. Would you expect as much?"

"I uh . . . Thought to live a sinless life. I am not a thief. You are looking at things from the wrong perspective."

"It is my perspective. I can never see things as you do."

She quirked a brow at that cryptic statement.

When he touched a slip of her spiked hair, she inhaled. She'd never stood so close to a man before. Not counting slow dancing with Howard Leeds in eleventh grade, but that had been a lesson in avoiding roaming hands and she hadn't looked at his face once.

Blackthorn had no scent, which bothered her. Yet he possessed the room, the very air, with his stature, his definite there-ness. No other place he should be right now, but right here, before her, preening over her hair, her face, her clothes.

You don't do things like this. Connect.

It felt good. Was that allowed?

"Blackthorn?"

"Yes," he whispered.

"What are you doing?"

"Waiting for you to look at me."

"I . . . can't."

His shoulders sagged and a sigh followed.

She'd let him down. So she put back her elbows and bounced on her heels, because that's what she did when the world tried to pry down her walls. "I never promised you anything."

"No, but I had thought the handshake a deal-clincher," he said.

"I just wanted to touch you. Feel if you were real, or maybe cold like an angel whose blood is blue."

"You've met an angel?"

"No, but I know things." Like that angels bled blue and demons stalked the Fallen ones with blades forged from divinity. Her grandmother had taught her. But granny had never mentioned handsome Soul-bringers who would hold a mirror up to her life.

"Okay, listen." She dropped the bravado. "I have one more job to do and then I promise you I will never eat sins again. I swear it to you. And I never break a promise."

"Never?"

She shook her head adamantly. His eyes were as black as his name. Filled with something so immense. Like centuries, or even millennia. Everything in there. Even her.

Nova gulped and looked aside. "That is, if you're still willing to give me that kiss."

He touched her chin and directed her gaze to his. "You know two days in advance of a dying soul? I thought your job was an on-call basis?"

"I . . ." How *did* Scottie know he was going to die on Saturday at noon? The only way a man in prison could possibly know something like that was . . .

"Desdenova?"

Suddenly shaking, she sensed Blackthorn's hug, him pulling her against his chest and cooing softly as her vision blackened. Felt too good, like a dream.

Her last fleeting thought was of the mournful cry as a soul is put to death for the heinous crimes its body has committed.

Blackthorn laid the sin-eater on her bed and pulled down her skirt to cover her knees. The room was another exercise in bohemian excess. The red lacquered dresser was crowded with framed photos. Family, he decided, comparing the little girl in various pictures to that of mother and father. A family she no longer had, for he felt her loneliness.

Did he want to save Desdenova Fleetwood? Or would it be far wiser to save his own hide and ensure the devil got his due?

Blackthorn had lived uncountable millennia. He'd gone beyond the everyday thoughts and trivialities of mortal life. He had become a vessel that ferried souls. Yet, he existed on the earthly realm and had perhaps even loved.

Loved? Maybe not.

But he understood the concept, and knew it was what kept most mortals alive. The emotion of everything being right and in its place. Of belonging. Of intimacy and respect. The mortal soul actually required love to beam brightly.

To be honest, when standing so close to Nova he'd felt something akin to want. To needing to belong. To existing again.

Why should he be denied simple pleasure when he served his holy and unholy masters so well?

Glancing to the bed, he noticed that her body wore a nimbus of moonlight. He wanted to kiss her pale lips. Lips tainted by multitude sin. Lips formed from the sweetness of innocence he'd never known. And though she was innocent – or believed herself to be – the woman was steeped in evil for some sins cleaved to the sin-eater's soul ever after.

And who would eat *her* sins? Not any sane sin-eater.

The woman needed rescuing. But he was no knight.

He shimmered away from her and got caught in the stream of soul cries that beckoned for his attention.

Four

Nova owned far too much stuff. She made connections with inanimate things more easily than with the living and breathing.

But he had breath. You felt it on your face.

She wanted to feel it again.

She splayed her fingers over the books on the shelf. Memories of heroes and heroines would always be hers; she didn't need the physical pages. The furniture in the living room echoed her bohemian aesthetic, but who needed a couch when they were dead?

Kicking aside the packing boxes half-filled with books she had labelled for the library and kitchen utensils she'd donate to charity, she settled on the floor, sinking against the wall.

The family photos peered at her from the bedroom dresser. Packing those felt like sacrilege.

"I am the queen of sacrilege," she muttered, "according to the Soul-bringer."

Could he be right? Was she the real thief?

An insistent knock at the door prompted her to call out, "It's open, Blackthorn." She didn't get company. Ever. So he was the only possibility.

The Soul-bringer stepped through the doorway and swept the room with his dark eyes. He wasn't much of a smiler. Yet his snazzy vest chased away the dour. He had stepped out of a different time period. Perhaps he had lived them all. Had he made connections in all those periods of time? Or was she a unique intrusion into his life?

"You intending a move?" he put out.

Nova sighed.

The man accepted her silence, wandered around the boxes, and circled back to Nova. Squatting before her, he pressed the heel of his palm to the wall over her shoulder and replicated her world-is-ending sigh.

"You cannot go through with your task tomorrow, Desdenova."

"Who are you to tell me what to do? And what makes you think you know what I'm going to do?"

"You are going through your things. It is as if you do not expect to be around after tomorrow."

"So what if I'm not? We all gotta go some time."

"I can agree that Scott Weston must leave this realm tomorrow at noon. But you have a choice."

"Don't you find it interesting a man can know his exact hour of death?" she pondered, avoiding his eyes. "And because of that knowledge, suddenly I've been given the hour of my death."

"Nova . . ." He didn't know what to say. Did he feel as uncomfortable as she, so close to one another? Did he want to taste her breath on his lips? "You don't need to do this. You cannot."

"I made a promise."

"Is breaking a promise a sin?"

"It is if I believe it a sin."

"You have to believe in a god to subscribe to sin."

He had her there. She did believe in a higher power – in Heaven – and redemption.

"My word is good, Blackthorn. I would never say something and not carry through with it. And if I had no intention to do something, then I would never say it."

"You've more integrity than ninety-nine per cent of the world's population."

"I don't know about that."

"I admire your honesty," he offered.

No one had ever admired a thing about her. Why did something interesting have to happen to her now, when her end was so near?

"Then don't ask me to break a promise. I'll stop eating sins right after Mr Weston. You don't think my soul will go to Heaven?"

"I cannot know. Your sins will be judged by your maker."

"You got that right." Bravery was getting heavier to bear.

Blackthorn dipped his head and looked aside. "What gives you the right to steal sin? You cannot be any man's judge. Only your god is allowed such mastery over the human soul."

She'd had this argument with herself before she'd begun sin-eating at thirteen. "People make mistakes, Blackthorn."

"Murder, dozens of times over, is not a mistake."

And was thirteen too young to know any better? It should be.

"Nova." His sighs sparkled within her when they should have made her sad. "There is a sinister delicacy to the human soul. Once tainted by evil it is very difficult to clean, no matter the circumstances that brought about the taint."

"Even if those circumstances involved taking other people's sins," she stated, not liking the reality of her profession. Thievery, indeed.

She took his hands in hers and smoothed her thumbs along them. They were strong and calloused. A man's hands. What would they feel like wrapped around her?

Nova cleared her throat and her wandering thoughts.

"When I first started," she said, "I ate the sin from a man who had dropped his crippled mother down the stairs. It was an accident. He had been carrying her from the bath to her bedroom. Her head hit the tile landing and she died instantly. He spoke to me a week before he died of cancer. He thought he was guilty, couldn't get beyond it, even after the police had ruled it an accident.

"I am there to calm worries, Blackthorn. To take away guilt for things that should never cause guilt. In a sense, we are all sin-caters. We sit beside our loved ones when they are dying, ease their discomfort, grant them absolution for simple things."

"Yes, but you've the power to erase sin, Nova. It should not be wielded without great care. The only worry this serial killer has is that you won't make it there in time. He bears no remorse for his crimes. His soul belongs Beneath. It is not for you to decide."

"Nor is it your decision."

She tugged her hands from his and drew her knees up to her chest. "I will quit after this last one. I promise."

"The Receiver of Beneath will take your soul if he is not satisfied."

Nova grimaced. "The devil wants to take my soul? Bring it on."

"And then he'll kill me. But only after I have watched him torture you."

She flicked a look at him. "Why? Do you care about me so much it would cause you pain?"

He touched her cheek, stroking his thumb along it. The touch was so intimate it made her want to lunge forward for the kiss she so desperately needed.

"Desdenova, you and I, we don't get to love."

Swallowing, she looked aside. "I know that."

"Love is a cruel emotion."

"So says the guy who probably doesn't even understand guilt and honour and . . . and emotion. You've no capacity to love, do you?"

"I see that love hurts those who cared about the deceased. They are torn apart. Why do you insist love is so good?"

"Blackthorn, love is the reason we are here on earth. To love, and be loved."

"I am aware that love feeds the soul." He explained, "I know how to love. I know how to want, to desire, to pine for something. I ignore that evil."

"Don't call something so perfect evil."

"It is something you pine for."

"I do."

"Is it more important to you than honour and truth?"

"I think so. I had it once, from my parents."

He nodded, pleased. "That is not your ego talking, but your truth."

"You're missing a lot if you don't feel it," Nova said.

"You think so?" He sat beside her and took her hand between his. "If love can be a distraction, you are it."

A blush warmed her cheeks.

The moment felt so freakin' normal. It wasn't as if some immortal man who had the ability to enter Above and Beneath sat beside her. He was just a guy. A handsome, warm, wonderful guy she wanted to kiss all day and night until she had to leave this world.

Leave her entire life behind. All because of a ten-year-old's naive promise.

"I won't allow this to happen," he said. He kissed her knuckles and held them there at his lips.

"I won't let you force me to break a promise."

"Keep your promise. Go to that bastard tomorrow."

She turned and clutched his vest, the fine silk too soft and rich. "Don't screw things up for me. If I steal these sins from you—"

"I'll be fine. But you . . . The devil will not have your soul," he said with determination. "Nova, trust me."

"I don't even know you."

"I like you." He winced, as if the words had cut his tongue. Or maybe it was such an odd declaration, he didn't know what to think of it.

"You like me? Like . . . romantically?"

Nova liked him, too. And she didn't have a reasonable explanation either, other than that he appealed to her. He made her want to know more about him. To want to show him that love was not always cruel.

"You're not frightened of me," he said. "You were born into a family tradition, and yet you face it with remarkable courage. There's not a sin-eater in this world who doesn't revel in sin and indulge because he knows the taint in his soul will see him Beneath when death calls his number."

"I may be tainted with the sins of others, but it's not my sin. I believe the greater power – be it God, Allah, Buddha, whoever you want to name – sees only those sins that belong to the person, not others."

"Interesting theory."

"You know otherwise?" *Please say no, please say no.*

"No."

She relaxed. She would have enjoyed getting to know this guy if she'd more time. But she couldn't mourn the things she'd miss if she hadn't yet had them. Things like love, desire and sex.

He clutched his heart. This time the wince creased his forehead. "Sorry. I've to go."

"Souls?"

He nodded. "You will see me tomorrow."

"I know. But it better not be until after I've done the deed."

Blackthorn's smile disappeared like the Cheshire cat's as he shimmered away from her side, leaving Nova shivering for the lack of warmth, and the thrill of new desire.

Five

Nova walked up the pristine sidewalk to the penitentiary. Not a bird chirped, there was no breeze to cool her sweaty palms. The sun was so bright it bleached the sky white. The prison's red brick walls made it look a schoolhouse, if not for the chain-link fence, razor wire, floodlights and towers with armed guards.

"Farewell," she whispered, knowing it sounded dramatic, but feeling it in her marrow, "to all my earthly attachments and my family."

And then there was Blackthorn Regis. Talk about wrong place and wrong time to find Mr Right.

Heck, she didn't know enough about him to decide if he was right or wrong. Probably a smart woman would say *wrong* because the man could never be around all the time.

Yet he believed in her. He accepted Nova held her own beliefs, and didn't try to make her something she was not. That was something no girl should let slip from her grasp.

She started to wonder how painful it would be, dying. It was never a picnic vomiting up sin. What followed after she'd performed the eating today was going to be that, multiplied by a hundred.

"Stop it," she muttered. Her black sneakers tracked the sidewalk. "Focus on the now. You can't change any of this."

Yet Blackthorn believed she could.

Certainly, she could make a different choice. But any choice other than this one would see her promise broken.

She had to respect a promise, no matter that it had been made fifteen years ago. Then she'd honour the promise made to Blackthorn.

The door to the prison opened with an ominous creak and shut so quickly Nova wondered how many had skinned a heel if they hadn't stepped in fast enough. A steely-eyed officer wearing full uniform and a gun at his hip waited for her to approach. This was no reception area playing muzak and offering magazines while you waited.

"I'm Desdenova Fleetwood. I have an appointment to see Scott Weston, er . . . after?"

"Right, the religious liaison," he said, noting something on the schedule before him. "Here to view the body and bless it, eh? The killer's dying wish. Sweet."

She nodded, nerves keeping her silent, for to speak she would have to reveal the truth. It wasn't her lie; it had come from Weston.

He pointed to the right. "You'll need to go through security."

"Thanks."

Shouldn't a dying man's last wish be honoured?

You have too much integrity.

At what point did a man lose his rights if he had taken the lives of so many? Truly, *did* he deserve a dying wish?

Nova was not the person to make that call. She was simply here to do a duty.

You've no right to be their judge. You are a thief.

Blackthorn had a point.

Nova clutched her neck. Was this wrong? She needed someone to tell her what to do. She was one person. One soul who followed her beliefs. But who was to say those beliefs were the right ones?

She glanced over her shoulder. Where was her rescuing knight?

You're letting him influence you, to sway you. Be strong. Don't succumb to base attraction. The man could never be right for you. He isn't even mortal.

Summoning courage, Nova walked onwards.

The security check was tedious. She was frisked from head to toe. It was embarrassing, even with a female officer doing the frisking. Nova thanked a God she wasn't sure existed for the freedoms she had enjoyed all her life.

Must a Soul-bringer lead a tethered life? He was always at the beck and call of souls waiting to be collected. A man couldn't possibly develop meaningful relationships that way.

They were two alike, in so many ways it heartened her. She wanted to know him. She wanted more time with him.

"Ma'am?"

Nova jumped and started towards the door to her right, but the female officer harrumphed loudly.

"Your bag."

"Oh. Sorry."

She set down her bag and the officer upended it. A glance at the clock showed two minutes to noon. Nova didn't have to show up while Weston was still breathing. Her work started after his heart stopped.

And no Soul-bringer had better beat her to it, either.

Yes, please, beat me there. Stop this thief before she sins again.

Oh, hell, Nova, you *are* the one in the wrong. You take away the judgment owed all men. And you will be judged yourself.

The officer shoved her empty bag towards Nova. "Stay right here."

Nova glanced at the wall. The clock's long hand clicked across the twelve at the same time the short hand did. She eyed the fluorescent lights. Would there be a power surge?

No, silly, that was only in movies. Besides, they gave lethal injections nowadays.

"You can enter the waiting room, Miss Fleetwood. The decedent will be brought in shortly."

Six

Dead bodies did not bother her. She ate the sins. Nothing bizarre happened. She didn't feel the sin go into her with a thud or shock. It was a non-event. Until she puked it up later.

Nova ate the last bits of salted bread from the plate she had set upon the unmoving chest. The corpse was dressed in a white cotton jumpsuit and no shoes. Scott Weston didn't look as she remembered him fifteen years ago. As always, the decedent merely looked asleep, caught in reverie.

Tears rolled down her cheeks. She'd never allowed emotion to contaminate an eating. Nor had she allowed conflicting thoughts to interfere.

This is your last meal, kept pinging the surface of her brain. And then – *Blackthorn didn't get here first.*

She dropped her arms to her sides and glanced to the guard standing inside the small room. A nod from him and she collected her bag from the floor beside her feet, and walked out.

Simple as that. Salt the bread. Eat it. Think pure thoughts (or try to). Leave.

Her footsteps quickened as she anticipated the inevitable violent purge.

Once outside, she ran towards her car, bag clutched to her chest and tears spattering the air. Slamming her hands to the trunk of her yellow VW Bug, she huffed and panted. She'd learned Weston had murdered eighteen women after raping them. This was not going to be pretty.

How dare she steal those sins? Was a promise so much grander than theft? Than murder?

Closing her eyes, Nova bent her knees and sank against the wheel well, the tyre digging into her hip. She should have parked at the back of the lot, next to the line of weeds under the chain-link fence. Towers dotted the high brick walls, capped with curled razor wire. Guards would see no matter where she positioned herself.

Soon the heat would rise through her muscles and skin and bring up her bile.

"I'm not ready," she said in sniffling sobs. "I can't die here. Alone. I've made a mistake."

The smell of hot tarmac should have dizzied her, yet the scent reminded her of summer. Gasoline fumes fixed her to real time, the now.

Thoughts were too clear. She did not feel out of sorts, as if her stomach billowed up to her throat. She did not feel . . . anything.

A pair of legs materialized beside her. Nova followed the elegant black trousers up to the snazzy vest.

She jumped up to face Blackthorn and clutched his jacket. "You stole from me!"

"I stole nothing," he said calmly. "I heard the soul shout and arrived to collect it."

"Before I was allowed in to eat the sins. You were waiting for it."

"Not at all. I cannot know when a soul is ready until the actual death. Nor am I aware who has, or has not, visited the body before my arrival. Nova, I am sorry. Had you actually eaten Weston's sins, you would be the real thief."

"Don't touch me." She stepped away from his touch. "I don't want to be a thief! I hate you!"

Scrambling around to the driver's side, she hopped in and fired up the engine. Blackthorn no longer stood in the parking lot when she drove out.

So he had lost the girl. And had he ever even wanted her?

"Yes," Blackthorn whispered.

He sat on the flat, pebble-frosted rooftop of a building across the street from Nova's apartment complex. Considering her emotional temperament, he'd been worried about her getting home safely.

Keep telling yourself that, buddy.

He hadn't stolen Weston's soul from her. He'd been doing his job. He had pleased the Receiver – and life went on.

Yet had he stolen Nova's integrity?

He knew he had not, but did she?

A shadow passed before the picture window fronting her apartment. No lights on inside. She'd packed all her things, had been prepared for death because she believed in her heart that her way was the right way. A woman like her stood alone. She could do so many great things if she stepped away from the abysmal darkness of sin-eating.

But who was he to judge? Without adversity life would be dull. If he had not the sin-eater's challenge he would not now be pondering his own heart. She had made him suddenly . . . not nothing.

Had he the capacity to love? At the very least, to care about a mortal soul still firmly affixed within a body? And not just a body. A simple, beautiful woman who required nothing more than a kiss – and trust.

He wanted to know things about her. Like, what was her favourite book on the shelf full of many? How had her grandmother smiled as she'd taught her granddaughter a craft? Had Nova known how great was that love?

Something lighted on his shoulder. Blackthorn started, and turned to find Nova beside him. Dressed in jeans and a soft blue sweater, she sat close, her arm hugging his and drew her knees up and propped her chin there.

"Sorry," she said. "I don't hate you."

"You've every right—"

"No, I don't. You were doing your job. I wanted it to happen that way, but denied the truth when it was granted. I've had a good talk with myself. I have no right to make judgments. I can't worry about what happens with my soul when it leaves this world. I want to live, Blackthorn. Right now. Tomorrow. The next day. What are you doing today?"

"Me?" Blackthorn drew her hand up to his mouth. Fragile fingers capable of caressing his hardened heart closed about his. "I think there's a deal I have to pay up on. Something about a kiss?"

"I was hoping you hadn't forgotten. But let me."

"Let you?"

"I'm going to kiss you."

He turned his body towards her. "I have never been warned about a kiss before."

"It's not a warning – well, maybe it is. You look the sort who will be surprised."

"Nothing surprises me, Nova. I have lived and experienced far too long."

Nova pushed her fingers through his hair and leaned to touch his mouth with hers. Yet she didn't connect immediately. Instead, the two of them lingered there, face-to-face, breaths blending, hearts pounding.

Becoming. Two learning.

She was the first to move forward and brush his mouth with hers. Warmth burnished more than her lips, perhaps her very soul. She wanted him to have a soul, to know this exquisite connection.

His touch drew her into the dark, sweet glimmer of alluring passion.

Want. It was a simple thing, laced with yearning and desire.

Sinful? That all depended on who was doing the judging. Nova didn't want to judge; she simply wanted to live. To take what life offered her.

When she pulled back, his eyelids flickered and his dark irises gleamed.

"You're surprised," she said.

"So I am." He held out his hand and Nova threaded her fingers through his. "That was a splendid kiss."

She laid her head on his shoulder. "So I didn't actually break my promise today."

"You went to the penitentiary with intention. It was not your fault the soul cried out before you got to the body. But you do know perhaps only monks live sinless lives?"

She nodded. "I understand now that sin-eating is sin in and of itself."

"Well-intentioned."

"I'm not going to worry about it. There are much better ways to occupy one's time." She tilted her head against his shoulder. "Do you date, Blackthorn?"

"You mean, a steady girl? I've never tried it."

"Maybe you should. It's good to make connections, and have friends. Love, well, it is important to survival."

"The soul's survival. I admire you. When I look at you my glass heart pulses."

"It's glass? That means you're a—"

"I was once."

"Wow."

He hugged her against him. "You understand me, Desdenova. Perhaps we could give it a try?"

"Would you disappear during the middle of a date to go collect souls?"

"Probably. But when I am not on a task I would be with you. Always."

"Kiss me again, Soul-bringer."

Fragile Magic

Sharon Ashwood

A wingtip brushed Selina's ear. She yelped, a short, sharp cry of surprise.

Jolted out of her grocery-shopping stupor, Selina whipped around. Her skin tingled where she'd felt the whisper of suede-soft skin. The sensation rippled down her neck like tiny fingers.

What the . . . ?

With a thunderous *smack*, the cereal aisle exploded in a storm of frosty, flaky goodness. Seconds later, the air filled with the sound of cereal pattering back to earth like the inside of a break-fast-food snow globe. Selina scanned her surroundings, trying to make sense of it all.

She squinted at the mess. There were certain things she expected to encounter in the grocery aisle. A gargoyle flounder-ing in a drift of Toasty-Os was not among them.

"What is that thing?" a man demanded, picking up a jar of peanut butter like an offensive weapon.

"It's hideous," someone else said.

"Is somebody going to call animal control?"

"It's just a gargoyle," Selina put in.

They were one of the many oddball species that had started popping up lately, some humanoid and some – like the gargoyles – definitely not. It had started happening during Y2K, when the vampires had swanned on to the talk show circuit and revealed themselves to the world in an emo tell-all. After that, being a plain old human was just so last century. Paranormal was instantly the new black. More and more supernatural species were emerging from the shadows and signing up for cell phones, credit cards and cable TV.

Which was exciting unless, like Selina, you'd rather *not* be special. Having a fey daddy and three fey sisters was enough to drive anyone to the relative sanity of business college. Nothing said "get that magic wand out of my face" like an MBA and a pinstripe suit.

Thankfully, she'd managed to tune out most of the media monster madness – until now. There, between her and the Toaster Tarts, was a gargoyle: pointy ears, beak and all, right where she couldn't ignore it.

Man, that is one ugly critter.

She wanted to back away but morbid fascination made her stare. Gargoyles were, for want of a better description, animals. Its hind feet – two claws front, one back – were made to perch on medieval architecture. Sadly, the Save-It Store lacked flying buttresses. Now the creature couldn't get its footing on the treacherous Toasty-Os and it squawked with cartoonish alarm. One wing drooped, perhaps injured in the collision with the display unit.

"What's it doing here?" the man asked, still clutching the jar.

Selina shrugged. "Some people keep them like dogs."

"Sick monster-loving jerks." The guy took off down the aisle with his peanut butter.

"Whatever." She checked her watch, her mind back at the gallery where she worked. She'd been dragged from the back offices to cover for the owner during his illness. As a result, she was slammed with appointments. This sideshow in the cereal aisle was going to make her late. Selina gripped the handle of her cart, a wave of grumpiness overtaking her.

Seconds later, a man in a green apron advanced with a broom and a scowl. At the sight of him, the gargoyle began flapping its one good wing, making a frantic noise somewhere between a *cheep* and the belch of a hairballing cat.

From the look on the clean-up guy's face, the gargoyle was about to be scrubbed out of existence. Selina pulled her cart to one side, willing the critter to make a break for freedom. *Do not pass go, do not collect Klub Kard points. Flee, little monster, be free.*

No such luck. It cowered before the broom guy, wings pathetically askew. It had big, round eyes the colour of lime Jell-o. Her heart began to hurt for it.

"I think it's a juvenile," Selina blurted. "It's kind of small."

Mr Clean-up poked the gargoyle with the head of the huge push-broom. The gargoyle staggered, its round body overbalanced. She could feel its panic like a wave of electricity, millions of sharp needles pricking her skin. That was her dreaded fey blood talking but even a plain old human could see the creature's distress.

The guy just jabbed it again.

"Stop that!" she snapped, coming out from behind the cart. Selina was small and slight, but outrage made her bold. *So I'm going to be late back to the office. I can't just leave the poor thing sitting in a pile of cereal.*

Broom Guy gave her the once-over, taking in her smooth blond hair and smartly tailored business suit – then turned away without interest. His expression said he preferred skinning baby monsters with his pocket knife.

"Damned thing probably got away from the pet store next door," he ground out, voice filled with as much light and laughter as the dirty floor tiles. "The flying rats figure out how to get the cage doors open." He knocked the gargoyle again. It toppled over with a moaning rattle.

Selina felt her skin growing hot with anger, her silk blouse sticking as she marched forward. "Why don't you just take it next door and give it back?"

"I'm not touching that thing. Have you seen that beak?"

"Coward." She didn't like touching supernatural creatures either – they stirred her own powers to life – but this was an emergency. Selina scooped up the gargoyle, cradling it against her chest. Its grey, wrinkled skin was soft as kid leather, warm and slightly fuzzy. It grabbed on with its front paws, digging tiny claws into the wool of her jacket. *That had better not leave holes.*

"Whatever." Deprived of a monster to bully, Broom Guy took a swipe at the Toasty-Os. "Pet store's to the left of the front door."

The gargoyle snuggled, making an odd little gurgle. One wing was definitely crooked. It looked broken to her. She could feel its panic fading to desperation as it curled against her, seeking the comfort of her warmth.

Selina turned on her heel and walked out, snatching up her purse as she abandoned her cart.

Half an hour later, she left the pet store with a shocking Visa bill, a carry-bag of canned food, and a *Getting to Know Your Gargoyle* info folder, complete with feeding instructions and veterinary referral.

She hadn't been able to stand the sight of the tiny wire cages along the back of the Exotic Pet Emporium – especially once the gargoyle had started to keen and cling to her. Its panic came back in hammering waves that sent her fey senses spinning. Other animals – some golden Lab puppies and a baby griffin – gave her big, sad eyes as she stood there hovering on the knife-edge of guilt and temptation. It was hard not to take them all.

"Congratulations," said the pet store cashier, all smiles as he rang up the sale. "You've got a great guard animal there. He's only eight weeks right now but they grow fast. This little guy will get to be about 120 pounds."

Oh, no way! She was so not keeping a gargoyle for a pet. She was just rescuing him until she could find a better owner. If she had a pet, it would be something like a fish or a canary – something that stayed in its cage and didn't break anything. Something that didn't kickstart the empathic powers she'd buried beneath a cartload of accounting texts and sensible shoes.

Dismay settled over her as she crossed the parking lot to her car. *A hundred and twenty pounds?*

Selina tossed the back-seat clutter – a woollen car blanket, a map book and some binders from work – on to the floor and made room for the gargoyle. It hunkered down until it was wedged between the seat back and the passenger door. Every few seconds, it worried its crooked wing with its beak, poking at the injury.

Selina pulled out her cellphone and dialled the gallery with one hand while, with the other, she fished in the pet store paperwork for the vet's address. The card was stapled to the inside of the folder and gave an address about ten minutes away. The vet's name was simply listed as "Dr Jake." What kind of a name was that?

Sounds like a frontier medical man, scalpel in one hand and bar room floozy in the other.

Meanwhile, the phone at The Old World Art and Antiques Gallery went to voicemail. The recorded message jerked her back to the present. Her boss, Richard Janos – still at home after heart surgery and grouchy as a bear – was too sick to run the gallery but still trying to micromanage from afar. He wouldn't be happy that she was MIA, especially right now.

In a little over a month, collectors were coming from three countries to attend Old World's exhibition and sale of eighteenth-century French antiques. There was a lot left to arrange, even though Selina had taken over the planning when Janos fell ill. She'd always shied away from working with the public, never wanting to advertise the fact that she was anything but a numbers gal, but this was an excuse to show off what she could do. Fey were the ultimate party planners, with a flair for turning the dullest affair into a smash hit. Combined with her human knack for financial detail, Selina was bred for the job. Not only was the show hotly anticipated, clients had started asking for her by name.

Hopefully, her recent successes would buy her some slack. Selina pushed a button to get the admin assistant's voicemail inbox. "Hi, it's me. Listen, would you please cancel the one-thirty with the caterer and tell him I'll be in touch tomorrow. Reschedule my two o'clock with Mrs McAdams to five and would you please call the framers and tell them I'll be by in the morning? Something personal's come up. I'll explain when I get there."

She disconnected before anyone could pick up. Sighing, she leaned back against the seat, trying to relax for a split second before tackling the next problem. She was getting a headache.

Part of the reason was that Selina could feel the gargoyle's anxiety like something gnawing at her belly. Instinctively, she reached out with her mind. If she could just steal away the animal's distress – that was her magical talent, the one trick her half-fey blood could sometimes manage. On a good day, she was just empath enough to catch emotion and blow it out like a candle.

But she was rusty, her fragile magic sluggish from disuse. It felt like moving blocks of concrete by will alone. *Can I do this?*

Selina opened her eyes, realizing she'd been squeezing them shut. Gasping a deep breath, she wiped her eyes and glanced in the rear view mirror. The gargoyle was staring at her, round-eyed, but the look was now adoration instead of fear. *It worked!*

On the other hand, she didn't look so good. Sweat dewed her face, tendrils of her blond hair darkened where they clung to her damp cheeks. Her expression looked bruised.

She'd sworn off using her talent for a good reason: it sucked. *And people thought being a fey meant dancing in dew circles with a mushroom cap on your head. Yeah, right.*

With shaking fingers, she stabbed the key into her car's ignition.

With a final glance at the back seat, Selina pulled out of the parking lot. The gargoyle whimpered as the car moved. It crawled down to the floorboards, doing its best to hide under the folds of the blanket. *So much for taking away his fear.* That only worked if there was nothing new to be afraid of. Car rides were no fun for any animal. *Must get one of those dog carriers.*

Which would only make sense if I was keeping him. Involuntarily, she twitched. One bad landing, and he could take out her collection of rare Chinese vases. And who knew what those claws could do to the Louis Quatorze escritoire? She'd bought that piece with an eye to her retirement plan. A good antique just kept gathering value – at least it would until Gary the Gargoyle smashed it to smithereens.

Gary. It sort of suited the little guy, who was now sending up an occasional pathetic moan. She hoped that didn't mean he was about to be car sick.

She turned into the Bayside Vet Clinic, wedging the car into one of the three visitor spaces. The building was showing its age – low, white and plain except for tattered green awnings. Selina got out of the car and walked around to the passenger side. She opened the door, ready in case the gargoyle made a run for it. It didn't. It flattened to a whimpering pancake.

Selina reached in, picking it up under the forelegs and catching an unpleasant smell. It had piddled on the plaid wool car blanket. It looked away, the picture of guilt, and hid its face against her arm. *Oh, damn. Poor little guy.*

She kicked the car door shut and, cradling the gargoyle, carried it into the vet's office. Dr J. Hallender's name – Dr Jake? – was the only one stencilled on the door, right above a line of bold lettering that read: *Everyone deserves the very best care. No furry friend too unusual.*

Selina wondered how much more this act of mercy was going to cost her.

The receptionist, identified by her name tag as Tracy, looked up as Selina came in. "Hi, can I help you?"

"Broken wing, I think."

"Are you one of Dr Jake's clients?"

"As of now I am."

Tracy gave a grudging smile. Selina eyed her. The young woman had a sharp, hungry look that wasn't quite human. Werewolf? Werewolfism wasn't contagious but did that matter once you were digested?

"How soon can we see Dr – um – Dr Jake?"

Tracy leaned across the reception desk, gently scratching the gargoyle's head. Selina could feel the heat of the she-wolf's skin even though they never touched. Shape-shifters seemed to run at a higher temperature than humans.

An affectionate look softened Tracy's features. "What's his name?"

"Um, Gary."

"Hey, Gary." She ran a finger down the crooked wing.

The gargoyle flinched into Selina's chest, gripping the front of her coat for dear life. He turned pain-filled eyes up to her.

A thin line formed between Tracy's brows. "Yeah, there's something wrong there, poor baby. Go right into Exam One. There are a few people waiting, but I'll make sure Jake sees this little guy right away."

Tracy pointed down the hallway. The sign for each exam room was clearly visible.

As she walked down the hall, Selina took quick peeks through glass windows into the other rooms. There was a storage space filled with surgical equipment, cages, and shelves of medical supplies. Another held a woman and what looked like a giant lizard. In a third, an ordinary-looking guy was pacing the room in a stew of anxiety. There was no pet in sight. *Hm.*

Exam One was empty. Selina went in and carefully set Gary on the table. He didn't want to let go, but he was getting heavy. *The little guy has to be a good twelve pounds.*

Fortunately, there was an open jar of dog treats on the counter. As she bribed him on to the table, he grabbed the cookie with paws that reminded her of a raccoon. *No wonder they break out of ordinary cages.*

"Don't give him too many of those," said a soft male voice from the doorway. "You should really be looking for grain-free products."

Selina felt like a mom caught feeding her infant french fries. Heat flared in her cheeks as she wheeled to face the door. "I'm sorry, I didn't know."

Oh! She caught sight of the speaker. "Dr Jake, I presume?"

He was young, in blue jeans and a navy T-shirt under a rumpled lab coat. The look was more outdoorsy than doctorish, his footwear sturdy hiking boots. His eyes and wavy hair were both a rich brown that made her think of dark chocolate fudge.

"Jake Hallender," he offered a hand.

"Selina Pearson." As she grasped his hand, she felt the same heat that had radiated from the receptionist's skin. *Wolf.* She resisted the urge to flinch away. It wasn't hard. His smile was filled with easy-going, good-humoured amusement, with just a pinch of mischief. There was nothing *obviously* threatening about the vet, unless one could weaponize male charm.

I bet he knows he's cute. He has that look, like he could get away with anything and you'd forgive him. Who knew male arrogance crossed species lines? The doctor's gaze was travelling up her body, eventually coming to rest on her face. From his expression, he liked what he saw. She took back her hand and turned pointedly to the exam table, avoiding inspection.

Gary was poking at his wing again. He'd abandoned the treat.

"I think my gargoyle's wing is broken," she said, getting right down to business.

"How long have you had him?" Dr Jake picked up a stethoscope and hooked it into his ears.

"About an hour."

He stopped short. "An hour?"

"Yes, I got him this afternoon," Selina looked at her watch. "And, I'm sorry, but I need to be back at the office by five for an appointment. I've already put it off once."

The vet all but rolled his eyes. "If you've got a full schedule, maybe you should adopt a cactus instead of a pet." Although his tone was polite, there was a sudden edge of frost.

She felt the heat in her cheeks deepen. "I didn't set out this morning to adopt anything. It was an accident."

Dr Jake gave her a curious look before pressing the end of the stethoscope against Gary's back and stomach, making him squirm. "An accident, huh? Gargoyles need at least some attention, and they're not small. This boy will grow to seventy-five pounds or so."

"Well, that's a relief."

Dr Jake raised an eyebrow. "A relief?"

"The pet store said one-twenty."

"Stores often don't know what they have. The big gargoyles are the European breed. The greys like yours are smaller. Friendlier, too."

As if to demonstrate, Gary made a gentle squawk into the stethoscope, grabbing it in one paw and then trying to stuff it into his beak. The vet winced, pulling the earpieces out and hanging the instrument around his neck. "Well, there's nothing wrong with his heart or lungs. You're lucky. Domestic specimens are often so inbred there are birth defects. Your boy's just fine." He turned Gary around and began examining his damaged wing. Gary chittered a protest, but didn't try to bite.

Selina watched Jake's square, competent hands as he worked. Firm but gentle. What else were those hands expert at?

He administered a shot, explaining it was to freeze the wing. Then he cast her a sideways glance. "So what made you accidentally buy a gargoyle?"

"I rescued him from a guy with a broom. Gary was on the lam from the pet store and took a dive into the cereal aisle at the Save-It Store."

The vet looked at her with new interest, one that went beyond physical appreciation. Rescuing Gary had obviously scored her points, which should have been a good thing. For Selina, not so much. Her empathic gift told her more than she wanted to know. She could feel his attention like a klieg light. That was the difference between a human and a wolf. When a wolf chose to notice you, he really *looked*. But Selina spent her life flying under the radar, and that much scrutiny was uncomfortable.

"I'm not sure I can keep a pet," she said flatly, hoping that would put him off. "I work in an antiques gallery. I'm gone most of the day and I live in a small apartment."

"Does the landlord allow pets?"

"I guess so. The lady next door used to have a parrot." She watched him dab what looked like a gel on the back of Gary's wing. Despite herself, she leaned closer to get a better look. "What is that stuff?"

"Glue, actually. It will help immobilize the wing while the bone heals." He carefully folded the wing into a natural, closed position. "Can you hold him just like that?"

Selina slipped her hands next to his, conscious of the warmth of his skin and the soft fuzz of Gary's hide. Dr Jake began binding the closed wing against Gary's back, wrapping the bandage just below the creature's armpits. "The worst habit baby gargoyles have is a tendency to swallow small objects. Rings, erasers, marbles—"

"Stethoscopes."

He laughed, a quick flash of white teeth. "Yeah. You have to watch them pretty carefully. Otherwise, they're excellent company. Easy to house train. As long as they have a window and somewhere to perch, they're pretty content to watch the world go by."

"Good to know," Selina replied. "How long is it going to take the wing to heal?"

He caught her eye, a smile lurking at the corners of his mouth. He brushed her hands more than was strictly necessary as he fastened the bandage. "About a month. There will be follow-up visits."

Selina caught the teasing tone in his voice. "Is that so?"

He gave her puppy dog eyes. "Several."

He held her gaze. She felt like ice cream slowly turning to a sticky puddle. *Don't go there. Really. Do. Not. Encourage. Him.*

Jake's smile was taking over his face, one dimple at a time.

Dammit. "Are you flirting?" *Stupid question.*

"Would you like me to?"

"I didn't think wolves dated humans."

"But you're fey."

Selina's whole body jolted with shock. *Oh, crap.* She was busted.

"Ah, sorry," he said, smile fading. "From the look on your face, you'd rather keep that private."

"I'm only half fey," Selina countered, feeling her heart skitter. "You're the first person in town who's guessed." *And you'd better be the last!*

"I knew quite a few fey back in my home town. I recognized your scent."

"Guess I'd better wear heavier perfume."

"Your secret's safe with me."

"There are professional reasons . . ." *No one does business with a fey. The humans think we're all tricksters. I'd lose my job.*

"Say no more."

"Please . . ."

"Don't you trust wolves?" His eyebrows arched. "Why don't I try and convince you of my honesty over coffee?"

Selina's shock morphed into exasperation. *This guy just won't quit!* "Aren't there professional ethics about seeing your patients?"

"I don't want to ask your gargoyle out for dinner." He stroked Gary's head. "As a species, they're sweet-tempered but deathly short on conversation."

Selina opened her mouth but struggled for words, outraged and intrigued at the same time. *I heard wolves moved fast.* She suddenly felt less articulate than Gary.

A crash came from outside the exam room door. The noise was metallic, as if a tray of medical instruments had fallen. It was followed by a loud thump.

Dr Jake pulled off his stethoscope and set it on the counter, his movements quick and precise. Selina read tension in the bunched muscles of his shoulders. "Stay here." He stepped outside, closing the door behind him.

What's going on?

Gary started bobbing up and down, squeaking like a rusty pogo stick. Automatically, she picked up the gargoyle to comfort him, stroking the soft skin of his back. The bright white bandage made him lopsided, his injured wing bound tight.

Cuddling him, Selina stood to one side of the exam room door and tried to peer through the narrow window. She could see part of the hallway and, sure enough, a rolling cart of supplies had crashed into the wall. It leaned drunkenly, a trail of surgical tools marking its path to collision. One of the other exam room doors stood open, blocking the rest of her view. She heard Dr Jake's voice. "Tracy! A little help here!"

Wasn't that the room where the ordinary-looking guy had been pacing? Selina tried to remember as she set Gary back on the table. The gargoyle cheeped, reaching for the dog cookies. Selina gave him one, hoping it would keep him busy for a moment. "You be good," she admonished.

Gary blinked his lime green eyes, the picture of innocence, and stuck the cookie in his beak. Selina opened the door, cautiously peeking out. Common sense told her the thumps and growls coming from the exam room were bad news, especially in a clinic like this. She stepped into the hall, pulling the door shut.

Tracy stumbled backwards into the hall. She caught sight of Selina. "Get back in the room!" she snapped. "We've got a first-timer in here." Her voice sounded rough, as if her wolf were lurking just beneath her human mask.

A first-timer! Someone – usually someone adopted as a kid – meeting their inner beast for the first time. Selina had heard horror stories about those poor shlubs who went through life as Grade A human, and then one day succumbed to a genetic time bomb that turned them into ravening fuzz balls. The late onset was due to a mysterious complex of factors – hormones, no pack socialization, human diet – but the outcome was predictable. Even if their bodies survived, their minds usually didn't. Unexpectedly turning into a wolf wreaked havoc with the psyche.

"But it's not full moon," Selina said.

"Don't believe everything you see in the movies. Full moon isn't the only time the change can happen."

Selina stood mute for a moment, fighting a dread so strong it felt like nausea. Some of it was hers, some came from outside. She took a breath, forcing her stomach to hold steady. "I think I can help."

"Yeah, right." Tracy flashed her a look of contempt. "Get back in the room or get out the door. This is going to be ugly."

The receptionist lunged for the rolling cart and began rummaging through the jumble of supplies. Two more bodies exploded from the room, hitting the worn carpet with a thump of bone and flesh. Selina jumped back. They rolled, momentum smacking them into the baseboard. Dr Jake was on top, kneeling on his opponent's back and wrenching the other man's arm into a hammer lock. The vet was a big man, but the other was surfing supernatural adrenaline. He threw Jake off and scrambled to his feet, roaring with fury and confusion.

Selina had seen the change just once before. It had been fast and fluid, like a ripple in water – one moment a man, the next a wolf. This guy looked like he'd become stuck. He was hairy more than furry, one eye blue, the other yellow. The bones in his head looked all wrong, and there were definitely too many big, sharp teeth.

The wolfman and Dr Jake noticed Selina in the same instant. The vet was on his feet again, scrambling to put himself in front of her. Jake was starting to look a little wolfy himself, his teeth bared and shoulders hunched.

"Get back," he said to the other man in a low voice. "Stay away from her."

The wolfman sprang at the vet, teeth snapping.

"Watch out!" yelled Tracy.

Jake rolled into the motion of his attack, throwing his attacker to the floor with a practised flip. The man's foot caught the edge of the cart and it went down with a crash, scattering supplies. Jake leaped on top.

Tracy crouched beside him, wrenching the wolfman's shirt aside and jabbing a syringe into his shoulder. The drug was too little, too late. Black, curving claws thrust from the wolfman's fingers in a spray of blood. He shrieked in pain, the sound cresting in an inhuman howl that tore through Selina.

A wave of hot nausea slammed into her. Choking it down, she pushed forward.

"Get back!" snarled Jake. He made a move to get up, to stop her, but checked himself because it was his strength alone that was holding the wolfman down.

"Cool it," she snapped. "I know what I'm doing."

"Yeah? What?" Jake puffed, forcing the wolfman's shoulders to the floor.

Selina wanted to run so badly her legs twitched under her. Tracy grabbed her shoulder, but she shook her off. *I don't want to do this. I moved a thousand miles so that no one knew I could even try.* She fell to her knees by the wolfman's head, fighting dizziness.

"The drugs aren't working," she said.

"No shit," Tracy snarled.

Selina opened her mental shields a crack. The wolfman's eyes were squeezed shut, tears streaming down his hairy, malformed cheeks. But even sightless, he could sense she was there – fresh, tender meat. He twisted his head, neck craning toward her, nose twitching to scent her. Selina leaned closer, letting him catch her aroma, letting her awareness drift closer to his.

"Are you crazy?" Jake looked aghast. "Get out of here!"

"Forget it," said Selina. Terrified, she damned her sense of obligation. There was a reason she worked where she did, with logical spreadsheets and beautiful antiques. They weren't live creatures filled with volatile, wrenching feelings.

She grabbed the wolfman's head, one hand on either cheek, and felt the black hole inside him. It was a dark whirlpool of pure terror. Her mind teetered on the edge, in danger of falling into the vortex of madness.

I can't. She snatched her hands back, her heart hammering in her mouth. She could feel Jake next to her, the heat of his body prickling against her skin. Their shoulders brushed, their breath mingling. Close enough for his werewolf senses to pick up on what she was trying to do. Because her mental shields were open, she felt the jolt of his realization. "You're an empath!"

"Sort of." There was no time to explain how her magic didn't always work right. Her hands clenched, as if her very skin shrank from touching the wolfman again. What if Jake talked? Or Tracy? Everyone would know what she was. She'd lose everything.

What possessed her to come here? She should have left Gary in the grocery store.

What if she screwed up?

What if . . .

Enough! She grabbed the wolfman again, pressing his face between her hands. His eyes, wild with horror, stared into hers. With a sick fascination, she felt his thoughts pour into hers. His name was Steve Collins. He was watching his body twist and deform, turn into something sickening and foul that he didn't understand. When the first symptoms had started a month ago, he'd thought the changes were signs of some degenerative disease and that he might die. Then he'd started to guess what was happening and came to the one doctor who might know how to help. But help how? Death would be better. He'd had a wife, a job. They were as good as lost.

His body was . . . the sheer terror of it was driving her mad. He was *hungry*. The smell of blood was revolting and good and he'd looked at his wife, wanting to touch her and eat her at the same time. He'd reached for her and she'd screamed and he'd run out of the house. *I didn't mean it!* and he was so sorry, sorry, sorry . . .

Selina pulled the plug on his conscious state, putting him instantly to sleep. She bit her lip, holding all those emotions in, putting them out one by one by one . . . like all the candles on a birthday cake from deepest Hell.

Dear God! The anguish was killing them both. Slumping back on her heels, she closed her eyes and released a huge, pent-up breath. Tears of anger and sorrow leaked from beneath her eyelashes. *So many losses.* The enormity of Steve's suffering was too big for one heart to hold.

I can't do this!

But she'd already done what she needed to do. Steve lay unmoving, his body slowly reverting to his human form. Jake let go of him, releasing a sigh of his own.

"Holy crap," said Tracy.

"Call the pack," said Jake in an exhausted tone. "We've got to put him in lock-up until this is over."

Tracy moved swiftly to the reception desk and picked up the phone.

Selina lifted her head. It was starting to pound, the hangover of embracing all that fear and rage. "Lock-up?"

"Sort of house arrest, until he changes all the way to wolf form. Once that happens, usually everything's okay. It's like the body learns what to do and can start developing some control."

"How long is that going to take?"

Jake shook his head. He looked as exhausted as she felt. "Hard to say. He has to stay aware to gain wolf form. A lot of first-timers keep passing out from sheer terror. It takes a few times before they make it through."

"This wasn't his first try, was it?"

"I don't know. This guy had just come in for initial tests. Really didn't want to talk. I had no idea his situation was this far advanced, or I wouldn't have had him sitting in the office."

Selina heard the defeat in Jake's voice. She guessed past cases hadn't gone well. "Isn't there a sedative? Something to relax him but not knock him out?"

"Not so far. We try new drugs as they come on the market, but the werewolf body does odd things during the change." His warm brown eyes were serious. "What you just did took serious guts."

Selina didn't feel brave. She felt depressed and slightly, inconveniently turned on by the concern in his gaze. Guys wanted her, but usually vanished once they got a whiff of her magic. Dr Jake Hallender wasn't a coward. Then again, he wasn't a human, either.

She managed a small smile, but it quickly faded. "I'm glad I could help. On the other hand, I guess I didn't. He needs to change. I stopped him."

Jake shook his head. "That wasn't going to happen today. He was too afraid. Besides, we need to get him someplace safe – for himself and others. You gave him that." He touched her shoulder, the contact light yet comforting as an embrace.

Selina dipped her chin, looking sadly at the now-human Steve while Jake gave some instructions to Tracy. Selena looked at her watch, realizing how much she used the gesture as a shield. Being busy kept people at a safe distance.

"I need to go. Please don't say anything about what I did here. I have to be able to pass for human." She swallowed hard, feeling suddenly awkward.

Jake nodded, his expression filled with understanding, but that intense gaze dimmed to a socially acceptable wattage. He was giving her space. The wolf no longer looked out of his eyes, just a tired man.

His withdrawal was a relief, but a disappointment at the same time.

The transition from the vet's office back to her normal life was disorienting. It was like leaving *Friday Night Fright Night* and landing in an episode of *Antiques Road Show*. Not that she wasn't grateful for the upgrade, but it was a weird segue.

Selina dropped Gary off at home. She made him a nest of towels in the bathtub where he couldn't hurt himself or anything else, filled bowls with food and water, and shut the bathroom door. She'd gargoyle-proof the rest of the apartment when she got home later and had more time.

As it was, she barely made it back to her office in time to meet with Mrs McAdams about the sale of her snuff box. An ivory oval no more than an inch and a half long, it was decorated with a coat of arms in delicately worked gold. Though small, it would be one of the attractions of the gallery's upcoming show – if she could get the elderly widow to part with it.

Despite the afternoon's drama, or maybe because of it, Selina presented the gallery's offer with extra elegance and passion. She'd always been content to work behind the scenes, but today she sparkled as Old World's negotiator. Some day, she thought breathlessly, *I might even have a gallery of my own.*

But not if you keep tempting fate. You have secrets to keep. What do you think you're doing, stirring up your magic like that? You know better than to play with other monsters!

Selina pushed her nightmares and daydreams aside, returning her attention to Her Lady of the Snuff Box. "It's a very good offer," Selina insisted.

"I just don't know, dear," Mrs McAdams wavered – more a negotiating tactic than any sign of weakness. The old lady was herself a keen collector and one of the gallery's best clients. "The box has been in my family for generations. It would stay in the family if only I'd been lucky enough to have children. Are you planning any children, my dear?"

"Not right now. But did I tell you about my new gargoyle?"

"Once or twice since I arrived," Mrs McAdams nodded. Laughter softened the sharp, shrewd look in her eyes. "I think your new pet is going to be a keeper. You seem happier than I've ever seen you. Much more chipper than old Janos."

"But about the box – what if I sweetened the deal a little?"

Selina was tempted to add a pinch of fey charm to her smile, but wouldn't give in to the impulse. She just smiled with all the happiness she'd felt rescuing her new housemate.

Not even Mrs McAdams could resist that.

After the papers were signed and her client shown to a cab, Selina hurried home, conscious that for once someone was waiting for her. It was nice, even if he was short, fuzzy, and an odd shade of grey.

She stopped at the Pet Play Barn to buy a few more supplies. It was a good thing she was warming up to the idea of keeping him. So far Gary had cost as much as the pair of really nice designer shoes she's been eyeing at that cute downtown boutique.

As she lugged a large driftwood perch up the stairs of her elevator-free apartment, she tried to focus on the fact that shoes weren't cuddly. Nor did they require squeeze toys, organic Gargy-Treatz at ten bucks a bag, or a freaking thousand-pound perch that shed slivers like a porcupine shooting quills. She was used to flying solo, not catering to another creature's needs.

That thought ricocheted her mind to Dr Jake and his capable hands. *What am I thinking? That whole* Hairy Met Sally *thing would never work.*

She unlocked the door and switched on the apartment light. When she opened the bathroom door, Gary was still burrowed into the terry cloth heap. He cheeped when she came in.

"Hey, champ, how's it going?"

Gary reached up. She picked him up, careful of his bandaged wing. He tucked his head under her chin, snuggling close. To her alarm, he was burning hot. *Do gargoyles get fevers?*

She went straight to the phone, where she'd left the number for Dr Jake's after-hours pager.

Gary clung to Selina, refusing to let go of her blouse, so she stood in front of the big balcony window, looking out at the twilight. With her arms full of baby monster, there wasn't much else she could do.

She thought about facing Jake again. She normally tried to stay away from other supernaturals because, like him, they could sense her fey blood. Everyone assumed the fey were cheats, which was unfair. Sure, their species had different cultural concepts about bargaining. Back in the day, they'd pay in gold that turned into dead leaves or horses that became a pile of straw – but they only did that to people who deserved bad luck. Plus, this was the twenty-first century. Everyone played by human business rules. She hadn't charmed the snuff box out of Mrs McAdams; she'd negotiated the price fair and square.

Unfortunately, old ideas died hard. Janos certainly wouldn't keep her if he knew what she was. If Selina wanted to work in a human company, she had to bury half her identity.

By living a lie, was she cheating? Or was she cheating herself? Why, oh, why had she used her magic on Steve? For all the right reasons, her soft heart had dragged her into a mess – with a vet who knew she was fey just by her scent. She felt horribly exposed.

As if picking up on her mood, Gary fussed, restless and uncomfortable. Selina paced back and forth, hoping the motion quieted him. One by one, lights in the surrounding buildings came to life.

The apartment buzzer rang, making Selina jump and Gary chirp. Selina pushed the intercom button to the downstairs door.

"It's Jake Hallender."

"That was quick," Selina said.

"Fast, furry and fabulous."

That surprised a laugh out of her. "Your self-esteem is doing okay, too."

Selina pushed the button to unlock the downstairs door, dismayed to find her stomach fluttering like a schoolgirl's before a big date. *Give me a break.* Then she opened the apartment door, still holding Gary like a security blanket. Jake arrived dressed in a sweatshirt and jeans and carrying an old-fashioned doctor's bag.

"Hi," he said.

"Hi." Selina swallowed. "Come on in."

He did, filling the room and making her antiques seem small
and flimsy. "You said Gary had a fever?"

Selina suddenly felt feverish, too. "Just feel him. He's burning
up."

Jake put his bag down and took Gary from her. The gargoyle
resisted, nearly taking Selina's blouse with him. Finally, Jake
nestled Gary into the crook of his arm. "A fever's not all that
unusual after an injury."

"Is there an infection?"

"There was no open wound. It's more likely the stress of
today's adventures. I can give him something to take his temperature down but the real medicine will be rest and good food."

Jake's eyes met hers. "Don't look so worried. Gargoyles were
bred to protect sacred places. They can take knocks and bumps
better than most creatures." He saw the perch and smiled. "I
guess you're keeping him."

Selina sighed. "Yeah, I guess I am."

The smile turned to a grin. "I'm glad. He really likes you."

Jake set the gargoyle down on the driftwood arm of the perch.
Gary's bird-like hind feet clamped around it, leaving his front
paws free to reach for the array of toys that Selina had hung
from the perch's other arms.

"So, how are *you* doing?" Jake asked Selina. He opened his
bag and pulled out a stethoscope and thermometer. "I can't
apologise enough for what happened back at the office."

Selina watched him calmly examine the gargoyle. She could
hear the regret in his voice, but also resignation. Maybe wrest-
ling wolfmen was just a day in the life of a veterinarian to the
supernatural.

On the other hand, he was opening the door to more than pet
owner chit-chat. Part of her wanted to hide, like she always did.
A larger part of her wanted to talk to *someone* about everything
that had happened, and Jake was the only choice. *No one else
knows my secret.*

"I'm fine. A little stirred up. Glad what I did for poor Steve
went okay. Being a half-breed, I don't risk using my magic much."

"Risk?"

She grimaced. "An empath's powers are fragile. At the best of
times, they're sort of – well – sometimes they just go sideways.

One time my older sister was dating a vampire, and I kept thinking *Ew, this guy is dead.* Suddenly, he was."

Jake looked shocked and a little amused. "Dead? You killed a vampire? That's not exactly empathy."

"Like I said, my magic is wonky. And I don't know that *killed* is the right word. I sort of de-lifed him for a while. And there he was, rotting on the kitchen floor, half an hour before prom. I don't think my sister ever forgave me. I mean, he was supposed to be the hottest guy around, all pale skin and tousled hair. Suddenly he was Mr Stinky in a cummerbund. I was *so* in trouble."

Jake shook his head, laughing softly.

Selina slouched miserably against the wall. "Hey, it wasn't like I *meant* to do it."

"What does your family do?"

"My dad and sisters are sorcerers for hire. My magic wasn't reliable enough for that."

"So you struck out in your own direction." He gave Gary a treat and then slipped the gargoyle a shot when he wasn't looking. "I did that too. There were four boys in my family, and three of us wanted to be alphas."

Selina squirmed. It was a strange conversation to be having with a near stranger but Jake listened with the same intensity with which he looked at her. She could tell he was absorbing every word. *It must be something to belong to a wolf pack, if they're all like this.*

She'd never been so very much the centre of attention. She could feel herself craving it, like an instant addict – and the gentle, clever way he handled Gary was mesmerizing. *Whoa, slow down there, kiddo. Don't make this more than it is.*

"Where does your family live?" he asked.

She cleared her throat, drawing herself up. *Distance yourself.* "A long way away. I've kept what I am a secret up until now."

Jake put his medical instruments away. "Don't worry. I get it. The business world is fey-averse. I won't tell a soul."

The way he said it made Selina feel bad about involving him in her lie. "Sorry."

He snapped the bag shut, his expression suddenly tight. "It's not just the fey who've got a bad rep."

"But we're the only ones who can't join the Chamber of Commerce, or get an import/export licence, or bid on government contracts. Wereanimals aren't treated that way. Neither are vampires." Selina heard the heat in her voice, but couldn't help herself. "Not all fey are leprechauns, you know. Most of us are honest."

Jake shook his head. "Some humans still think my people carry lycanthropy. I wanted to be a doctor. Only the vet school would accept my application. Of course, to a werewolf, vet and doctor are pretty close to the same thing. Then again, I might have tried to be a cop and ended up the dogcatcher." He laughed ruefully.

"So you don't even get the prestige of being an M.D.?"

Jake continued to smile, but something more serious lurked in his eyes. "The prestige I can live without, but I wish I had more resources. There's a lot of work to be done in supernatural medicine. As you saw first-hand, no one has even discovered an effective sedative for people like Steve."

Selina swallowed. Her clients could drop a fortune on an antique vase. How much research would those dollars buy? "You'd think people would do the research just for the sake of science." The moment she said it, she realized how naive that was, coming from a businesswoman.

For a moment, it looked like he struggled with how much to say. "The medical community doesn't understand us, and doesn't want to. I even had to fight to get a veterinary licence. The board was seriously afraid I would eat some old lady's chihuahua. Get serious. One of those things wouldn't even cover a piece of toast."

Selina smiled at his jibe, but she could hear his bitterness. She dropped her shields a notch. His emotions were clear: frustrated, passionate, but also relieved to be sharing his feelings. That threw her. He was the perfect listener, but he also needed to be heard.

But why me? Why was he talking to her, a half-fey recluse?

The answer wasn't hard to find. As an empath, she could feel what he felt in her own body. Jake faced the world with squared shoulders, feet firmly planted, his muscles braced to take everyone's burden. He was the go-to guy for his community, always on call, always ready to answer someone else's needs. He didn't get much chance to let his fur down. *An alpha.*

She was isolated by choice, he by responsibility. Suddenly, they had something very important in common.

"Do you want to get a pizza?" she said impulsively. "I know a good place that delivers."

Selina felt suddenly faint. The impetuous move had taken her breath away.

His eyebrows lifted. "Are you sure? I didn't think you were into wolves."

She looked out the window, unable to meet his eyes. "I'm more of a cat person, but I'd feel better if you stuck around for Gary's sake."

"I'm happy to be of service but, uh, Gary's going to be just fine."

She gave him a sidelong glance. She felt that hot, hard focus again, as if every cell of his being were paying attention only to her. It was unnerving, but there was something incredibly attractive about finally being seen. All at once, she wasn't the family misfit or just the numbers gal. She was, judging from Jake's expression, someone wonderful. *Go, me.*

"What do wolves take on their pizzas?"

"This one likes pepperoni. The hotter the better."

Selina ordered two huge pies, and it was a good thing. Werewolves were bottomless pits. So were baby gargoyles. Gary revived enough to flop off his perch and waddle over to the Victorian-era clawfoot side table, where Selina and Jake had put the pizza boxes while they watched a baseball game on her woefully tiny TV.

Jake, it turned out, had a thing for the Mariners. Gary had a thing for pepperoni, napkins, hand wipes, and anything else that would fit in his beak. Selina was grateful when Gary finally slumped against her side and started to snore. She'd begun to daydream about duct taping him to the perch before he choked on the remote control.

Jake wiped the gargoyle spit from the remote on to his jeans and muted the commercials. "So, I've got a question."

"What?" Selina asked around a mouthful of pizza.

He frowned, lacing his hands behind his head and stretching out his long legs. He was utterly at ease, taking up as much space as he wanted. "I totally understand wanting to hold down a humans-only job, but did you give up magic just for that reason?"

She chewed and swallowed. "My magic's not very good. I have the family talent but not always the strength to control it." She could feel her powers now, moving of their own accord, testing the atmosphere. They sometimes did that when her emotions were aroused.

"But you can help people. I don't just mean like Steve, but you can tell what people really need or want. Doesn't that apply no matter what you do?"

She stopped and took a swallow of cola, telling her magic to go back to sleep. "I don't need superpowers to do my job. I'm successful in the human world."

He pinned her with that hundred-watt stare. "But your non-human talents?"

"Spending my day around beautiful art and antiques makes my fey side happy."

"Is that enough? Doesn't it bother you having to hide who you are?"

"I'm fine with things the way they are." The lie tasted ashy. "Someday I want a gallery of my own. I have to play by the rules."

"You can partner up with other people. Other supernaturals, maybe. Get them to buy the import licences."

The idea momentarily stunned her. She'd been so set on living as a human, that this was an option she'd never considered. It flew in the face of the things that made her feel safe: working alone, and hiding who she was.

"I've made it this far on my own."

Jake flashed an amused grin. "You're very determined. I like that."

Selina was suddenly breathless again. "And I order a mean pizza, too."

"I think your pizza is the soul of kindness." He leaned forward, bringing those intense brown eyes of his closer and closer.

His lips were so soft that she wasn't certain when the kiss started, but she sure knew when Jake ramped it into high gear.

If his gaze was as intense as a searchlight, his kiss was . . . search turned to rescue. Or maybe that was surrender.

She tasted pizza and cola and something darker, the essence of wolf. It spiced his scent, the texture of his dark hair, the way he finally released her mouth only to place feathery nips along the shell of her ear. Her blood rushed with eager desire, suddenly hot with the need to know exactly how well a werewolf played doctor.

Selina subsided, yielding to Jake's weight. Gary squawked an indignant protest. They'd forgotten he was cuddled between Selina and the arm of the couch. Selina and Jake froze mid-swoon. Selina bit her lip, then cleared her throat.

"I guess not in front of the kids."

Wordlessly, Jake pulled her to her feet, leaving the gargoyle in possession of the warm couch cushions. Gary waded to the softest spot and curled up into a sleepy ball.

Jake slid his hand down Selina's back, his touch so slow and precise that she nearly felt every ridge of his fingertips through the silk of her blouse. She wound her arms around his neck, resting her head just under his chin.

Empathy and dating were normally a bad mix. First dates – and who knew at the start of the evening that this would be one? – were sucky enough without brutal truths. But, with the same impulse as squinting through her fingers while watching a horror movie, Selina couldn't help it. She peeked into Jake's emotions.

Of course, she could feel his sexual interest. It was all male. But, beneath all that was admiration. He was curious. Intrigued. Fascinated. He saw her as worthy.

And so is he, her powers whispered. Her mind understood that he was smart, handsome and kind. Her body knew something wild inside him made her heart pound. The knowledge was instant, as immediate as a touch or sound.

Jake popped the top button of her blouse, letting his lips roam. She thrust her fingers into his thick hair, feeling the springy texture of it. He smelled wonderful; his mouth on her throat felt soft and dangerous at once. Dizziness spun her senses. She let them. The pure, strong enjoyment of a new lover was too good to miss.

"I can feel your magic tingle over my hands," he whispered. "You've the taste of the fey, sweet like wildflowers, but you're also warm and earthy, like a human."

"All the better to eat me?"

"All the better to keep you close. You can't hide from me."

His kiss brought her to her toes. His fingers skimmed the silk of her blouse, lingering over her ribs, then closed over her breasts. Selina made a noise somewhere between a sigh and a cry of protest. He was moving too slow and too fast at once. Her own hands reached downward, finding the rough cloth of his jeans. Her palms felt incredibly sensitive, the denim the most fascinating texture she'd ever touched.

Her magic was riding his desire, multiplying it by her own, and feeding it back to both of them in an ever-stronger loop. She'd opened her shields after that first doozy of a kiss, and now her magic was running amok. Fey power crashed through barriers that would have prolonged the dating ritual for weeks before she'd have allowed this kind of heat. *Oops.*

"Guess what," she murmured in Jake's ear.

"Hmm?"

"I think my magic has got us on the fast track."

"Better than striking me dead on the kitchen floor."

"I don't want to take advantage of you."

He gave her a toothy grin. "Concern duly noted. Now, do you want to play Red Riding Hood or a really twisted version of Three Little Pigs?"

The gallery opening finally came on a clear, moonlit May night. Selina arrived early for two reasons. One was to deal with last-minute details – Janos had resumed complete command of the gallery and everything had to be perfect. The other was that Mrs McAdams had asked to meet Gary, and an antiques collector of her calibre couldn't be denied. Not when her request was so easily fulfilled.

"Here he is!" said Selina, carrying Gary to where Mrs McAdams was standing by the plinth with her snuff box. Nearby, a waiter hovered with a tray of hors d'oeuvres. Another passed out flutes of champagne.

Gary blinked his big, green eyes and stretched out one of his front paws to the old lady. The appealing gesture melted everyone who saw it.

"Oh, he is adorable!" Mrs McAdams exclaimed, clapping her hands together.

The sound disappeared beneath the low murmur of conversation. It was still early, only half the expected guests present, but the champagne was already causing the sound level to rise. The gallery looked wonderful, its gilded plasterwork lit by candles and artfully concealed track lighting. The space had once been the lobby of an Edwardian hotel and still had the original high, coffered ceiling and marble floors. The rest of the fixtures were spare and modern, showing off the French antiques and artwork with no distractions.

Except for one baby gargoyle. Gary rapidly became the main attraction, especially with the ladies. They crowded around, cooing like a flock of diamond-studded doves. As they all watched, Mrs McAdams fed Gary a mini-quiche. He stuffed it in his beak and chirped happily, looking around for more. A collective "aw!" filled the air, drowning out the string quartet.

More guests crowded around, asking questions.

"What's his name?"

"What a cute little tail!"

"What's with the bandage? Is something wrong with his wing?"

"Where did you get him?"

"Does he eat caviar?"

It was at that moment that Selina saw Jake approaching, looking handsome in a dark suit and crisp white shirt. He'd even put on a maroon silk tie. Selina caught her breath. She'd expected him to dress up a bit, but this was above and beyond for a guy who lived in boots and old jeans. *This is worth putting on a hundred of these shows!*

They'd been going out for a month – movies, dinners, checking all the right dating boxes – and she'd caught plenty of glimpses of his alpha wolf side. But this was the first time she'd seen Jake on display, dominating a room. The guests turned as he walked past, their expressions both admiring and cautious. If Jake wasn't that far from the wild, neither were humans. Their instincts still knew a potential predator, even when one walked by with a happy smile on his face.

That confidence was contagious. Just by being around him these last weeks, she could feel herself getting bolder, thinking far beyond her mind's usual neat rows and columns. She'd broken her own rules and let her liaison with a supernatural boyfriend become public. After all, no red-, blue-, or green-blooded woman would miss an opportunity to point to Jake Hallender and say, "He's mine!"

"Caviar would be too rich for a gargoyle's digestion," Jake replied, pitching his voice perfectly to carry over the cocktail hour din. "The consequences would be unpleasant."

All attention, including Gary's, switched to Jake. The gargoyle reached out, and Jake took him from Selina's arms. She brushed the wrinkles out of her dress, thinking for the thousandth time how nice it was that Gary didn't shed. Although it had cost her a mint, she'd broken out of the pin-stripe fashion rut for the opening. She was wearing a bolero of heavy Tibetan cream silk over a grey-green halter dress. The full skirt was cut on the bias and moved like water, kissing her knees in sensuous swishes. She felt beautiful and exotic, her fair hair piled on top of her head in a mass of loose curls. From the look on Jake's face, the outfit was a hit.

Janos chose that moment to stroll in. Tall, with iron-grey hair and a stern brow, he looked like somebody had ordered him from the Tycoons "R" Us catalogue, complete with the extra-grumpy options.

"Good evening, Selina," he said, giving Gary an evil look.

"Good evening."

"I must admit, for an accountant you've done a fine job with the show." Janos took a step over to the plinth where the snuff box was displayed on a black velvet cushion.

"Thank you, sir."

It didn't take an empath's powers to tell that her success had irked him. Janos needed to be top dog – quite a contrast from Jake, who simply *was* the first among his pack.

Janos turned back to face her. "I'm not certain, however, how your gargoyle will do anything but distract our clientele. I would prefer that you put it away and circulate among the guests."

She'd planned to do that anyway but refused to make excuses. "Understood, sir. I'll put Gary in my office."

"Thank you."

"She brought Gary at my request," Mrs McAdams said with an edge in her tone. "I thought it was kind of Selina to make the effort to please an old lady."

Janos gave a slight, old-fashioned bow. "I would expect nothing less of my staff."

Jake passed Gary to Selina with a look just short of an eye roll. He bent to whisper in her ear. "Just give the word and I'll get the whole pack to pee on his Jaguar."

Smothering a laugh, she shouldered the gargoyle in time for Jake's cellphone to ring. He answered it as she watched Janos stride away in search of more employees to harangue.

Gary struggled, trying to lean out of her arms and snag more of the mini-quiche. Selina turned the other way, facing Gary away from temptation, and watched Jake's face. Phone calls often meant problems with a patient. She hated the possibility that he'd have to rush off. This night was her triumph. She wanted him there to share it.

Waiters pushed through the double doors at the far end of the room, bearing trays with more food and drink. Like a school of fish, the guests drifted in their direction, leaving Selina and Jake behind.

She began to pace back and forth from table to plinth, waiting for Jake to get off the phone.

"Selina!"

She jumped. It was her boss, glowering and pointing. Jake abruptly hung up his phone.

"What?" Selina glanced down just in time to see Gary stuffing the snuff box into his beak. *Oh, shit!* Gary's wing was still broken. She couldn't exactly whack him on the back.

"Stop him!" Janos snapped.

Jake solved the problem by grabbing Gary's beak and prying it open before the gargoyle could swallow. With one quick sweep of fingers, Jake pulled the snuff box off the gargoyle's pointed black tongue. He dropped it, sticky with spit, back on the plinth.

"Get that animal out of here!" Janos snapped. "Get it out before I put it out."

Jake wheeled on him, a sudden blast of irritation breaking through Selina's shields.

"Jake, don't," Selina said quickly. "I'll put Gary in the back right now."

The gargoyle burrowed against her, hiding his face. Janos and Jake glared at each other. Jake's eyes narrowed, an eerie stillness settling over him. *This is bad. This is really bad.* The guests were starting to drift back their way, fresh glasses of bubbly in hand.

"Jake?" She touched his arm.

He blinked and was suddenly back to normal. "I'm really sorry. There's an emergency and I have to go."

Disappointment stabbed through her. "Okay."

He saw her look and gave a small, apologetic smile. "I was hoping this wouldn't come up tonight. I really wanted to be here, but . . . it's Steve. It's his last chance, and it's not going well."

She suddenly felt sick. "Oh, no."

Jake held her gaze. "Come with me. He – I – both of us could use your help."

"Don't you dare," growled Janos, who'd been eavesdropping but was obviously unmoved by anyone else's emergencies.

Jake's eyes flickered in her boss's direction, then back to Selina.

"Selina?" Janos took a step forward.

"What happens if Steve doesn't make it?" Selina asked quickly.

Jake gave a quick shake of his head. "Then he really doesn't make it. His time's running out."

Damn. Selina bent to kiss the top of Gary's head, breaking his gaze. She resented Janos for being hard to deal with and resented Jake for asking so much of her. For a moment, she even blamed Steve for being an incompetent werewolf. They were pushing her into a corner.

Janos glared at her. "If you leave, you're fired."

Shock stabbed through her, but she knew Janos wasn't kidding. This was about control. It didn't matter if she was a valuable employee – she was committing the double sin of stealing the limelight away from her boss, and then valuing something other than the job he bestowed on her.

"Don't do this," she begged.

"Trust me, you're on thin ice right this minute. Choose wisely."

How can I? The decision boiled down to her life – the gallery and everything she'd worked for – or Steve's. *No, there's more to it than that. It's my human and fey sides at war all over again.*

It was the life she'd built with her own hard work versus all the traumas and disappointments of her early years. It was the freedom to be all she could be, or the freedom to be who she truly was.

Neither choice would give her a complete victory, but turning her back on Steve wasn't possible. Just like success based on living a lie wasn't really success.

She looked around at the magnificent gallery that she loved, and the show she'd worked so hard to put together. She could tell by the smiles on the faces of their clients that the event was a hit. *And some of that was because Gary charmed their socks off. Supernatural is the new black. Cute supernatural just ups the appeal. A smart businessman would be taking notes, not kicking me out the door.*

It all flashed through her head in an instant. The next moment hummed with trepidation. *I'm throwing my life away on a newbie werewolf I don't even know.* But behind Steve's plight was her own. She was caught between two species herself, hiding what she was under a placid, human face.

She was sick of it. Sick of being on her own. Sick of never being honest.

She couldn't blow Steve off when he needed her.

Jake was right. Why *didn't* she get business partners and strike out on her own? All she'd lacked was confidence enough to think outside the box. Money wasn't the problem. She'd led the life of a hermit and saved enough to bankroll her own gallery.

Selina felt a thrill of defiant pride as she looked Janos in the eye.

"Buh-bye."

They took Jake's vehicle. He'd installed a gargoyle carrier in the back, which looked like a large, felt-lined box with barred windows. As Jake sped down the country road, Gary cheeped every time they hit a rut.

Selina sat in silence, doing her best not to let her anxieties spiral out of control. *What am I doing?* Leaving Janos was a bold

stroke, but Selina was left with a feeling of free-fall, kind of
nauseating and exciting all at once. *What am I doing? Everything
I've worked for just went poof!*

Jake had kissed her once and then left her to her thoughts,
silently supportive. That was fine with Selina, who needed the
space to come to grips with her sudden freedom. His phone
rang twice more before they reached their destination. The news
wasn't encouraging.

Selina cracked open a window, letting the night air wash over
her. Finally, they pulled into what looked like a farm. The driveway forked and they went left. The path wound through a dense
stand of cedar trees, finally coming to a dead end at the foot of
a steep rise. Jake threw open the door of the Explorer and ran
up the tree-covered hill. Selina went more slowly, wincing as
the kitten heels of her fawn suede sandals sank into the spongy
earth. She laboured up the slope, grateful when Jake turned to
grab her hand.

As they crested the hill, she saw that a clearing spread under
the shifting night sky. Cedars ringed much of the space, hissing
in the fitful wind. Clouds drifted across the full moon, morphing
from shape to shape like skaters bending, stretching, spinning
in a slow ballet. Selina shivered, the thin bolero nowhere near
warm enough. Her feet were freezing and ached from trying to
balance on heels on rough ground. Jake's hand was the only
solid, comforting thing.

A couple of battery-operated lanterns had been left at the
edges of the clearing, adding sharp shadows to the moonlit
glade. As they drew nearer, Selina blinked rapidly, realizing the
dark shapes beneath the cedars weren't bushes or clumps of
grass as she'd first assumed. Wolves ringed the space, a huge,
hairy form every six feet or so. There must have been twenty. Or
thirty. Eyes glinted like scraps of fire as they stared into the circle,
but that was the only movement. Otherwise, they remained as
statues. She wondered which of them she'd met in human form.

Selina pressed closer to Jake. "I had no idea there were so
many werewolves in town," she whispered under her breath.

"It's not like we're in the phone book under W." He slipped
an arm around her waist and drew her to the edge of the circle.
A thin grey wolf stood and moved to one side, making room for

them to join the ring. As Jake guided her forward, Selina could see the object of their attention. Steve sprawled in the middle of the clearing, half-changed just as he had been in Jake's office. The wind rippled through the grass, wavelets of silver through the darkness. He seemed to float, marooned on a restless sea.

"What's going on?" she whispered.

"He passed out partway through the change." Jake swore. "I had hoped this would work."

"What would?"

"We put him in the full light of the moon."

"I thought the full moon didn't make wolves change."

"But it helps, especially when you're new at it."

Selina shivered. "And he dies if he doesn't go all the way?" Her heart seized with pity. So much more than distance separated Steve from the circle of watching wolves. They were on a safe shore. He was on a perilous journey.

Jake looked uncomfortable. "He could. Or he could stay like this forever. There's no question he'd go crazy."

She remembered the terror in Steve's mind. "I know."

"He's dangerous in this state. All those old horror movies didn't come out of thin air. That's why so many wolves are here. We can't let him get away."

At the moment, Steve remained perfectly still. He wasn't going anywhere.

"Stay here." Jake turned away, leaving her to go look for something in the pile of coats and shoes left heaped by one of the lanterns.

Selina felt his absence as if she had suddenly been set adrift. There was nothing to anchor her in that shifting sea of cloud and grass and whispering cedars.

Last time I knocked Steve out and that wasn't the answer. How can I help now?

Then Steve began to stir, and she understood. As consciousness returned, his emotions rippled like a shockwave, slamming into her with all the force of an atomic blast. Steve had blacked out from pure terror, and he couldn't turn unless he was awake and aware. She had to keep him calm enough to complete the change. Magic had to be the sedative science hadn't invented.

Selina felt a sudden urge to vomit. Sharing Steve's fear long enough to see him through the change would be like falling into that churning vortex of panic. If Steve didn't tear her to shreds first. She started to shake. *I'm not a coward. I'm not a coward.*

Jake rejoined the circle, holding a weapon big enough to atomize an elephant.

"Please tell me it's a tranquilizer gun," she rasped.

Jake looked stricken. "Sedatives didn't work on him, remember?"

"Why do you have to shoot him? You're a doctor."

"I'm also the pack leader." He said it in a voice meant to end debate. "I have to bear the responsibility."

She could feel Jake's heart breaking as he said it. Selina's mouth went dry. "Steve's just afraid."

"That's the problem." Jake's mouth flattened.

"I'm scared, too." She couldn't help saying it.

"I know," he said. Regret and desperation warred in his voice. "But I have this rifle, and thirty-two werewolves are ready to tear his head off if he so much as growls at you. You'll be safe, but that doesn't mean the magic won't be ugly. He's terrified, so I know it's going to be hard on you. I'm sorry."

Selina gulped air. Jake was right. Steve radiated a slimy film of panic. Her heart began to beat faster, making his fear her own.

No, no, no! She'd left the supernatural community to get away from her unpredictable magic. Jake was making her face it again. She really, really didn't want to do that.

But Jake had asked, and Steve needed her, and – as hard as it was to admit it – Selina needed to be whole again.

Now Steve was getting up, his limbs not quite working properly. His feet had an extra joint, making him wobble worse than Selina did in her high heels. He fell forward to all fours, the motion jerky with pain. Craning his neck, rising up on his haunches, Steve let out a moan that grew and swelled and shivered into a howl. A handful of the wolves responded, filling the chill air with a sound that seemed to fall in veils, layer on layer of mournful, haunting notes.

They were encouraging Steve, helping him along, but they were grieving with him, too. Tears streamed down Selina's face, her whole body aching to take away that sorrow. It was the loss of everything Steve had known, even his own flesh.

And the loss of everything I worked for.

Jake, on the other hand, had raised the muzzle of his gun. Selina grabbed the barrel, forcing it down. "What are you doing?" she hissed.

"If he's going to rush us, it'll be now."

Selina swore long and hard enough that several of the wolves looked astonished. She wiped her face with the back of her hand, not caring anymore if her makeup smudged. She had a sudden flashback to Gary crashing into the cereal boxes at the grocery store, helplessly floundering because there was no one willing to pick him up.

She had dealt with Gary. She would deal with Steve.

But Steve *was* the terrifying black vortex. Nevertheless, she stepped forward. Jake stepped with her, rifle at the ready.

"Back off," she said.

"You're not doing this alone."

"I'm not doing this with you hanging over my shoulder. I'm trying to get rid of his fear. You're pointing a gun at his head."

"But—"

Selina turned on him. "Trust me. Do what no one else has done for me and trust my magic!"

Jake said nothing, but he lowered the gun. His eyes held all his objections.

Selina ignored them.

Steve was silent now, slumped in an awkward squatting position. He was panting, globs of drool and blood stringing from his malformed jaws. Fangs had punched through his gums like ivory razors.

She slowly approached, dropping her shields a bit at a time. Emotion blasted from him with a bonfire's heat. Fear. Pain. Despair. She realized he recognized her and knew she was the one who had helped him at Jake's office. She had made the change stop.

Steve reached out with one imploring, claw-tipped hand. The gesture said everything. *Make this nightmare end.*

Trembling so hard her teeth chattered, she took his hand. *You just need to go a little further and everything will be all right.*

The moment she touched him, she felt the undertow of his
panic sucking at the edges of her mind. The black whirlpool
churned with sickening speed. Survival instincts screamed at her
to back away. Selina felt her shields closing down, the reflex as
inevitable as squinting against the sun.

No! Steve's hand – paw – tightened around hers, the strength
of his terrified grip grinding the bones of her fingers together.
Don't leave me.

Selina's consciousness flowed into Steve's mind. Before,
she'd snuffed out his fear like flame, but this time there was
only the dark panic filling his soul. She felt it as their thoughts
collided, hurtling her into a chasm of fear. He gave a wrenching,
ragged scream, a creature forever snared in a merciless trap. His
thoughts grabbed her, a suffocating embrace.

Hold on! Selina cried. His terror sucked her down, like a
drowning man dragging his rescuer under. Selina fought with
sheer willpower, struggling against the undertow of raw emotion.
We will not go under.

But she was losing.

In the physical realm, Jake closed the distance between them.
Selina felt his presence like a shadow across the moon, distant
from the place where she strained to anchor Steve. He put a
warm hand on her shoulder.

Jake was urging her, offering something. Her conscious mind
was confused, but her powers were intuitive. They clutched
at him, seeking the information Steve's body required. They
needed the template to change. *Show us how.*

Within the three-way link, energy began to flow, as if a dam
had washed away. All at once, she felt the change come over
Steve, fur flowing, bones reshaping themselves. Her physical self
felt the shift. The hand she held was suddenly a hand no more,
but a broad, powerful paw.

Through her, Jake showed Steve how to finish the change.
Unfortunately, while Steve's body was ready, his senses lagged after.

What's happening? Steve demanded. Human needs were falling away, wolf thoughts crashing into their place. A hunger for
meat and flesh tangled with thousands of scents, each a puzzle to
be decoded. Steve's thoughts stuttered, unable to sort through it
all. Overwhelmed.

The panic had slowed for an instant. Now it came lurching back.

The sudden jolt made Selina falter, and her half-fey strength wasn't enough to hold on. Everything she'd feared came true. In an instant, she was in his panic, going under like the spars of a wrecked ship. With a plaintive wail, her own psychic scream joined Steve's.

But Jake caught them, pouring his strength into the web her fragile powers had spun. Behind him were the others, the pack a solid wall of energy waiting to be tapped. Cautiously, Selina drew in that strength, filling her magic with the cool, silver energy of the wolves.

She opened her eyes to find her face buried in the wild grey ruff of Steve's neck. She pulled back, gasping as she saw the great yellow eyes, his long snout, and the strong limbs. A perfect, magnificent beast.

Steve nuzzled her cheek, the cold, wet shock of it snapping her fully awake. He rose, bumping her playfully, the rough brush of his tail slapping her arm. Then he took off with a bound, racing to greet the members of his new pack.

Tears blurred her eyes. She blinked them back, fighting a sudden, painful lump in her throat. She'd never been able to save a life before. She'd never been able to make that kind of magic. *Now there's a way to help the first-timers!*

With a blink of surprise, she realized Jake's gorgeous suit was on the ground, paw prints squashing the supple fabric into the grass. Jake himself, a huge, brown wolf, was sprawled before her.

"The magic pulled you over, too?" she asked.

He shimmered, and suddenly there was a naked man on the grass, his chin propped on one hand. Selina couldn't stop her gaze from roaming over all that muscled flesh. She was in a mood for celebration, with Jake as the party favour.

He gave a lazy smile. "So, was that good for you?"

Selina fell on to her side, bringing her face close to Jake's. Her hair was in shambles, her dress a ruin, but she felt magnificent. "I've never been strong enough to do magic like that before. I don't think anyone's ever blended wolf and fey power before. This is entirely new."

He kissed her, digging his fingers into the tangled curls of her hair. "You're magnificent."

"I had a lot of help. I needed the power of the wolves."

Jake gave her a serious look. "Everyone needs help, but don't sell yourself short. Your human side is a brilliant business-woman. Your fey side is a brilliant healer. I honour both sides of you. If a little wolf gets thrown into the mix well, hell, that's so much the better for me."

Selina thought naked and serious was a good look on him. "I can't turn my back on what I am anymore. I can't deny that I'm part of the supernatural world. Not after Gary, and not after you. Especially not after tonight. What we did together was amazing. Important."

"So you're ready to be fey again?"

"Half-fey – but I still want my own gallery. No one has opened one with exclusively non-human artists." She rolled on to her back, the grass cold and damp beneath her. "There are plenty who need representation. You should see some of the vampire portraits. Dark, but so gorgeous. The art world will eat it up with a spoon."

They were silent for a moment. Selina watched rags of cloud drift across the full moon. Jake's breath brushed her cheek, warm and familiar.

"You up for a werewolf partner?"

She grinned. "Who do you think is going to help me hang my first show?"

"Gary?"

She swatted at Jake, but he caught her around the middle and flipped her on top of him. The strength in his long, sculpted limbs made her shiver. His eyes were playful, but wild as the distant howls of his kin.

He slid his hand up her thigh, under the flowing fabric of her skirt.

"What are you doing?" She whispered it because the night was too dense, too charged for talking out loud.

"Thinking up new kinds of magic."

NightDrake

Lara Adrian

People are strange.

A twentieth-century philosopher once said that, or so I've been told. As I drove my rig through the rain and sludge towards the docks in Port Phoenix, I couldn't help thinking how apt the observation was. Especially now, some 300 years after Earth hiccupped on its axis in 2066 and brought about all manner of changes to the world mankind once knew.

The waters rose in many places; vanished in others. Landmasses shifted, ripped apart by earthquakes and volcanic eruptions, or drowned by mudslides several storeys deep. Once-great cities toppled, technology and infrastructure were swept away overnight.

Kingdoms and governments, corporations and institutions were all rendered impotent with the sudden, irreparable, global financial crash. Survivors of the planet's changes – a population estimated to be only in the tens of millions – fled across borders that no longer existed to rebuild their lives and form new communities.

And, after some long millennia of hiding, living in the safety of the shadows, a small number of other survivors came out of the dust and rubble of this altered new world.

They are the Strange.

Shapeshifters and telepaths, nymphs and hobgoblins.

Goddamned freaks of nature, I thought to myself as I rolled to a stop at the dockyard entrance and glanced through the box-truck's window at a pair of grey-skinned gargoyles squatting atop the tall pillars of the gate. I stared for a long moment, if only to let them know that I had no fear of them. The disdain between the Strange and me is well-known, and definitely mutual. As I rolled down the glass, one of the hideous creatures perched overhead sneered down at me through the dark and drizzle of the cold summer night.

"Nisha the Merc," he hissed, obviously recognizing me while I reached out and pulled the rope on a copper bell, then waited for the guard on duty to come over and let me inside. Above me, the beast crouched lower, dropping his voice to a gravelly whisper. "Nisha, the cold-hearted bitch."

Amused, the other gargoyle chuckled quietly and shifted on his taloned feet, rattling the heavy iron manacles that ensured he and his companion remained at their posts. Even if they weren't shackled in place, these two Strange beasts couldn't touch me and they knew it. Harming a human was punishable by death.

But they could hate me.

They could despise that I made my living as a mercenary, although I've always preferred to think of myself as a *facilitator*. Generally speaking – and for the right price – I was a problem-solver. When something needed to get done quickly and quietly, no questions asked, folks with the money and the means usually turned to me to make it happen.

Tonight's job was no different. I had been hired to pick up and transport a cargo shipment for someone who preferred to keep his business at the seedy Port Phoenix dockyard confidential. Not that any of the lowlife humans working the yard, or the even lowlier Strange enslaved there as labourers, would give a damn what was coming or going from the supply freighters that arrived from all parts of the globe.

Still, my client had his reasons, I supposed, and that was good enough for me. I didn't need to know who he was or what I was moving. All that mattered was the two rough-cut diamonds currently tucked into the fur lining of my boot and the three that would be given to me after I'd delivered tonight's cargo to its destination.

The big human guard humped out of his shack near the gate, a long black rifle slung across his body from a wide leather shoulder strap. I leaned out and he peered at me through the rusted iron bars, recognition lifting the heavy brow visoring small, avid eyes that made my skin crawl. "Back so soon, eh, Nisha?" He grunted, leering now. "You sure are a woman in high demand these days. Not that I'm complaining about that, of course."

I gave him a smile that a smarter man might have recognized as loathing. "What can I say? Business is booming."

He grinned as he unlocked the gate and let me drive through. "Which slip is it tonight?"

"Three-East," I said through the open window, the designation indicating the docks where cargo from New Asia arrived. When the guard hopped up on to the truck's running board alongside me, I gave him a flat look. "I know the way."

He dropped back down with a scowl. "That freighter just came in about an hour ago. They're still unloading. Could be a while before they're done, so if you need to get out of the cold, you come on up and I'll let you sit with me in the guard house."

I waved him off without looking back. The icy rain was turning to sleet, pelting the windshield like tiny pebbles. Burrowing deeper into the hood of my parka, I drove towards the deep-water port that had long ago been desert lands and city skyscrapers – before the planet's shift had cracked a wide salt-water chasm between the island of Mexitexas and the shrunken coastal borders of North America. As I neared the enormous ship moored at the slip marked 3E, the stench of brine and steel and belching exhaust fumes blew into the open window, cling-ing to my throat and stinging my eyes.

I slowed to a stop near the loading ramp, where four big, tusked trolls were carrying a tarp-covered crate across the plank to the dock. They shivered in the bad weather, their clothing sodden, their long braided beards dripping water with each lumbering step. The workhorses of the Strange, trolls were built like tanks and able to labour tirelessly in all kinds of climates. These four walked gingerly – almost reverently – with the large rectangular container, one of them on each corner, taking great care with it. A human supervisor waited at the end of the ramp, closely monitoring their progress.

"Be careful with that, you brainless clods!" he barked. "One slip and I'll have your bloody hides!"

I got out of my rig and walked over to the dock boss. "I take it this one's mine?"

He grunted in acknowledgment and wiped the back of his filthy hand under his runny nose. That same hand then reached out to me, palm up. "I'll have my payment now, Nisha."

I dug into the pocket of my coat, withdrew a chip of cloudy pink stone and dropped it into his waiting hand. "There you go. One quarter-carat raw ruby, same as always."

His greedy fingers closed around the paltry gemstone that represented a fortune to him. The little rock disappeared an instant later, and I didn't follow his hand to see where he'd stuffed it. "Whatever's in that thing, it's got my labourers spooked," he told me, staring through the sleet as the container neared the end of the ramp. "What the hell are you picking up tonight?"

"Don't know and don't care," I said. "I don't get paid to care."

He scoffed. "No, I reckon you don't. Most folks say you'd sell your own mother if the price was right."

"Harsh," I replied, wholly unfazed. The insult was based on reputation, more than fact. All of which served me just fine.

As for my mother . . . it was harder to remain unaffected by the thought of her. She was killed years ago, when I was just a young girl. The nightmare of that day still haunted me, sometimes even when I was awake. Her death had haunted my father too, until his heartbreak had finally claimed him.

The dock boss said nothing more, watching with me as the trolls carefully brought the crate off the ramp and set it down in front of us. The contents shifted slightly as the box came to rest on the ground, something metal clacking quietly from within. Whatever was inside must have been valuable, given that it was protected from the elements in an enormous sheet of rare, extremely expensive plastic.

Guns, I guessed, having transported a fair share of munitions in my line of work. I stepped up to the corner of the crate to check the bindings on the plastic tarp. Although they looked secure, I wanted to be certain before I gave the okay for the trolls to load the container into the back of my rig.

As I reached out to test the straps, something growled and began to move inside the box.

Something big.

Something mired by what sounded to be heavy chains and shackles, but something very much alive.

A couple of hours later, I was sitting atop an empty grain barrel in the back of my truck, eating a tin of hydrated soymeal for supper while I waited for my client's people to come to the private warehouse where I was parked and relieve me of my newest cargo. I had to admit, if only to myself, I was eager to be rid of it.

I'd never moved live goods before and, despite my willingness to transport all manner of other things without batting an eye, I was suddenly wondering if the three diamonds waiting at the end of this job were payment enough. More than that, I was wondering about the contents of the container sitting just a few short paces away from me in the truck. Speculating on just what was shuffling around inside there and what my client could possibly want with it.

I picked up the instructions the dock boss had handed me before I'd left Port Phoenix. They were written on a small square of dried animal skin that had been affixed to the container at its point of origin. I'd read the directions already – three succinct orders, penned in a bold hand:

> *Keep the crate and contents dry at all times*
> *Do not insert anything into the crate*
> *Do not open under any circumstances*

I set down my empty soymeal tin and hopped off the barrel. From where I stood, I saw there were small tears here and there in the plastic tarp. I knew whatever sat inside the large box had been watching me the whole time I'd been in the back of the truck with it. I'd felt eyes on me – shrewd, predatory eyes. Now, as I walked closer to the covered crate, the fine hairs at the back of my neck rose in warning.

"They say you are colder than ice," came a deep, cultured male voice from behind the concealing plastic and confining wood. "No one ever mentioned that you were also very beautiful. As dark and enticing as night itself . . . Nisha, the Heartless."

I didn't say anything at first. Shock stole my breath and I stood there for a long moment, dumbstruck and unmoving. I hadn't expected to hear my cargo speak to me, let alone know my name. Oh, I'd assumed it was some kind of beast in the crate – even now, I knew that he was something Strange, more than likely – but the smooth tone and elegant voice took me aback completely.

"What are you?"

"Come closer and see for yourself. I have no wish to harm you, even if I were able."

I snorted, snapped cleanly out of my stupor by that treacherous invitation. "The only way I'd come any closer to one of the Strange is to put a pistol up against its head."

"Ah, yes," he said, exhaling a quiet sigh. Chains clinked and straw rustled as he moved about in his tight prison. "How you love your weapons, Nisha. Particularly when they are used against my kind. Many have died because of the weapons you've put into the hands of bad men."

"I do what I have to in order to survive," I said, unsure why I felt the need to defend myself to him. "I'm in the supply-and-demand business, that's all. My clients pay me to deliver things they want. What they do with those things is not my concern."

"Hmm." He shifted inside the crate again, and I could feel that assessing stare locked on me still. "So, you're saying that you would just as easily sell your weapons for war to me – to one of the Strange – if I had the wherewithal to meet your price?"

I wouldn't and we both knew it. I glared at the covered crate. "I don't need to justify what I do, least of all to someone like you."

He released a heavy breath. "No, you don't. And it was pointless to even ask it. My kind has no desire to wage a war against man. We never did."

"You'd never win anyway," I pointed out flatly. "You have too few numbers, for one thing, and most of you are indentured, besides. Wars take more than guns, you know. They take vision and determination. They take leaders, and that's something your kind has lacked all along. If the Strange were going to fight, they should have done it long ago."

"Yes. You're right, Nisha." I heard regret in his voice now, and told myself I had no reason to feel guilty for that. "But there are those among my kind who believe that, in time, there will be peace."

I exhaled a humourless laugh. "That's why you're sitting in a crate in shackles, about to be shipped off to who knows where and for what purpose."

"I know what lies ahead for me," he replied, that velvety deep voice as calm as I'd heard it so far. "I won't be enslaved. That's not why they took me. My capture will have only one outcome."

"Death," I whispered, ignoring the twinge in my chest. I wanted to see his face in that moment – whether or not it was Strangely hideous – to determine if the thought of dying scared him even a little. It didn't seem to and I held my ground, fisting my hands at my sides instead of reaching out to move aside the tarp that hid him. "You know you will be killed."

"Eventually, yes," he said, without a trace of fear or sorrow. "I feel my death might serve a higher purpose."

I shook my head, unsure if he could see me or not. For some reason, despite everything I knew and felt about his kind, his resignation bothered me. More than bothered me, it pissed me off. "You're just giving up. Don't try to pretend it has anything to do with honour."

"Sometimes, Nisha the Heartless, there is a greater good to be gained in dying than there is in living. For me, certainly. I go to my fate willingly."

I barked sharply. "Well, then, I guess that makes you either very courageous or very stupid."

I reminded myself that he wasn't my problem. His fate – whether or not he welcomed it with open arms – sure as hell was not my concern. I walked over and picked up my empty soymeal tin, my movements tight with aggravation.

"I've had enough thought-provoking conversation for one night," I told him, more than ready to spend the rest of the wait up front in the cab by myself. "Get some rest. Your other ride should be here soon."

I jumped out of the back of the truck and closed the doors, sealing him inside.

★　　★　　★

I fell asleep in the cab.

The dream woke me, as it always does. Not the violent nightmare I'd had since my parents' deaths, but the dream that started soon afterwards and visited me more often than I liked. This time, everything seemed more vivid – so real I felt as though I could sweep my hand out before me and touch it.

Sunlit skies. Glittering azure ocean. And me, soaring high above it all, twisting and gliding on a gentle wind towards an infinite horizon.

I jolted awake, trembling and breathless.

It was the usual reaction. Just the thought of flying terrified me. The act itself was unnatural, whether achieved in the thunderous, now obsolete, metal machines of decades past, or as performed by those rarest of the Strange who'd needed none of man's inventions to aid them. Flying was nothing I'd ever done, or ever wanted to know anything about.

Desperate to purge the troubling sensations, I pushed myself up in the driver's seat of the cab and fumbled for the wristwatch I kept fastened to the steering wheel. It was an ancient wind-up type, the only time-keeping devices that still functioned in the post-technology age. I checked the gloved hands on the smiling black-and-white mouse.

"Shit." I'd been asleep for more than two hours.

The truck was quiet. No movement at all in the warehouse and no sign of my client's people coming to take the Strange cargo off my hands yet.

"How much longer before I can collect my pay and get out of here?" I grumbled, climbing out of my rig to go and check on things around back.

I heard the dry, choking rasp as soon as I opened the doors.

"Are you all right?" I asked, climbing in and stepping cautiously towards the covered crate. There was no reply, only a further round of coughing and a terrible-sounding wheeze. "Are you hurt in there?"

I realized I didn't even know his name, not that I needed to. Nor did I need to run for my water canteen when he started to dry heave, but that's precisely what I did. I told myself it was only reasonable to make sure Mr Honour-and-Higher-Purpose stayed alive long enough for my client to kill him, since that's what he'd claimed he wanted so badly.

I returned and jumped into the back of the truck. He was gasping now, sucking in air, each breath sounding deathly parched. Canteen in one hand, I hurried to the crate and tugged loose a corner of the tarp. "I have water. You need to dr—"

My voice fled as I lifted the plastic sheet from the front of the wooden container. A liquid gold gaze peered at me through a slim crack between the nailed planks of the box. It startled me, penetrating and intense, sending a swift, unbidden heat into the core of my being. Just as quickly, the golden eyes were shuttered as they turned back into the darkness of the cell and the prisoner's wheeze grew more violent.

"Stay away," he rasped from deep within the shadows. His throat scraped with every syllable, sounding as dry as cinders. "Leave me. This will pass."

I muttered a curse, low under my breath, knowing he was in far worse shape than he wanted me to think. I walked around the crate, pulling off the tarp as I went. The few gaps that separated the wooden planks were so tight not even my little finger would be able to slip through them. No way could I get the canteen to him without breaking open the box. And that was out of the question.

"Hold on," I said. "I have an idea."

Slinging the canteen strap over my shoulder, I hoisted myself up on to the side of the crate and clambered to the top of it. I brought the canteen around and took out the stopper. Beneath me, his bright citrine eyes followed my every movement through the narrow breaks in the wood. Every nerve ending in my body tingled, warning me that something Strange and powerful lurked just beneath me.

"Come closer, bring your mouth up to me," I told him, more a command than request. "Stop being noble, and take a drink."

"Nisha." My name was barely a whisper in the shadows below. "You know the rules."

I swallowed, recalling very well the instructions I'd been given for this job. Instructions that all my logic and experience told me to follow. But then he coughed again – a deep, shredding heave of his lungs – and neither logic nor experience had prepared me for the concern I had for him in that moment.

I leaned down and brought the mouth of the open canteen to the largest gap in the top of the crate. "Drink."

I thought he might refuse again, but then I heard him moving – sensed him drawing nearer to where I waited. His eyes locked on mine. I felt a warm rush of breath puff through the crack and skate across my hand. White teeth gleamed as he parted his lips near the break in the wood and waited for me to pour the water into his mouth.

I gave him only a trickle, not wanting to rush him before he was ready. His lips closed on a deep growl that vibrated through the crate and into my bones. And then the growl became louder. The crate rumbled beneath me, shuddering and shaking.

I leapt off – just in time to watch the whole thing explode before me, wood planks splintering in all directions like nothing more than toothpicks.

The Strange being within the container erupted out of the wrecked crate in a blur of gleaming, iridescent blue-and-black scales and immense, talon-tipped wings. The great head of the dragon swung toward me, massive jaws agape, those golden eyes looking far fiercer in the light of my rig than they had in the dark confines of the box.

Terrified, I scrambled backwards, then pushed to my feet and fumbled for the pistol holstered on my belt. Hands shaking, I chambered a round and lifted the gun up in front of me to take aim on the beast.

But he was gone now. In his place was a man. A shapeshifter. Breathtakingly handsome, and utterly naked. He was tall and muscled, his skin a warm, sun-kissed bronze. Blue-black hair fell down around his shoulders in thick, glossy waves. Ageless citrine eyes seemed to bore straight through me as he strode forwards, undeterred by the weapon I held squarely in line with his head.

"Stand down, or I'll shoot," I warned him. "Don't think I won't kill you."

He gave a mild shake of his head and kept advancing, easy paces that devoured the distance between us. I didn't fire on him, and I suppose he guessed I wouldn't. With gentle strength, he brought his hand up and wrapped his fingers around the barrel of my gun, slowly lowering it to my side.

"You tricked me," I muttered, wondering why I should feel such a sting at that.

"No," he replied, his voice as tender as I'd heard it all night. "My captors had denied me water and I was dying of thirst. You saved me. You . . . surprised me. It's been a very long time since I've been surprised by goodness, particularly in a human."

He smiled and stroked my cheek. When I turned my face away, ashamed of the pleasure that raced through me at just his praise and light touch, he caught my chin and gently drew my gaze up to his. "I think, Nisha the Heartless, that despite what you lead others to believe, you are, in fact, very kind."

His hands were warm and firm as he cupped my face and brought me towards him. He kissed me – a sweet, tender brush of his lips across mine. All of my senses reached for him as though I'd been starving for this – this Strange kiss – all my life. I could have kissed him all night.

Perhaps I would have, if not for the sudden rumble of an approaching vehicle outside the warehouse.

"My client," I managed to gasp as I broke away from the shapeshifter I was expected to surrender to his would-be killers that very moment. I heard the crunch of gravel, the sharp squeal of brakes . . . the hard *thump-thump* of two vehicle doors being closed. "They're coming for you."

He nodded solemnly and stepped back from me. Back towards the splintered remains of the cargo crate and the broken shackles that had fallen off him during his change. He wasn't going to fight the men who were coming for him now. Wasn't going to threaten me or attempt to bargain his way out of capture.

He was noble and proud, and I'd never been so livid in my life.

"What the hell do you think you're doing?" In truth, I should have been asking myself that same question. I had but a split-second to decide my next move – a decision that would set the course of my future, right then and there.

Did I surrender my Strange cargo to his captors, collect my pay, then roll on to the next job and the next one after that? Or did I throw everything away to help one crazy shapeshifter escape a death he neither feared nor resented?

I swore under my breath and ran over to grab some clothing from the personal supply chest I kept in the back of my rig. The wool tunic I found was moth-eaten in places, and the ancient blue jeans had last been worn by a dead man, but both were big enough to cover him. Whoever he was.

"What's your name?" I asked him, hastily pulling the clothes out of the chest. Outside the warehouse, I could hear my client's men nearing the door. I threw a hard look at the Strange man behind me. "Your name, dammit!"

"I am Drakor," he replied, scowling at me.

I threw the sweater and pants at him. "Get dressed, Drakor. We're getting the hell out of here."

His golden eyes were grim with understanding. "You do not know what you're doing, Nisha."

"Tell me about it." I shoved my gun back in its holster as he shrugged into the clothing. "We need to hurry if we're going to outrun these guys."

"Nisha." He came to me, dressed like a pauper, yet his handsome face was serene. I was even tempted to call it regal. "This could be a very costly mistake for you."

I shook my head, hoping to dismiss some of my own misgivings, slim as they were. "We need to go now. Come on, Drakor. Follow me and don't argue."

He growled something dark in a language I didn't understand, but when I jumped out of the back of the truck, he was right beside me. I slammed the doors and threw the lock bar into place. I motioned him towards the cab as I ran around to the driver's side. I hopped in, and he took the passenger seat.

"You'd better hang on," I said, glancing in my side mirrors. The men started to open the warehouse receiving gate behind us. I threw the rig into reverse and watched as their faces lit up with surprise – then fear, when they realized what was about to happen. I looked over at Drakor, sitting beside me in silent observation. He probably thought I had lost my mind. Heaven knew, I was beginning to wonder myself. "All right, here we go."

I stomped on the gas and the truck rocketed backwards out of the place, sending my client's men scrambling for cover. I righted the rocking vehicle and put us on the road, heading off into the cold, dark night. The two of us . . . together.

*   *   *

We were six hours north of Port Phoenix before I dared slow down even a little.

The rig's dim headlights piercing deep into the darkness ahead of us, I glanced out the side windows, trying to get some idea of where we might be. The night was fathomless on all sides. Nothing but stars overhead and vast forest wilderness encroaching on the broken pavement of the seldom-used highway.

No one behind us, either, which I figured was about the best luck we could hope for at the moment. I didn't suppose it would hold out forever. Tonight I had put a giant target on my back. I had been in business with powerful, dangerous people long enough to know that a stunt like the one I'd just pulled would not go uncontested.

"You look tired," Drakor said from the seat beside me.

He'd been quiet most of the trip. Pensive, I thought, having caught him staring out into the dark more than once since we'd been on the road. I knew he had to be as exhausted as I was; he'd confided in me during the drive out of Port Phoenix that his body was depleted after being starved of food and water during his captivity. Breaking out of the crate had drained him even further.

But I didn't think it was any amount of physical fatigue that had him so still and brooding. His mind was burdened, perhaps his heart as well.

"I'm fine," I told him. "And we need to keep moving."

"No, Nisha." In my peripheral, I saw his dark brows lower over those shrewd canary-yellow eyes. "I want you to have rest. Find some place to stop the vehicle now."

There was an air of command in his voice that almost made me obey simply on instinct. *Almost.* "We can't afford to stop until we've put more distance between them and us. They could be following even now. We have to push onward."

He reached across the cab, his strong, elegant fingers closing over my hand where it was locked in a death grip on the wheel. "Nisha, we go no farther until you rest. It is not a request."

I gaped at him, astonished by his arrogance. "Last I heard, I was the one calling the shots around here. Unless someone died and made you king, I'll thank you to sit back and let me handle the situation."

He removed his hand from mine and I found I instantly regretted the emptiness left in its place. Drakor settled back into his seat and gazed out the window. "My father passed 157 years ago, after centuries of a peaceful, noble reign."

I threw a sharp look at him. "Excuse me? Are you saying what I think you're saying?"

He sighed remorsefully and glanced back at me. "My father's death made me King of the Strange. Or would have, if I'd actually been worthy of accepting that mantle of responsibility. Either of my elder brothers would have been far better suited, but they had both been killed in wars with mankind by the time my father took his last breath. I was little more than a stupid boy, unfit to rule."

I hit a rut in the ruined old road and had to jockey to keep my rig on course. When I was able, I stared at him again, incredulous. "If you haven't assumed your father's place in all this time, who has?"

"I was twelve years old when I relinquished my power to his court. I believed our kind would be better served by someone other than me." He grunted then – a soft, wry exhalation. "Apparently someone in my homeland felt the need to make certain I could never change my mind. I suspect it was a member of the court who betrayed me to the person who hired you."

I was outraged – not only by the thought of Drakor being sold out by a traitor, but also by the notion that he would have so readily accepted it. "So, you are willing to let yourself die rather than risk failing as king?"

He looked at me for a very long moment, a storm seeming to brew beneath the burnished gold of his gaze. "I *was* willing."

"And now?" I asked.

"Much has changed since I was shackled inside that box and shipped across the ocean to this place, Nisha. Now I find myself questioning quite a lot of things."

Although he was contemplative and hard to read, I sensed the flicker of determination beneath his calm demeanour. He would make a dangerous adversary, I had no doubt. His kindness and intellect would make him a formidable but fair ruler.

"It seems to me that you could better serve your people by being a leader, Drakor, not a martyr."

"Indeed?" He smiled at that, only the subtlest curving of his sensual mouth. "I think you may be wiser than any of my long-lived counsellors and advisors, Nisha the Heartless."

For some reason I didn't care to examine, it bit somehow to hear him refer to the cold reputation I'd prided myself on for so long. I wasn't heartless – not when it came to him. I looked at Drakor and felt as though my entire being was made of awakening emotion and sensation, not the logic and fear and mistrust that had been drummed into me from a very young age.

I cared for him.

If I didn't watch my step, I worried that I might very easily find myself in love with him.

"Do you have somewhere that you can go?" I asked him, needing to steer my thoughts back to the situation at hand. "It won't be safe for either one of us to be on the road any longer than we have to be."

He nodded, grim. "There is a hidden enclave of my kind in this region of the new continent. They haven't yet been discovered by man. No human has been near their settlement, but if I asked it of them, they would provide us shelter."

I wasn't sure I was ready to rely on the Strange for any form of protection, but I didn't tell him that. "Do you know specifically where they are?"

"The place was once called Colorado."

"It's not far from here," I said, recognizing the old name from the time long before I'd been born, when most of this land had comprised unseen borders hemming in and uniting areas known as states. "I can take you there."

Drakor seemed to consider for a moment. "In the southwest region of that place, there are ancient dwellings built into the side of a cliff. Tribes of humans once lived there, before their modern brothers drove them out and used the dwellings as parkland. Now the Strange hold it."

I nodded and looked back out to the road. Even though I wanted to put another couple of hours behind us before we stopped to rest, my arms were heavy and my eyes were burning from staring into the darkness.

"I have some old maps in the back," I said. "Maybe we should pull over and have a look."

Drakor gave me a silent nod of agreement. I slowed the truck and detoured off the empty highway, taking us toward a thicket of woodlands several hundred yards from the road.

I lit a candle lamp and brought it over to where Drakor was studying one of the dozen or so historical maps I kept on hand in my rig. I sat down next to him on the floor.

"This is about where we are right now," I said, pointing to the area above a ghost town known, a couple hundred years ago, as Flagstaff. I moved my finger across the map and his sharp gaze followed the northeasterly, diagonal path I indicated on the worn and brittle swatch of paper. "This is the old state border of Colorado. The area you told me about would be roughly around this corner. The roads between here and there aren't the greatest. It will probably take me a couple of days to get you there."

When he looked up at me, I felt a question burning in his unsettling eyes.

I slowly shook my head, answering before he could ask me. "I won't be staying once we arrive there. I can't. I'm human and I wouldn't belong."

His black brows lowered. "What if I said I wanted you to stay? What if I demanded it?"

I smiled, unwillingly pleased by his possessive, imperial tone. "I would remind you that you may be King of the Strange but I'm not one of your subjects."

He reached over and cupped my cheek. "What if I told you that I don't think I'll be ready to let you go in a couple more days?"

I barely resisted the urge to turn my face into the warm cradle of his palm. With a strength I didn't realize I had, I drew away from his touch and put my focus back on the open map. "We'll need to stop for fuel sooner than later. Usually someone in the villages has a tank or two that can be bartered for—"

"Nisha." He cast aside the map, forcing me to look at him. "If you don't accept my help, then where will you go? You can't go back to your home. Your old life is gone now."

"I know," I said. "I can't go back to anything I knew before. Word of what happened tonight will travel fast. All I can do is keep moving now, figure out how to make my way. And I will.

I'm not afraid of the unknown, Drakor. I know there's bad in the world. I've survived the worst. I won't run and hide from anything ever again."

My eyes stung with memories from my past. I tried to blink away the tears, but he saw them. He stared at me, his strikingly handsome face tender. "What did you lose, dear Nisha?"

I shook my head, ready to dismiss the question before it could tear my heart wide open. But Drakor's eyes were warm and caring, his hands comforting as he stroked my hair. The memories swelled inside me until I couldn't hold them in.

"My mother," I began, then took a steadying breath. "She was killed when I was four years old. She and my father and I were living in the country at the time. One day hellhounds broke into our home and chased us out to the woods."

"Hellhounds." Drakor's expression hardened. "Ah, God, Nisha. They are vicious creatures, the worst of our kind."

I knew all about them, of course, as did most of mankind. Hellhounds lived for blood sport and were most commonly employed as trackers. With their hideous double-heads, razor-sharp claws and incredible speed, there were few that could escape them – human or Strange.

"My father ran with me in one arm, his other hand wrapped around my mother's wrist." I blew out a quiet sob. "One moment she was with us, the next, she was gone. She turned back and tried to lead the hellhounds away from us. I can still hear her screams in my nightmares."

Drakor gathered me to him and I didn't have any strength to resist. I leaned against his chest, listening to the steady drum of his heartbeat. His arms were strong around me, his lips gentle as he pressed a kiss to the top of my head.

"My father was destroyed over the loss of my mother. I think seeing me only made it worse because I reminded him too much of her. My father blamed himself for putting her in danger, but he never really told me what he meant. We lived in fear of all the Strange after that. He drilled into me that I could trust no one. That no matter what, I should always only look out for myself."

"And so out of your despair, you arose courageous and strong," Drakor murmured as he lifted my face up toward his. He kissed me, long and slow and deep. When his lips left mine,

I saw hot need in his gaze. "You are such a beauty, Nisha. You are as exotic as the night for which you were named."

I reached up and stroked his bold, square jaw. "My mother named me in her language. She was called Jariat."

Drakor brows arched almost indiscernibly and he gave a soft, amused-sounding grunt.

"What is it?"

"Nothing," he said, caressing my cheek. "It's a very old name, from a very old people. A beautiful name."

"Is there anything you don't know?"

He leaned down and kissed me once more. "I have been around for a long time. One cannot help but learn a few things. But you . . . you are a marvel to me, Nisha. I am amazed by all I'm learning from you. I never dreamed I could care so deeply for a human."

"Nor I, for one of the Strange," I whispered, my heart aching with emotion, my body thrumming with desire.

Our lips met again, with a passion neither of us seemed able to deny. Drakor undressed me with maddening care, his mouth tasting each naked inch of my skin. His own clothing came off in a hurry, and then he was poised above me, his thick shoulders and arms bunched with muscles, his bare chest smooth as velvet under my roaming fingertips.

I put my hand around the back of his neck and pulled him down on top of me. His mouth claimed mine with fierce need as our bodies came together, hot and yearning. He filled me up, gave me more pleasure than I'd ever known.

We tossed about in a slick, delicious tangle of legs and hands, insatiable for each other, even after we'd both come down from a shattering release. He was wild and magnificent, and even if I'd spent a thousand nights in his arms I knew I'd still crave more. I hungered for all of him, and for all we'd never have again once we reached our destination and said our goodbye.

As we lay together side by side, he stared into my eyes with the same unspoken longing I felt weighing down my own heart.

"Nisha," he murmured. "My God, I never expected you. I never expected to feel any of this. I shouldn't feel it. You are human, and I am not."

"I know." I nodded, tried to smile even though it hurt.

He brushed his lips across mine, a sweet, tender kiss. "You are human . . . and I don't care. I want to be with you, wherever you need that to be. I love you, and none of the rest matters."

I swallowed, uncertain I'd heard him correctly. "You what?"

"I love you," he said, and kissed me again, more firmly now. A claiming kiss that burned through me like fire.

I started to tell him that I felt the same way, but then I heard something terrible ring out in the distance. A low howl, coming from somewhere in the dark outside. Then another, and still another.

All the blood seemed to drain from my head and settle into my stomach as cold as ice.

Drakor looked at me, his gaze stark. "Hellhounds."

We barely had time to dress and jump back into the cab of my truck before the beasts' howls had grown dangerously close.

I turned the engine over and swore when the damned thing sputtered and choked. I tried again. It coughed to weak life, rattling as though it were on its last legs.

And that's when I noticed the needle on the fuel gauge.

"Shit." I reached into the dash and tapped the temperamental old gauges, hoping the needle had merely gotten stuck as it so often did on relics like the one I was driving. After a few knocks, it did move a couple of degrees – deeper into the negative. "We're practically out of fuel."

In my haste to get us out of Port Phoenix, I'd neglected to do even the most basic systems check. And, in my state of fatigue after so many hours behind the wheel, I'd managed to drive us smack into the middle of nowhere. With hellhounds on our tail.

Another bone-grating howl went up somewhere in the darkness outside.

"I think we can make it another ten miles or so. We can head deeper into the wilderness and try to outrun them." I grabbed the gearshift and started to put the rig into drive. Drakor's hand stopped me.

"Nisha, there isn't time. The truck will only be a hindrance in the end." He took my hand in his and pulled me across the seat to slide out the passenger side door with him. "Let's go."

"We'll never make it," I said as we raced away from the sound of the gaining hellhounds. "Are you strong enough to fly?"

"I am," he replied. "But I wouldn't be able to carry you very far yet. We have to run."

I tried to pull myself free of his hold, but he wouldn't let go. "Drakor, listen to me. You have to get away. You have to leave me here and save yourself."

He swore something dark and nasty and pulled me into a faster pace. The forest was pitch black, a maze of tall pines and thorny bramble. We tore through it, uncertain where we should go except as far away from the hellhounds as possible.

But each second that I felt hopeful we might elude them, it seemed the Strange beasts sounded closer. Their howls and snarls echoed in the woods, coming at us from several directions.

"Drakor, please," I whispered fiercely. "We can't both get away from them. They're going to catch up to us."

"Then I will stand and fight them," he muttered tightly, not slowing his gait.

No sooner had he said this than one of the two-headed hounds erupted from out of the darkness and launched itself at him. I lost his hand in the sudden crash of colliding bodies. I heard the gut-wrenching sounds of the struggle, the snapping of animal jaws. The tearing of vulnerable flesh and sinew.

"Drakor!" I cried, anguished to think of his suffering.

All at once, flames shot up into the night. In the abrupt illumination, I glimpsed Drakor in his dragon form, the thick forest in front of him, nothing but endless night at his back. He hissed a plume of fire at the attacking hellhound, incinerating the beast. Another one came at him with both sets of jaws gnashing and was similarly torched.

Two of the awful creatures were down, but three more were right behind them.

And Drakor had already shifted back into a man.

He was panting and sweating, strain showing in the taut lines of his face. My heart sank like a stone in my breast. The shift had drained him of his power.

"Nisha, behind you!"

I swung around and met with two sets of feral eyes staring out at me from the heads of an enormous hellhound who stood just an arm's length away. It bared its terrible teeth and fangs, massive hind legs coiled and ready to spring into a leap.

I couldn't run. There was nowhere to go. I went for my gun, but it was too late.

The hellhound leapt at me.

It knocked me off my feet, sent me reeling through the dark night air. I waited to feel the crushing blow of the ground coming up to meet my spine. It didn't materialize. Instead, I fell and fell and fell . . . into a black void. A chasm so deep and wide it was all I could see.

"Nisha!" Drakor's voice roared from somewhere high above. It echoed off the stone walls of the abyss that surrounded me. "Nisha, no!"

All my fears of flying – that inexplicable terror at finding myself airborne – pressed down on me like a lead weight. I plummeted faster.

From somewhere deep inside me, I knew it was my fear that would destroy me. Not the hellhound that had pitched over the ledge with me and had since dropped out of my sight. Myself alone.

I thought of my mother, who sacrificed herself so that my father and I could live.

I thought of my father, who died of a broken heart because fate had torn her from his arms.

And I thought of Drakor, the Strange and noble man I didn't want to love but couldn't live without. I didn't want him to know my father's pain. Selfishly, I wanted to spend the rest of my days in Drakor's sheltering arms, however long destiny might grant us.

Far above me now, I heard him call to me again. I saw him leap over the cliff's edge, not in dragon form but as the man I loved.

I screamed, heartbroken and horrified.

Something fell away from me in that moment. I felt my fears dry up and swirl off on the breeze that rushed up all around me. I watched Drakor diving toward me in the empty darkness, and something deep within me shook free of its tether.

I closed my eyes, and when I opened them again I wasn't falling anymore. I was floating. I was flying, suspended on the night wind, my arms and torso covered in glorious white feathers.

And there was Drakor beneath me now, his massive wings spread out as if to catch me, hovering as I was in the middle of the immense canyon that gaped as far as the eye could see.

In silent understanding, we flew together to the far side of the canyon, leaving the hellhounds to stare after us in disappointment.

Drakor and I touched down on solid ground as one. He shook off his scales, and I watched in amazement as the snowy plumage that covered me from my glossy beak to the tops of my taloned feet dissolved back into skin.

"An eagle," Drakor said, wonder in his deep voice. "I might have guessed."

"How could you have?" I asked. "I didn't know myself."

His smile was rather smug. "Your mother's name, Nisha."

"Jariat?" I shook my head. "I don't understand."

"As I told you, it is a very old name, a mythical name. According to legend, Jariat was a beautiful bird who became a human for love of her offspring."

It took me a moment to process. "You're telling me that my mother was Strange? The Jariat of legend?"

He bent his head and kissed me with so much love it made my heart ache. "We have a lifetime to figure all of this out. We could share forever, Nisha, if you'll have me."

I smiled up into his handsome face. "I like the sound of that."

"There's just one other thing." He grew very serious then. "I will be making some changes in the way my father's court is run. I will need someone courageous, someone honourable, whose opinion I value over any other, to stand beside me when I reclaim my father's throne."

I swallowed, proud of him and hopeful for the future we might build together. "You want me to be part of your court?"

His assenting nod couldn't have been more regal if his head had been wreathed with a jewelled crown. "I cannot imagine becoming king unless you are with me, Nisha. As my queen and chief advisor."

I threw my arms around him and caught his mouth in an elated kiss.

"I'll take that as a yes?" he chuckled.

"Yes!" I cried. "I love you, Drakor. So, yes, yes! Yes to whatever you desire of me."

He growled with purely male interest. "Now, *I* like the sound of *that*."

Drakor and I spent two weeks with the Strange enclave that dwelled in the hidden cliffs of what had once been southwestern Colorado. Once he'd regained his strength and recuperated from his kidnapping, we travelled back to the coast together, towards his homeland of New Asia.

The air was crisp that day, but the sun was high, its warming rays stretching down to touch us as we stood at land's end and stared out at the vast blue ocean ahead of us. Drakor's hand was clasped easily around mine.

"Are you ready, Nisha?"

I looked up into the face of my lover, my mate, my king, and I smiled. "I'm ready."

He gave me a nod and let go of my hand.

With a shrug of his mighty shoulders, he transformed. I joined him in shifting, giving a shake like a dog throwing off water and watching with still-fresh wonder as my white feathers sprouted into glorious plumage.

My dragon looked at me, and I thought I could see him smile. I gave him a nod of my beaked head. Together we stepped off the steep edge of land.

And we flew.

The Sons of Ra

Helen Scott Taylor

One

Chateau Montgatine gleamed in the sun like a spun-sugar palace. Colourful flower borders laid out in the pattern of Egyptian symbols trimmed either side of the long gravel driveway. Tricia knew about the mystical floral design even though it was only visible from above. Twenty-two years ago, Christian Lefevre, the Comte de Montgatine, had taken her up in his private plane to show her.

The years telescoped, taking her back to the first time she'd set eyes on the chateau as a naive eighteen-year-old. She'd felt like a fairytale princess, dreamed of romance and happy endings. She'd grown from a girl to a woman during her month in France and learned that happy endings were strictly for fairytales.

She pushed the button on the intercom by the gate.

"*Bonjour.*" A man's voice gabbled a few incomprehensible sentences through the crackly speaker.

"*Bonjour, monsieur*. I have an appointment with the Comte."

"Ah, *oui, oui*. Welcome back to Chateau Montgatine, Mademoiselle Tricia."

Tricia's heart skipped as she recognized the voice of Christian's butler. "Monsieur Benoit, is that you?"

"*Oui, oui*. Still here, mademoiselle, still here. We talk in a moment."

The latch on the gate clicked open and the wrought-iron sections swung inward. Tricia jumped back into her rental car and started the engine. Her pulse sprinted as she drove to the chateau. She might be forty now, a different person to the teenager who'd given her heart away, but the prospect of facing her first love left her breathless with nerves. If only there had been someone else she could have turned to for advice.

The front door opened as Tricia grabbed her briefcase and climbed out of the car. Monsieur Benoit stood on the top step beaming a welcoming smile. "You have not changed at all, mademoiselle." She intended to tell him that he should call her *madame*, but before she could speak, he hugged her, pressing the customary three kisses to her cheeks.

"You're too kind, Monsieur Benoit. You haven't changed either." He must have been forty when she'd stayed in a cottage near the chateau over two decades ago, but he certainly didn't look sixty now. He barely had a grey hair.

A strange little flutter of unease passed through her as she glanced around the chateau grounds. Two gardeners were busy weeding, lizards sunbathed on the limestone walls and swallows swooped and circled over the garden, snatching insects from the sun-drenched, fragrant air. If it hadn't been for the briefcase clutched tightly in her damp hand and the small Citroën rental car, she could almost believe she'd been transported back in time.

Tricia shook herself and followed Monsieur Benoit into the cool interior of the chateau. Her sense of déjà vu continued. The intricate coloured patterns on the walls and ceiling were unchanged, the furniture exactly as she remembered. Tricia laughed, mainly to relieve some of the tension clogging her throat. "You haven't redecorated I see."

"Oh no, no. The Comte, he does not like change."

He'd been quick enough to change his feelings for her. Tricia pressed her lips together. Now was not the time to dredge up old hurts. She couldn't change the past. She could only make the most of the present and her present involved her passion for her job at the Bristol Institute of Art. This meeting was business, not pleasure. She'd best remember that.

She smiled at the butler. "May I see the Comte now?" The name "Christian" whispered in her mind, but she had no right to call him by his given name. Twenty-two years apart had made them strangers again.

"Oh, of course, of course. He waits for you in the library."

Tricia's breath eased out in relief. She and Christian had never spent time together in the library, so she would not be haunted by memories. Maybe that was why he'd chosen to meet with her in that room.

After following Monsieur Benoit to the library door, she passed through with a smile when he opened it for her. She breathed slowly, evenly, stared at the rows of old leather-bound books. *Calm and professional*, she repeated in her head. The click of the door closing made her heart trip; then she heard a rustle of clothing.

"Madame Cole. Tricia."

The sound of her name spoken in the deep, achingly familiar voice from her memories drew her gaze inexorably to the man on the far side of the room.

She froze. Shock pounded in her chest, echoed in her temples, beat a drum of startled panic through her body. The briefcase dropped from her nerveless fingers to the floor.

Framed by the elegant marble fireplace, Christian stared back at her wearing his familiar linen suit, his hair neatly trimmed, his eyes green as emeralds, his skin supple, bronzed, *smooth*.

He hadn't aged at all.

Lines formed between his eyebrows. He moved towards her. "Are you all right, Madame?"

Tricia's hand pressed over the frantic beat of her heart. "You're so . . . young," she breathed in a strangled voice.

Understanding flashed across his face, followed by pain. "No one has told you. I'm sorry. My father passed away ten years ago."

Tricia blinked, his words skating around her brain, making no sense. She grabbed for a chair back. He hurried over to support her elbow, help her into the chair. Then he pulled another seat up and sat facing her.

Tears pricked the back of her eyes. Although Christian had sent her away, knowing he was living out his life in the same world as she had given her some kind of comfort. Too late, she realized that deep inside she had still dreamed he might want her back.

But now . . . "Dead?" she whispered, daring to look this doppelganger in the face. He was the spitting image of his father. His eyes were the exact same shade of green; his hair the same light brown with sun-kissed streaks. Could a son resemble his father to such an extent? Even identical twins had some differences, didn't they?

"I'm so sorry, Tricia. Remy must have forgotten to tell you."

"How old are you?" she whispered. Even as the words passed her lips, she realized it was rude to ask such a direct question. Especially of a *comte* she'd only just met. But every cell in her body was shocked into confusion. Instinct told her she knew this man. Everything about him was familiar.

"I believe I was born the same year you visited France."

A shaft of pain caught her breath. So there had been another woman in Christian's life even as he romanced her. A woman carrying his child. He must have married the other woman, or her son would not have inherited the title.

"How do you know which year I visited?" she asked, hoping he had made a mistake.

The Comte rose and fetched something from a desk under the window. He held out a small wooden frame containing a photograph of her sitting on the edge of the fountain in the secret garden, smiling at the camera. An exquisite butterfly hair clip decorated with diamonds and rubies glinted against her dark hair. She'd almost forgotten the romantic afternoon when Christian had taken her along the maze of tiny paths overhung with roses and given her the gift. She'd treasured that precious butterfly for the grand total of three days. When he sent her away, she'd thrown it back in his face.

The Comte pointed to the date written in the corner. "My father kept this photograph on his desk."

Why would he keep a photo of her? Christian had been the one to end their relationship, claiming she was too young for him. Even though he had only been in his early twenties. Although at times he'd seemed much older than his years, just as the young man before her did. Christian's son could only be twenty-one, yet his assured manner belonged to a man twice his age.

The Comte rose and filled a tumbler with amber liquid from a decanter. He returned and held out the glass. "You've had a shock. Cognac will steady your nerves."

Tricia barked a sharp, disbelieving laugh. "Christian gave me cognac when I was stung by a bee once and . . ." Her words choked off with emotion as the memory rose from the deep recesses of her mind. After a long moment staring at his lean fingers holding the cut crystal, she accepted the glass. The smooth liquid burned a path down her throat.

"A predilection for Cognac is in the Lefevre genes," he said wryly.

By the time she'd downed the contents of the glass, a warm fuzzy sense of unreality filled her head. "You look so much like your father. I'm finding it difficult to . . ." She rubbed her temples. "Maybe if you tell me your name it'll help."

He rose, placed her glass on a silver tray, then stared out the window for a few seconds, his shoulders tense. "It's Christian, I'm afraid . . . after my father."

Tricia's sense of unease flared again as this young Christian, who could have stepped out of her dreams, turned to look at her. For long moments, his emerald gaze perused her face, her body, as if he wanted to memorize her. "Still so beautiful," he said softly.

Her breath escaped on a tiny gasp. "What?"

He curved an elegant hand towards the photo. "Compared to your picture, Madame, you've aged well, like a fine wine."

Her heart tripped, flickers of awareness racing through her in response to his appreciative gaze. She stared at her hands gripped tightly in her lap. Being attracted to this man was wrong. He was little more than a teenager; the son of the man she'd loved.

He picked up her briefcase and placed it beside her chair, then sat before her again, suddenly all business. "If you're recovered from your shock, perhaps you'd like to tell me why you came all this way to see me."

"I came to see your father."

His shoulders lifted in a small shrug. "I might be able to help you."

He must have inherited his father's possessions. Perhaps he would recognize the *objet d'art* about which she wanted information.

A sense of purpose infused Tricia as she unfastened her brief-case. She took out the photograph of the strange transparent pyramid that had been bequeathed to the Institute. "We can't find anyone who knows what this is." She handed the photo to Christian. "The base of the object is twenty-four inches square and the thing's very heavy. There appear to be flames inside it, but it must be a clever special effect. I'm hoping you'll be able to tell me what it is because I saw something similar here years ago."

"When?" The young Comte's gaze snapped up from the image and pinned her in place. His eyes flickered like green fire. For the first time in years, Tricia's cheeks grew hot. This young man hadn't even been born on the day she'd crept into the chateau uninvited, hoping to beg Christian to take her back. She had found no sign of the man she loved, but the memory of the mysterious pyramid full of green fire that she'd found in his bedroom was seared into her mind.

"Years ago." She pushed away her sense of embarrassment and tapped a finger on the photograph. "The pyramid the Institute has contains blue fire rather than green, apart from that, it's the same as the object I saw here. The transparent material is definitely not glass, it's crystalline."

The Comte's gaze had fallen to the image again. Now his eyes rose to interrogate her with an authority that looked strange for one so young. "Has anyone touched it?"

Tricia nodded. "Of course. It's been uncrated and examined."

"Did *you* touch it?"

A tremor of apprehension passed through her at the alarm in his voice.

"Why shouldn't I touch it? It's fascinating. The flame inside looks real, but the pyramid appears to be sealed. Real fire can't burn without oxygen."

The Comte banged his fist on the arm of his chair, making her jump. "*Ça alors!* After all I gave up to protect you."

"What are you talking about?" Christian's son hadn't done anything to protect her. She hadn't met him until today.

"Where is the *ben ben*?" At her frown, he gestured impatiently at the photograph. "I mean the pyramid, Tricia, where is it?"

"In the secure area beneath the gallery at the Bristol Institute of Art."

"I need to see it."

Tricia found herself shaking her head in confusion. "Can't you just explain what this *ben ben* is? Once I know, the Institute can value it and decide whether or not to put it on display."

"The *ben ben* must be kept hidden." The Comte surged to his feet, paced to the door and wrenched it open. "Remy!" When Monsieur Benoit hurried up, Christian issued rapid instructions in French. Then he returned to her and stared intently at the pyramid's photograph. "We depart for England immediately. You will not leave my sight, Tricia. We're lucky you have not already been claimed."

Tricia rose to her feet unsteadily. Irritation stirred across her shocked thoughts. The emotional meeting and his strange reaction had left her shaken, but she did not intend to let this young upstart take over and treat her like an idiot. "You're welcome to come and view the pyramid, my lord, but I can look after myself. There's no reason why I should be in danger."

"*Non?*" His breath hissed out between his teeth. He closed his eyes for a second and flexed his shoulders, making a visible effort to relax. When his eyes opened again, he surprised her by reaching for her hand. He raised her knuckles to his lips and pressed a warm kiss to them.

Streamers of tickly heat fluttered through her belly, leaving her breathless with mortification at her response. She must not react to him like this. She was old enough to be his mother.

His glittering green gaze caressed her face and a tiny smile caught at the corners of his mouth. "My noble intentions are undone, *mon amour*. I gave you up to protect you from danger, but danger has found you anyway. I should be sorry, but my heart sings now fate has given you back to me."

Two

Christian piloted the helicopter from France to Bristol Airport in the UK. The emotional roller coaster of the last few hours had left Tricia lightheaded. Was it only this morning that she'd set out from her hotel in the pretty French market town of Montgatine?

Could this young Comte really be the man she'd lost her heart to twenty-two years ago?

Dusk had fallen by the time they landed. After their passports had been checked, Christian guided her to a black limousine and they headed off to the Institute of Art.

Tricia huddled in a corner of the back seat, staring at Christian, confusion unravelling her thoughts. The highlights in his hair shone guinea gold in contrast to the black trousers and black leather jacket he'd donned for their night foray. He smiled, his green eyes glittering with gold flecks. Instead of taking the far seat, he slid up beside her as the car moved off. "I'm sorry to have upset you. Do you forgive me?"

A tight little laugh burst from her throat. "No! You lied to me." She'd thought she knew the man she loved but she hadn't known him at all.

He gave a small resigned nod of understanding. "I did not break up with you because you were immature as I alleged but because I wanted to protect you from the dangers in my life."

"Yeah, well, I'm not immature now. I'm old enough to be your mother."

He took one of her hands and gripped it tightly in his warm palm. "Believe me, looks can be deceiving."

"I'm forty. You were masquerading as twenty-one a few hours ago. That makes me old enough to be your mother."

"You'd have been a very young mother," he said with a teasing smile.

"Stop splitting hairs." She yanked her hand away from him. Despite her protestations, she felt more like an ignorant child. "Why haven't you aged?"

He angled his head, searching her face for her reaction as he answered. "I do age. My secret is that I can renew myself."

"Huh? So you've discovered an elixir of eternal youth?" Sarcasm edged her words.

"I renew myself with fire, Tricia. The fire inside the crystal pyramid you have at the Institute of Art is the life essence of a man like me. My race was at its most powerful in ancient Egypt. We're the Sons of Ra."

His words zapped her befuddled brain to full alert. Her job had taught her a lot about Egyptian history. Ra the sun god was supposed to die every evening when the sun went down only to be reborn when the sun rose again in the morning. His followers had worshipped him in a temple called the Mansion of the Phoenix.

Sun, fire, rebirth.

Her breath trembled. Was Christian telling the truth?

If she believed him, then that meant the transparent pyramid in the Institute's basement contained the essence of a man. It also meant that the green fire she'd seen in the pyramid in Christian's room all those years ago had been his life essence. The idea was impossible to comprehend.

Full dark had fallen by the time the limousine drew up outside the Institute. Tricia stepped out into the pool of illumination beneath a street light. Panic caught in her throat as she mounted the steps to the impressive entrance of the Victorian building. She retrieved her keycard from her purse and swiped it before tapping in the access code.

Christian glanced over his shoulder then followed her into the building. The security lights blinked on when they sensed movement. "Make sure you lock this door behind us," he instructed.

The serious tone of his voice made her pause to stare at him. "Are you expecting some kind of trouble?"

"Let us say it pays to be careful."

Christian prowled around, his gaze darting down the shadowy side corridors. How had she ever fallen for the story that he was only twenty-one? Everything about him screamed experience and power. He returned to her and placed a hand on her back. "Take me to the *ben ben*."

"I need to check in with security first."

Christian gave a single nod. "I'll come with you."

Even the hollow sound of Christian's footsteps behind her held the ring of authority.

Once the guard had deactivated the alarm system on the basement level, Tricia led Christian down the narrow stairs that had originally been used by domestic staff back in the days when the building had been a private mansion.

"The *ben ben* didn't come down these stairs. Is there another way in?" Christian asked.

"The old servant's entrance gives access at basement level.

The doorway's been enlarged to allow crates to be delivered that way."

"How are the objects in the basement moved up to the gallery?"

"There's a service elevator."

Christian paused at the foot of the stairs to glance around. "Any other exits? Maybe doors that aren't normally used."

"There's a fire door on every floor, leading to the fire escape at the back of the building. Except on this level."

He gave another of his quick nods. "Show me the *ben ben*, please."

Tricia stared at him while his gaze tracked around the space. His eyes glowed an inhuman golden green in the muted light. That did more to convince her he had told the truth about the Sons of Ra than anything he'd said. "What will you do with the pyramid?"

"I'll decide when I see it."

Not the answer for which she'd hoped. She just wanted him to crate the thing up and take it away so she could be done with all this weirdness.

She led him into the assessment room where all new pieces of doubtful origin were checked before being logged on to the system. So far, the only official record of the pyramid was a delivery note.

Tricia snapped over ten switches on the lighting control panel. Spotlights beamed on to the transparent pyramid in the centre of the room.

Christian stilled beside her. For long seconds he didn't even appear to breathe. The blue-tinged flames in the heart of the artifact danced and flickered, as real as any fire she'd ever seen. "*Merde*. That shade of blue belongs to Benedict Rothswell's family."

A jolt of shock rooted Tricia to the spot. She sucked in a breath. He couldn't mean . . . "Are you talking about the Duke of Buckland?"

Christian wheeled around to face her. "You know him?"

"He's the Institute's patron. He owns this building." She flung out an arm to indicate the mansion. "He owns half of Bristol actually."

"And you touched the *ben ben*?" Christian's gaze narrowed. "We have a serious problem."

"I have to concur, Lefevre," a deep masculine voice said. "I take a very dim view of your entering my territory without invitation, or even permission."

The smooth, deep baritone of The Duke of Buckland made Tricia turn, her heart thumping. "Your Grace. I'm sorry. I didn't realize you were here." She winced inwardly at the stupid comment. He'd obviously arrived unannounced in the middle of the night to avoid discovery.

The duke's flaring blue gaze made her step back. She'd met him five times as part of the management team welcoming him to an event at the Institute, and they had never exchanged more than a polite greeting. Tall, with hair the colour of polished ebony, and a cut-glass British accent, he exuded breeding and authority from every inch of his powerful frame. He had the compelling attraction of a large predator. He strode purposefully towards her.

Christian was suddenly in front of her, blocking her view of the duke, yet she hadn't even seen him move. "She's mine, Rothswell."

"You haven't claimed her yet, Lefevre and she's in my domain. Ergo, she is mine."

"I discovered her twenty years ago."

The duke laughed, a dark chuckle edged with primeval hostility that did not belong to a civilized man. "Negligent of you, Lefevre, not to trap the pretty butterfly before now. I have males in my family who would fight for her. Why should I let you walk away with something so rare?"

"As the price for my help."

An electric tension hummed in the room as the two men faced each other down. Tricia stepped back and pressed herself to the wall, mute with disbelief at what she'd just heard. They sounded positively medieval. The duke glanced at the pyramid spotlighted in the centre of the room and annoyance flashed across his face.

"I'm guessing that *your son* rests inside that *ben ben*," Christian said softly. "You'll need help if you plan to force him to renew. Let me take the butterfly back to France and I'll lend you my power."

Tricia's pulse beat so fast the blood vibrated in her temples. It wasn't difficult to understand that she was the butterfly they were discussing like a couple of Neanderthals vying for the right to drag her away by her hair. She could just about understand why Christian might want her now, after all, he had desired her twenty years ago. But the concept that the Duke of Buckland knew men who would fight over her was absurd.

A coppery flush painted the duke's cheekbones. When he glanced back at Christian, his eyes glowed blue. "You win this time, Lefevre. But I'm warning you, claim the woman or my family will take her from you and make her ours."

Tricia did not intend to be claimed as a possession by any man, even a wealthy, handsome, titled man. She edged along the wall towards the door, her breath coming in shallow snatches as the two men approached the pyramid.

Christian stripped off his leather jacket and tossed it over a chair, while the duke removed his charcoal-grey suit jacket and red tie.

The duke ran his hands over the four surfaces of the transparent shape, searching for something. "Here," he said at length, turning to Christian. "Careless as usual, my son's left a fault that will give us a starting point."

Tricia's retreating feet halted and she stared, unable to drag her gaze away as both men stepped back and extended their arms. A four-foot long sceptre with a flat head and forked tail appeared in each man's hand. They both pointed the tops of their sceptres at the pyramid. "Cover your ears and look away," Christian called over his shoulder to her.

A moment later, a blast of gold-green fire from his sceptre hit the pyramid at the weak spot. The duke's gold-blue fire streamed out, targeting the same spot.

Tricia slapped her hands over her ears at the agonized screaming sound like metal straining under impossible force. She squinted through the shadow of her dark lashes, unable to look away from the terrifying spectacle. The pyramid started to glow so brightly her eyes hurt and the heat warmed her from across the room. The floor beneath the melting crystal had to be getting hot. She sidled closer to the door and scrabbled blindly for the fire extinguisher she knew was there.

"Your son's resisting the rebirthing," Christian shouted.

"He's bloody lazy and doesn't want to wake up," the duke replied.

Tricia released the fire extinguisher from its panel and peered at the instructions. Why had she never bothered to find out how the damn thing worked?

Slowly, the transparent pyramid melted. When the trapped blue flames burst forth into the air, Christian and the duke stopped their assault and pulled back.

The fire from inside the pyramid licked the ceiling. Tricia hefted the extinguisher, ready to douse the flames. Before she could press the trigger, the last traces of the pyramid disappeared and a man's naked body materialized.

Tricia hugged the extinguisher like a lifeline to normality as the man's face appeared. With his dark hair and blue eyes, the young man closely resembled his father.

Christian hurried back to her and wrapped an arm around her shoulders. "Buckland can clear up his mess. Let's get out of here."

"Cover yourself up," the duke growled at his naked son. He cuffed the young man on the side of the head, sending him stumbling into a computer desk, then tossed a dustsheet at him.

Christian eased the extinguisher out of Tricia's death grip and placed it on the ground.

"Where am I?" The young man asked, blinking in confusion.

"Up to your neck in trouble, boy. As usual." The duke grabbed his son by the arm and propelled him past them and out of the door. The boy looked barely more than a teenager. His bemused blue gaze snagged hers when he passed and her sympathy welled.

The duke paused and seared her with his stare. "Not a word of this to anyone, Lefevre, or the woman's mine."

Three

Tricia shrugged Christian's arm off her shoulders the moment the duke and his son disappeared. As her fear receded, her anger flared. She hurried up the steps from the Institute's basement and through the silent echoing Victorian hallway to the front door. Her legs felt weak, but she wasn't going to admit as much.

"The immediate danger is over, Tricia," Christian said in a soothing tone.

"Wonderful. You can go away then."

She stomped out of the front door and, despite her bravado, her heart gave a little leap of relief when she saw the black limousine still waiting for them outside. Although she was hurrying in front, Christian managed to pass her and have the car door open for her when she reached the road. She climbed in and crossed her arms.

Once the vehicle was moving, Christian slid closer to her with a disarming grin and ran a fingertip down her arm. There was no hint left of the formidable man who'd stood up to the duke. Instead, he behaved like the charming Comte she'd known years ago, a man who'd spent his days inspecting his vineyards and romancing her. She should be frightened after seeing him blast fire from a sceptre that appeared out of thin air, but her mind couldn't summon fear. This was her Christian. The man she'd loved. But did she still love him? Was it possible to forgive him for hurting her?

"You know I would never let Buckland take you, don't you?"

"*I* won't let him take me," she retorted, knowing full well after what she'd seen tonight that the duke wouldn't ask for her permission. She'd admired the Institute's patron as a strong, powerful man who got things done. Now the thought of his attitude to her made her temper simmer. "Why did the duke call me a butterfly?"

Christian's breath sighed out and he laced his fingers through hers. "Buckland is old school and rather medieval in his attitudes. Butterfly is normally a term of endearment, *mon amour*."

The limo pulled up outside Tricia's small house.

"May I come inside?" he asked.

"You haven't answered my question."

"The term butterfly for a woman was coined centuries ago. The Sons of Ra are all male as the name suggests, but there are women who carry the gene. These women are always drawn to us, like moths to a flame." He smiled. "I don't know if someone confused butterflies and moths, but that's where the term originated."

"So I carry the gene? Any son I have will be like you?"

"Only a son fathered by one of the Sons of Ra."

Tricia stared at the back of the driver's seat her eyes losing focus. She and her ex husband had tried unsuccessfully for five years to have a baby. "If that's why the duke thinks I'm worth fighting over he needn't bother. I can't have children."

She expected Christian to express shock, sorrow, offer the usual platitudes. Instead, the gentle stroke of his fingers continued brushing her arm. "You'll only be able to conceive a child with one of us."

"What?" Tricia's temper shot to boiling in an instant. She elbowed him away, pulling on the door handle.

"Wait, Tricia."

She jumped out of the car and rounded on him. "Why didn't you tell me?" Tears filled her eyes, ached in her chest. By keeping quiet, he'd sentenced her to years of heartbreak trying for a baby she couldn't have. She'd lost her husband through the strain the experience had put on their relationship. "When you sent me away, you knew I wouldn't be able to have a child with another man because of this bloody gene. But you didn't think that fact was worth telling me?"

She pivoted away from the car and ran up the steps to her front door, fumbling for the key in her purse.

"Tricia, calm down." Christian gripped her shoulders and she ducked away from his touch.

"Get lost. You had a chance to tell me all this twenty years ago. Instead of helping me to understand, you cut me off with no explanation, even though you knew it would affect my life."

"I was trying to protect you."

"From what? From jerks like the duke? Strange that I've been working for him for the last twelve years then, isn't it?" Her fingers finally closed around her key and she jammed it in the lock. She tried to squeeze through the door and shut Christian out, but he wedged a foot in the gap.

She gave up trying to exclude him and retreated to the kitchen, flicking on all the lights as she went. The front door closed and she heard the deadlock click and the security chain engage. "We'll stay here tonight," Christian said, following her into the kitchen. "You're tired and distressed. Buckland has enough on his plate this evening dealing with his son. I doubt he'll come for you."

"You're not staying with me," she snapped.

Ignoring her, he found two mugs and started to make coffee. She stood on the opposite side of the kitchen, watching him. His lithe perfectly balanced body radiated youthful energy. His skin was smooth, not a line or wrinkle in sight. His thick hair gleamed gold under the kitchen spotlights. She turned and stared at her reflection in the glass cabinet doors. She'd kept her figure because she hadn't had children. Only a few grey hairs had invaded her brown locks. At a pinch, she might pass for thirty-five. Even that age difference might not have mattered, but she would continue to age and he wouldn't.

Once she would have sold her soul to be with Christian, but times changed. Whatever his reasons, he hadn't wanted her enough to be honest with her twenty years ago. If the Duke of Buckland had realized she had the magic gene, he'd have spirited her away to some private estate and paired her off with one of his men like a brood mare. When Christian turned her away, he'd left her vulnerable. She didn't owe him a thing. She would not return to France with him. The damn Duke of Buckland didn't own the whole of the UK. There must be a place outside of his control where she could live.

While Christian had his back to her, she removed her shoes and walked quietly down the hall, up the stairs and into her room, shutting her bedroom door firmly behind her.

Tricia prepared for bed like an automaton, her mind numb with shock and fatigue. Wearing her oversized T-shirt, she switched off the light and snuggled under her covers.

A knock sounded on the door. "Tricia, I have your coffee."

She didn't answer, hoping Christian would think she was asleep and leave her alone.

"I know you're awake." The door opened. Christian stood in the gap, the masculine angles of his body silhouetted against the hall light.

Her treacherous heart lurched. They had never been in a bedroom together. Although they'd been inseparable during the six weeks of her stay in France when she was eighteen, he had always been a gentleman, never taking advantage of her.

"I don't want coffee. Go away."

He ambled in and placed the mug on her nightstand, then switched on the bedside lamp. "A hot drink will do you good. You haven't eaten anything since you arrived at the chateau this morning."

"I've already cleaned my teeth."

Christian sat on the edge of her bed and she made a performance of dragging the covers higher to show she was annoyed. He placed a hand on the pillow on either side of her head and leaned closer. Tricia froze, trapped in the flare of green fire in his eyes. Twenty years dropped away and her body tingled in expectation. "I won't come to France with you."

The corners of his lips tucked up as if he were trying not to smile. "I'd forgotten how stubborn you are." He ducked his head and pressed firm, warm lips over hers. Her eyelids fell at the silky slide of his mouth. Even as she pledged not to touch him, her palm curved around his stubbly cheek. She'd dreamed of this endlessly, before she met her husband, while she was married to her husband, and after the poor man left. She'd always blamed their divorce on her infertility. In truth, it had more to do with her attitude. Her husband had never replaced Christian in her heart. She doubted anyone ever could.

Christian kicked off his shoes and stretched out on top of the covers at her side. His fingers traced her features with a feather-light touch. "I've missed you every day since you left, *mon adorée*. After I lost you, I spent weeks in cleansing fire to kill the pain. When I emerged I was younger and stronger, but my heart hurt as much as ever."

"Why didn't you come to find me?" After they'd parted, she'd prayed every night that Christian would realize he'd made a mistake and come after her.

"I thought I was doing the best thing for you by letting you go. I wanted to spare you the sort of experience you had tonight. My world is full of danger."

Tricia closed her eyes and pressed her cheek against his, felt his lips brush her neck. She breathed in the uniquely French fragrance of the sun and rich earth tinged with ripening fruit that clung to him like a memory of perfect happiness.

"What shall I do, Christian? Returning to the Institute is out of the question now."

"Come to France with me, *mon amour*. We've been apart too long."

She sucked in a breath, revelling in his fragrance, while images of Chateau Montgatine, the vineyards and gardens flickered through her mind. She would have Christian and a beautiful place to live. But how would she feel in twenty years when she was sixty and looking her age? How would Christian treat her then?

"I'm not sure," she whispered, not wanting to voice her concern because she knew he'd just brush it aside.

"Let us talk of this tomorrow when you're rested," he said softly against her ear, his fingers stroking tantalizing circles on her neck and shoulder. "Sleep now."

The feel of Christian's arms around her gave her the security to relax. Time drifted and she was nearly asleep when he tensed beside her. The warmth of his body withdrew. She blinked and pushed up on her elbow to squint into the darkness.

In the moonlight, he stood like a statue staring at the door. "Do you smell that?"

Tricia rubbed her eyes, disoriented. Then the bitter tang of smoke reached her nose and the fuzziness of sleep fell away.

Four

"What the hell?" She jumped out of bed and raced towards the bedroom door. Christian grabbed her arm and pulled her to a halt. "My bag is downstairs with my credit cards and driver's licence."

"They're replaceable. You're not."

Smoke trickled in under the door and rose in a grey wispy curtain like a ghost. Tricia pressed a hand over her nose and stumbled back, the taste of burning plastic on her tongue. Christian strode to the window, unlatched it and peered out.

Tricia pressed up beside him, flutters of terror in her chest when she felt the heat rising outside. Flames licked out of the downstairs windows.

"*Merde*! We're trapped."

"Surely *you* can't burn?" Tricia asked through the sweater she'd pressed over her nose.

"You can." His jaw clenched. "There's only one way out. Dress warmly."

"Why."

"Just do as I ask. Quickly." The urgency in his voice stimulated her into action.

She yanked on her old sweat pants and jersey, then turned to him.

"Socks, shoes, gloves, hat," he barked.

She frowned to herself but rooted through her drawers to find what she needed. The smoke had thickened, stinging her eyes and making her cough. Christian guided her to the window so she could breathe cleaner air. He pushed yet another sweater over her head, dressing her as though she was a child. Maybe he thought all the clothes would cushion her landing when she jumped out.

"Stand back." He raised a foot and kicked out the window frame, sending wood and chunks of masonry crashing to the ground.

Tricia had wound a scarf around her face to filter the air and shield her eyes. As she squinted through the weave, Christian's black jacket seemed to melt away and something bright and glittering took its place. He reached for her, but she stumbled back in confusion, bumped into the nightstand, and sent the lamp crashing to the floor. Strong hands gripped her, pulled her to the window. She coughed, her chest aching as she struggled for breath.

Christian dragged her against his body. His torso was covered in something hard and shiny and her gloved fingers rubbed over a pattern on his chest. He stepped out of the window. Tricia braced to fall. Instead, the smoke disappeared, and the city lights faded to be replaced by stygian darkness.

Cold scraped razor sharp across the small areas of exposed skin around her eyes and neck, drove icy needles into the marrow of her bones. She shivered, her teeth chattering so hard her jaws cramped. Her skull ached as though in a vise. Her eyes froze shut; her breath jolted in short painful snatches of arctic air. She tried to press tighter against Christian, but she couldn't reach his heat. His arms held her close, but his body was as hard and cold as ice.

A scream echoed in her head but only a pitiful whimper passed between her chilled lips.

Just when she couldn't stand the pain any longer, the air expanded around her. Her feet touched ground and the warm scent of night in the Loire Valley trickled into her nose.

Her legs folded beneath her, but Christian's arms were suddenly warm and strong. He caught her up and laid her on a bed before bundling covers around her. "You'll be all right, *mon amour*. You'll be all right."

She heard a door open and Christian shouted. "Remy, we need cognac."

Tricia's body trembled with cold but at last she managed to crack open her eyes. All she could make out were blurred colours. The rushing sound of water blended with the thud of footsteps. A knock on the door. "Chris, *mon ami*? You are hurt?" Monsieur Benoit's voice.

"I had to bring Tricia through the ether. We need to warm her quickly."

She huddled in a shivering bundle beneath the bed covers. When she tried to speak her lips cracked and she tasted blood.

"Shh, Tricia. Shh." The bed dipped at her side and a glass pressed to her lips. A burning trail of brandy ran down her throat, until she had fire in her belly and a spinning head.

She managed to open her eyes enough to see him bend over her to pull off her shoes and socks. Then her sweat pants disappeared.

"What . . . ?" she whispered.

"Warm water, my little butterfly. That will do the trick."

He peeled off her gloves, then pulled the two sweaters over her head, leaving her naked. He scooped her into his arms and swept through to the bathroom. Tricia hadn't heard Monsieur Benoit leave, but the bath was full and the butler nowhere in sight.

Christian lowered her into the oversized tub of bubbly warm water. Her eyelids fell. A sigh of relief hissed over her lips as the gentle heat chased away the last of the chill.

"You didn't suffer frostbite, thank goodness." At Christian's words, she opened her eyes to see him step into the tub with her. He'd stripped to the waist, keeping on his black trousers.

He settled at her side and gently rubbed her arm. "Are you feeling better?"

"Much." Her head lolled back and her eyelids drifted down. She had dreamed of such a scenario. Suffering the painful cold might be a price worth paying to feel his hands on her body. He massaged up her arm, then shifted to her other side.

Languid heat coursed through her veins and spread across her skin. Her breasts became heavy, her nipples tight and tingly. She knew exactly where she wanted him to massage next.

He leaned his back against the side of the round tub and lifted Tricia to sit between his legs, her back pressed against his chest. He worked his fingers over her neck and shoulders. Her head flopped forward. The chill long forgotten, she lost herself in the wonderful sensation of Christian's hands massaging her muscles. "Pure bliss," she whispered in a husky undertone.

The regular movement of his fingers paused, then continued more gently. "Are you recovered, *mon adorée*?"

"Mmm." Tricia wriggled her bottom back snug into the vee of his thighs. Twenty years ago she'd been innocent and taken her lead from him. She wasn't eighteen any more. She placed her palm on Christian's thigh and squeezed the firm muscle.

"Tricia." His breath whispered across her neck, sparking nerves beneath her skin. She didn't know if she would stay with him, but she had dreamed of making love with him so many times; she had to take this opportunity.

She rose, water and bubbles cascading off her body, and stepped out of the bath. The room was warm. She didn't cover herself but stood naked in invitation, waiting for him to follow.

Christian climbed out, his wet trousers clinging to his skin. She feasted her eyes on the sculpted muscles of his torso, his lean hips and powerful thighs.

A lopsided grin settled on his lips. "I'd forgotten you are . . . more experienced now."

"Twenty years will do that for a girl."

His hand rested at her waist and pulled her a step closer to him. He stroked the long dark strands of wet hair from her face.

He angled his head and kissed her with slow, thorough exploration until she was light-headed and breathless.

"Does this mean you'll stay with me?" he asked against her lips.

Tricia leaned back, ran her hands over his chest, and looked up into the green-gold flames burning in his eyes. "That depends how good you are in bed," she teased.

Five

Tricia lay in the centre of Christian's bed, tingling with anticipation while he eased his clingy, wet trousers down his thighs.

He stretched out beside her and trailed his hands over her curves as if learning her shape. "You're more beautiful than I imagined."

Pulling him closer, she pressed herself against him. His mouth claimed hers in a tender kiss while her fingers explored the silky skin of his back. His face was the epitome of youthful masculine beauty, but he had the well-muscled body of a mature man – a tantalizing combination.

She had yearned for Christian for so long; being here with him in his bed was like a dream. She wanted the moment to last forever, but she was as hungry for him as he was for her. Their eager hands teased and claimed with frantic need. He shifted on top of her with a growl of desire and she wrapped her legs around him, urging him to hurry.

Her fingers dug into his shoulders as pleasure shimmered through her, sweeping away her fears and worries until nothing mattered except loving him.

After they had finished making love, he collapsed on his back beside her, breathing hard. She snuggled up to him, little aftershocks of pleasure racing through her. "The Duke of Buckland is out of luck." She imagined a scowl on the duke's arrogant face and smiled. "Will you tell him you've claimed me?"

Christian rolled on his side to face her and kissed her fingertips. "I haven't claimed you yet, *mon amour*. That's something different."

"So the duke would still take me from you, even though we've made love?"

"Let's ensure he doesn't have a reason to try." His gaze roamed her face and he ran the pad of his thumb over her lips. "I'll never give you up again, Tricia. I shall claim you now."

"You haven't told me what's involved in the claiming yet."

"I'll bind you to me in a way that means I'll be able to sense you, keep you safe. You'll be marked as mine, untouchable by any others of my kind."

Tricia shifted uncomfortably. "Sounds as though you're about to hang a tag around my neck with your phone number on it in case I stray."

He chuckled. "The connection between us will go a lot deeper than that. You have a dormant gene that the claiming activates to attune you to my energy."

Tricia was no biologist, but she knew that *every* cell in her body contained genes. "You're talking about something pretty drastic here, Christian. You're spooking me."

He slid his fingers into her hair and kissed her. "I promise you there's nothing to worry about. The experience is special . . . intimate. Something I've only ever shared with one other woman."

Right now, she did *not* want to hear about the other woman with whom he'd shared this special intimate thing. "Just tell me how you do this transformation."

"Simple. I bathe you in my fire."

"Whoa." Tricia pulled back out of his grip and reflexively snatched the sheet to her chest. "No way."

Christian sat up and angled his head, assessing her. "You're frightened."

"Any sane person would be."

"I won't hurt you. My fire renews."

"Your fire's hot. Don't try to tell me it's not because I watched you melt that pyramid at the Institute. I felt the heat from across the room."

Christian sighed and rubbed the back of his neck. "I would never hurt you. You're going to have to trust me on that."

And there lay the rub. He had already hurt her so badly he had shattered her teenage confidence and left her broken-hearted. His definition of hurt didn't tally with hers. And it sounded as though once he'd claimed her there would be no going back. He'd have some kind of psychic tag on her for the rest of her life.

Tricia rose from the bed, tugging the sheet with her to cover up, and walked to the window. Dusk had fallen. The scent of evening flowers filled the air while tiny bats circled the terrace below.

"I need to claim you to protect you, Tricia. I suspect whoever set the fire at your home will pursue you here. The followers of Set and Anubis hunt our women and kill them when they can."

"Great. So if the duke doesn't take me some nutty pagans will try to kill me."

"I'm afraid they're more than nutty pagans. Apart from Ra, Set was the most powerful of the old gods. He's evil incarnate and he arms his followers with powers that challenge even the Sons of Ra."

Tricia plopped down on to the window seat and stared at him. "Are you telling me the Ancient Egyptian gods are still alive?"

"A few, but you only need to worry about Set and Anubis."

"Oh, great. Well that's all right then." She rolled her eyes.

"Now you understand why I sent you out of my life to protect you, *mon amour*."

"Actually, I don't. If I'm a target, you should have at least warned me."

"They only found you because *you* drew attention to yourself."

"Well forgive me for wanting a job and a life." She turned her back on him, her heart pounding with indignation.

A rustling sound warned her he had climbed off the bed. His hand settled gently on her shoulder. "After I sent you away, the odds of you encountering another Son of Ra or of touching a *ben ben* were close to zero. Will you keep punishing me for a choice I made with the best of intentions?"

Tricia squeezed her eyes closed and let her head drop forward. Was she being childish and vindictive? Did she want to hurt him for a decision he'd made twenty-two years ago?

She rose and turned into his waiting arms. He eased her head against his shoulder. His warm hand splayed soothingly on the small of her back. "Remy knows the touch of my fire. He'll confirm it doesn't hurt." His lips brushed her ear. His hand on her back pulled her closer; the evidence of his arousal pressed against her stomach. "Come back to bed with me, *mon amour*. We'll discuss the claiming tomorrow."

In the middle of the night, knocking intruded on Tricia's sleep. Drowsy with the languor of sexual satiation she barely roused at the sound of Remy's urgent words.

"I've been called to Egypt," Christian whispered. "I'll be back in the morning."

But when Tricia woke the following day, Christian hadn't returned.

She had warm croissants and hot chocolate for breakfast in the kitchen but didn't ask Remy about Christian's fire. She'd realized that men like Christian and the duke were unlikely to harm the rare women who carried their magic gene. She was more bothered about being tagged like a dog and losing her independence. Christian had spoken about the claiming as if the process was romantic, but the Duke of Buckland, for all his arrogance, might have been more honest. Once one of them claimed her, she would effectively become their property.

After breakfast, Tricia wandered the familiar path through the garden to the vineyards, meandering along the dusty trail between the neat rows of grape vines to the edge of the River Loire. Memories tumbled back of strolling hand-in-hand with Christian. Years ago, she'd thought love was the answer to everything.

She sat on a wooden bench under the trailing branches of a weeping willow where she had spent blissful afternoons with Christian and stared at the rippling water.

Two days ago, her main concern had been the cost of her mortgage. Now her home was probably a burnt-out shell containing the debris of her worldly possessions. Tears glazed her eyes and she blinked them away. Crying wouldn't solve anything. When she returned to the chateau, she would make a list of everyone she needed to call to sort out the disaster her life had become.

A blast of chilly wind stirred goose bumps on her skin. Ten feet away a dark rent opened in the air and a man stepped out. She recoiled, then slithered off the side of the bench and crawled behind it.

The man's intimidating blue gaze fixed on her, but she took a moment to identify him as the Duke of Buckland. Gone were the trappings of modern man; instead, he paced towards her clothed like an ancient warrior out of a fantasy film. Wide bands of gold bearing Egyptian symbols enclosed the bulging muscles of his biceps and his forearms. Gleaming plates of armour protected his torso, the breastplate decorated with a blue, jewel-studded image of the eye of Horus. His powerful thighs flexed beneath a short armoured skirt. In one hand, he held a wicked curved blade dripping blue fire, while in the other he held the sceptre that he'd used to melt the *ben ben* at the Institute of Art.

"Where's Lefevre?" he demanded.

She cowered behind the bench, staring at him with a stunned sense of unreality.

He halted when he reached her. "The bloody fool hasn't claimed you yet. He's had his chance. Now you're mine."

He tossed the curved blade aside. A small rip parted in the air and swallowed the weapon. While she was staring at the spot where the blade had disappeared, his hand closed around her wrist and he pulled her to her feet.

Sense rushed back in a panicked burst of adrenaline. She yanked against his grip. "No. It's my fault. I didn't let him."

"*You* shouldn't have a choice."

"I love him."

The duke paused and his jaw tightened. His blue eyes narrowed on her face. For the first time she had the sense that he saw *her* rather than simply a woman with the right genes. His breath hissed out in a frustrated rush and he released her. "Love is not enough in our world. You're in danger because he hasn't done his duty by you."

He stepped back and raised his arm. The curved blade reappeared in his hand.

"Tricia!" Christian's worried shout came from between the rows of vines. A moment later, he ran up and pulled her into his arms.

"Claim her *now*, Lefevre. Then next time you'll be able to find your woman before I can."

"I didn't want the claiming to be hurried like this," Christian framed her face in his hands.

A blast of arctic air whistled around them, dragging at her skirt and hair.

"*Merde*." Christian pivoted to face the direction of the wind, pushing her behind him.

"Too late, you bloody fool," the duke bit out with a scathing sideways glance.

Christian's trousers and shirt melted to be replaced by garb similar to the duke's. His biceps bunched beneath thick golden bands as he raised his arms. A curved blade and sceptre appeared in his hands.

Twenty feet away, a hole opened in the air sending the temperature plummeting. With a terrifying howl, a sinewy dog-shaped beast the size of a horse bounded out of the ether. The creature crouched, muscles tensed, claws raking the dirt. Saliva dripped from wickedly sharp canines as its lips drew back on a growl. Tricia's teeth chattered and she stumbled back against the trunk of the willow tree.

"Anubis," Christian whispered, his tone thick with disbelief.

Tricia pressed a hand over her mouth. She recognized the black jackal form of the Egyptian god from ancient drawings. But it couldn't be real; it couldn't be hunting her.

"Take her to safety and claim her now," the duke barked.

"You won't be able to tackle Anubis alone. Call the others," Christian replied.

"One of them will take your woman."

"No they bloody well won't."

The duke cut Christian an oblique look. "Your call, Lefevre. Don't say I didn't warn you."

The duke sketched a string of Egyptian hieroglyphs with the top of his sceptre, leaving a pattern of blue fire hanging in the air. He spoke a couple of sentences she didn't understand and the symbols melted away.

Anubis sprang at her with a blood-curdling growl. Christian and the duke pointed their sceptres at the beast and streams of green and blue fire poured over its head. But the creature kept coming. Christian stepped back, shielding her with his body while the duke charged forwards and hacked at Anubis' neck with his blade. An arc of dark blood splattered across the sunbaked earth between the rows of grapevines. The animal pulled back, flickers of blue fire sizzling in the wound.

Tricia huddled between the tree and Christian, wishing she

was anywhere on Earth but there. Cold blasted her and other men appeared, four, five; she lost count. She retreated behind the tree and watched from behind the trunk while the riverbank became a battleground. Anubis was bloodied and weakened but he kept trying to reach her. The Sons of Ra surrounded the beast, striking it with their blades and blasting it with fire from their sceptres. Mingled with Christian's green fire and the duke's blue were flaming streams of gold, turquoise, red and purple.

Angry words ricocheted back and forth between the men as they fought. Although she couldn't understand everything the men said, they were obviously angry with Christian.

She was wondering if she should make a dash for the chateau when she sensed the air behind become heavy and still. Warily, she turned her head and gasped.

Six

A tall Egyptian man stood a few yards away. His long black hair was tied back, framing the classic perfection of his bronzed features. Deep brown eyes outlined with black and turquoise narrowed on her. Gold glittered at his ears and jewels sparkled on every finger. A heavy gold torque set with turquoise and rubies glinted at his throat. He wasn't dressed like the Sons of Ra, instead a midnight blue robe decorated with gold hieroglyphs hung from his broad shoulders, fastened with a sash around his narrow hips.

She rose, keeping her back to the tree trunk, acutely aware of the sounds of battle from the other side of the tree.

The weight of his gaze pressed against her like a physical force. Some primeval instinct warned her that this man was as dangerous as the slavering monster Christian and the other men were fighting.

The man's nostrils flared. Deep, commanding words fell from his lips like the rumble of distant thunder. Her pulse raced and her breath shortened. But she couldn't answer. She had no idea what he'd said.

She risked a glance around the tree and called out to Christian. He must have heard the note of panic in her voice because he broke away from the other men and ran towards her. She expected him to leap in front of her protectively as he had done before. Instead, the moment he saw the man, he went down on one knee.

"Down," he whispered. "Kneel down."

A few days earlier, she'd have refused. She had thought nobody deserved such veneration. Strange how the threat of death altered one's beliefs. She crouched slowly and put one knee to the dry dirt, keeping the man in view through her lashes.

"Is he on our side?" she asked under her breath.

"Sometimes."

The man spoke again in a voice that resonated with the rise and fall of civilizations.

Christian answered before interpreting for her. "He wants to know why we're fighting Anubis."

"Who is he?"

"Runihura, the destroyer of gods."

"Never heard of him." But with a name like that, she thought she should have.

"Think of him as a powerful, immortal policeman." Christian shuffled closer to her while the other Sons of Ra joined them on their knees. Tricia glanced around anxiously but there was no sign of Anubis.

She turned back to find Runihura's fathomless dark gaze on her. A warm wind stirred her hair and the scent of the desert swirled around her. He beckoned to her. At Christian's nod of encouragement, she rose cautiously and stepped forward. The aura of power surrounding the Egyptian prickled her skin.

"You are the source of this conflict," he proclaimed in his epic voice.

Great! Someone had burned down her home and tried to incinerate her; a giant dog that shouldn't even exist had attacked her and this misogynistic immortal wanted to blame *her*.

"It's not my fault if I have a gene that makes Anubis want to kill me."

Runihura flicked a hand at her in a gesture that clearly said *women should be seen and not heard*. "Who claims this woman?" he demanded.

Christian rose. Tricia's gaze jumped to the Duke of Buckland, tension gripping her throat. His eyes flicked up to her but he didn't rise as she'd expected, instead he remained on his knee, the only movement his shoulders rising and falling as he caught his breath. Had the duke relinquished his claim to her because he knew she loved Christian? Maybe he wasn't as bad as she'd thought.

Her sigh of relief whispered over her lips a moment too soon. The golden-skinned Son of Ra with the red fire stepped up on her other side, his dark brown eyes glinting with golden flame. "I would have this woman for my family."

Christian rounded on him. Suddenly the curved blade was back in his hand, spitting green sparks. "She belongs to me, Luca."

He didn't say, "I love her" or even "I need her". This was all about staking his claim on something valuable. Feelings didn't come into it. Certainly not her feelings.

"I don't want to be claimed by any of you," she snapped.

Runihura's gaze drilled into her, dragging every scrap of her attention to him. Against her will, she took a stumbling step towards him, followed by another.

Her insides quivered as eddies of hot air raced around her. The sound of Christian's shouts faded.

"Please . . ." *Don't hurt me.* Words circled in her head but her mouth wouldn't obey.

A ball of pure white fire flared in Runihura's cupped palm. She tried to raise her arm to protect her face, but her muscles didn't respond. He lifted his hand and dropped the fiery sphere on to the top of her head. Her pulse raced as a shroud of glittering white sparks cascaded over her and penetrated her skin.

Her rush of panic faded as the fire whispered through her with a silky caress. She swayed and her breath hissed out on a little moan of pleasure. On the edge of perception, she heard Christian's angry shout and a scuffle. She didn't remember closing her eyes, but when she opened them, the Duke of Buckland and a golden-haired Son of Ra were holding Christian down on his knees as he scowled up at Runihura.

The immortal stared at her for a moment, flickers of white fire dancing across his golden skin. "You are protected," he said. Then he stepped back and disappeared. No blast of cold or rips in the air, just there one moment, gone the next.

A string of French curses rent the air as the two men released Christian.

"I warned you that another would claim her," the duke said.

"This is your fault," Christian pointed at Luca, the man who'd challenged him for her. But if he wanted a fight, he was out of luck. Luca shrugged, then stepped back into the ether and disappeared.

The other Sons of Ra departed, including the duke, leaving her and Christian alone. The sudden silence and peace seemed unnatural after the terror and noise of battle.

Christian's strange garb shimmered. She blinked and he was clothed in a pair of tan trousers and a blue shirt. He walked away from her and dropped down on the bench where she'd been waiting for him before Anubis attacked.

His gaze ran over her incredulously. "He renewed you so fast." He snapped his fingers. "Twenty years gone in a second."

"What?" Tricia touched her face. The skin felt smoother. The twinge in her knee had vanished. "My god, are you saying he's knocked twenty years off me?"

"I would have done this for you, *mon amour*. If only you'd let me."

Her pleasure at her newfound youthfulness faded at the look of desolation on his face. If she hadn't rejected him last night, he'd have already claimed her. There would have been no need for Runihura to bathe her in his fire. Part of her regretted hurting Christian, but another part was relieved that she wasn't his property. Twenty-two years ago, the blind devotion of teenaged love would have made her give up everything to be with him, but she'd have felt trapped in such a relationship.

"I still want to be with you, only now it's my choice. Isn't that better?"

"You don't understand, Tricia. You belong to Runihura. I can never touch you again."

"You don't seriously believe *he* wants *me*?" She snorted at the idea. "He was simply protecting me so I didn't cause him any more trouble." And giving her the freedom to choose her own man. Maybe Runihura wasn't such a misogynist after all.

She sat beside Christian on the bench and reached for his hand. He snatched his arm clear and jumped up. "Don't! The pain is excruciating."

The blood drained out of her head as understanding dawned. "It'll hurt for us to touch?"

"Of course. Didn't you listen to me?"

"No, you . . ." Her words trailed away when she remembered what he'd told her the previous night. *You'll be marked as mine, untouchable by any others of my kind.* She hadn't understood he'd meant it literally.

"Have you ever tried to touch a woman claimed by another Son of Ra?"

His angry gaze snapped to her face. "That is forbidden."

"Then how do you know it's true?"

His breath rushed out in irritation. "Luca touched my countess when he tried to save her life. They both suffered for his noble act."

His countess? "What happened to her?"

"She lost her head to Madame Guillotine." Christian pivoted away from her and paced to the river. That must have been the woman he'd mentioned the previous night. Tricia pressed her temples, feeling rotten. Had Runihura bathed her in fire as punishment for defying their customs, knowing it would prevent her from touching Christian again? She hadn't sensed anger in the Egyptian.

"Runihura isn't a Son of Ra, is he?" she asked, thinking aloud.

For long moments, Christian didn't answer. Then he swung around with a frown. "No. He's one of the old ones."

"Perhaps his fire's different. He summoned it as a ball in his hand rather than from the end of a sceptre."

Christian shook his head but the tension on his face had faded and a spark of hope lit his eyes. He came to stand before her and held out a finger. "One fingertip only."

She swallowed, spooked by the talk of excruciating pain. Her finger hovered in the air a fraction from his. He closed the distance. As their skin touched, a sound like distant wind whistled in her ears. A rushing sensation flowed through her body. White fire burst from her fingertip and engulfed Christian's arm.

She squeaked with surprise and yanked her hand back.

"Tricia, are you all right, *mon amour*?" Christian dropped to a crouch before her, his face a mask of concern.

"It didn't hurt," she assured him, embarrassed that she'd made such a fuss.

"When you cried out, I thought you were in pain." Christian levered himself on to the bench beside her. Before she had time to think, he pulled her into his embrace; his lips pressed against hers. The rushing feeling gradually eased until it was no more than a gentle tickle across her senses. Christian pulled back, blinking in astonishment. Flickers of white fire danced all over him. "I've never seen the like. Runihura did more than protect you; he's given you fire that eclipses mine."

Tricia stared at him, totally nonplussed. "Why?"

Christian shrugged. "He moves in mysterious ways. What matters is that I can touch you; we can be together."

He pulled her on to his lap and nuzzled her neck. Tricia giggled at the sudden release of tension. She held out her hand to see if she could summon fire. Instead, a curved dagger with a mother-of-pearl handle appeared on her palm, white fire skating along the blade. She dropped the knife in shock and it disappeared again. "Good gracious, what does Runihura expect me to do with that?"

Christian rubbed his thumb over her lips and flickers of sparkling white fire danced between them, tingling against her skin.

"We have the rest of our lives to find out, *mon amour*."

Eve of Warfare

A Marked Story

S.J. Day

"By warfare and exile you contend with her."
— Isaiah 27:8

One

"You want me to babysit *cupid*?" Evangeline Hollis' fingertips drummed against the wooden arms of her chair. "You can't be serious."

"That is not what I said, Miss Hollis."

Raguel Gadara's reply was laced with the compelling resonance unique to archangels. He sat behind his intricately carved mahogany desk in his expansive office with a leisurely sprawl that didn't fool Eve for a minute. Gadara was watching her like a hawk from beneath slumberous lowered eyelids.

From her seat in one of two brown leather chairs that faced him, Eve raised both brows in a silent prompt for him to explain. The eternal fire crackling in the fireplace to her left and the portrait of the Last Supper decorating the space above the mantel were tangible reminders that her formerly agnostic view of the world was shattered forever.

Her secular world was behind her, displayed to breathtaking effect by the wall of windows overlooking Harbor Boulevard. Gadara Tower sat a few blocks south of Disneyland and

California Adventure, just outside the city zoning that ensured no skyrises were visible from inside the amusement parks.

"I said 'cherub'," the archangel reiterated. As he leaned back in his chair, the diamond stud in his right ear caught the light. "We received a report of suspicious activity in San Diego. Zaphiel has been sent to address it and requires an escort."

Eve's guard went up. Raguel's job on earth was to manage the infestation of Infernals in North America. Why would a cherub intercede? And why wasn't Raguel more upset about that? All the archangels were intensely ambitious. It didn't make sense for him to concede any power to anyone, even an angel of considerably higher rank. "I get that pairing him with me instead of giving him a full contingent of your personal guards sends a message that you're annoyed, but as far as impact goes, it's more of a 'meow' than a 'roar'."

"I send no message," Raguel denied, attempting to look innocent, which was impossible.

"Right." Diplomacy and showmanship were utilized just as often in the celestial underground as they were in the secular world. The cherubim topped the angelic hierarchy. Even the seraphim ceded rank to them. Exposing such a high-level celestial to her bad demon karma was stupid enough to have a really clever motive behind it.

"I asked for you."

The rumbling masculine voice was dangerously soft. Eve turned her head, knowing a small, childlike figure just didn't fit that mature voice but she was still unable to shake the image of a chubby baby with tiny wings and a big diaper.

Catching sight of Zaphiel, she blinked. *Holy shit.*

He was massive. Ripped with muscle and terribly beautiful, with eyes of the same blue hue found at the heart of a flame, and golden hair that hung past his shoulders. Fan-fuckin-tastic. There was only one reason angels and demons went out of their way to get to her: they wanted to irritate the two men in her seriously screwed-up romantic life – Cain and Abel. They went by the names Alec Cain and Reed Abel in present day, but they were the infamous brothers of biblical legend nevertheless.

She glanced at Gadara. "This *really* isn't a good idea."

The archangel smiled. That flash of pearly white teeth within the framework of coffee-dark skin told her he had an ulterior motive for agreeing.

"I have every faith in you," he said, practically purring.

Oh boy. Not too long ago (back in her old life) working for Gadara Enterprises had been a career dream of hers. Raguel Gadara was a real estate mogul rivalling Donald Trump and Steve Wynn, with property developments all over North America just begging for an interior designer of Eve's calibre. In reality, however, the dream turned into a nightmare. Her years of interior design education and experience had been relegated to the sidelines of her "real" job: demon bounty hunting.

"Time to go, Evangeline," Zaphiel said, jerking his head imperiously toward the private elevator that would take them down to the lobby level. The deliberate use of her name cemented the suspicion that she was – yet again – being used as a pawn in a bigger game.

It was a game she didn't play well; something the cherub would be figuring out soon.

Eve stood. In her former life, she'd be sporting Jimmy Choo stilettos and a svelte pencil skirt. As a Mark – one of thousands of sinners cursed with the Mark of Cain – she was wearing Doc Martens and worn jeans. The thick, straight black hair she'd inherited from her Japanese mother was pulled back in a simple ponytail. Dressing for the job was 24/7; Marks never knew when they'd be called out to vanquish a rogue demon.

She walked to the cherub, expecting him to shift/teleport them to wherever it was he wanted to go, but he just smiled smugly.

"You will drive me," he pronounced.

"O-kay . . ." Moving on to the elevator, she pressed the call button.

Within minutes, they were buckling into her red Chrysler 300. When she glanced at him for directions, he told her to drive toward Anaheim Hills. As he spoke, a pair of sunglasses appeared on his face, reminding her that he was yanking her chain by making her drive to their destination.

She pulled out of the shadows of the subterranean parking lot and into the bright Southern California sunshine. Grabbing her Oakley sunglasses from the centre console, she put them on.

"Why are you not with Cain?" he asked.

"He's busy and I'm babysitting you."

His lips pursed at the dig. "I am not speaking of the present moment. You are in love with him, yet you are not involved with him romantically."

She made no effort to deny her feelings. It would have been pointless, considering how pivotal her prior relationship with Alec was to the existing state of the Marked system. "It's too complicated, *and* none of your business."

Cain was the original and most bad-assed Mark of them all. He functioned outside the Marked system hierarchy as an autonomous hunter taking orders directly from the Almighty. He was a revered and polarizing figure for other Marks, a lofty and undefeated ideal that each of the archangels longed to exploit for their own advancement. Eve's attachment to Gadara's firm came with Cain as a bonus. Cain gave the archangel a massive advantage over his fellow firm leaders.

"I could further your cause," the cherub said. "Cain's advancement to archangel was only supposed to be temporary."

Her grip on the steering wheel whitened her knuckles. "Don't you dare take that promotion away from him and blame it on me! Alec is right where he wants to be."

"Without you? The archangels are barred from feeling romantic love."

"I'm sure there's a reason for that." Her voice was tight and she made a concerted effort to relax. Zaphiel was rubbing salt in her wounds, knowing damn well that she'd broken things off with Alec because he was no longer capable of loving her the way he used to. He admired her, lusted after her and was determined to remain faithful to her, but her unreciprocated love was a huge liability to them both. "Killing demons has a high mortality rate, if you hadn't noticed."

"That is not why you resist the attraction. Perhaps Abel's affections are enough to console you?"

She stomped on the brakes. The car behind them lay on the horn and swerved around her with tyres squealing.

Don't let him get to you, Reed Abel warned, his thoughts crossing over the connection that existed between Marks and the *mal'akhs* – common angels – who meted out their Infernal-hunting assignments. Like the American judicial system, there were bondsmen (the archangels), dispatchers (*mal'akhs*), and bounty hunters (Marks like her). It was a well-oiled system for the most part. It was her rotten luck that her romantic entanglements with Cain and Abel made her the squeaky wheel.

Easier said than done, she shot back.

Zaphiel is always a prick. Despite the subject matter, Reed's velvety smooth voice was a delight to hear.

Her not-quite-a-relationship with Alec Cain's brother was one of the many complexities in her life. Alec had ridden into her life on a Harley when she was almost eighteen and by the time he left, he'd taken her virginity and her heart. She was still comparing other men to him ten years later when Reed Abel entered her life and branded her with the Mark of Cain. That had been the start of a triangular relationship she'd once thought would be impossible for her. How could she feel so strongly for Reed when she was absolutely certain that Alec Cain was the love of her life?

"I would prefer that you not injure yourself unnecessarily," Zaphiel said calmly.

Twisting in her seat to face him, she asked with equal calm, "What's your problem?"

"I have no problem."

"I'm a single unit. Got it? Not that you need to know, but asking about Cain and Abel is pointless. They've got their personal lives, and I have—"

"—none," he finished.

"Drop it. Now." Alec was her mentor, her friend and one of only a handful of people in her Marked life whom she trusted to have her best interests at heart. He was an integral, daily part of her life; they shared the same sort of mental connection she had with Reed. Through that bond, she felt the wall inside him that blocked his love from her. It was the worst sort of torture to be linked to him, yet farther apart than they'd ever been.

Smiling, Zaphiel looked forwards. "I will say no more."

With an imperious wave of his hand, he directed for her to continue. Eve fumed for the next quarter of an hour until they began to climb the side of a steep hill. Then her attention was caught by the size and elegance of the mansions they passed on their ascent to the top. The space between homes grew wider until they stopped seeing any houses at all. The last mile was marked only by the road.

Eventually, they reached a gate that blocked further public access. A guardhouse stood on the right from which a burly male in an athletic suit stepped out. Zaphiel lowered the window and his sunglasses disappeared, revealing his face. Wary recognition shadowed the guard's features before he stepped back and hit the remote that opened the two heavy wrought-iron gates.

The drive up to the main house from that point was at least a half-mile. Security cameras were prominently positioned along the way in gaps of approximately twenty feet. When the manse itself came into view, Eve was so taken by the simplistic beauty of its organic architecture that her foot lifted from the gas pedal and the car decelerated to a gentle rolling stop behind a silver Bentley. The residence scaled the side of the hill in three tiers that boasted wide wrap-around balconies. Distressed wood siding, rock terraces and exposed wooden beams enabled the house to blend into its surroundings.

Zaphiel exited the car. Eve turned the engine off and jumped out, catching his questioning gaze over the roof.

"I'm going in with you," she said preemptively. Her interior design sensibilities were sharply engaged by the cohesiveness between the building and its surroundings. She was eager to examine the interior but, more than that, he'd dragged her all the way out here. Maybe having her play chauffeur, followed by irritating her in the car had been the reasons for that – she wouldn't put the desire for petty amusements past any angel – but she damn sure wasn't going to leave empty-handed when faced with such an architectural marvel.

"As you wish." Zaphiel followed her gaze to the two guards flanking the double front doors. Rounding the front of the car, she drew abreast of him and they approached the entrance in tandem.

The door opened before they reached it, revealing a man who stopped Eve in her tracks. Dark hair, caramel skin and the flame-blue eyes of an upper echelon angel combined to create one hell of a gorgeous male. He stood in his bare-feet, his long legs sheathed in loose-fitting faded jeans, his torso clad in an un-tucked white button-down shirt with rolled-up sleeves and an open collar. The casual elegance of his attire only emphasized his unrestrained sexuality. It also said he felt no threat from his visitors, despite the tangible tension now radiating from Zaphiel's powerful frame.

Eve's head tilted to the side as her curiosity grew.

Zaphiel spoke first, with a notably harsh edge to his voice. "Adrian."

"Your interference is unnecessary."

"Since you just lost your lieutenant, I beg to disagree."

Adrian stiffened. A haunted look ravaged his handsome features, passing so swiftly Eve wondered if she'd imagined it.

She re-evaluated Adrian, looking deeper beneath the elegant exterior. As with Alec, there was a dangerous edge to the man, a sharpness in the way he regarded people that betrayed him as a hunter. But in another respect, he wasn't like Alec at all. Alec struck like a viper – in and gone before anyone knew it, leaving little evidence behind. Adrian had a far different air about him . . . a weighted expectancy like the calm before a storm. She suspected there was an aftermath when he unleashed violence, a razing of the landscape that left no doubt he'd been there.

With a theatrical and mocking sweep of his arm, Adrian invited them into his home. Zaphiel brushed past as if he owned the place. Eve paused in front of her host. Her stance was relaxed with her shoulders rolled back. Bravado went a long way in throwing Infernals and Celestials off their game.

Removing her sunglasses, she thrust out her hand and introduced herself.

Adrian's mouth lifted on one side before he accepted the greeting. The half-smile didn't quite reach his eyes and his grip was stronger than required. "Adrian Mitchell."

She felt a power surge from his palm to hers. Considering his reluctant deference to Zaphiel's arrogance, she guessed he was a seraph. She wondered why one of the seraphim was living among mortals. They were the angels responsible for sending kill orders to the archangels; it was through the seraphim that the firms knew which demons to hunt. The job didn't require being stationed on earth. In fact, the seraphim so rarely visited the firms that an appearance by one of them usually heralded a storm of trouble.

Adrian's expression softened. "Losing someone while they're still with you is painful, I know."

It took her a moment to realize he'd intruded into her mind and read her. She yanked her hand back. "I hate it when you guys do that."

"I'm sure." Genuine amusement crossed his face, softening him. It elevated him to a whole new level of hotness. Even Eve, as madly in love as she was, could appreciate it.

Preceding him deeper into the house, she saw that the expansive foyer descended into a living room via three wide but shallow steps. The massive space spreading out from that point was furnished with oversized burgundy leather sofas and roughly hewn wooden accent pieces. The river rock-faced fireplace was large enough to hold a Mini Cooper, but it couldn't compete with the wall of windows and its stunning vista.

When Adrian moved to sit, Zaphiel said, "I have no intention of staying long. If I am to see to your failures, I must begin immediately."

Eve stopped moving, hoping to become a fly on the wall. Knowledge was power and direct knowledge from the upper echelon angels was nearly impossible for Marks to come by.

Adrian's arms crossed. "Begin what?"

"Hunting the vamp who killed your second-in-command."

Her brows rose. Vampyres were one of the many classifications of Infernals that Marks dealt with. Gadara and the firm should be handling any problems in that area. Having a cherub and seraph digging into the situation set her teeth on edge. The more fingers in the pie, the bigger the clusterfuck.

"I've got a handle on it," Adrian said coldly.

"You do not." Zaphiel examined his fingernails. "And it pleases me not at all to know that lives have been lost due to your negligence."

"You think I'm happy about it?"

"I do not care how you feel. I am here to tell you to stay out of my way. The rest is no longer your concern."

Adrian laughed without humour. "Whose concern is it, if not mine?"

Zaphiel lifted his hand and pointed at Eve. "Hers."

Two

After returning Zaphiel to Gadara Tower, Eve headed home with plans for a hot shower and an evening alone. A feel-good movie while curled up on the couch sounded like heaven to her. She usually preferred blow-'em-up action flicks but she'd had enough real-life explosions to last her for a good long while. Maybe *Becoming Jane* would do the trick or something stupidly funny like *Blades of Glory*.

She stood for a long time beneath the pummelling spray of the shower, telling herself that she had no business wondering why Alec wasn't at home in his apartment next to hers. She'd given up the right to know what he did at night and she shouldn't second-guess that decision, especially after today. No one should end up stuck in the middle of a feud between a cherub and a seraph. She wouldn't wish it on her worst enemy.

After drying off, she tossed her towel over the laundry basket and belted on a thick white terry cloth robe. Then she went on the hunt for comfort food. It was a boon of the Mark that her body ignored any attempt on her part to screw it up, including wanton snacking; otherwise her breakup with Alec would surely have given her a fat ass by now.

She was turning into the kitchen when the stereo in her living room inexplicably came on. Stevie Nicks' beautiful "Crystal" replaced the silence, freezing Eve mid-step.

On her deltoid, the brand of the Mark of Cain – a one-inch in diameter triquetra surrounded by a circlet of three serpents, each one eating the tail of the snake before it – tingled and flooded her bloodstream with adrenaline. Her senses sharpened so quickly it was nearly a rush, the world around her bursting into a vibrancy she'd never experienced as a mere mortal. The Mark made her faster, stronger and quicker to heal. It also enabled her to identify the man in her living room from where she stood – sight unseen.

Eve started forwards again with a shiver of anticipation, continuing to where the hall emptied into the living room. The sheer curtains that framed her sliding glass doors billowed from the ocean breeze. Beyond her balcony lay the sands of Huntington Beach, a coastal community that was home to hundreds of demons. That number was just a fraction of the worldwide population of Infernals living undetected among mortals. Such was the life she lived now, having her groceries bagged by incubi and her Big Mac served by faeries.

The clink of shifting ice against metal drew her eye to the silver champagne bucket on the coffee table and the napkin-wrapped bottle it held. Two half-full flutes waited nearby.

The man at her entertainment centre turned to face her. She was struck again by how gorgeous he was. So like his brother in physical traits – smooth olive skin, black as night hair, and espresso brown eyes – but completely different in every other way. His resemblance to Alec had first drawn her to him but Reed Abel continued to hold her attention all on his own. She was halfway in love with him, which confused her and caused all sorts of trouble.

"Hi," he said. Although he appeared casual and relaxed, his dark gaze was avid.

"Hi, yourself."

"I hope you don't mind that I popped in." His choice of words was apt, considering his angelic gifts enabled him to shift from one location to any other in the world in the blink of an eye.

"You're always welcome. Nothing is going to change that."

He caught up the flutes as he came towards her and a cool stem was pressed into her hand. She looked down, catching sight of something circular glittering at the bottom. Her breath caught.

"I'm glad to hear that," he murmured. His warm fingers wrapped around hers. "Because I have a question to ask you . . ."

"Reed." A stunningly large diamond graced an engagement ring covered in tiny champagne bubbles. It was the kind of ring women turned pea green over; it shouted the wealth of the man who'd given it and the value he placed on the woman wearing it. The ostentatious piece was totally Reed, a man known as much for his Lamborghinis and Ferraris as he was for the calibre of his work.

The ferocity of her response was enough to rock her backward a few steps. The last few months of confusion coalesced into one shining moment of perfect clarity. She felt a similar jolt of reality startling him before rippling across the connection between them.

He spoke too quickly. "Zaphiel is here to investigate the recent death of a seraph. He wants you to assume a cover and move into one of Raguel's resort communities as a resident."

"O-kay . . . How is that supposed to work? The Infernals will smell me coming." Infernals reeked of rotting souls; Marks smelled sickly sweet. Alec said it was similar to deer smelling the wolves coming – it was "fair". Eve called it a "what-the-fuck". She couldn't understand why God would draft an unwilling army of sinners to fight his battles against demons, only to announce their arrival by making them stick out in a crowd.

"We're not dealing with Infernals," Reed said. "But we'll get to that in a minute. Raguel wants you undercover as part of a team, not solo, which means you'll need a husband. Hence the ring."

Relief flooded her. "Oh, gotcha. Geez, you scared me for a minute. The whole champagne and music—"

"When Raguel explained the assignment to me, I realized the idea of marrying you had some merit." He shifted on his feet and shoved his hands into the pockets of his Versace slacks. "So, why propose twice when I can do it right the first time?"

Eve gaped. "We're not even dating at this point!"

"Because you're hung up on Alec," he shot back.

"And you're a commitment-phobe."

"Bullshit." Reed glared down at her. "You know I want more than you're giving me. *You're* the one holding back."

"The moment I saw the ring in the glass, I felt you freak out. I did, too." She'd also wanted, with every fibre of her being, to love him the way he deserved to be loved, but that wasn't something she could control.

"Because it was *me* offering the ring," he accused. "Alec's a dead-end. You know that."

Eve wished she was wearing something more substantial than a robe while having this conversation. "Everything about being a Mark is a dead-end, Reed. I don't see the point of trying to have a relationship when everyone is pursuing conflicting goals. You and Alec want to advance; I want to find a way back to my old life. There's no way to make it work."

He rocked back on heels. His jaw set at a stubborn angle. "I want you. That works."

Her mouth curved with wry affection. "Sexual attraction has never been our problem. You won't hear me saying there's anything wrong with really great sex with someone you admire and like spending time with."

"But . . . ?"

"But that's not enough for me to commit to the life of a Mark, and that's exactly what I'd be doing by committing to someone inside the system."

"It could be hundreds of years before you earn off the Mark," he said coldly, knowing she refused to accept that possibility. "No way are you going to be celibate that whole time and you're not the casual sex type."

"So marriage is your solution to getting into my pants?"

Reed shrugged. "Yours are the only pants I want to get into."

She set her flute down on her glass-topped coffee table. "Putting the whole demon-hunting lifestyle aside, we've got other issues. I've never been to your house. I don't even know if you live in Orange County, or if you shift to some other continent for a change of clothes. We've never gone anywhere together that wasn't work related; you come to my place and that's it. You join my life when it suits you and you disappear when it doesn't. What we had was a working relationship with benefits."

"Whatever, babe," he scoffed, running a hand through his precisely cut hair. "You wouldn't let it be more than that. Playing house is just what we need."

Noting the sullen set of his mouth, Eve knew it was time to change the subject or argue pointlessly for hours. She took a seat on one of her cream-coloured down-filled sofas. "About playing house . . . Explain what's going on to me. Since when are vampyres not Infernals any more?"

There was no outward show of it, but she felt the relief that moved through him. "Vampyres with a 'Y' are demons, yes. Vampires with an 'I' aren't. You weren't trained about the second kind, because Marks aren't supposed to deal with them. You'll be the first."

All Marks went through a comprehensive training program, something like a boot camp for recruits. Every classification of demon was discussed in depth, with a focus on how best to kill them.

"Of course," she said dryly, not at all surprised that she was getting stuck with another *crap-tas-tic* assignment. Jerking her around was Entertainment #1 for angels of all ranks. "If vampires-with-an-I aren't demons, what are they?"

Reed adjusted his slacks and sat beside her. "You've been taking a crash course in the Bible since you were Marked. Remember reading about the Watcher angels?"

"Two hundred angels were sent to observe human behaviour but they started fraternizing and doing other naughty things, including breeding children called Nephalim, etcetera."

"That's the ones. Once Jehovah saw what was going on, he sent an elite team of seraphim warriors – the Sentinels – down to punish the fallen Watchers. The Watchers lost their wings and became known as the Fallen. Wings and souls are connected, so without one they lost the other. Following?"

"Soulless, wingless fallen angels. Got it."

He nodded. "Seraphim rely on their souls to survive. They don't eat or drink the way mortals do. They absorb energy from the life-forces on earth."

"So they starved to death?"

"I wish. No, they discovered they could feed from life in a more direct manner—"

"They started drinking blood," she finished. "Okay. So there are two kinds of vamps – those who are demons and those who were angels? That's why Adrian lives on earth? To hunt and kill the Fallen angels?"

"Jehovah has never ordered the death of an angel. Sammael wouldn't be alive otherwise."

"True . . ." Satan was thriving. And she often wondered why, but that was a question no one seemed to have an answer for.

"The Sentinels are supposed to contain the Fallen to areas where they can't get into too much trouble."

"And Southern California is trouble galore. How many Sentinels are there?"

"Not enough."

"Why send in just two of us undercover then? Wouldn't more Marks be merrier?"

"I would think so, but this isn't my call. Marks can't sniff out the Fallen."

"No souls translates into no smell?"

"You got it. We can't afford to have too many Marks tied up indefinitely, plus the cost of housing, a decent cover story, and so on. Our resources aren't limitless."

"So we're hunting someone who blends perfectly into the surroundings with nothing to give them away." She made a frustrated noise. "What's our cover?"

"We're Mr and Mrs Kline. We're renting the resort space because I have to be in town on business and you're a trophy wife."

She shot him an arch glance. "You're a bit high profile for undercover work, aren't you?"

"I'm a travelling businessman, babe. Aside from a car in the driveway at night, I won't be seen."

Basically, he wasn't assuming a cover at all then. As long as she'd known him, he was always popping in and out. He came when she called, but otherwise, seeing him was a random thing.

Using his *mal'akh* gifts, Reed shifted the ring from the bottom of her glass into his hand, then slid it on to her finger. "This could be real, Eve. Think about it."

He left without warning, disappearing before her eyes.

Eve collapsed into the sofa back with a groan.

Alec exhaled harshly and sank to the floor with his legs stretched out before him. He leaned into the shared wall between his condo and Eve's, and closed his eyes.

Reed's half-assed proposal had been too close for comfort.

When Eve had come knocking on Alec's door earlier in the evening, he'd known about it even though he was far from home. She could have spoken to him through the connection between them, but she'd wanted to see him face-to-face. Ignoring that need had damn-near killed him, but he'd been deep into a negotiation he couldn't interrupt. He'd bargained with the only thing he had of value – his willingness to do the dirty jobs no one wanted to be associated with – so he could have what he wanted most.

His hand rubbed at the numbness in the centre of his chest. Every day it became more difficult to remember how loving Eve felt. She'd been the only joy and comfort in his life and she still was, but he was hollow without the ability to love her back. Lust and admiration were there, but being "just friends" with her was killing him. It was killing her, too. She was closing herself off from everyone in the Marked system, avoiding building connections in the hope that she would find the leverage to shed the Mark. He'd once intended to help her, but now . . .

"Now, you can't walk away," he whispered. She couldn't turn her back on unsuspecting mortals being preyed upon by demons and she'd never be able to send her children to school with Infernals she couldn't smell or identify. Reluctant as she was – and he didn't blame her for that – she was too big-hearted to leave any underdog unprotected. No, she'd seen the darkness behind the veil and she could never un-see it.

Alec pushed to his feet. *Be careful what you wish for* . . . He'd wanted to advance to archangel and helm his own firm, but he hadn't considered what that goal would cost him.

His humanity was slipping from him every minute and if he didn't get Eve back, he was afraid of what he would become without her.

Three

Eve stood on the patio of her new resort condominium and watched two undercover Marks offload boxes of household goods that didn't belong to her. Gadara had provided the furnishings from one of Arcadia Falls' model homes for her use while undercover. The pieces were tropical in style – lots of wicker and floral patterns – which wouldn't have been her choice but weren't offensive either.

The condo was the middle unit of three adjacent properties. It was two-storeyed and sported the same red tile roof as all the other homes in the housing community. There were four available floor plans and a strict set of CC&Rs that ensured a uniform look over the entire property. The decorative lawns were all beautifully landscaped and maintained, and the streetlights resembled bamboo, which she thought was an interesting touch.

Grabbing a duffle bag out of the back of a Gadara Enterprises-owned Jeep Wrangler Limited, Eve wondered how the hell she was supposed to find a vampire who didn't smell and wasn't affected by sunlight. He or she could be anyone living in any of the 100 condos around her. She didn't even know if she was looking for one vamp or a coven. She didn't know how long she was expected to stay in Arcadia Falls or what she was supposed to do when she identified her quarry. And Reed wasn't talking. He'd been notably silent in her mind all day. It wasn't a great start to their front as a happily married couple.

"Hello!"

Eve straightened from the back of the Jeep and caught sight of a petite blond approaching from the sidewalk. "Hi."

"Welcome to Arcadia!" The woman extended a hand tipped with french-manicured acrylic nails. Dressed in khaki cargo pants and a white tank top, she showed off a great tan along with her youthful fashion sense. "I'm Terri Anderson, president of the homeowner's association and your next door neighbour."

"Hi, Terri." Eve returned the handshake. "Eve Kline."

"Angel?"

Evangeline. Eve. Angel. It was a pet name only Alec ever used.

She turned to find him. He came from the direction of the house, his long legs eating up the distance between them with his familiar sultry stride.

"Hi," he said, in the deep voice that could turn a reading of *A Brief History of Time* into an erotic experience. "Alec Kline."

He gifted Terri with one of his easy, sexy smiles and she flushed as she introduced herself in return. It was a reaction Eve recalled all too well, even though the Mark now negated her physical reactions to most stimuli.

Alec Cain was prime grade eye candy. Deliciously defined biceps were showcased in a semi-fitted white tank, and long, muscular legs made his knee-length Dickies shorts look really damned good. His glossy black hair was slightly overlong, giving him a bad boy look that drew women like bees to honey.

What are you doing here? she asked.

You have to ask? You're mine, angel. He winked, radiating confidence and predatory anticipation. The thrill of the hunt was in his blood, and his favourite prey lately was her.

She was in so much trouble.

Terri rocked back on her heels. "I'm having a barbeque tonight with some of our neighbours. We'd love to have you join us."

How lucky are we? Alec asked.

We're not. This isn't going to work, she argued. *You're the poster boy for the Celestial team. Everyone knows who you are!*

"Do you have children?" Terri asked.

Alec replied. "Not yet."

Eve winced. One of the driving forces behind her desire to get her old life back was because she wanted a family. A husband, two and a half kids, a dog and a white picket fence. Considering the Mark's side-effect of sterility, she had no chance of having children unless she found a way out of the Marked system.

"We don't have any either, so we'll have drinks, too." Terri rubbed her hands together. "Six o'clock work for you?"

Alec nodded and tossed his arm over Eve's shoulder. "Sounds perfect."

Pretending to be married to him was going to be excruciating. Playing house with Reed didn't have near the amount of baggage. All these years later, Alec's affect on her was the same – she saw him and something inside her said "mine". Something that couldn't let go, even though it was best for both of them.

Terri pointed across their lawn. "There's your other neighbour now."

Eve turned her head as a late-model Camaro pulled into the driveway next door. A tall brunette male unfolded from the low front seat, then waved.

He reached them and extended his hand to Eve first. "Tim Cotler. Great to meet you."

Alec growled. *I can't believe he looked at you like that when I'm standing right here.*

It was nothing.

The two men introduced themselves, with Alec making a point of staking his claim.

He was so possessive, which was an impossible situation when she was so crazy about him. Her unrequited love left her too vulnerable, too hopeful. Not to mention all the trouble it caused Alec, who felt guilty and responsible for her, forcing him to concede, bargain and negotiate away his talents in order to protect her.

Terri waved over another set of neighbours and made the introductions. "These are the Mullanys – Pam and her daughter

Jesse. They live in the next building over. You'll want to know where that is, because Pam is our resident Avon cosmetics lady. And the guy helping your movers unload is Gary Reynolds. He lives on the other side of Pam."

Alec went to say hi to Gary, while Eve extended her hand to Pam.

It didn't escape Eve's notice that everyone was exceptionally attractive. Gary was blond, tanned and notably strong and agile, as evidenced by his quick save of a heavy box tumbling from the back of the moving truck. Pam Mullany was a lovely redhead with brilliant emerald eyes and gorgeous skin. Eve couldn't see a freckle on her, which was rare for natural redheads. Jesse Mullany was a girl of about sixteen, with dyed black hair and visible red roots. She had a pierced nose and red-stained lips, and when she returned Eve's smile she displayed a perfect pair of pearly white fangs.

"Love the fangs," Alec said, returning with a grin sure to disarm any female.

Pam toyed with one of her short red curls and sighed behind her daughter's back. "Her dad bought her veneers on her birthday. Scared me to death when she came home."

"Leave it alone," Jesse said sharply, her smile fading. She looked at Tim and rolled her eyes.

"He could have asked," Pam argued.

"How? You're not talking to him. Besides, he doesn't need your permission."

Ah, the joys of teenagers, Alec murmured.

One of the Marks shouted for Eve's attention. Alec went to deal with him, but Eve decided to go too use the excuse while it was available. She wanted to know just what, exactly, Alec thought he was going to accomplish here. Besides blowing her cover and driving her crazy . . .

"I'm sorry," she said. "I've got to give these guys some direction so they can get out of here. What should I bring tonight?"

Terri shook her head. "Just yourselves. You've got enough to worry about just moving in."

Tim backed away. "I've got some stuff to take care of before I can call it a day. I'll catch up with you all over dinner."

Eve waved goodbye and made her way over to Alec, who was

signing a paper on the Mark's clipboard. Their cover had been so carefully crafted – new car, boxes of stuff that didn't belong to them, rental papers on the breakfast bar . . . All that prep work seemed pointless now that Alec had stepped in.

As soon as the moving truck backed up and pulled away, they moved into the house.

They crossed the threshold of their open double front doors and she dug in. "Listen . . . unless the Fallen have been living under a rock on Mars, they're going to know who you are the moment they see you. You can't go undercover if everyone knows your real identity."

"That's a problem, I agree." With his hand at her lower back, he steered her towards the stairs.

"So . . . ?"

"So what? If you think I'd ever let Reed play house with you, you're nuts."

They reached the top landing. Sunlight flooded the hallway from the open doors of the three bedrooms on the floor. A decorative alcove was filled with a custom table and superior quality fake flowers in a blown glass vase. The only other decor-ation in the space was moving boxes.

Alec waved his hand in the direction of the master bedroom.

"I'm nuts?" she shot back, taking his cue and preceding him down the hallway. "Reed taking on the role was a stretch, but he wasn't planning on being seen by anyone. You, on the other hand, just shouted 'Cain's in the house' from the rooftops!"

A few boxes blocked the entrance into the room. He skirted her and pushed them aside with a powerful, yet graceful swipe of his booted foot. "I asked for the assignment and they gave it to me, so it must work for someone. And if it doesn't work for the vamp, I'm not going to complain about that. I don't want you doing shit work like this anyway. You're better than this."

"What's the point of these boxes? Why go through the trouble of getting the minutia of our cover story right, then use you as—" Eve lost her train of thought when she spotted the man lying atop the bed.

Alec made a low noise. "What are you doing here?"

"You *are* working for me," Zaphiel said, remaining in his reclined position with his head propped in one hand. He was such a large man that the California king-sized mattress seemed too small for him. "It is in my interests to ensure you both have the best chance for success."

"We know how to hunt."

Zaphiel straightened and swung his long legs over the side of the bed. "But you cannot hide without assistance."

Eve's brows went up. In the time it took for her to blink, the cherub had shifted to a position directly in front of them. He grabbed her arm and Alec's. A rush of sensation flooded her body, centring on the Mark that lay beneath his palm.

Alec cursed in a foreign language and shoved Zaphiel back into the bed. The cherub sprawled across the mattress on his back, chuckling.

Eve dropped to the floor on her knees, gasping and dizzy. She felt numb everywhere, as if she'd been shot up all over with Novocain. "Oh man . . ."

"Angel." Alec crouched beside her, setting one hand over hers on the floor. His fingers were shaking, which horrified her. Nothing fazed Cain of Infamy.

Lifting her head, she met his gaze. "W – what the hell was that?"

"I think . . . we're mortal."

Eve sat at the oblong wooden table in her new dining room and glared at the innocent-looking cherub sitting across from her. The rapacious gleam in his eyes set her teeth on edge. She noticed that his irises seemed less blue than before, like dull glass. Everything around her seemed muted, less vibrant and alive.

"This is a seriously stupid plan," she argued, accepting the glass of water Alec handed to her. "Are you trying to get us killed?"

"Of course not."

"How are we supposed to defend ourselves without our super senses?"

"Super senses?" He shot Alec a mocking look. "Your mentorship is unique."

Alec's voice came tight with strain. "Mortality wasn't part of our deal."

"Deal?" Eve glanced over her shoulder at him. His answering look was hotter than she'd seen it in a long time and it took her breath away. "What deal?"

"Cain wants a demotion," Zaphiel explained.

Alec silenced anything she might have said with a firm grip on her shoulder. "We can talk about that later," he murmured.

She sat stunned, knowing he wanted a demotion because of her. Because he couldn't love her while he was an archangel.

Zaphiel's smile was smug. "When I explained the situation, he agreed to step aside."

"He did?" She didn't know how to feel about that.

You don't know how you feel about anything, Reed snapped. *You need to get your head on straight about Cain. You have to choose, Eve.*

"I can still hear him," she said, looking back at the cherub.

Alec growled. "Yeah . . . me, too. What the fuck? You take away the benefits and still leave us with *him* in our heads?"

The three of them were connected in a singular way – Reed Abel to her and her to Alec. For other Marks, the mental connection to their mentors was severed when they connected to their *mal'akh* handlers. Alec's ascension to archangel had screwed that up for her, making her brain the brothers' closest connection since childhood.

Zaphiel shrugged. "Raguel insisted that he be able to reach you both. Aside from that caveat, I have provided the perfect opportunity for Eve to make the decision Abel demands of her. As a mortal, Cain no longer has the restrictions imposed on archangels. He loves you again."

"For now," she snapped, her fingertips flexing over the polished wood surface of the table. She noted that her freckles were back, as well as the scar on her knuckles that she'd gotten as a kid. The Mark took care of such blemishes, so the sight of the flaws was a visible acknowledgment of her lack of celestial enhancements. "How are we supposed to find a vamp in this condition?"

"You are not searching for anything. You are here to be found."

"What?"

"There is some concern that there is a growing demand for angel blood in the Fallen community."

"Oh my God." She waited for the chastizing sting of the Mark, which acted like a behavioural-modification dog collar. When the burn didn't come after taking the Lord's name in vain, she found some of the fog in her brain lifting. *She'd lost the Mark.* "You want bait for a trap. That's why you wanted to use Reed. Because he's a *mal'akh*. When Alec offered himself, you figured an archangel is better than an angel. Especially an archangel that's immediately recognizable."

"Something like that," the cherub agreed smoothly.

"So why the hell did you strip Alec of his powers?"

Zaphiel leaned back in the chair, making it creak. "Well, we cannot risk actually losing angel blood until we know what they want it for."

"And you say you don't want us dead."

"No one will suspect that Cain does not have what they want," he argued. "And the blatant nature of your presence here will make them overconfident."

"Why can't you leave this to Adrian?" she shot back. "This is his business, not ours. In case you hadn't noticed, I have enough trouble keeping up with the Marked system."

"It has been left to Adrian for centuries, but he refused to use a Sentinel as a lure, so it is left to me—" he smiled, "—and you. Sentinels prefer to use their dogs on the front line, but lycan blood is not what the Fallen want."

"Lycan?" Eve looked at Alec. "Werewolf?"

"Some of the Fallen made a bargain to serve the Sentinels to regain their souls and avoid vampirism," he explained. "They were turned into lycans and now they work like herding dogs to keep the other Fallen in line. What Zaphiel isn't saying is that the Sentinels haven't been reinforced since they arrived. They're forbidden to reproduce, so their numbers have shrunk with every casualty. The lycans can breed, but they're not immortal, so their numbers have grown very slowly. The Fallen, however, are immortal and they can spread vampirism to mortals so their numbers have exploded over time. Adrian can't afford to risk any of his Sentinels as bait. That's why he didn't agree to Zaphiel's plan."

"And lycans are what?" she asked. "Werewolves of the angelic variety?"

"Right."

Eve exhaled harshly. "You know . . . Whether you Celestials like to admit it or not, Heaven and Hell are just opposite sides of the same coin."

His mouth curved. "Where do you think Sammael got ideas for creating Infernals? He saw what Jehovah was cranking out and got inspired. His versions have a few defects: his vamps are sensitive to sunlight and blessed objects, and his weres are forced to change forms at certain times of the month. But unlike the Fallen, the Infernals have souls . . . even if they *are* rotting."

"Lucky them," she muttered, turning her attention back to Zaphiel, a being she doubted had a soul himself.

The cherub gestured to a dagger that had appeared on the table. "This silver-plated blade will kill the vamp, if the situation gets that far."

Eve just stared at him, incredulous. Alec's hand on her shoulder tightened in warning, as if he knew just how close she was to lunging across the table and strangling Zaphiel.

"We should continue this conversation later," Alec said tightly.

The cherub lifted one shoulder in an offhand shrug, then disappeared.

Four

Alec pulled out the chair beside Eve and sat.

"Are all angels sadists?" she muttered. She was flushed, bright-eyed and really pissed off.

And he was madly in love with her. Where he'd felt hollow the night before, he now felt too much. The surge of emotion made it damned hard to think clearly.

"You're being generous," he said gruffly.

She pivoted on her seat to face him head-on. He caught her face in his hands and sealed his mouth over hers. It took her the length of a heartbeat to catch on, but when she did, it was no holds barred. She tilted her head and licked deep, knowing just what he liked, responding to the cues he gave with passionate enthusiasm.

Groaning his approval, Alec pulled her closer, his mouth slanting feverishly over hers, his tongue stroking in the way he knew drove her crazy with lust.

They were made for each other. He believed that with absolute certainty.

Eve gripped his wrists and gave as good as she got. He was inflamed by the smell and feel of her, a completely new experience now that he had only his own mortal senses. As long as he'd known her, the Mark of Cain had been fogging things up with preternatural sensations.

"I love this," he growled, tugging her into his lap. "I love you."

The ache of longing in his chest made it hard to breathe. He'd been her first lover and he would damn well be her last.

His hands roamed, moving from her face to her breasts, cupping their weight and kneading until her back arched into his touch with a moan. He nipped her lower lip with his teeth, then soothed the sting with a soft stroke of his tongue, reminding her of what it felt like when his mouth was engaged in other, more private places. He loved to lick her all over, every silken inch, every curve and crevice. It was an activity he wanted to engage in right here. Right *now*.

"Alec—" Eve tore away and hugged him hard, trapping his greedy hands between them so they couldn't move.

"Don't stop," he said hoarsely, adjusting her so that she felt the press of his erection against her thigh.

"Aren't you worried about what Zaphiel is up to?" she gasped.

"I'm worried he's going to change his mind before I can fuck you. I need to feel you from the inside while we're like this." He looked at her from beneath heavy-lidded eyes. She was flushed and damp with perspiration, easily the most sensual-looking creature he'd ever seen. An exotically beautiful Asian goddess who couldn't be more perfect for him. "If we miss this chance, I'm not sure I'd survive it."

"I'm freaked that you're not going to survive, period!" She made a frustrated noise. "You're *mortal*, Alec. There are a gazillion Infernals dying to get a piece of you, and now you've got Fallen angels, too."

He rocked his hips, letting her know the brain running the show was still the one between his legs. "I want *you* dying to get a piece of me."

"Alec." She straightened and moved away, denying him the pleasure of feeling her up. "I need you alive."

Shoving a hand through his hair with a smothered curse, he pushed to his feet and walked into the adjacent kitchen. He went to the sink and splashed water on his face. "You don't want me dead, but you won't live with me either."

"Don't change the subject."

"It's the same subject." He shut off the faucet and leaned against the counter with his arms crossed. He let her see all the love and lust and longing that ate at him. "We're in love with each other, Eve. We always have been. Why aren't we together? Sharing a house, a bed, a *life!*"

She straightened her shirt, her gaze deliberately averted. She was running away without moving, but he was done giving her space. It was time to pick a path and stick with it.

"You know my dad," she prevaricated, wincing because she knew she was copping out. "He'd kill me for living with a man before marriage."

"So let's get married."

Eve's face drained of colour. She shook her head and walked out of the room.

"Angel . . ."

She kept going, tossing her reply over her shoulder. "You're not my favourite person right now."

"You're my favourite person," he said calmly, following her. "I want to spend the rest of my life with you."

"All fifteen minutes of it? If you're lucky."

"You could get lucky," he drawled. "Right now."

"You're starting to sound like your brother," she snapped. "Except his marriage proposal had some romantic trappings to it."

He smiled. His off-the-cuff proposal had the desired effect of cracking her shell. That she was hurt made her a hypocrite, considering she was the one who'd broken off their relationship, but he wasn't going to point that out.

"Them's fightin' words," he said instead.

She gave a careless wave over her shoulder. "I don't want to fight with you. That's why I'm walking away."

Navigating through the boxes in the living room, she reached the foyer and made a beeline for the stairs.

"Turn left," he said.

Eve turned right towards the stairs.

"If you don't turn left," he warned, "I'll toss you over my shoulder and haul you where I want you."

Exhaling harshly, she turned left and entered the family room. She drew to an abrupt halt on the threshold. Alec deliberately crowded behind her, pressing the length of his body against her back.

He'd scoped out every room in the house before deciding on this one. He guessed it would be her favourite, décor-wise. An overstuffed sectional sofa in soft brown and accent pieces in red and gold made the space warm and inviting, which was the way he saw her. He'd added the fire in the fireplace and the white satin duvet on the floor in front of it, which he had covered in red rose petals. Their first night together had been on white satin, and when he had returned to her ten years later, he had used white satin again. He'd found the sheets in her linen closet, and knew she would have bought them with memories of him in mind. She had haunted him the same way. He fell in love with her the moment he saw her and every day that passed, even the ones when they'd been apart, he'd grown to love her more.

Eve stared at the makeshift bed in front of the fireplace and felt tears sting her eyes.

This is Alec, she thought, swallowing past a lump in her throat. She saw now that his proposal in the kitchen had just been a way to bait her into revealing more than she wanted to. He now knew that she'd wanted him to ask her at least enough to get upset about the way he got around to doing it.

She should have known better. Alec wasn't the kind of guy who jumped without looking, especially into something as monumental as marriage. He was a tender romantic, a man of grand gestures and thoughtful considerations. Reed was the one who had knee-jerk reactions to unexpected events and his idea of seduction was pinning a woman to the nearest flat surface and banging her to oblivion.

"I can nail you to a wall," Alec whispered, nuzzling the spot below her ear. "Any time you want."

She choked. "Stay out of my head."

"I don't need to be in there to know that you've been comparing me and Abel since you met him. You and I both know he's too self-absorbed to be what you need, but being with him comes with less pressure and expectations. He doesn't let anyone in, so there's no chance of a real future, which means less risk for you."

"Don't analyse me."

"I'm just saying what you thought the moment you saw that ring in your wineglass. I *was* in your head then." He wrapped his arms around her and caught up her left hand. With a gentle tug, he removed Reed's ring from her finger. "I'm a huge risk, because committing to me is forever and it means sticking with the Mark for the long haul."

"Alec . . ." Turning in his embrace, she hugged him tightly and listened to his heartbeat. "We have so many fundamental differences between us. You're devout, and I'm . . . not. You're an archangel and I'm hoping to get out of this mess and have kids one day. I want baseball games and sleepovers and Girl Scout cookie sales and family vacations—"

"And I want you to have those things." His warm breath ruffled the hair at her crown. "You know I do. But I can't let you have those things with someone else, not when I know I'm the guy you want."

"I can't have those things with you. I can't even have you."

"That's your fear talking."

"I'm not—"

"You're trembling," he pointed out wryly, tightening his arms around her. "And I get why. You're trying to distance yourself, so if something happens to me it hurts less."

"Can you blame me? You have demons and angels of all persuasions gunning for you."

"We're not together now. Does that make it easier for you to deal with the risks of me being mortal?"

Eve's fingers flexed restlessly into the hard muscles on either side of his spine. *Easier?* She didn't want to let him out of her sight. "No."

"I've regretted every minute that we haven't been together. They're all missed opportunities for happiness in a life you know is damned fucking hard." His lips brushed across her temple. "After dealing with the shit we do all day, I want to come home to you and just be *me* for a few hours. Aren't you tired of being a Mark 24/7 with nothing in your life to make you feel human? Don't you want the freedom of sharing your life with someone who knows and loves you for who you are in your private moments?"

"I get it." She'd been letting her life as a Mark overtake whatever was left of the mortal she'd been before. Her personal and professional lives were both being moulded around her goal to get her former life back, which – until now – had been only a distant possibility. She had a family: two parents, and a great sister and brother-in-law with two kids Eve loved madly. The thought of them growing old and dying while she lived for years afterwards was crushing. Just thinking of it made it hard to breathe. But was that selfish of her? Wouldn't she be more useful to them as a protector than not?

Pulling back, Eve looked up at him. "You need to shelve the proposal for a bit."

"Ouch." He grinned, knowing her too well to take offence.

Still, she explained. "You're mortal and until we deal with the safety issues around that, I can't think about what you're asking me."

"I still know how to protect us. Taking away the power doesn't take away the skill."

Her thoughts rewound through the events of the day before, then rushed ahead. "Zaphiel took me with him to meet the head guy who's in charge of cleaning up after the Fallen. Adrian. I just can't see him missing a vampire in his own backyard, especially one living in a place like Arcadia Falls where the neighbours are unusually friendly. Adrian seemed too sharp, Alec. He's definitely not someone I'd ever want to piss off."

"You have to understand Zaphiel. He has a problem with the seraphim, so he likes to fuck with them, with or without a valid reason. He believes they've been given too much power, to the point that they're encroaching on the cherubim."

"What kind of power?"

"Like elevating a Mark to archangel."

"You." She began to pace, which helped her think. "You're saying this is about the deal you struck with Sabrael for your promotion?"

Alec's ascension to archangel had come at a price – he'd agreed to perform some unspecified future service for the seraph who had promoted him. That bargain gave Sabrael a tremendous advantage over everyone else in the angelic hierarchy: the seraph had at his command the greatest weapon since Satan.

Watching her, Alec nodded. "The only way to break free of my deal with Sabrael was to go higher up the food chain, but I had to be careful not to position myself as the sole target of retaliation."

She understood. "If you went to God, Sabrael couldn't take it out on the Almighty, so he'd have to vent his anger on you."

"Exactly. When I heard that Zaphiel was coming to see Adrian about a recent Sentinel killing, I made sure Raguel knew that I didn't want to be an archangel anymore. I figured he'd be only too happy to find a way to knock me down a rung or two and if Sabrael gets pissy, he can take it up with him."

He was playing a dangerous game, pitting angels against each other to achieve his aims. And he was doing it for her. So he could love her again. She'd been so determined to keep distance between them, while Alec had been trying to find a way to close it . . . even at the cost of his own dreams of promotion.

She scrubbed at her tearing eyes, aware that she didn't have time to be emotional if she was going to keep Alec alive. "So that's your side of what's going on – you wanted out of the advancement and your obligation to Sabrael, and you knew Gadara and Zaphiel would make it happen. But it's looking like knocking you down isn't enough for them. It makes sense now why Zaphiel made me drive him out to Adrian's place. At the time, I figured he was just trying to mess with you or Reed by making me play chauffeur. Then this assignment came up and I reconsidered. Maybe he wanted me to know where Adrian lived or what he looked like. Maybe there was something he wanted me to see."

"Maybe he wanted to insult Adrian by sending a Mark to do a job an elite seraph couldn't manage."

"I think it's because I was supposed to be *seen*, by someone who'd follow me and find you stripped of the archangel gifts that help keep you safe." She stopped moving and faced him dead-on. "Adrian Mitchell isn't in hiding. I Googled him last night, because I knew that house he owns must have garnered some press. I found out he owns Mitchell Aviation, one of the largest aeronautical companies in the world. He's been on the cover of *Forbes* and his home has been showcased in a dozen architectural magazines. The Fallen know exactly where he is and if they're smart, they're watching his place."

Alec crossed his arms. "So we're waiting for the other shoe to drop. In the meantime . . . Marry me, angel."

"Alec—" She groaned and starting pacing again. "Are you paying attention to me at all?"

"Some things are still sacred. Marriage happens to be one of them. Whatever happens from this moment forward, no one could break vows we make before Jehovah."

" 'Let's get hitched before I die and lose the opportunity'? Is that what you're saying?"

His smile was breathtaking. "You know I'm too valuable to kill, or I'd already be dead. They might want to see me knocked around a bit, just for shits and giggles, but it won't go farther than that."

"I'm already a huge liability to you. Moving me up in status from 'piece-of-ass' to 'wife' is just going to make that worse."

"You've never been a piece of ass to me and everyone damn well knows that." He caught her as she passed. "Right now, we can't control whether or not Sabrael promotes me again. We can't stop Raguel from yanking you around to piss me off. We can't do a damn thing about Zaphiel hanging us out as bait. They've got all the power, but it doesn't have to be that way. We can make a commitment to each other that no one could break. If Sabrael promotes me again, he can't take my love away. If Raguel wants to toy with you, he'd have to think twice about it, because interfering in a marriage is a damn sight trickier. And Zaphiel won't let anything happen to you, knowing the censure he'd face from Jehovah."

"So wedding vows supersede or take precedence over everything?"

"Always." He let her go. "I was late getting here today, because I stopped by your parents' place and talked to your dad. He gave me his blessing."

Eve moved towards the fire, noting the blue at the heart of the gas flame, the same flame-blue she saw in the irises of cherubim and seraphim. The hue seemed murkier now, everything around her did except for Alec. The loss of the Mark was like listening through water, feeling through gloves and smelling through a head cold. Maybe she'd acclimatize to the loss of heightened sensation after a while, but for now, she felt disconnected and out of sorts. It would take her more time to be sure, but she was resigned to the fact that she'd turned a corner somewhere and she couldn't go back. Without the Mark, she'd always be looking over her shoulder and second-guessing everyone she crossed paths with, wondering if they were an Infernal because she no longer possessed the senses required to identify them.

She heard him come up behind her. He set his hands on her shoulders and gently turned her around.

Groaning, she dropped her forehead against his shoulder. "I need to talk to Reed. This is happening so fast and he needs to know what's going on."

"He knows. If you think he avoids eavesdropping for politeness, you're way off base. I'll admit that you're probably the closest he's ever come to caring more about someone else than himself, but that's not your problem. You don't have to be the only hope he's got of being happy. He has to figure that out for himself."

"I don't think you know him as well as I do."

"I know I'd kill him again before I'd let him have you," he said fiercely. "See if he'll make the same effort before you say your vows to me."

Reed, she called out. *Talk to me, please. We need to discuss this.*

She waited for long moments, but he didn't answer.

Alec dropped to one knee and her heart stopped beating. She forgot to breathe until the room tilted, then she sucked in air with a huge deep breath. He reached into his back pocket and withdrew a ring box. The moment the lip snapped open, she covered her mouth with her hand. A solitary princess-cut diamond sat within a simple platinum band. Sized around two-carats, it so perfectly fit her tastes she wanted to weep at the sight of it. Her reaction to the ring was just as ferocious as the one she'd had the night before, but for a very different reason.

"Angel, would you—"

"Yes."

Five

The phone rang less than five minutes after Eve left a message with Adrian Mitchell's secretary.

She answered immediately and shivered at the sound of the smooth, warm voice on the other end of the line. The power the man wielded caused a tangible response, even without the Mark's enhancement to her senses.

"Eve," he said. "Adrian Mitchell."

"Hi. We've got trouble." She explained how Zaphiel had stripped her of the Mark. She didn't mention Alec's lack of power, unable to say it aloud out of fear for his safety. *If something happened to him* . . . "Assistance would be appreciated."

"I already have someone on you, although I doubt Cain needs the help."

"You do?" She looked at Alec with brows raised. "Did you have me followed?"

"Of course. Changing to the Jeep threw us off a bit, but as it turns out, I would have found you anyway." His tone was wry. "I'm told you're a former agnostic, but I'm sure you've learned by now that some things fall into place despite the odds."

Since she was living that fact now, she couldn't disagree. "Thank you."

"Not necessary. You got stuck in the middle of a pissing match that has nothing to do with you."

"Yeah," she said wryly. "That happens to me a lot."

It was five minutes after six when Alec rang the Andersons' doorbell.

The smell of barbeque on the grill and the sounds of conversation and laughter had begun a half-hour before, but Eve and Alec had spent time getting the house ready for any unwanted visitors.

The door swung open and revealed Pam, who looked smart in a pair of white capris and a sage green shirt that matched her eyes. "Hey. Come on in. Terri's in the kitchen being an overachiever."

Eve held up a bottle of wine, Alec carried a six-pack of Blue Moon.

"My kind of neighbours," Pam said, grinning. "Come this way, Eve. Alec, if you want to head outside, that's where the men are."

Eve followed Pam through the living room to the kitchen, while Alec headed out the sliding glass door that led to the back patio.

"I was hoping I could come by tomorrow," Pam said, eyeing her avidly. "I have a new catalogue and some great samples."

Remembering that Pam sold cosmetics, Eve smiled. Certainly Pam would be familiar with many of the Arcadia residents. Perhaps Pam was using her consultant business as a cover for a darker purpose. If not, Eve could use their acquaintance to do so. "Sure. I'd love to have you over. You'll have to forgive the boxes."

"I can help with that while Jesse's in school."

"Thank you. I'd like that."

They entered the kitchen where Terri stood tossing a salad at a large granite-covered island. "Enjoying the new house so far?" she asked Eve.

"We're thrilled."

Jesse looked up from her task of slicing strawberries and smiled, then glanced out the backdoor longingly, as if she'd much rather be outside.

"Can I borrow a corkscrew?" Eve asked. "I need to let this Merlot breathe a bit."

Terri gestured with a jerk of her chin. "There's a wine bar in the family room. You'll find all the accessories – glasses, wine charms, corkscrew – in there."

Heading into the family room, which was easy to find since the floor plans were so similar, Eve made a point of checking out the house. She had no idea what she was looking for, but knew she'd recognize something off if she found it.

She'd just located the corkscrew in a drawer when Tim came into the room.

"Hey," he greeted her.

"Hi." She noted that he looked different, then figured out what it was. His eyes weren't blue so much as a muted grey, similar to how dull Zaphiel's irises became after she lost the Mark.

"I was hoping to catch you alone."

Something about the way he approached her set her on edge. There was a sharp focus to the way he watched her and the balance of his footfalls – light and on the balls of his sandalled feet – was inherently predatory.

Although he was dressed innocuously in navy board shorts and a loose-fitting white tee, she altered her stance and her grip on the corkscrew. She may not have the speed and power of the Mark, but she still knew how to fight.

He smiled. "We have a mutual acquaintance."

Eve absorbed that. "Oh?"

"Adrian."

Her head tilted to one side. "Wings or fur?"

"Definitely not furry." He wagged his finger at her. "Be careful who you call a lycan. Those who aren't one, don't take it well."

"Point taken. How are you with corkscrews? I've been known to get cork in the wine."

He moved to the other side of the bar and took over. As he deftly uncorked the bottle, Eve looked around the room, noting the same lack of wall adornment she'd picked up on in the living room. Almost as if the Andersons hadn't quite moved in yet . . . or were ready for a quick move out.

"How long has Terri lived here?" she asked.

"I have no idea. I haven't been here long myself."

Eve looked at him. "Is this home permanent for you? Or just for now?"

"Nothing's permanent." He tossed the cork in the trash and rinsed off the corkscrew before tossing it back in the drawer. "I get in, get what I came for, and get out."

"I know what that's like."

"I'm surprised Cain is getting involved in Adrian's business."

"That's my fault. I got suckered into this and I'm flying blind. I didn't even know the Watchers . . . the Fallen . . . vampires – whatever were still around until last night and I've been scrambling to catch up. Since he's my mentor, he has to tag along, too."

"He looks a bit more invested than that."

"Yeah . . ." She smiled, but kept her personal life to herself. "It's complicated."

"Which is why I work alone." He poured a half-glass and set it in front of her.

Eve toyed with the stem a minute, then asked, "Why are we both here in Arcadia Falls? Is the location tied to the hunt in some way?"

"I'm here because of the resort rental situation. No one expects me to keep regular hours or stick around long term. If the vamp is here in the community, it's because Adrian, Raguel, and Cain are all running their operations from Anaheim, so there's a high concentration of angels in the area. Since Raguel owns this property, maybe the vamp thinks that ups his chances of catching an angel here. As for you, I don't know. Maybe Raguel knows something about this location that roused his suspicions?"

"I wouldn't know. He enjoys withholding vital intel from me." Eve took a drink and was surprised to feel warmth as the alcohol moved through her. The mark prevented mind-altering substances from having any affect. "Do you know why angel blood is in such demand?"

"No, but it has to either cause a rush – like a drug – or be power-enhancing, because it's commanding a hefty price on the black market."

"I'd expect so, considering the risk."

"There's no risk to you," he said, his handsome face austere. "I've got your back."

"I appreciate that. Thank you. Do you have any leads?"

"I've been looking at Jesse. I know *Twilight* is all the rage with kids these days, but she might be emulating someone else with those veneers of hers. One of her girlfriends? Or a boyfriend, maybe? I've been trying to figure out who she's hanging out with, but it's tough to ask questions about a girl that age and not look like a pervert."

She glanced aside at him. "I can help with that."

"I was hoping you'd say that."

"In the meantime, we'll be better guarded from tomorrow night onward," she improvised, taking the first steps towards the door. "I doubt anyone will come for us so soon after we've moved in."

Tim fell into step with her. "I agree. There's reckless, and

then there's stupid. I don't think we're lucky enough to be dealing with the latter."

"Figures." She smiled at him. "At least the neighbours are
nice."

It was three o'clock in the morning, the devil's hour, when Eve
knew her house had been breached. The security system was on
and silent and all the doors and windows were locked, but she
felt the disturbance in the goose bumps that covered her arms.
She slid her legs off the side of the bed and looked at Alec, who
reclined against the headboard beside her.

His gaze met hers and he reached for her hand, his arm flexing in an inherently graceful display of taut muscles rippling
beneath olive-coloured skin. He offered a reassuring smile, but
it didn't reach his eyes. He was worried about her. She wished
he'd be more worried about himself.

Eve stood and padded barefoot towards the open bedroom door.
She was dressed in clothing that gave her a full range of movement – loose flannel pants paired with a spaghetti-strapped bra top.
She'd prefer to have her Doc Martens on, but they needed their
visitor to be as unguarded as possible. They were mortals trying to
trap an immortal; they needed all the help they could get.

Moonlight from the guestroom windows cut alternating
swathes across the carpet, affording her enough illumination to
walk without fear of running into anything. That didn't mean
she wasn't afraid of something happening to Alec while she was
helpless to protect him. Her heart was racing and her palms were
damp; physical reactions that the Mark would have prevented.
She missed the rush of aggression and bloodlust that came from
the Mark, as well as the heightened senses that would have
allowed her to hear even the minutest of noises and to sniff out
her quarry. As it was, she wasn't blind in the strictest sense, but
she was definitely guessing.

A shadow darted across the landing in front of her. Eve stilled
and played the role she and Alec had agreed upon. "Hello?" she
whispered. "Is someone there?"

Behind her, Alec faked a loud yawn and called out, "Angel?
What are you doing?"

"Nothing. Getting some water."

Jesse materialized before her, a slender figure dressed in black with a serrated blade in her hand. She put a finger to her lips, then smiled, showing her fangs.

A brush of air against Eve's nape caused her to pivot slightly. Pam stood between Eve and the master bedroom, her petite figure hunched in an abnormal way. Her fingers were splayed and curved, revealing thick claws. Eve's gaze shot back up to the woman's face, noting a feral snarl and pointed canines.

Jesse made a soft noise to catch Eve's attention, then beckoned Eve forward with her knife.

As Eve moved again, the fine hairs on her arms stood on end and her breathing quickened. She was a step away from reaching the landing at the top of the stairs when an arm snaked out from one of the guestrooms, grabbing her by the biceps and yanking her backwards into a rock-hard torso.

"Back off, bitch," Tim snapped. Whether he spoke to Jesse or Pam, Eve couldn't tell. But then he wrapped his hand around Eve's neck and she felt the razor sharp nails at the tips of his fingers.

The teenager blew a bubble of gum and popped it. "What now?"

Pam growled, her gaze darting back and forth.

Alec appeared in the master bedroom doorway. He leaned into the doorjamb, crossed one ankle over the other, and drawled, "Which one of you wants to get their ass kicked first?"

Jesse looked at Tim. Eve felt him move, then a plastic bag and tubing sailed past her, tumbling through the air from his free hand to the teenager. Jesse caught the package deftly.

"Get his blood," Tim said.

Eve hadn't expected that. She looked at Pam. "Are you with them?"

The sound that came from the other woman's throat was agonizing to hear. Eve looked at Alec, but his face gave nothing away. He was better at bluffing under pressure than she was, but then, he'd had a lot of practice. Still, he wouldn't look at her. She knew he couldn't while she was absolutely vulnerable and in the hands of a vampire. He'd go nuts and that would put her in more jeopardy than she already was.

"Those aren't veneers, are they, Jesse?" Eve asked.

"Nopc."

"Jesse . . ." Pam's voice was sandpaper rough. "Why?"

"Because I wanted to," Jesse said, continuing towards Alec.

Pam blocked her way. "I can't let you touch him, Jess."

"Can't?" the teenager cried, sounding both furious and plaintive. "Because Adrian ordered you to be a good doggy and do what you're told? Fuck him, Mom. Fuck all the Sentinels. We have a right to do what we want."

"We have a responsibility to do the right thing."

"What is 'the right thing'? Protecting him—" she gestured at Alec, "—and the other angels that treat us like animals? Just because our ancestors crawled back to the Sentinels and became work dogs, doesn't mean we're stuck with their choice. We can still join the Fallen. We can still be immortal."

"I'd be happy to turn you, Pam," Tim purred. "Lycans take the Change better than mortals. You'll like it."

He sounded far too smug for Eve's tastes, but she'd heard enough anyway. She shoved her hand between them and grabbed his balls. Vampire or not, testicles were always a good target. He roared and stumbled back. Startled, Jesse dropped her guard. Pam tackled her daughter, falling to the floor just as Alec vaulted over them.

Eve hugged the wall, knowing better than to get in his way.

Launching into the vampire, Alec caught him up and smashed him into the far wall. They grappled, the combatants discernable only as a flurry of violent movement in the dark. Then a body was hurled over the bed, crashing into the closet door in an explosion of shattered wood.

A figure stepped into the moonlight slanting through the window. Tim's face was revealed, his handsome features contorted by both his vampirism and fury. Eve hunched low, prepared for a blow.

The muffled report of a silenced gun had Eve dropping to the floor. She watched, wide-eyed, as Tim's body erupted into flames. He writhed against the wall, his claws ripping into to the drywall as if trying to crawl out of his own skin. His flesh sizzled off of his bones, dropping to the floor in burning chunks.

An outstretched hand came into her line of vision, snapping her out of her horrified fascination.

She looked up and found the gate guard from Adrian's place.

"Adrian sent me to help Pam," he explained.

Alec climbed out of the ruins of the closet. "I forgot how bad it hurts to be mortal."

The guard arched a brow as he helped Eve to her feet. "Adrian didn't mention that part."

"I didn't tell him." Which turned out to be a good thing. If he'd known, then Pam would have known, and then Tim would have known through Jesse.

Pam . . .

Eve scrambled into the hallway. She hit the light switch. The sudden flood of illumination revealed walls splattered with crimson. Jesse lay on her back, chest heaving. Half her throat was missing. Blood gushed in rhythmic pulses from her ruined neck, spreading across the floor in a thick, glistening puddle. Beside her, Pam sprawled with eyes open and sightless. The handle of Jesse's dagger protruded from her heart.

The guard joined Eve in the hall. Dressed in loafers, slacks and V-neck sweater, he looked too polished and powerful to be anyone's pet.

He lifted his arm and pointed his gun at Jesse. "Your mother will be missed."

"Fuck you, lycan dog," she gurgled, blood running from the corner of her mouth. "Tell Adrian . . . we're both free."

He pulled the trigger.

"You are like a tornado, Ms Hollis," Raguel began, staring at Eve. "You always leave a path of destruction and chaos in your wake."

Alec's mouth kicked up on one side. They were presently crammed into the guest bedroom nearest the upstairs landing. Zaphiel sat on the mattress, while Eve stood at the foot of the bed next to Raguel. Alec grabbed a corner and settled in to enjoy the show. No one flustered Raguel like Eve did.

He watched as the archangel pointed at the blood in the hallway, then at the destroyed closet, then at the burn marks that shadowed the torn wall.

"Hey," Eve complained. "I didn't do any of that!"

"You arranged this confrontation, did you not?"

"Noooo . . . You and Zaphiel arranged this mess." She looked at the cherub. "What exactly did you expect would happen when the vamp came after us?"

"I expect you to clean this up," Raguel interjected. "Since I need you both to stay under cover to manage the neighbourhood reaction to the mysterious speedy departure of three residents at once, you can oversee the repairs during that interim."

"Thank you for your help," Zaphiel said, before shifting out.

Raguel moved towards the door. "You may use your expense account, Ms Hollis, to pay for the necessary repairs. I expect it will take at least three weeks to cement your cover story and settle the other residents. I will speak to Abel about removing you from rotation during that time."

The archangel shifted away as quickly as the cherub had.

Alec frowned. "That's it? Raguel usually likes to lecture us for an hour or more."

"I knew it," she said quietly. "The whole thing was too convenient. Too fast. Too easy."

"Speak for yourself, angel. Seeing you in the hands of one of the Fallen damn near killed me."

She looked at him sombrely, worrying her lower lip between her teeth. "We didn't get our Marks back. We're still mortal."

"Lucky for them." He pushed away from the wall. "They wouldn't want to see how pissed I'd be if I didn't get you into bed first."

Eve began to pace, which meant she was thinking hard.

"What's wrong?" he asked, hating to see her upset. "Are you still worried about me?"

"When we lost all the bonuses of the Mark, did we lose all the restrictions, too?"

"I hope so. I could use a drink right now."

She gave a shaky exhale and glanced at him. "Tim gave himself away. Why? Pam was the backup Adrian talked about on the phone and she didn't reveal herself. Tim was the one we were looking for and he walked right up to me at Terri's party. He said he worked alone. If he'd been one of Adrian's seraphim, he would have had a lycan or two with him somewhere. Wouldn't he naturally assume I'd know that."

"What are you thinking?"

"If he wanted his soul back . . . if he wanted to go back to Heaven after all these years on earth sucking blood, would he make a deal with an angel to earn his way back into God's good graces?"

Alec inhaled sharply. "Maybe. But what would Raguel or Zaphiel get out of it?"

Stopping suddenly, she faced him head-on. "You and me alone in a house for a month with no Mark standing between us. No restrictions to the normal workings of male and female physiology. What would the natural course of events lead to, God willing?"

As understanding dawned, he grew very still. It took him a moment to find his voice. "Angel . . ."

Eve's heart was racing. The roaring of blood in her ears was nearly deafening. She felt short of breath, bordering on panic. She was standing on the edge of a very sharp cliff and she was gearing up the courage to jump.

Alec's sudden slow smile did crazy things to her equilibrium. It was joyous, outrageously sexy, and made her weak in the knees. He was gorgeous, wonderful and in love with her. He was also God's primary enforcer, he killed demons for a living, and he had an ex-wife from Hell . . . literally. But what man didn't have his faults? Her mother always said it wasn't about finding the perfect guy; it was about finding a guy whose faults you could live with.

Then there was the fact that when it came to making babies, he was the only man she'd ever imagined having kids with. If one child was all they could finagle out of this damned mess of Marks, demons and manipulating angels, she'd count herself blessed for the first time in her life.

"We can damn well try," he said, with a hoarseness that betrayed how the idea affected him. He came to her and pulled her close. His hands weren't steady.

"Some people are afraid to bring children into the regular, screwed up world." There was a tremor in her voice she couldn't hide. "We're talking about bringing one into Hell on earth. And we're giving Raguel and Zaphiel what they want," she warned. "We have no idea what their motives might be, what their intentions are—"

"Bring it on." He wore an expression that dared all comers.

"We're giving ourselves what *we* want, angel. We can handle whatever we need to when the time comes."

The tension left her in a rush, leaving her boneless. She sank into him and held on tight.

Alec pressed a kiss to the top of her head. "Who says we can't have it all?"

They decided to get married in the house, because it was quick and there was a bed nearby. Alec called in Muriel, a *mal'akh* they both knew and trusted, to perform the ceremony. Eve asked the angel to fetch a simple white crocheted summer dress from her closet at home, but she told Alec to stay just the way he was. He was exactly as she wanted him, no formality necessary.

When he protested, she explained that they'd have to marry again for her family and friends and he could wear a tuxedo then. For now, the need for haste was of paramount importance. She'd finally made up her mind and she was ready to get on with her new way of living – accepting her Marked fate and taking what joy she could from it. Everyone else was enjoying having her in the Marked system, because it benefited them. It was time for her to get something out of it, too. And really, getting married to the man she'd loved her whole life, with an angel presiding over the ceremony, was all any girl could ask for . . .

. . . except for maybe a bit of closure with the guy she was walking away from before they ever really got started.

But Reed was ignoring her. Whatever it was they had, it deserved a farewell and an attempt at separating with no hard feelings. He was her handler, the *mal'akh* responsible for assigning her to hunts. They'd be working together indefinitely, as well as sharing thoughts and emotions for many years to come.

Through the open bedroom window overlooking the back patio, she heard Alec and Muriel laugh over something. He'd looked so boyish and carefree when she accepted his ring, and she felt a soul-deep surety that this was exactly what she was supposed to do. There were no doubts left, which gave her a sense of freedom the likes of which she hadn't experienced since becoming Marked.

Since they had the house for another few weeks, she intended to live all of her old dreams in that limited time span, making the most of every moment.

Then she and Alec would create new dreams to go with her new life.

Turning around, Eve took one last look at her appearance in the cheval mirror. When she saw the man reflected in the glass, she very nearly jumped out of her skin.

"You scared the crap out of me!" she cried, her hand lifting to shelter her racing heart.

Reed didn't smile. He sat on the edge of the mattress with legs spread wide and his elbows resting on his knees. Dressed in a black shirt and slacks, he looked like he was in mourning. His gaze was hard and lacked any emotion.

"You make a beautiful bride," he said without inflection.

Eve faced him directly. It was easy to say there was nothing permanent between them when they were apart. When she was faced with his presence, however, the attraction was undeniable. "Thank you. I suddenly feel like shit."

"Don't," he said tightly. "Fuck the doubts and guilt and all the other crap I feel stirring around in you and give this marriage everything you've got. You wanted Cain and now he's yours. You better damn well enjoy it."

She intended to, but that wasn't the issue. "Don't be sarcastic. It stings."

"I'm not." He shifted to a spot right in front of her. "I mean it. I'm not going to have what I want from you until you've reached the end of the road with him. I've got all the time in the world. I can wait 'til you get there."

"We're getting *married*, Reed."

The look he gave her was both scathing and mocking. "You have to. I didn't realize that until last night."

"Reed—"

He grabbed her right hand and pushed the pink diamond engagement ring over the knuckle of her fourth finger. "Cain gave it back to me, but it's yours."

The fit was snugger on her dominant hand. Not uncomfortably so, but enough to make her very aware of the ring's presence.

Dropping her hand as if it burned him, he stepped back.

"Marriage isn't an unbreakable contract, Eve. Cain's been married before."

Her hand fisted, testing the weight of the massive stone.

"I have something you need and want," Reed bit out. "I'm damned if I know what it is between us, but I do know it's not going away, and neither am I. You and I are unfinished business, and you won't be able to live with that forever. You'll come back to me some day. And when you do, we'll both know you're ready."

She opened her mouth to reply, but he shifted away. There one second, gone the next. As ephemeral as smoke, just as he'd always been. She sucked in a deep, shaky breath and felt a huge weight slip from her shoulders. He had given her a blessing of sorts, something she hadn't realized she wanted until she had it. And Alec was right; Reed wasn't putting up a fight. That spoke louder than words.

Eve left the bedroom in her bare feet and hurried down the stairs towards her future.

The Majestic

Seressia Glass

Rinna walked past the row of crimson stools at the Majestic's well-used counter, heading for a table in the back corner. The Art Deco diner had been an indelible part of the Poncey-Highland neighbourhood just east of downtown Atlanta since 1929. Open twenty-four hours and every day except Christmas, the Majestic catered to an eclectic crowd of humans and hybrids alike.

At this time of day, the diner was mostly empty. That would change as night fell, then at midnight. That was when the Majestic became a prime people- and hybrid-watching venue.

She wasn't there to watch, though. No, she'd arrived an hour early to gather her thoughts and prepare to make her case to a man she hadn't been able to forget for two years.

She looked up as the waiter placed a menu, a glass of water and tableware in front of her. "Hey Sam. Getting in touch with your feminine side this cycle?"

Sam flashed a sharp-toothed grin, pushing her green-tipped black fringe off her forehead. "Thought it wouldn't hurt to take a walk on the wilder side," the hybrid confided. "You wanna look at the menu, or do you already know what you want?"

"I'll flip through it, and just start with a cup of black coffee, thick."

Sam placed a laminated menu on the table. "Gotcha. Back in a bit."

Rinna tapped her fingers as she looked through the menu, trying to quell her nerves. Two years. After two years, it would finally happen. She'd finally see him again.

Sam returned with coffee. "Today's the day, eh, Rinna?"

"Yes." She fidgeted. "At least, I hope so."

"Of course it will be. How can Bale resist you?"

"Easily." Rinna wrapped her hands around the coffee mug to prevent tapping a hole into the table. "Our people can really hold on to grudges, down to the smallest slight. Bale and I didn't exactly part on the best of terms."

Best of terms. She'd run away from Bale like a weak *banring* afraid of being exposed to die by her crèche mother. All because she'd discovered Bale's clan affiliation. A clan he no longer recognized, much as she'd left hers for a new life in Atlanta two years ago.

"He'll come," Sam assured her. "Didn't the Chaser tell you so?"

"Yeah, she did." Rinna had taken a huge risk approaching the Shadowchaser, especially given the circumstances in which they'd first met. Besides, Shadowchasers were a hybrid's version of the boogeyman, a tale used to frightened the young. All she'd heard growing up was that Shadowchasers hunted hybrids and Shadowlings, trapping or killing them on sight. And that they loved to munch on young misbehaving *banrings*. It didn't matter what you did or didn't do, the fact that you existed made you the Shadowchaser's enemy.

She'd learned that wasn't the case, thanks to Bale. She'd learned a lot of things, thanks to the male *banaranjan*.

Two Years Earlier

A pulsing beat thundered through all three tiers of the DMZ's main room, forcing Rinna's heart to keep pace. It was a great night to party. It was an even better night to hunt.

Not that she needed to hunt. Many *banaranjans* made do with synthesized human adrenaline delivered via autoinjectors or served over dry ice in mixed-clientele clubs like the DMZ. It did what it needed to do, but nothing compared to sampling the epinephrine directly from the source. In a place like this, there were always plenty of volunteers around.

The Goth club looked like a cross between the Roman Coliseum and a factory from the start of the Industrial Revolution, perfect for its diverse clientele. Those who walked in Light gathered on Rinna's left, though all three levels seemed sparsely lit with the blue-violet-white flickers that denoted Light beings. *Maybe they're all at a convention*, she thought.

On the right, occasional flashes of yellow lit the deep dark of the Shadow side of the club. Plenty of beings on that side, Rinna noted. Most club-goers, human and otherwise, spilled over the middle ground between the two camps, the most neutral of the neutral territory inside the club.

Finding a nightspot that catered to hybrids and humans alike had been essential to her successful relocation to Atlanta – that and the Majestic, of course. The DMZ was a demilitarized zone masquerading as a bar that allowed anyone, of any walk of life, to enter as long as they didn't draw weapons. Rinna couldn't see the protective shielding that radiated from every bit of the club's infrastructure, but she could feel it. She knew it was quick to take care of anyone careless enough to display aggression. Rumour had it that even the Shadowchaser had to remove her weapons before she entered.

Rinna wasn't sure about that, but if it was true, it only confirmed her belief that she'd made the right choice relocating to Atlanta. A diverse club, the lack of a major *banaranjan* community and the presence of a Gilead Commission unit meant Rinna had a chance of a decent home and a reasonable life expectancy. Much better odds than where she'd been before.

Rinna took a final sip of her cocktail before discarding the plastic cup. She hoped she looked like most of the human females in there. Strappy stilettos, form-fitting jeans and a blouse with a plunging neckline seemed to be standard-issue attire for most of the women. It had taken months to perfect her human persona, practising in secret then making clandestine trips to test her abilities. Once she could pass for human and feed without detection, she'd made her escape.

Rinna leaned over the rail that ringed the first level. A live band played on a round stage in the centre of the club. The Pit circled the stage, a seething maelstrom of Shadow and darkness in which the DMZ's non-aggression rules didn't apply. Anywhere else in the club, if you drew weapons or called your power, wards would flash an orange warning, giving the perpetrator about two seconds to dial down or die. In the Pit, however, hybrids were given free rein, as long as no one got killed. Humans could go into the Pit too, but not without a little hassle. Since Rinna had been visiting the DMZ, she'd never seen a Light being enter the cauldron of violence. The humans who dared to had to sign a waiver before descending the stairs to the gated entrance.

She breathed deep, eyes sliding closed. Adrenaline wafted through the air, not enough to attempt to filter. For that, she needed more humans in the Pit or one male to show interest. She exhaled, releasing a simple banaranjan pheromone lure, and waited.

"Hey."

She turned away from the railing. A human male with spiky blond hair, pale jeans and a dark navy shirt smiled at her, the prerequisite bottle of beer dangling from his fingers. Nice.

"Hi yourself." She smiled, revving up her charm. *Draw him in slowly*, then *get his heart racing*.

"Would you like to dance?"

"Sure."

"Sweet."

The club was too crowded to move further along the dance floor, so they carved out a bit of room along the rail. Rinna lifted her arms and gave herself over to the frenetic music pouring from the stage. She kept the unnamed blond in her sights, smiling and flirting while dancing close, spiking his adrenaline.

He leaned forward, careful not to spill his beer. "My name's Cade."

"Nice to meet you, Cade," she called out over the lead singer's growling vocals. She leaned close, brushing her body against his. "My name's Rinna."

His heart pounded loud enough for her to hear it. "Rinna. A cool name for a hot chick."

She laughed. "Does that line get you laid a lot?"

He gave a self-deprecating shrug. "It may be a line, but it's still true."

She placed a hand on his shoulder. He flinched from the contact, then sighed. Rinna knew humans felt something between fear and pleasure from a *banaranjan*'s touch, an involuntary reaction to the epinephrine flooding their system.

The hormone was ambrosia to a *banaranjan*, not necessary to live, but coveted all the same. While many of her kind had no problem scaring adrenaline out of humans, Rinna much preferred to seduce a rush from her "samplers".

Cade trembled again. They had moved closer to the safety barrier that prevented dancers from accidentally falling into the Pit. Rinna pressed against him, running her hands over his back just above his kidneys. "So Cade . . . have you ever been down in the Pit?"

His heart triple-beat in his chest, and another burst of adrenaline hit his blood. *Delicious*.

"Sure, babe. I go in all the time," he said, false bravado clear in his voice. "What about you?"

She pinned him with a stare, hoping her eyes hadn't flickered yellow with excitement. "I've gone in a couple of times. It's a surreal experience."

"Yeah." Something flitted across his expression, something apprehensive, dark, and excited. "It's definitely something else."

Rinna nodded, but decided to trust his body instead of his words. People had called her type adrenaline junkies long before extreme sports became vogue. While *banaranjans* didn't need adrenaline for daily sustenance, it was a necessary component of their survival. She didn't think humans needed to jump out of airplanes or fight bulls or watch horror movies, but they did. When they did, *banaranjans* were there to collect the carelessly released adrenaline for themselves.

Cade was probably an adrenaline junkie. He certainly looked the part with his carelessly spiked hair and athletic build. Rinna had seen plenty of guys like him base jumping, free climbing, and free running. It was all about the rush, the brush with death. For these junkies, if there wasn't a near fatality, they didn't feel alive.

If Cade wanted a brush with death, Rinna would be happy to oblige him.

He jerked his head toward the Pit. "Wanna go in?"

Rinna sucked in a breath. Enough humans had finally entered the Pit to spike the thick club air with the musky sweetness of adrenaline and other hormones. She could filter more if she went in herself, but she wasn't ready for that. Not that she couldn't hold her own; she knew how to get in, get what she wanted, then get out. But there were plenty of hybrids and Shadowlings in the black maelstrom who would be thrilled to fight her for her human companion. Plenty of beings much bigger, much meaner, and much more disposed to push the club rules.

The music crescendoed, then stopped. Rinna turned toward the stage, cheering and applauding with the other club-goers. "Looks like it's last call," Rinna told Cade. "People are coming out of the Pit."

They watched, silent, as several humans staggered up the stairs to the main floor. Ripped shirts were the least of the injuries. One man had to be helped up the stairs by two others, the left side of his head bloodied. Club employees immediately gathered to help the humans to small recovery rooms out of sight.

A quick movement caught Rinna's attention. She looked over Cade's shoulder, her gaze falling on a darkly handsome man in a rust-coloured shirt coming up from the Pit. Where most of the others staggered and clearly showed evidence of the brutal experience the Pit could be, this male looked as if he'd thoroughly enjoyed his time in the lawless underbelly of the club.

As if he felt her gaze, the man turned to look at her. Rinna didn't need the yellow glint in his black eyes to tell her he was a hybrid. Tiny hairs stood up along her arms, and her own heart kicked into a faster rhythm.

He was a *banaranjan*, gorgeous and in his prime. She'd seen him around the club before, but she'd always kept her distance. She had no way of knowing his clan affiliation, which meant she had no way of knowing whether he was friend or enemy. Since she'd come to Atlanta specifically to escape confrontations like that, she'd decided avoiding the male *banaranjan* was prudent.

Apparently he had a different opinion. His gaze flicked to her left, to the human beside her. If the menacing frown was any indication, the male *banaranjan* didn't like what he saw. He changed direction, making his way towards them.

By Hetache's flame, no, Rinna thought. She did not want to be intercepted by this guy, or the DMZ's security wards. It was time to go.

Cade's heart rate increased, distracting Rinna from the other *banaranjan* approaching. The blond man's expression balanced somewhere between fear and aggression. "Friend of yours?"

Rinna blinked, turned her attention back to the irritated human. "Not even."

"Good to know." He caught her hand, his smile returning. "This is supposed to be the part where I ask for your phone number so I can call you later. But that would mean saying goodbye, and I'm not ready for that yet."

Rinna hid a smile. She hadn't put out a strong lure, but she hadn't needed to. If she were into humans, this man would be high on her list of suitors. She hadn't taken in nearly enough adrenaline to satisfy her craving, but she wasn't a fool. She had no intention of going any farther than the parking lot with the handsome blond, but getting away from the other *banaranjan* was definitely a good idea. "Neither am I."

"Awesome. What do you say I buy you breakfast or a cup of coffee at the Majestic?"

Rinna considered it for a hot second. There was only one place to go after a night of feeding off human energy at the DMZ: the Majestic. At three a.m., a good mix of humans and hybrids crowded the landmark twenty-four-hour diner in Virginia-Highland, most drunk on one thing or another. It was unofficial neutral ground after midnight, simply because most patrons were too tired, too hungry, or too high to be confrontational.

"Sure. A little Majestic sounds good."

They made their way through the middle doors, joining the bulk of the crowd making its way out of the bar. The sky hung dark and glittering above the DMZ's protective shields, tinged fluorescent orange by the city's ambient light. It was one of those travelogue-worthy spring nights in Atlanta in which the pollen count was down but the temperature was up. It was close to three in the morning, the time when Normals relinquished the night to the things that liked to "go bump".

Cade surveyed the mix of club-goers clogging the sidewalk – an eclectic mix of hybrids that passed as human and humans who looked liked hybrids.

They headed southeast from the club, leaving others behind. The club's parking lots filled quickly most nights, and Rinna had learned to park a couple of blocks away to avoid the traffic dumping out on to North Avenue. The distance made it easy to determine if someone had followed her out of the club, and it enabled her a final chance to walk through throngs of club-goers to filter their hormones one last time.

Rinna kept her attention on Cade's adrenaline levels. His excitement was a palpable thing, filling the air between them. She breathed deeply, drawing the heady pheromone into her throat. *So tasty. Much better than that stale, synthetic stuff.*

"There's something about you, Rinna," Cade said softly, his face turned up to the sky. "Something that tells me you're different from other women in the club."

"Thank you."

He scrubbed at his gelled hair. "I mean, when I saw you, I was like, 'whoa'. I mean, you're hot, smoking hot, but it's more than that."

She could tell. His heart was beating at a rapid pace, his chest rising and falling with his quickened breath. "Uhm, is there a compliment in there or something?"

"Yeah, yeah." He darted a look at her. "Back in the club, you touched me, and I felt like I'd just nailed a front double cork."

"I figured you were a sports fanatic. So what's a snowboarder doing in Atlanta when there's still plenty of snow on the ground up north?"

"I like all kinds of action," he told her. "Not just on snow."

"Only extreme sports, or an adrenaline junkie too?"

"Both." He spread his hands. "Among other things. What about you?"

"I'm not into sports beyond watching them, and I'm not an adrenaline junkie."

"So what are you then?"

She slowed her steps. "Excuse me?"

He stopped, turned to face her. "Come on, Rinna. You go to the DMZ, a place that's a little dicey most of the time. You say you've been in the Pit, a place that nobody but daredevils or drunks taking a dare would go into."

He brushed his cheek along hers, sniffed. "And that perfume works better than anything else I've ever inhaled. I'm betting you're not human."

By Hetache's flaming nostrils. Rinna knew the human male was unusual, but most of them, after discovering they weren't at the top of the food chain, either tried to run or tried to kill. Or, in an effort to show how open and progressive they were, they asked way too many personal questions.

Cade just stood there, the carefree frat boy demeanour gone. "I know humans aren't it," he said, his voice even. "I've travelled a lot, seen a lot more. It's cool with me if you're not human. I just wanted to know what you are exactly."

"You're an unusual human," she finally said. "As for me, I'm a *banaranjan*."

"A *banaranjan*." He nodded. "What sort of demon is that?"

"I'm not a demon, I'm a being born of this earth just as you are," she insisted, barely refraining from rolling her eyes. Human prejudices lasted long past their short lifespan. "*Banaranjans* are a race of beings who need to sample a little adrenaline now and then."

She didn't really feel like sharing too much with the strange human. One just couldn't predict what he'd do with the knowledge. She only knew the stories her crèche mother had told her, mainly horror stories to ensure her obedience. None of the tales involving humans and hybrids ended well, which was why most of the supernatural community preferred living in secret. Humans couldn't even get along with other humans. Every hybrid knew what would happen if the general population discovered the truth. Humans craved knowledge, but given the chance to create or destroy, most of the time they'd destroy.

Eagerness lit Cade's expression. "So you're adrenaline feeders. Do you take it like vampires drink blood?"

The night was going south like a runaway freight train. Her need to feed dissipated on the warm night air. She stopped beneath the dark bare branches of a large oak, a couple of blocks from the club, in an area that quickly gave way to empty buildings and overgrown lots. She was unwilling to go any farther with the human. All she wanted now was to go home. Alone. "I don't attack people, and I definitely don't bite. I only take what's freely given."

He snorted. "Yeah. I bet the people you're chomping on don't see it that way. Doesn't matter to me, though. I still think we can do this, don't you?"

"What are you talking about?"

"You and me. Hooking up."

Rinna's stomach knotted. "No. By the Dark Abyss, no." She'd be better off with the male *banaranjan*.

"Why not?" He stepped closer to her. Even in the late night darkness, she could see that his features had tarnished into something bare and ugly. Even his adrenaline didn't taste the same. "I like to feel adrenaline hitting my blood. You can make me feel that, you can feed off it. It's the perfect symbiotic relationship."

She backed up a step. If she had to defend herself, she'd need room. "Sorry, Cade. I'm not into fetish fulfilment. If you just wanted to get with a hybrid for bragging rights, you should have picked someone else."

He looked crestfallen, sticking his hands deep into his pockets. "That's a shame. Guess I'll have to get my rush some other way."

"I guess so." Rinna backed away, wondering how she'd made such a screwed-up choice. Too focused on the hormone and not the human. "Good night."

"It was nice dancing with you. See you around." He turned, heading back towards the club.

Rinna watched him head off, then turned and resumed her walk to her car, angry with herself. She should have just sifted for epinephrine in the club, but no, she had to have a direct source. From now on, she'd attend a couple of sporting events when she needed to feed, and learn to like the taste of the synthesized stuff.

The blond's adrenaline was strong though. So potent. It would have been nice to have a steady source like that. Then again, the guy was an admitted adrenaline junkie. No telling what extremes he'd go to just to—

She had just a split-second to react. She spun down in a crouch, hissing a warning, wings bursting from her shoulder blades.

He crashed into her before her wings could completely unfurl, sending them both rolling along the cracked sidewalk. Pain skittered along her nerves as something snapped in her left wing. Shock raced through her. It wasn't the male *banaranjan* attacking her, but the human, Cade. *What in the Abyss . . . ?*

Sharper pain exploded in her left shoulder. She ignored it, concentrating all her energy on landing blows on her attacker, wishing she had super-hybrid or even super-human strength. They rolled into a deserted darkened lot, Cade wrapping his hands around her neck.

She got her legs between their bodies then pushed, jettisoning him. He landed with a hard, satisfying crunch.

Stumbling to her feet, she clawed at her shoulder, pulling a syringe free. He'd stabbed her! "What the hell is this, you bastard?"

He spat out a wad of blood and a tooth, then rolled to his feet. "Call it an equalizer."

"For what?"

"Told you I was into extreme sports. Hunting demons is about as extreme a sport as you can get."

She'd fallen into a trap. She'd been warned that something like this could happen, but she'd chalked it up to another wild story about dangerous humans. Now she knew better. "You're a monster!"

He laughed. "And you're a demon. Told you we were compatible."

"Why you—!" Her vision swam, then shimmered yellow as her body fluctuated between her human and natural form. Shaking with rage and the drug he'd injected her with, she threw the syringe at Cade, hitting him square in the stomach.

He pulled the needle free with a pained grunt. "You're gonna pay for that!"

He reached for something. She didn't take the time to determine what. Instead, she launched herself at him, struggling with her disabled wing, every instinct screaming that she wrap her hand around his throat and mine his fight or flight response for very ounce of adrenaline his heart could pump out before it stopped.

A thick arm caught her about the waist in mid-strike. She howled in outrage, only to clam up swiftly as she caught the clove scent of male *banaranjan*.

"You play a most dangerous game, *banring*," the male said, arms locked about her.

"Let me go!" she snarled. "I am not new from the crèche!"

"Could have fooled me," another voice said. A female.

Rinna stared. The female was human, but the most unusual human she'd ever seen. Black braids hung past her shoulders. In the darkness Rinna couldn't tell what shade the woman's skin was, only that it was lighter than the dark vest she wore without benefit of a shirt beneath. Sinewy arms, lightly muscled, and grey cargo pants. The woman looked breakable, as if she was a dancer. But she held the human male on his knees with just one hand clamped to his forehead. A pale blue glow emanated from the woman, brightest at her hands, brighter still on the blade in her right hand. Even with her vision swimming in and out of focus, Rinna had no doubt as to the woman's identity.

Shadowchaser.

Cade groaned, then slumped over face-first. The Shadowchaser released him, shaking her hand as if to flick away grime, then turned to Rinna. "How badly are you hurt?"

"Since when is a Shadowchaser concerned with the health of her enemies?" Rinna blurted out. The male *banaranjan* squeezed her ribs in warning.

"I'm not," the Chaser noted. The light surrounding her dagger slowly faded. She shoved it back into its sheath. "Trust me, if you were my enemy, you would know it."

The male holding her spoke. "Is that him?"

"Yeah." The Chaser shook like a dog dislodging water from its coat. "You don't want to know what sort of sport he had in mind for this little one."

"And she walked right into it." The disapproval in the male's voice was palpable. If Rinna weren't injured, she would have struggled against his superior strength.

The Shadowchaser pulled gloves out of her back pocket, slipped them on. "Thanks for the head's up, Bale."

Bale? *Banaranjans* rarely gave their names, simply because clan offences ran deep and fights could break out over centuries' old slights.

She twisted around to the other *banaranjan*. He dipped his

head. "I call myself Bale," he said, deliberately leaving off his clan name. "What do you call yourself?"

"Rinna." She, too, left off her clan name.

"Rinna, that is Kira Solomon, the Shadowchaser for this area," Bale said. "Your date calls himself Cade, and he's been linked to the disappearances of quite a few hybrids in and around this town."

Rinna stared at the unconscious human male. Her body was using quite a bit of the harvested adrenaline to fight her injuries and the drug, leaving her brain sluggish. "He hunts hybrids . . . for sport?"

"He tends to prey on solo hybrids, female ones, because he thinks they're weaker," the Chaser said, nudging the human male with one booted foot. "He uses his physical assets in an effort to have some sort of liaison and if that doesn't work, he'll resort to drugs."

Rinna felt the Chaser's gaze, cool and assessing, quite like her crèche mother determining which of the *banrings* were weakest and should be put out to die of exposure. Since a *banring* didn't have wings, death was usually quick if they were eaten or slow if left to the elements. "He injected me in the shoulder," she told them. "And I think something's wrong with my wing."

"You have a tear, and one joint is dislocated," Bale explained. "The syringe probably contained something that could drop an elephant. You will need a couple of days of down time to work the tranquillizers out of your system and to heal your wing. I can take care of it for you, and give you a place to stay."

Rinna stared up at him. Their people were territorial to the point of obsession. Tribes didn't intermingle without deadly consequences. Accepting his offer might be the same as leaping out of the crèche and into the fire. "I – I don't think that's a good idea."

"Your judgment isn't worth much right now," the Chaser said bluntly. "Besides, quite a few people saw you leave the club with this guy. Laying low isn't a bad thing. Go with Bale. He can tend to your wing, and teach you a thing or two about living here."

Rinna lifted her chin. "What if I refuse?"

The Shadowchaser didn't so much as curl her lips. "You have two choices. One: you go with Bale and allow him to help you."

"What's the second?"

"I put you into a Gilead holding tank. The problem with that is that those who go in usually don't come out."

"Rinna," Bale's warning voice was a low hiss. "Did your crèche mother teach you nothing? Do not antagonize a Shadowchaser. Especially *that* Shadowchaser. Let me offer you my hospitality."

The Chaser squatted until she was at eye level with Rinna. "Why did you come here, *banaranjan*?"

"Because back home it was time to join the feud, and fight," she replied, folding her arms across her chest. She wanted to lean against Bale, appreciate his warmth and inhale the reassuring scent of cloves. But she couldn't be vulnerable, not yet, not more than she already was. "I didn't want to fight."

The Shadowchaser looked to the male. "And you, Bale. Want to tell her why you came here?"

"Fighting without good reason is a waste of time and energy. 'Just because' isn't reason enough." His voice was a low rumble against Rinna's back.

Rinna flinched when the Chaser trained her gaze Rinna's way. "Seems to me like you've got more in common with Bale than you may think."

Kira straightened. "Bale does a lot of work in the hybrid community, particularly for those without other affiliations for one reason or another. If you want to be a successful part of this community, Bale will help you. Of course, if you don't want to be a successful part of this community, you then become my problem."

The Chaser split her gaze between Rinna and the male as Bale helped Rinna to her feet. Rinna held her ground, but just barely. This Shadowchaser was younger than her. But the Chaser's heart beat a normal rhythm; no adrenaline pumped through her veins. Kira frightened Rinna more than facing her clan's wrath, and the Chaser hadn't so much as threatened her.

"I came here to live my life as far from *banaranjan* politics and intrigue as I can get. But I'm a hybrid, and I obviously have a lot to learn. I think I've experienced enough stupidity for one night. I gladly accept your offer."

Bale helped her to her feet. Rinna gritted her teeth but her wings refused to retract. It was Bale who gently folded her wings back snug against her shoulder blades, but the pain was still intense. Somehow she bore it, using the agony to drill clarity into her adrenaline- and drug-soaked skull.

"I guess I won't be driving tonight."

"I'll get you some place safe," Bale assured her, "then return for your car. On my word, you will be safe in my care. I've promised the Shadowchaser."

She looked at the Chaser. Without the blue glow suffusing her skin and the small smile curving her lips, the Chaser looked almost normal.

Rinna turned her attention to the human male. "What are you going to do with him?"

The Chaser's smile faded. "I don't take well to rogues running loose in my town. I don't care what side they're on. Your friend will be made to see the Light."

Rinna shivered. The way the Chaser said it, Rinna didn't think she meant a pleasant conversation leading to reason and understanding. She was glad she wasn't on the woman's Chase list.

"Thank you, thank you both for your help." With danger averted, her body wanted rest, despite her mind's will to the contrary. "I will find some way to repay my debt to you. I will—"

Her next words were lost to the Abyss as she slipped headlong into unconsciousness.

Rinna spent days in Bale's care, healing her wing, learning about her adoptive city, listening to Bale talk about the need for communication and understanding among the disparate hybrid communities in Atlanta, especially with a Shadowchaser and Gilead Commission watching and waiting.

She spent nights face down on a thick featherbed, her face cradled by a down pillow, careful not to disturb her healing wing. Not that much could disturb her in sleeping quarters like this. The bed linens felt soft and luxurious against her skin, quite unlike the nettles lining the *banring* crèche she'd called home for her first decade of life. Even her bed in her apartment didn't feel half as wonderful, and she'd made sure nothing about it reminded her of her old life.

Bale's place was a two-bedroom condo with floor-to-ceiling windows giving an unobscured view of the Midtown Atlanta skyline. When he wasn't helping hybrids, he worked as a sports agent and talent scout, a gig that enabled the male *banaranjan* to get his adrenaline fix and make a living.

The more she listened to Bale, the more star-struck she became. He was unlike any *banaranjan* she'd ever known, male or female. It was easy to give her imagination free rein, to envision founding a new clan with him, a clan that didn't make a habit of pursuing conflict just because storm clouds filled the air.

Even without the thought of establishing a new clan here in Atlanta, Rinna wanted to experience Bale in all his glory. Banaranjans coupled with the strongest or the fastest partner during a mating flight in order to produce offspring with the greatest chance of survival. Love and other tender emotions were aberrations, and not necessary to producing healthy young.

Rinna had left her clan and in doing so, had left old beliefs and ways behind. She was free to explore her tender feelings. Free to act on them.

Unfortunately, Bale didn't seem to share her sentiment. He was a male in his prime, strong, fierce, well-formed. He could have his pick of female *banaranjans* if he wanted. Perhaps he already did, even without sharing his clan affiliation.

"Did you hear me, Rinna?"

She shook herself out of her reverie. She had perched atop one of the red leather barstools that lined the kitchen counter while Bale examined her wing. "I'm sorry. Too busy thinking. What did you say?"

She could feel him manipulate the wing, testing the spread, the membranes, each joint, the touch of his fingers sure and warm. "I said it looks like your wing has healed up nicely. Can you fold it down?"

Rinna concentrated, calling her magic to fold her wings snug, then curl them in to her shoulder blades, hiding them beneath her human glamour. She spun on the barstool until she faced him. "It didn't hurt. Thank you!" Impulsively, she threw her arms about his shoulders.

He stepped into the embrace, meaning her thighs flanked his own. "You're welcome," he said, his voice gravelly. "You'll be night flying in no time."

She drew back enough so that she could whisper in his ear. "I haven't been night flying before. Don't suppose you'd be interested in taking me?"

He drew back further, to stare into her eyes. "Surely you've been . . . ?"

"With human males, yes," she answered. "Never night flying with a *banaranjan* male, though."

Thunder chose that moment to rumble over the building, sending the expansive windows vibrating as rain began to pelt the glass. "It's going to be a hell of a storm," he told her, yellow eyes sparking. "Care to fly with me?"

Flying in the midst of a storm was to *banaranjans* like catnip to cats. With Bale, it would be more than just flying. It would be much more. She saw the clear intent in his eyes and thrilled at the prospect.

But if her wings couldn't support her, couldn't take the force of diving and banking, she'd be all but useless. "Do you think my wing will be all right?"

"Don't worry." He held out a hand to her. "I'll catch you if you fall."

He led her over to the balcony. Fifteen storeys up gave a decent view of Midtown Atlanta, the Fox Theatre south of them with its marquee like a beacon in the storm. This time of night, in a storm like this, few humans would be about. Few hybrids would venture into the rain, lightning and potential hail. It was a perfect time to be a *banaranjan*, a perfect night to go flying.

Grinning with the joy of being alive, she quickly stripped, her skin tingling as electricity gathered in the blue-black clouds. She dropped her glamour next, magic running over her like raindrops, changing her skin from peach to copper satin. Her wings unfurled, supple leather, filling the balcony. "Why don't you try and catch me now, Bale?" she dared him, then leapt out into the night.

His laughter rang out behind her, trilling along her nerves as she reached for the sky. Her wings obeyed the involuntary command, beating huge gusts of air to thrust her skyward. Blue-white lightning arced overhead, fat drops of rain biting into her skin. Adrenaline flooded her system, giving her body a slight glow. Bale was out there somewhere, stalking her, waiting for the right moment to pounce.

As soon as she thought it, he was there, magnificently elemental and male. Her breath caught as he banked in front of her, courting her with his flying prowess. She appreciated the effort, but she'd wanted him for days. Still, it wouldn't hurt to make him work for it.

She climbed higher, up into the storm clouds. He followed, she could sense it, feel it, see the adrenaline glow of his body through the clouds and rain and lightning.

Her heart thumped as he caught her, arms tightening about her. Instinctively she thrust her arms around his neck and folded her wings. His eyes burned brilliant yellow, power radiating from him. She wrapped her legs around his waist.

She threw back her head as he entered her, sensations pummelling her as lightning rolled through them and around them; wild, driving, a tumult of power and pleasure as Bale drove them higher and higher. Suddenly they broke through the storm, to a place where everything slowed. They hovered there at the edge of the earth for a couple of wingbeats, hearts pounding, pleasure peaking, souls bonding. She touched his cheek, wonder and something more fragile blossoming.

Then Bale folded his wings and dived down, back down, back into the chaos, the frenzy. Wind screamed past them as they fell, causing them to spin with the force and speed of their dive. Rinna shrieked as pleasure exploded through her body, launching spikes of lightning. Bale joined her a moment later, thunder booming with their ecstasy.

The snap of Bale's wings opening was louder than a thunderclap. They jerked upright, his wings beating fiercely in a fight against gravity. She realized then how far they'd fallen in their pursuit of pleasure as Bale flew *up* to reach his balcony.

She slid away from him, and then missed him immediately, still shaking and lightheaded from the experience. He folded his wings away, then wrapped a large palm around the back of her neck and pulled her closer for a kiss, their first kiss. They stood there, kissing, steam rising from their bodies as the ferocity of the storm and their passion subsided.

They broke apart, fighting to regain their breath. "That was wonderful," Rinna whispered. "Thank you."

"No, thank you, Rinna." He squeezed her, then turned to slide open the balcony door. "By the wings of Keterach, that was an amazing flight!" He headed into the darkness of the main room.

Rinna froze in shock. *Keterach*. Her clan's most-hated enemy. *Banaranjans* preferred war to peace on the best of occasions. With Shadowchasers and the Gilead Commission now policing the preternatural community, her race had long ago turned the love of battle into the art of grudge-holding, taking to thunderous skies to settle disputes under cover of storms.

Sweet Darkness, she had taken to the skies with her mortal enemy! Worse, she had mated with him. If her clan found out, she would be worse than dead.

Did he know her clan affiliation? Surely not, or he wouldn't have stepped in to save her. Then again, he had been careful to not give his clan name when they first met. Maybe he already knew. Maybe healing her and taking her out into the night was all part of some sort of plot to gain leverage over her, or make sure she could never rejoin her clan again.

"Rinna?" Bale came back for her. "Is something wrong?"

"No," she lied. "I'm just worn out. I could really use some sleep."

He scooped her up. "Sleep, yes. Then we'll reenact our flight without the pyrotechnics. Then talk."

Rinna bit her lip. She wanted this, wanted Bale with the same intensity that she'd wanted to escape her clan. She fought a swell of panic. Somehow she had to make it through, then find time to think. No matter what, she had to get away from Bale, even if it was a mistake. Because if it wasn't a mistake, her life was in danger.

* * * *

"Rinna?"

She snapped out of her reverie, raising her head as a man approached the table. He looked the part of a successful human business man, dressed for the mild late spring weather in dark khakis and a burgundy-coloured dress shirt.

"Bale." She immediately covered her eyes with her palms, a traditional *banaranjan* greeting to another of higher rank, skill, power or age.

"That's not necessary, Rinna."

"Perhaps not to you," she replied, lowering her hands, "but necessary to me. Will you join me?"

He took the chair opposite hers, facing the entrance. He looked good, still fit and in his prime, dark hair curling thickly about his ears, brows like two wide slashes above dark brown eyes lit with flecks of otherness yellow, the strong chin, stronger nose. Even his mouth hinted at his power. Taken separately each feature could be overwhelming, but Bale's features fit him perfectly. A strong, striking face, the face of a man secure in his abilities.

She remembered his eyes the most. Those eyes had regarded her with gentleness, with compassion, with consternation, and then with intimate heat. Now, those eyes stared at her with cool civility, no trace of the passion that had surprised and disturbed them both two years ago.

Bale broke the awkward silence. "Chaser Solomon called me, said that you wanted to see me."

"Yes."

"You know you didn't have to go through the Chaser to meet with me," he admonished. "She's got enough to deal with right now."

Rinna stared down at the table, her heart sinking. Not that she'd thought Bale would wrap his wings around her and lift her off the floor in a *banaranjan* lover's embrace, but this cool distance was disconcerting and disheartening.

"I thought if the request came from the Shadowchaser and not from me, that you would be more inclined to come," she said. "Chaser Solomon didn't seem to mind."

"Either way, I am here." He leaned back in his chair. "What do you wish to talk about?"

The rehearsed words fled her mind. "I wanted to thank you again, for what you did for me two years ago."

He waved a hand. "You've already thanked me for that. There's no need to rehash it."

She shook her head. "I don't mean just saving me from the

hunter," she said softly. "Though that was huge. You helped me a great deal that night. And afterwards."

He nodded. "I did. Then you left."

"I had a valid reason."

"Yeah." He sat back. "The classic 'I-need-to-find-myself' letter that humans have used for centuries. You didn't have to do that, Rinna. I would have helped you."

"You helped me enough. I needed to help myself. I was almost taken out by a human thrill killer, I was mouthy with a Shadowchaser, and I ran away from you – twice." She sighed. "I was childish. Thinking that I could survive the way I was back then proved it."

"But you have survived," Bale pointed out. "You're here now." He paused. "Why are you here?"

"To ask you for another chance." She leaned forward. "I actually took some training while I was away. Studying for a psychology degree. I know the classes are geared to human psychology, but I've been thinking of how to customize some of the information for the hybrid community. In particular, to displaced, outcast or lone hybrids who need a sense of belonging."

She lowered her gaze again. "Not having a place to belong, a group to belong to, can be very isolating for those of us used to being part of clan dynamics."

He nodded. "It can make us make mistakes, do things we deeply regret later."

"Yeah." Did he have regrets? She fiddled with her coffee cup, struggled gamely on. "There can also be issues for hybrids used to being loners, issues with being able to trust others in times of need. Even simple things like coordinating knowledge of threats against us from within and without can be beneficial."

She reached for her messenger bag, pulled out a thick notebook in a binder. "I have some other suggestions, just ideas for outreach and stuff like that. Not anything particularly earth-shattering or radical, but I think it might be good for those of us who don't want to be on the wrong end of the Shadowchaser's blade." She slid her binder to him.

He pulled the notebook closer, then opened it. Rinna watched him as he flipped through the sections. "Why did you do all of this?"

"I want to work with you to help the hybrid community here. I don't want what nearly happened to me to happen to someone else because of fear or ignorance."

She took a deep breath, then added, "And I hope it's a way of showing I can be of value to you."

"You are of value to me, Rinna," he finally said, closing the book. "Obviously I didn't do a good job of showing you that."

"You did, but I wasn't sure of what I felt or what you felt. Then I discovered that you descend from Keterach. I descend from Hetache. It's an enmity that goes back centuries, so far that no one knows the cause. All I know is that we're supposed to be mortal enemies."

"Duels to the death on sight, the nursery rhymes used to say." His gaze raked over her. "Do you want to fight me now, Rinna?"

"No. A duel to the death between two *banaranjans* would level most of Virginia-Highlands."

"Not to mention a fight like that would come to the Shadowchaser's notice."

"Yeah." She shuddered. "I'd really rather not be on her bad side if I can help it."

"I seem to recall you saying that the reason you came to Atlanta was because you didn't want to fight," he said then. "My reasoning was, and still is, the same." He sighed. "I know how hard it is to be alone, to try to find a place different from what you've been taught all you life. Seeing you, a lone female, triggered the clan instinct in me. When you left with that human male, I was angry. Seriously angry. Only the DMZ's protective shielding prevented me from confronting you in the club. And the Chaser stopped me from immediately going after you when you left."

He spread his hands. "Luckily, my anger turned to concern when I realized who the human was. Call it the clan instinct or male arrogance, I don't know. But I only knew that I had to take you from him. After the danger passed and you healed, I couldn't shake the instinct or desire, or whatever, to make you mine."

"Really?" She hadn't known. "You did a good job of keeping that to yourself."

"To be blunt, I did a piss-poor job of suppressing it. Which is why I'm glad you left like you did."

"You are?"

He nodded. "I couldn't tell if I wanted you because you're Rinna or because you're a lone *banaranjan* female. I also wasn't sure if your attraction to me was an after-effect of your ordeal with the hunter or because you were interested in me. I would have ignored those doubts for as long as possible if it kept you with me. Eventually though, I think it would have soured every-thing. And I didn't want to sour anything between us."

"Bale."

"So I'm glad you left. You had things to learn about yourself, and I had things to learn about myself."

"What did you learn?" She could barely get the question out.

Dark brown eyes flared yellow as they bored into hers. "I learned that I want you even more now than I did two years ago."

If she'd had her wings out, they would have shivered with pleasure. "I was afraid you'd be angry, angry enough to refuse me. We are grudge-holders, you know."

"I've no grudge against you." He reached out, lacing their fingers together. "I think we've already proved that we're not like other *banaranjans*."

"We're most definitely not." She smiled.

Bale returned her smile. "Then why don't we start over? Have a little breakfast here at the Majestic and talk about your ideas, and where we go from here?"

"I'd like that, but I don't think we have to start over *completely*. For instance, I really enjoyed that night-flying manoeuvre."

"Good." Heat crept into his gaze. "Because I plan on doing a lot of night-flying with you."

"Sam!" Rinna called. "We need to order. Something tells me I'm going to need some energy!"

Answer The Wicked
A Story of the Shadow Guard

Kim Lenox

Late afternoon, London, 1883

"I shall have a visitor today," Mr Rathburn quietly announced.

Malise Bristol turned from the upper drawer of the walnut clothes press, where she arranged her elderly patient's nightshirts. One of the hospital's perpetually out-of-breath, red-faced laundresses had delivered them only moments before. The linen was still warm to the touch.

Mr Rathburn's quietly spoken words had startled her – startled her because in the nearly two years she had been assigned as his personal nurse at Winterview, he had never once received a visitor. The other residential patients of the exclusive, elegantly appointed home for the aged often had visitors, even if only barristers with papers to be signed or family members with stylish hats in hand, begging for an increase in their allowances.

"A visitor, sir?" she enquired, closing the drawer.

He sat in his wheelchair peering out the window, which was framed by vertical swathes of burgundy silk. In the dim afternoon light, the silk appeared almost black in contrast to the grey sky on the other side of the pane. He appeared gaunt today. Frailer than in days before, and nearly swallowed by his green silk dressing robe.

"Indeed," he answered, offering nothing more in the way of explanation.

"A member of your family?" she enquired hopefully. Though neither of them was an excessive conversationalist by nature, she had grown very fond of Mr Rathburn and wanted him to have a loving family. Only why wouldn't they have made an appearance before now? *Because*, her mind supplied, *they were obviously a terrible, useless lot.*

"No, not family," he answered evenly, sounding not the least bit disappointed.

"Business?"

"Thank God, no."

"A friend then," she prodded gently.

He was quiet for a long moment. "I suppose."

Malise's heart warmed with a vision of two elderly gentlemen, whiling away the remainder of the afternoon reminiscing about younger days. A visit from a friend would do Mr Rathburn good. She should not be his only companion in his final days.

Even from her perspective, as his nurse, a visitor would be a welcome distraction. Their days together followed a rather monotonous pattern, each day nearly identical to one before.

First, there was breakfast, then she would push Mr Rathburn in his chair for a walk about the grounds. If weather did not allow for such an excursion, they walked the halls instead. Next, the elderly gentleman would spend a few quiet hours squinting through his brass-rimmed spectacles at one of his many old books. Sometimes he would ask her, ever so politely, to read to him. Then it was time for luncheon and another walk. Afterwards, she would tidy his suite or draw in the sketchbook he had given her for Christmas while he wrote in silent concentration in one of his many leather-bound journals. Then, after a light repast of tea and whatever staid culinary selection the kitchen sent up, the male attendants would come and assist him into bed and she would retire to her tiny room in the hospital attic – except for Saturday evenings when she took the train into Chelsea. Sundays were her day off.

She made no complaints about the quiet predictability of their time spent together. Her life before coming to Winterview had been more eventful than she cared to remember.

Still, admittedly, she was more than a little curious about her elderly patient's visitor. Anson Rathburn was an elegant, dapper old gentleman. His belongings – an exotic mélange of carved masks, primitive weaponry and foreign texts – suggested a life of adventure. There were also a few tintypes, some showing a smiling, handsome and young Anson Rathburn. But strangely, he had never spoken of his life before Winterview. She, as his hired nurse, had never presumed to press too invasively for details.

A sudden question occurred. How did Mr Rathburn know to expect a visitor? He had received no letter. No telegraph.

It was then she realized he did not simply look out the window now, at nothing in particular. His gaze was fixed on something there.

She crossed the room to stand beside him. Drops tapped against and drizzled down the panes, offering a distorted view of the grounds. The early spring rain had cleared the rolling, green lawn of patients, staff and guests, save for—

Stone benches lined Winterview's central drive, and upon the furthest of these, nearly concealed by a thick canopy of trees, sat a dark-clad figure. The man wore a long raincoat and a wide-brimmed Western style hat that concealed most of his face, everything but a stalwart jaw and pursed lips. One leg was bent at the knee, its foot planted against the ground, while the other leg jutted straight on to the path before him. His hands rested against his thighs, completing a pose of pensive reluctance. Though difficult to tell much more from such a distance, she perceived a broad, well-turned pair of shoulders and fitted trousers over long, athletic legs.

"Is that your visitor, sir?" she asked, a bit breathlessly.

"It is."

Excitement shot through her. Why? She couldn't exactly say, other than that the "old friend" she'd imagined in her mind was very different than the apparently much younger man sitting in the rain outside.

"Would you like me to go down and invite him inside?"

Mr Rathburn smiled. "Not just yet."

His answer relieved Malise. She supposed he was correct, and that his friend would come inside from the rain whenever he decided to do so.

And yet a half hour later, Mr Rathburn's visitor had still not seen fit to call. He had, however, over time, moved from one bench to the next so that he narrowed the distance between himself and the front steps. Malise knew this to be so because she had passed by the window to steal a peek at least a half dozen times. Astoundingly, Mr Rathburn appeared to have forgotten all about him. He sat in his wheelchair at his desk, quietly reading. Another quarter of an hour passed before he lifted his blue-eyed gaze from the page. His eyes sparkled with humour.

"I do believe he must be soaked through by now. What do you say, Nurse Bristol?"

"That must certainly be true, Mr Rathburn."

"Please do invite him up."

"Yes, sir."

Malise crossed the carpet, smoothing the folds of her white nurse's apron, and turned the knob. The colder air in the hallway chilled her skin.

"Nurse Bristol?" he called.

"Yes, sir?" She paused, turning back.

"Don't forget the umbrella." He peered at her over his spectacles. "And his name is St Vinet."

"Mr St Vinet," Malise repeated, nodding. She took up the umbrella from the stand, and pulled the door closed behind her.

In the hallway, she glanced into the gilt-framed mirror, and caught a glimpse of herself: a brown widow's peak, visible from beneath the centre fold of her white nurse's cap; brown eyes, and a small, pale face. Invisible. She had long ago become invisible. It was why she didn't pause for more than a glance, or to pinch her cheeks or smooth her hair. She had learned her lesson. A handsome man who charmed with smiles and sweet words was just as likely a monster as a Prince Charming. It was why she preferred the sanctuary of this place and the company of men too old and infirm to do her harm.

Winterview had once been a private residence and did not feel like a "hospital" at all. Though the pointed arches and exaggerated buttresses proclaimed it to be a gothic villa in style, certain modernizations had been made for the comfort of the wealthy, aged residents. One such modernization was the electricity and another was the lift. A metallic rattle and hum came from inside the shaft, indicating the elevator was in-use, so rather than wait, she descended down three flights to the ground floor. Here, a number of small sitting areas graced the far corners of an expansive tiled floor and a fire burned on opposite ends of the space, in two matched fireplaces. Finches chirped in large cages. A few residents and visitors occupied the lobby. A number of new nurses had been hired of late. Several of them followed dutifully behind Nurse Henry, the newly hired Head Nurse, making their way toward the kitchens. Her crisply issued instructions echoed in the cavernous space. Only at Winterview a few weeks, she'd already made her mark as a strict taskmistress. She expected perfection from her staff, and strict adherence to all rules and regulations. So far, Malise had been fortunate enough not to draw Nurse Henry's attention or ire.

Nurse Alice, a round-faced woman nearly a foot shorter than Malise, carried a covered silver tray towards the stairs. Just two weeks before, she and Alice had become roommates, sharing a boarding house room in Chelsea on their nights off.

"Where are you going in that rain, Nurse Bristol?"

"Just outside to the drive. Mr Rathburn has a visitor."

The young maid smiled. "Mr Rathburn? A visitor? Well that's something, isn't it? Good for him, I say. See you at the train station for the ride in." Her smile stretched into a grin. "Tick tock, it won't be long now. We're almost free of this place, at least for a day."

"Yes, I shall see you there."

At the double doors, Malise paused. Mr St Vinet, the mysterious visitor would be on the other side. She assumed a pleasant smile and pushed through the doors –

The afternoon light dimmed.

Intense warmth touched her skin. She gasped in confusion. For a moment, it seemed a thousand dark wings fluttered around her, battering her, blinding her in shadows.

In the next breath, the sensation was gone, moved past her. She stood on the front steps, gasping, the umbrella gripped in her hand. Rain fell from the sky at a hard slant, splattering against her skirt and apron. She spun round to see what had pushed past her, fully expecting to see that dark flock of birds, but saw nothing.

Perhaps she had simply grown faint. She could think of no other explanation for the sensation of heat, weight and darkness that had passed over her so quickly, and then disappeared. Certainly that was it – a simple change of temperature, the shock of going from a warm hospital out into the brisk cold. Only she'd never been one to grow light-headed over such minor things, nor did she lace her corset too tightly, as some of the other nurses certainly did.

Water sluiced off the umbrella. Ah, Mr St Vinet.

She peered down the long drive. He was nowhere to be seen. She scanned the grounds, her heart slowly sinking into the pit of her stomach. Clearly he'd been reluctant to come inside and see Mr Rathburn, but to have simply departed without explanation? She prayed her gentle patient would not be terribly disappointed. She understood disappointment. The soul-deep, life changing sort. She wished the feeling on no one.

Inside, she climbed the stairs and made her way back to the uppermost floor. Weighted by regret, she turned the knob and reentered Mr Rathburn's rooms. Voices touched her ears.

"Oh—" The exclamation escaped her mouth before she could stop it.

Mr Rathburn sat in his wheelchair in the small sitting area. His visitor, Mr St Vinet, sat in the chair opposite him, his hat on his lap. He had dark brown hair, worn just long enough to curl behind his ears. Raindrops glistened on his shoulders and dripped off the edge of his coat on to the carpet. Even seated, he towered over Mr Rathburn. She read agitation, even anger, in the rigid line of his shoulders, and the sharp downward turn of his lips. He glanced at her with the irritated expression of one confronting an unwanted intruder.

Mr Rathburn did not appear the least bit troubled by his guest's demeanour. "Nurse Bristol, please be introduced to Mr St Vinet."

She was staff. Truly just a servant. Not even a real nurse with formal medical training. A simple companion. As such, she had not anticipated a formal introduction. She half-curtseyed. "Good afternoon, sir."

"Pleased to make your acquaintance, Nurse Bristol," St Vinet murmured, barely offering her a glance. But then his chin halted, and his eyes narrowed and he *did* look at her, and piercingly so, as if reading her every feature.

Heat crept up her neck and flooded her face.

He looked sharply away.

She returned the umbrella to its stand, and subdued the impulse to back out of the room and only return when she was sure Mr St Vinet had departed. It was his direct stare. Something in his eyes. It was almost as if he had reached out and touched her. For someone who had not been touched in a very long time, her physical and emotional reaction was unexpectedly profound.

She reminded herself of her position and her purpose in the room. "Sir, ought I to prepare tea?"

She did not return her glance to Mr St Vinet but felt the pinpoint heat of his gaze on her.

Mr Rathburn answered, "Thank you, Nurse Bristol, tea would be most welcome."

A copper kettle warmed on the narrow metal shelf of the wall stove. The men spoke, but they kept their voices low, so their words remained unintelligible to her ears. Within minutes, she'd prepared the tea tray and returned to serve them.

"How could I not come?" St Vinet hissed, his jaw and mouth tensing even more than before. "You summoned me. I have never been one to deny my duty."

Malise kept her expression bland as she lowered the tray to the marbled-topped table between them. A leather case sat on the carpet next to Mr St Vinet's booted foot. It was the sort a doctor might carry on a house visit.

"Duty?" Rathburn steepled his fingertips and peered, half-lidded, at his younger companion. "You warm my soul with such heartfelt sentiments. You could have come before, you know, without my summoning you. Why did you not?"

A dry laugh rattled from St Vinet's throat. "To see you like this? You *know* how I feel about *this*." He pointed at Rathburn, zig-zagging his finger in agitation. "You, being pushed around in that damn chair, by a damn nursemaid, for God's sake. And this place," he spat. "It's like a coffin. Your coffin. And you expect me to come and watch as you die before my very eyes, all because of *her*—"

Malise's temper flared protectively, and she glared at St Vinet, not caring that he was a gentleman and she only the hired help.

Leaning forward to give him his cup of tea, she whispered, "Mind your manners, sir."

His gaze, as grey as gunmetal, lifted to hers, and locked. Simmered. His cheeks were ruddy with emotion.

"What was that, Miss Bristol?" asked Mr Rathburn of her back.

A long moment of silence passed.

"No, Nurse Bristol," murmured St Vinet, his nostrils flared, and his pupils dilated. "I require no sugar or cream. Thank you."

Mr Rathburn interjected, "Miss Bristol, I've only just now realized the clock on the mantle says four-thirty, which I know very well is usually the time you leave for your day off. I have no wish to intrude upon your personal time. Please go on and do enjoy yourself."

She poured his cup of tea and made sure he had a firm hold on the saucer before releasing it to him. "Are you certain, sir? I don't mind staying."

"As always, you have done more than your job requires and this old man is grateful for that. I've left coins for a hansom cab in the dish by the door."

"Mr Rathburn, you oughtn't—"

He raised his hand and shook his head. "I don't like the idea of you walking in the rain."

St Vinet listened to them silently, his hands curled into fists on his thighs.

Though she was curious to see what else would pass between the two men, she realized she had no good excuse to remain.

"Thank you, sir." She took up her coat and bag, and the coins from the dish, and let herself out. "I shall see you Monday morning then."

In the hallway, she buttoned her coat. She removed her nurse's cap and replaced it with the small taffeta and straw bonnet she kept in her reticule. A narrow door led to the service stairs, and she descended to the ground floor, emerging into another narrow hall. The staff physicians kept their offices here, as well as the administrators of the facility.

"*Nurse Bristol.*"

It was Head Nurse Henry.

"Yes, Nurse Henry."

"Please step inside my office."

Malise did so, holding her reticule tight against her ribs. "Would you prefer that I sit?"

Nurse Henry's eyebrows had been drawn on her forehead in brown grease pencil. The twin arcs crept up her forehead. She shrugged, and stated briskly, "Sit or stand, your choice makes no difference to me. What I have to say will not take long, so I will not dally with empty words. Plain and simple: your employment has been terminated."

The word echoed in Malise's head.

"Terminated?" she whispered.

"Don't make me repeat myself. You know what that word means."

Her chest felt as if a boulder had been dropped upon it. Barely able to breathe, she blinked through tears. "Yes, of course I do, but why?"

"Mr Rathburn has insisted upon it."

Mr Rathburn had insisted on her termination? She had come to trust her elderly patient. This place had become her haven.

"Are there no other positions available here in the hospital?"

"No."

"I would even consider a housekeeping position."

Nurse Henry's eyes narrowed to slits. "To keep you here after a valued patient has requested you be released would be awkward, to say the least. Do you have all your belongings with you?"

Malise looked down at herself. A dress, shoes, coat and a reticule. "Yes."

Nurse Henry slid an envelope across the desk. "You'll find a week's severance pay inside. That is all. You may go."

Numbly, Malise left by the service door at the back of the hospital. She'd followed the rules. Done everything she was supposed to do. She'd stayed invisible. How could this have happened? Where would she go? She had only enough saved earnings to stay in the boarding house for three, perhaps four days. Crossing her arms over her chest, she shivered and walked beneath the metal gate, into the street. A hansom sped past, but she did not hail it. She would not squander the coins given to her by Mr Rathburn, not now when every shilling meant survival. Why would he have done something so thoughtful, such as give her coins for a hansom, when he knew she would never return? Guilt, perhaps? In her mind, that explanation made no sense. None of this made sense. She looked back upon the stone façade of the hospital, to his bay window. No face peered down at her, only the faint glow of lamplight.

A horse pulling a large open wagon rattled into view. Crowded with occupants, the vehicle radiated with laughter and song.

"Stop! Driver, stop!" shouted a woman's voice. The horse and wagon veered toward the curb, nearly barrelling over Malise. "Nurse Bristol!"

A score of boisterous male and female voices mimicked the original caller by shouting her name. Another time, she would have smiled at their good humour but tonight their attentions left her feeling exposed. She perceived the dark glimmer of more than one bottle being passed to and fro inside. A familiar face emerged from all the others – Nurse Alice. She grasped the side rail of the wagon, and hoisted herself half-over, pink-cheeked and smiling. The scarlet roses on her straw hat had come unfastened and dangled near her left ear. Her eyes were bright. Drunkenly bright.

"I worried when I did not see you at the station. You're only just now getting away?"

Malise now saw that several of the newly hired nurses were passengers in the wagon as well. With such an audience, she couldn't bring herself to share her unfortunate news. Not just yet. Instead, she forced a smile. "I had to stay a bit late."

Alice tsked. "They'll work us to death if we let them. Come on. Get in. There will be no train t'night. Something about the tracks and emergency repairs. Everyone pitched in a few coins for the wagon."

Malise hesitated. Though she was in no mood to climb into a wagon full of raucous strangers, the distance to Chelsea was too far for her to undertake on foot. Returning to the hospital was out of the question. Coldness seeped through her coat and into her bones. Fog hovered above the surface of the roadway.

Nurse Alice held up a dark brown bottle, and grinned. "Come on, it'll be fun."

"The woman says ta' get in!" one of the young men shouted.

"We're freezin' our arses off," hollered another.

Numbly, Malise nodded and allowed herself to be pulled inside.

Nightfall

"He's here, St Vinet."

Dominic did not pretend for even a moment not to know of whom Anson, the man who had once been his mentor and closest friend, spoke. Everything inside him tensed.

"How do you know?"

"The same as before. When night comes, I hear his laughter. He taunts me. Soon, he will come for me, just like he did for her."

It no longer mattered what differences had come between them four decades before. The Seether had come out of hiding, as they had always suspected he would. A myriad of visions from the past filled his mind. Terror. Violence. Blood.

He responded with vehemence. "I will stop him."

"I have become an old man—"

"Truly? I hadn't noticed," he responded snappishly.

Rathburn's fists curled. "I can't help but believe he's been out there waiting and watching all along, until I grew so old and infirm that I could no longer defend myself." He whispered, "Back then, it was my greatest wish to Reclaim the Seether, to be the one to dispatch him to Tartarus where he belongs."

Inside Dominic's chest, the old anger surged anew. "You should have thought of that before you so foolishly relinquished your immortality for the love of a mortal woman – a woman the Seether promptly murdered, just to show you he could."

"Speak no more of it!" shouted Rathburn, clasping his hands to his face. More softly, he repeated. "Speak no more of it, please."

"How long has he been here? How close is he?"

Rathburn shook his head resignedly. "I no longer have the instincts or the powers to know. That is why you must go into the city and find him. He will be there, you know. Amidst the people of the streets and alleyways. Growing stronger from the misery and wickedness of others, as all Transcending souls do."

St Vinet nodded. "Tonight."

"Did you bring all that I requested from the Inner Realm?"

Once Rathburn became a mortal, he could no longer return into the protected Inner Realm of the Amaranthine immortals. Dominic touched the case. "I did."

"Even the vial of Demeter's tears?"

"She nearly scalped me for taking them, but yes, everything is here."

"Good." Rathburn slid a folded slip of paper across the table, past their now-tepid cups of tea. "Here are the formulas. You must mix everything precisely. My hands, they shake . . ."

St Vinet read carefully. "This one, with mud from the deepest crevice of the river Styx—"

"Is to Reclaim the Seether. The other, made with Demeter's tears, is to reverse the effect on any innocents he has claimed."

An hour later, and the numerous vials had been emptied, measured and mixed and resealed into slender glass ampoules. Dominic tucked most of them into the breast pocket of his overcoat but one remained on the table beside Anson. Just in case . . . just in case the Seether came to Winterview. Dominic lowered his hat on to his head. Shadow slashed across his eyes.

He pondered the door, but decided on the window. Standing there, he unlatched the lock, and turned to Anson. "Until tomorrow."

"Dominic . . . we were the best of friends once."

"Once." St Vinet clenched his teeth. But his anger faltered. "*Still.*"

"I must elicit one additional promise from you."

"Tell me then."

"The girl . . . my nurse. I fear that because of my fondness for her, she may become a target, much as my darling Lavinia did."

St Vinet shrugged, attempting nonchalance. Nurse Bristol. There was something about her that, in the moment he had looked into her eyes, had stolen his breath. A rare occurrence, that. Clearly she attempted to hide her beauty, but unfortunately, he saw beyond the staid nurse's uniform and cap, to the jewel which lay beneath. Intriguing. Alluring. He'd instantly wanted more of her, mind, body and soul. But she was a mortal woman, and no good thing could come from falling into a delirium of passion with one such as her.

Rathburn clasped his eyes shut. "I don't wish for Nurse Bristol to die the same death. I do not know where she goes on these nights, but grasp hold of her *trace*. Follow her. Find her. Watch over her this night and the next, until this thing is finished. Until I can be certain of her safety, how can I ever pass from this life in peace?"

Dominic did not answer, but he nodded. With his next breath, he changed. Transformed.

In shadow, he descended the outer stone wall of the hospital. Almost instantly, he discovered Nurse Bristol's *trace* threaded upon the cool air, as rich, sweet and seductive as currant wine.

She ought not to have drunk of the wine. She'd taken only a few sips, but the sweet stuff already affected her. The night spun about Malise, disorienting her. Disjointed visions flashed through the dark, of yellow-orange gaslight, pale faces and tall buildings. The young man beside her had already tried to kiss her three times but she'd planted her hand against his chest and shoved him away. He had laughed good-naturedly and turned his attentions to Alice, and had been much more successful there. She knew not how long the wagon bounced and creaked and jerked along.

At last the wheels jerked to a stop.

"Come on," said Alice. "The driver says we get off here."

They climbed down into the midst of a crowd. Unsteady on her feet, Malise closed her eyes until the spinning stopped. Opening them again, she walked alongside Alice. The three other nurses followed along behind. In the wagon Malise had learned they had all taken rooms at the same boarding house as she and Alice. People danced in the street – young, bright-eyed women with their hair streaming free, and smiling men with their shirts half unbuttoned. There were musicians and magicians. Tom-tom drums thudded and tambourines jangled. The aromas of fresh cakes and roasted nuts scented the air.

"Oh, it's a street festival," gushed Alice, clapping her hands. "Let's see what's about."

Malise wanted to be free. To dance like those other young women, and laugh and flirt. Not so long ago, she had been like that. Happy and carefree. She'd married young, a clever young doctor in her small fishing village in Scotland. He'd been handsome and charming, but soon after they were wed, she'd learned of his penchant for violence and sexual terror. Her widowed father, the local schoolmaster, had refused her pleas to return home. He was proud to have a doctor in the family – his status had been elevated in the community. One night, bloodied and humiliated, she'd escaped as her husband slept. She'd begged rides on farmers' wagons, and stowed away on a train, eventually arriving in London. Her limited knowledge of medicine, gained in the short time living with the monster she called her husband, had been enough to get her the job at Winterview, the first place at which she'd enquired after getting off the train at the outskirts of London. Now, with no references, she had no idea where she would find another position, and quickly enough to save herself from destitution. In this moment she was in no mood for revelry.

She touched her friend's shoulder. "Alice, you enjoy the entertainments with the others. I think I'll go on to the room."

"Go to the room?" Alice's eyes widened. "It's early still. Oh, Malise, please," she begged. "Please stay. I don't know the other girls as well as I know you."

Malise relented, allowing Alice to weave her arm into the crook of her own, and lead her into the thick of the crowd.

"Everyone's going this way," said Alice.

Two large metal barrels bracketed either side of an alleyway, rusted sides cut into faces, like jack-o'-lanterns. Flames inside them illuminated their triangular eyes and mouths, lined with jagged teeth. Voices in the crowd proclaimed—

Magician.

They passed between the barrels. For a moment, utter darkness consumed them as if they spiralled without foothold into a bottomless crevice. But then light burned in the distance . . . embers in the night. Torchlight.

A small stage had been set up with wooden boards and behind this was parked a large enclosed wagon, painted in colours of turquoise and orange. On the side were painted the words,

"S. E. Ether & Son" as well as a placard advertising liniments, healing spirits and apothecary services. Several young women, with long hair, tightly laced bodices and saucy smiles bustled in and out of the wagon, accepting coins from the crowd in exchange for an assortment of green and brown bottles and small pouches.

But at the centre of the stage, a tall man in a green velvet great-coat and tall stovepipe hat paced the centre boards. Long, blond hair fell in waves over his shoulders, in shocking, almost naptha-bright contrast to the velvet. With his bright green eyes and high cheekbones, he boasted a lithe, cat-like male beauty.

He moved with his arms extended out to his sides, "—even now, my assistants are filling your orders for our miraculous healing elixirs." Fervency burned in his eyes. "For those of you who have not yet decided, *believe*. I beg you to believe. Just one sip of our carefully formulated potion will ease the persistent pain in your intestines and repair the unsteady beat of your heart. Yes. Yes. Come forward good sir."

The crowd pushed forward.

"Oh, what's that?" the man shouted, cupping a slender hand at his ear, and looking towards the wagon. "My assistant tells me it's time for another of our entertainments."

A roar of applause and verbal encouragements sounded all around Malise.

Alice exclaimed, "Let's get closer to the stage where we can see."

With her arm still through Malise's, she pulled her forward. They lost the other nurses somewhere in the press of bodies. Soon, they stood at the edge of the stage. Others, also trying to get closer, pushed and elbowed them from the side and from behind.

"All I need is another pretty girl to do the honours. This time, instead of one of my assistants, let us call someone out of the crowd." The tall blond man surveyed the multitude.

Young women surged forward, raising their hands to him. "Me. Me, *please*."

"You? Or you?" he teased them, his handsome lips curling into a broader smile. "No . . . I think . . . *you*."

Malise's eyes widened on the tip of his finger, which was undeniably pointed at *her*.

"Go on, Malise! It will be fun."

"I really don't wish to—"

Arms grasped her elbows and her waist, lifting her on to the stage.

The man's face appeared very close to hers. His hand pressed against her lower back. "Welcome to my show. I am Dr Ether."

Her pulse beat a frenzy. She whispered, "Really, I decline. I've never been one for dramatics."

He stroked a hand down her cheek, his smile widening. "Never fear, the part is small and involves no dialogue."

"No, truly—"

Dr Ether disappeared and his assistants surrounded her, jostling her to the far edge of the stage, laughing and cajoling and praising how daring she was. Behind her, something weighty and creaky rolled against the wood, as if on wheels. The cold firmness of wood pressed against her back, and leather straps circled her wrists and ankles. She struggled but it was too late. The girls danced away, leaving her strapped to a large circular panel. They clapped their hands and encouraged the crowd to do the same.

Dr Ether approached again. Her gaze fell to his sides, where he clenched a cluster of gleaming, foot-long blades in one hand. "I think everyone has a bit of actor in them. All it takes is getting oneself into the right frame of mind." He spoke to her softly, as if oblivious of their audience. "Take the emotion of fear, for example. Even if one is on stage and with full realization there is no danger to one's person, the successful actor must put themselves into a believing state of mind."

He tossed one of the blades from his crowded left hand to the palm of the empty right.

Her pulse staggered. "Sir, truly, I don't wish to participate—"

"Shhhhh," he soothed. "You must forget the existence of the audience. And the stage, and the curtains, and the ropes and pulleys, and the orchestra . . . and convince yourself to believe you just might be a breath . . . away . . . from *death*."

He bent and with a growl of effort, slammed the tip of the blade between her ankles. She shrieked. The blade pierced through the layers of her skirt and petticoats, into the wood panel.

"For your modesty," he growled, low in his throat. "Your skirts around your head would no doubt incite the crowd into a frenzy but that's not at all the effect we're going for."

She recognized something in the gleam of his eyes and hidden in his handsome smile. A potential for cruelty.

He backed away, three remaining blades in hand. Reaching the far end of the stage, he offered her a dramatic, assessing glance. "Too easy. That is too easy, what do you say my friends?"

The shouts from the crowd filled the alleyway, deafening in their intensity.

"*Too easy.*"

"*Spin the wheel.*"

"What was that?" he asked. "Spin the wheel?"

A unified chant emerged. "*Spin . . . the . . . wheel. Spin . . . the . . . wheel.*"

"No!" shouted Malise but her protests were drowned by the enormity of the sound.

He grinned at his adoring audience. "If you insist."

A young woman appeared beside her, someone familiar. One of the new nurses. The one named Jane. Only Jane had shed her coat. Her hair shimmered in long curls around her shoulders and her lips had been painted bright scarlet.

"*Spin . . . the . . . wheel.*"

"Jane?" Malise gasped, now not just frightened but panicked.

"I'm sorry but do I know you?" laughed Jane, a stack of golden bracelets jangling on her arms. Her hands gripped the wooden handle above Malise's head and with a lusty shout she *pulled*. Everything moved. Spun.

THUNK.

Malise struggled against the force of movement, bent her neck to see. A blade jutted out, a half inch from her right side.

"No more!" she screamed, her hair loosening, and swinging about her face.

THUNK.

She froze. That one, *just beside her ear.*

A sudden roar filled the alley. A flash of light blinded her and heat scorched her skin.

"Seether!" a voice bellowed.

THUNK.

Midnight

"Bloody hell," cursed Dominic. "Your hair."

Nurse Bristol pushed up, and rubbed her eyes. She lay half-sprawled on the grass, her bodice torn and her undershirt parted, which bared the lovely swell of her breasts. Her hair, now streaked with silver moonlight, fell in soft disarray over her shoulders. After Ether and all of his new followers had disappeared, screaming, growling and hissing into the night, Dominic had brought her here to this empty field.

Recognizing him, her eyes widened. "You."

His mouth went dry. God, had he done the right thing? He threw the now-empty ampoule into the darkness.

"Why is my bodice wet?" She paused. "Ugh. That's . . . blood."

He nodded. "Yours, Nurse Bristol."

"Malise. Call me Malise." She searched her body. "But I'm not hurt."

"You were, though." He reached out and with his fingertips, touched her bare skin at the centre of her chest. "Here. The knife went in here."

She pressed her hand over his, holding his palm against the swell of her breast. She appeared interested. Not at all shocked.

"That makes no sense. But . . . I believe you. I feel so different. Unafraid. You don't know how that feels," she whispered, her lips slowly forming a smile. If he'd found her beautiful before, she was that, tenfold, now. "I am oddly unconcerned that apparently something momentous has happened to me that I can't explain. Would it have anything to do with the awful taste in my mouth?"

St Vinet lifted the empty ampoule. "It was meant for them. There was enough for everyone in the crowd who drank or ingested Ether's false elixirs."

"Those things never work. He's a liar, only taking advantage of their hopes and stealing their money."

"Oh, but his elixirs do work. Only they don't heal. They enslave." He pushed himself up from the ground.

She, too, stood, brushing the grass from her rumpled skirts. "Like opium turns people into addicts?"

"Much, much worse, Malise. His victims are transformed into Seethers, who then grow ravenous for the emotion of misery. They prey upon weaker mortals. They exploit and kill, in terrible ways."

"But I didn't drink any of his elixirs" she said softly.

"I didn't even consider that. I just . . . couldn't let you die and hoped this might heal you somehow. Things went further than I expected. You are more than healed now. You are . . ."

He closed his mouth.

"What? What am I?"

"Bloody hell, I'm not ready to say," he growled.

She did not shrink away, but stepped closer, so close her skirts brushed his trouser leg. "You didn't know what its effect would be?"

"Rathburn formulated it. We did not go over every possibility for its use."

"Rathburn . . . he called you an old friend. But he is old, and you are not. What will you tell him now? Mr St Vinet, what will you tell me?"

"That I have, without your permission or consent . . ."

"Yes . . ."

"Turned you into an immortal."

Unable to watch her reaction, he gave her his back, and strode a few feet across the grass to snatch up his hat from the ground. He lowered it on to his head, and waited for the disbelief. The stuttered questions. The curses.

Her hands and arms were around his waist. Something flared, deep inside his chest.

He twisted round, facing her.

She smiled up at him. "Do you know what it's like to be unafraid? Do you understand this gift you have given to me? It is as if I have been freed from a lifetime of imprisonment. I feel as if I am capable of anything."

Her words assuaged much, but not all, of his guilt. Even so, to his pleasure, her hands spread across his chest and came up to his neck and his jaw. He had heard, but never observed for himself, that when the rare mortal was transformed into an immortal they experienced a wild euphoria for days, one that included . . . certain urges.

She whispered, "St Vinet . . . I can't explain it, but I want nothing more than to be closer to you . . . I *need* to be close to you . . ."

He needed no further invitation. Amaranthines were a lusty lot, indulging when natural impulses struck. But with Malise there was something deeper. So deep he experienced only anguish that it had taken this long for them to stand face to face, breath to breath, when until now experience had told him he must forever stay away. From the moment their eyes had met, in Rathburn's rooms at the hospital, she had captured him, heart and soul.

Their lips and bodies met in a mutual frenzy of desire. Within seconds, they fell to the cool grass, a tangle of limbs, garments and bared skin.

St Vinet lifted his head. "Agh! Wait. Stop."

"What is it?" she asked dazedly.

"We've no time for this—"

Malise nodded. "The Seethers . . . they are still out there."

"Yes." He nodded. "The newer Seethers, the Ancillaries, usually hibernate for a good two days before starting their mayhem, so there's time to track them but I need more of Rathburn's elixir in order to save them all. It's Ether I've got to find tonight."

"Let me help you." She re-buttoned her bodice. "He put a blade in my heart. Revenge sounds like a rather sweet pursuit."

"*Rathburn.*" Dominic spun away from her, staring into the night.

"What is it?"

"I must go to him. Immediately."

"How do you know?"

"He has summoned me."

"I thought he was mortal."

"He is mortal. If I were to attempt communication with him, he would never perceive my efforts but when his emotions are intense and insistent, I can sense them across land and sea. He knows this and in this way he has called out to me."

"What is wrong?"

"I don't know. All I know is that he's in danger. It has to be the Seether."

"Ether," whispered Malise.

They crossed the park and emerged on to the cobblestones. Dominic shook awake the driver of a hansom and instructed him to convey them to Winterview. The streets were near empty, so their travel occurred with speed. As they grew nearer to the hospital, an orange light illuminated the sky, the distinct colour of flame.

The hansom shook and jerked to a stop. Even from this distance, Malise felt the heat on her skin and smelled the smoke. She leaned forward in her seat and grasped the door handle. St Vinet seized her arm, holding her back.

"Stay here, Malise."

"No, I won't. I care for him too. Perhaps even more than you."

Stepping down from the hansom, they raced across the lawn, passing residents in their nightclothes, seated in chairs and bundled up against the chill. Nurses moved to and fro, tending to the elderly residents. Three different fire brigades directed thick streams of water into the blaze.

"Nurse Bristol," shouted a nurse.

"Where is Mr Rathburn?" Malise enquired, her voice husky with urgency.

The nurse stared, wide-eyed. "You . . . you look so *different*."

"Mr *Rathburn*! Where is he?" shouted Malise, gripping the woman's arm.

"We got everyone else out." The nurse peered toward the upper floors. "Everyone but Mr Rathburn. Nurse Henry said she would bring him down. She and that visiting physician, Dr Ether. They were so very brave, going straight up into the flames."

Dominic strode toward the burning structure. Malise joined him.

He growled, "I suspect Nurse Henry is an Ancillary, here to set the stage for Ether's arrival."

Malise added, "There were other nurses too, only recently hired. They helped Ether bind me to the wheel."

They grew closer to the hospital. The heat intensified but did not scorch Malise's skin. In that moment, a great crash sounded, and the lower floor buckled. The roof sagged and collapsed inward. Flames blazed out from the gaping hole.

"Oh, my God," Dominic's face paled. "We're too late."

"No!" Malise cried, tears glazing her eyes. "Mr Rathburn!"

St Vinet's arm came round her, bringing her close to his side. Bending down, he pressed his lips to her tears. Winterview was now nothing more than a great burning heap. Rathburn, his mentor and friend, was dead.

A stream of carriages arrived and soon all of the residents were whisked away to other lodgings. Their cause lost, the firemen retreated. Wagons returned to the street, they rolled their hoses and prepared to depart.

A voice sounded behind them. "Don't tell me you're going to stand here all night when there's a Seether to be Reclaimed."

Malise turned. A tall figure strode towards them, a charred, still-smoking leather case in hand. As he drew nearer, the light from the flames illuminated his features – those of a young man in the prime of his life. She recognized him from the tintypes in Mr Rathburn's room.

In shock, Malise broke free of Dominic's embrace and raced towards the one who approached them.

"Mr Rathburn," she exclaimed, reaching out to touch his face. "It's you."

He dropped the case, and seized her up into his arms.

"I like the hair," he murmured. "It and immortality suit you."

"What in the hell?" Dominic demanded, the intensity of his fury hotter than any inferno. "You played me for a fool. All these years, you were simply playing a part."

Anson released Malise and turned towards him. "No, I truly aged. There's a way, little known and I begged the approval of The Primordial Council. But the method is dangerous. A gamble. I was never certain once I'd let things go this far that I'd be able to return from the brink. But remember, St Vinet, the process by which we are all given our immortality. We are baptized in fire – and fire reversed the process of my aging and returned me to my true, immortal state."

Dominic said, "But you gave up your immortality when you wed the mortal woman. Once you've relinquished your immortality, you can never go back."

Anson shook his head. "I never relinquished my immortality. I simply allowed my physical body to age. I loved Lavinia. She wanted someone to grow old with. She deserved that much. By then, you were already so furious with me for marrying her – curse your bloody temper – I let you believe as well. Then Ether returned, seeking revenge. I thought I'd already Reclaimed him with one of my elixirs but the formula was faulty. Though weakened, he murdered Lavinia, then disappeared. Disappeared so completely, I feared I would never have my revenge upon him. So I took a chance. The chance that he hated me so greatly that as he regained his strength, while he was watching and waiting, he would one day reappear when I was at my oldest and my weakest."

"And he did, and you Reclaimed him," exclaimed Malise, gazing at him in admiration.

"No, he's still out there."

"Still out there?" growled Dominic. "We've got to stop him, then. Tonight."

Malise added, "And there are still his victims who must be saved. Returned to their normal state."

Anson took up the case. "Then let us be on our way. He can't escape the three of us. Though not a Shadow Guard with final Reclamation powers, Malise can still join in the hunt."

Dominic rested a hand on Anson's shoulder. "When this is all over . . ."

"I know. You're going to kick my arse. Do your best."

"The Primordial Council will be furious that we've turned a mortal."

"Let me do the talking, then."

Their gazes held. "I'm glad you've returned."

"So am I." Rathburn lowered his voice. "But if you ever kiss my nurse again—"

Malise looked to St Vinet and then to Rathburn, and laughed.

Author Biographies

Lara Adrian
New York Times and *USA Today* bestselling author of the Midnight Breed vampire romance series from Bantam Dell Books. To date, Lara's books have been translated into fourteen languages and have sold more than a million copies worldwide.
www.laraadrian.com

Sharon Ashwood
Author of The Dark Forgotten contemporary paranormal series. *Ravenous*, book 1 in the series, won the 2010 Golden Quill award in the Paranormal category. She is a freelance journalist, novelist, desk jockey and enthusiast for the weird and spooky.
www.sharonashwood.com

Sonya Bateman
Urban fantasy author of *Master of None* (4.5 stars, *Romantic Times Book Reviews Magazine*), with the first in a new series featuring an original take on the djinn.
www.sonyabateman.com

Gail Carriger
Author of the Parasol Protectorate series (*Soulless, Changeless* and *Blameless*), urbane steampunk fantasies with comedy and romance thrown in. When not moonlighting as an archaeologist, she lives on a vineyard in Northern California surrounded by fabulous shoes. She drinks too much tea.
www.gailcarriger.com

Karen Chance

New York Times bestselling author of urban fantasy, including the popular Cassandra Palmer and Dorina Basarab series.
www.karenchance.com

Shirley Damsgaard

Author of the acclaimed Ophelia and Abby paranormal mystery series, she resides with her family in small-town Iowa where she has served as postmaster for the last twenty years.
www.shirleydamsgaard.com

S.J. Day

Author of the Marked urban fantasy series S.J. Day is the pseudonym of Sylvia Day, national bestselling and award-winning author of paranormal and historical romances.
www.sjday.net

Sherri Browning Erwin

A graduate of Mount Holyoke College, Sherri writes contemporary and historical fiction with a paranormal twist. Her latest book is the horror mashup *Jane Slayre* (Gallery Books), a timeless tale of love, devotion and the undead.
www.sherribrowningerwin.com

Seressia Glass

Award-winning author of contemporary and paranormal romance, Seressia made her urban fantasy debut with *Shadow Blade*, book 1 in the Shadowchasers series, which is set in her hometown of Atlanta.
www.seressia.com

Ava Gray

The 2008 PEARL award-winner for Best New Author, Ava Gray is the romance pen name for national bestselling author Ann Aguirre. She lives in Mexico with her family.
www.avagray.com

Nathalie Gray

Award-winning author of over thirty novels of speculative fiction ranging from steampunk to fantasy. She has been featured in *The Independent* (UK), *RT Book Reviews* Magazine, and *Realms*

of Fantasy. A former soldier and avid renovator, Nathalie makes her home in an impregnable fortress beneath the Nordic ice sheets, where she plots to one day take over the world.
www.nathaliegray.com

Michele Hauf

Author of dark paranormal romance, action/adventure and fantasy, her story in *Paranormal Romance 2* is part of her Of Angels and Demons series available from Silhouette Nocturne.
www.michelehauf.com

Jackie Kessler

An urban fantasy and paranormal romance author who likes to write about demons, angels, the hapless humans caught between them, superheroes and the supervillains who pound those heroes into pudding. Along with her books for adults, she writes novels for teens under the byline Jackie Morse Kessler.
www.jackiekessler.com

Kim Lenox

The award-winning author of the Victorian-era paranormal Shadow Guard series. She was a 2008 *Romantic Times* Magazine nominee for Best First Historical, and winner of their 2009 Best Vampire/Shapeshifter/Werewolf Historical award.
www.kimlenox.com

Moira Rogers

Author of dark paranormal romance and romantic urban fantasy.
www.moirarogers.com

Helen Scott Taylor

Winner of the *American Title IV* contest, Helen writes paranormal and fantasy romance. The first book in her Magic Knot Fairies series was chosen as a *Booklist* Top Ten Romance for 2009.
www.helenscotttaylor.com

Elissa Wilds

Award-winning of sexy paranormal romance novels *Between Light and Dark* and *Darkness Rising* from Dorchester Love Spell.
www.elissawilds.com